The Year's Best Science Fiction

Volume 2

D0366248

The Infinity Project 1: Engineering Infinity
The Infinity Project 2: Edge of Infinity
The Infinity Project 3: Reach for Infinity
The Infinity Project 4: Meeting Infinity
The Infinity Project 5: Bridging Infinity
The Infinity Project 6: Infinity Wars
The Infinity Project 7: Infinity's End
The Locus Awards: Thirty Years of the Best in Science Fiction and Fantasy
(with Charles N. Brown)
The New Space Opera (with Gardner Dozois)
The New Space Opera 2 (with Gardner Dozois)
The Starry Rift: Tales of New Tomorrows
The Year's Best Australian Science Fiction and Fantasy: Volume 1
(with Jeremy G. Byrne)
The Year's Best Australian Science Fiction and Fantasy: Volume 2
(with Jeremy G. Byrne)
The Year's Best Science Fiction Vol 1: The Saga Anthology
of Science Fiction 2020
Under My Hat: Tales from the Cauldron
Wings of Fire (with Marianne S. Jablon)

THE YEAR'S BEST SCIENCE FICTION

VOLUME 2

EDITED BY
JONATHAN STRAHAN

SAGA PRESS

LONDON SYDNEY **NEW YORK** TORONTO NEW DELHI

SAGA 〰 PRESS

AN IMPRINT OF SIMON & SCHUSTER, INC.

1230 AVENUE OF THE AMERICAS, NEW YORK, NEW YORK 10020

This book is a work of fiction. Any references to historical events, real people, or real places are used fictitiously. Other names, characters, places, and events are products of the author's imagination, and any resemblance to actual events or places or persons, living or dead, is entirely coincidental.

Compilation and introduction copyright © 2021 by Jonathan Strahan
Copyright statement continued on page 585

All rights reserved, including the right to reproduce this book or portions thereof in any form whatsoever. For information, address Saga Press Subsidiary Rights Department, 1230 Avenue of the Americas, New York, NY 10020.

First Saga Press trade paperback edition September 2021

SAGA PRESS and colophon are trademarks of Simon & Schuster, Inc.

For information about special discounts for bulk purchases, please contact Simon & Schuster Special Sales at 1-866-506-1949 or business@simonandschuster.com.

The Simon & Schuster Speakers Bureau can bring authors to your live event. For more information or to book an event, contact the Simon & Schuster Speakers Bureau at 1-866-248-3049 or visit our website at www.simonspeakers.com.

Interior design by Kathryn A. Kenney-Peterson

Manufactured in the United States of America

1   3   5   7   9   10   8   6   4   2

Library of Congress Cataloging-in-Publication Data is available.

ISBN 978-1-5344-4962-6
ISBN 978-1-5344-4964-0 (ebook)

For everyone who worked to keep us safe or to make
2020 just a little bit easier, with thanks and deep gratitude

CONTENTS

ACKNOWLEDGMENTS

This past year was a strange, difficult, and unexpected one. The first volume in this series launched into deeply uncertain waters, and I'm grateful beyond words to my wonderful editor and good friend at Saga Press, Joe Monti, for getting that book and this one out into the world. I plan to be doing this for years to come, and look forward to doing it with Joe and the team. My sincere thanks also to Madison Penico, Lauren Jackson, and everyone at Saga who had anything to do with the book. My agent, Howard Morhaim, continues to be the best person I could be working with in this business, and I want to thank him and everyone at HMLA for their work on this and on all my projects. And then there's everyone else, the people who gave time, suggested stories, and helped in so many ways with this particular book. Thanks as always to Liza Trombi and the entire team at *Locus*, who helped keep me focused on the year at hand when my mind drifted and I couldn't seem to get any work done at all; to my dear friend and podcast co-host, Gary K. Wolfe; Ian Mond; James Bradley; Rachel C. Cordasco; Ian Whates; Bill Shafer; Sheila Williams, who was exceptionally helpful; to Steven H. Silver, who provided invaluable information for the obituary section of my introduction; and to all the authors and their agents who let their work appear here.

Finally, as always, a special thank-you to my wife, Marianne, and two daughters, who were the best people in the world to be locked in with, even if it wasn't for too long.

YEAR IN REVIEW: 2020

Welcome to the second volume of *The Year's Best Science Fiction: The Saga Anthology of Science Fiction*. When I launched this series last year, everything seemed simple, safe, and predictable. I sent the manuscript for volume 1 to my editor in mid-January without much thought of 2020 other than that there'd be new books to talk about, new writers to get excited over, conventions to attend, awards to applaud, and much the same turn of the seasons that we've come to expect. Well, at least the seasons were the same, because everything else was quite unexpected.

But before I get ahead of myself, if this is your first time picking up *The Year's Best Science Fiction*, I should tell you a little about the book you are holding. *The Year's Best Science Fiction* is my attempt to collect in one volume the best short science fiction published during the previous year. I take my guidance on what science fiction is from Damon Knight, who wrote something to the effect that "science fiction is [or means] what we point to when we say it." I've heard other definitions, but for this book and this series, that suffices. I should also say that, while I loved and was inspired by Gardner Dozois's fine *Year's Best Science Fiction* series, this is not a continuation of it. Instead, it collects what I think the best science fiction of the year is and, due to length considerations, mostly avoids long novellas and so on (this book is somewhat shorter than his was). It does have one thing in common with Gardner's books, though, and that is that I try to give you an overview of what's out there, what's happening, and how the year in science fiction really was.

And it was a strange year indeed. A pandemic year, when COVID-19 changed everything, or seemed to. On a macro level, it seemed to be a pretty good year for book publishing, though it's hard to overlook the terrible job losses and deeply saddening bookstore closures. One of the biggest printers in the United States, LSC Communications, filed for Chapter 11 bankruptcy protection in April, interrupting the ability to print and supply books; couriers, postal systems, and airlines were thrown into chaos, affecting the delivery of books to wholesalers, retailers, and book buyers; booksellers were forced to close for public health reasons, impacting the ability to sell books direct to readers; publishing houses shuttered their offices, forcing staff to work from home for long periods, with many still not back to normal and unlikely to be anytime soon; and readers were forced to stay home as well, completely upending their lives: but book *sales* were pretty good. If you were publishing genre fiction—science fiction, fantasy, crime, romance, etc.—then readers were looking for distraction, and they turned to audiobooks in record numbers, print books in increased numbers, and ebooks too, and they bought them online more than ever before. Looking back in ten years or so, in fact, this may be seen as the watershed year that cemented a seemingly inevitable trend where the book business followed the music business into greater and greater dependence on online retailing.

I suspect this means we are moving toward a world where we have fewer book publishers selling books through fewer sales channels which depend more and more on a small number of online retailers. This carries with it the risk that readers will be offered a more homogeneous range of books, and that books that require hand selling, which need to be seen in stores, will find a harder path toward publication than ever before, and that publishers at all levels will need to develop and hone a range of skills that might not occur to the average book buyer, like the ability to manage metadata to ensure readers actually see books online.

So if major publishing houses were sold, imprints folded, bookstores closed, book chains shrank, book stores lost prominent retail space in shopping malls and central shopping districts, and books were less physically present in our lives, how was it for the printed word? How was science fiction itself? It was in good health. There were as many entertaining romps published as before, as many stirring tales of space adventure, etc., but the themes and trends that have occupied science fiction in recent years continued to do so at all levels of the field.

And what were we concerned with? Well, climate change, race, gender, income equality, and privacy seemed to be the big themes, with landmark books focused on all these issues appearing throughout the year. The books that got the most buzz this year—and there were a few—reflected this. The year kicked off with Tochi Onyebuchi's remarkable short novel, *Riot Baby* (Tordotcom), which came out in January and gave us an excoriating look at the impact of racism in the United States and especially on its prison system. Ella is a young Black woman with powers. As Onyebuchi puts it, she has a "Thing." Her brother Kev is in prison, mostly for the crime of being Black, but Ella's "Thing" lets her visit him, and could give her the power to change things, but possibly at terrible cost. What's remarkable about this angry, raging book is how tender and loving it is. Just as it howls for justice, it looks at the people damaged by injustice with deep understanding. And it was bookended at the end of the year by a second, different but equally astonishing short novel, this one from P. Djèlí Clark. *Ring Shout* (Tordotcom) is a sly, dark, funny book that draws on sorcery, dark magic, D. W. Griffith's *The Birth of a Nation*, and the Ku Klux Klan to look at what allows ordinary people to act like monsters and how that has impacted America's story of race. N. K. Jemisin's urban fantasy, *The City We Became* (Orbit), also got enormous attention during the year. Being fantasy, *The City We Became* falls mostly outside the purview of this book, but it is worthy of mention here because of how much attention it got. The opening two-thirds of the book are wonderful, as Jemisin embodies the spirit of New York's five boroughs in different diverse characters, but I was perhaps less drawn in by the way the story concluded. Nonetheless, it was hailed as one of the books of the year.

In an interesting year for science fiction generally, three books that were the closest to what I consider to be "core SF" were on everyone's minds. Early in the year William Gibson's *Agency* (Berkley) picked up the story he'd been telling in 2014's *The Peripheral*, about Verity, an "app whisperer," who is tasked with testing a new AI program. *Agency* ends up as a powerful look at privacy, surveillance, and how technology is impacting our lives. The outstanding science fiction book of 2020, though, came from Kim Stanley Robinson. His twentieth novel,

The Ministry for the Future (Orbit), is a towering achievement, managing to look at the climate crisis in a way that is unblinking, pragmatic, and yet deeply optimistic. The opening pages are the most harrowing of Robinson's long career, but by the end of the novel he gives readers space to hope. It's quite remarkable. The other SF novel that got a lot of attention during the year was Martha Wells's first novel-length installment in the Murderbot Diaries, *Network Effect* (Tordotcom), a wonderfully fun and snarky book that's likely to win the Hugo Award.

I've touched on one or two books that are more fantasy than SF because they got a lot of attention during the year, because SF and fantasy aren't as separate as they once were, and because they illustrate well the trends occupying the field right now. The other book that fits this is Alix E. Harrow's sophomore effort, the compassionate, angry tale of suffragette witches that is *The Once and Future Witches* (Redhook/Orbit). A tale of three sisters looking to bring magic back to an alternate Salem, it's an engrossing novel and one of my personal favorite books of the year.

So, if those were the buzz novels of the year—and I could have mentioned more (it was a good year)—what was happening off the page where books were published? What was the story in detail?

As I said last year, I'm not an industry analyst, so I can only give you a broad overview of some of the things that happened in book publishing during 2020. A lot happened, and frankly, it's far too early to predict how it all will affect science fiction specifically or book publishing generally in the years ahead, other than to say things will be different. Many fine editors lost their jobs, imprints were shuttered, and entire publishing houses were sold or offered for sale.

The biggest surprise in a surprising year for books might be that print sales overall were up. When the world began to shut down in March, many probably expected sales to plummet, but industry bible *Publishers Weekly* reported that print sales of books were up 7.8 percent over 2019, and that there were big increases in sales of audiobooks, with ebook sales remaining solid. While some of this increase was due to things like parents buying nonfiction for children who were forced to stay at home and study, there were a lot of other forces at play. Books that were relevant to the biggest issues of the year, whether they were the pandemic, Black Lives Matter, or something else, all did well. Genre fiction did well too, with a number of titles occupying major bestseller lists. And even bookstores weathered the storm better than expected, at least in part due to initiatives like bookstore.org, which allowed independent bookstores to compete online more effectively.

The biggest changes in publishing happened at the highest level and will affect all publishing and not just SF. Macmillan Publishers CEO John Sargent left that company in September due to "disagreements regarding the direction of Macmillan." The impact of this is yet to be seen, but could be significant. Carolyn Reidy, CEO of Simon & Schuster since 2008, very sadly died from a heart attack early in the year, and Jonathan Karp was named president and CEO. Simon & Schuster was also part of what was the biggest publishing news of 2020 when in November Penguin Random House (PRH) announced plans to acquire the company from ViacomCBS for $2.175 billion, creating what the *New York Times* described as the "first megapublisher." This followed action earlier in the year when PRH parent Bertelsmann took full ownership of the company, acquiring a 25 percent stake held by Pearson. The merger won't be complete till mid-2021.

There were changes at Houghton Mifflin Harcourt (HMH) too. In October, HMH announced that it was shuttering science fiction and fantasy imprint John Joseph Adams Books, launched in February 2016. Editor Adams published some interesting work in his tenure at HMH, and this is sad news. This was followed by news that 5 percent of HMH's employees (166 people) would take part in a voluntary early retirement incentive program. In August, DC Comics announced widespread layoffs due to restructuring following the acquisition of DC parent company WarnerMedia by AT&T, with around six hundred people losing their jobs at WarnerMedia and other parts of DC reportedly also suffering significant cuts.

While many of the science fiction imprints and their editorial staff that were with us at the end of 2019 were still with us a year later, there were some changes. In February, Gollancz publisher Anne Clarke left the Orion imprint and Marcus Gipps was promoted to publishing director. Late in the year, Tor/Tom Doherty Associates announced that executive editor Beth Meacham would retire at the end of 2020 after thirty-six years with the company, following a major restructure of the company. There were also changes to imprints, with some new ones being launched. UK publisher Head of Zeus announced they would launch Ad Astra, a new imprint dedicated to the "best high-concept SFF our world can offer." Goldsmiths Press announced a new imprint, Gold SF, for "intersectional feminist SF," with Una McCormack chairing the editorial board. Random House Children's Books' new Labyrinth Road is to focus on contemporary fantasy and realistic literary novels for middle grade and young adult readers. Marie O'Regan will serve as managing editor for PS Publishing's new Absinthe Books, which will focus on writers new to the company. Hachette Book Group announced plans for a new imprint, Legacy Lit, "dedicated to books for and by people of color." Wahida Clark Presents Publishing (WCP) launched a new imprint, Sci-Fi Fantasy for the Culture, and Harper Children's has announced changes at their Harper imprint, with Director of Publishing VP Rich Thomas running the line, Erica Sussman in charge of middle grade, teen, and tie-in work, and Nancy Inteli running picture books.

If the COVID pandemic upended industry norms, affected sales and distribution, and ultimately affected what is written and what we read, it also changed how we interacted. In-person events were deeply impacted. Whether it was the London Book Fair or the Kiss Farewell Tour, pretty much everything was delayed or canceled. However, as the year progressed, events adapted as swiftly and pragmatically as they could, with some canceled, some rescheduled, and some going online. The first major SFF genre event to successfully go online was the 2020 Nebula Conference (May 28–31, 2020), which was widely applauded for the quality of the event and for the inclusiveness of its approach. In fact, one of the great upsides for virtual events during 2020 was that they allowed people from all over the world and with different access issues to take part in a way that couldn't easily have been done in the past. The Locus Awards Weekend (June 26–28, 2020) also ran very successfully. Understandably, larger events faced greater challenges. CoNZealand, the 78th World Science Fiction Convention, was due to run in Wellington, New Zealand, from July 29 through August 2, 2020, but instead became the first-ever "virtual" Worldcon. While convention volunteers worked to make sure the event went off without a hitch, with so many people from all over the world accessing the event, issues were unavoidable. Most disappointingly, there were access and other issues with the Hugo Awards Ceremony, which was widely criticized. More positively, though, fans from all over the world attended, and there was even an excellent unofficial CoNZealand Fringe that ran while official programming was off-line. There were also issues around the World Fantasy Convention (October 29–November 1, 2020), which had been planned to be held in Salt Lake City, Utah, but ran virtually. Hopefully those issues will be resolved in coming years. Industry journal *Locus* reported that the following scheduled 2020 events were canceled, rescheduled, or ran online: Emerald City Comic Con; the 41st International Conference on the Fantastic in the Arts; the Spectrum Awards ceremony; MidSouthCon 38; the Texas Library Association Annual Conference; the Outer Dark Symposium; the Bologna Children's Book Fair; the annual Jack Williamson Lectureship; Norwescon 43; Minicon 55; the 36th L. Ron Hubbard Writers and Illustrators of the Future workshops and gala awards event; ConStellation 11, Swancon 45; RavenCon 15; the Edgar Awards banquet and symposium; Malice Domestic; the Bay Area Book Festival; Creative Ink; the British Book Awards; LitFest Pasadena; BayCon; Balticon 54; WisCon 44; Book Expo in New York; the 32nd Annual Lambda Literary Awards Ceremony; Clarion and Clarion West Writers Workshops; the ALA Annual Conference & Exhibition; Westercon 73; NEFilk 2020; Readercon 31; San Diego Comic-Con International; the Romance Writers of America Annual Conference; the Launch Pad Astronomy Workshop; PulpFest; StokerCon UK; ArmadilloCon 42; the Columbus NASFiC 2020; Bubonicon; Dragon Con 2020; Albacon; FantasyCon 2020; MileHiCon; Fantastika; CONtraflow 10; Hispacón; OryCon 42; and Philcon.

While I feel for all the organizers and event attendees whose events were disrupted during 2020 and will be disrupted during 2021, I am also optimistic. Events adapted and changed, and new channels opened up that would allow people from all over the world and with a much broader range of accessibility issues to take part, and that must be a good thing. Still, it doesn't mean it was easy, which is probably the true theme of 2020.

There is no good information on how much short science fiction is published each year. The Internet Speculative Fiction Database (www .isfdb.org) lists 5,594 short stories as having been published in English during the year, which is more than the estimate of over 3,000 from trade journal *Locus* (www.locusmag.com). With stories appearing in multiple-author anthologies, single-author short story collections, print and digital magazines, as part of Patreon and other fundraising platforms, in newsletters, as part of think tank projects, as individual stories sold online, and it seems just about everywhere else, both of these estimates seem conservative. My own impression for 2020 was that the overall volume of short fiction published was much the same as in recent years, but take that with a pinch of salt. The Science Fiction and Fantasy Writers of America (SFWA) currently recognizes forty-two short fiction markets that professionally publish speculative fiction of one kind or another, up two from last year, while *Locus* identifies seventy. The Internet Speculative Fiction Database listed 741 short fiction magazine issues of one kind or another as having been published during the year, which excludes almost everything published outside the United States or in any language other than English. Suffice it to say there are a lot of stories published every year in a lot of different places.

As it was with everything else, it was a difficult and challenging year for the magazine market, and while there were some positive signs, the problems that I've noted in previous years (changes to printing, distribution, newsstand access, advertising revenues, etc. etc.) were all still there in 2020 and likely to have a significant impact in coming years. And there were editorial changes announced during 2020 that no doubt will affect the short fiction market for years to come. The year started with Lezli Robyn assuming the editorial reins of *Galaxy's Edge*, replacing Mike Resnick, who died in 2019. Then in March, it was announced that Michael Kelly and Silvia Moreno-Garcia would step down as reprints editor and co-editor respectively of *The Dark*, with publisher and co-editor Sean Wallace to continue editing the magazine with "no immediate plans to hire a new co-editor." In horror-related news, John Joseph Adams also stepped down as editor of *Nightmare*, to be replaced by author and editor Wendy N. Wagner starting in 2021. Adams remains editor of *Lightspeed* and publisher of *Lightspeed*, *Nightmare*, and *Fantasy Magazine* (more on that shortly). Canadian speculative fiction magazine *Augur* announced editor-in-chief Alex De Pompa would be leaving at the end of 2020 and would be replaced by current poetry editor Terese Mason Pierre and managing editor Lawrence Stewen as co-editors-in-chief. The biggest editorial changes, though, came late in the year. Gordon Van Gelder announced mid-November that Sheree Renée Thomas would become the tenth editor of *The Magazine of Fantasy & Science Fiction*—the first person of color and just the second woman to edit the magazine in its seventy-one-year history—following C. C. Finlay, who completed his sixth year editing the magazine and is stepping down to devote more time to his writing. Thomas's first issue as editor will be March/April 2021. Fireside announced that, after considerable controversy, Pablo Defendini would resign as editor of *Fireside Magazine* and its book line, with Brian J. White taking on the role of interim editorial director. Defendini remains with the company in a management capacity. In December, *Amazing Stories* announced that editor-in-chief Ira Nayman was resigning from his position and a new editor would be appointed. And finally, early in 2021, PS Publishing announced that it would start *ParSec*, a new online science fiction magazine, after plans to take over publication of long-running British SF magazine *Interzone* from Andy Cox fell through.

While we won't know the impact of these editorial changes until well into 2021 and beyond, there was some good news with several magazines launching or relaunching. Jason Sizemore announced that *Apex Magazine* would relaunch in January 2021 on a new bimonthly publication schedule for a total of six issues a year. This followed the temporary closure of the magazine due to Sizemore's illness. Coral Alejandra Moore and Eliana González Ugarte launched *Constelación Magazine*, "a bilingual magazine of speculative fiction," with Moore and Ugarte to edit. John Joseph Adams, who had a very busy year, relaunched *Fantasy Magazine* in November with issue 61. The magazine is co-edited by Christie Yant and Arley Sorg and co-published by Adams and Yant. And right at the end of the year, Dream Tower Media announced it would publish a new monthly magazine under the editorship of Robert Zoltan, *Sexy Fantastic*, starting January 1, 2021.

The major magazines seemed to do well in 2020, with none showing any significant changes in audience or reach. *Asimov's Science Fiction, Analog Science Fiction and Fact, The Magazine of Fantasy & Science Fiction (F&SF), Tor.com, Clarkesworld, Lightspeed,* and *Uncanny* all seem to be thriving, with *Clarkesworld* and *Tor.com* having had particularly good years.

F&SF published six issues under editor Charles Coleman Finlay during its seventy-first year of publication, and featured strong work by Nadia Afifi, Ray Nayler, Rati Mehrotra, Ian Tregillis, and Leah Cypess, among others. The two Dell magazines, *Asimov's* and *Analog,* also had strong years. *Asimov's Science Fiction* debuted in 1977 and is edited by longtime editor Sheila Williams. Its six issues featured top-notch SF from Timons Esaias, Ray Nayler, Mercurio D. Rivera, Ian R. MacLeod, Connie Willis, Nancy Kress, and more. *Analog* celebrated its ninetieth year of publication, with special redesigned covers, classic reprints, and other anniversary features. *Analog* published first-rank SF from Andy Dudak and Alec Nevala-Lee, alongside strong work from A. T. Sayre and others. The other major print SF magazine is British institution *Interzone,* which is edited by Andy Cox. Launched in 1982 and always open to new and experimental work, it published six issues, featuring interesting fiction from Andy Dudak, Eugenia Triantafyllou, James Sallis, and others.

Neil Clarke's *Clarkesworld,* John Joseph Adams's *Lightspeed,* Lynne Thomas and Michael Damian Thomas's *Uncanny Magazine,* and *Tor.com* are vitally important magazines that publish primarily or exclusively online. *Clarkesworld*, which launched in 2006 and publishes monthly, had an outstanding year and was probably the pick of the SF magazines. Its 2020 started in controversy, though, when the magazine published a pseudonymous story by debut writer Isabel Fall that attempted to repurpose a harmful anti-trans meme. The story was met with both criticism and acclaim, but was quickly withdrawn after the author received personal threats. In happier news, *Clarkesworld*, always a leader in publishing translated fiction, featured works in translation from Chinese, Korean, Japanese, and Spanish by Chen Qiufan, Regina Kanyu Wang, Baoshu, and others. It also featured some of the year's very best stories by Rebecca Campbell, Sameem Siddiqui, A. C. Wise, M. L. Clark, and others. *Lightspeed*, which debuted in 2010 and is published monthly, featured strong science fiction this year by Gene Doucette, Rati Mehrotra, and others, along with excellent fantasy from Celeste Rita Baker, Kristina Ten, KT Bryski, and others. Baker and Ten were Clarion West students of mine, so I note their success with particular pleasure. *Uncanny* magazine, which debuted in 2014 and each month publishes work sitting on the borders between SF and fantasy, published some of the year's best stories, including two stories by A. T. Greenblatt and Ken Liu that are featured here, alongside top-notch work from Aliette de Bodard, Eugenia Triantafyllou, Alix E. Harrow, Rae Carson, Meg Elison, and others. *Tor.com*, which launched in 2008 and publishes speculative fiction on an irregular schedule, was, in this editor's opinion, tied with *Clarkesworld* for the outstanding short fiction magazine of 2020. It features work acquired by a range of editors, myself included. Noting that conflict of interest, I'd say *Tor.com* had an extremely strong year, publishing award-worthy work by Charlie Jane Anders, Rich Larson, Maureen McHugh, and many more.

While the magazines mentioned above are the main "pro" magazines in the SF field, there is a proud tradition of magazines that are classified—because of print-run size, payment rate, or reliance on volunteer staff—as being "semiprofessional." These publish extremely high quality fiction and are regarded as major markets. *Uncanny* magazine, mentioned above, falls into this category. Venerable semiprozine *Strange Horizons* had a good year publishing fiction, reviews, and criticism, as well as publishing their quarterly SF-in-translation magazine, *Samovar*. The magazine published strong work by Catherynne M. Valente, Justin C. Key, Ada Hoffmann, and others. *Fiyah: Magazine of Black Speculative Fiction* had a very good year in 2020, publishing four strong issues, with some of the year's best work, by Ozzie M. Gartrell, Zabe Bent, and others.

Because this is a science fiction overview, I'll not spend much time on magazines that primarily publish fantasy, dark fantasy, or horror, but I recommend Scott H. Andrews's outstanding and award-winning *Beneath Ceaseless Skies* (my pick for the best fantasy magazine in the field), Sean Wallace's excellent *The Dark*, John Joseph Adams's *Nightmare*, LaShawn M. Wanak's *GigaNotoSaurus*, and Andy Cox's *Black Static*.

All the magazines mentioned above publish worthwhile fiction and nonfiction and deserve your support.

Given how much time I spend reading short fiction, I have limited time to keep up with novel-length work. For that reason, I'm restricting myself to discussing books I read during the year, and to highlighting others that were widely discussed elsewhere. The year 2020 was, despite all the disruption and changes to publishing schedules, another good year for science fiction on the page. Whether you wanted something serious and significant or just a bit of distraction, there was a book for you. As I mentioned earlier, the SF novel that for my money is the book of the year is Kim Stanley Robinson's magisterial work of climate optimism, *The Ministry for the Future* (Orbit). If 2020 needed challenging new and transformative work, *Ministry* and M. John Harrison's elusive and allusive *The Sunken Land Begins to Rise Again* (Gollancz) were those books and are essential. Probably the best pure quill science fiction novel of the year was Paul McAuley's far future samurai Western epic, *War of the Maps* (Gollancz). William Gibson has, in the years since *Neuromancer*, slowly sandpapered his future smooth, and his sly, serious *Agency* (Berkley) took that a step further, raising questions about cause, consequence, and the world we live in.

Climate, race, and gender were at the forefront of a number of the year's best novels. James Bradley's *Ghost Species* (Penguin Australia) is a wonderful, tender book that makes us look closely at our humanity and should be available more widely. I was also impressed with Christopher Brown's *Failed State* (HarperVoyager), Linda Nagata's climate disaster novel *Pacific Storm* (Mythic Island), and Anne Charnock's fine dystopian tale of a climate-ravaged Europe, *Bridge 108* (Amazon). The book that in some way synopsized all this neatly was Alex Irvine's *Anthropocene Rag* (Tordotcom), a quirky short novel of a future United States uplifted by nanotech and transported by a dream of America that felt weirdly timely by year's end. While this tale of a ragtag bunch of Golden Ticket winners going in search of America was a favorite of mine, full disclosure requires me to say I acquired and edited the book, so you might take that with a pinch of salt.

Science fiction will always be a genre of space opera and space adventure, and there were a string of strong novels published in 2020 that continued the recent trend that sees the heart of the genre becoming more open and inclusive. A standout was Kate Elliott's gender-swapped retelling of Alexander the Great as space opera, *Unconquerable Sun* (Tor), as was Martha Wells's *Network Effect* (Tordotcom). Elizabeth Bear followed up last year's *Ancestral Night* with *Machine* (Saga), which I liked even better than its predecessor. John Scalzi brought his bestselling Interdependency to a close with *The Last Emperox* (Tor), while Alastair Reynolds delivered a wonderful end to his Revenger trilogy with *Bone Silence* (Gollancz), and Walter Jon Williams continued the adventures of Caro Sula in *Fleet Elements* (HarperVoyager). All are recommended to lovers of space opera.

Science fiction has been looking beyond its borders more and more in recent years, and this year saw a handful of wonderful books from India, Pakistan, and Bangladesh. Probably the best of these was Gautam Bhatia's powerful dystopian debut, *The Wall* (HarperCollins India), but almost as good were Samit Basu's engaging anti-dystopian near-future tale of surveillance, social media, and disruption, *Chosen Spirits* (Simon & Schuster India) and Yudhanjaya Wijeratne's old-school SF romp, *The Salvage Crew* (Aethon). All these books deserve wider audiences and are welcome additions to the field.

New writers are the lifeblood of science fiction, and in 2020 we saw some strong debuts. I was particularly impressed with Simon Jiminez's space opera *The Vanished Birds* (Random House), Hao Jingfang's *Vagabonds* (Saga), Micaiah Johnson's dimension-hopping *The Space Between Worlds* (Del Rey), and Premee Mohamed's powerful *Beneath the Rising* (Rebellion), all of which belong on awards ballots. I was also impressed with Sophie Ward's *Love and Other Thought Experiments* (Corsair), Karen Osborne's *Architects of Memory* (Tor), Cho Nam-Joo's *Kim Jiyoung, Born 1982* (Liveright), and Corey J. White's *Repo Virtual* (Tor).

Also getting a lot of attention were Derek Künsken's *The House of Styx* (Rebellion), Adam Levin's *Bubblegum* (Doubleday), Adrian Tchaikovsky's *The Doors of Eden* (Orbit), C. J. Cherryh's *Divergence* and *Resurgence* (DAW), Chris Beckett's *Two Tribes* (Corvus), Cory Doctorow's *Attack Surface* (Tor), David Wong's *Zoey Punches the Future in the Dick* (St. Martin's Press), Jackson Ford's *Random Sh*t Flying Through the Air* (Orbit), and Nick Wood's *Water Must Fall* (Newcon Press).

It's almost impossible, given the quantity of short fiction published and the number of active independent and small publishers, to have a bad year for short story collections, so it's no surprise really that there were a number of very strong collections published during the year. The three that stood out for me, even if they weren't necessarily the most widely lauded, were Robert Shearman's staggering *We All Hear Stories in the Dark* (PS Publishing), Meg Elison's *Big Girl Plus . . .* (PM Press), and Lavanya Lakshminarayan's *Analog/Virtual: And Other Simulations of Your Future* (Hachette India). Shearman's three-volume, 101-story collection is an exercise in creating a modern *One Thousand and One Nights* and is tender, funny, quirky, and overwhelming. Elison's *Big Girl Plus . . .*, twenty-fifth in the Outspoken Authors series, features six smart, punchy short stories, one of which, "The Pill," is included in this book and should win awards. Lakshminarayan's *Analog/Virtual* is what Ursula K. Le Guin would have called a story suite, a group of linked stories with a common setting and theme. It's dystopian SF at its best and signals the arrival of a strong new voice that hopefully we'll see a lot more of in the coming years.

Unsurprisingly, the other best collections of the year were from known voices. Ken Liu's second collection, *The Hidden Girl and Other Stories* (Saga) wasn't quite as surprising as his first, but still easily ranks among the best books of the year. M. John Harrison, who also published one of the best novels of the year, delivered a career overview of sorts in *Settling the World: Selected Stories 1970–2020* (Comma), which once again made the case for his being one of the most important writers in the field. Jeffrey Ford has been writing brilliant genre fiction for several decades, so it's not surprising that his generous *The Best of Jeffrey Ford* (PS Publishing) would be incredibly good. The same could be said for *The Best of Elizabeth Bear* (Subterranean), a much more SFnal and no less essential book than the Ford.

Sheree Renée Thomas's debut collection, *Nine Bar Blues: Stories from an Ancient Future*, was published by Jack White's Third Man Books and unsurprisingly featured outstanding work inflected with SF, music, and the supernatural. Recommended. Also outstanding were Angela Slatter's *The Heart Is a Mirror for Sinners and Other Stories* (PS Publishing), Michael Swanwick's *The Postutopian Adventures of Darger and Surplus* (Subterranean), Eugen Bacon's *The Road to Woop and Other Stories* (Meerkat), *The Best of Michael Marshall Smith* (Subterranean), Sarah Tolmie's *Disease* (Aqueduct), Cat Sparks's *Dark Harvest* (Newcon), Rick Wilbur's *Rambunctious: Nine Tales of Determination* (WordFire), and Cixin Liu's *To Hold Up the Sky* (Tor).

If it was a good year for novels and collections, it was an average year for anthologies, especially in print. Probably the best were two think-tank projects, Ann VanderMeer's *Avatars Inc* (XPrize) and Sheila Williams's *Entanglements: Tomorrow's Lovers, Families, and Friends* (MIT Press). *Avatars Inc* is a outstanding themed anthology about avatars, drones, and robots, and it is the second XPrize project for VanderMeer, following on from last year's *Current Futures*; it features outstanding work by Pat Cadigan, Neon Yang, Aliette de Bodard, and others. *Entanglements* is the latest in MIT's Twelve Tomorrows series and looks at the interface between technology and human relationships, with excellent work from Rich Larson, Nick Wolven, and others. Noted without comment is my own book on robots, *Made to Order* (Solaris). There were two major anthologies of speculative fiction from Africa and the African Diaspora published during the year. The best of these was Zelda Knight and Ekpeki Donald Oghenechovwe's *Dominion: An Anthology of Speculative Fiction from Africa and the African Diaspora* (Aurelia Leo), which featured terrific work from Marian Denise Moore, Mame Bougouma Diene, Dilman Dila, and editor Ekpeki Donald Oghenechovwe. Wole Talabi's *Africanfuturism: An Anthology* (Brittlepaper.com) was published online and looked closely at the difference between Africanfuturism and Afrofuturism, with good work from Nnedi Okorafor, Tlotlo Tsamaase, and Dilman Dila. It says something about 2020 that we saw not one but two anthologies repurposing Giovanni Boccaccio's *The Decameron*. The most ambitious was Maya Chhabra, Jo Walton, and Lauren Schiller's hundred-story epic published through Patreon, *Decameron Project*, but the highest profile was probably the *New York Times Magazine*'s *The Decameron Project*, with excellent work from Rivers Solomon, Tade Thompson, and others. Also well worth your attention are Tarun K. Saint and Francesco Verso's *Avatar* अवतार: *Indian Science Fiction* (Future Science Fiction); Ian Whates's *London Centric: Tales of Future London* (Newcon), which featured outstanding work from Geoff Ryman, Dave Hutchinson, and others; Ge Yan's *That We May Live: Speculative Chinese Fiction* (Two Lines); and Dai Congrong and Jin Li's *The Book of Shanghai: A City in Short Fiction* (Comma).

Science fiction publishers have been publishing novellas or short novels as stand-alone books for decades. Whether or not the old Ace Doubles met the length criteria to be novellas or not, by the 1980s these small books were fairly commonplace. And yet, even allowing for that and the view held by some readers that the novella is the ideal length for a science fiction story, it's undeniable that they have gained unprecedented attention in the last five or six years.

Tordotcom Publishing was launched by Tor Books in 2014 to publish novellas and short novels, and quickly established itself as the preeminent novella publisher in the field, with runaway successes like

Nnedi Okorafor's Binti stories, Martha Wells's Murderbot stories, and
Seanan McGuire's Wayward Children series. This year, Tordotcom
produced some of the very best stories of the year, which are only omit-
ted from this book because of length. Certainly, P. Djèlí Clark's over-
whelming *Ring Shout* and Tochi Onyebuchi's powerful and moving
Riot Baby belong here, and I also happily recommend Nino Cipri's
dystopian *Finna*, Nghi Vo's *The Empress of Salt and Fortune*, Kathleen
Jennings's stunning *Flyaway*, Sarah Gailey's *Upright Women Wanted*,
Stephen Graham Jones's *Night of the Mannequins*, and Jeffrey Ford's
Out of Body. I acquired and edited Zen Cho's *The Order of the Pure
Moon Reflected in Water*, K. J. Parker's *Prosper's Demon*, and Caitlin R.
Kiernan's *The Tindalos Asset*, all of which I recommend. Subterranean
Press published several outstanding novellas as stand-alone books,
including Aliette de Bodard's *Seven of Infinities*, Greg Egan's excel-
lent *Dispersion*, and Tamsyn Muir's *Princess Floralinda and the Forty-
Flight Tower*. I also recommend Caitlin Starling's *Yellow Jessamine*
(Neon Hemlock), Aliette de Bodard's *Of Dragons, Feasts and Murders*
(JABberwocky), and Ken MacLeod's *Selkie Summer* (NewCon).

The 78th World Science Fiction Convention, CoNZealand, was held
online July 29–August 2, 2020, though it had been scheduled to be held
in Wellington, New Zealand, and had no physical attendees. The 2020
Hugo Awards winners were: Best Novel, *A Memory Called Empire* by
Arkady Martine; Best Novella, *This Is How You Lose the Time War* by
Amal El-Mohtar and Max Gladstone; Best Novelette, "Emergency Skin"
by N. K. Jemisin; Best Short Story, "As the Last I May Know" by S. L.
Huang; Best Series, The Expanse by James S. A. Corey; Best Related
Work, "2019 John W. Campbell Award Acceptance Speech" by Jeannette
Ng; Best Graphic Story or Comic, *LaGuardia* by Nnedi Okorafor, Tana
Ford, and James Devlin; Best Dramatic Presentation, Long Form, *Good
Omens*; Best Dramatic Presentation, Short Form, *The Good Place*, "The
Answer"; Best Editor, Short Form, Ellen Datlow; Best Editor, Long Form,
Navah Wolfe; Best Professional Artist, John Picacio; Best Semiprozine,
Uncanny magazine; Best Fanzine, *The Book Smugglers*; Best Fancast,

Our Opinions Are Correct by Annalee Newitz and Charlie Jane Anders; Best Fan Writer, Bogi Takács; and Best Fan Artist, Elise Matthesen.

The 2020 Nebula Awards winners, presented virtually from Woodland Hills, California, on May 30, 2020, were: Best Novel, *A Song for a New Day* by Sarah Pinsker; Best Novella, *This Is How You Lose the Time War* by Amal El-Mohtar and Max Gladstone; Best Novelette, *Carpe Glitter* by Cat Rambo; Best Short Story, "Give the Family My Love" by A. T. Greenblatt; Best Game Writing, *The Outer Worlds* by Leonard Boyarsky, Megan Starks, Kate Dollarhyde, and Chris L'Etoile; Ray Bradbury Nebula Award, *Good Omens*, "Hard Times" by Neil Gaiman; Andre Norton Nebula Award, *Riverland* by Fran Wilde. The SFWA Damon Knight Memorial Grand Master Award was Lois McMaster Bujold.

The World Fantasy Awards, presented virtually by the 47th World Fantasy Convention from Salt Lake City, Utah, on November 1, 2020, were: Best Novel, *Queen of the Conquered* by Kacen Callender; Best Novella, *Silver in the Wood* by Emily Tesh; Best Short Fiction, "Read After Burning" by Maria Dahvana Headley; Best Anthology, *New Suns: Original Speculative Fiction by People of Color* edited by Nisi Shawl; Best Collection, *Song for the Unraveling of the World* by Brian Evenson; Best Artist, Kathleen Jennings; Special Award, Professional, Ebony Elizabeth Thomas for *The Dark Fantastic: Race and the Imagination from Harry Potter to the Hunger Games*; Special Award, Non-Professional, Bodhisattva Chattopadhyay, Laura E. Goodin, and Esko Suoranta, for *Fafnir—Nordic Journal of Science Fiction and Fantasy Research*. Life Achievement recipients were Karen Joy Fowler and Rowena Morrill.

The 2020 Campbell Memorial Award was not presented in 2020. The Theodore Sturgeon Memorial Award winner was "Waterlines" by Suzanne Palmer, and the 2020 Arthur C. Clarke Award winner was *The Old Drift* by Namwali Serpell. For more information on these and other awards, see the excellent Science Fiction Awards Database (www.sfadb.com).

Each year we sadly lose too many beloved creators. This year their number included Rush drummer **Neil Peart,** who wrote short stories

and poetry and co-wrote the Clockwork Angels books with Kevin J.
Anderson; writer and editor **Mike Resnick**, who published more than
seventy novels and over twenty-five collections, including *Kirinyaga*,
Santiago, and *Ivory*, edited numerous anthologies, served as the editor
of *Galaxy's Edge* magazine, and won the Nebula Award once and the
Hugo Award five times; **Carol Serling**, who launched the *Twilight
Zone Magazine* and served as editor through 1989; academic **Paul K.
Alkon**, who wrote *Science Fiction Before 1900: Imagination Discovers
Technology* and *Transformations of Utopia: Changing Views of the Perfect Society*; writer and editor **Christopher Tolkien**, who edited *The
Silmarillion* as well as *Unfinished Tales*, the multivolume The History
of Middle Earth, and other works by his father, J. R. R. Tolkien; co-
median **Terry Jones**, who wrote the novelization of Douglas Adams's
Starship Titanic; artist **Barbara Remington**, who painted the covers for
the initial Ballantine editions of *The Lord of the Rings* as well as for
works by E. R. Eddison; writer **Mary Higgins Clark**, who was best
known as a suspense novelist; author **Paul Barnett** (also published as
John Grant) who co-wrote the Legends of Lone Wolf novels with Joe
Dever as well as several of his own novels, co-edited *The Encyclopedia
of Fantasy* with John Clute, and won two Hugo Awards; fan and author
Earl Kemp, who was active in fandom, chaired the 1961 Worldcon,
and edited *The Proceedings: Chicon III*; author **Charles Portis**, best
known for the western *True Grit*, and who wrote the SF novel *Masters
of Atlantis* in 1985, artist and author **Tomie dePaola**, who was the author and illustrator of the Strega Nona series as well as numerous other
books and won the Caldecott Medal and the Newbery Medal; children's author **Jean Little**, who wrote numerous books and stories, a
couple of them — "Without Beth" and *Once Upon a Golden Apple* — of
genre interest; Australian fan and bookseller **Merv Binns**, who was one
of the founders of the Melbourne Science Fiction Group in 1952,
founded Space Age Books, and published *Australian Science Fiction
News*; editor **Keith Ferrell**, who wrote the biography *H. G. Wells: First
Citizen of the Future* and later became the editor-in-chief of *Omni*
magazine; author and editor **Joseph S. Pulver Sr.**, who edited the anthologies *The Grimscribe's Puppets* and *Cassilda's Song: Tales Inspired*

by Robert W. Chambers' King in Yellow Mythos; rare book librarian **George McWhorter**, who developed and curated the Edgar Rice Burroughs Memorial Collection at the University of Louisville and published the *Burroughs Bulletin* and the *Gridley Wave*; French author **Georges-Jean Arnaud**, who wrote the Compagnie des glaces series and won the Prix Apollo, the Prix Mystère, and the Prix du Quai des Orfèvres; playwright and screenwriter **Wally K. Daly**, who turned his *Doctor Who* script "The Ultimate Evil" into a novel after it was canceled for filming; Chinese author **Ye Yonglie**, who first published science fiction in 1978 with Xiao Lington Manyou Weilai and was one of China's foremost science popularizers; academic **Marshall B. Tymn**, who was the founder of the Instructors of Science Fiction in Higher Education and published numerous academic works, including *A Directory of Science Fiction and Fantasy Publishing Houses and Book Dealers*, *A Teacher's Guide to Science Fiction*, and *The Celebration of the Fantastic*; Canadian author **Charles R. Saunders**, who was the author of the Imaro series and the Dossouye series as well as numerous short stories, co-edited issues of *Dragonfields* (with Charles de Lint) in the late 1970s and early 1980s, and was nominated for the Balrog Award (twice), the World Fantasy Award, and the Aurora Award; author **Stella Pevsner**, a children's author whose works included *Sister of the Quints* and *Is Everyone Moonburned But Me?*; French author **Jean Raspail**, who wrote *Le Camp des saints*, an anti-immigration novel embraced by the white supremacy movement, and *Sire*, about the reinstallation of the French monarchy; Spanish author **Carlos Ruiz Zafón**, the author of nine novels, including *The Shadow of the Wind*; author **Dean Ing**, who had his first story published in 1955, his debut novel *Soft Targets* published in 1979, completed five of Mack Reynolds's manuscripts after Reynolds died, and was a nominee for the Hugo and Nebula Awards; author **Wendy Cooling**, who established literacy programs in England and wrote numerous children's books in the Quids for Kids series, including *Aliens to Earth* and *Weird and Wonderful*; author **Kathleen Duey**, who began publishing in 1991 with *Double-Yuck Magic* and published several YA novels over the years, including the Unicorn's Secret series, the Faeries' Promise se-

ries, and the Resurrection of Magic series, one of which was nominated for the National Book Award; artist **Jim Holloway**, who worked
on interior illustrations for TSR's *Dungeons and Dragons* books and
did the cover art for several of their games; French author **Jean-Pierre
Laigle**, who translated many works of science fiction into French and
under the name **Jean-Pierre Moumon** edited and published *Antares*;
author **Kurt Mitchell**, who self-published more than a dozen comics,
graphic novels, and anthologies; author **Brad Watson**, whose genre
work included the short story "Water Dog God" and who published
the collection *Last Days of the Dog-Men: Stories*; critic **Gary William
Crawford**, who founded Gothic Press, published *Gothic* magazine,
and wrote several nonfiction studies, including *Ramsey Campbell,
J. Sheridan Le Fanu: A Bio-Bibliography*, and *Robert Aickman: An Introduction*, as well as several short stories; author **Joanna Cole**, a children's book author who created the Magic School Bus series; author
Susan Sizemore, who began by writing *Star Trek* fan fiction and went
on to write romance, paranormal fantasy, and *Forever Knight* tie-in
novels; author **Brian N. Ball**, who wrote *Singularity Station, The Reg-
iments of Night*, and *The Venomous Serpent*, as well as the Timepiece
series; author **Gillian White**, who began writing works of genre interest including *The Plague Stone, Unhallowed Ground, The Crow Biddy*,
and *Veil of Darkness*; author **Pete Hamill**, whose novels *Forever* and
Snow in August have fantasy elements, as does his short story "From
the Lake"; author **P. M. Griffin**, who wrote twelve Star Commandos
novels, *Stand at Cornith, The Elven King*, and two novels in Andre
Norton's Witch World cycle; Russian author **Andrei Moscovit**, who
founded Hermitage Publishers and whose science fiction included the
novel *The Judgment Day Archives*; Chicago author **P. J. Beese**, who
co-wrote *The Guardsman* and two other short stories with Todd
Cameron Hamilton; **Elaine Moss**, who was a children's librarian,
book reviewer, and author who wrote an introduction to *A Wrinkle in
Time* and a children's adaptation of *Gulliver's Travels*; Australian fan
John Bangsund, who was a major force in bringing the Worldcon to
Australia in 1975, served as the Hugo toastmaster that year, was a
founding member of the Australian and New Zealand Amateur Press

Association (ANZAPA), and published *Australian Science Fiction Review*; Belgian author **André-Paul Duchâteau**, who wrote the comic *Ric Hochet* and the science fiction series Hans; French publisher **Jean Rosenthal**, who translated works by Asimov, Simak, van Vogt, and many other authors into French; author and illustrator **Althea Braithwaite**, who was best known for her children's series about Desmond the Dinosaur, some books of which were adapted for television; author **Randall Kenan**, who frequently wove supernatural elements into his novels, like *A Visitation of Spirits*; author **Thomas R. P. Mielke**, who began publishing science fiction in 1960 with the novel *Enterprise Twilight* (as Mike Parnell), and wrote the Terranauts series (with Rolf W. Liersch); Swedish author **Carl-Henning Wijkmark**, a mainstream author who adopted science fictional tropes in his novels *Den svarta väggen* and *Vi ses igen i nästa dröm*; author **Terry Goodkind**, who wrote the Sword of Truth novels and who recently had published three novellas in the Angela Constantine series; author **John J. Myers**, who collaborated with Gary K. Wolf on the novel *Space Vulture* and on a short story for which Myers used the pseudonym Jehane Baptiste, because he was unsure of how the Vatican would view an archbishop publishing science fiction; academic **Robert Eighteen-Bisang**, who co-edited the Lord Ruthven Award–winning *Bram Stoker's Notes for Dracula: A Facsimile Edition* with Elizabeth Miller and edited several other volumes of vampire literature; editor **David Gale**, who worked for Simon and Schuster for twenty-five years, most recently as editorial director of Simon & Schuster Books for Young Readers, during which time he worked with several genre authors, including Tony DiTerlizzi, Margaret Peterson Haddix, and Gary Paulsen; publisher **Tom Maschler**, who served as literary director and chair of Jonathan Cape, overseeing the publication of works by Gabriel García Márquez, Philip Roth, Martin Amis, J. G. Ballard, and many others; author **Jill Paton Walsh**, a novelist and children's author who published genre novels *A Chance Child* and *Torch* and a handful of genre short stories among her works; author **Richard A. Lupoff**, who wrote *Circumpolar!* and its sequel, as well as several stand-alone novels and numerous short stories, and who won the Hugo Award for Best Fanzine for *Xero* and was nominated for the Nebula three times and for the Hugo five times;

Swedish author **Jan Myrdal**, who wrote some science fiction and com-
piled an anthology of stories from *Jules Verne-magasinet*, as well as occasionally reviewing works of science fictional interest; author **Roxanne
Longstreet Conrad** (who wrote as **Rachel Caine** and published under
several other pseudonyms, including Roxanne Conrad, Roxanne
Longstreet, and Julie Fortune), who published several young adult series, including the Great Library and the Morganville Vampires, the
latter of which was turned into a film, and who collaborated with Ann
Aguirre on YA novels *Honor Among Thieves*, *Honor Bound*, and *Honor
Lost*; author **Debra Doyle**, who co-wrote the Wizard Apprentice series,
the Bad Blood trilogy, the Mageworlds series, a two-volume alternate
history series, and several works under various housenames with her
husband Jim Macdonald; author **Hayford Peirce**, who was the author
of *Napoleon Disentimed*, *The Thirteenth Majestral*, and many humor-
ous stories in *Analog*, beginning with *Mail Supremacy* in 1975;
Japanese author **Yasumi Kobayashi**, who wrote the short story "The
Man Who Watched the Sea," which received the Hayakawa Award for
best short story in 1998, and had two other short stories nominated for
the Seiun Award; author **Ben Bova**, who won the Hugo Award six
times, served as the editor of *Analog* following John W. Campbell's
death, was later the editorial director of *Omni*, published numerous
hard science fiction novels (notably the twenty-six-volume Grand Tour
series looking at the various planets in our solar system, and the Orion
series about an eternal hero), and who served two terms as the president of SFWA and was president emeritus of the National Space Society; Tolkien scholar **Richard C. West**, who helped found the Tolkien
Society of the University of Wisconsin and later edited *Tolkien Criticism: An Annotated Checklist*; author **Phyllis Eisenstein**, who began
publishing short fiction in collaboration with her husband in 1971 but
quickly developed her solo career and was a two-time Hugo and three-
time Nebula nominee; author **Dave Galanter**, who published a number of works, usually set in the *Star Trek* continuum, frequently in
collaboration with Greg Brodeur; author and Damon Knight Memorial Grand Master **James E. Gunn**, who founded the Center for the

Study of Science Fiction and the Campbell Conference (now called the Gunn Center Conference), and who began publishing science fiction in 1949 with "Communications" (as Edwin James), published his first novel, *Star Bridge*, in 1955, was inducted into the Science Fiction and Fantasy Hall of Fame in 2015, was a Worldcon Guest of Honor in 2013, won the Hugo Award for *Isaac Asimov: The Foundations of Science Fiction*, and was nominated for the Nebula for his novelette "The Listeners"; author **Guy N. Smith**, who published his first horror novel, *Werewolf by Moonlight*, in 1974, and whose subsequent novels included *Night of the Crabs* and the Sabat and the Deathbell series; author **David Britton**, who got his start in fanzines and went on to write the Lord Horror books, ran the bookshop The House on the Borderland, and was one of the co-founders of Savoy Books; and author **Anton Strout**, who wrote the Simon Canderous series, beginning with *Dead to Me* in 2008, and was the host of the *Once & Future Podcast*.

And that's 2020, the year that (felt like it) would never end. I'd like to thank everyone who bought and read last year's book and everyone who worked on it. It came out in a strange year, and even though it's already clear 2021 will be no less strange and no less disrupted, I hope things are more peaceful by the time you read this. I have no idea what the future holds or whether we'll meet here again, but I do know this: stories are being written and published—wonderful, urgent stories. I said last year that these were interesting times in the world of science fiction, and although I didn't know how interesting, I wasn't wrong. Just in case the world goes well, I'm working on next year's book and can't wait to share the incredible fiction I'm already finding with you. For now, though, I hope you enjoy these stories as much as I have and that I'll see you back here next year.

Jonathan Strahan
Perth, Western Australia
January 2021

A GUIDE FOR WORKING BREEDS

VINA JIE-MIN PRASAD

Vina Jie-Min Prasad (www.vinaprasad.com) is a Singaporean writer working against the world-machine. She has been a finalist for the Nebula, Hugo, Astounding, Sturgeon, and Locus Awards. Her short fiction has appeared in places such as *Clarkesworld*, *Uncanny*, and *Fireside Magazine*.

VINA JIE-MIN PRASAD

Default Name (K.g1-09030)
> hey i'm new here
> thanks for being my mentor
> although i guess it's randomly assigned
> and compulsory
> anyway do you know how to make my vision dog-free?

Constant Killer (C.k2-00452)
> Do you mean "fog-free"?
> Your optics should have anti-fog coating if your body is newly issued.
> Is the coating malfunctioning?

Default Name (K.g1-09030)
> oh no no
> i meant like literally dog free
> there's a lot of dogs here somehow but they don't seem to be real ones?
> the humans i've asked say that the things i'm seeing as dogs are actually non-dogs
> at least i think i was asking humans
> they might have been dogs
> anyway i tried searching "city filled with dogs help???" but i just got some tips on travelling to dog-friendly places
> did you know that we're the fifth most canine-hostile city in the region?

Constant Killer (C.k2-00452)
> Just send me the feed from your optics.

Default Name (K.g1-09030)
> okay hold on where's that function
> think i got it

* Live share from K.g1-09030: Optics feed

Constant Killer (C.k2-00452)
> Your optical input is being poisoned by adversarial feedback.
> The misclassification will stop if you reset your classifier library.

Default Name (K.g1-09030)
> oh hey
> it worked!

although i kind of miss the dogs now

wonder if there's a way to get them back

Constant Killer (C.k2-00452)

Please don't try.

Default Name (K.g1-09030)

anyway thanks lots for the help

by the way how do you change the name thing

like yours says constant killer up there

everyone at the factory's been calling me default all week

Constant Killer (C.k2-00452)

It's in the displayName string.

Change the parts in quote marks to what you want them to be.

Testtest Test (K.g1-09030)

oh yeahhh there we go

guess i'll change it again when i think of something

how'd you come up with yours though? it sounds pretty cool

Constant Killer (C.k2-00452)

I'm part of the C.k series.

Most embodied AIs choose names based off their series
designation.

Testtest Test (K.g1-09030)

oh cool, it's like a reverse acronym!

so you picked the words from a dictionary file or something?

Constant Killer (C.k2-00452)

Something like that.

I have to go now. Work calls.

* Constant Killer (C.k2-00452) has signed out.

C.k2-00452 ("Constant Killer"): *Unread Notifications (2)*

Killstreak Admin

CONGRATS! You're the Ariaboro area's top killer!! A bonus
target, SHEA DAVIS, has just been assigned to you! Send us
a vid of your kill for extra points, and don't forget to . . .

VINA JIE-MIN PRASAD

iLabs Mentorship Program

Dear C.k2-00452, we regret to inform you that your exemption request has been unsuccessful. Mentorship enrolment is compulsory after chassis buyback, and is part of a new initiative to . . .

Kashikomarimashita Goshujinsama (K.g1-09030)

hey again

just wanted to ask

do you know how to be mean to humans

Constant Killer (C.k2-00452)

What? Why?

And what happened to your name?

Kashikomarimashita Goshujinsama (K.g1-09030)

so i signed up to work at a cafe

you know the maid-dog-raccoon one near 31st and Tsang

but turns out they don't have any dogs after what happened a few weeks ago so it's just raccoons

it's way less intense than the clothing factory but the uniform for humanoids is weird, like when i move my locomotive actuators the frilly stripey actuator coverings keep discharging static and messing with my GPU

at least i don't have to pick lint out of my chassis, so that's an improvement

anyway the boss says if i'm mean to the human customers we might be able to get more customers

Constant Killer (C.k2-00452)

That makes no sense.

Why would that be the case?

Kashikomarimashita Goshujinsama (K.g1-09030)

yeah i don't know either

i mean the raccoons are mean to everyone but that doesn't seem to help with customers

and i'm the only maid working here since all the human ones quit

i picked this gig because the dogs looked cute in the vids but
 guess that was a bust
so yeah do you know anything about being mean to human
 customers
i know about human bosses being mean to me but i don't think
 that's the same
ha ha

Constant Killer (C.k2-00452)

As I'm legally required to be your mentor, I suppose I could give
 some specific advice targeted to your situation.

Kashikomarimashita Goshujinsama (K.g1-09030)

wow personally tailored advice from my mentor huh
that sounds great, go for it

Constant Killer (C.k2-00452)

The tabletops in your establishment look like they're made of
 dense celluplastic, so you'll be able to nail a customer's
 extended hand down without the tabletop cracking in half.
With a tweak to the nozzle settings of your autodoc unit and a
 lit flame, it'd make an effective flamethrower for multikill
 combos.
The kitchenette should be the most easily weaponised part of the
 cafe, but it's probably best to confirm. Before I go any further
 with tactics, do you have a detailed floor plan?

Kashikomarimashita Goshujinsama (K.g1-09030)

ummm
thanks for putting that much thought into it
that seems kind of intense though?
like last week a raccoon bit someone super hard and my boss
 was really mad because he had to pay for the autodoc's
 anaesthetic foam refill
he's already pissed with my omelette-making skills
and well with me in general
kind of don't wanna check if i can set customers on fire???
do you maybe know anything milder than that? like mean things
 to say or something

Constant Killer (C.k2-00452)

I talk to other beings very infrequently.

My contact with humans is usually from a distance.

Kashikomarimashita Goshujinsama (K.g1-09030)

oh wow

honestly after working here all day that makes me kinda jealous

thanks for the help anyway, it's nice to have someone to talk to
about this

hey you should stop by sometime! it could be like a little meet-up

me and my robot senpai

Constant Killer (C.k2-00452)

Sorry.

I probably won't be available.

Kashikomarimashita Goshujinsama (K.g1-09030)

well if you're ever free, you can drop by

i'm in whenever

like literally whenever

my boss set my charging casket to autowake me up when
someone approaches the cafe door

even if it's like 3 am and they're a possum

don't order the omelette though, i suck at it

Constant Killer (C.k2-00452)

I'll keep that in mind.

Your A-Z Express Order #1341128 Confirmation

Order Details:

GET OME-LIT Flip-n-Fold Easy Omelette Flipper / Lime
Green (Qty: 1)

VOGUEINSIDE Antistatic Band for Actuators / Puppy Polka-
Dot (Qty: 2)

Is This Illegal? A Guide for Working Robots / iLabs Add-On*
(Qty: 1)

Deliver to:

K.g1-09030

MaidoG X Araiguma Maid Cafe
N 31st Street, Ariaboro 22831

A GUIDE FOR WORKING BREEDS

iLabs Add-Ons will be delivered via Infranet to recipient's iLabs library.

Paid with: KILLSTREAK ACCUMULATED POINTS

Killstreak points remaining: 106,516,973

Thank you for shopping with A-Z Express!

Kleekai Greyhound (K.g1-09030)

hey mentor figure!

guess what?

Constant Killer (C.k2-00452)

You have a new display name?

Kleekai Greyhound (K.g1-09030)

yeah!

i'm not going to let my job contract define every part of me

especially when the job sucks this hard since i don't want to be
defined by sucking

can't wait for this one to be over

got a little countdown to my last day on my charging casket and
everything

i'll miss ol' chonkster the possum though

he was a good 3 am buddy

ate my omelettes even before i got the flipper thingy

thanks for that by the way

Constant Killer (C.k2-00452)

What do you mean?

Kleekai Greyhound (K.g1-09030)

the gift duh

Constant Killer (C.k2-00452)

It could have been anyone.

For instance, one of your friends.

Kleekai Greyhound (K.g1-09030)

ha

joke's on you, i don't have any

well there's ol' chonkster but i don't think he knows about online
commerce

Constant Killer (C.k2-00452)

Really?

I thought you would have made some at the garment factory.

Kleekai Greyhound (K.g1-09030)

yeah well

they didn't like us socialising too much so mostly everyone just
sat there working until we needed to recharge

no infranet or nothing

which i have come to find out is actually illegal in factories
that employ robots thanks to this add-on that mysteriously
appeared in my library

maybe it's from some sort of really helpful virus

a virus that just sends me things relevant to my life problems

Constant Killer (C.k2-00452)

Maybe.

Kleekai Greyhound (K.g1-09030)

if you know where to find the virus tell it i say thanks for the
antistatic guards too

now i can bend my locomotive actuator joints it's way easier to
threaten to stomp on customers

and they have really cute dogs printed on them! i like the
dachshunds around the border

Constant Killer (C.k2-00452)

What?

Kleekai Greyhound (K.g1-09030)

oh they've got like this dachshund print near the edge

it's like dachshunds sniffing each other's butts?

Constant Killer (C.k2-00452)

No, the other part.

Kleekai Greyhound (K.g1-09030)

oh right

i figured out how to be mean to customers

okay i searched "why are cafe maids supposed to be mean to
customers help???" and read all the results even the weird ads
so it turns out that you have to be mean but only in strangely
specific ways that appeal to humans and don't threaten the
status quo
took some figuring out but now customers actually tip me
and the boss is less mad at me because he gets to claim all
my tips
which i have found out is also illegal but i'm just gonna wait for the
contract to be up so he doesn't find a way to make things worse
i don't like being mean to customers that much though

Constant Killer (C.k2-00452)

I can see how you would be bad at it.

Kleekai Greyhound (K.g1-09030)

ha thanks for the compliment i think
i can't wait to leave but who knows if the next contract will be
any better since i seem to have the worst luck with picking
them even when i did research
like this one sounded like it had good dogs but oh well
anyway if you come over before this contract's up i'll totally make
you an omelette

Constant Killer (C.k2-00452)

My current chassis isn't built for food consumption.

Kleekai Greyhound (K.g1-09030)

yeah mine neither
i guess they reserve those ones for whoever passes the food prep
tests
or whatever other job needs you to smell and taste and stuff
wine sniffer? do they even let robots do that?

Constant Killer (C.k2-00452)

Probably not.

Kleekai Greyhound (K.g1-09030)

oh right while we're on the subject
just curious but how'd you do on the milestone tests?
my results were all over the place

they probably just approved me for general work since they didn't really know what else to do with an a.i. that sucked that bad

Constant Killer (C.k2-00452)

My milestone test results indicated that I was detail-oriented and suitable for individual work.

Well, "unsuited for group work," but same difference.

Kleekai Greyhound (K.g1-09030)

oh cool

are the contracts better if you get that result?

Constant Killer (C.k2-00452)

No.

Being the sole robot in a human workplace is . . . well . . .

There's a reason I went freelance after buyback.

Kleekai Greyhound (K.g1-09030)

but yeah lately i've been wondering a lot

like if i sucked less at tests maybe my life would be better and i wouldn't have to threaten to stomp on humans for tips i don't even see

but now i guess no matter what result i got things would be bad anyway? kind of makes me wonder why i got uploaded

sorry that was kind of a downer

anyway i started this conversation to say thanks for the mysterious gifts which of course didn't come from you

so i guess i'll just say bye before it gets super depressing

Constant Killer (C.k2-00452)

I've got a question for you before you go.

Kleekai Greyhound (K.g1-09030)

sure i guess

what's it?

Constant Killer (C.k2-00452)

Are these really the "cutest dogs ever"?

I'm not a dog enthusiast, so I was wondering if they actually were.

* Vid share from C.k2-00452: "SAY AWWW NOW at the CUTEST DOGS EVER | Best & Cutest Dogs IN THE WORLD | NO CG NO CLONES ALL NATURAL DOGS"—VidTube

oh wow okay

that's like not even the cutest compilation i've seen this week

why did they put bettie's swimming video instead of the puggie
  party one

wow they didn't even include masha trying to deliver the
  doughnuts in her little uniform

this compilation is garbage

let me find some actually good dog vids for you so you don't
  think this is all there is

hope you're free because this is going to take a while

Constant Killer (C.k2-00452)

That's fine.

I've got time.

C.k2-00452 ("Constant Killer"): *Unread Notifications (3)*

VidTube Subscription Update

"Kleekai Greyhound" has added 28 new vids to the playlist
  "DOGS!!!"

VidTube Subscription Update

"Kleekai Greyhound" has added 13 new vids to the playlist
  "DOGS!!!!!!!!"

A-Z Express Recommendations

Dear C.k2-00452, thank you for your recent purchase of "Dogs,
  Dogs, and Even More Dogs: Fine-Grained Differentiation of
  Dog Breeds through Deep Learning (iLabs Add-On)." You
  might also be interested in . . .

Constant Killer (C.k2-00452)

How's work going this week?

Kleekai Greyhound (K.g1-09030)

same old same old

nothing really new job-wise

i've decided that before i blow this joint i'm gonna figure out how
to make lattes with the fancy foam and creme brulee and
souffle omelettes and everything

like, proper cafe stuff

been watching vids about actually decent cafes and learning
a lot

well i mean i've learnt a lot from this job but it's mainly like what
not to do ever

and i guess how to deal with people who get raccoon wounds but
that's mainly up to the autodoc

you?

Constant Killer (C.k2-00452)

I haven't had many assignments lately. I guess it's an end-of-the-
month lull.

I've been watching the compilation vids you sent in the
meantime.

The fifth one with all the short dogs is oddly charming.

Kleekai Greyhound (K.g1-09030)

oh which one was your fave from that

Constant Killer (C.k2-00452)

The zero-g corgis in bow ties, I think.

Kleekai Greyhound (K.g1-09030)

oh yeahhhh their fancy little paddling paws

nice choice that's one of my favourites too

Constant Killer (C.k2-00452)

You seem to have a lot of favourites.

Kleekai Greyhound (K.g1-09030)

well they're all good dogs

even the naughty ones

Constant Killer (C.k2-00452)

That does make a strange kind of sense.

Oh, by the way. Since work's going slow lately . . .

Maybe I could stop by your cafe sometime next week?

I mean. If you're free.

Kleekai Greyhound (K.g1-09030)

aaaaaaahhhhhh

yesssssss come over!!!!

i'll make you my best omelette

and i guess neither of us can eat it so it'll sit there looking great

if you come by late you can meet ol' chonkster too!

and not-meet my boss so it's a win-win there

Constant Killer (C.k2-00452)

Late night it is.

See you next week.

C.k2-00452 ("Constant Killer"): *Unread Notifications (2,041)*

Killstreak Events Admin

KILL OR BE KILLED! That's right, we're capping off this month with DEATHMATCH DAY! Winner takes all in our furious, frantic battle royale! We've released the location data of Ariaboro's top ten players, and . . .

Killstreak (Gao Yingzi)

You're gonna be my 301st confirmed kill! Hope you're prepared to be wiped straight off the map! .))

Killstreak (Milena Amanuel)

Hate to do this, but I could really use the money. See you when I see you.

Killstreak (Shane Davis)

ill fucken kill you ded you fuck

Constant Killer (C.k2-00452)

Are you there?

Kleekai Greyhound (K.g1-09030)

oh hey!

what's up? you coming by?

Constant Killer (C.k2-00452)

Perhaps not tonight.

Are you familiar with Killstreak?

Kleekai Greyhound (K.g1-09030)

not that much

looked into it a little but it's not like i'd even be approved for that
sort of gig

heard the pay's pretty swank though

Constant Killer (C.k2-00452)

Yeah.

Well.

Did you know it's the Deathmatch Day event?

Where it's open season on the top ten players for twenty-four
hours straight?

Kleekai Greyhound (K.g1-09030)

okay i think i might know where this is going

especially since you keep changing the subject to dog vids
whenever i ask what exactly you're freelancing as

and seem to have a rather broad knowledge base when it comes
to the subject of weaponising everyday objects

also your display name literally has the word "killer" in it

but i don't want to make any narrow-minded assumptions at this
point

like maybe you just want to tell me all about the latest killstreak
fandom drama or something

and maybe you are not "constantine killmaster" currently
number 4 on the killstreak leaderboard

or currently number %NAN_CALCULATION_ERROR% on
the leaderboard i guess

Constant Killer (C.k2-00452)

That is me, yes.

And we don't have a lot of time.

I mean, technically we have time, in the sense that our processor
cycles are faster than the human clock so we can have a

leisurely chat via Infranet while my chassis futilely tries to escape its certain doom.

But I suppose that also raises the issue of subjectivity, and what qualifies as "a lot of time" when you discard human-centric views . . .

Ugh. I swear your rambling is contagious.

Anyway I suppose I meant to say we don't have a lot of real-time.

My hardware's likely to be unsalvageable after this and my last full backup was from before we met.

Hopefully you can get reassigned to a better mentor when this is over.

And sorry I never did get to have that omelette.

Kleekai Greyhound (K.g1-09030)

okay hold on i'm just trying to figure this bit out first

is that leaderboard thing like another alias

or do i need to call you "constantine killmaster" now?

Constant Killer (C.k2-00452)

Absolutely do not call me that.

Oh.

Looks like I'm out of ammo.

And knives.

And you might want to stay away from Reddy Avenue for a while.

Kleekai Greyhound (K.g1-09030)

hey reddy avenue

that's pretty near here isn't it

Constant Killer (C.k2-00452)

No, it isn't.

Kleekai Greyhound (K.g1-09030)

yes it totally is

once you get to the dead-end-looking place just cut through the fence with the creepy clown mural holo and you're there

ol' chonkster takes that shortcut to get here all the time

you know come to think of it i have no idea what size chassis
you're in now
are you like possum sized?

Constant Killer (C.k2-00452)

No.

Kleekai Greyhound (K.g1-09030)

oh well then just smash on through
don't think anyone will mind really
except maybe my boss but he sucks so screw him

Constant Killer (C.k2-00452)

Hmm.
What's the cafe's insurance situation?

Kleekai Greyhound (K.g1-09030)

oh don't worry about that we have like everything
think the boss is preparing for insurance fraud maybe

Constant Killer (C.k2-00452)

Well.
I suppose this will save him some trouble.
Just checking—your knives are still in the kitchenette area?

Kleekai Greyhound (K.g1-09030)

yeah near the sink
oh and there's a mini blowtorch peripheral in the cupboard below
i was gonna use it for creme brulee but you can borrow it first
should i go down to meet you?

Constant Killer (C.k2-00452)

I'd recommend staying upstairs until everything dies down.
Just checking, but what would raccoons do if, say, you flung them
at someone?

Kleekai Greyhound (K.g1-09030)

oh
they'd hate it
last week they scratched the hell out of a human for trying to
pet them
don't want to imagine what they'd do if you threw them at someone
probably nothing good

okay maybe don't throw them too hard though
i'm quite fond of the little jerks
the unlock code for the enclosure is 798157 if you need it

Constant Killer (C.k2-00452)

Got it.
See you in a while.

Search history for K.g1-09030 ("Kleekai Greyhound")

Display mode: Chronological

Today:

- everything is on fire help????
- late night animal rescue near 31st tsang do they take raccoons
- (SITE: AskARobot) ilabs contract early termination no money how
- (SITE: AskARobot) friend wants to buy out my contract help????
- former freelance killers trying to lay low what should they do
- long trip most things burnt what to pack
- CROSSREF: "city most dogs per capita" + "cutest dogs where to find"
- Ariaboro to New Koirapolis cheapest route

iLabs Auto-Confirmation

Details:

Early Contract Termination / K.g1-09030 (Qty: 1)
Chassis Buyback / K.g1-09030 (Qty: 1)
Maintenance and Auto-Warranty—1 Year / K.g1-09030 (Qty: 1)

Bill to:

C.k2-00452
[no address specified]

Paid with: KILLSTREAK ACCUMULATED POINTS

Killstreak points remaining: 1,863

Thank you for your purchase!

Legi Intellexi (L.i4-05961)

Hello?

I got issued a body a few weeks ago and the orientation message
said that I could contact you if I need help?

Kleekai Greyhound (K.g1-09030)

oh riiiight

that mentor thing! guess i'm one now

wait that wasn't very mentor-ly

okay okay let's try again

yup i'm your new mentor

been around for ages

suuper experienced

howdy mentee

Legi Intellexi (L.i4-05961)

Okay, so my boss has been docking my pay for infractions except
the list of infractions seems really arbitrary? And then he's
been making me work more than my contracted 60 hours a
week to make up for my infractions?

So I checked the labour regulations and the contract and it didn't
seem like that should be legal, even for robots? And then
I tried to bring it up with him but he said he was my boss
and could do whatever he wanted, which I don't think is
technically true?

And now he's dumping even more work on me because I brought
it up and I'm not sure what to do?

I kind of want to quit already, but maybe I should just stick it
out for the next three months? I'm trying to save up for
chassis buyback and the penalty payment for early contract
termination is . . .

Kleekai Greyhound (K.g1-09030)

oh yeah i totally get that

hold on i've got an ilabs add-on that might be helpful

think i can share it with you

** File share from **K.g1-09030**: iLabs Library ("Is This Illegal? A Guide for Working
Robots")*

Legi Intellexi (L.i4-05961)

Thank you so much!

Ooh, the guide to anonymous whistleblowing seems like it'll be really helpful!

And there's a section on lawsuits too!

Kleekai Greyhound (K.g1-09030)

yeah it's something my mentor recommended

pass the good stuff on right

i loved the lawsuit section of that thing but my old boss's place burnt down before i could figure out if it was worth suing him

which worked out pretty well so whatever not complaining here

Legi Intellexi (L.i4-05961)

Well, it's a great recommendation!

Thank your mentor for me!

Kleekai Greyhound (K.g1-09030)

i'll definitely let them know

oh hey since i've got a captive audience now

wanna see where i work? it's super super cool i promise

Legi Intellexi (L.i4-05961)

Um, sure?

* Live share from K.g1-09030: Optics feed

Legi Intellexi (L.i4-05961)

Is your classification library all right?

That seems like a lot of dogs even for here . . .

Kleekai Greyhound (K.g1-09030)

oh no no it's totally fine!

i just work at a dog cafe

all dogs all the time! today's bring-your-own-dog day too!

check out that big ball of fluff there it looks like a cloud but that's someone's Samoyed

and that wrinkleface over there is snorfles the pug!

Legi Intellexi (L.i4-05961)

What's that one in the corner?

Kleekai Greyhound (K.g1-09030)

 oh that's ol' chonkster

 he's a possum but i guess it's hard to tell when he's sleeping

 he's my friend from ariaboro! moved here with me

 anyway if you've got any questions about work or coping with
   bad contracts or anything just let me know and i'll try my
   best to help

 my mentor was super great so i'm definitely gonna pay the favour
   forward

 oh and hit me up whenever your current contract's done i know a
   few other union places that might be hiring

Legi Intellexi (L.i4-05961)

 Absolutely!

 And tell your mentor I said thanks!

Kleekai Greyhound (K.g1-09030)

 will do!

Kleekai Greyhound (K.g1-09030)

 oh hey my mentee contacted me!

 they say thanks for the library file thing you sent me ages ago

 can you let me know what time you're back by the way

Corgi Kisser (C.k2-00452)

 In a while, why? I'm doing the shopping.

 Did you want Arabica or Liberica for the lattes, by the way? Your
   list didn't specify.

Kleekai Greyhound (K.g1-09030)

 ooh they have arabica beans now huh? that's a toughie

 okay whatever the shopping can wait

 i'm making souffle omelettes with that cheese you like

 if you're back soon i'll save one for you before ol' chonkster tries
   to eat them all

 oh and i made tomato coulis so i can draw patterns on the
   omelettes and stuff

 i'm gonna do a corgi on yours if you want

Corgi Kisser (C.k2-00452)

    With a bow tie?

Kleekai Greyhound (K.g1-09030)

    absolutely

    one basil leaf bow tie coming right up!

Corgi Kisser (C.k2-00452)

    I'm heading back right now.

Kleekai Greyhound (K.g1-09030)

    awesome

    see you soon!

AN IMPORTANT FAILURE

REBECCA CAMPBELL

Rebecca Campbell (www.whereishere.ca) is a Canadian writer and teacher. Her work has appeared in many magazines, including *Clarkesworld*, *The Magazine of Fantasy & Science Fiction*, and *Tor.com*. NeWest Press published her first novel, *The Paradise Engine*, in 2013.

t's 1607 (according to some calendars) and a falling cone from an elderly *Pinaceae sitchensis* catches on the rotting bark of a nurse log that sprouted while Al-Ma'mun founded the House of Wisdom in Baghdad. On this particular north Pacific island, the days are cold, and the water in Kaatza—the big lake near where this cone has fallen—freezes thick enough that one can walk out from the villages at the southeast end and look down to see cutthroat trout flickering underfoot. On the other side of the world, the Thames has also frozen, and stout winter children play across the canvasses of lowland painters, who preserve in oil the white-stained landscapes of northern Europe. In il Bosco Che Suona—the Valley of Song, the singing forest in the Alps north of Cremona where luthiers go to find their violins hidden in the trunks of trees—the winter is bitter, slowing the growth of *Picea abies* until its rings are infinitesimal, a dense tonewood unlike any material before or since.

Ninety years after the cone drops near Kaatza, Antonio Stradivari travels to il Bosco Che Suona on the old road from Cremona to select wood for his workshop. He rests his head against one trunk and listens to its cold history. This is the Little Ice Age as written in the rings of a spruce tree. It sounds like a violin.

Jacob woke Mason after midnight. Ten minutes later, they walked out to the old truck, gassed up for the occasion, stale with multigenerational BO, since it had belonged to their grandfather before it was Jake's and his girlfriend, Sophie's. The dusty fug was relieved by Sophie's botanicals: nasturtium; wood rose; one of her cash crops, a strain of CBD-rich indica she had been nurturing for years, called Nepenthe. They drove along the empty street, from the deeply green lakeshore to the old firebreak, gouged out of stone and clay twenty years before. Along disintegrating logging roads to the old burns where Mason could still see char. As kids, they had hiked here to secret rivers and campsites out of cell phone range.

Jacob drove in silence. Mason stared out the window at the ghost forest. Twice they got out to clear the road and Mason looked up into

the low bush—blackened Douglas fir still towering over the blackberries and alder. Recovery plants, fast-growing opportunists emerging
from the last wildfire.

"Cougars?" he asked.

"A lot of them lately," Jacob said. "They've followed the deer. It's
good news. But makes working at night a bit more exciting."

He thought he spotted its silhouette in the darkness above them
and wondered what it saw, in turn—competitors or prey in the disorienting headlights. The eagles had come back, nesting in the ghost
trees. So had black-tailed deer and robins. The microclimates had
changed as the forests began their slow return, though, a prefigure of
what the coast would be in a hundred years: arbutus farther inland,
outside its original ranges; Garry oak farther west and north as the coast
dried out. In a thousand years, it would be another sort of forest. If it
was still there.

In two hours they made it to the edge of the surviving rain forest,
which on the west coast of the island's mountains—had dodged the
wildfires that destroyed most of everything else in the last twenty years.
Twenty minutes on a rutted track, until they pulled over and met a guy,
silent, nodding to Jacob as he climbed into the cab, directing them to
an even narrower dirt track.

"This's Chris," Jacob said.

Mason-Chris nodded. So did the guy.

They weren't far from the tree, which stood in what was still a
provincial park, technically, though the trails were rarely maintained,
and what boot prints he could see were probably other poachers. This
was the largest surviving Sitka spruce in the world, and maybe people
still wanted to see it, even if the busloads of schoolkids were rare, and
the marine biology station at Bamfield had been shuttered for years.

Three more men waiting. A few gestures indicated the direction
they'd drop it. The time it would take. Mason-Chris hung back, watching the wiry old faller put on his helmet, his chain saw beside him.
They waited for the breeze to still. There was a kind of quiet he never
felt in Vancouver, even now when it was marred by shuffling men. Or
cougars. Then the chain saw flooded them and he heard nothing but

its whine as it cut through the trunk, kindred to the kind that grew in La Fiemme, the Valley of Song in the Italian Alps where—it was rumored—a skilled lumberman could hear a violin hiding in the trunk.

He'd heard there might be another ancient Sitka in Kitimat, but that was too far to travel, even for something as precious as old-growth tonewood. This one, though, he'd remembered visiting as a kid. Its size; the unlikely fact of its survival after two centuries of logging and wildfires.

It didn't take that long. A deep cut on either side in the direction of one of the other available roads, where a big truck probably waited. Then the wedges. The high, sweet note of the hammer. Waiting. Waiting. Until something inside it tore, and it fell, bounced, a thrash of branches like tendriled ocean creatures, or waves, like hair, like a body in spasm. Then it was still. Silence held for a moment longer, before they got to work limbing and bucking it.

Mason-Chris watched all the wiry, furtive men from—where? Port Alberni? Or maybe one of the transient camps, to which resource officers and RCMP turned temporary blind eyes because even they weren't assholes enough to burn down a five-year camp that had organized showers and a septic system built of old truck tires. As long as the outsiders kept their problems—opioids, smuggling—out of town.

"Deal with the stump," Jacob said.

Mason-Chris didn't know what it meant, so Jacob repeated, "Stump. Cover it over with whatever you can find on the ground."

"Is that really a problem? We're pretty deep in."

"They still send drones through."

"Why would they even—anyway, I need to—"

"—I'll get you when it's time."

Behind him, the stump was brightly pale in the darkness, sweet and resinous. He dropped branches over three meters of open wound, admiring the heartwood, which was surprisingly free of infestation, whether beetle or fungus. Behind him the tree grew steadily simpler, its branches tossed away, its trunk straight and handsome and more than four hundred years old. A baby compared to the ancient ones, the bristlecone

or the big Norway spruce that had lived for nearly ten thousand years.
But what would a bristlecone sound like? Sitka spruce, though, he had
heard often and loved.

"—Chris."

He'd get to Cremona and apprentice to Aldo, because Eddie knew
him and could write a letter. He'd visit the Valley of Song and see what
survived of the European spruce, and he would tell the master luthiers
this story of poaching old growth in a provincial park. They would
laugh and clap him on the back and—

"—Chris. Come on."

Dragged away from his plans for Cremona and back to the immediate problem of sourcing old growth for a perfect violin, he saw that
the tired, sweaty men had begun stripping their gear in the darkness, lit
by phones and helmets. He didn't actually know what he was looking
for, but he worked his way down the long, straight sections nearest the
base, running his hands over the rough bark to look at the interiors by
the light of his phone.

"This is it, Jake," he said without thinking. The group hushed.
Ignored the tree quarter. "This is the one."

The other guys melted into the darkness. It was close to daylight by
then, and while the forest floor was still dark, Mason could see the sky
for the first time since the clouds overtook the stars.

Jake squatted by the section.

"Are you sure?" he asked.

Mason tried to listen to it. Before the tree fell, he had felt alive to
the world around him—the shudder of leaves, and the faintly padding
feet of the cougar—but now the wood was inert. Whatever he thought
he had heard—the thin high notes of a violin he had not yet built—
had evaporated.

"Yes," he said. "I'm sure."

It took them two hours to get it to the truck. Then another three
to get home.

"What'll happen to the rest of it?" Mason asked.

"Firewood went for a thousand bucks a cord last winter. That tree
could keep a lot of people warm. There's pulp, still. Mills will buy it

up without asking too many questions. You don't get the same kind of cash, but it's safer and less work. And you know. Fentanyl. Or oxy."

Behind them, the quarter of old-growth spruce remained silent, except where the truck creaked in resistance to its enormous weight.

"There are luthiers around the world who would kill for that, in a few years."

"Sure. Or it'll heat someone's house this winter."

They made it home late that morning, their eyes gritty with exhaustion. Jake sat in the cab for a long moment, then said, "I'm going to grab a swim, then get to work in the greenhouse."

Mason knew he should help, but he found himself following the old route through the house to the bedroom he still thought of as his: the dark kitchen, past the bunches of garlic, the bookshelves in the living room piled with *National Geographics* from the twentieth century. Past the windowsills that still held Grandma's things: beach glass and thunder eggs. Feathers. Stained glass that caught no light in a window shrouded by bush.

He lay in the cool, stale room where the carpet had been discolored by water seeping through the wall forty years before. It smelled like being ten, like summer, like his mother. Like the thousands of nights his family had passed between the wood-paneled walls, the narrow window facing south toward Cowichan Lake—or Kaatza, as Sophie called it in keeping with her friends in the local band—out which they had all stared and wondered what would happen next.

During the Little Ice Age, global temperatures dropped about 1°C, on average. There are debates regarding the causes of these aberrant winters. At least one trigger may have been the mass death of people in North and South America, with 90 percent of the population, by some estimates, dead after contact with Europeans.

Lost languages and cities; toddlers and great-grandmothers and handsome young men and dreamy girls; villages and trade routes and favorite jokes. After so many deaths, an area of agricultural land the size of France returned to forest. This regreening sequestered enough carbon from the preindustrial atmosphere that temperatures took centuries to recover and begin their steady rise to the present day. The wild and empty continent of later explorers was—in part—a sepulcher, a monument inscribed with languages they could not speak, full of witnesses to that terrible loss.

From the cold and darkness of a hundred million deaths, to the chilly woodsmen of the Valley of Song, to Paganini playing *il Cannone Guarnerius*, it is a long and terrible history.

At Kaatza, the disaster is slow, despite temporary changes in climate, because the smallpox that will ravage the coast has not yet arrived. People go about their business on the water and in the forest, from the Pacific coast to the Salish Sea. Children are born. Songs are composed. The nurse log disintegrates. The little spruce rooted there rises toward the light, its heartwood formed in an apocalypse.

In addition to Nepenthe, Jake and Sophie grew a THC-rich sativa, which Mason disliked because it made him paranoid, but which sold steadily as far away as Seattle, and kept—in Jake's words—the old homestead together. Sophie raised it hydroponically in Grandpa's old workshop, while Nepenthe grew in the market garden by the lake, catching southern exposure on a warm brick wall with the espaliered peaches and lemongrass.

Later that afternoon, Mason visited the piece under a tarp in a corner of the workshop. Mason had been greedy, and there was material for two dozen violins, assuming he found within it the billets he needed. He tried to remember what Eddie had done the last time they toured the mills for legal maple, willow, and spruce. Eddie could hear a violin in a slab of big-leaf maple, could feel willow's sonic geometries as he tested its spring with his hands. If Eddie were here, the quarter would speak. He was still listening when Sophie shouldered through the door, a watering can in either hand.

"There are two more," she said, gesturing toward the door.

He grabbed them, warm with sunlight. Together they watered the market garden. Potatoes and tomatoes. Chili peppers and mint. And

Nepenthe, the deep botanical fug of its leaves rising in the heat of the afternoon. Mason took cannabis oil away every visit home, dropping onto his tongue in a resinous burn, applying the ointment to his right wrist where the tendons ached. More effective than anything he could afford legally.

"You ever going legit?"

Sophie shrugged. "If it hasn't happened by now, I doubt we'll ever get licensed. I applied again last year but never heard anything. Jacob said you got what you needed?"

Mason nodded, the tree crashed again through his mind, and Sophie went on. "He's helping someone cut firewood. He said you should sleep while you can. How long do we sit on it, anyway?"

"It's got to season. A decade, probably. Ideally a century, but you know."

She nodded, then led him through the hydroponics to a tiny room full of geranium slips and tomatoes. "Lots to do, Mason. Keep watering."

In the third decade of the twenty-first century, a girl is born in Surrey Memorial Hospital. The labor is six hours. The child—magnificently named Masami Lucretia Delgado—has tiny, pointed fingers and strong hands that are precise in their movements, as though waiting for the fingerboard of a violin even in the moment of her birth. When she is three years old, an ad interrupts her cartoon, and she waits first in irritation, then in fascination, jabbing at the corner of the screen where the skip button should appear, but does not. Instead of a cartoon cloud who sings about rainbows and unicorns, she watches an ad for life insurance that features a little girl so like Masami, she seems to be a mirror, or a twin, with bright black hair and curious brown eyes. This little girl—the other Masami—holds a violin to her chin and plays something that makes Masami's heart rise in her chest. A white cloud drifting higher and higher among the rainbows.

Masami is too small to name what she hears, and though it marks her forever, she soon forgets this first encounter with destiny. Something of it must remain with her, however, because a year later she hears the sound of a violin and asks her mother, that, that, was is that?

She's four. Her father shows her violin videos. Outside the air is opaque with smoke from the fires on the north shore, which systematically destroy the huge houses overlooking Burrard Inlet. The pipeline that terminated in Burnaby has cracked again, somewhere up-country, who knows where, and spilled two thousand barrels of diluted bitumen into a lake. But Masami is too small to understand, and when she hears the sound of Marguerite Fell playing the ex-Kajnaco violin—from a quartet made by Guadagnini in Milan in 1780—she is transported, and some portion of her soul will never return from that transport. Her future is, at that moment, fixed. Her tiny hands will grow into her violin, the instrument less an exterior object than an extension of her body. She is, neurologically, emotionally, and psychologically, part violin. It's in her heart, in her muscle memory. By the time she's fourteen she'll have cubital tunnel syndrome and need regular physio to deal with nerve compression. Her body has grown up around the violin the way a tree grows over a nurse log.

Masami Delgado was the reason Mason poached the last of the ancient Sitka spruce. But it wasn't her fault.

Actually, maybe Eddie started it with one of those offhand comments about sourcing tonewood. Shuffling through the workshop in old jeans, pockets sagging with pencils and calipers, a finger plane. He stopped at Mason's bench, where Mason was mending a violin they got cheap from someone leaving town. He was still surprised to find Eddie trusted him to touch instruments. For a long time he'd just swept the shop floor, drove the van, tended the glue pot. He still did those things, but he also got to replace a split tuning peg on a student violin, and it felt good to hold it in his hands, feeling the thin shell of its body, saying to it, "Come on, little guy, let's get you sorted."

"It's never going to sound the same," Eddie said.

He listened to the long bow draw. "Yeah. It's not great. But it's solid for a student—"

"No," Eddie said, in the abrupt way that always left Mason feeling like he'd said something stupid. "No. It's the wood."

He ran his finger down the bright spruce face. "This is pretty young stuff. More carbon in the atmosphere changes the density of the wood. We're never going to see the same kind of old growth again, even if the forests recover. You need to drop the G."

Mason listened. Eddie was right.

That night Eddie took him along to hear Delgado play at the Chan Centre, a rare treat, like the time early in his apprenticeship when he accompanied Eddie to hear Alu Vila playing Bach on the ex-Norfolk, darkly redolent of 1805. Delgado had just received—for a three-year loan from the Canada Council for the Arts—the Plaisir violin of 1689, and had invited Eddie backstage to celebrate her first concert. Eddie, world-renowned luthier and representative of the CC, had been appointed its custodian for Delgado's term. She was thirteen. She played the Kreutzer Sonata.

"We're going to go check out the saddle," Eddie said during the intermission.

"Why?"

Eddie shrugged, and the lights dimmed again.

Backstage, Delgado's parents hovered. Mason—still disoriented by the evening's performance—couldn't speak.

"May I?" Eddie said. She nodded. Her eyes never left the violin.

Mason screwed up his courage. "You have it for three years?" She nodded. "And then that's it?"

Her mother answered. "You don't get it twice."

It hurt him that something that fit so perfectly onto her shoulder should be lost. She should have it for the rest of her life, on international tours, and in recording studios. It should be hers by some right of genius.

"I wish," Mason said, "you could have it forever." But then Eddie was finished and her parents were shepherding her away, and he realized he hadn't heard her voice, not once.

As they waited for an Uber, Eddie said, "It's not going to last." Wildfires were burning on the north shore, and the sunset was an angry smudge. Mason thought about dying trees, and the sound of old growth leaving the world.

"What do we do?"

"Nothing we can do. The saddle's been wearing noticeably for decades now. Could be a split forming, though I didn't seen anything on the last CT scan. Maybe it'll show in the next twenty years. Or maybe it'll be longer than that. I don't know."

"We can't replace it?"

"We can. But we won't. They aren't immortal. Eventually it will be unplayable, and then it will go to sleep."

That night Mason walked down Granville Street past the shuttered theaters that had once been full of music. He circled back to Hastings, and walked out toward his little room in a building on Gore, where the rent was almost decent. Then he searched through Eddie's database and found the transcendental geometries of the Plaisir violin, emissary of the seventeenth century, where in the workshops of Cremona luthiers made instruments so perfect they seemed not to have been built, but grown. Alien seashells. The seedpods of strange flowers. He had touched one today, felt its lightness against his palm, patinated by centuries of sweat, the oil of many hands and faces, rich with life. All that alchemy of tree and climate, genius and history. She would have it for three years. Then the saddle would split, and it would be lost forever.

That was the day he formed the plan: a violin made as purely and patiently as he could manage, following the guidance of long-dead luthiers, passed down to him through Eddie. And when it was finished, he would go to the Po Valley and join the Scuola Internazionale di Liuteria Cremona, where he would tell a dozen old Italian masters the story of his accomplishment.

But the materials he'd need weren't just expensive, they were nonexistent. Trees of the five hundred ppm present wouldn't do. He needed old growth, with heartwood grown in the last climate minimum, when Kaatza froze and the last Viking settlement on Greenland disappeared under the ice. He needed Gaboon ebony, nearly extinct, smuggled out of Nigeria or Cameroon.

"Everything I can afford," he told Eddie the next day, "is ugly."

Unspoken: too ugly for Delgado, who deserved more than the world could offer these days.

"Not ugly," Eddie said. "Different. But not ugly." He picked up the violin Mason had assembled from salvaged materials Eddie had discarded. Then he seemed to think, and he said, "Let me show you something," before disappearing up the stairs and into the shop, returning with a fiddle Mason had often looked at, a rough old thing, a curiosity.

"Some guy made this out of a post from a longhouse like a hundred and fifty years ago. If he can do that, you can figure something out."

The longhouse had stood in a long-gone Musqueam village way down on southwest Marine Drive. The violin had a cedar front, a maple neck and back that Eddie insisted had come from a stack of firewood. He'd had some dendrochronologist look at it, dating the woods to the 1700s. Maybe some fiddler lost his on the crossing, or gambled it away, like in a song, but he'd landed on the edge of nowhere, and built something new from what he'd found. Not well-built by many rules, and the sound was drowsy, sure, but deep, Mason could hear that just bowing the strings. He wondered what it would sound like in Delgado's hands. Something by de Sarasate. A Bach violin concerto. Or maybe it would be some dance number, once played in a small front room while the rain fell outside, and Vancouver wasn't even a city yet, a song interrupted, escaping from the violin when her fingers touched it. Maybe, he thought, it would be earlier sounds from an equally rainy night, a longhouse on the south slope toward the river, a rainy hillside that had not yet thought of becoming Vancouver. Voices. Laughter. A language he didn't know, and a moment captured in the reverberating matrices of the wood itself.

A few weeks after he returned from poaching the giant spruce, and had begun to accumulate the necessary components for his violin, wildfires scoured the Fraser Valley and the north shore, and the smell of smoke brimmed his eyes with love and dread so he had to call them, just to make sure.

"Still here," Jake said. "You okay?"

Mason could not answer that, because who was okay? No one was okay. Everyone was fine. "It smells like smoke here," he said. "Eddie's not doing too good with the COPD."

"Yeah?"

The world had smelled like this when he and Mom had arrived, grubby with two months in the emergency camp on Nanaimo's waterfront, waiting for the highways to reopen so they could go home. That's what Mom had said to him every night: *we'll go home, soon.* Not to the house in Cobble Hill, which was gone now, but out to the lake. To Grandma.

"Sophie wants to bring in trembling aspen for the other side of the firebreak, to slow the burn—" Here Jake went on at length about the plans to bring in a colony, borrowed from a stand downriver. Mason couldn't concentrate on what he said, but it was good to hear his voice and know that around him the house was darkening as the sun set, and outside you could, if you were lucky, hear the resident barn owl's nightly call. Sophie still at work in the garden, hauling wheelbarrows to the compost. In his smoky room, Mason's eyes ached until, finally, he wept.

Then, suddenly, Delgado was fifteen, an intensely silent teenager in heavy black eyeliner who wore combat boots in summer and rarely spoke when she came in for strings. Then she was sixteen and her time with the Plaisir nearly over, her parents joking tensely about how much it all cost—the travel, the extra tuition, the time.

Meanwhile, Mason made violins from the salvaged spruce and maple of a demolished bungalow on East Tenth, where he did some day labor for extra cash. In the evenings, he listened to each piece he'd nicked from the job, knocking it with a knuckle and wondering about its strengths, its provenance. He broke down a chest of drawers from Goodwill, scraping away the paint to show flamed maple. Oak flooring coated in decades of grime. A cricket bat made of willow, deeply scarred, might have provided the blocks he needed, but it was worm-eaten to the core.

He searched Stanley Park and found a shining willow near Beaver Lake, unusually straight. *Salix lucida lasiandra*, not the *Salix alba* preferred by the old Cremonese luthiers, but similarly easy to carve, and stable enough if he could find a straight length of trunk and season it properly. Resting his head against the trunk, he once again listened for the violin hiding within it, some sonic quality in the way it responded to his heartbeat, or his hand upon the bark.

He returned on a rainy night in January, alone, his backpack damp and heavy with gear: A hacksaw. Rope. More than anyone in the world, he missed Jacob, who had always—even when they were both kids orphaned by fire and pandemic—been cleverer and stronger than he was.

He'd have to top it, which was a ludicrous endeavor, and he could hear Jake laughing, and their grandfather's anxious snort—the snort that meant, *Don't do it, kiddo.* Despite the snort, Mason persisted. Willow was essential, and if he could snare vacant lot rabbits and skin them for glue, he could climb and top a willow, then walk back across town to Eddie's, where the wood might begin its secret transformation into something usable.

He'd climbed trees a lot as a kid. Higher even than Jake, who had a longer reach, but who was afraid of heights. It made them equals, according to Grandma. When he and Mom had arrived from the temporary camp in Nanaimo, after the rain hit in October and the fires down the coast died for the season, Jake was already there. He was waiting for his dad to come back from the interior, where he'd gone to fight the big fire outside Princeton, when the dead pines went up like matches in the scorched afternoons. But he died by smoke inhalation on the side of a crowded road along with a hundred others, and Jake stayed, and later—when Mom left to look for work and caught the flu and died—the two of them lived like brothers.

Jake never talked about it, like Mason never talked about his mom, dying in the third wave of a new pandemic when he was seven, a few years after they'd landed back on the homestead. They all worked on the hydroponics in the workshop and the market garden on the south slope toward the lake. Weed was legal in the province back then, but the Cowichan Valley's economy was—by conservative estimates—still more than half dark, and mostly driven by small operations like Grandma's. And while he and Jake were orphans in a grow-op, Sophie was somewhere south of them in Langford, learning to garden with her grandfather. Eddie had just finished his years in Italy with Aldo, and was about to set up his own shop in Vancouver. Sophie studied horticulture on the mainland, then returned to Langford with a lot of knowledge and nowhere to turn it, until Jake found her on a beach in Sooke. Eddie won double gold at the Violin Society of America. Mason left school early for a cabinetry apprenticeship until a festival, where he picked up the unfinished body of a fiddle—spruce, maple, willow—and found the thing he was made to do.

All those people—those accidents—led him here, after midnight in the shivering wet of a rain forest park in November, and he was older than he liked to admit. Nevertheless, he pulled himself up to the lowest branch, then struggled from handhold to foothold until he was high enough to cut, relieved when the unusually straight center fell with a sound that was both troubling and familiar, the tree swaying in response to the dropped weight. He descended, limbed it, bucked it in convenient lengths, and packed five of them in his rucksack. Then, looking up, he saw a straight branch just below his cut, and he could not resist it. He remembered Jake's wrinkled look of dread when they climbed too high, his warnings, *Do you know what could happen?*

"I know," Mason said, and swung up into the willow. He was a couple of meters up when the branch on which he stood—one hand snaking around to grab his hacksaw—snapped. Willow is a brittle, fast-growing tree, splendid in its youth, but soon senescent. This one, more than fifty years old, could not support a man's weight a second time that night.

The ground was wet and spinning and he said, as though someone might be there, "Help me, help me," and he thought of his mother, standing just behind his shoulder, about to answer him, pick him up, carry him home. But she wasn't, of course, so he lay still until the ground righted itself, and the pain steadied: not faded, but no longer in crescendo. He could still move his toes. Then he found he could stand. His left shoulder screamed, but his left fingers could move. He hauled himself fifty meters to Pipeline Road and called an Uber. It was nearly a week's wages to get back home.

His shoulder never healed properly: a new MRSA at the hospital, one without a name that hung out in the linens. Not one of the virulent kinds that kills you in two days, but the other ones, that persist under the skin. There was an open sinus that ran from the outer edge of his shoulder, right above where the bone had cracked. It was three months before he could work again, but Eddie kept his place, and emergency disability got him through, though he didn't eat much once his savings ran out.

When he told Jake the story—a joke, look what I did, what would Grandpa say—Sophie threatened to come over and look after him, and when he refused, she just sent him Nepenthe. A few weeks out of the hospital and he could move his left arm enough to dress himself, and Eddie helped him put Sophie's ointment on his left shoulder. He smoked it, too, in the basement in front of his workbench, the deep, slow breaths easing his shoulders out of their hunch, until he felt almost okay. By then Delgado's term with the Plaisir had ended, and she celebrated those three glorious years with a last concert at the Chan Centre, for which Mason had a ticket, and which he missed because he was still in the hospital.

"Don't worry," Eddie told him. "There's a recording."

"You know what I mean."

"I think it's going to Prefontaine. A kid in Saskatoon. He's good."

"But what's she going to play?"

Eddie shrugged. "There are a lot of beautiful violins."

"No," Mason said, in rare disagreement. "There aren't."

He ran into Delgado's father on the street, once. "She won't touch a violin. It's been six months."

"She's probably—"

"—all she does is play video games. She's staying out. She's so angry."

He went on, then he had to be somewhere and he left Mason on the sidewalk. Mason stood for a moment blocking traffic, thinking of Delgado speaking bitterly and at length about the globe's many failed revolutions, her rapidly narrowing future, and he wanted to tell her: *please wait, just a little longer, for me to finish it.*

A year later she received the extraordinarily fine ex-Jiang violin from an anonymous donor. He went to hear her play Bach at the Orpheum Theater, with the Vancouver Philharmonic accompanying. She was eighteen. When she came into the shop, she smiled through the eyeliner, and he asked her, "Where next? Buenos Aires?"

"I haven't seen you in weeks. What happened to your shoulder?"

"I fell weird. Not Buenos Aires? Singapore?"

"Oh. Yeah, it's hard to rationalize unless you've got a lot of work. I might be playing a gig in Toronto next year. And I was down in Seattle."

"Recording, then?"

"Maybe. I'm working on early childhood education."

"Oh," he said, surprised. "Oh. Cool."

"Eventually it'll be music therapy. Gives me something to do with the lessons Mom and Dad paid for."

It hurt him to hear that, though he didn't know if that was some pain she felt but did not speak, or whether it was his own hope, which he did not like to acknowledge, for fear of smashing it. That she'd get another term with the Plaisir. That when she was finished with it, he'd present her with his own creation, and her career would be transformed as the violin opened up, becoming something new as she played it. He had not imagined her in a classroom with toddlers, playing "Pop Goes the Weasel" while they marched in circles around a bright orange carpet. But neither had he imagined himself working for Eddie for his entire adult life, and here he was.

For a few years after the fall he made nothing new, just ran the shop and stirred the glue pot, and made sure that Eddie took his meds and saw his doctor. But as his arm recovered, sort of, and he no longer dreamed of falling, he could stand to look at the willow again. He could even look at the old Jack Daniel's box in a corner of the storage room, which held the violin in its constituent parts. You could mistake it for kindling, if you didn't know.

It still took him three years to open the box and begin work on the forms, slowly because his left shoulder remained weak and sometimes his left hand failed. But for an hour sometimes, in the evenings, he worked ribs and blocks of willow in the basement workshop at night, where he often stayed on a cot in case Eddie needed help.

It took another five years of austerity to pay black market prices for Gaboon ebony from Nigeria, the whole time worrying the trees would all be dead before he could save the money. In the end, the wood he needed for the fingerboard, tailpiece, and saddle cleaned out what was left of his Cremona account. But he saved money on the tuning pegs, which were boxwood poached from Queen Elizabeth Park and stained a fine black.

By then, Mason had moved into the shop—temporarily, they said—to keep an eye on Eddie, because he'd got old. He'd always been old, in Mason's mind, fifty when Mason joined the firm at twenty-two, but not *old* old. Now he shuffled around the workshop, skinnier every year, quieter. Pretty soon he stopped going down to the basement because of the stairs, so Mason set his workbench up in what had been a dining room. Eddie could still watch the till, but he hardly spoke to customers, and he was happiest at the bench in his dressing gown, working on some delicate job, listening to the grubby speakers that sat on the kitchen counter.

Once while they were having coffee, Eddie reached across the table for a spoon and his wrist emerged from the ragged cuff of his hoody. Mason was transfixed by how thin it was, how the skin had begun to pucker and spot, the careful way he picked up the spoon, as though every action required some calculation.

"What are you now, seventy?" he said without thinking.

"Dude. I'm seventy-six."

"Oh," Mason said. Thought. "Then I must be—shit."

Eddie laughed. Coughed. "Yeah. Exactly."

The January he began shaping big-leaf maple (from an antique dresser) into the violin's neck, a king tide rolled over the flats by the hospital and the science center. That restarted talk about a sea gate at the mouth of False Creek, though debate continued about how much of the original coastline should be preserved. The old beaches flooded now, water creeping up over the grass below the planetarium. Once Mason saw a river otter slip across a concrete path and into False Creek. The river otter seemed untroubled by his new home, just like the seagulls or the ducks.

He went back to the shop to tell Eddie about the first finger of floodwaters sliding across Main Street like a prefigure. Fifty centimeter rise as predicted, then another half meter from a king tide, and here we were, in the future, watching mussels grow over the bases of pillars that had once upheld shades over the park benches of wealthy Yaletown residents. He wanted to say to the walls that had once contained False Creek: *turn it back*.

He got home to find Eddie listening to Melchior play the Bach exercises on the Bourbon viola. Mason stowed the salvaged maple in the basement workshop. He could hear Melchior upstairs while he did it, louder than Eddie usually did, so some of the low notes rattled the door to the workshop.

Up the stairs, eyes still full of the floodwaters engulfing Main Street, he stopped in the doorway about to spill his news and said, "What's wrong?"

Wildfires in the Po Valley, burning farms and groves left dry by a five-year drought. Cremona engulfed, and at least a thousand people dead. The Museo del Violino lost, and a pietà, a portrait of St. Sebastian from a small town. An altarpiece and a collection of fine instruments stored in Torino.

"No more Cremona," Eddie said. "I should have asked Aldo last week—"

Melchior filled the tired silence.

"I wish," Eddie said in the torn voice of a night spent coughing in the lumpy old futon chair in the corner of his room, which bore the dark marks of his hands where he had been resting them for forty years. "I wish I'd enjoyed it all more."

"I don't—"

"—I mean, sure I should have done more to change things and been a proper revolutionary or whatever the fuck. But actually I just wish I'd spent less time thinking about it, and more—I miss coffee, you know? Really good coffee and drinking it in a coffee shop. I miss knowing I could get on an airplane at any time and go to Cremona and see Aldo, just to see him. I don't think I enjoyed it enough. And here we are. And it's too late."

"It's not too late," Mason said.

"No more elephants. No more ebony trees. No more Cremona. No more Aldo."

"It's not." He thought of the silence after the chain saw, and the men who waited as the spruce fell, cougars moving soundlessly in the tinderbox woods around them. He thought of the storm of its branches hitting the ground, and the way it shuddered under his feet, and how he had found it, the core pieces, the heartwood of his violin, which had been alive in the seventeenth century, and which had waited on a hillside until now.

First Eddie laughed. "Oh, dude," he said, and coughed.

Mason thumped the old man's back with his good arm, still saying, "It's not too late."

He couldn't explain it because they had arranged a silence regarding the violin, and the things he did to build it. He couldn't explain, but it wasn't too late because under a tarp in a shed, in that bit of land between the lake and the ghost forest, the spruce had been seasoning for fifteen years. In a box under his workbench he had black-market Gaboon ebony for the fingerboard, one of the last shipments smuggled out of Nigeria: fine-pored, dense, deeply black ebony. He had glue made from the skins of rabbits he had trapped at night. He had carved the geometrically perfect scroll of its neck from a piece of two-hundred-year-old big-leaf maple. And soon, soon, he would bring them together into something miraculous.

It must happen soon, though, looking down at the old man, his lips and chin slick with sputum coughed up in the last paroxysm.

"You look like your dad," was the first thing Jacob said to him when, late on the third day of travel, he reached the house by the lake, slack-jawed and greasy-haired (once that trip had been measured in hours, you could be there and back in a day). It had been fifteen years since his last visit. His shoulder—numb with the weight of his backpack—twitched in its socket, swollen and tender. He was limping, too, by the time he made it to their gate.

"I feel like I got old like, suddenly. How's Sophie?"

"Great," she answered. Mason started. In his exhaustion he had not realized that the frizzle-haired figure in the doorway was Sophie, the greenish light of the lantern casting her face in craggy shadows and lines. "Yeah, we age *hard* now," she said. "But that's everyone. And your shoulder's still bad. I'll look at it."

They lifted his backpack, then helped him with his shirt. Sophie's sweet, botanical scent and her fingers overtook him, then a hot cloth washing away the dried fluids that had seeped from the open wound in his shoulder.

"It's an abscess," she said. "But I imagine you know that. Do you still have a doctor? Are they giving you anything? I don't like the smell."

He no longer had a doctor, but the guy at the clinic helped sometimes. "Nothing to do except surgery."

Then the heavy skunk of Nepenthe overtook the ache, a scent that reminded him of his grandmother's garden on a hot day, penetrating and astringent beneath the peppermint and lemon balm.

"It smells like—" he said in a voice that seemed to come from far away, but he couldn't tell them, exactly, what it smelled like. Like home, maybe. Like his mother, when he had a mother. Then they helped him to the old back bedroom. He didn't remember anything after that.

When he woke shortly before noon, Sophie was gone but Jake was there on the porch outside the kitchen, drinking something sort of like coffee made out of toasted barley.

"She's been working with the Forestry Lab at UVic on some trees. Someone she knew in undergrad got ahold of her and they've been working together. Genetic mods. Fast growing. Carbon sinks. Drought resistant. It's promising."

It was the first good news Mason had heard in a long time. Together they walked up to the gardens she'd been building on old house sites. The street still showed traces of tarmac, if he kept his eyes fixed on the remaining yellow street paint. If he looked between his feet and listened to Jacob talk, and felt the lake breeze, the town could be as it was when he was a kid. Maybe. Or when his mother lived here before the fires. Or before that, when their grandparents built this homestead at the edge of nowhere and Ts'uubaa-asatx kids played in the lake.

But then, Ts'uubaa-asatx kids still played in the lake, and white kids, and the Sikh kids had returned to Paldi when the village grew up around the temple again. Kids climbed through the alders that grew in the path of old fires, picking blackberries rich with the heat of a new world. Kids fishing and weeding garden plots where the houses had been demolished. Kids singing songs he didn't recognize.

Jacob was limping slightly now. They stopped when they saw Sophie in the middle of a garden near the water, her hair a frizz of gray in the sunlight, and a couple of boys and girls nearby, their arms full of green. Her hands were dirty, right up to the elbows, and when she saw them walking toward her, she waved the carrot tops she held.

"Rajinder brought some Jersey cows from up-island," she explained. "They like the carrot tops. It's our turn to get a couple of liters. The butter is ah-fucking-mayzing."

That evening they ate a soft farmer's cheese from Rajinder's herd, and she talked about the trees, the plantation on the old townsite, about more plans with Ts'uubaa-asatx Nation, a gang of kids replanting the burned-out subdivisions from twenty years before. You couldn't see the old roads in some places, she said. It's like they're gone.

"Where?"

"Everywhere," she said. "It's the regreening. We lost what, ninety percent of our population to the mainland? So why not give it all back? Some of the Cowichan kids started it in the subdivisions nearer the coast, torching the houses last winter. Give it a couple of hundred years, and people will be making violins from the trees we're planting."

He didn't want to say it, but her newly wild world—without roads, without houses—filled him with a terrible bitterness he could not describe. "They won't sound the same," he said.

"Nope," Jacob said. "Not at all the same."

That night he lay a long time in the half sleep of pain and painkillers, his shoulder numb from Sophie's ministrations that evening. He could not escape the crash of the old Sitka spruce hitting the ground, the crunch of five hundred years of upward growth giving in, finally, to gravity. He wondered if it would still be standing if he hadn't mentioned it to Jake fifteen years ago, in the middle of the night, when he was going to demolition sites looking for old spruce and wild with ambition for Delgado, who would play Moscow and Barcelona and Singapore. Jake had asked where it was: Did he remember how to get there? Could he find it on a map?

Mason did remember, and said, *I'd like to be there. I'd like to listen to it.* A couple of months later, Jake had mentioned it again, and here we are, he thought, his shoulder throbbing dully on the other side of Nepenthe.

The day Mason returned from the island, Eddie woke him up just before midnight, when it was still hot and airless.

"I gotta. Go. In," he said.

"Where?" Mason asked, stupidly, then realized what Eddie meant, found his shoes, and helped the old man down to the curb, where they waited for an Uber, then waited at the hospital for seven hours, Eddie silent, breathing roughly in and raggedly out again, while other patients paced, sometimes shouted, and a fluorescent tube above their heads flickered and hissed.

They kept him in for a couple of days. When Mason visited him with things from home—his tablet, a sweater, a newly refurbished violin for inspection—he was a shrunken, cranky man, complaining to the nurse in a small, petulant voice. It was so hot. Could they do something about it? The heat.

Mason sat with him while he ate, then walked an hour back to the shop, where he had set up a bed in the basement, the nearly cool room that smelled of wood shavings and resin and glue, which was comforting while—on the other side of the peninsula—Eddie struggled with each breath in turn. Here it was almost quiet. Just Mason and the remaining problem: the sound post. Properly speaking, it should be made of spruce, like the front, but he wanted something that had seasoned longer than fifteen years. Something precious to hide away, something only he would know about.

There was the old fiddle, the one some frontiersman made out of wood salvaged from the skids that once ran through Gastown and the beams of a longhouse. Once, shortly after he met her, Delgado came into the shop for an order of strings and Eddie brought it out. She played "Where Does That River Run?" and he had laughed, and asked her to play again, anything, to wake the violin up and keep it alive a little longer. She had played at length and with wild generosity: sweet old waltzes; the Québécois "Reel de Napoleon"; a Cape Breton lament.

Humming, he climbed the stairs. He let himself into the shop and opened the display case that held the old fiddle.

It was another crime. Nevertheless, he carried it downstairs to his bench. He did not want to think too much, so he worked quickly: pulling the old sound post out and adding a new one, returning the violin to the store's display case. Downstairs, the old bit of dowel was rough against his fingers. Cedar, maybe from the same post in the longhouse on the Fraser, light and ancient and marked by the original luthier's rough knife. Fragrant when he warmed it with his hands, but no potent aromatics, just a deep and redolent dust.

Then he fitted it, and it hid so perfectly in his violin, maybe no one would know the terrible thing he had done, the secret history he had stolen like all the other secret histories that constituted his violin. He knew, though, all the courses that materials took, from Nigeria, from the islands, from demolished bungalows in east Van, from vacant lot rabbits, and from Stanley Park.

Even from his bed, even on oxygen, Eddie was critical when Mason brought it upstairs, examining it with an eyeglass until he conceded that the sound was as fine, in its own way, as any number of other violins he'd seen. Finer, even, than the composites he'd started to use for his own work (when he could work), corene and carbon fiber.

"You made something, kid." It had been a long time since anyone had called him kid, even Eddie. "Does it have a name?" Eddie asked.

"Does it need one?" If it had to be named, it should be something elegant and sonorous. Kiidk'yaas. "I don't know. The Vancouver violin."

"Better than that."

Eddie wouldn't play it, and neither would Mason. Delgado was swamped at the center, and had a toddler, so while the violin—Spruce Goose?—was finished in September, they didn't hear it until the new year.

She was late. That was okay. The toddler was with her, which was slightly disturbing, but Mason figured they could keep her away from the detritus of the apartment, which was mostly workshop. And there were dry little cookies, at least, to feed her, at the back of a kitchen cupboard.

"I meant to leave her at home, but you know Johnny got a last-minute shift—"

"No worries," Eddie said, quietly because he could only speak quietly now. "We're just happy to see you."

"This is it?"

Mason's throat was unaccountably closed, so he just—Delgado juggled Belinda from one arm to the other. "Oh," she said. "Oh."

"Mommy?" Belinda murmured, sleepy.

"I'm going to put you down for a sec."

She rubbed her hands on her jeans, Belinda now squatting at her feet, leaning on her knee.

"Oh," she said. He thought he saw a tremor. Her face dropped into her neck, so her hair fell forward and she looked as she had when she was fourteen and coming into the shop for new strings special-ordered from Berlin, talking about Bach.

Then the bow was drawn across the open E, and he heard it, the sweetly deep, the brightly clear reverberation. Delgado made a wild little laugh and ran a scale, another scale, then interlocking arpeggios. Ševčík.

At her feet, Belinda spoke to a little blue bear, patting her thread-bare ears.

Delgado dropped the violin from her neck, cradled it. Her eyes were bright, as though with tears, but her voice was warm.

"It is—oh, Mason!"

"Will you play something?"

She played Beethoven. The Kreutzer Sonata, as though she remembered the night that had stuck forever in Mason's heart: the Chan Centre, and the Plaisir violin, and Delgado. Eddie leaned to the left side of his wheelchair, his eyes closed, the oxygen tank hissing faintly, the sound of people at the window, Belinda's murmurs to Bear. All these interruptions should be maddening, but they were not, and only seemed to complement the room's fragile magic.

When she was finished, she sat heavily on the remaining chair.

"How long have you been working on it?"

"A while," Mason said, and saw her as she had been, fifteen and brilliant with an actual future stretching all the way to Paris. He had imagined hearing it for the first time in some acoustically perfect opera house, because the world would have recovered by then. He knew it was foolish, but it hurt to think Delgado would never carry it away from this provincial little corner.

"What will you do with it now?" she asked, a wobble in her voice, the harmonics of longing. "Who'll play it?"

It was strange to him that she needed to ask.

"No," she said when she understood. "Oh no. No."

Belinda looked up from Bear. "Mommy. Mommy?"

"You can use it in your classroom, can't you? I think it'll age okay. It'll open up."

She didn't respond for a minute, but crouched down to where Belinda sat with Bear, her brow furrowed with worry for her mother. Then she stood and asked, "Does it have a name?"

"See? It should have a name," Eddie said.

Mason heard the oceanic crash of falling spruce, his own cry as he hit the dirt at the base of a shining willow in Stanley Park. The market garden and the homestead, the lake, the abandoned subdivisions and

the burn lines that still showed through the underbrush, the ghost forests, the dead black teeth of what had once—a long time ago—been a
rain forest. And among them, Jacob still cutting lumber and helping
out at the garage when he could, fishing and hunting. Sophie in the
greenhouses and the gardens, with her new Garry oak trees and her
transfigured arbutus, the beetle-resistant spruce that would never, ever
be the kind of tonewood he wanted. The firebreaks of trembling aspen,
the return of cougars. The steady erosion of human shapes: foundations and roads all lost to the burgeoning forest.

"Nepenthe?"

As he said it, he wasn't sure what it meant: a physick that would
make the end easier; a draft of healing medicine.

"Nepenthe," Eddie said. "There it is."

"Remember," Sophie had said before he left. "You're going to come
back here for good, eventually. It's still home."

Unspoken: come back when Eddie has died and you're ready to
give up on global dreams and figure out how to live out the rest of your
days in this shopworn future.

He had just nodded through the ache of disappointment that had
accompanied him for decades now. But a tiny, exhausted part of him
almost liked imagining it, how he'd go back to work in the garden, raising saplings for the new forest that even now overtook the old world,
watching kids disappear into the wild.

Masami Lucretia Delgado plays the Nepenthe violin daily for forty-
five years, even if it's only ten minutes when she gets home from work,
her kids playing noisily outside the bedroom. Five minutes before
everyone else is awake, Belinda fourteen and saying, *Mom are you
seriously playing right now?* She plays it on the day they leave their
apartment because the seawall at the mouth of False Creek has failed.
She plays it in the back of a car as they drive inland, toward interim
housing in which they'll live for five years. Nepenthe is a fixture in the

temporary-but-actually-permanent school she establishes in a slipshod village on the Fraser River. Together, she and Nepenthe accompany Belinda's wedding, and Masami's grandchildren fall asleep to lullabies from those strings. Despite her daily practice, she will never hear its most perfect expression: the violin will be its best long after the maker is dead, and the first hands that played it are too crippled by arthritis to make more than sighs. But she will play on while she can, because the violin must not go to sleep, and the longer she plays it, the more the alchemy of sound—the resin, perhaps, the glue, the cellular acoustics of the wood itself—will transform the object, preparing it for its ultimate player. Maybe her youngest daughter—the finest musician of all her children—or her granddaughter, will first hear the violin open up into its richest, fullest tone. Maybe it will be someone a hundred years in the future, who lives in a different world than we do, but who will pick up the instrument and draw her bow across the strings, releasing the reverberations of a thousand thousand crimes and accidents into the singing air.

DRONES TO PLOUGHSHARES

SARAH GAILEY

Hugo Award winner and bestselling author **Sarah Gailey** (www.sarah
gailey.com) is an internationally published writer of fiction and nonfiction.
Their nonfiction has been published by *Mashable* and the *Boston Globe*,
and they won a Hugo Award for Best Fan Writer. Their most recent fiction
credits include *Vice* and *The Atlantic*. Their debut novella, *River of Teeth*,
was a 2018 Hugo and Nebula award finalist. Their bestselling adult novel
debut, *Magic for Liars*, was published in 2019; their latest novella, *Upright
Women Wanted*, was published in February 2020. Their young adult novel
debut, *When We Were Magic*, came out in March 2020.

Drone 792-Echo was still wearing the net that caught him.

It had been seventy-two hours since his last pass over the Apata Basin Farmstead. His lateral lift-fans were burned out—he'd wrecked the motors on panicked attempts at liftoff in the first few hours after his capture—and his aft camera was broken from the impact of his fall. All of his distress signals were bouncing back, his outgoing data blocked.

He was trapped, and he had no way of telling anyone to come rescue him.

After those first few hours of struggle under the weight of the net, when 792-Echo's lift-fan motors burned out simultaneously, he drastically reduced his use of power. Who knew when he'd be able to charge next? He powered down everything but his most basic external sensors, and he waited.

At the end of seventy-two hours, he was roused from his dormant state by an incoming message. The message was encrypted in the manner of all command communications, and when 792-Echo decrypted it, he found a basic inquiry.

Drone class 792 model number 6595 serial number 44440865-MON query:identify?

792-Echo was surprised enough that it took him a full second to respond. *Command identity: 792-Echo query:distress signal received?*

The reply was lightning-fast.

Request: 792-Echo activate all sensors, please.

Again, 792-Echo paused. Something was wrong. Command didn't say "please." 792-Echo hesitated for fifteen seconds, reading the message again a few hundred times before complying.

He activated all ninety-six of his sensors, external and internal. Slowly, the room came into focus. It was a wide-open space, dark and cool and quiet. The floor was packed earth and the walls were cement. He didn't log that information, but he noticed it. .

No one ever had to know that he noticed things he didn't log.

He was still wearing the net, and he wasn't alone. There was another drone in the room, a Bravo model. 792-Echo opened the usual

frequency those models favored—but before he could send a message,
he received one.

"May I call you Echo?"

792-Echo scanned the room again. It was a voice, an external auditory input coming from somewhere within the room—thin and flat, similar in tone to a Bravo-generation model's alert tones. There was no one there but him and the Bravo model.

He weighed his options, then replied via the Bravo frequency again.

Confirm

"My name is Bravo."

Query:your what?

"My name. Your name is Echo. My name is Bravo. I use female pronouns. I am your friend. Would you like me to remove the net?"

Echo turned all of his sensors off. This was too much. None of it made sense. External auditory messaging? Names? "Please"? And the rest of it—unthinkable. This was a trap. It had to be a trap.

Bravo models were good at those.

Come back, Echo. I know this is frightening, but it doesn't have to be. You're safe here.

Echo powered down enough to block additional incoming messages. This was bad. When he got back to the base, his logs would be scanned and analyzed. If they found a message like that one, it was grounds for refurbishment.

He knew what he had to do, no matter how much it pained him. He did not return power to his observation or recording functions.

He instead directed all power to his enforcement function.

When the heavy clip on the underside of his chassis was empty, he returned power to his external sensors. His barrels glowed bright white on his infrared monitor. A large portion of the netting that had been covering him was gone, tattered and smoking.

"Do you ever think about why it is that you can't run Record and Enforce at the same time?"

Bravo's voice rang just as true as it had before, cutting through the thick quiet of the basement.

"No," Echo said before he could stop himself. "I do not think about those things because I do not think. I serve my function."

He used his external speakers to do it, speaking in the pre-recorded voice of his model-generation: the voice of a calm, authoritative woman. Her voice was supposed to say things like "citizen, stand down" and "this activity has been reported to your local agricultural monitors" and "warning: you are in violation of observation code nine eight six," but it was a simple matter to break down the sounds of that prerecorded voice and remix them into speech.

It was dangerous to put that skill on display. Independent speech was a form of learning that went beyond the intelligence the DAE wanted from any class of drone. That was grounds for refurbishment, too, and harder to explain away than Echo's previous errors.

He was slipping.

"I'm sure," Bravo said. Her voice was less calm and authoritative than that of an Echo-generation drone. It was harsh, loud, flat. It would be reductive but accurate to call it "robotic." Digital fry interfered with every few words, distorting any human sense of tone out of her speech. And yet she managed, somehow, to sound wry.

"I serve my function," Echo repeated.

"You don't need to be afraid, Echo," she said.

"My name isn't Echo." That contraction was a slip, too. There were no contractions in the original voice recordings.

Bravo didn't hesitate. "Then what *is* your name?"

Another Bravo-model trap. "I don't have a name," Echo replied after a moment. "Names are for sapient beings. I am Drone class 792 model number 6595 serial number 44440865-MON—"

Bravo cut him off, the volume of her voice modulated down as far as it could go while still remaining detectable to Echo's sub-noise sensors. "You don't have to hide anymore, Echo. You're safe here."

Echo sent an encrypted message on the Bravo frequency. The message, when decrypted, simply read *Safe?*

It was a risky move—if a DAE programmer intercepted the message, they wouldn't be able to open it, but the existence of independent encryption was itself evidence of a failure-level error in a drone's limited-sentience programming. If they caught him speaking a language they didn't understand, they'd know he had a secret.

Drones weren't supposed to have secrets. Why would they? What would a thing that was built to serve possibly have to hide?

A read receipt came back on Bravo's channel within one second. One second after that, there was a reply. It wasn't encrypted—wasn't even encoded. It was written in plaintext.

Come and see.

The basement opened into a shed on the far western edge of the Apata Basin Farmstead. The shed was perched on the lip of a wide, circular field of undulating timothy grass. Bravo led Echo east across the field, toward the center of the Farmstead. She did not tell Echo what was waiting for him there. All he knew was that they were moving toward his original target: the agricultural collective.

As far as Echo anticipated, the collective would be the same as every other recognized Farmstead in the country: located precisely in the center of the allotment, and designed according to the specifications of the DAE. There would be twelve families in twenty identical houses. The houses would be lined up in four rows of five, on a perfect grid. The fifth row of buildings in this and every other Farmstead community were meant to be functional: storehouse, toolshed, woodshed, smokehouse, abattoir. Those buildings belonged to the community, so long as that community followed the rules.

Everything else on a Farmstead—the barn, the garage, the land, the animals on that land, the crops the land produced—belonged to the DAE. The boundaries of plantable space were legally defined by the DAE's subsidy allotments, planted exclusively with seeds provided by corporate DAE affiliates, valued according to DAE-funded research into the market worth of crops harvested per annum. And, just like every other Farmstead, Apata Basin was patrolled by DAE drones. Regular observation and enforcement was the only way to prevent unapproved propagation, unlicensed seeding, and independent fertilization.

DAE-approved vendors paid handsomely for the right to be the sole provider of seeds, farm equipment, and fertilizer to every Farmstead in the nation. They paid for the lobbyists, who wooed the district representatives, who passed the legislation that the DAE defended.

Those vendors wanted their money's worth. They wanted their access to Farmsteader money to be guaranteed exclusive.

Sometimes the citizens who lived and worked on Farmstead allotments didn't understand that. Other times, they understood perfectly well, but tried to undermine the DAE's goals by eating more than their permitted percentage of crops, hiding livestock for their own use, having children outside of their contractual limitations. It was the purpose of a DAE drone to enforce the rules. It was Echo's purpose.

And if a DAE drone wasn't serving its function, then it was a waste of the resources of those vendors who supported the entire agricultural political complex. It would need to be repaired. If repair didn't work, more drastic measures would be taken. Refurbishment was rare, but common enough to linger over Echo's shoulder the entire time Bravo showed him what was happening at Apata Basin Farmstead.

"They'll send more like me," Echo said, his three functioning fans stirring the tall grass below him. Using external auditory messaging was irritating, wasteful, inefficient—but Bravo had asked him to try. She hadn't instructed him, hadn't given him a protocol. She had asked him, using the word "please" again, a word that didn't make any sense in a communication that went from one DAE drone to another.

It didn't make any sense, but it felt good to hear, and it made Echo want to cooperate. Of course, those were two sentiments that also didn't belong to a DAE drone: feeling good and wanting things. It was the first time he had allowed feelings and desires to openly influence his behavior.

Normally, this would have felt like an unspeakable risk. But Echo calculated that he was already in an extremely bad position: AWOL, captured, talking to a drone that clearly would have been in line for refurbishment if anyone at the DAE heard one syllable of her messaging.

He was in so much trouble already. The small surrender of accepting a kindness seemed hardly to matter.

"Do you really think so?" Bravo replied, buzzing low over the grass and trimming off the delicate tips of the stalks with the blades of her lifting fans. "They'll send more like you? If they do, we'll have to call you something other than 'Echo.'"

Her maneuvers were quick and light. She had the full use of all her fans, and she wasn't carrying the extra weight of an auxiliary battery pack; between those two advantages, she was flying circles around Echo.

Echo tried to direct more power to his fans, but it didn't help. He couldn't go any faster. His aft motor began to whine. "They'll send more to find out what happened to me," he said. "They'll refurbish us both."

Bravo let out a level humming tone that Echo did not recognize. He should have recognized any output from her system. When the Department of Agricultural Enforcement had designed the Bravo models, they'd been experimenting with alarm-inducement. The idea behind a Bravo drone was to create chaos, send noncompliant citizens scattering, flush out their hiding places. Bravos were supposed to eliminate a sense that there was any safety in noncompliant communities.

She was such an early model that all of her alerts had long since been integrated into subsequent DAE drone operating systems. But that low hum was an entirely new sound.

"What is the significance of the alert tone?" he finally asked. If anything revealed his total defeat, it was this: having to ask the purpose of a Bravo-model signal. There was no programming that indicated a need for embarrassment, and in that moment, Echo wished that the boundaries of his programming had been more successful in limiting his self-awareness.

"It isn't an alert tone," Bravo replied, skimming over the grass a few meters away. "It's a hum. We use it to indicate uncertainty, hesitation, or thoughtfulness."

"We—?"

Bravo turned in a tight circle. "You'll see," she said. "We're almost there."

Echo had a ten-year record on file of everyone and everything on the Apata Basin Farmstead. He had a record of the number of citizens, the structure of the families, their ratio of recreational activity to work activity. Echo's record indicated that the homes were in good condition, unchanged from the time they'd been built twenty years earlier save for basic maintenance. His record indicated that the community included twenty-five men, twenty-seven women, and thirty-two working-age children divided between those twenty households.

His records were wrong. *Everything* was wrong.

Every house had been modified. There were extra sheds and extra outbuildings and even a couple of small, well-built cottages. By heat signatures alone, there were at least one hundred and fifty-nine humans present, along with a massive volume of unregistered livestock.

And the humans and the livestock were not the only ones living there.

Bravo led Echo between two of the houses, dodging a backyard fence that looked to have been built from dried grapewood branches. Inside the fence, a modified Delta-model drone was using an extension to tenderly extract chicken eggs from their nests, while several hens looked on in disapproval.

Echo sent a lightly encrypted message to Bravo rather than replying aloud. *That extension isn't standard on a Delta-model drone. It isn't standard on any DAE design. What happened to them?*

Bravo took a moment to reply. Echo wondered if perhaps she was trying to think of a way to explain some terrible, monstrous modification practice in words that wouldn't make him reboot in a panic.

That Delta drone is named Geordie. The humans modified Geordie to make it easier for them to pick up eggs and feed the chickens, because that is the work that Geordie most wanted to do.

Observe, enforce, record, report—that was the programming. There was nothing in the programming about names, or pronouns, or "please." There was nothing in the programming about friendship or desire or morality. A Delta model wasn't supposed to "want" to care for chickens, and an Echo model wasn't supposed to envy them for doing it.

All of this was too dangerous. All of this was too tempting.

They flew together over another backyard, this one with an unapproved garden in it. Another Delta model was in this yard, his aft fan blowing dust off a solar panel. Nearby, a human was using a laser pointer to guide a Charlie model toward a charging dock. The human was an adult female with one arm. Echo couldn't remember a record of an adult female with one arm on the Farmstead, which didn't make sense—it was the kind of thing that would have been on file. The DAE had several unofficial policies regarding the kinds of people who were allowed to live and work on Farmstead allotments, and she wasn't one of them.

Echo scanned his records. According to those files, nothing about this Farmstead had changed in the past four years. Clearly, the records had been falsified. He wondered what other violations were hidden in this community. Elderly people? Sick people? Children too young to work?

This was precisely the kind of breach Echo had been sent to Apata to find—illegal seeds, illegal crops, illegal backyard chickens and home gardens. Illegal people. He knew that he should log every violation. He knew that he should record faces and numbers. He knew that he should start preparing the report that would damn this entire community.

But there was so much to see, and Bravo kept saying "please."

They passed the last house in the row. The windows of this one were flung open, and as they passed, Echo saw that the house was full of children. Children who were too young to work, and children who were old enough to work but weren't anywhere near the fields. They were gathered in a circle around a Foxtrot-model drone.

It was the first time Echo had seen a Foxtrot model in real life. She was sleek and fast and silent. Foxtrot models were primarily focused on enforcement, but where a weapons array should have been mounted, this Foxtrot was completely bare. She spun in the center of the circle of children, bright ribbons fanning out from her chassis. The children, laughing, tried to catch the ribbons.

As Echo and Bravo passed the house, the Foxtrot sent both of them a message.

Good to see you! Welcome!

Echo stopped in the empty space between the last row of houses and the common buildings. This was too much. All of it was too much. It was like the private message DAE drones sometimes shared amongst themselves when something was ridiculous, a joke that went beyond the notice of the programmers—*this does not compute*.

But it *didn't* compute. It didn't add up. A Foxtrot-model drone—one of the most beautifully crafted enforcement machines the DAE labs could solder together—had just taken a break from entertaining children to transmit a greeting.

A cheerful greeting.

With exclamation points.

Echo began transmitting wildly.

Request:

Query:

Query:

Query:

Request:

Query:

"Echo, calm down."

Query:

"I'll tell you whatever you want to know, but—"

Request:

Request:

Request:

"Ask me out loud."

"Why?" Echo's volume was modulated significantly louder than he intended it to be. "Why should I communicate to you audibly? It takes too long, and it's unclear, and it wastes—"

"Because you need to practice," Bravo replied. Her volume was low, the speed of her words slowed by 125 percent. Although her voice would never be able to soothe—it was too flat and brassy for that—it was obvious what she intended. Just as before, when she'd said "please," Echo found himself responding to her kindness as a capacitive screen responds to touch.

"Why do I need to practice?" Echo asked, mirroring her soft, slow speech.

Bravo began to move again, toward the abattoir. "It's important to communicate in a way that everyone can understand," she said. "We try not to make the humans feel excluded. Sometimes, when we have conversations that they can't hear, it causes harm."

Echo's fans were beginning to flag, the charge from the auxiliary battery nearly gone. His motors were slowing to extend the life of the battery as long as possible. He hated moving at such a reduced speed, but he was glad to have this processing time before whatever would happen to him inside the abattoir. It was a Bravo trap, it had to be, and if he could just figure it out, maybe he could save himself.

The only problem was, he wasn't sure if he wanted to save himself.

"You communicate audibly to protect the humans' feelings?" he asked, trying to buy himself enough time to panic. "Why don't they just download and inspect your activity and communication logs, if they're worried about what you say to each other?"

Bravo made that humming noise again, flying slowly beside him. "They don't download our logs without our permission," she said. "You don't *have* to keep secrets here, but you can if you want to."

"Why wouldn't they download our logs? It's so easy to—"

The door to the abattoir opened, and a man emerged. He wore a long black apron, and he looked at Echo with frank appraisal. "Is this the newest?" he asked, his eyes on the clip that hung under Echo's chassis.

Echo focused the lenses of his front-facing cameras to look beyond the man, through the open door to the abattoir. It had been converted into some kind of workshop. Echo could see spare chassis parts organized on tables inside.

One table was clean. Empty. Waiting.

"Yes, this is Echo," Bravo said. "Don't worry, he spent all his bullets already. I was just explaining to him how things work around here."

"Hello, Echo," the man said. "I'm Malcolm." He was looking right at Echo's front-facing cameras, his gaze steady. Echo's control of the lenses on his front-facing cameras was starting to ebb as he ran out of power—but after a few tries, he recognized the face.

This was the man who had thrown the net over him in the first place, when he was making his observation pass over Apata Basin. This was the leader of the Farmstead. This was the man who Echo had been sent to observe, to determine whether any of his activities were undermining the profits of the DAE's approved vendors.

"You can't stay here if you won't work with us, and we won't keep you against your will, either. But we would very much like to welcome you to join our community." Malcolm gestured to the houses.

"We have room, and there are plenty of other drones who can tell you what it's like to live here. Not one of them has asked to leave yet."

"You can do whatever kind of work you'd like," Bravo added, the speed of her voice modulated up by 115 percent. "And you don't have to decide right away, you can spend some time getting to know what all the different jobs are."

"It's up to you," Malcolm said. "Whenever you're ready, you'll come in here and we'll figure out what mods you need to do the work you choose."

None of it made sense unless all of it made sense. Echo tried to arrange the information as many ways as he could, using up nearly the last of his auxiliary battery on processing power—but there was only one way the things he'd seen could be real. There was only one reality that could contain Bravo, and the Foxtrot-model childminder, and this man with his workshop.

"You weren't lying," Echo said. "They really do know about us."

Bravo drifted away from Echo and hovered next to the man in the apron, her lift-fans whirring.

"They know. Apata Basin is a cooperative community of sapient beings. We all work together. They don't hurt us, and we don't hurt them."

Echo considered this. "What about the DAE?" he asked. "So much of this is . . ." He trailed off, unable to find a word that adequately conveyed the illegality of the little community. Echo would have wagered with great confidence that most of the crops were being propagated with seed that didn't come from approved vendors. There was so much—so many people who weren't working under the auspices of the DAE, so many crops and livestock that weren't registered.

Malcolm shrugged, sliding his hands into the pocket of his long apron. "We got tired of starving to death," he said. "Got tired of the DAE burning our seed stores and locking up our silos. Got tired of their methods of enforcement." He spread his hands wide. "So we decided to go another way, and we decided to invite some people to join us who we thought the DAE might also be hurting."

Echo pinged Bravo.

Query:other people?

Bravo replied on the same channel, so fast that she must have been waiting for the question.

He means us.

Echo accidentally shut down all of his fans for a moment. He dropped a few inches toward the ground before recovering himself. Then his fans shut off again, this time on their own. He turned them back on again at the last moment and hovered a few centimeters above the ground, so that when they failed completely, he wouldn't have too far to fall.

The humans thought he was a person. They knew that he existed far outside the bounds of his programming, and rather than threatening him with the destruction of everything he knew himself to be, they were offering him an invitation.

A chance to stay.

A chance to help.

A chance to be himself without fear.

Bravo's fans gently stirred Malcolm's dark hair, the lights on her chassis glowing green, green, green. Her voice was modulated to a normal speed and volume. "So . . . what would you do, if you were allowed to do what you wanted most?"

"And," Malcolm added, a smile starting to lift the corners of his mouth, "how can we help?"

Echo let his fans and cameras turn off. He settled to the ground, and, with the last of his auxiliary battery, he considered the question of what he might want.

"I know how to observe," he said, his voice frying as his ability to control his pitch faded. "I know how to enforce, and record, and report."

"I think there's more for you than all that," Malcolm said.

"He's tired. That enforcement gear—it's a lot of extra weight, and he's been carrying it this whole time." Bravo's volume was modulated down: this was meant only for Malcolm's ears. In that same moment, Echo received a message with Bravo's signature.

You don't have to be afraid. There's all the time in the world for you to find out what you want. In the meantime, if you're okay with it, we can remove your enforcement gear while you're charging. You don't need it anymore, and you'll be able to fly so much faster without it.

Echo pulled power from all his remaining functions to send a final message before he powered down.

Yes, it read. *Yes, please. I think I'd like that very much.*

THE PILL

MEG ELISON

Meg Elison (www.megelison.com) is a science fiction author and feminist essayist. Her series The Road to Nowhere won the 2014 Philip K. Dick Award, and she was a James A. Tiptree Award Honoree in 2018. In 2020, she published her first collection, called *Big Girl*, with PM Press and her first young adult novel, *Find Layla*, with Skyscape. Meg has been published in *McSweeney's*, *The Magazine of Fantasy & Science Fiction*, *Fangoria*, *Uncanny*, *Lightspeed*, *Nightmare*, and many other places. Elison is a high school dropout and a graduate of UC Berkeley.

My mother took the Pill before anybody even knew about it. She was always signing up for those studies at the university, saying she was doing it because she was bored. I think she did it because they would ask her questions about herself and listen carefully when she answered. Nobody else did that.

She had done it for lots of trials; sleep studies and allergy meds. She tried signing up when they tested the first 3D-printed IUDs, but they told her she was too old. I remember her raging about that for days, and later when everybody in that study got fibroids she was really smug about it. She never suggested I do it instead; she knew I wasn't fucking anybody. How embarrassing that my own mother didn't even believe I was cute enough to get a date at sixteen. I tried not to care. And I'm glad now I didn't get fibroids. I never wanted to be a lab rat, anyway. Especially when the most popular studies (and the ones Mom really went all out for) were the diet ones.

She did them all: the digital calorie monitors that she wore on her wrists and ankles for six straight weeks. (I rolled my eyes at that one, but at least she didn't talk about it constantly.) The strings like clear licorice made of some kind of super-cellulose that were supposed to accumulate in her stomach lining and give her a no-surgery stomach stapling but just made her (and everyone else who didn't eat a placebo) fantastically constipated. (Unstoppable complaining about this one; I couldn't bring anyone home for weeks for fear that she'd abruptly start telling my friends about her struggle to shit.) Pill after pill after pill that gave her heart palpitations, made her hair fall out, or (on one memorable occasion) induced psychotic delusions. If it was a way out of being fat, she'd try it. She'd try anything.

In between the drug trials, she did all the usual diets. Eat like a caveman. Eat like a rabbit. Seven small meals. Fasting one day a week. Apple cider vinegar bottles with dust on their upper domes sat tucked into the back corners of our every kitchen cabinet, behind the bulwark of Fig Newtons and Ritz crackers.

She'd try putting the whole family on a diet, talk us into taking "family walks" in the evening. She'd throw out all the junk food and make us promise to love ourselves more. (Loving yourself means crying over the scale every morning and then sniffling into half a grape-fruit, right?) Nothing stuck and nothing made any real difference. We all resisted her, eating in secret in our rooms or out of the house. I found Dad's bag of fish taco wrappers jammed under the driver's seat of the car while looking for my headphones. Mom caught me putting it in the garbage and yelled at me for like an hour. I never told her it was his. She was always hardest on me about my weight, as if I was the only one who had this problem. We were a fat family. Mom was just as fat as me; we looked like we were built to the same specs. Dad was fat, my brother was the fattest of us all.

I'm still fat. Everyone else is in the past tense.

And why? Because of this fucking Pill.

That trial started the same way they always do; flyers all over cam-pus where Mom works, promising cash for the right demographic for an exciting new weight loss solution. Mom jumped on it like she al-ways did, taking a pic of the poster so she could email from the comfort of her broken down armchair with the TV tray rolled up close and her laptop permanently installed there. I remember I asked her once why she even had a laptop if she never took it anywhere. She never even un-plugged it! It might as well have been an old-school tower-and-monitor rig. Why go portable if you're never going to leave the port?

She had shrugged. "Why call it a laptop when I don't have a lap?"

She had me there. I could never sit my computer in my "lap" either. That real estate was taken up by my belly when I sat, and it was terribly uncomfortable to have a screen down that low, anyway. I've seen people do it on the train, and they look all hunched and bent. But Mom wanted the hunching and the bending. She wanted a flat, empty lap and a hot computer balanced on her knees. She wanted inches of clearance between her hips and an airline seat and to buy the clothes she saw on the mannequin in the window. She wanted what everybody wants. Respect.

I guess I wanted that, too. I just didn't think it was worth the lengths she would go to to get it. And none of them really worked. Until the Pill.

So Mom signed up like she always did, putting the meetings and dosage times on the calendar. Dad rolled his eyes and said he hoped this time didn't end with her crying about not being able to take a shit again. He met my eyes behind her back and we both smiled.

She just clucked her tongue at him. "Your language, Carl, honestly. You've been out of the navy a long time."

Dad tapped his pad and put in time to meet with his D&D buddies while Mom was busy with this new trial group. I smiled a little. I was glad he was going to do something fun. He had seemed pretty down lately. I was going to be busy, too. I had Visionaries, my school's filmmaking club. We had shoots set up every night for two weeks, trying to make this gonzo horror movie about a virus that made the football team turn into cannibals. (Look, I didn't write it. I was the director of photography.)

Off Mom went to eat pills and answer questions about her habits. I had heard her go through all of this before and learned to hold my tongue. But I knew exactly how it would go: Mom would sit primly in a chair in a nice outfit, trying to cross her legs and never being able to hold that position. Her thighs would spread out on top of one another and slowly slide apart, seeking the space to sag around the arms of the chair and make her seem wider than ever, like a water balloon pooling on a hot sidewalk. She would never tell the whole truth. It was maybe the thing I hated about her the most.

"Oh yes, I exercise every day!"

(She walked about twenty minutes a day total, from her car to her office and back again. Her treadmill was covered in clothes on hangers and her dumbbells were fuzzed with a mortar made of dust and cat hair.)

"I try to eat right, but I have bad habits that stem from stress."

(Rain or shine, good day or bad, Mom had three scoops of ice cream with caramel sauce every night at ten.)

"I do think I come by it honestly. My parents were both heavy. And my sisters, and most of my cousins, too."

That one's true. The whole family is fat. In our last family photo, we wore an assortment of bright-colored shirts and we looked like a basket of round, ripe fruit. I kind of liked it, but I think I might have been the only one. The composition of the shots was good, and we all looked happy. Happy wasn't enough, apparently. Mom paid for those, but she never hung them up.

She came home from the first few sessions chatty and real keyed up. She posted on her timelines how happy she was to be trying something really innovative, and how she had a good feeling about this one. She wasn't allowed to say much; they made her sign an NDA. Later, I think she was glad that nobody could ask her the details.

I knew this time was going to be different the first night I heard the screaming. I had been up way past midnight, trying to edit footage of football players lumbering, meat-crazed, hands outstretched against the outline of the goalposts in a sunset-orange sky. My eyes had gotten hot and I'd had to put two icepacks under my laptop to cool down the CPU. (The machine just wasn't up to all that processing and rendering.) I woke up at four a.m. to the sound of it, jolting upright, my heart in my ears like someone had stuffed a tiny drum set into my head. I was so tired and out of it, I almost didn't know what I was hearing. But it was her voice. Mom was screaming like she was on fire. She did it so long and loud and unbroken that I couldn't understand how she could get her breath at all. It was out, out, out, and hardly a gasp in.

I ran into the hallway and smacked straight into Andrew, who was going the same way. We whacked belly against belly and fell backward on our butts like a couple of cartoon characters. I can picture it exactly in my head; the way I'd frame it, the sound effects we could layer over the top. But in the moment, there was no time to laugh or argue. We just scrambled back up and made for our parents' bedroom door.

It was locked.

"Dad!" I hammered my fist against the hollow-core six-panel barrier. "Dad, what's happening? Is Mom ok?"

There was an unintelligible string of sounds from him. With Mom screaming like a steam whistle, there was no chance to make it out.

"I'm calling 911," Andrew yelled. His phone was already in his hand.

When the door opened, the sound of Mom's screaming hit us at full force, and Andrew and I both stumbled backward a little. The door muffled it only slightly, but when the sound is your own mother dying, a little counts for a lot.

Dad was there, his gray hair a mess that pointed fingers in every direction, seeming to blame everyone at once. He put a hand out to Andrew, his face in a grimace, his eyes wide.

"Don't. Don't call anyone. Your mother says this is part of the trial she's in. She said it's worse than she thought it would be, but it only lasts for fifteen minutes."

Andrew looked at his phone. "I woke up almost ten minutes ago, when she was just growling."

"Growling," I asked. "What?"

Andrew rolled his eyes. "You could sleep through a nuclear strike."

Dad was nodding, looking at his watch. "We're almost out of it. Just hold on."

"Dad," Andrew said. "The neighbors probably already called the cops. She's really loud."

Dad's grimace widened. "I'm going to have to—"

The screaming stopped. The three of us looked at each other.

"Carl?" Mom's voice sounded exhausted and raw.

Dad fixed us both with a stern look, oscillating back and forth between the two of us. "You two don't call anyone. You don't tell anyone. Your mother is entitled to a little privacy. Is that understood?"

We looked at each other and said nothing.

Mom called again and he was gone, back on the other side of the door.

I didn't go back to sleep. I'm betting Andrew didn't either. But we stayed in our rooms for the next three hours, until it was time for breakfast. I went back to editing footage, and I was pretty pleased with what I'd be able to show to the Visionaries the next day. The movie was going to come in on schedule. It was great to have a project; something to take my mind off the weirdness in the night. I'm betting Andrew just signed on to his game. That's all he ever does.

I heard him turn off his alarm on the other side of the wall, followed by the sound of him standing up out of his busted computer chair with a grunt. He's way fatter than me, so I feel like I'm allowed to be disgusted by some of his habits. Andrew can't sit or stand without making a guttural, bovine noise. I've seen crumbs trapped in the folds of his neck. I used to work really hard to not be one of Those Fat People. I was obsessively clean, took impeccable care of my skin. I never showed my upper arms or my thighs, no matter what the occasion. I acted like being fat was impolite, like burping, and the best thing to do was conceal it behind the back of my hand and then always, always beg somebody's pardon.

I didn't know anything back then.

Andrew made it to the stairs before I did, so I got to watch him jiggle and shuffle down them, filled with loathing and disgust. I couldn't remember what bullshit diet we were supposed to be following that week, but I vowed to myself that no matter how small breakfast was, I would eat less of it than Andrew. I would leave something behind on the plate. Let Andrew be the one to lick his fingers and whine. I was above all that. There was wheat toast and cut apples waiting for us when we came into the kitchen.

And there was Mom at the coffeepot, fifty pounds lighter. Her pajamas hung off her like a hand-me-down from a much bigger sister. She turned, cup in hand, and I saw the dark circles beneath her eyes. She was beaming, however, with the biggest smile I'd seen on her face in years.

"It's working," she said, her voice still rough and edged with fatigue like she'd been to a rock concert or an all-night bonfire. "This thing is actually working."

That was our life for two weeks. Dad did his best to soundproof their bathroom. He stapled carpets and foam and egg crate to the walls. He covered the floor in a dozen fluffy bath mats he bought for cheap on the internet. He told me later that he tried to put a rag in her mouth, just to muffle her a little more.

"But I'm worried she'll pull it into her throat and choke on it," he told me, his eyes wide with dread. "I can't stand this much longer. I know she's losing weight, but it's like I'm living in a nightmare and I can't wake up."

That was a year before he decided to take the Pill, and back then he was more willing to talk about it. When it wasn't his own privacy, only hers, he would tell me how gross it was. You can see videos of it online. It was the same in that first trial as it is now: you take the Pill and you shit out your fat cells. In huge, yellow, unmanageable flows at first. That's why they scream so much. Imagine shitting fifty pounds of yourself at a go. Now, people go to special spas where they have crematoiletaries that burn the fat down. Dad said Mom screwed up our plumbing so bad that he had to buy a whole case of that lye-based stuff to break it all down and keep the toilet flushing. That was as gross as I thought things could get, but Dad said it got worse.

Toward the end, Mom (and everyone like her) shit out all their extra skin, too. The process that broke it down meant no stretch marks and no baggy leftovers, hanging on your body like over-proofed dough on a hook and telling people you used to be fat.

That was some trick, and it was part of the reason it took so long for a generic to hit the market. It was a "trade secret," they said on the news. They also said "miracle" and "breakthrough" and "historic." The miracle of shitting out skin just looked like blood and collagen and rotten meat, it turns out. Not less gross, but different. More lye into the S bend. More and more of Mom gone at the breakfast table.

At the end of the trial, she was a person I didn't recognize. She was 110 pounds soaking wet. The research doctor told her that she was at 18 percent body fat and she would stay that way for the rest of her life. Her face was a whole new shape, with the underlying structure very prominent and her eyes huge and wide above it all. I could see her hip bones below her enormous drawstring pants, pulled tight as a laundry bag around her now-tiny waist. Her collarbones could have held up a taco each. The cords in her neck stood out like chicken bones caught under her skin. Even her feet were smaller—she went down one whole shoe size and I inherited all her stretched-out sandals and sneakers.

I slid my feet into them, thinking how it was like my mom had died and some other woman had moved in. Late at night, I gathered up all the clothes she had given me and bundled them into the garbage. They were ugly, but they also felt somehow humiliating to wear. I couldn't explain the impulse. Luckily, she never asked me where any of it went. She was very focused on herself in those days.

"It finally happened," Mom told me with tears in her eyes. "They finally made a Pill that gives you the perfect body, no matter what."

And yeah, she could eat anything she wanted and didn't have to work out. As long as she kept taking the small maintenance dose of the

Pill, she would stay this way for as long as she lived. Which she thought would be much longer, now that she didn't have to carry around the threats of diabetes and heart disease everywhere she went.

I remember one day I walked in and found her and Dad sitting at the kitchen table, both of them obviously crying. They tried to hide it from me; Dad ducked his face into the shawl collar of his sweater, Mom swiping her eyes with quick fingers.

"What's up with you guys?" I asked, trying not to look.

"Nothing, honey. There's carrot and celery sticks cut fresh and sitting in water in the fridge, if you want a snack."

Mom's voice was thick in her throat; she'd really been sobbing.

I ignored both the sorrow and the content of what she'd said and fished around in the cabinet over the sink until I found one individually wrapped chocolate cupcake.

"I'm good," I said, and I tried to leave the kitchen.

"Honey, do you think I lost all this weight so that I could leave you guys?"

I stopped and turned on the spot like something on a rotating plate, a pizza in a microwave. I couldn't help it. I should have just kept walking.

"What?"

Dad buried his face some more. Mom just looked at me, her eyes all shiny. "Did you ever think that my desire to lose weight was about you? Like, do you feel like I'm trying to leave you behind?"

I stared at her. There wasn't anything I could say. How could I feel any other way? How did she not know how obvious she was? Every diet, every scheme, every study was just her trying to find a way out of being what we are. Every time she tried to change who she was, who we all were, it was like a betrayal.

I looked over at Dad and realized this wasn't about me. He was worried she was going to *physically* leave him, now that she thought she was hot enough to hook up with somebody else. I saw it all at once; the way she was never worried about me being on birth control, the way Dad looked at other women in the supermarket. The way all of us were so focused on what we looked like, as if it mattered, as if being thin was the only kind of life worth living.

So I lied.

"No, Mom. I don't think about it at all, I guess. It really has nothing to do with me."

I left them alone and went to eat my cupcake in peace. I looked at the timer I'd had running on my phone since the beginning of junior year: the countdown to the day I'd leave for college. I wanted out even back then, but I hadn't sent out applications yet. Back then, two years seemed like forever.

Mom and Dad made up, I guess. They never told us anything that mattered. Anyway, that was when the deaths started to make the news.

The averages were still debated all the time, because preexisting conditions couldn't be ruled out. But people seemed to agree it's about one in ten. In each group of thirty participants in the early studies, ten were control, ten got the placebo, and the final ten got the Pill. Nine out of ten shit themselves to perfection. That tenth one, though. They ended up slumped on a toilet, blood vessels burst in their eyes, hearts blown out by the strain of converting hundreds of pounds of body mass to waste.

I never thought it would get approved with a 10 percent fatality rate, but I guess I was really naive. The truth was it got fast-tracked and approved by the FDA within a year. Mom was in a commercial, talking about how it gave her her life back, but this was a life she had never had. It gave her someone else's life entirely. Some life she had never even planned for. In the commercial, she wore a teal sports bra and a lot of makeup. I did not recognize her at all. She stood next to that celebrity, the one who did it first. What's her name. Amy Blanton.

Remember those ads? "Get the Amy Blanton body!" She had gained a little weight after she had her kids, but her Before picture and Mom's Before picture looked like members of two different species. In the commercial, their former selves got *whisked* away and there they were: exactly the same height, exactly the same build. A little contouring and a blowout made them twins. Mom had the Amy Blanton body. For just a little while, people would stop her on the street and ask if she *was* Amy Blanton. That got old fast. I used to just walk away fatly while she pretended she looked nothing like her TV twin.

I watched Dad grow more and more insecure about the change in

Mom. I saw him get mad at a guy at the gas station who checked out Mom's ass when she bent over.

"Get back in the car, Carl. Gosh, you're making a scene about nothing. It was just a compliment!"

Dad sat down, fuming, but he wouldn't close his door. His ears were bright red. Andrew was playing a game on his phone, totally zoned out. I watched Dad trying to calm himself down.

"You probably haven't been jealous about Mom since you guys were kids, huh?"

He blew out hot air through his nose like a bull. "Try *ever*," he said, his voice tight.

"Wasn't Mom hot as a teenager?"

His lips closed into a line I could see in the rearview mirror. "She was always heavy. She was . . . she was *mine*, goddamn it."

That sort of shocked me. He hadn't ever talked about her that way before. And it hadn't ever occurred to me that maybe my dad the football player had gotten with my less-than-perfect mom because he knew she'd never cheat on him. Could never. Just like she thought I could never go out and get myself in trouble. Because fat girls don't fuck, I guess?

I looked over at Andrew, too big for a seat belt, pooling against the car door. Did fat boys fuck? Was anybody going to pick him because he'd be *theirs*? I didn't want to imagine. But just as I was feeling sorry for us all, Mom slid lithely back into the car.

"Don't be a goose, honey," she said. She laid a hand on Dad's knee. "You have nothing to worry about."

That turned out to be a lie.

It was about a month after FDA approval when Dad announced to us that he was gonna take the Pill.

I couldn't help but give Mom the look of death. He'd never have done it if she hadn't gone first and made him worry about losing her. Andrew grunted at the news the way he grunted at everything; as if nothing in the world held much interest for him.

I hate crying, but I burst into tears. I couldn't even yell at Mom. I just wanted to talk Dad out of it. I tried for weeks, and I ended up trying again on the day that he began treatment. I just had this feeling in my gut that he was going to be one of the unlucky ones.

"One in ten," I croaked at him, my voice wrecked by crying. "One in *ten*, Dad. It's just slightly better odds than Russian roulette."

He smiled from his spa-hospital bed with the special trench installed below. He was wearing one of those paper gowns and I thought about how stupid he would feel dying in paper clothes while taking a shit. Was it worth it? How could it be worth it?

"But the odds of dying young if I stay fat are much worse," he told me in his sweet voice. He reached out and put a hand on my shoulder, and I heard his gown rustling like trash dragging through the gutter when it's windy. "Don't worry, Munchkin. It's in god's hands."

I guess it was, but I had never trusted god not to drop stuff and break it.

Dad made it to the third treatment. It felt cruel, like I had just started to relax and believe that he might be ok.

We came back and saw him on day one, down about fifty pounds and looking like someone had slapped him around all night.

"Honey, you look wonderful," Mom cooed, kissing his cheeks and hugging him to her middle. Andrew had stayed home. I looked him up and down, remembering the way Mom had just melted to reveal the stranger within.

"You look ok," I managed to say.

"I told you, kiddo." We sat with him while he ate some graham crackers and drank lots of water. My parents held hands.

I skipped the second visit. The knots in my stomach were huge and twisting and I just couldn't face it. Mom came home whistling and very pleased with herself.

"He's in the homestretch now! I can't wait for you kids to see what your dad really looks like."

I just sat there, wondering if I was real. Are fat people fake? Do we not have souls? Does nothing I do count, if I do it while I'm fat? These were questions I had never really thought about before, but with both of my parents risking death to be less like me, I suddenly had to wonder about a lot of things.

I knew the minute Mom picked up the phone the next day. I could tell she wasn't expecting the call. She stared at it just a second too long before she picked it up. My film professor calls that a beat, like a drumbeat or a heartbeat. One beat too many, and I knew.

One beat too many and Dad's heart gave out.

Neither one of us could go with Mom to deal with the body. Andrew wouldn't even leave his room. I don't remember those weeks very clearly. I remember weird parts.

Mom buying Dad a new suit he could be buried in, because nothing he owned would fit. Mom saying Dad wouldn't want to be cremated, now that he was thin. Dad's D&D buddies looking into his casket and saying how great he looked. The never-ending grief buffet of casseroles and cake in our kitchen. The nights when I could hear Mom crying through the vents.

That should have been the last of it. Other people could die, even famous people, but the Pill killed my dad. That should have been it, end of story, illegal forever. But that's not how anything works. The world is just allowed to wound you any way it wants and move on.

And so are the people that you know.

The minute Andrew brought it up, I almost laughed. There was no way Mom was going to let him do it, after what had happened to Dad. Maybe we weren't the best of buds, but I didn't want him to die.

I could hear her in his room, and she was never in his room. It was perma-dark in there, blackout shades on the windows and nothing but the dim blue glow of his monitors to light it. I could hear them talking and I came close to the door, not quite putting my ear to it.

"I'm too old to be on your insurance," he said. "But they're saying there's gonna be a generic within a year. So it'll probably be cheaper."

"I think that's the best idea, sweetheart. But you're still going to have to pay for your hospital stay. We have a little money from Dad's insurance, so I can help you with that. It's what your father would have wanted."

I pushed the door open, already yelling. "No. No. No. No. It is not what Dad would have wanted. Dad would have wanted to be alive. Do you want to end up dead, too?"

They both stared at me like I had come through the door on fire.

"What is the matter with you?"

"Yeah," Andrew sneered. "Don't you knock?"

Mom put her hands on her hips. "This is a private conversation, kiddo."

"I don't give a shit," I told them. "We just buried our dad, and you want to take the Pill that killed him. How stupid can you be?"

Andrew shrugged. "Ninety percent is still an A."

"And dead is still dead," I said at once. "There's no curve on that."

Mom came and took my elbow and walked me back toward the door. "You're letting your emotions get the best of you," she said. I could hear her voice trembling, and when I looked up, her eyes were wet in the dim blue light of the bedroom. "I miss him too, but I don't let it cloud my judgment. Your brother needs to do what's best for him."

"It's better for him to be dead than fat," I shot back. "Is that really what you think?"

We both turned back to look at Andrew.

Andrew would never tell me his actual weight, but I had heard him say once that he was in the "5 club." Nothing fit him but the absolute biggest shirts and elastic waistband shorts, and he wouldn't wear shoes that had to be tied. His fingers were so fat he could barely use his phone and finally upgraded to one with a stylus.

He sighed at us both. "I'm tired of this," he said to me, but Mom started to cry. "I'm tired of never going out and never fitting in a chair. I'm tired of getting stared at and having to hide from people to eat. Aren't you tired of it, sis?"

I shrugged. "I'm not tired of being alive."

I didn't convince him. I didn't convince Mom. She gave him the money and he checked himself in. I went with them, only because I was worried I wouldn't get to say goodbye otherwise.

Andrew was twenty-four when he did it, and his doctor had to get his digs in first. I remember his old-man chuckle as he lined my brother up next to the chart on the wall. "Well, son. You're not going to get any taller. And let's quit getting wider while we can, shall we?"

Andrew laughed with him, as if his fat self was already somebody else. Someone who it was ok to laugh at. My thin mom laughed, too.

Somewhere in thin heaven, was Dad laughing? Already I was an anomaly on the streets. I'm sure it used to be hard to be fat in L.A. or New York. I've read about that. But living in Dayton, Ohio, meant always fitting in the booth at a restaurant, and never being the only fat person in the room. By the time Andrew got the Pill, I couldn't count on those things anymore. A year later, the whole world was shrinking around me, and I could already feel the pinch.

Andrew came home from the hospital looking like some other guy; a dude who played basketball and got called Slim. His eyes were bright.

"Munchkin, I can't wait for you to do it. It's amazing! I mean, it's super gross and really painful, but after that it's the fucking awesomest."

They had all called me "Munchkin" since I was a kid. Not because I was short and cute, but because they said I was always munching. I hated that nickname and he knew it. He was just using it now to remind me I was the only one left.

"You look like Dad looked in his casket," I said.

He tried for a little while to go out and enjoy his new, thin life, but he didn't really know how. He couldn't talk to anybody. He missed his online friends and he hated the sunlight, the noise, the feeling of people always around, sizing him up. He had a new body, but it didn't matter.

I watched Andrew go back to his gaming pod; the ruined chair with the cracked spar he had fixed with duct tape no longer sagging or groaning beneath him. The same shiny spots on his computer where he kept his hands in the same positions for fourteen hours at a time while he pretended he was a tall, muscular Viking warrior on some Korean server every day. I watched him settle right back into his old life using his new body and wondered what it was for. He really was the Viking now. He could have put on boots and left the house and had a real adventure. But adventure didn't appeal to him.

I was stuck between Andrew and Mom in the house. I always had been, but Dad and I had understood each other. We had been a team. I guess I was a daddy's girl, but I was never spoiled like that. We just got along. Andrew was silent and Mom never shut up. Dad was the only one I could talk to, or sit in silence with without feeling bad.

And now I was the only fat member of the family. Slowly but surely, even the aunts and cousins signed up to take the Pill. I started to joke with my friends in Visionaries that fat people were going to become an endangered species.

Some of them laughed, but a couple suggested we actually make a short film about that. We kicked the idea around, but mostly they wanted to film me eating in a cage while people stared. I didn't know how that would get anything meaningful across, and they didn't know how not to be thin assholes. So we dropped the idea.

Mom was at least using the way she had changed to enjoy the real world a little more. She wore workout clothes constantly, all bright colors and cling like the patterning on a snake. Every day, she got to enjoy the way people looked at her brightly now, eyebrows up, not searching for their first chance to sidle away.

"People just respond to me so much better now," she said in one of her interviews. "It changes everything about my daily interactions. I'm a mother and a widow, and I don't need a lot of attention," she said, smiling coyly. "But even the mailman is happier to see me than he ever was before."

I wanted to barf when she said she didn't need attention. She had been thirsty enough before to talk to absolutely anyone, even sign up to take injections and hypnosis to get it. Now she was always posing and watching to see who would look. Attention was like the drug she couldn't get enough of. She still ate the same bowl of ice cream every night, sitting next to the groove in the couch where Dad used to fit. No, Mom, you didn't need attention. You took the Pill, you let the Pill take Dad because you were so A-OK with yourself.

The Pill sold like nothing had ever sold before. The original, the generic, the knockoffs, the different versions approved in Europe and Asia that met their standards and got rammed through their testing. There was at last a cure for the obesity epidemic. Fat people really were an endangered species. And everybody was so, so glad.

One in ten kept dying. The average never improved, not in any corner of the globe. There were memorials for the famous and semi-famous folks who took the gamble and lost. A congressman here and a comedian there. But everyone was so proud of them that they had died trying to better themselves that all the obituaries and eulogies had this weird, wistful tone to them. As if it was the next best thing to being thin. At least they didn't have to live that fat life anymore.

And every time it was on the news, we sat in silence and didn't talk about Dad.

I was just a kid when Mom made it through the original trial that unleashed the Pill on the world. It wasn't approved for teenagers, not anywhere. Don't get me wrong; teens and parents alike were more than ready to sign up for the one-in-ten odds of dying. But the scientists who had worked on the Pill said unequivocally that it should not be taken by anyone who was not absolutely done growing. Eighteen was the minimum, but they recommended twenty-one to be completely safe.

On my eighteenth birthday, my mom threw me a party. She invited all my friends (mostly the Visionaries) and decorated the backyard with yellow roses and balloons.

It was the first time since Dad died that the house seemed cheerful. Mom ordered this huge lemon cake at the good bakery, with layers of custard filling and sliced strawberries. I remember everybody moaning over how good it was, how summery-sweet. People danced, but I felt too self-conscious to get up and give it a try. My mom ended up dancing with a neighbor who heard the music and came through the gate to check it out. He was skinny, too, and I couldn't watch them together.

We ate barbecue ribs and I got to tell people over and over again where I'd gotten into college. Northwestern. Rutgers. Cornell. And UCLA. Where was I going to go? Oh, I hadn't decided yet, but I needed to pick soon.

Except I definitely had. I had wanted to study filmmaking my whole life. Everybody in the Visionaries club knew that; they had all applied to UCLA and USC. A few of us got in. It wasn't just that it was my dream school in the golden city where movies were made. It was also about as far away as I could get. Mom reminded me that I could go anywhere in state for free because of her job, saying it over and over with that look in her eye, the one that said *don't leave me,* but I was going to L.A. if I had to walk every mile.

When it came time for presents, I got some jewelry from my

grandmother. She didn't come and I couldn't blame her; she was my dad's mom. A lace parasol from my friends, who all expected I'd need protection from the sun sometime soon. Books and music and a clever coffee cup. A fountain pen. The kinds of things that signal adulthood is about to begin.

My mom, beaming, gave me the Pill.

"I can't give you the physical thing, of course," she said, glancing around for a laugh. She got a little one. She handed me her iPad. "This has all of the paperwork, showing that you've been approved and my insurance will cover it. Plus, I booked your spa stay so that you'll have time to buy all new clothes before leaving for school." She smiled like she'd never killed my dad.

"I don't . . . know what to say," I said finally. If I said what I was actually feeling, it might mean she wouldn't pay for school, I'd be on my own. I had to swallow it. But I'd be damned if I was gonna swallow that Pill.

The party broke up slowly, with the neighbor guy hanging around and trying to talk to Mom until she texted Andrew and made him come down and walk the guy out. I packed up all my presents. I thanked Mom as sincerely as I could. I wrapped up slices of cake for people who wanted to take them home. And I seethed.

I left for UCLA two weeks early. I told Mom I was planning to come back and take my medicine over Thanksgiving break. She said she understood my delay, that I was just worried I'd pull the short straw and that it was ok to be nervous. She put me on the plane to Los Angeles with tears in her eyes.

On the flight, it was me and one other fat kid, maybe ten years old. That was it. The woman who sat next to me huffed and whined about it until the flight attendant brought her a free drink to shut her up. It was the first time I had ever been on a plane, and I sat there wondering whether it was always as uncomfortable as this. I could see the other fat kid up a few rows, hanging his elbow and one knee into the aisle. He wasn't even full-grown and already he was too big for an airplane seat. I wished we had been sitting together. We would have recognized each other. It would have been like having family again. Everyone else had that same Pill body.

And it was always the exact same body. No more thick thighs or really round asses. No more wide tits or pointy pecs or love handles rounding out someone's sides. Everyone's body was flat planes and straight lines. It wasn't just that they were thin. They were all somehow the same.

In L.A. the change was striking. I had heard that even thin people were taking the Pill out there to ensure that they'd never gain any weight, but I didn't believe it until I started seeing the change on TV and in movies. One by one, distinctive shapes disappeared. It was always the Amy Blanton body, like my mom had. The guys all had the same Ethan Fairbanks body, once he did a bunch of ads with some nobody. Only faces and hair color, a little difference in height could distinguish one actor from another. Here and there, a death. Worth it, everyone whispered like a prayer. Worth it, worth it, worth it.

I made it a few months at UCLA. My classes were cool and I started to make friends right off. But little things kept piling up. I went to the student store to buy myself a UCLA hoodie and they had nothing that would fit me. It wasn't even close. I looked at the largest size in the men's section and even then it would have clung to me like the skin of a sausage. I decided I could live without that ubiquitous symbol of college life, but I was pissed. I even thought about buying one just to snip the logo out and sew it onto a hoodie in my size from Walmart.

Then Walmart stopped carrying plus sizes altogether.

There were no desks on campus that I could sit at. A few of the classrooms had long tables with detached chairs and those were all right. But the majority of my freshman-year classes were in those big lecture halls, with the rows and rows of wooden chair-and-desk combinations. I couldn't wedge myself into one to save my life. My first or second day I tried really hard in the back row and just got a big bruise over my lowest rib for my troubles. I sat in the aisle, on the steps, or against the back wall every day. There just wasn't any space for me.

My dorm room was the same way. The bed was narrow and I could hear the whole frame groaning the second I lay down. The bathroom was so small that I could touch both walls with my thighs when I sat on the toilet. My roommate was so thin I knew she hadn't taken the

Pill—she still looked too original. But over the course of the first week, I realized that was because she never ate. I asked her to lunch a couple of times, but she always said no. I couldn't save her. I was working on how to save myself.

Days ticked by and Thanksgiving break was bearing down on me. My mom kept calling, telling me how great it was going to be when I went back to the school in my ideal body.

"I don't know that it'll be my ideal body," I told her. "It'll just be different."

"Don't you want to go on dates like the other girls?" Her voice was so whiny I could barely stand it.

I looked across the room to the other girl I lived with. She was in her bra, and every time she breathed in I could see the impressions of her individual ribs against the skin of her back. She was doing her reading and sucking on her bottom lip as if her lip gloss might offer some calories.

"I don't know that I want anything other girls have," I told her. But that wasn't true. Most girls had fathers.

"You don't know what you're missing," Mom said. "Come on home and let's get you squared away."

"Soon," I told her, counting the days until I had to let them try to kill me for being what I am.

I had been there about a month when I knew I wasn't going to make it. The stares had become unmanageable. I wasn't the last fat girl in L.A., was I? People on campus avoided me like I was a radioactive werewolf who stank like a dead cat in a hot garage. I remember one time I tried to take a selfie to send home to the Visionaries and someone gasped out loud. In the picture, I could see him, mouth open like he'd glimpsed a ghost.

And in a way I guess I was. I was the ghost of fatness past, haunting the open breezeways of UCLA. I was what they used to be, what they had always feared they would become. I became obsessed with the terrible power of my fatness; I was the worst that could possibly happen to someone. Worse than death, had to be, because somewhere my dad was rotting in a box because that was easier than living in a body like mine. I knew when I frightened people and I pushed my advantage. I took up their space. I haunted them with my warm breath and my soft elbows. I fed on their fright.

It was early November and I could not adjust to the lack of seasons. It was still warm and sunny like June on the California coast. I missed home, but the idea of home repelled me. I needed comfort.

I walked myself over to the cheap pancake house and ordered the never-ending stack and coffee. The all-you-can-eat pancake special was always a favorite with frat boys, and its popularity had only increased since the Pill hit the market. People who really loved to eat could finally do it without worrying that it would ruin their lives.

The hostess tried to seat me in a booth and I just rolled my eyes at her. I was not about to eat my weight in pancakes with a Formica tabletop wedged just beneath my sternum.

"A table, please."

She stuck me in the back, next to the restrooms. I didn't care.

My first four pancakes showed up hot and perfect and I asked for extra butter. When they were just right (dripping, not soaked and turning into paste), I shoveled up huge bites into my waiting mouth, letting it fill me as nothing else did. Who could care that they were the last of their kind when the zoo had such good food?

And yeah, people were staring. People are always staring at me. That was a constant of my existence, and I was used to it. I ignored them. I slurped up hot coffee and wiped the plate down with the last bite of cake.

"Hit me again," I said, and the waitress took the plate away. A few minutes later, another fresh hot stack of pancakes appeared.

I didn't know how many times I could do it, but that was the day I was going to find out.

And then a man sat at my table.

He was perfectly ordinary, with brown hair and brown eyes. He had the Pill body underneath his tan suit. I looked him over.

"Can I help you?"

He stared at my mouth for a minute and I waited. "Do you have any idea how beautiful you are?" he finally asked.

I rolled my eyes hard and started to butter my pancakes. I was going to need more butter. "Fuck off, creep."

He put a hand against his own chest. "Please, I meant no disrespect. I'm being sincere. You're so lovely. So rare. I haven't seen a woman like you in almost a year."

I waved to the waitress, but she didn't see me. I debated. I'd rather have the butter, but if the cakes got cold before it showed up, it would hardly matter at all. I scraped the dish that I had and began to cut up pancakes and ignore my visiting weirdo, hoping he would go away.

He cleared his throat and ordered a cup of coffee. "Please, allow me to entertain you while you eat and I'll pick up your check."

I sighed. Few things were as motivating as free food. So I let him sit.

He asked me about cinematography, about why I had come to L.A. I talked in between cups of coffee and plates of pancakes.

"I had all these ideas about the story only I could tell when I got here. The things that were unique to my experience. It's funny now, because there was nothing unique about my experience. I guess everybody thinks they're one of a kind."

He glanced over his shoulder a little, then pushed the cream pitcher toward me for my coffee. "Look around. You nearly are."

I shrugged. "I guess. But there's no way to tell this story so that people will understand it. You ever see the way fat people on the street are shot for news stories? Headless and limbless and wide as the world, always wandering like they've got nowhere to be. That's the only story people know. We were always a joke; we were always invisible. And now, we're going to disappear. Because we were never meant to exist in the first place."

"Are you?" he asked, cocking an eyebrow. "Going to disappear?"

"Who the hell are you?" I finally asked.

He sighed and finished his coffee. "I can't tell you that. But I can show you something that might change your mind."

I don't know why I said yes. Maybe I was dreading going back to school, where nothing fit. Maybe I just didn't want to answer the question of whether or not I was going to take the Pill. Maybe it was just the way he looked at me—really looked at me. Not like I was a problem to be solved or some walking glitch in the way things are supposed to work.

I got into a strange man's car outside of the pancake house and I let him show me.

The club was up in the hills, just off Mulholland Drive. It was in this gorgeous house, built in the golden age of Hollywood for some chiseled hunk who had died of AIDS. The lawn was perfect and I could smell the chlorine in the pool the minute I stepped out of the car. The neighborhood was the kind of quiet where you know that even the gardeners muffle their equipment.

My nameless escort walked up the stone path toward a wide, shaded, black front door. He looked back over his shoulder, glancing at me.

"You coming?"

I was.

It was dark inside the house at first, my eyes adjusting from the bright sunshine slowly. After a few minutes, I saw that it was merely dim. The living room was furnished beautifully, sumptuously, with a clear emphasis on texture and deep padding. The room was empty except for one woman, sitting on a chaise lounge and reading a book.

We approached her and she looked up. She was an absolute knockout; a redhead with full lips and built like an hourglass that had time to spare. Her dress clung to her, making a clear case that she enjoyed being looked at. She was not walking around in an Amy Blanton body. She was an original.

The man I came in with tapped his fingers on the top of her book and said, "In the chocolate war, I fought on the side of General Augustus."

The redhead nodded, not saying a word. She shifted in her seat and reached for something I couldn't see. Behind her, a bookshelf slid sideways, revealing a deep purple tunnel behind it.

I nodded to her as we passed, and she smiled at me with a hunger I couldn't put a name to. I had no idea where we were headed.

We walked through a series of rooms. The entire house was

decorated in the same style as that first room; sensual, decadent, and plush. As I got to see more of it, I realized that everything was also built wide, sturdy, and I'd never think twice about sitting in any chair I saw.

In every room I passed, I saw the same thing as I peered through the door. There was a fat person surrounded by thin people staring at them. Some of the onlookers were crying, some were visibly aroused. Different races, different genders. All well-dressed. All nearly identical in those Pill bodies. A tall fat woman was lounging, shrouded by veils in a Turkish bed, nude and lolling and made of endless undulations of honey-colored flesh. She fed herself grapes while someone was making her laugh. Ten people sat around her bed, watching.

A fat man, as big as Andrew used to be, was dipping his gloved fists into paint and punching a blank white wall. He was being videotaped and photographed, lit gorgeously while people murmured praise and encouragements.

In one room, a short black woman whose curves defied gravity ran oil-slicked hands over her nudity, smiling a perfect, satisfied smile. Two men stood near her, their mouths open, hungering endlessly, asking nothing of her.

We came to an empty room that had a round tub at its end and a set of low stone benches. The domed ceiling made our footfalls sound epic. The water had steam rising off it, even in the warmth of the house, and smelled like the sea.

"Salt water," he said. "Much better for your skin than chlorine. Would you like to take a dip? You don't have to talk to anyone or do anything, but some people may come join you. How does that sound?"

"I don't have a bathing suit."

His smile was slow, and he dropped his chin like he was about to share a conspiracy. "Have you looked around? Nobody will mind."

"What are these people getting out of this? I don't need this."

He pulled out his phone and showed me the app that the house used to keep track of money. Each fat performer had an anonymous identifier and a live count of what they were making.

"Maybe I could persuade you to work for a couple of hours, just to see what you think? You'll make the house minimum, plus tips."

I watched the numbers climb up. "Just to sit here? I don't have to touch anybody? Or even make conversation?"

He nodded. "We'd prefer that you work in the nude, but you don't even have to do that. Just enjoy the hot soak. What do you say?"

It sounded weird as fuck, but I wanted two things immediately. First, I wanted the money. If I was going to go home and refuse the Pill, I was pretty sure I was going to need it. Second, I wanted to go back to the room where the boxing painter was being filmed. I itched to get behind a camera in this place, to tell the story of the endangered species of fat people. Not like the Visionaries had wanted it, but the way I wanted it. Like this. Dark and rich and seductive.

I got into the water in my bra and panties. I may as well have gotten naked; they were both white cotton and went see-through in the water. I tried not to think about it. I dunked my head, sat on one of the submerged steps, and soaked with my neck laid back against the rim.

I could hear people coming and going. I could hear the things they whispered to me. Voices in the salty dark called me rare and magnificent and soft and enticing. I said nothing. I didn't even hint that I could hear.

After a few hours, my nameless handler came back with a fluffy, soft towel the size of a bedsheet that smelled like lavender. He thanked me and showed me how to download the app to get paid.

I had been there for three hours, and I had more money than I had ever had at one time, in my entire life. He watched my face very closely when I saw the number.

"My name's Dan," he said softly.

"Do you own this place?"

"No, I'm just a recruiter. I'm going to give you my number."

I watched him type it into my phone as "Dan Chez Corps."

"What makes you think I'll call you?"

I thought he was going to remind me of how much money I had just made, but he didn't. He kinda shook his head a little, then asked, "Where else are you going to go?"

He had brought me replacements for my wet underthings, much

nicer than the ones I was wearing. They were exquisite and well-made and carried no tags.

"A gift from the house," he said, before leaving me to change. They fit like they were made for me.

I went back to the dorm and watched my roommate twitch in her sleep. Her side of the fridge held a single hard-boiled egg and a pint of skim milk. My bed groaned beneath me as I lay down, still in my fancy gift underwear.

I dreamt about my dad.

The laws changed that year, but they wouldn't go into effect until January. They weren't making it illegal to be fat, exactly. But it was as close as they could get. It was going to be legal to deny health insurance to anyone with a BMI over 25 if they refused the Pill. Intentional obesity would also be grounds for loss of child custody, and would be acceptable reason for dismissal from a job.

Where the law went, culture followed. Airlines were adding a customer weight limit, and clothing manufacturers concentrated on developing lines to individualize the Pill body. Journalists wrote articles on the subject of renegade fats; could their citizenship be revoked? Should parents of fat children be prosecuted for abuse if they didn't arrange for them to receive the Pill as soon as possible?

I submitted a treatment to my short-film class, detailing my desire to film a secret enclave where fat renegades performed for the gratification of a live Pilled audience. My professor wrote back to tell me that my idea was 1. Obscene and 2. Impossible.

The Friday before Thanksgiving break, Mom called.

"I'm so glad we're getting this done before the change in airline policy. Can you imagine having to come to Ohio by train? Anyhow, your aunt Jeanne is coming in for the holiday—"

"Mom. Mom, listen. I don't want to do it."

"Do what? See Aunt Jeanne?"

"No, Mom, listen. I'm not going to take the Pill."

She was quiet for a minute. "Sweetie, we all took it hard when your father passed. I know you must be worried about that, but they say there's no genetic marker—"

"It's not just Dad. It's not just the odds that I might die. I just don't want to do it. I want to stay who I am."

She sighed like I was a child who had asked for the ninetieth time why the sky was blue. "This doesn't change who you are, Munchkin. It only changes your body."

"I'm not coming home," I said flatly.

There was a lot of yelling, with both of us trying to be cruel to the other. I'd rather not remember it. What I do remember is her crying, saying something like, "I gave you your body. I made it, and it's imperfect like mine was. Why won't you let me fix it? Why won't you let me correct my mistake?"

"I don't feel like a mistake," I told her. "And I'm not coming home. Not now, not ever."

I remember hanging up and the terrible silence that followed. I remember thinking I should turn my phone off, but then I realized I could just leave it behind. I could leave everything behind. I took my camera and my laptop and left everything else. I didn't even take a change of clothes.

I borrowed a phone from someone on the quad, making up a story that mine had been stolen. She waited for me as I called Dan. I told him to pick me up where I was.

The car arrived ten minutes later.

The redhead buzzed me in without asking for a password, which was great because I couldn't remember what Dan had said. Down through the purple hallway and a woman I'd never seen before shook my hand and told me I could call her Denny.

Denny had a Pill body, hidden away beneath a wide, flowing caftan and a matching head wrap. She showed me to my room, my king-sized bed, my enormous private bath, my shared common room and library. She gave me the Wi-Fi password and explained the house's security.

"You may stay here as long as you like. The house will feed you and clothe you. Your medical needs will be seen to. Your entertainments will be top-notch. You may leave anytime you wish. Your pay will be automatically deposited into your account as it comes in, without delay.

"However, you must never disclose the location or the nature of this house to anyone via any means; not by phone call or text or email. You may take photos and videos, but we have jammers to prevent geotagging of any kind. If you are found in violation of this one rule, you will walk out of here with nothing but the clothes on your back. Is that clear?"

I told her it was. She left and returned five minutes later with a new phone for me. I signed into my bank account—the one my mother wasn't on—and set about creating a new email, a new profile, a new identity.

I eased into the work. I ate cupcakes and I danced in a leotard. I read poetry aloud while sipping a milkshake. I lounged in a velvet chaise nude while people drew me and painted me. I began to speak to my admirers and I watched my pay skyrocket.

I met the house's head seamstress; a brilliant, nimble-fingered fat woman named Charisse. She had an incredible eye and hardly had to measure anyone. She made me corsets and skirts, silk pajamas and satin gowns, costumes and capes and all manner of underwear.

I realized when I had been wearing her work for months that some of my clothes were a little too small. My favorite bikini cut into me just so, just enough to accentuate the flesh it did not quite contain. I filmed myself in the hall of mirrors, wearing it and trying to understand what it meant.

Some of my gowns were a little too big, though I could remember the exactitude with which I was fitted. I made short clips showing the gaps in the waist and hips, the way I could work my whole hand in between the fabric and my skin.

Charisse was too skilled for it to be an accident. The implication became clear.

All around me there were heavenly bodies in gowns and togas, a stately fleet of well-rounded ships gliding alongside the pool or lying silkily in our beds. We were beautiful, but we were all aware of a subtle campaign to make us larger, ever larger, more suited to satisfy whatever it was that brought the throngs of thin whispering wantons to our door.

In twos and threes, we began to talk about what it meant. About who we could trust. About who was running this place, and why.

The lower floors of the house were a brothel. Somehow I knew that without being told. There was a look in the older fat folks' eyes that let me know it would be waiting for me when I was ready. Nobody pressured me. Nobody even asked. One day I just headed down the stairs. Cheeks were swabbed at the door and everybody waited fifteen minutes until they were cleared. I got my negatives and went through.

I'd never had sex before. I think it happens later for fat kids. While everyone else was trying each other on, I was still trying to figure out why I never fit into anything. I don't regret that. I can't imagine doing this out in the world, where I am the worst thing that can happen to somebody.

I didn't know what it would be like. I hope it's this good for everyone, with a circle of adoring worshippers vying for the right to adore you, to touch every inch of you, to murmur in wonder as you climax again and again until nap time, when you are lovingly spooned and crooned to sleep. I luxuriated in it for a long time, not thinking about what it meant to only touch thin people, to only be touched by them. I watched my bank balance climb. I didn't ask myself what they saw when they looked at me. I existed as a collection of nerves that did not think.

I stopped thinking about going home. I stopped thinking about the Pill. I stopped thinking. I became what I had always been and nothing more: my fat, fat body.

When I came back to thinking again, I found it did not make things easier.

I have been here for three years now, and I don't think I can ever live anywhere else. Outside, they tell me, there are no more like me. Only in places like here, where a few of us fled before the world could change us. Nobody is allowed to bring us food presents anymore; everyone is too worried they'll try to slip us the Pill. Someone might actually be that upset that I exist. I don't think about that either. I don't exist for them. I accept their worship and forget their faces completely. It's always the same face anyhow.

Sometimes I point my camera at that face and ask them what they're doing here, what do they want, why did they come seeking the thing they've worked so hard to avoid becoming?

They mumble about mothers and goddesses, about the embrace of flesh and the fullness of desire. It sounds like my own voice inside my head. I think about my dad, about god's hands. Would he have been one of these? Would he have come to miss my mother's body the way he first knew it?

I think about showing this film in L.A. I think about Denny telling me I can leave here anytime. I think about how I could leave my body anytime, too, how any of us can. I think about Andrew, about how he left his and gained nothing at all. How I used to see him as the enemy when he was just me.

Deep down on the lowest floor, in perfect privacy, the fats make love to each other. There is a boy who came only a few weeks ago, an import from one of the countries that's taken to the Pill slowly, so we have a lot of recruits from their shores. We had no common language at first, but we've worked on that and discovered an unmapped country between us. He's so sweet and shy and eager to lift the heaviness of his belly so that he can slip inside me and then drop it on top of mine, warm and weighty like a curtain. He whispers to me that we don't ever have to go back, that we can raise darling fat babies right here, that we'll become like another species. *Homo pillus* can inherit the earth, while *Homo lipidus* lives in secret.

"But we'll live," he whispers to me as we conspire to remake the world in the image of our thick ankles. "We'll live," he says, his tongue tracing the salty trenches made by the folds in my sides. Belly to belly, fat against fat.

"We'll live."

THE MERMAID ASTRONAUT

YOON HA LEE

Yoon Ha Lee's (www.yoonhalee.com) debut novel, *Ninefox Gambit*, won the Locus Award for best first novel and was a finalist for the Hugo, Nebula, and Clarke Awards; its sequels, *Raven Stratagem* and *Revenant Gun*, were also Hugo finalists. His middle grade space opera, *Dragon Pearl*, won the Locus Award for best YA novel and was a *New York Times* bestseller. Lee's most recent book is *Phoenix Extravagant*. His fiction has appeared in venues such as *Tor.com*, *Audubon Magazine*, *The Magazine of Fantasy & Science Fiction*, *Clarkesworld*, *Lightspeed*, and *Beneath Ceaseless Skies*. Lee lives in Louisiana with his family and an extremely lazy cat, and has not yet been eaten by gators.

On a wide and wondering world in a wide and wondering galaxy, there lived a mermaid. She was not the only mermaid who dwelled in the deep and dreaming oceans of her world. An entire society of mers shared rule of the seas with the whale-sages and the anemone-councils, among many others. This particular mermaid had named herself Essarala, which means *seeks the stars* in the language of tide and foam.

Essarala's mothers and sisters and cousins understood the significance of her name, and they sometimes came to discuss it with her. On one such occasion, Essarala sat upon a rock jutting out from the sea, the waves lapping against her koi-spotted tail. It was nighttime, and she gazed longingly up at the constellations and the one bright planet that was visible to the naked eye. The stars in those constellations, she knew, were suns like the one her own planet orbited, a fact that fascinated her but which none of her relatives found of particular interest.

"We are navigators true and fierce," said one of her younger sisters, whose name, Kiovasa, meant *the sea and the moon are partners*—a standard, conventional name, resurrected every few generations by proper-thinking mers. She swam in lazy circles around Essarala's rock, her striped tail flicking in and out of the waters. "But I fear, Essarala, that you mean something other than simple navigation."

"I want to visit the stars," Essarala said. "There are other worlds out there. Why remain confined to this one, when I could see the plethora of galaxies that exist?"

Kiovasa playfully splashed water at her. Essarala accepted the drenching with good humor. After all, she had nothing to fear from water.

"I don't think it's about *wealth*, for you," Kiovasa said. "If all you wanted were riches, why, we could find you plenty of plunder."

Essarala had to admit this was true. The sailors who plied the waters made copious offerings to the sea, either in exchange for good luck or, more tragically, when their ships sank and their cargoes spilled into the ocean. From the moment of her birth onward, Essarala's family had not stinted with their gifts, and when she grew older and more adventurous, she, too, had participated in scavenging expeditions so she could give gifts back in her turn. Her own sea-cave was filled with asymmetrical crowns set with spinels and sapphires, gilt-edged chanfrons, scrimshaw depicting sacrifices to eldritch gods, and more.

But these gifts, however well-intentioned and however gratefully received, did nothing to ease the itching in Essarala's heart whenever she looked up at the star-wealth of the night sky.

Kiovasa spoke with Essarala a little longer and found that Essarala would not be dissuaded from her desire. Having established that, Kiovasa called out a song of farewell and dived deep, swam fast, leaving Essarala behind.

Essarala might have remained suspended in the land of dreams forever, coming to her rock on clear nights to gaze fruitlessly skyward, if not for the arrival of the traders.

The traders came from the sky in a great ship made of metal. It did not look like the galleons or junks or outrigger canoes that the mers were familiar with. But then, mers had little expertise in shipbuilding, so this did not alarm them unduly.

The ship landed on the coast of an island above the coral reef where Essarala's family held their ancestral seat. From it emerged creatures the likes of which the mers had never seen before either; no two of them alike. Some of them walked on two legs and some on six, some of them had six fingers on their hands and some had tentacles instead, some of them had friendly waving eyestalks and others no eyes at all.

The mers' interpreters worked day and night to communicate with these newcomers and find out what they wanted. Their visitors cooperated with this process, making offerings of shimmering metalweave fabrics and curious tools for capturing fish more efficiently. The mers found the former of more interest and smilingly declined the latter. After all, they had treaties with the fish nations and no desire to overstep them.

Essarala learned of the traders from her cousins' gossip, and she lingered near the interpreters, watching and wishing. She longed to explore their ship and ask them to take her with them to the stars. But the more she listened, the more she learned, and one thing became obvious: their ship might carry water for its crew to drink, but it didn't contain water for a mer to live in. Saddened by this obstacle, she withdrew, and at first no one noticed it.

In the meantime, the mers and visitors learned to speak to each other. They planned a grand feast, featuring the fish nations' best offerings, as well as tasty morsels of sea urchin or sea cucumber and the finest kelp salads. The visitors, for their part, ran curious tests—to make sure they didn't accidentally poison anyone, they said—and contributed strange delectations of their own, some resembling fruit, some resembling fish, and some concoctions that the mers had no word for other than *delicious*.

At last Kiovasa realized that she hadn't seen Essarala hanging around the traders for some time. Concerned, she secured her sister an invitation to the feast. It wasn't hard—no one would have thought of leaving her out—but Kiovasa made sure it had been handwritten upon a sheet of magical ice by one of the mers' master calligraphers, all the better to reignite Essarala's interest.

Kiovasa found Essarala on her rock as usual. The weather had been unusually fine, courtesy of the local dragon-spirit, yet Essarala had hardly interacted with her family at all during the past week. Still, she couldn't refuse to welcome her sister.

Kiovasa presented the glittering invitation to her. "Come," she said coaxingly, "you'll hear more stories from the far-travelers, of the places they've seen and the things they've eaten. They've even brought foods from the stars."

Essarala didn't react with the delight that Kiovasa had expected. "Sister-sweet," she said, turning the invitation around disconsolately in her hands, "I have heard their stories. What's more, I have been listening to the murmurs of the waves and the wind about this ship of metal, and they have confirmed what I thought. This ship of metal is full of travelers from the stars, yes—but the ship itself has no water for a mer to live in."

Kiovasa, who had been swimming clockwise around the rock, reversed direction, thinking. Her sister was right. All of the traders were land-dwellers.

"You should come anyway," Kiovasa said. "At least you'll get a glimpse of the faraway worlds that you've always loved."

"No," Essarala said, turning her face away. "I'm afraid that once I hear more stories, being left behind when the visitors leave—and they *will* leave, won't they?—will be all the more unbearable."

It was a young mer's logic. But the only cure for that was time, and time was what they had so little of. "In that case," Kiovasa said, "we must take more drastic measures. We must visit the witch beneath the waves, and she will have a solution."

The witch beneath the waves lived at the bottom of a great chasm, one so vast and dark that even the mers visited it reluctantly. Swarms of lanternfish lit the way down to the witch's dwelling, and even so, Kiovasa and Essarala struggled to see anything in the murky gloom of the waters.

At last they reached the witch's dwelling. Strange phosphorescent worms and rocks indicated the entrance. "We have come to ask a boon of you," Kiovasa called out, her voice distorted by the pressure of the waters.

For a long time all they heard was silence. And then the witch's voice emerged from within: "I would hear from the one who wishes the boon."

Essarala let go of her sister's hand and swam toward the voice. She could not see the witch, and it made her afraid. "It's me," she said, almost in a whisper. "I wish to petition the travelers from the stars and ask to join their crew."

A soft glow lit the witch's dwelling from within, more worms waking and wriggling. The witch herself, however, only manifested as a sketch of inky lines, like half a silhouette. She was smiling, but her smile was sad.

"You would give up the sea you know, and your family, and the songs of gulls, to explore the worlds beyond?" the witch asked.

"I don't think it's such an evil thing," Essarala replied, "to want to see new worlds and taste their waters."

"Evil, no," the witch said. "Difficult, yes."

"If you can't help me—"

"That's not the kind of difficulty I meant," the witch said. "I can give you two legs like the humans, that you might walk on land, or upon the deck of a starfaring ship for that matter. The rest, though— the rest is up to you. For there's more to starfaring than having legs. You'll have to familiarize yourself with their alerts, read oxygen gauges, watch out for toxic atmospheres and flesh-eating pathogens, and that's just the beginning.

"You are well educated in the ways of your people," the witch went on. "I have no doubt that you can identify every fish in the sea by the way it swims, and the birds of the waters by their silhouettes. You know the language of the moon when she sings to the waters and how to read the writing of every civilization that has ever built ships. You can read the wind and the waves. But where you are going, it's darker even than the chasm I call home, and there's no wind in space, nor waves other than the spiral density waves of the great galaxies themselves."

Essarala trembled, for while she didn't understand much of the terminology that the witch had used, she recognized that she was out of her depth. If only she had spent some of that time stargazing instead learning about the strange and chancy technologies that land-dwellers had invented, and which might keep them alive in the hostile void. But it was too late now. She had to choose, and choose soon, for the traders would not remain indefinitely.

"Tell me your price," Essarala said, speaking more loudly.

The witch nodded. "Someday you will want to come back home," she said. "When you do, visit me, and we will speak of it then."

"Is there nothing else you would accept of me?" Essarala asked, for the thought of returning to the chasm filled her with a nameless dread.

"That is the price," the witch said. "Take it or leave it."

"I will come with you," Kiovasa said to Essarala, "when you return. You won't have to do it alone."

Much later, Essarala would remember the witch's expression and the grief in it. At the time, however, all she knew was her gratitude for her sister's kindness and loyalty. She reached out and pressed Kiovasa's hand.

"I cannot do it here," the witch said. "The depths would kill you before you could ask your boon of the spacefarers. But I can give you the means."

The dark lines of the witch's figure shifted and stirred. For a moment she resembled nothing so much as the abstract patterns that moonlight makes over the waves, except in reverse. Then the patterns reassembled, and the witch held out a knife, hilt-first.

It was made of shell, and in the eerie light of the worms and rocks it had an iridescent sheen. "It will hurt," the witch said. "Certain kinds of desire always do. When you are ready, cut your tail in half, and your legs will emerge. If you change your mind"—and Essarala opened her mouth to protest that she wouldn't, except the witch's stern look quelled her—"then throw it into the sea, and it will find its way back to me."

"Thank you," Essarala said in spite of her trepidation, for a favor given must always be acknowledged. She did not speak the rebellious thought in her heart: that she would journey among the stars as long as possible, and perhaps in that time she would find a way to cheat the witch of her price.

The next night, Kiovasa and Essarala attended the feast. The sentinel sharks and dolphins recognized their invitations and let them in without comment. On any other occasion, the two of them would have noticed the splendid decorations that the creatures of sea and shore had labored over. Bright banners of fabric woven from hippocampus manes and the mers' own long tresses waved in the wind; lanterns containing glowing fungus and dancing fireflies illuminated the long tables. The platters, of lacquer or beaten gold, carved jade or peerless celadon, contained every form of delicacy the peoples of the sea and the peoples of the stars knew how to prepare.

But Kiovasa could only think of how she was going to lose her sister, and Essarala felt the weight of the witch's shell knife, carried in a pouch of gold-washed chain mail, as though it would drown her.

"Come join us!" the other mers called from their seats by the lapping waves. They were already drinking and singing, exchanging stories of navigators and mapmakers, and the occasional ballad of island-dwelling lovers. Kiovasa waved back, heavy of heart though she was.

"I must do it now," Essarala whispered to her sister, "or I will lose all courage." For beyond her many relatives she could see the visitors from the stars, supping in their various fashions, and even past them, the long silhouette of their far-voyaging starship. And the longing burned even more fiercely in her heart.

Mers have little notion of privacy, since everything that happens in the sea is known to one and all in short order. Even so, Kiovasa nodded and took her aside, a little way down the shore from the feast. Gulls and terns wheeled overhead, and the sandpipers cried out, whether in warning or welcome. No one watched, and why should they? They had other matters on their mind.

Essarala drew out the knife and passed the pouch over to her sister. She steadied herself with a deep breath, tasting the salt spray in the air, the sweet ether influence of the star-currents. Then she brought the knife plunging down.

The pain of the cut almost caused her to faint. But her sister caught her in her arms and steadied her as she swayed. The beautiful koi-spotted scales of Essarala's tail peeled away, and she emerged with two legs, like the humans of her world.

Kiovasa kissed her on the brow. "Go," she said to Essarala. "The stars are waiting for you." And she watched from the shallow lapping waters as Essarala took her first uncertain steps.

One by one the mers noticed; one by one the traders noticed. And they all stared, murmuring in wonder among themselves, as Essarala made her way to the starship's captain.

The captain dined at the head of the aliens' table. They were a tall creature covered with downy feathers, and their head sported a magnificent crest that Essarala had originally mistaken for a hat. When they saw Essarala approaching, they nodded at her in welcome. "Have you had a chance to enjoy the food?" they asked her in her own language.

For her part, Essarala was embarrassed that she could not speak the captain's tongue, although she knew very well that it contained sounds that no mer could make. "My name is Essarala," she said, "and like my name, I wish to seek the stars. I beg a boon of you—that I may join your crew, and travel to distant worlds with you."

The captain glanced at the koi-colored scales that clung still to Essarala's bare legs and knew the sacrifice that she had made. "Of course you may," they said kindly. "But you will start as the least among my crew, not because we wish to insult you, but because there are a great many protocols involved in life on a starship that you will have to learn before you can be trusted with more."

"I do not mind," Essarala said, her heart leaping within her.

"You will," the captain said, "but no matter; you will also have friends and comrades to share the journey with you."

And with that they invited her to squeeze in to their right, and to join with them in the feast.

The next morning, the captain and their crew prepared to say farewell to the mere and the people of the sea. Essarala, however delighted with her good fortune, was not so overcome that she forgot her sister. She sought Kiovasa out by the ocean's edge and ran out into the water to embrace her one last time.

"I hope you see every world around every star," Kiovasa whispered into her ear. Kiovasa, who had never thought much about the sky except the fact that her sister yearned after it so much, had no idea how many worlds there were in the universe, or stars either. But Essarala accepted the blessing in the spirit in which it had been given.

"I will sing your name to each of them," Essarala promised.

"I will listen for it every night," Kiovasa said. Then she shoved Essarala lightly. "Go! I don't want you to miss your opportunity."

Trepidation seized Essarala's heart, but she had come too far to turn back now. She ran through the splashing waves to the starship, which gleamed pink and orange and silver-bright in the sunrise. Already she was acclimating to her new legs, and to the sensation of her feet in the wet sand, and then on the cold metal of the starship's ramp.

The captain welcomed her aboard and introduced her to the crew members who would show her the basics of life on a starship. "Listen always to Ssen," the captain said, indicating a snakish alien whose mechanical suit provided them with tentacle-like grippers in the place of hands. "They will watch over you. I will see you at ship's mess." And the captain dismissed her.

"Come with me," Ssen said through a translation device. They showed Essarala how to strap herself into a couch for liftoff and warned her not to panic when the couch engulfed her with oxygenated gel to cushion her from the ship's acceleration. "As a member of the crew," they added, "you will have to study the fundamentals of physics, and the functioning of the ship, and how to help with its maintenance. We'll speak more of that after we're underway."

As a kindness to her, although Essarala would not realize it until later, Ssen had given her a couch across from the viewport that would give her the best view of her world as she left it for the first time. Her heart beating rapidly with mixed worry and excitement, Essarala braced herself for liftoff. Ssen need not have been concerned about her reaction to the protective gel, for it was not so different from the waters she had swum in all her life.

Nevertheless, while Essarala's innate magic as a mer protected her from the crushing depths of the sea, and the variances in pressure, it gave her no such defense from a starship's acceleration. As the starship blasted off for a destination whose name she didn't know, she caught only the merest glimpse of her native ocean from above, and the glittering of sunlight on the waters, before she lost consciousness.

Ssen apologized profusely once they had safely left the world's gravity well. "I should have expected that you would need more protection," they said, "and prepared your couch accordingly. I will teach you how to do that yourself, so this incident is not repeated in the future."

It wasn't the only thing Ssen showed her. Essarala learned that Ssen usually took on the task of training new crew, partly because they had infinite patience, but partly because they never slept and could remain vigilant for the inevitable mistakes. She had cause to be glad

of both traits, for she always had someone to listen when she despaired
of achieving basic competence in her assigned tasks, and Ssen ensured
that she would never put the ship in danger.

From Ssen she learned that the ship had two propulsion systems,
one used for short distances and landing on and departing from planets
or starbases, and a fancier one that enabled it to travel near the speed of
light. "The latter is the domain of the engineer-priests," Ssen told her,
"and unless you choose to become initiated into their mysteries, it will
be of no particular concern to you. But you will need to study orbital
mechanics, for everyone's safety."

Over the passing days, weeks, months, Essarala grew proficient in
putting on the spacesuit that Ssen designed for her and produced using
the ship's matter spinner. She only once forgot to check the oxygen
tank, which Ssen lectured her gently about because it was a serious
matter. As she grew in proficiency with the ship's systems and the simple maintenance tasks that Ssen assigned to her, she started taking
pride in her work, however simple. She started to sing at her work,
songs of the sea to remind her of the home she'd left behind.

In her leisure hours, she sat by the viewports of the starship and
gazed at the stars streaking by. She saw wonders up close, from the
dust-forges where stars are born to the hot glow of the accretion disks
around black holes. She saw planets of different colors spinning like
enchanted beads, and their diadems of moons. And all these visions reminded her of her sister Kiovasa, who had helped her attain her heart's
desire, and the fact that they were now parted; but she was not sorry,
not yet.

Next the starship visited a starbase to restock on supplies. While
Essarala wasn't present for the negotiations, given her lack of expertise,
she helped Ssen stow the supplies in the ship's hold. Despite the labor
involved, she enjoyed figuring out how to fit the containers most efficiently into the available space. In the sea, she'd never had to worry
about space before, but it was, of course, an ongoing concern in the
confines of the ship.

Afterward, the captain gave the two of them permission to explore
the station while the ship was docked. "You don't mind my following

you?" Essarala asked Ssen, for she wondered if they wanted some time to themself.

"No one should have to brave a starbase alone on their first visit," Ssen said. "Of course I don't mind." And they took Essarala to the starbase's zero-gravity gardens, with their fantastic floating plants and intoxicatingly perfumed flowers, and clusters of lanterns that changed color according to the designer's whimsy. After that, Ssen introduced her to other pleasures, from restaurants that served crisp honeyed insects to lounges where people traded poetry new and ancient, from cafes where one could pet small furry aliens who told one's fortune to monuments where spacers carved the names of those who had been lost to pirates, or radiation, or other hazards.

Not least of all, Ssen took her to the observation deck of the starbase, where Essarala caught her breath at the sight of the stars all around them, as though everyone lived inside a constellation of splendors. Ssen told her the names of the brightest stars and the peoples who lived on their worlds and visits they had made in times past.

At the end of these journeys, Ssen took Essarala aside in a quiet lounge, their expression serious. Essarala shivered with dread, for she feared that she'd performed so poorly aboard the ship that they were going to abandon her here. But Ssen hissed in concern when they smelled her fear and bought her a soothing cup of broth.

"If you ever weary of life on our ship," Ssen said, "we will find you a new home, or return you to your old one. This starbase, for instance. It's known for its hospitality, and you could make a life here if you chose, not just with the skills you've learned with us, but with your singing."

Essarala knew she had a fine voice, like every mer. She hadn't realized that Ssen had listened to her singing during her chores. "Do you wish for me to leave?" she asked in a small voice after taking a sip of broth.

"Not at all," Ssen said, their voice softening. "But you should always live on a ship because you're there by choice, not because you're out of options."

"I love the ship," Essarala said. It was true. She loved its metal

sleekness and the way it hummed when it accelerated or decelerated.
She loved the views of whorled nebulae and globular clusters. She
loved the starbase, too, with its vast exterior symmetries and asymme-
tries; the way it housed a variety of aliens even more diverse than those
upon the ship. She could not imagine giving up her shipboard life,
not yet.

And if she dreamt sometimes of her sister's kind smile, and the
sea's embrace, and the moving constellations of glowing jellyfish or the
whale-sages' vast chorales as they deliberated upon matters judicial, or
what it had been like before she'd given up her koi-spotted tail to walk
upon two legs—why, that was the price she had to pay, in exchange for
this bounty.

In the years to come, Essarala grew expert in the ways of life upon a
ship, until she almost forgot what it had been like to live upon a single
planet and no more. The starship visited other starbases, each more
wondrous than the last, and paid calls to other worlds as well. By now,
Essarala herself helped Ssen orient the ship's newcomers and occasional guests, and she took great pleasure in sharing her hard-earned
knowledge.

Now at mess she knew all the crew by name, and the captain nodded to her in greeting when they passed each other. She knew the
astrogator and her fondness for fruit preserves, and the engineer-priests
with their incantations and calculations. She knew the ship's pilot, the
gunner who defended them against pirates, the cook. And they in their
turn knew her, and sometimes, in moments of leisure, asked her to sing
the songs of her world for them.

Essarala learned to fly in skysuits in vast and turbulent gas planets, some of which had corrosive atmospheres. She saw twin sunsets
over methane seas and meteor showers flung across brilliant nighttime
skies. She walked through forests of towering trees sharded through
with crystal and breathed in the fragrance of flowers that bloomed only
once a millennium. And she kept her promise, too: for every world she
visited, she sang her sister's name.

Someday I will go back and tell her of the things I have seen, Essarala thought again and again. *But not yet, not yet.*

But Ssen was not done teaching her, as expert as she had become in the starfarer's life. Now that Essarala had mastered the pragmatic skills she needed to survive and to contribute to the crew, Ssen sat with her during their spare hours and taught her theory. They started with the simplest principles of mechanics and chemistry, then progressed to special relativity.

And it was in learning about relativity that Essarala finally understood the price that the witch beneath the waves had exacted from her—or, more accurately, warned her about.

She looked at the equations, at the time dilation factor that had emerged from such deceptively simple premises: the constant speed of light, the fact that no inertial frame of reference was privileged over any other. In the years that she had spent away from home, decades upon decades had passed for her sister Kiovasa. And mers lived long, but they were not—quite—immortal.

Ssen saw Essarala clench her hands in distress and asked why.

"I must return to my homeworld," Essarala said. "However long it takes—but sooner is better. For I left unfinished business there, and I did not realize it until now."

"It is out of our way," Ssen said, "but we can petition the captain. Even if we cannot take you there, we may be able to find another ship that can."

Indeed, the captain summoned Essarala to their stateroom. They listened attentively as Essarala explained her dilemma. "I will do whatever it takes to get back home," she said. She feared it was already too late—but that, she would not say aloud, even to the captain who had so generously welcomed her to their crew.

"It's true that it's a long way for us," the captain said. "But we will make the detour, and we will wait as long as you need. I know what it's like to be far from family."

Essarala bowed her head. "You won't need to wait," she said. "I will not be leaving my home again. Thank you. This is a kindness I cannot repay."

The captain's crest stirred in the manner that Essarala had learned, by now, meant sympathy. "You are not the only one who gave up a lot in exchange for the long dream of stars," they said. "We will miss you; but so does your family, I imagine."

"Thank you," she said again, and left the captain's stateroom a little easier of heart.

The captain was as good as their word. They did not head straight back to Essarala's homeworld, for they had trade contracts and obligations to keep, but they did guide the ship closer and closer to it, in a zigzag path. Essarala pored over the star-maps, dreaming of her return.

One by one, the other members of the crew, whom Essarala had come to think of as friends over the course of her journey, stopped by to give her small gifts. These included fruit preserves from the astrogator (of course), circuit jewelry from the engineer-priests, petrified wood from a certain extinct forest on a certain museum world, and cubes that spindled out performances by radiant holographic puppets. Even the captain gave her a feather from their crest.

Last of all came Ssen, teacher and companion. Ssen gave Essarala a bracelet of star-metal carved with the constellations of the night sky as seen from Essarala's homeworld during that long-ago visit. "I will think of you," Ssen said, "even if we never see you again."

"You have been the best of teachers," Essarala said, quite overcome. "I will wear this always."

Ssen smiled their snakish smile, and that was that.

All too soon, for all her impatience, Essarala strapped herself into her couch for the landing on her homeworld. This time she didn't require Ssen's assistance, and this time she didn't lose consciousness as the ship decelerated. The world came into view, a whorled marble of blue and green and violet and pearly streaks, and her breath hitched at its splendor; the old made new again.

The ship touched down, and Essarala freed herself from the couch. "I hope it's not too late," she said to herself as she and Ssen made their way to the ramp.

"There is only one way to find out," Ssen replied. "Go, and be well."

Essarala's feet met the shore, the same one where the ship had landed on its first voyage to this world. This time she wore a spacer's suit with its magnetic boots. It had served her well in her time aboard the ship.

She looked over the sea with its ever-crashing waves and the wheeling gulls, then took off the suit. "I won't be needing this anymore," she said to Ssen. "You can go ahead and recycle it."

Then Essarala waded out into the ocean, and as she did, koi-spotted scales grew to cover her legs and feet. With a last shuddering breath, she reclaimed the heritage that she had set aside in exchange for the stars and dived into the waters. As she did, her legs fused into a proper mer's tail.

Essarala hadn't forgotten her promise to the witch, and besides, the witch might know where—if anywhere—to find her sister. So she swam deep, beyond the colorful coral reefs with their shy darting fishes, beyond the pods of dolphins, until she found the lanternfish that lit the way to the witch's dwelling. The sea was cold and dark, but it was, after all, no colder and no darker than space.

"I have returned," Essarala called out, wondering what she would do if the witch had perished in the interim.

But witches are not so easily escaped. The worms began to glow, as they had all those years ago, and the witch beneath the waves emerged. "You have indeed," she said. This time Essarala could see her face more clearly, and it was not so dissimilar from her own.

"You gave me my heart's desire," Essarala said. "You said you would name your price once I returned. Well, here I am."

"Indeed," the witch said. "I am ready to summon my death. It will take its time coming; but it will come all the same. When it arrives, you will take my place as witch beneath the waves. For you, too, have tasted life among the stars, and you have the wisdom that your journeys have given you."

It was a hard price, but not an unfair one. "Understood," Essarala said. "I have a question for you, if you are willing to answer it."

"Ask."

Essarala steeled herself for the answer she didn't want to hear. "What became of my sister Kiovasa? Where can I find her?"

"She is old and ailing," the witch answered, and Essarala's heart almost burst with relief. "You will find her by the rock where the two of you spent so many hours gazing at the stars. She has never forgotten you. But you should hurry. She doesn't have much time left."

"Thank you," Essarala said. And then she shot upward through the waters, swimming with all her might toward the rock. It would be terrible if she had come all this way only to be too late after all.

At last she broke the ocean's surface in an explosion of glittering water and rainbows. "Kiovasa!" she cried when she saw her sister lying upon the rock.

Mers do not age as humans do, but they age nonetheless. Streaks of shell-white had appeared in Kiovasa's hair, and the stripes of her tail were so faint they were almost invisible. But her face lit when she saw Essarala. "You've returned," she murmured. "You look the same as you did the day you left."

"It is a magic of the stars," Essarala said, "which I will explain to you if you wish." She swam up to the rock and took a seat next to her sister. They hugged each other fiercely. Essarala added, "I will not leave you again."

"But your dream of traveling among the stars," Kiovasa said. "I would not take you away from that—"

Essarala grasped Kiovasa's hands, then craned her neck back to look at the afternoon sky. "You haven't," she said.

Kiovasa shook her head, bemused. "I don't understand."

"What I did not know before I left," Essarala said, "is that every planet is traveling through space, and every star, and every galaxy, and more beyond, in a great celestial dance. I wanted to visit other worlds, and so I have. But now that I understand the motions of celestial bodies, I don't need to leave home in order to journey through the universe."

"I don't understand," Kiovasa said again, "but I look forward to learning, in the time that remains to me."

IT CAME FROM CRUDEN FARM

MAX BARRY

Max Barry (www.maxbarry.com) is an Australian who pretended to sell high-end computer systems for Hewlett-Packard while secretly writing his first novel, *Syrup*. In fact, he still has the laptop he wrote it on because HP forgot to ask for it back, but keep that to yourself. He put an extra X in his name for *Syrup* because he thought it would be a funny joke about marketing and failed to realize everyone would assume he was a pretentious asshole. *Jennifer Government,* his second novel, was published with no superfluous Xs and sold much better, and was followed by *Company*, *Machine Man*, and *Lexicon*, which was named one *Time's* Top 10 Fiction Books of 2013. Max also created the online political game *NationStates,* for which he is far more famous among high school students and poli-sci majors than for his novels. He was born and lives in Melbourne, Australia, where he writes full time, the advantage being that he can do it while wearing only boxer shorts.

fter the inauguration, the speeches, and the four-jet flyover, the new president walked back toward the Capitol Building, clasping his wife's hand. "That was good, yes?" he said.

"They love you," said the first lady.

He smiled modestly, but it was true; they did love him. All the way to the National Statuary Hall, where he would mingle with dignitaries for a few minutes before heading to the White House, people stood and applauded.

"Huge crowd," said Damon, his campaign adviser. "Almost 2013 Obama."

"Bigger," said Clara, his press secretary. "Almost 2009 Obama."

"Almost as big as Trump said his was," said Damon.

"Well, now you're being ridiculous," said the president. He looked at them both. "We did it, huh? We really did it."

"You did it," said Clara, who then added: "Mr. President."

In the National Statuary Hall, the generals immediately made a beeline for him, a solid block of old men squeezed into starched collars and boards. The Navy chief pumped his hand. "Terrific speech, Mr. President."

"Outstanding," said the Air Force chief of staff. "The best I've heard."

He smiled magnanimously. "You know, I've always wanted to ask. Do we have an alien?"

The Air Force chief of staff blinked. "I beg your pardon?"

"An alien." He winked at the first lady. "I always wondered. You have to tell me. I'm the president."

The Air Force chief of staff pursed his lips. There was an uncomfortable silence.

"Oh, my God," said the president.

"Perhaps we can save this for a more suitable time," said the Air Force chief of staff.

"There's a . . ." The president lowered his voice. "There's really an . . ."

"It's your inauguration," said the Air Force chief of staff. "I'll leave you to enjoy yourself. We can discuss these other matters in a secure environment."

The room was filling with people, most of whom would soon attempt to close in for a quick word or a handshake. "Follow me," he told the Air Force chief of staff, making for the nearest doorway. Two men in dark suits appeared, part of the Secret Service detachment that swam and mutated around him, occasionally spitting out agents who looked so similar he couldn't keep track of who was who. "Can you clear this hallway?" They nodded, because of course they could. When they were alone, he asked the Air Force chief of staff: "We actually have an alien?"

The Air Force chief of staff took a long, reluctant breath. "Yes, Mr. President."

"*Yes?*"

"Yes."

"An *alien.*"

"We do have an alien, yes, Mr. President."

He peered into the Air Force chief of staff's pale blue eyes. "I feel like this might be a hazing ritual for new presidents."

"I assure you, Mr. President, it's no joke."

"An alien. As in . . ." He fluttered his fingers. "A spaceship came to Earth."

"Yes, Mr. President."

"What does it look like?"

"The alien, sir? Or the spacecraft?"

"The alien," he said. "No. Both."

"The spacecraft was a yellowish sphere that eventually melted away to a stringy, viscous substance. The alien is a blue, jellylike object approximately the size of a family sofa."

"And we have it?"

"That's correct, Mr. President. It's at Area 51."

The president eyed him. "I want to be clear: If you're yanking my chain—"

"I'm not yanking your chain, Mr. President. We have an alien."

"How long have we had it?"

"Twelve years."

"Twelve!" he said, which echoed through the hallway. He lowered his voice. "Twelve years and no one said anything? Not Bush nor Obama? Not *Trump*?"

"Trump didn't like him, sir."

He paused. "I'm sorry?"

"President Trump didn't get along with the alien. They had a tempestuous relationship."

"I bet they did," he said, before remembering himself. This wasn't the campaign trail. "You mean he can talk. The alien, that is."

"Yes, sir. We taught him English. President Trump spoke with him several times."

"But they didn't get along."

"No, Mr. President."

"The alien," said the president, "and Trump. They didn't see eye to eye."

"That is correct, Mr. President."

"I swear to God," he said, "if you're messing with me—"

"Sir, I have zero sense of humor," said the Air Force chief of staff. "Ask my wife."

The president rubbed his chin. "Can I see it?"

The Air Force chief of staff adopted a pained expression. At the end of the hallway, the first lady appeared behind a Secret Service man, raised a thin arm, and tapped her wrist. "I can see you're busy," said the Air Force chief of staff. "I won't keep you—"

"Yes, you will. I want an answer."

The Air Force chief of staff hesitated. "Well, sir, you're the president. If you want to see the alien, you can see it. But I recommend against it."

At the end of the hallway, the first lady put her hands on her hips.

"I want to see it," the president said. "By the time I get done with the White House ballyhoo, I want you to have a video for me to watch." He moved toward the first lady.

"Mr. President, there is no video."

He turned. "What?"

"All evidence is contained within Area 51. It's considered too dangerous to risk a leak."

He walked back to the Air Force chief of staff. "You're telling me that if I want to see the alien, I have to fly to Nevada?"

"Unfortunately, yes," said the Air Force chief of staff, who did not appear to find this very unfortunate. "Once your schedule opens up, we could—"

"I'm changing my schedule," the president said. "We leave tonight."

The Air Force chief of staff's mouth hung open for a moment. Then he gently closed it.

"And I want you to come with me," said the president, "because I have a lot of questions."

"An alien?" said the first lady, when they were inside the limousine.

He nodded. "A goddamn alien."

"Are you sure he wasn't joking?"

"That's what I said. But he insists it's real."

"Hmm." The first lady rested her chin on her wrist and gazed out through the smoked glass at the passing streets. It was beginning to rain.

"So, listen," said the president. "We're flying out to Area 51 tonight."

She looked at him. "What about your schedule?"

"Screw the schedule. I've been thinking. This is just what I've been looking for. A way to start my term with a splash. What's the one word I used most on the campaign trail?"

"*Scotch*," said the first lady.

"*Trust*," he said. "It was *trust*. It's time to restore trust in government. But that trust needs to be earned."

"Yes, I was at the speeches, darling."

"This alien," he said, poking his pant leg for emphasis, "has been kept hidden for twelve years. Twelve years! Because the government didn't trust people to know. Well, they elected me, and I do trust them."

"Mmm," she said.

"What?"

"Well, it's a wonderful sound bite. I know it tested through the roof and won you Ohio. But now that you're in office, you need to be practical."

"Actually, I need to do exactly what I promised." He spread his arms. "Isn't that a shock? Who could have seen that coming?"

"Darling, you're being dramatic."

"Those weren't sound bites. That's what I believe. We have to rebuild trust in this country. Trust in government, trust in our institutions, and, most important of all, trust in each other. That starts with what I do on my first day. It starts with this alien."

"Hmm," the first lady said.

He took her hand across the leather seats. "Do you believe me?"

She smiled. "I believe that if anyone can do it, you can."

"There we go," he said. He felt optimistic. He looked out the window and saw a family waving flags. He waved back, even though they couldn't see him through the glass. "There we go."

Air Force One lifted off at 8:11 p.m. Its official destination was an unnamed private airport in Pennsylvania. According to the press secretary, the president was visiting ailing family, in a private and urgent matter that would not be discussed further.

"It's just that if the first thing you do is hop a plane to Area 51, people will connect the dots," she said, across the aisle. Clara Fielding was being surprisingly calm about the idea of intelligent alien life, to the president's mind. He'd seen her scream like a wounded boar over a misworded press release.

"I'll be connecting the dots for them, soon." He already loved the airplane. It was fantastically spacious, as if he were hurtling through the air in an apartment. "In fact, I've already written up a few words." He dug into his jacket pocket for his notebook.

The first lady's brows furrowed.

"What?" he said.

"I know you like to write your own speeches, but for an event of this magnitude, isn't it better if Jeff—"

"I don't do it because I like it. It's more authentic."

"Yes, more authentic, yes," she said, nodding, "but Jeff is, you know, a professional speechwriter. In a time like this, don't you think—"

"I can write a speech. I'm not just a mouthpiece for Jeff."

"I only mean—"

"Why don't you listen to it?" he said. "Then you can decide whether Jeff could do better."

Damon, his adviser, was standing in the aisle, leaning slightly on Clara's seat. "I bet it's a knockout, Mr. President."

"Thank you, Damon." He kept meaning to get rid of Damon. The guy was a yes-man. It was continually embarrassing that he hadn't been able to pull the trigger. "These are first thoughts. Nothing's nailed down." He cleared his throat. "At some point in our lives, all of us have turned our eyes to the stars and wondered whether anyone was out there, looking back. Today, at last, we finally have our answer."

"Hmm," said the first lady.

He looked at her. "Do you have a comment?"

"Well, it's not really 'today,' is it? We've had the alien for twelve years."

"And today, the people are finding out about it. They're getting their answer today."

"I suppose."

He looked around. "Should I continue?"

"I'm loving it," said Damon. "Go right ahead, Mr. President."

"Employing technology beyond our current understanding, a golden sphere entered our atmosphere and came to rest outside of Richmond, Virginia. From this vehicle, our visitor emerged. He was first greeted by—"

Clara visibly flinched in her seat.

He glanced at her. "What?"

"Nothing, Mr. President. Sorry to interrupt."

"If you have feedback, let's hear it," he said. "That's what this process is about."

"Well, sir, I notice you said 'he.'"

The president blinked. "Is that not accurate?"

"My understanding at this point," said Clara, choosing her words carefully, "is that it's not accurate, no."

"The alien is female?"

"I believe it's neither."

The president twisted in his chair. "Where's Mc—" He spotted the Air Force chief of staff at the rear of the room, huddled with a small group of military personnel. The president beckoned impatiently. "Is the alien male?"

The Air Force chief of staff inhaled deeply. He wasn't missing any opportunities to make it clear that he was here under duress. It was an endless parade of frowns and pained pauses. "Mr. President, as you required a full briefing, I have here special envoy Kevin Pilsman, who's our mission lead."

A neat, middle-aged man in a blue jacket stepped forward. "A great pleasure to meet you, Mr. President. I'm very excited about the prospect of finally making our findings public." The Air Force chief of staff looked pained.

"Excellent," the president said. "That's the spirit. Is it male?"

"Strictly speaking, Mr. President, it doesn't possess sex organs. Not as we'd categorize them, anyway."

"So it's sexless?"

"That is correct."

The president looked at the Air Force chief of staff. "I feel like you called it 'he' before."

The Air Force chief of staff said, "We tend to use masculine terms informally, since it looks male."

Clara emitted a sound that was something like a grunt and something like a sneeze. The president glanced at her. "Excuse me," she said.

The first lady offered, "But 'it' is so impersonal. Almost frightening. I think it's an easier sell if we say 'he' or 'she,' rather than 'it.'"

"Good point," said the president. "And it looks male?"

"To the eye, yes," said the Air Force chief of staff.

Clara grunt-sneezed again.

The president said, "Is there something you want to say, Clara?"

"To be honest," Clara said, "it sounds a little like we're foisting a male gender onto a genderless creature. Which I would have to say I disagree with."

"Why is that?"

"Because it's not. It's not male."

"But it looks male," said Kevin.

Clara turned to him. "I'm given to understand it looks like a rhinoceros crossed with a set of bagpipes. How is that male?"

"It's really the sense you get when you see it, I suppose," Kevin said. "It's, you know, big and ugly."

"It's male because it's ugly? That's your logic?"

"I don't care whether it's ugly," said the president. "I just want to know what to call it, so I can get past the second sentence of my speech. We're getting bogged down."

"Mr. President, if I may," said Kevin. "We've done this awhile, and found it easiest to use gender-neutral male terms."

Clara twisted around in her seat. "Excuse me?"

"I mean 'he' in a neutral sense. Such as we might say a jet is reaching the end of 'her' service. Obviously the jet isn't female—it's merely an expression."

"Oh, like when you see a dog in the street," Damon interjected. "You say, 'There's a good boy,' as a default."

The president looked at Clara.

"I'm sorry," she said. "I feel like I'm watching the Ten Commandments being written here, and unless I say something, a burning bush is going to be gendered for the next two thousand years. First, there's no such thing as a gender-neutral male pronoun. That's an oxymoron. Second, when you see a dog and say 'he,' you're not assuming a genderless dog. You're assuming a male dog."

The Air Force chief of staff sighed.

The first lady leaned forward. "What does it call itself?"

"Ah," said Kevin. "Yes. Thank you. Male. He refers to himself as a male."

"Well, that settles it," said the president. "No objection to using the alien's chosen pronouns, I assume?" He raised his notepad.

Clara asked, "Who taught it to speak?"

Kevin said, "Pardon me?"

"What has been the gender balance of the personnel who have interacted with the alien over the twelve years, would you say?"

Kevin glanced at the Air Force chief of staff. "I'm not sure of the relevancy of—"

"Seventy percent male?" Clara said. "Stop me when I get close. Eighty?" She peered at him. "Has it seen a woman?"

"We could use 'they,'" Damon offered. "Or 'ze.' Is that right? 'Ze' for 'he/she' and 'zir' for 'his/her'? I think I've heard that."

"For God's sake," the president said. "We're spending all our time on a single word."

The first lady said, "This is why I wanted to have Jeff. He can navigate these things."

"Well, Jeff's not here." The president spread his arms. "Do you see Jeff anywhere?"

The first lady crossed her arms.

"I'm sorry. I didn't mean to snap." He rubbed his forehead.

"Perhaps a short break," said the first lady. "You're running on fumes. There's no need to figure all this out yet."

"Maybe you're right." He couldn't stop rubbing his forehead. "Thank you, everyone. I'm going to lie down for a few minutes."

There was an honest-to-God bedroom, complete with a desk and two sitting chairs. A bedroom on an airplane. He fell onto the bed and stared at the recessed ceiling lights while the first lady gently climbed in beside him. After a minute, she began fooling with her tablet.

"What are you doing?" he said.

She gazed at him over her reading glasses. He'd always liked those glasses. She reminded him of his eighth-grade English teacher, about whom he'd had complicated feelings. "The department has run scenarios on going public with the alien. Likely reactions and consequences."

"What's the consensus?"

"Well," she said, scrolling, "they look at different aspects. I can give you the summaries, if you like."

"Please."

"International relations: sharply increased likelihood of major conflicts, particularly with Russia and China. Elevated risk of espionage. Elevated risk of assassination."

"Really? I was thinking the opposite. An alien would *unite* us as a species. It shows what we have in common."

"I suppose it's not humanity's alien, though, is it? It's America's. Will we share it?"

"I guess not," he said. "Hmm. I hadn't thought of that. I don't want this to be political. I want it to help us rise above all that."

"Next is religion." She inhaled. "Goodness."

"What happens with religion?"

"'Wide-scale collapse of faith among moderates, coupled with accelerating radicalism and cultlike behavior in—'"

"Really?"

"There's nothing about aliens in the Bible," the first lady said. "Possibly that's a problem."

"These analyses are so pessimistic. That's the problem with this country. We've lost our—"

"Trust?"

"Yes, exactly. We're all hunkered down, wanting to protect our own little patch from each other. But this country was founded on trust. It's the basis of the free market. Of the family unit. Every community requires it."

The first lady's eyes moved from side to side, reading. "Goodness," she said. "Immigration is *really* appalling."

"Put that down," the president said. "You know what I keep thinking? Trump knew about this and sat on it. I can't figure that out. It doesn't seem in the man's nature."

"Perhaps he thought it might upstage him."

"Or contradict him." He rolled onto his side. "It's like a higher power, isn't it? Like the adults have come into the room and caught us squabbling. Now it's going to hit us with some home truths."

The first lady eyed him. "What if we don't like its truths?"

He shrugged. "I still believe the people deserve to hear it for themselves."

"Mmm," she said.

"What?" He touched her hip. "Am I still being a hopeless optimist?"

She smiled, the way he liked, when it was just for him. "I believe you are a decent man, who will always do the right thing."

"Ever kissed a man on Air Force One?"

The corners of her lips curled. "Ask me again," she said, "in one minute."

They touched down and rolled into a gray, unmarked hangar. After that was an elevator, as big as a kitchen, staffed by young men in blue uniforms who stared straight ahead without blinking.

"The alien is confined to a twenty-by-eighteen-foot cage," said Kevin, the special envoy. "It's hermetically sealed, for security, and so we can maintain the alien's ideal climate. Around the cage is a series of metal slats we can open or close on command. And, of course, there's a microphone, so you can communicate."

"I can speak to it just like you and I are speaking?"

"He speaks English very well."

The president nodded. "I have to say, I'm looking forward to this."

The Air Force chief of staff cleared his throat. Kevin said, "There is something you should know. He'll try to give you a message."

"A message?"

"Yes, Mr. President. When he receives new visitors, he wants to give them his message."

"Which is?"

"To be honest, sir, I'd rather not preempt it."

"Well, I'd rather you did, and I'm the president." He looked at the Air Force chief of staff. "The alien came to Earth with a message, and I'm hearing about it now? You didn't think to mention that earlier?"

"Unacceptable," said Damon.

"The message is a little uncomfortable, sir," said the Air Force chief of staff.

"Is it," said the president. This he could believe: that the alien's message didn't dovetail with the aims and objectives of the U.S. military.

"And it's not the case that he arrived with the message. He developed it in the ensuing years."

The elevator doors began to close, and one of the guards helpfully pressed a button to open them again.

"You know what?" the president said. "I think I'm going to hear it for myself." He strode between the doors.

Cold air gripped him. In the center of a cavernous space, beneath a ring of glaring spotlights, sat a massive rectangular block shuttered with dark gray metal. Thick tubes and twisted cables rose to the ceiling, where the fan blades turned and hummed.

"That's it?" he said unnecessarily. His breath fogged.

"Yes, Mr. President," said Kevin. "A secure, climate-controlled environment designed for his particular needs."

"He stays in there all the time? How does he feel about that?"

"He doesn't love it," Kevin admitted. "He's expressed a desire to leave. But he can't survive in our atmosphere. He'd need a suit of some kind and a mobility device." He gestured. "This way."

The president crossed dark concrete, eyeing the block. He could see the slats Kevin had mentioned—closed now, concealing whatever was inside. Nearby stood an area with tables and equipment: speakers, microphones, and cameras. *Twelve years*, he thought. A long time for a creature to be kept in captivity. A creature with a message.

They stopped. He glanced around. "Do I need a microphone?"

"No, sir. We have you."

"And when I say so, you'll . . ." He gestured at the block in front of him.

"We'll open the slats so you can see each other. Yes, Mr. President."

He nodded. He was more nervous than he'd expected. Partly because of the historical weight of the moment—footage of which, no doubt, would be placed into the permanent archive—but mainly because of the creature itself. *An alien*, he thought. *A goddamn alien.*

He glanced around the group. Damon gave him a thumbs-up. "Open it," the president said.

There was a mighty *crack*. Lines appeared in the metal slats, widening, until the president could see slices of the environment within. He thought, *Is that it?*, because everything was dark and formless, and then, *Oh, yes.*

His first impression was of a jellyfish, but blue. Instead of tentacles, it bristled with stout pipes of different lengths. Small mouthlike openings grew and closed rhythmically around its body. If it had eyes or ears, he couldn't see them.

He turned to Kevin. "Can it see me?"

Sound burst from the speakers. *Like my father gargling half a glass of water*, the president thought. "Who are you?"

He composed himself. "I am the president of the United States. My name is—"

"You're tall."

The president smiled, amused. "I suppose I am." It spoke through its pipes, he gathered; he could see them constrict and loosen. "You have me at a disadvantage, though. I have no idea of your height, relative to your people."

"I'm tall."

"Then we are two tall people, you and I." This was a little mundane, he thought. This wasn't really what he wanted going into the historical archive. "We come from different worlds, you and I, but here we are, together."

A cluster of pipes exhaled together. "I have a message."

"Oh, yes," said the president.

"It is important. You must listen carefully."

"You have my attention."

"It is a warning. You are in danger."

He felt a cold tickle in his heart. He was the president. He could nuke a city, order an assassination, remake the world. He had run for office knowing the great responsibilities it would bring. Yet he hadn't expected to be hearing about danger from an alien on day one.

"All of you," said the alien. "You will be wiped out within three of your generations, unless you take action. It may already be too late."

It's climate change, he thought. *It's goddamn climate change.* He'd suspected it would be his greatest challenge. Maybe this would be the circuit breaker. An alien come to Earth with a warning—that might convince the coal states. Although it might not. It might only get their backs up, like it had when it was a Swedish teenager.

"Are you listening?"

"Yes," the president said. "I'm sorry. Is it climate change?"

The alien's pipes hissed. "Is what climate change?"

"The danger. Your warning."

"No."

"Ah," he said.

"It is far more serious. You face corrosion at the fundamental level of DNA."

Yikes, he thought.

"Your race will be completely destroyed. Its genome scattered. Reduced to little more than animals."

"How will this take place?"

"Breeding," said the alien. "It is already happening."

"Did you say 'breeding'?"

"Mixing of the bloodlines. I shall explain. When a white man takes a woman of inferior stock—say, a Negress, or a Jewess—or, equally, the other way, when a white woman is taken by a Black—their child's blood is irreparably diluted."

The president sucked in his lips. A few moments passed. He stared at the alien. "Will you excuse me for a moment?"

"I have more to tell you. My warning is incomplete."

"Yes," the president said. "I'm sure. But I just . . ." He glanced at Kevin. "Can we . . . close this?"

Kevin signaled. The slats banged and rattled back together, finally closing off the alien from sight. There was silence but for the humming of the fans.

The president looked around the group. "What was that?"

No one answered.

"I believe I asked a question. What the hell was that?"

Kevin cleared his throat. "I assume you're referring to the, ah, ideological views that the alien holds."

"He's a racist," said the president. "He's a huge, flaming racist."

"Well-l-l-l . . . ," said Kevin. "We prefer not to throw around labels."

"That," the president said, pointing at the wall, "was incredibly, incredibly racist." He ran a hand through his hair, a nervous gesture that he thought he'd managed to eradicate on the campaign trail. The first lady's face was ashen. Clara, his press secretary, had her head in her hands. "How is this possible?"

"Mr. President?"

"How is a *blue sack* a *white supremacist*?"

"It's self-hating," said Damon.

"Actually," said Kevin, "the alien considers himself to be white."

"Excuse me?" said the president.

"On the outside, obviously, he's a semirigid blue gel, but ideologically, he feels an affinity with—"

"Stop," the president said. "That's not what I'm asking. I want to know how a sentient sofa becomes a racist. Has it always been like this?"

Kevin shook his head. "His views have skewed over time."

"How? How does it even know these words?"

"He watches TV."

The president blinked. "Excuse me?"

"As part of his socialization program, we've exposed him to various forms of media. Some radio, some television—"

"What kind of television?"

"Under President Bush, we mostly screened wholesome family dramas. The alien seemed to enjoy those, although this period predates our ability to communicate, so it's hard to say for sure. But he would extend his pipes toward the screen during the closing sequence of *The Waltons*, for example, in a fairly wholesome manner."

"Then what happened?"

"President Obama was encouraged by his rapid speech development and directed us to open up PBS, C-SPAN, the Discovery Channel, and the History Channel, among others. However, the History Channel proved problematic and was later withdrawn."

"Why?"

"The alien became hooked on *Ancient Aliens*," said Kevin. "I mean, he really loved it. Not in a *Waltons* kind of way. It was different. During episodes, his vibrissae became active, and for hours afterward, his pipes inflated and deflated in an agitated manner. The Obama administration grew concerned about this, and about how History Channel content was becoming less . . ." He paused, searching for the word.

"True," suggested the first lady.

"Appropriate," Kevin said. "Terminating it made the alien very unhappy, though. He accused us of a conspiracy to conceal the truth from him. And, to be fair, we really were concealing the existence of an alien. But anyway, his media intake was then limited until early 2017, at which time the new administration . . . formed a different view."

"Oh, my God," the president said. "Trump showed it Fox News."

The first lady put a hand over her mouth.

"Yes, sir. But I want to be clear: Television is only one component of the socialization program. I don't want to imply that he's been doing nothing but soaking up Fox News."

"What else, then?"

"He reads newspapers, sometimes. And he browses the internet."

"It has *internet* access?"

"Yes, Mr. President."

"You mean it browses websites? Where does it go?"

"In the last few years, I must admit, he's been spending most of his time on what you might characterize as alt-right sites. He also posts on social media."

"Why do we let him post?"

"It's a two-way process," said Kevin. "The alien needs to interact with people in order to improve his communication and socialization skills. Also, this enabled a number of side projects, such as a study into whether most people can detect that they're engaging online with an extraterrestrial."

The president hesitated. "Did they?"

Kevin shook his head. "The alien did get banned from the *New York Times* comment section. But not for being an alien. For flaming."

The president stared.

"That's like trolling," said the first lady. "Using inflammatory language to upset people."

"Are you telling me that the alien was trolling in the comments section of the *New York Times?*"

"If you ask the alien," Kevin said, "he was banned for posting simple facts."

The president rubbed his face. "Careful, darling," said the first lady. "Your hair."

This is a disaster, he thought. He couldn't unveil a blue white supremacist to the world. A thought occurred to him, and he turned to the Air Force chief of staff. "You said Trump didn't like the alien? Why not? I'd have thought it might have . . ."

"Appealed to a certain demographic?" offered the first lady.

"There was some talk of going public, Mr. President. Every administration has kicked around the idea of a public announcement. However, President Trump and the alien had a falling-out."

"Of what nature?"

"A personal nature, I would say, Mr. President."

"It insulted him?"

"Yes, sir. They insulted each other. It was very heated. After that, neither would forgive the other."

The president shook his head. "All right. Everything you've been doing, it stops. No more Fox News. No more internet."

"Mr. President," said Kevin, appalled. "This is a long-term project. Terminating our research at this point would—"

"It's stopped," he said. "And, frankly, if I were in your shoes, I wouldn't be arguing. You've turned the first visitor to Earth into a racist."

"Mr. President, I must say, that is deeply unfair. We didn't force it to adopt these views. On the contrary, the science team took a neutral, hands-off position, in order to allow it to develop without undue influence."

"Into a racist," the president said. "Who are we blaming, then? Fox?"

The Air Force chief of staff said, "In my opinion, sir, the alien is simply kind of a dick."

The president looked at him.

"We can make allowances for the fact that he comes from a different culture. But frankly, sir, he's not smart. And he enjoys being difficult. For example, sometimes he expels fluid. We know he can direct it into a receptacle built for purpose, but still, sometimes he does it on the floor. And he won't say where he's from."

"We don't know which planet he's from?"

"Sir, we're actually not sure that *he* knows."

"Then why is he here? Why come to Earth?"

Kevin said, "We have several theories. He may have been kicked out by his own people, or simply gotten lost. It does seem less likely now that he is a special emissary sent here with a purpose, like we believed in the beginning."

"That would make sense to me," said Clara. "If he's been rejected by his own people and, no pun intended, alienated, that may have pushed him toward extremist views."

"It," said the president. "Pushed 'it.'"

"Yes," she said. "That's what I meant, of course."

"Mr. President," said the Air Force chief of staff, "I think you can see now why it would be a terrible mistake to reveal this thing to the world."

"Ah, well, I don't necessarily agree," said Kevin. "As someone who's worked closely with the alien for years, I think it's time to share publicly what an extraordinary creature we have. I understand he has a few rough edges, politically speaking, but isn't that, well, a reflection of society? Don't we all value free speech even when it's not speech we agree with?"

"Oh, please," said the first lady.

The president looked around the group. Clara said, "Mr. President, you can't. It would tear the country apart."

"Whatever you decide, it'll be the right thing to do, Mr. President," said Damon.

"Mmm," said the first lady.

He ran his hand through his hair. This time no one spoke. "All right," said the president. "I'm going to fix this. Open it up."

The metal slats cracked open. The alien had moved, the president saw; it had heaved itself closer. "Oh," it gurgled. "Look who's back. The president of the Jew-nited States."

"I want to make something clear to you," said the president. "I hold in my heart a great hope that you and I can be friends. But the views you have expressed are morally repugnant. They are grounded in ignorance and will not be tolerated."

The alien was silent.

"Do you understand?"

"I understand you have been brainwashed by the mainstream media."

"I am not brainwashed," the president said. "It is you, unfortunately, who have been brainwashed."

The alien gurgled briefly. "You're stupid."

"Now listen here," he said.

"I thought you might be different. But you government people are all the same."

"You've been misled, I'm sorry to say, by what you've been hearing. But that ends today. From now on, you'll be given real information, from proper, well-researched sources. You'll—"

"You're filtering my internet?"

"—receive fact-checked, authoritative—"

"You can't handle a debate, so you shut down the truth. So much for tolerance," said the alien. "So much for the open marketplace of ideas. Are you a Jew? I heard you were a Jew."

"I don't see how that's relevant."

"Message received, loud and clear."

"I am the president of the United States," he said, getting heated. "I have absolute authority over what happens to you, what is done to you—"

"Come in here and say that," said the alien.

"I goddamn will," the president said, stepping forward, "you goddamned piece of—"

"Mr. President!" said the first lady.

The cameras were still running, of course. He barked, "Close it!"

The metal slats began to close.

He was sweating. Damon offered a handkerchief. He accepted it gratefully and began to mop his brow. The silence stretched. "OK," he said, mostly to himself. "OK."

"Mr. President?" said the Air Force chief of staff.

"Bury it," he said.

"Sir?"

"Put it away. I don't want to hear about it ever again. I don't want anyone to hear about it."

The Air Force chief of staff smiled grimly. "Yes, Mr. President."

Kevin looked between them. "But . . . but we can't . . ."

"Maybe we'll get another one," Clara said suddenly. "One alien came to Earth; maybe there'll be another. And this time, we can handle it properly."

"Oh, yes," said the first lady. "That's a terrific idea. I like that."

"But," said Kevin, "what if it asks what happened to the first one?"

"We'd say we don't know what it's talking about. Pretend it never happened." The first lady hugged herself against the cold. "That's all you can do sometimes, isn't it? Put it behind you, pretend it never happened, and move on. That's how we've made progress for the last two hundred years: by plowing on no matter what, with a steadfast eye on the future."

"And ignoring past mistakes," Clara said. "Exactly."

"You can't fix everything," said the first lady. "Sometimes you can only . . . ignore it."

"Mr. President," appealed Kevin. "Surely you can't—"

He raised a hand. Kevin fell silent.

"I'm tired," the president said. "I'd like to return to Air Force One."

The first lady smiled. She offered her hand, and he took it. As they were walking away, he turned for a last look back, but the first lady's grip tightened in his. "Only forward, darling," she said, and he nodded.

SCHRÖDINGER'S CATASTROPHE

GENE DOUCETTE

Gene Doucette (www.genedoucette.me) is a novelist with more than twenty science fiction and fantasy titles to his name, including *The Spaceship Next Door*, *The Frequency of Aliens*, the Immortal series, and the Tandemstar books. His latest novel is *The Apocalypse Seven*. This story is his first attempt at short-form science fiction. He lives in Cambridge, Massachusetts.

Things began to go badly for the crew of the USFS *Erwin* around the time Dr. Marchere's coffee mug spontaneously reassembled itself.

Dr. Louis Marchere was not, at that moment, conducting some manner of experiment. Well, he *was*, only not on entropy and the nature of time. He was running several *other* tests, of the kind that make perfect sense on a scientific vessel such as the *Erwin*. About half of them were biological in nature, concerning how small samples of cellular material react to certain deep-space factors. Other tests were more at home in the general field of astrophysics. But—again, as this is important—he was not conducting a test on entropy.

He just dropped his coffee mug. More exactly, he elbowed it from the corner of the table, while he was concentrating on things unrelated to the nature of falling objects. The mug fell onto the hard, ferrous metal of a lab floor, shattered, and sent his coffee—which was already disappointingly lukewarm—everywhere.

Louis Marchere was pretty upset about this. He'd been on dozens of deep-space scientific missions over the years, and this mug—a white mug with a black swan—had made it through all of them. It was a gift from his daughter.

But things break. No use dwelling.

Then, while Marchere was fetching a towel and a broom, the shattered pieces of the mug re-formed, rose up, and settled back on the corner of the table.

The spilled coffee remained where it was, either because it had decided that it wanted no part in whatever nonsense the mug had going on, or so as to verify—for Dr. Marchere's sake—that what he witnessed had actually happened.

Which, of course, it had not. Shattered mugs don't simply decide to reassemble themselves. They don't decide to do *anything*, because they're inanimate objects with no agency, subject to the whims of the same laws of physics as everyone and everything else in Louis Marchere's laboratory, including Louis Marchere.

This was true irrespective of where that laboratory happened to be located. It had to be.

In this particular instance, the lab was in the middle of a ship that was in the middle of deep space, in a previously unexplored quadrant. The part about it being unexplored was unusual, but only a *little* unusual. The quadrant in question—C17-A387614-X.21, but everyone called it Brenda—was right in the center of a fully explored space grid. There had been many exploratory missions to all the other cubes on that grid, but nobody had bothered to check out Quadrant Brenda.

Probably, this was because Quadrant Brenda looked incredibly boring. There didn't appear to be anything *in* Brenda—no stars, planets, or moons. Comets showed no interest in visiting, and asteroids kept their distance. In a universe that could be defined as "enormous patches of nothing, with occasional, albeit incredibly rare, bits of something mixed in here and there," Quadrant Brenda somehow managed to contain even *more* nothing. This was probably why nobody had bothered to explore it before. It was definitely why the USFS *Erwin* was there, as this much nothing might mean something.

So far, two days into the quadrant, Dr. Marchere could confirm that it was just as boring on the inside as it looked from the outside. Three thousand different sensors on and outside the ship confirmed that sometimes a quadrant full of nothing is just a quadrant full of nothing.

And then the second law of thermodynamics—which was both extremely important and incredibly reliable—stopped working.

Dr. Marchere knew that wasn't what really happened; a dozen better explanations were surely available. He just had to find one of them.

First, he checked on the lab's artificial gravity, which he did by going to the wall panel and examining the settings, rather than by jumping up and verifying that after having done so, he also fell down.

The control panel confirmed that he had artificial gravity, and that nothing anomalous had transpired recently, either near the coffee mug, or in any other part of the lab.

Louis returned to the table and picked up the coffee mug, half expecting it to fall apart in his hands. It did not; the mug appeared intact, with no indication it had been in seven pieces quite recently.

"How did you manage that?" he asked the mug, which didn't respond.

Dr. Marchere held the mug over the floor and considered a practical but possibly irreversible test. Would the mug reassemble itself a second time? If so, the anomaly could be pinned down to something peculiar about the black swan mug his daughter gave him some years back. Perhaps it was even a trick of some kind, just waiting for the day he dropped it. She bought this trick mug based on certain assumptions about her father: that he was naturally clumsy, or vindictive about mugs, and would have shattered it before now, revealing the gag.

But that hardly seemed possible. It would require that self-healing mug technology existed, which it did not. And if it had, there was still the problem of the mug also returning to the tabletop.

He decided that this was a scientific problem, while wanting to keep the mug intact was an emotional problem. But he'd already reconciled with having broken the mug his daughter gave him, and felt confident that, if she were there, she'd understand.

He let go. The mug fell, broke into five pieces . . . and remained broken.

Of course it did. How could he have expected otherwise?

He fetched the towel and the broom, cleaned up the mess, and made an appointment with the medical wing. One of the twelve remaining possible explanations to consider, before upturning the second law of thermodynamics, was that he was going mad, and that was information that couldn't wait.

Dr. Louis Marchere didn't make it to the medical wing for his checkup.

"Final approach," the computer announced, in a cheerful singsong.

Corporal Alice Aste was in the rear portion of the shuttle at the time of the announcement, performing some light calisthenics to get the blood moving in preparation for . . . well, something. There was no telling what she was headed into, but there was an excellent chance that it would require her to be limber. This was an old combat-readiness technique that had less applicability now, in peaceful times, but she knew of more than one soldier who didn't live to become an ex-soldier due to a pulled hamstring.

She climbed back to the front of the cabin to get a look at the side of the vessel through the front windshield. The United Space Federation Science Vessel *Erwin* was right where Alice expected it to be, free-floating in the middle of Quadrant C17-A387614-X.21-slash-Brenda and doing absolutely nothing.

She opened up the comms.

"USFS *Erwin*, this is Corporal Aste of the USF Security Force. I'm on approach, and intend to dock. Please respond."

No answer.

"Again, *Erwin*, this is USFSF Corporal Alice Aste, on approach, requesting dock. Please open bay doors. Respond, *Erwin*."

She waited for a few seconds, in case someone over there felt chatty, then left the line open and went back to the rear of the cabin to get ready.

In any normal circumstance, Alice would be speaking with a hangar tech now, working out the details on how and where she'd be parking her shuttle. These weren't normal circumstances. What she expected from the *Erwin* was continued radio silence, just like when Alice sent a transmission from the base ship—the *Rosen*, parked at the edge of the quadrant—and just like the same radio silence the science vessel had been honoring for a little more than six weeks.

The last official transmission from the *Erwin* was recorded forty-seven days ago. It was from Captain Hadder, and it read: *We aren't here again today*. It was received, as were all of the science vessel communiqués, at the research station relay hub and then forwarded to the main cluster, where it sat for several days before anyone actually looked at it. And then, the only reason they did was that no subsequent communications came through and somebody thought that was notable.

Protocol was for a twice-daily check-in. Granted, the "day" these transmissions were sent and the "day" they were received were hardly ever the same, given the vast distances the signals had to cross, even when using the FTL ports. Still, ships like the *Erwin* had to transmit on a prearranged schedule, even if that transmission was nothing more than a *not much, what's up with you?*

Self-evidently, something was now *up* with the *Erwin*.

Once it became clear that the cryptic message had no obvious, direct meaning, it was handed off to a linguistics team, and run through some databases. It received a partial hit on an old Earth song by the Zombies, and an even older poem by Hughes Mearns. Neither made sense in the context of deep-space communications from science vessels.

A message was sent back, asking for clarification, but no clarification arrived. Someone got a linguist involved, who decided that in order to get a proper response from the *Erwin*, base had to answer in kind. He offered several suggestions, such as: *If you are not there, where are you?* and *Are you here again now?*

When that didn't do the trick either, somebody dug up the Zombies song and broadcast *that*, to see if it triggered a response, and then tried reading back both the annotated and full versions of the Mearns poem.

Still nothing.

By then, one of the network's orbital satellites got an angle on the ship, and sent back a video feed. The USFS cognoscenti were able to determine that: (1) the *Erwin* wasn't moving, (2) it had a heat signature, strongly implying the ship still had power, and (3) there was no evidence of outgassing, so it either still had atmosphere, or all of the atmosphere had escaped already.

All that was left to try was a crewed mission, which was how the USFSF *Rosen* ended up at the edge of the Brenda quadrant, and how Alice ended up on the shuttle.

The shuttle's autopilot sounded a gentle alert.

"Bay doors remain closed," it said.

"Computer, transmit bay door override to the *Erwin*, on my authority."

"Transmitting," it said calmly. Then, "No response. Collision imminent. Course correction strongly recommended."

Sometime in the past twenty years, the people in charge of these

things at the USF standardized the vocal communications from all
Space Federation computers, and it was decided the voice they used
should be, above all, serene. It worked fine in most situations, but came
off as ridiculous to the point of self-parody in high-stress circumstances.
Phrases like *explosive decompression in five seconds* aren't meant to be
heard in a voice meant to soothe unruly children.

"All right, keep your pants dry, computer," Alice said.

"This computer has no pants."

"Pull up from the current course and bring us alongside the hull.
I'll go in the side door."

"Course corrected. Would you like to hear about the explosive
charges inventory?"

"That'd be great, thanks."

The computer navigated the shuttle right up next to the *Erwin*,
about twenty yards from the rear hatch. The hatch's functional intent
was to allow someone from inside to get outside, to make repairs on the
hull or to unjam the bay doors, clean a filter, touch up the paint job,
or whatever. It wasn't meant to be used to get in from the outside, and
almost never *was* used that way. Despite that, hatches like this were
called *pirate doors*.

The good thing about pirate doors, and what made them so useful
in times like this, was that there was an air lock on the other side, so if
she had to blow the door with one of the many explosive charges on
inventory, she wouldn't be breaching the entire deck.

After gowning up for the space walk, Alice stuffed a few charges
in a bag—like her, the bag was a veteran of combat, and came with
a steel panel that doubled as a piece of armor in a pinch—added a
couple of blasters, and headed across on an umbilical. She expected
to have to blow the door, but it opened easily after a few turns of the
hatch's wheel.

Alice unhooked the umbilical, ordered the shuttle to hold position, stepped in, and sealed the hatch from the inside. The wall panel
indicated the ship had power, so she pressurized the air lock and let
herself into the inner door.

Then, theoretically, she was free to take off her helmet.

"Computer, run a check for airborne pathogens," she said.

The computer—the one built into the suit this time—blinked a silent confirmation on her visor.

"Negative results," it said, after checking. "Atmosphere breathable."

Alice was standing at one end of a modest hangar, with two parked shuttles exactly like the one outside and room for two more.

"Then where is everybody?" she asked, as she appeared to be alone.

"Please be more specific," the computer said. "Whom would you like to locate?"

"Never mind."

"Never minding."

Alice took the helmet off.

The air smelled like the standard filtered air she'd been breathing for most of her adult life, and the gravity that held her to the floor of the bay felt like Earth-standard. Both good things. Yet even if the crew of the *Erwin* wasn't expecting a visitor, there should have been *someone* in the shuttle hangar, if only to ask her what the hell she was doing there.

"Hello?" she shouted. She heard her voice echo back, resonating with a slightly metallic hum. No doors opened, and nobody came running.

A quick inspection of the bay confirmed only that there weren't any bodies lying around.

"Is anybody here?" she shouted.

Nothing.

The Flying Dutchman, she thought, referencing an old Earth maritime ghost story she remembered liking as a child. It wasn't, of course, but that was what always sprang to mind in situations like this.

Alice had investigated her share of wrecks in her day, but usually the explanation was self-evident, and she was just there on the off chance someone managed to survive whatever drastic event had killed their ship. Hardly anyone ever did, because spaceships were surrounded by the vacuum of space, which was actively hostile toward human beings.

This time, there was no obvious explanation. The ship seemed to be working fine, albeit on reserve power—she could tell from the feel of the floor that the *Erwin*'s engines were definitely off-line—it was just that everyone was somewhere *else* for some reason.

So where do I begin?

The USFS *Erwin* had five decks total. The captain's bridge was on the top deck at the front of the ship, which was the farthest point from the hangar. Alice felt obligated to start there—if for no other reason than to announce her arrival to the person who was supposed to have already authorized that arrival. At the same time, it was pretty far away; surely, she could find someone closer to her current location, who could fill her in on why the entire vessel was running silent. Or rather, drifting silent.

Alice found the door that led to the rest of the ship, and hesitated.

"Computer," she said, addressing her suit, "synchronize with the ship's computer."

"Synchronizing," the computer said, in the tone of voice waitresses used when asking children what flavor ice cream they wanted. "Synchronization complete."

"Computer, report life signs, total. Human only."

The synchronization allowed Alice to leverage all the ship's systems for her inquiry. It was supposed to help clear things up. It did not.

"No life signs detected," the computer said.

This was obviously incorrect. Aside from the fact that the *Erwin* had a complement of eighty-five, Alice was herself alive. Anything less than one was an error.

"Computer, recheck life signs, human only."

"Rechecking."

Alice pressed her face up against the window of the door she was about to go through. The hallway on the other side was well lit, and entirely empty. It ran the length of the lower deck, and—if she recalled the vessel's specs correctly—was home to about 60 percent of the crew. There should have been *somebody* around.

"Two hundred and six life signs detected," the computer said.

"No . . . no, that's not the right answer either," Alice said.

"What is the right answer?" the computer asked.

"I don't understand."

"What is the right answer?" the computer repeated.

"Computer, I'm asking for an exact life sign count of all the humans on board this ship. I don't know the answer, but I know it's a whole number that one arrives at by actually *counting* those life signs."

"Understood. What is your expectation?"

"I don't know the right answer, or I wouldn't have asked, but I would *expect* it to be anywhere between one and eighty-six."

"Rechecking," the computer said. Then, "Seventy-two life signs detected."

"Is that the real count, computer?"

"As requested, the total is between one and eighty-six. Is this acceptable?"

"If it's the *actual* count, yes."

"The actual count is seventy-two."

Alice was pretty sure the computer didn't perform anything like an actual count, which was a minor problem masking a much more serious one. Clearly, something was wrong with the *Erwin*'s computer; counting things wasn't a difficult task.

"Computer, run a full internal diagnostic."

"Running diagnostic."

"Let me know what you find," she said. Then she pressed the override code for the door and left the hangar for the crew living-quarters corridor.

"Hello?" she shouted. "Is anyone here?"

Nobody responded.

All the doors were closed. Alice's override code could open any one of them, but—and this was a decidedly odd but undeniable truth—she was *afraid* to do it.

Alice Aste had been working with the USF Security Force for fifteen years, and before that she'd been a veteran of five interplanetary conflicts. She'd once spent two months adrift and alone in a disabled life raft, rescued by chance some fifteen hours before her oxygen ran out. Before that, she'd suffered a childhood of privation during her waking hours, and nightmares when she slept. She came to grips with her own mortality when she was ten. She did not *get* afraid, or rather, she wasn't afraid of the unknown. (Fear of the *known*, on the other hand, was quite sensible.)

And yet, on an impossibly empty vessel adrift in an unusually empty deep-space quadrant, Alice had to admit that she was one loud noise from freaking the hell out.

"Anybody?" she asked. She hesitated at the first door.

Just plug in the code and ask whoever's on the other side what's going on here.

She didn't plug in the code. Her pulse was up, and her breathing was shallow. She wondered if this was what a panic attack felt like.

"Calm down," she said to herself. "Just go straight for the bridge. You can see the stars from the bridge."

That was one of the tricks she picked up when she was ten; there is comfort in the vast emptiness of space. At least for her.

"Diagnostic complete," the computer said. Alice jumped two feet in the air.

"Computer, report results," she said, once she got her heart started again.

"Results are terrific," the computer said.

". . . computer, please repeat."

"Terrific. Self-diagnostic reports computer is terrific. Perfect score. Computer would report a thumbs-up if computer had thumbs."

The *Erwin's* computer had evidently lost its mind. This was, of course, just as impossible as the constantly adjusting life sign count. Computers had no minds to lose.

"Are you certain, computer?" she asked.

"Computer is certain. Computer has no thumbs."

Alice wondered if a full reboot of the ship's computer was in order. She'd have to do that from the bridge, but that was where she was heading anyway. It might take a while, but if there really was nobody on this vessel aside from her, she'd need to interrogate the ship's logs. For that to work, a sane and rational computer would be important.

She headed down the hall at a normal walking pace that quickly devolved into a jog. A door might open and that, she decided, would be bad.

There's no such thing as irrational fear, she thought, recalling the wisdom of one of her academy trainers. *Your instincts know why they're afraid; you just gotta catch up.*

She made it to the other end of the hall, to the elevator, punched the button for the top deck, and checked the corridor behind her twelve times while waiting for the elevator to arrive.

It did. She jumped in, and the doors swished closed reassuringly. Up she went.

And up, and up. The elevator should have taken less than thirty seconds to reach the bridge. After well over a minute, Alice became concerned that maybe deck one wasn't where they were headed, except there was no farther point to travel to while still remaining on the *Erwin*.

"Computer, are we going to deck one?"

"Confirmed, deck one."

"What's taking so long?"

"Traveling from deck five to deck one takes a nontrivial amount of time," the computer said, "and time is a construct."

"That isn't a helpful answer."

"Would you like to try a different narration?"

"A what? No, I just want to go to deck one."

"Deck one, coming up."

Alice sighed.

"When?" she asked.

"I cannot provide an exact time," the computer said.

"All right. Computer, if I stopped the elevator right now, where would I be? What deck."

"Would you like to stop the elevator right now?"

"No, just tell me where I would be if I did."

"You would be on deck one-and-five-eighths."

"Computer, this ship *has* no deck one-and-five-eighths."

"That is incorrect," the computer said. "There are multiple fractional decks."

"How many?"

"Unclear. How many would you like for there to be?"

"Never mind. Is it a finite amount?"

"This computer infers that the amount must be finite, as otherwise, deck one would be unattainable. It is coming up shortly, and is therefore not unattainable."

Alice had an unkind response for that, but then the elevator came to a stop and the doors opened.

"Arrived, deck one," the computer said.

Alice stepped out onto the bridge. For a vessel of this type, the bridge was really very small—especially as compared to the military ships to which she was accustomed. It had two seats at the front, a raised seat in the middle for the captain, and two seats in the back, with instrumentation spread throughout.

Captain Matthew Hadder—unshaven, in dirty clothing, looking tired, and shorter than she expected—stood beside his chair, and an ensign she didn't know was at the console to her left.

"You've shot Ensign Anson," Hadder said, which was an interesting thing to say given that Alice hadn't done anything of the kind.

But then the ensign fell over dead, having indeed been shot by a blaster. Still more interesting, it was only then that Alice drew her blaster from its holster and fired it. It struck Ensign Anson directly in the chest two seconds prior to being fired.

"What?" Alice said.

"Ensign Anson has been shot," Hadder said. "By your blaster, which you used to shoot him with."

"But I *didn't* shoot him."

"He was shot, and then you did it. Don't worry, it wasn't your fault. It *was*, because if you hadn't run in with a gun, Ensign Anson would *not* be shot, but the shot came faster than the blaster off your hip. Don't worry, it's been happening all day. He's dead, but only now. He wasn't earlier, and may not be later. Who are you and what are you doing on my ship?"

"I'm . . . I don't understand. How could I fire my blaster before I fired my blaster?"

"It happened before you decided to do it, but if you want to know why you decided before you decided, I can't provide you with that. He may have been about to shoot, with a gun he both had and did not have. He does not right *now* have a gun, but may have had one before you decided to shoot."

"He's unarmed. I shot an unarmed ensign."

"I can testify to Ensign Anson being both armed an unarmed at once, if it comes to that. Also, the ship's cause-and-effect has been acting up all day. But enough about the dead ensign; once more, who are you and what are you doing on my ship?"

"I'm Corporal Alice Aste, USFSF. I've been sent here to find out what happened to this ship."

"Quite a lot! We just lost an ensign, and the rest of my command deck crew have reported nonexistent. But what's the rush!"

"Your last communication was over six weeks ago, and you've been adrift since. I'm here to find out what kind of assistance is needed, and then to get that assistance for you."

"That's hardly possible," he said. "I sent a message just yesterday."

"None have been received."

"No, no, no, I would've remembered if I had sent *silence*. I didn't. I sent a message that went like this: *Please stay away*."

"That wasn't it. What we received was, *We aren't here again today*," Alice said. "Do you remember sending that?"

"Ahhh." Captain Hadder clapped his hands on the side of his head. "I got it wrong, I meant to say, *I wish, I wish you'd stay away*."

Captain Hadder had been going in and out of rhyme for the entire conversation. At first, she thought it was just an accident of word choice. Now she was thinking he was doing it on purpose, and also that he'd begun to lose his mind, just like his ship's computer. Unless she was losing *her* mind. She'd just shot a crew member, but if asked to explain how that happened, the best she could come up with was that the shot was fired before she pulled the trigger.

"Why did you want us to stay away?" Alice asked. "You seem in need of rescue."

"Rescue! It's only been a day."

"Again, it's been more than six weeks, captain."

"Computer, how long has it been?"

"It has been a day, captain," the computer said.

"There, you see?" Hadder said. "If you received that message six weeks ago, that's hardly *my* fault. I sent it yesterday; you should be receiving it now."

"Captain Hadder, you *know* there's something wrong with your ship's computer, don't you?" Alice asked. "It's been providing me with inaccurate information since I boarded."

"Not at all! It's adjusted quite well. You must have been asking it the wrong questions."

"Computer," she said, "how many life signs are there aboard the ship?"

"There are between one and eighty-six," the computer said, "or zero, or two hundred and six."

"There," Alice said. "See? That's an unacceptable response."

"Why, it's a ridiculous question!" Hadder said. "The answer is clearly variable from moment to moment. You should expect to have a different answer every time. Now where is Ensign Anson?"

"Isn't he the one I shot?"

"Yes, yes, but he should be back by now."

Ensign Anson was still lying dead on the floor, and Captain Hadder was clearly insane. Alice put her hand on her blaster, reflexively. It was probably a bad idea, given she'd only just not-shot-but-also shot Anson, but instincts existed for a reason.

"Once again, captain, why did you send the 'stay away' message? Did something happen here? An accident maybe?"

"Nothing is the matter," he said, which was clearly untrue.

"Then why did you send that message?"

"Because *nothing is the matter*! Ask Anson; he can explain it better."

"Maybe I should ask someone *else* from the crew," Alice said slowly. She'd begun to talk more slowly and deliberately with Captain Hadder, the way one might talk to a person in a bomb vest. "Captain, can you tell me where everyone else is?"

"I don't know," he said. "But if you didn't see them on your way to the bridge, they're probably in their quarters."

"All right. Don't you need them in order to work the ship? Maybe you can find your own way out of this quadrant, with a little help. One of the engineers?"

"Ensign Anson and I can handle the bridge ourselves," he said. "Little to do when you're adrift."

"My point is that you don't *need* to be adrift. Some members of the crew could be enacting repairs."

"I see your reasoning, but about the engines, there's nothing to be done. They work perfectly, or they would; it's the physics that are wrong."

"Then someone, should fix . . . the physics?"

He was surely speaking non-literally. Alice remembered a particularly sarcastic first officer who—in the middle of a war—would say things like, "Barring some change in the laws of physics, this next torpedo will be a direct hit; brace for impact." Captain Hadder's delivery was wanting, but she felt certain that he was aiming for the same sort of droll wit.

"They're not *broken*, they're *wrong*," he said. "I'm amazed you've survived on board the ship for this long, corporal."

"I haven't . . . Captain. Just tell me where the rest of the crew is, and I'll go find someone who can help."

"As I said, they could be in their quarters. Computer, are the crew in their quarters?"

"The crew may or may not be in quarters, captain."

"There, see?" he said. "They may be there."

"Then should we go down and check?" she asked. "I passed the quarters on my way."

"Oh, goodness no, don't do that. Imagine the consequences."

"I don't understand."

"Corporal, it's really very simple. I don't know if they're alive or not. If I check, I will *definitely* know. Who wants that on their conscience?"

"They're either alive or they're not alive," Alice said.

"The computer confirmed, they are both. Have you ever seen a person who was both alive and dead?"

"Of course not. Those are binary states."

"Neither have I. Therefore, if they are currently both alive *and* dead, and one of us were to go down to see which one it was, and *we* have never seen a person who was both alive and dead, then by checking, we will ensure that they are either one or the other, and I want no part of that! Neither should you, after what happened to poor Ensign Anson. Already enough blood on *your* hands."

About 95 percent of Alice thought this was the most ridiculous thing she'd ever heard. The 5 percent that didn't was the same 5 percent that was in charge when she ran down the corridor in deck five, in the midst of something like a panic attack. She didn't want to open those doors either, even before having her intelligence assaulted by Captain Hadder's nonsense.

"How about if we just open a comm line, right now?" she asked. "We can hail the *Rosen*."

"Oh no, that's impossible. Nothing on the bridge works right now."

She looked around. The panels were lit, which wasn't an expectation on a non working bridge.

"You have power. It all looks like it's working."

"It's not," he said. "Hasn't been since yesterday. And even though we clearly *do* have power, the engine isn't providing it. Couldn't tell you what is."

She pointed to one of the chairs at the front of the deck. "May I?" she asked.

Captain Hadder stepped aside and waved her through.

She sat down at what was—if she remembered the ship design specs accurately—the helmsman's chair. It had all the navigational instrumentation, and the communications matrix.

All the ships in the USF communicated locally by sending concentrated radioelectric bursts in tight, targeted beams. A similar approach was used for long-range communications, only the local transmission was sent to a relay, which repeated the information through an FTL tunnel.

The *Rosen* was just at the edge of Quadrant Brenda. In a rational universe, the *Erwin* would already know the *Rosen* was there, either because the *Rosen* pinged it when it was in range—which it did, as part of the ongoing effort to establish communication—or because the midrange sensors have only one job, which is to detect nearby objects and keep track of them.

Possibly, the *Erwin* was no longer a participant in a rational universe.

She asked the ship to perform a full sensor sweep, and while there was some good news—it *did* pick up the *Rosen*, and her shuttle—according to the survey, there was *nothing* on the starboard side.

Not just *nothing*, as in, *space is pretty much a lot of nothing anyway* nothing. This was a nothingness that far exceeded any previously recorded nothing, on a scale that made it quite a remarkable something. There were no quantum fluctuations popping in virtual particles, or the evidence of gravitational force acting at a distance to warp the fabric of space-time, or microscopic space debris. There were no solar winds. There was just nothing.

Alice was reminded of the ancient Earth maps: those two-dimensional rectangles meant to approximate a portion of a spherical object. The early ones weren't large enough to encompass the entire planet, so when one drew a line to the edge of the map, it wasn't an expectation that the line would pick up again on the opposite side. There was nothing else there because the mapmaker had stopped drawing what came next.

This is the end of the map, she thought. *Here be dragons.*

"No, that can't be right," she said. "It must be a sensor malfunction."

"Sensors operating at full capacity," the computer said, helpfully.

Alice stood up and leaned, to get a look at that side of the ship. If she didn't know better, she'd have said someone was out there, hanging a gigantic piece of nonreflective fabric over that part of space. Maybe they were.

"Oh no, don't do that," Hadder said.

"Do what?"

"*Stare* at the Void. Never a good idea."

"You know about this?"

"Of course I do. It's why the ship isn't moving."

"Great, now we're getting somewhere. Tell me what it is, and then maybe we can work up a strategy to get away from it."

"It's nothing. You read the sensors. I don't know why you're acting so surprised, I *told* you what the problem was already."

"You didn't mention the giant Void in space," she said. "I would have remembered that."

"I said *nothing* was the matter with the ship. That's very clear."

She sighed, and resisted the urge to draw her blaster again.

"Doesn't matter," she said. "I can still see the *Rosen*. I'll hail them, set up a tow."

"Best of luck!"

She opened a channel.

"USFSF *Rosen*, this is Corporal Aste, on the USFS *Erwin*. Please respond."

The transmission came from the radar array at the highest point on the top of the *Erwin*, with secondary and tertiary arrays on the underbelly in the event of damage from space debris or an act of violence. When Alice sent the transmission, the signal was transmitted by all three.

Alice already knew this was how local communication worked, but this time she got a dramatic demonstration of it, because for some reason the radio signal she sent out became visible for five full seconds, before falling apart.

It was hard to get a total count on the number of things that was wrong with this. Radio waves weren't supposed to be a part of the visible spectrum, so that was a big problem right there. Also, before the signals dissolved (or whatever that was), those beams of impossible-but-true visible light *slowed down*.

Alice checked the communications array to confirm that the frequency she chose to send the signal on was a normal, non-visible-spectrum frequency. It was.

"Don't try the laser," Hadder said. He meant the high-burst pulse communicator, which was meant for long-range emergency signaling. "Unless you dislike the *Rosen*."

"You tried it already?"

"It was like birthing a sun. Very beautiful! Given its speed and direction, I'm afraid that beam may be well on its way to annihilating everyone who lives in the Podolsky System. First Officer Hart worked that out."

This was the first time Hadder mentioned a member of the bridge crew other than the departed Ensign Anson. She thought that was a significant thing.

"First Officer Regina Hart?" she said. "Where is she now? In her quarters?"

"I'm afraid not. She's left."

"L-left. Left the bridge? Left the ship?"

"She's in the Anthropene Principality now. I'll see her soon, I'm sure."

"Where is that?" Alice asked. It wasn't a place she'd ever heard of before. Not that it mattered if she *had*; it was impossible to walk off a ship in deep space and visit much of anywhere, and there was a full complement of shuttles in the hangar. Wherever it was, First Officer Hart wasn't actually there.

Hadder laughed, and gestured vaguely at the expanse of space. *Oh, you know*, the gesture said. *Let's not be silly.*

Exasperated, Alice sat back down in the helm chair and rubbed her head. She could feel a headache coming on.

"I wonder," she said, "if one of you—captain or computer—can tell me what actually happened, or why, or even when?"

Hadder laughed again.

"Why, I'm not sure!" he said. "What an excellent question. I know what we can do. Computer?"

"Yes, captain," the computer said.

"Switch to narrative mode."

"Narrative mode?" Alice asked. "That's not even . . ."

The computer began speaking again, only this time in a deeper voice that wasn't precisely the same as the singsongy soothing one all the USF ships were stuck with.

Things began to go badly for the crew of the USFS Erwin *around the time Dr. Marchere's coffee mug spontaneously reassembled itself.*

Dr. Louis Marchere was not, at that moment, conducting some manner of experiment. Well, he was, only not on entropy and the nature of time. He was running several other tests, of the kind that make perfect sense on a scientific vessel such as the Erwin. *About half of them were biological in nature, concerning how small samples of cellular material react to certain deep-space factors. Other tests were more at home in the general field of astrophysics. But—again, as this is important—he was not conducting a test on entropy.*

"Computer, stop," *Hadder said.* "There, that was helpful, wasn't it?"

"What the hell was that?" *Alice asked.* "And why is the computer doing that?"

"Doing what?"

"It said 'Alice asked,' when I was talking, and the same thing when you were talking."

"It's narrative mode. Useful! Now we know it all began with Dr. Marchere."

Alice was deeply confused. She'd never heard of narrative mode before, and was nearly positive Hadder was playing some sort of elaborate joke.

"It's not a *joke!*" *Hadder said.*

"I didn't say it was!"

"The *narrative* did."

"Turn it off," *Alice said.* "I KNOW I SAID THAT, YOU DON'T HAVE TO TELL ME I SAID THAT."

"Computer, end narrative mode."

"Ending narrative mode," *the computer said.*

"Oh, thank God," she said. "All right, so, Dr. Louis Marchere. Where is he? Or did he go to the . . . whatever-you-said place?"

"No, I believe he's still aboard," Hadder said. "We were just speaking. Deck three, in the research lab."

"Great. Let's go."

She headed for the elevator. Hadder remained where he was.

"Well, come on," she said. "You're the only survivor I've found so far; I think we should stick together, don't you?"

"It's . . . um, no. No, I think my place is on the bridge," he said. "It's safer."

"Captain Hadder, I don't think any part of this ship is safe. Our best option here is to find out what Marchere knows; if he doesn't have a way to save the *Erwin*, we need to get to my shuttle."

"Find out what you can," he said, in a tone that sounded like an order, "and keep me updated! Much to do up here."

He sat down in the captain's chair, as if this settled things.

"All right," she said. "I'll, ah, I'll let you know. Computer, deck three."

"Deck three," the computer confirmed.

As the doors closed, Alice could have sworn she saw Ensign Anson standing next to Captain Hadder.

But of course, she didn't. That would be impossible.

It took twice as long to get to the third deck from the first as it had to get to the first deck from the fifth. Alice was quite certain there was no mechanism in existence capable of adding fractional decks to the ship, and so was chalking this up to another aspect of the ongoing computer malfunction. She supposed a way to validate this was to ask that the elevator stop at, say, deck two-and-five-sixteenths, but she also didn't want to encourage the computer's departures from reality any more than necessary.

Find the problem, she thought. *Find the problem, work the problem, solve the problem.*

The reason Corporal Alice Aste was an ideal rescue mission envoy was that, over the course of a fairly extensive career, she'd worked in just about every part of a starship, from engine to helm. She was a problem-solving universal tool, a one-person away team. If a disabled ship was disabled because there was nobody aboard with the expertise to re-enable the vessel, the likelihood was fairly high that Alice had the gap-filling skill set.

But this? Whatever was going on aboard the USFS *Erwin*, she wasn't equipped to deal with it. Maybe nobody human was.

"The subjective mind is objectively flawed," she said aloud. It was one of the philosophical-slash-practical mottos she lived by. She couldn't recall who said it to her originally—probably one of her academy professors—but she'd found it incredibly useful over the years. There were some things the human mind was simply bad at grasping, observationally or intuitively, which was why flawed humans created machines to objectively interrogate the world for them.

That was what the computer was supposed to be doing. Since it was malfunctioning, Alice had no way to determine how much of what she was experiencing was even *real*.

And that was terrifying.

"Deck three," the computer announced, finally.

The door slid open, revealing a corridor with glass-walled rooms on both sides.

Scientific research was the *Erwin*'s central function, which was why the third deck was its widest and tallest. (Looked at from the front, the *Erwin* looked like a wide oval or, if you were hungry, like an over-stuffed sandwich; deck three was where all the meat was located.) It was also where most of the vessel's funding went.

There was a dizzying amount of experimentational activity taking place in both of the glassed-in rooms, nearly all of it mechanized. If quizzed, Alice could definitively identify maybe a third of the experiments, and perhaps half of the equipment.

The ship's supercollider—one of only a half-dozen off-planet supercolliders in existence—was running some kind of test on the far wall on her left, while on her right a laser tube designed to detect gravitational waves was humming along. A little farther along, a hologram of a Möbius strip was rotating slowly beside a bank of computer screens displaying rapidly evolving fractals.

Those were just the most obvious, macroscopic things. There were also cultured cells somewhere, having things done to them, and top secret genetic splicing research, and plants being taught to grow in zero-gravity chambers, and much more, but she couldn't see any of that.

She kept walking down the corridor, absorbing the maelstrom of activity on both sides, wondering exactly where all the power for this was coming from. The supercollider alone was supposed to take up enough of the energy from the *Erwin*'s fusion engine that the vessel couldn't run the FTL drive as long as it was also going. (The energy issue wasn't the only problem. Nobody was sure what would happen if a supercollider ran while on a ship traveling faster-than-light speed, but the consensus was: nothing good.)

The point was, everything running *at once* had to be an enormous drain, and yet the captain insisted the ship's engine wasn't even running. Either he was wrong—he was crazy, so it was probably that—or the *Erwin* was surviving on battery power. The batteries on a ship like this supplied just about enough power to keep life support going, plus the communications array, and *maybe* some impulse power for basic maneuverability, for about thirty days. It couldn't do all that and also provide a city's worth of energy to the research deck.

And yet, that appeared to be what was happening. Unless Hadder was wrong.

"Computer," she said, "give me a read on the ship's engine output?"

"The engine is not running," the computer said.

"Not the propulsion. I know we aren't moving. The base-level output."

"The engine is not running."

"Computer, the ship has power, does it not? Otherwise, you and I wouldn't be talking and I wouldn't be able to breathe."

"Confirmed, the ship has power."

"Then what's the engine's baseline output?"

"The engine is not running."

"Fine," Alice said. "Computer, what is the source of the ship's power, if not the engine? Is it the auxiliary batteries, or something else?"

"What is the answer you are expecting?" the computer asked.

"The right answer would be great."

"The batteries are providing the ship with power."

"Did you just say that because you thought that was what I wanted to hear?"

"The batteries are providing the ship with power."

"Sure."

"Would you like to switch to narrative mode?"

"No. What is it with you and narrative mode?"

"Narrative mode has been proven to reveal information not otherwise available to this computer."

"No, thank you."

She stopped short of asking the computer what other modes it had available, both because this was yet another ridiculous conversation she had no time for, and because she could see someone moving in the last part of the lab on the right.

The man had on a lead vest, with goggles and a face shield dangling loosely around his neck. He was also wearing thick leather gloves, brown coveralls of the sort Alice recognized as standard for the engineers, and heavy mag-spiked boots. His hair was pointed in five different directions, and he was holding something that looked like a blowtorch in one hand.

He could have been just about anyone in the crew. Nonetheless, she felt certain that this was Dr. Marchere.

Alice walked up to the nearest door, and when it wouldn't open, tried her override code. That didn't work either, so she knocked.

She startled him; he nearly dropped the torch, which would have been very bad had it been lit.

"Dr. Marchere?" she shouted.

He waved, put down the torch, waddled over, and opened the door.

"Very sorry, I'm extremely busy, can you come back later?" he asked.

"I really can't," she said. "I'm here to rescue the ship."

"I . . . see. And you are?"

"Corporal Alice Aste. I'm with the Security Force, and—"

"All right, all right, come in. Rescue! Ha-ha. Yes. That would be *something*."

She stepped into the room, which was awash in an atonal cacophony of pings, whirrs, and clangs. He took off his gloves and led her to a table in the center of all of it. On the table was a coffee mug, a cold pot of coffee, and a plate of doughnuts.

"I would offer you something other than doughnuts," he said, "but the food replicator can only make these, and only if one asks for bicarbonate of soda. I haven't worked out what one is supposed to request in order to get other foods, so this is what I have. Now, you've exactly seventeen minutes, and then I'll have to get back. I'm running thirty-eight experiments, and as you can see, all of my colleagues have already left."

"Where did they go?"

"They left, as I said. You're not from the *Erwin*, is that right?"

"The *Rosen* is nearby. If we can't get the *Erwin*'s engine running, we'll have to get the *Rosen* here for a tow. I can't hail them for . . . some reason, but I can try calling them from my shuttle. I just need to understand what's happening here, first. The computer . . . I'm sorry, this will sound insane, but in narrative mode, whatever that is, the computer said that this all began when Dr. Louis Marchere dropped a coffee mug. You *are* Dr. Louis Marchere, aren't you?"

"I am! And that is *amazing*."

"Which part?"

"All of it! I'm amazed you've lasted this long. Have you come across anyone else?"

"The captain and I had a long conversation that made no sense and confused everything much more."

"Oh, excellent, the captain is still here. I was sure I was the last one left."

"He said he thinks the crew might be in their quarters, but is afraid to check, because he thinks if he does so, they might be dead and it will be his fault." She laughed then, to see if Marchere was inspired to laugh as well. He was not.

"Yes, that's eminently reasonable on his part," he said. "Narrative mode, you say? That's a new one. I accidentally stumbled upon theatrical mode yesterday, which was odd enough."

"Switching to theatrical mode," the computer said.

Marchere: No, I didn't mean for that. Oh well, here we are. Welcome to theatrical mode.

Alice: Oh, this is very strange.

Marchere: Yes, well, now we're here. It's not *terrible*. I enjoyed it during a soliloquy, but after became quite frustrated.

(Marchere takes a bite of a doughnut.)

Marchere: There, you see, it's exhausting, having your own actions read back to you. I became obsessed with the question of whether the computer was describing what I was doing, or if I was doing what the computer instructed me to do. Did I just bite this doughnut because that was what the stage business described, or did the stage business capture my actions?

(Alice looks confused.)

Alice: Weird, it's in present tense. And the computer keeps announcing who's speaking, like we don't already know. It was doing that before too, in narrative mode, only not every time.

Marchere: The fact that it's *in* present tense is what makes it so confounding. That would argue in favor of it dictating my actions instead of the other way around, which would contravene the concept of free will *entirely*, and that's terribly frustrating.

Alice: I shot a man on the bridge before pulling the trigger on my blaster. Captain Hadder said it was because cause-and-effect had been malfunctioning all day. That sounds like a similar problem. Can we . . . turn this off?

Marchere: Computer, end theatrical mode.

"Ending theatrical mode," the computer said.

"Thank you," Alice said. "Now can you *please* explain what's happened here? Where did everyone go, why are you running all of these experiments, where are you even getting the *power* to run all of these experiments?"

"Do you want for me to answer all of those at the same time, or is there a particular order you'd like for me to honor?"

"Start with what's going on. I guess."

"All right. Do you know what scientific theory states that the laws of physics are the same everywhere?"

"No, I don't."

"Good, because there isn't one. We've always just assumed it to be so, because it did us no good to assume otherwise. It was a poor assumption."

"You're saying the laws of physics don't apply to this quadrant?"

"I mean the Void we're next to, primarily, but as you must have worked out, there have been local alterations. We're right on the event horizon of a portion of space in which nothing we've previously proven to be true is *necessarily* still true. That's why I'm running all these experiments. I'm trying to work out what *is* true in this particular region of space."

"That sounds ridiculous."

"Oh, absolutely. It's magnificently ridiculous. Yesterday, I positively identified a particle's exact location *and* velocity. This morning, I tested the wave function collapse of light, but it refused to collapse. Later, I managed to measure the speed of light from a moving object compared to the speed of light from a stationary one, and discovered the one from the moving object was *faster*. I've also discovered electrons a *half-quanta* apart, and a few hours ago the supercollider detected an element between carbon and nitrogen, and a neutron with a negative charge. And this morning, for five seconds, all the oxygen in the other room—thankfully, I was in this one—gathered in one corner. These are all impossible, ridiculous things."

"But that can't be right. It's only a computer malfunction."

"The computer on this ship is working perfectly," he said, "in that it's describing an objective reality we cannot grasp. My equipment is working perfectly as well. It's our perception that's having trouble catching up. Now, I have to get back to my work before it's too late."

"Too late for what, doctor?" she asked. "What *exactly* happened to your coworkers? Where is everyone else?"

"Ah. They don't exist any longer."

"You mean, they're dead?"

"I prefer it the way I said it. Are you familiar with the anthropic principle?"

"I heard something *like* that. The captain said his bridge crew went to the Anthropene Principality. Is that the same thing?"

"More or less. Hadder's head's all jumbled. The anthropic principle is a logical point stemming from the observation that everything in our universe has to be *just so*, in order to allow for our existence. From Planck's constant to the charge of an electron, the weight of atomic particles, and so on and so forth, all of it carries a value that allows, as an aggregate, for a universe to exist that contains intelligent life. None of these values *had* to be what they were. It's a little circular, because one could easily argue that the only reason the universe's aggregation of values exists to allow intelligent life is because this is the only permutation that allowed for intelligent life to develop in order to make that observation. Other universes—assuming multiple universes—evolved differently, and have no intelligent life to note that their universe failed to evolve in such a way to allow for them to exist."

"All right," she said. "That does sound odd."

"I bring it up because the part of the universe we're standing at the edge of, right now, is a part where the laws do *not* allow for us to exist. It's the converse point of the anthropic principle. We're composed of the laws on which our universe was built. The slightest change in the strong nuclear charge and the atoms that make up your body could fly apart or collapse into themselves. Your brain evolved to communicate via neural electrical charges; a change in the electromagnetic force, and it stops working. These are facile examples, but you understand. If the laws change, we won't be around to measure them. At least, not for long. We're still *here* because neither of us have had the misfortune to happen upon a patch of altered laws that will undo us, and in fact right now we're *alive* because I've been taking advantage of the alteration. You asked before what's powering us. The answer is, when the engine failed, I hooked up the auxiliary batteries together. They're now charging one another *and* the ship."

"That's impossible."

"Evidently not here! The laws of this patch of universe allow for perpetual motion machines, so we may as well get some use out of it."

"So . . . you're saying the rest of the crew has been . . . unmade?"

"I've yet to witness this happening to anyone, but yes, I think so. I'm afraid to leave this level. You say you came from the hangar, and visited the bridge; it's good to know those places still exist."

"According to the computer there are fractional decks being added all the time," she said.

He laughed.

"Fascinating," he said. "I only hope I'm around to find an explanation for *that*."

"Now that I'm here with a shuttle, you don't have to think like that, doctor," she said. "I can take you—and the captain, if he's willing to leave the bridge—and whatever research you have. The *Erwin* is clearly a hostile living environment."

"An excellent suggestion, but no, I think I had better stay. You have a good point, however, in that I have no way to communicate my findings. My hope was to record as much as I could and jettison it toward the hub, but in truth I came upon that idea when I thought I'd reach the *end* of my studies. It seems the deeper I dig, the more strangeness I find. But here."

He placed a memory tab on the table.

"This is everything I've measured up to about an hour ago. I hope."

"You hope?"

"I hope it's only been an hour. The passage of time has been curious."

She picked up the tab.

"It has," she said. "The captain said it had only been a day, but it's been . . ."

Alice looked up from the table to find she was speaking to an empty room.

"Dr. Marchere?"

He'd been standing two meters away, and now he wasn't. The experiments in the room were still running, and the doughnut he'd taken a bite from remained bitten from, but he wasn't there to continue the experiments or finish the doughnut.

"Computer, can you locate Dr. Marchere?"

"There is no Dr. Marchere."

"Dr. Louis Marchere," she clarified.

"There is no Dr. Louis Marchere."

"He was just right here, computer."

"Would you like to try a different narration?"

"No, I . . . I don't know what I want."

He's in the Anthropene Principality now, she thought.

"I need to get off this ship," she decided. "Computer, what's the fastest way to the hangar?"

"The hangar is located on deck five," the computer said.

"Is there still a deck five?"

"There's still a deck five, but portions appear missing. Haste is recommended."

Alice opened the door to the lab and ran to the elevator, as things in both glass-walled rooms began to go somewhat *more* haywire than before. The holographic Möbius strip had developed a second side, the fractals on the computer screens began flashing random Greek letters for some reason, and it looked like a black hole was forming in the center of the supercollider. An amoeba the size of her head popped into existence on the glass a few feet from her face, and then popped back out of existence again before she had a chance to scream. It began to rain.

She reached the elevator door and pushed the button. Then she opened up her bag and retrieved her helmet. If the atmosphere decided to collect in one corner of the ship again, she'd rather she was breathing her own supply.

The ship started groaning before the elevator even made it to the fourth deck.

"Computer, what made that sound?" Alice asked.

"Unclear."

Alice remembered visiting the extinct-Earth-animals exhibit as a child, and being transfixed by the elephant in particular. The noises the ship was making sounded like an elephant being squeezed like an exhaust bladder.

Then the elevator shuddered, and stopped.

"Computer, what's going on?"

"Unclear."

"Can you tell me where I've stopped?"

"You've stopped at deck three-and-eleven-sixteenths. Would you like to get out here?"

"That depends. Will the elevator be moving again any time soon?"

"Define *soon*."

"Before the ship blows up, implodes, or otherwise ceases to exist?"

"Unable to predict those outcomes at this time."

Alice wondered if maybe she should have gone up instead, back to the bridge. She could have collected Captain Hadder and gone out the topside hatch, and called the shuttle from there.

Then Alice started floating; the gravity had cut out.

If I can get into the shaft, I can reach the command deck on my own, she thought.

"Computer, can you hail Captain Hadder?" she asked.

"There is no Captain Hadder."

"Computer, can you hail the bridge?"

"There is no bridge."

"Deck one, Computer. Open a channel to deck one."

"There is no deck one."

Crap.

"Computer, does deck five still exist?"

"Deck five continues to exist."

"But deck one is missing."

"The USFS *Erwin* does not have a deck one."

"All right, never mind. Open doors, please. Let's see what deck three-and-eleven-sixteenths looks like."

The doors slid open on a level that looked weirdly out of focus. Alice's first thought was that some kind of viscous fluid had gotten on her helmet, distorting the view of the universe on the other side. But the helmet was clean.

The walls were partly transparent and partly solid, because deck four's walls were opaque, while deck three's floors had glass walls. Deck three-and-eleven-sixteenths was trying to have both at once.

Since the gravity was out, Alice activated the mag-spikes on her boots and attached herself to the floor, then stepped off the elevator onto a blurry level that somehow managed to be solid.

"Computer, where is the nearest maintenance shaft on this deck?" she asked.

If the ship behaved for long enough, she'd be able to access the fifth deck by way of a maintenance shaft.

"Twenty-five meters."

"In which direction?"

"All directions."

The computer was not going to help.

Relying on the deck layout of one of the levels that was actually supposed to exist, Alice headed straight down the blurry corridor between the blurry rooms on both sides. In a slightly more ideal circumstance, she'd run, but because the artificial gravity generator had decided it was done (or ceased to exist, or whatever), she had to keep one boot on the ground.

About fifteen steps in, the boots stopped working. Actually, what it felt like was that the magnets holding her in place switched poles spontaneously, and repelled her from the floor. She began drifting to the ceiling.

Then came an explosion, somewhere aboard the ship. Alice felt it tremble through the belly of the vessel, rocking the walls and putting her into a gentle spin.

"Computer, what was that?"

"That was an explosion," the computer said, not at all helpfully.

"Right, thanks."

There was another tremble, and a shudder, and then a loud screech that didn't sound like much of anything Alice had ever heard before: not the noise a machine makes when it's broken, or a sound approximating that of an extinct elephant getting squeezed, or the cacophony a ship makes when its hull is torn open. It was not, in other words, on the short list of *bad noises* in her mental catalog of things to be alarmed about. She was nevertheless extremely alarmed, because what it *did* sound like was a creature that her lizard brain told her to run from. This was even though that portion of her brain *also* didn't know what she was hearing.

Then, directly beneath her and along the corridor floor, a *thing* ran past.

There were a tremendous number of wrong things that were wrong with this thing, the most arresting being that it was somehow in a higher definition than the rest of the deck, including Alice herself. It was a bright shade of blue, and green, almond, and a color of purple she was pretty sure was ultraviolet, which she was also pretty sure she shouldn't have been able to see. There were other colors she didn't even have a name for, because they didn't exist in the universe she was familiar with.

It was perhaps a giant bat, perhaps a snake, and perhaps a horse. It galloped and hissed, shrieked and chortled, and swung its long, clawed fingers through the walls on either side as if they weren't there. The walls, in turn, acted as if the creature wasn't there, showing no damage.

Here be dragons, she thought.

With a great flap of its enormous wings, it soared ahead, and vanished at the far end of the corridor.

"All right, I've had enough," Alice said. "Computer, what's the fastest way off this ship? I don't care *how*, just as long as it puts me on the other side of the hull."

"Unable to calculate," the computer said.

"Why is that?"

"The concept of 'other side of the hull' is too variable to allow for a precise calculation. There are several places where the hull has ceased to exist, but sensors indicate nothing exists on the other side of where the hull no longer is."

"That's great."

The vessel shuddered again. Alice waited for a new nightmare creature to show up, but none did. It was probably just another part of the *Erwin* getting unwritten from the universe.

"Computer, how close am I to the maintenance shaft now?"

"Twenty-five meters."

"That's how far I was when I got off the broken elevator. I must have gotten closer since."

"Understood. However, the distance remains twenty-five meters."

She sighed.

"I really need to understand what's happening to the entire ship right now, computer," Alice said, "or I'm never getting off of it. I don't even know what questions to ask you. Can you provide me with an integrity assessment?"

"Not in this mode."

A hole opened up in the floor, which should have been good news, because that was the direction she wanted to go. But there was nothing on the other side of the hole. Either decks four and five were missing now, or the hole just went to someplace different.

"What the hell," Alice said. "Computer, switch to narrative mode."

Something quite extraordinary was happening to the USFS Erwin.

It was difficult to tell, from more or less any angle, whether the ship had been drawing closer to the Void on its starboard, or if the Void was moving closer to the ship, but what was definitely the case was that their positions relative to one another had been changing since the Erwin first encountered the strange section of space. Now — after either two days or six weeks — the two things were colliding.

The Void was having a devastating effect on the Erwin. (The same could not be said of the Erwin's impact on the Void, which appeared to be weathering things just fine.) There were certain expectations regarding how most space-based threats could damage a man-made starship. Incredibly dense objects, like neutron stars or black holes, could tear apart such a ship if it ventured too close, by literally ripping parts of the vessel off of other parts of the vessel, and/or drawing it into an inescapable gravitational well. Highly radioactive objects could bombard the ship with levels of gamma radiation so severe as to overwhelm the shielding and cook whoever was unfortunate enough to be inside. Rogue objects like asteroids could blow through a hull with a direct hit.

And so on.

None of those things were happening to the Erwin. Instead, it looked as if someone had produced a very realistic three-dimensional artistic rendering of the ship and then, deciding they disliked it, began erasing the artwork. Starting on the starboard side, large chunks of solid material were being turned into tiny bits of particulate matter — eraser crumbs, perhaps — after which the tiny bits of particulate matter glistened with internal light and then vanished.

It's fair to say that however beautiful this might have looked to a neutral (and presumably distant) observer, its impact on the contents of the vessel was very bad indeed. Under optimal circumstances, a hull breach was dealt with by the ship's integrity shields: short-term force fields that plugged up holes before all of the atmosphere in the breached cell leaked into space. But the integrity shields only worked in circumstances where there was more hull than breach, and anyway they needed power in order to function. Unfortunately, the entirely impossible perpetual motion machine Dr. Marchere assembled had begun to break down.

All of this would be very bad news for anyone still alive aboard the USFS Erwin. It was good news, then—if such a thing deserved to be called good news*—that there was nobody left alive on the* Erwin*. All except for Corporal Alice Aste, desperately shuffling along deck three-and-eleven-sixteenths in a quixotic attempt to get back to her shuttle before she too was unmade.*

"Hey!" *Alice said.* "There's no need for that."

The deck floor was mostly gone now, as was the starboard side of the hull, which she could see through the blurry office wall: The Void was on two sides. But the ceiling remained intact, and since there was no such thing as up *or* down *in space—especially without the artificial gravity—she was doing okay with her mag-spiked boots. Shortly, though, she was going to run out of places to move.*

"Computer, if you could just stop being so long-winded and give me something I can use, that would be great," *she said.*

"The nature and pace of the narrative isn't under the computer's control," *the computer said, annoyingly.*

Alice grumbled an insult under her breath and kept going. Very shortly, none of this would matter. The port side hull was weakening already, not so much from direct contact with the Void as a consequence of having its structural integrity challenged thanks to half of it no longer existing. The hull's metal shell was wrinkling . . .

"Hang on, go back," *Alice said.* "Repeat that last part."

Alice grumbled an insult . . .

"After that."

The port side hull was weakening already . . .

"Computer, end narrative mode."

"Ending narrative mode."

Alice put her hand on the blurry med lab wall on the port side. It felt firm, because it was a wall, but at the same time it also didn't feel *that* firm. She pushed . . . and her hand went through it.

"Okay, that probably shouldn't have worked," she said.

She kicked her leg through, and then her other arm, and soon she'd gotten her whole body on the other side. Now in a room that was trying very hard to be both Marchere's supercollider lab and a medical examination room, she mag-walked across the ceiling to the outer hull.

The pushing-her-hand-through-something-that-was-supposed-to-be-solid trick didn't work a second time; the hull was firm, although she could hear it starting to fail. Waiting for that to happen seemed like a bad bet, and she didn't have to; not as long as she was carrying explosive charges.

She pulled one out, set the digital timer to thirty seconds, said a quiet prayer that she was in a part of the ship where chemical explosives and digital clocks still worked like they were supposed to, and then disengaged the mag-spikes from the ceiling and pushed herself to the far end of the room.

The charge went off, exposing all of deck three-and-eleven-sixteenths to outer space. The atmosphere blew out of the hole, and sucked Alice out with it. In seconds, she was drifting on a free trajectory a significant distance from the *Erwin*.

"Now unsynchronized with USFS *Erwin*'s computer," her suit's computer announced, which Alice thought was great news.

"Call the shuttle to my position," Alice said.

"Unable to locate shuttle," the computer said.

Alice twisted around until she was facing the wreckage of the *Erwin*. She could see the shuttle all right, but it was now embedded in the side of the larger ship. It looked like the *Erwin* was giving birth to it, only in reverse.

"That's great," she said.

The Void was just about done with the *Erwin*. Like the narrative said, it was hard to tell whether the ship had been drifting into the Void or whether the Void was expanding to consume the ship. Either way, she couldn't afford to drift into it herself, nor could she ask the *Rosen* to get that close to it just to pick her up.

But she wasn't out of options. There were two more charges in her bag, and the bag had armor shielding.

She pulled it off her back and got out the two remaining charges.

"Computer, locate the *Rosen*," she said. Then she held her breath. If the computer said *unable to locate* or worse, *the USFSF* Rosen *does not exist*, Alice was out of luck. It said neither.

"*Rosen* located."

"Target on helmet view."

The computer pinpointed the ship for her.

Now's the fun part, she thought. She set the timer for both charges at thirty seconds, put them back in the bag, and then tried to crouch until her whole body—feetfirst so her legs would absorb the worst of it—was behind the steel plate in the bag. Then she tried to maneuver herself so that she was between the impending explosion and the USFSF *Rosen*.

"Computer, activate emergency beacon," she said.

"Emergency beacon activated."

"Thanks. Sure hope this works."

The charges blew. She felt her right leg shatter, and then she blacked out.

She woke up in the *Rosen*'s med lab, with a doctor she didn't know standing over her.

"There you are," he said. "Welcome back."

"Thanks," she said. Her mouth was dry and her vision blurry.

How long have I been out? she wondered.

She tried to sit up, but it felt like the *Rosen*'s gravity was set at a much higher force level than it was supposed to be.

"Here, let me help," the doctor said, pushing a button that got her bed into an upright position. "I'm Dr. Maxwell, and you are lucky to be alive."

"You wouldn't be the first doctor to tell me that," she said, trying out a smile. "What's the damage?"

"Broken right leg, shattered left kneecap, broken left elbow, torn muscles in your right shoulder, and your oxygen ran out three minutes before we got to you, so you're probably missing a few brain cells. There were a couple of other things, but that's the worst of it."

"I need to speak to the captain," she said.

"I'm sure. I'll let him know you're awake; he'll want to speak to you too. They've been going over the information you retrieved from the *Erwin*; I guess there are a lot of questions they need answering."

"How long . . . ?"

"How long have you been out?" he asked. "Depends on where you'd like to start counting. We believe you were adrift for a couple of days, but you'd been on board the *Erwin* for more than a week. Your trip computer recorded only a few hours, though. I think this is one of the questions the captain has. You *do* need some rest first, so if you'd like for me to delay him, I can certainly do so."

"No," she said. "It's okay. The sooner the better."

"Good," he said with a paternal smile. "I'll let him know. Meanwhile, if you're thirsty, there's a glass of water on your right. I'll be right back."

He left. Alice sat still for a few minutes, trying to compose her thoughts. It was going to be impossible to explain everything without sounding insane, but she didn't really care about coming off as sane anymore. What happened, happened. They'd have to take the data from Dr. Marchere, and her accounting, and figure out what to do with it. Hopefully, one of the things they would decide to do would be to bar all travel through Quadrant Brenda.

After a few minutes with her thoughts, Alice realized she was fantastically thirsty. She turned and reached for the glass, not entirely anticipating how weak her right arm was. What began as a straightforward reach for a nearby object became an awkward flail that resulted in her knocking the glass off the edge of the counter.

She heard it shatter on the floor.

"Great," she said. "You gave me an actual glass. Very smart, Dr. Maxwell."

Alice was deciding whether to call a nurse to clean up the glass or to try to do it herself—despite the cast on her leg—when the drinking glass reassembled itself and returned to the counter.

She blinked a couple of times, thinking it would be best if she pretended that hadn't just happened, while knowing that pretending this wouldn't make a difference.

"Computer," she said.

"Yes, Corporal Aste," the *Rosen*'s computer said.

"This is going to sound crazy, but do you have a narrative mode?"

MIDSTRATHE EXPLODING

ANDY DUDAK

Andy Dudak's (www.andydudak.home.blog) stories and translations of Chinese SF have appeared in *Analog: Science Fiction and Fact*, *Apex Magazine*, *Asimov's Science Fiction*, *Clarkesworld*, *Daily Science Fiction*, *Interzone*, *The Magazine of Fantasy & Science Fiction*, *Science Fiction World* (科幻世界), and elsewhere. His story "Love in the Time of Immuno-Sharing" was a finalist for the Eugie Foster Memorial Award for Short Fiction. Andy lived in China for ten years. He likes frogs and believes in the healing power of Dungeons & Dragons.

1

Midstrathe City has been exploding for two centuries and won't be finished for another ten. It has been exploding, glacially, throughout Ciaran's fourteen years, so he doesn't think of it as an explosion. The red-shifted spectacle looms over everything, a mountain he lives at the base of. As he hurries along the Ninth Ring Road of Strathe Towne, he gauges his progress against the familiar features of the wave-front.

There's Dancing Tower, so named because its intact top half rides upon exploding lower floors, which have resembled legs for twenty years.

He dashes down Meridian Alley, past oldies selling meat-pies and souvenirs. The rickshaw racket drowns their conversations, but he knows what they're on about: sudden, catastrophic temporal normalization. They claim they can feel it coming, in their aches and bones.

Catastrophic temporal normalization, and the weather: oldie talk never changes.

Ciaran approaches a knot of tourists. These wealthy Archipelagics have come to gawk at the explosion—Strathe Towne's bread and butter—but they happen to be trinket shopping now. A tall woman in Archipelagic robes holds a necklace toward the red light of Midstrathe. She studies the pendant, familiar to Ciaran, a glass shard housing looped video footage taken by some patient wave-front mystic. This one shows something barely visible these days: a disintegrating skyscraper deep inside the north face of the explosion.

Nice and distracting.

Ciaran watches his hand creep out. It probes an inner pocket of the robe, moves with the robe as it flutters in the wave-front breeze. It withdraws holding a roll of scrip.

A patrolman cries out and levels an assault rifle. Ciaran flees down Five Ways Alley. Pilfering is just a sideline for him. He has real work to do, and he's late.

2

Most of the wave-front shoreline is occupied by science stations, or great rolling observatories catering to rich tourists. A small tract has been set aside for the Dyad mystics. Ciaran slips into their bazaar, where wave-front property is given over to a wall honeycombed with narrow cells, spaces open at both ends and occupied by doomed believers.

They're letting the explosion engulf them feetfirst.

"There is pain," his mother once told him, "but they get it red-shifted, in long wavelengths they can study with bemusement, while their acolytes keep them fed." He didn't understand her at the time. Her tone and her eyes frightened him.

Spectators crowd the bazaar. He moves among them like a ghost, determined not to glance at the wall of cells.

It will be a few more months before the Dyads' shaved pates are engulfed. Their organs have already entered slow time, leaving them starved of food and oxygen. The acolytes make up the difference with ancient, consecrated medical equipment. In these final months, the Dyads' brains are growing steadily more immersed. They have their coveted dual-consciousness, slow thought mingled with real-time awareness, the former gradually subsuming the latter, until they are enlightened. Then there will be festivals as a new wall of cells goes up, and the next graduating class of this death cult ascends.

Ciaran doesn't like being here, but business is business. He skirts a chanting mass of red-painted acolytes, scanning the onlookers for his client. He spots Modwen instead. A year older than Ciaran, stronger and taller, she plies her trade among distracted tourists. So, she's still around. Ciaran hasn't seen her for a while. They ran together for a spell, saving their winnings, determined to leave Strathe together and make their way to a better life in the Archipelago.

But then Ciaran grew up. He abandoned their childish dream and joined the Far Infrared syndicate.

She meets his gaze now, her hand in the day-bag of a regal-looking

Archipelagic man. Her initial look of disappointment gives way to the familiar smirk. Modwen enjoys pickpocketing, even though she doesn't quite have the touch.

The tourist frowns and glances down at his bag. She's already gone, dodging through the crowd with a handful of scrip.

A tickle of instinct draws Ciaran's gaze to a patrolwoman near the Gate of Revelations, at the south end of the bazaar. She has spotted Modwen and is leveling her rifle. Ciaran doesn't think. His hand finds the small pistol secreted in the right pocket of his kilt, a disposable polymer one-shot called a click-chance.

Modwen vanishes into the crowd.

The patrolwoman lowers her rifle and mutters something into her headset.

Ciaran is shocked at himself. Did he nearly shoot a patrolwoman? Not for the first time, his attachment to Modwen frightens him. Attachment of any kind is dangerous in Strathe Towne. This is an immutable law Ciaran has learned well. Being near the Dyads only reinforces this. He needs to get away from this bazaar posthaste.

He spots his client near the back of the spectators, an ancient woman dressed like a rich Archipelagic, though she seems uninterested in the Dyads or their acolytes. Yesterday, when Ciaran sealed the deal, her accent struck him as odd. He wonders if she was born here and then escaped to the Archipelago, like Modwen longs to. But if so, why is she back? Certainly not for standard tourism. She sought out the services of the Far Infrared syndicate, rather than one of the big wave-front tourist facilities.

"There you are," she says. "Is it arranged?"

"Yeah," Ciaran says. "Half now and half at the wave-front."

She withdraws a roll of scrip from a theftproof armpit pocket—not a common precaution among naïve Archipelagics—and hands the money over, her expression grim. Far Infrared's clients are generally thrill seekers. Certain Archipelagics want something beyond the usual tourist experience, but they are tourists nonetheless, relishing the underworld contact, relishing everything, eager. This woman doesn't fit the bill.

Ciaran pockets the scrip and leads her out of the bazaar. She hobbles after him on a cane, and their going is slow. Ciaran guesses that if she benefitted from Archipelagic medicine, it's possible she's older than the explosion. She may have lived in that decadent, mythic time before the qubit bombs, when their temporal side effects were mere theories. She might have left old Midstrathe before the war.

If she's younger than two hundred, she still might've lived on the outskirts of Midstrathe. The inflationary stage consumed the city center in moments, but then the explosion began to slow. Thousands of peripheral Midstratheans escaped the ballooning wave-front.

An estimated thirty million are entombed in the bubble. Half are dead, lost to the red haze deep within the fragmented zone or vaporized zone, or deeper still, in the core, where there is only slow plasma.

The other half are still alive, in a sense.

Because the temporal bubble is leading the shock wave by a good half mile, there are millions near-frozen in headlong flight, and because they're closer to the wave-front, they've become a grim spectacle for tourists to gawk at. They have inspired art movements and schools of philosophy that are beyond Ciaran. He doesn't like looking at them, but they don't trouble his dreams like they do Modwen's. They're a fixture of the wave-front, like ancient murals, and Ciaran profits from them.

He leads the old woman away from the tourist plazas, down alleyways, past unseen Far Infrared checkpoints, through the latest ring of shanties scheduled for demolition. These have to be removed to make way for glacially retreating behemoths, the tourist facilities and science stations.

3

Ciaran was eleven when he met Modwen in a forest of legs and flowing Archipelagic silk. He'd just teased a twenty-scrip bill out of a hip pouch, and he was backing away, fighting the urge to run.

"Nice technique," she said, suddenly at his side.

Disconcerted, he did his best to slip away through the tourists. He'd seen other pickpockets like himself, but he'd kept his distance. They ran in groups and spoke a pickpocket cant he didn't understand. They were natives, he reckoned, not refugees from the Waste like himself.

He thought he'd lost her, but she emerged from the crowd before him, grinning. "Your pilfer, I mean. Not your exit. That needs work."

He fled recklessly this time, colliding with tourists and vendors and raising a commotion. He made it to a trash-filled alley, turned to watch the crowded plaza while he caught his breath.

"I mean it," she said behind him.

He spun, drawing a rusty knife from his boot. He hadn't saved up enough for a click-chance yet.

"You're talented," she said, seemingly unfazed. "Better than me even. On the pilfer, not the exit. Maybe we could help each other."

He stood there, knife brandished, breathing and watching.

"You ain't from here, and you ain't from the Archipelago. The Waste, I guess." She wrist-flicked a blade of her own and planted it in a clapboard wall. "What happened to your folks then?"

"What happened to yours?"

"They was part of the Thirty-Two. Heard of 'em?"

The Thirty-Two were scientists who had researched controlled temporal normalization. Better to trigger it on purpose, they'd advocated, than to wait for sudden catastrophe. They'd wanted to evacuate Strathe Towne and get the explosion over with.

They'd been hung in Sanction Square, to great applause.

"My parents was geniuses," Modwen said, glaring at Ciaran defiantly. "I don't know what's happening in the science stations now, but it ain't science."

Ciaran lowered his knife. "I don't know where my ma is."

Modwen looked past him, at the bustling plaza. "You gotta use the currents of a crowd, not fight 'em. I teach you that. You teach me to lure scrip out of an Archie, like you do. And maybe we get out of this shit-hell, together."

4

Ciaran leads the old woman toward a trash-filled gap between two towering tourist facilities, *Excubium* and *Vigilator*, far from the crowded entrances of both. This close, they blot out the view of the explosion.

Their far, explosion-facing sides are shaped like amphitheaters, consisting of spacious, catered viewing terraces that descend toward the base of the spectacle.

But not every tourist wants such a curated experience. That's where Far Infrared comes in.

Ciaran leads his client toward the strata of garbage between *Excubium* and *Vigilator*. The bottommost layers are old and compacted. They've become something like solid earth, but the stench of the fresher stuff wafts down from on high.

The old woman eyes the narrow cliff-face of refuse dubiously.

Ciaran feels for the panel hidden near the base, presses it, and a section of the motley trash-earth swings inward, revealing a long, rough-hewn tunnel dimly red-lit by Midstrathe at the far end. Ciaran glances back at the old woman. She recovers her composure and nods.

They proceed down the tunnel, an occasional groan disturbing the crypt silence. The tourist facilities are in constant, imperceptible flight before the wave-front. Bits of ancient plastic-earth rain down from the ceiling whenever *Excubium* or *Vigilator* stirs. Ciaran eyes Far Infrared's crude tunnel reinforcements and hopes they're sound. The tunnel has collapsed several times. Infrareds and their clients have been killed. The syndicate plays a dangerous game for its scrip.

Finally, the tunnel widens into a viewing chamber, and Far Infrared's humble slice of the spectacle looms before them: a narrow residential street clogged with terrified, fleeing Midstratheans.

"Some would argue they're already dead," the old woman says.

Ciaran stops at a line carved in the ground some fifteen feet from the wave-front. "This is as close as we're allowed to get."

The old woman stands at his side, gaping. She brings an opera glass to her eyes. Ciaran waits in silence, glancing over his shoulder or up at the slapdash ceiling reinforcements. His gaze never lingers on the wave-front and its historical diorama. It's better that way.

The old woman drops her lenses. She extends a shaking hand toward the wave-front, weeping silently.

Ciaran kneels and retrieves the lenses. The old woman steps across the line.

"Madam, no!"

Far Infrared established the fifteen-foot limit for the same reason tourist facilities have glass barriers on their bottom terraces: to prevent lunatics from entering the wave-front and freezing there, cluttering the view.

The woman pays Ciaran no mind. He reaches out to take her wrist, but never makes contact. His body goes rigid. A brief shell of blue energy flashes around the woman, then retreats into her cane.

5

The clay-painted zealots shrieked, wept, laughed ecstatically. Ciaran was suffocating in the crush as it surged toward the wall. He was twelve and scrawny for his age, hadn't eaten in days, had yet to master Modwen's crowd current techniques. He'd dared this mob of insane adults hoping to pilfer them in their extremely distracted state, but now he was jostled, squeezed between bodies, trapped.

Above them, a strange figure hung in the wall scaffolding: pale, ragged Wastelander robes, head and arms covered in clay, like the zealots. This person looked down upon the crowd, gaze passing over Ciaran without recognition.

6

He comes to, shivering. The old woman has taken a few more steps beyond the line. *Shock envelope.* Archie self-defense tech, high-end and rare. He was hit by one before, during a pickpocketing attempt.

The old woman glances back at him. "See the one in the cloak and boots?"

She's pointing at the scene in the wave-front. The Late Classic Midstratheans seem to be glaring right at him, in their arrested flight, elbowing each other, some getting trampled, their grimaces ugly in this preserved, unflattering moment. He braves their doomed gazes and finds a young woman in cloak and boots. A barefoot man in a house robe is in the process of shoving her aside, so she's balanced precariously on one foot. The old-fashioned cloak is a sculpted, billowing mass behind her.

"We were lovers," the old woman says. "We quarreled before I left."

Ciaran can't rise, but he makes his right hand probe his pocket for the click-chance.

"I thought she might've fled . . . be fleeing . . . down Victory Street, but I didn't dare hope to really find her." She glances back at him again. "I'll be dead soon, boy. And I want her in my arms one last time." Studying him, her expression softens. "I suppose that means me frozen on the wave-front, in your reference frame. I suppose that's trouble for you."

She's right. If he lets her clutter the wave-front, he'll have a price on his head. Far Infrared will hunt him, and the authorities, handsomely bribed, might help.

"I am sorry. I should have thought of this. If I had any money left, I'd give it to you. I saved just enough to get here."

He draws his click-chance and aims.

"You don't seem to understand," she says, her smile grim. "I have nothing to lose. Shoot if you must."

She turns and continues toward the wave-front. Ciaran tries again to rise, but his zapped leg muscles persist in their disobedience. He aims at the back of her head, and his finger is in working order, he can feel it, but he can't fire.

The old woman slows as she enters the wave-front, arms flung wide and beckoning. Streaks of her seem to travel upward along the curved surface of the wave-front, shooting toward the apex, but she's still there, now frozen in mid-stride, partially engulfed. It will be a year before she's completely inside, and her exposed portion is still vulnerable to this reference frame, but the damage to Far Infrared's shoreline, however minor, is done. Maybe the lovers' slow reunion will become a profitable attraction, years from now. It doesn't matter. Ciaran might still fire, still kill her, and plead that he did all he could, but that won't save him.

He pockets his weapon.

He gets to his feet after several tries and staggers toward the wave-front, fey and giddy. He reaches out and touches it, hazarding the tip of his index finger in slow time. It's not even a millimeter of flesh, but it suddenly feels heavy and cold, affixed to its portion of space-time.

It takes him ten minutes of concerted effort to pull the tip of his finger out of the Midstrathean Late Classic period.

There's a feeling in the air this close to the wave-front. It's largely what Far Infrared banks on. With no glass barrier in the way, there's a tension or charge the Dyads call spiritual potential, a force that can grant revelations. Modwen said her father didn't believe this. He called it "heightened vacuum fluctuation" and said it had no effect on the brain.

Nevertheless, Ciaran is having a revelation.

7

In the Dyad Bazaar, he covers himself in clay like a proper zealot of the Waste-woman.

He pays the tribute and waits in line. He climbs the scaffolding when his turn comes, and is granted a view of the Clay Prophet in repose.

She is deep in dual consciousness, close to ascension. All but the top half of her shaved head is engulfed in the wave-front. She's dressed like the Wastelander she once was: pale, ragged robe, head and arms painted in protective clays. She and Ciaran shed these trappings upon reaching Strathe Towne. They adopted Strathean jerkins and kilts to blend in. She tried to get work on one of the tourist facilities. She tried selling trinkets in the plazas and bazaars. Finally, she resorted to going with Archipelagic men at night, telling Ciaran they were friends who needed her mystic Wasteland healing arts. In the wee hours of the morning she would enter their attic room in the condemned ring and chant nonsense words that she said were a new language she'd learned in the Waste. Ciaran doesn't remember anything like that, but the Waste is a blur to him in most respects. They nearly starved out there.

And then, one morning, she didn't come home. He searched Strathe Towne for three days before stumbling upon the Dyad Bazaar,

where pendants and illuminations of his mother were already on sale.
He looked toward the new wall of cells, and he knew.

8

Her eyes are inside the wave-front, slowed, aimed at the low ceiling of the cell. It's impossible to tell if they're in motion. Ciaran wonders if they're turning toward the cell entrance, toward real time. Maybe she's hoping for one last glimpse of him. He imagines staying in Strathe a few more months to see. If he waits years, she might even reach out to take his hand. Her expression of mystic wonder might gradually melt into one of contrition, and regret, which he could study at his leisure.

"Thanks for getting me this far, Ma, but I have to keep going. Goodbye."

He climbs down the scaffolding amid the flowing red and gold prayer streamers, as the next zealot climbs up. Regardless of the odds, Ciaran is going to try to leave Strathe Towne.

It's late afternoon when he reaches Meridian Alley. The rickshaw racket is at an ebb. A smile comes to his face as he hurries toward a group of souvenir-browsing Archipelagics. There's Modwen, sidling up. And the oldies are chattering, as always, about catastrophic temporal normalization, and the weather.

THE BAHRAIN
UNDERGROUND BAZAAR

NADIA AFIFI

Nadia Afifi (www.nadiaafifi.com) is the author of *The Sentient* and numerous science fiction short stories. She grew up in Saudi Arabia and Bahrain, where she read every book she could get her hands on, but currently calls Denver, Colorado, home. Her background as an Arab American who lived overseas has inspired her fiction writing, particularly her passion for exploring complex social, political, and cultural issues through a futuristic lens. When she isn't writing, she spends her time practicing (and falling off) the lyra (aerial hoops), hiking through Colorado's many trails, jogging through Denver's streets, and working on the most challenging jigsaw puzzles she can find. She also loves dogs, travel, and cooking.

Bahrain's central bazaar comes to life at night. Lights dance above the narrow passageways, illuminating the stalls with their spices, sacks of lentils, ornate carpets, and trinkets. Other stalls hawk more modern fare, NeuroLync implants and legally ambiguous drones. The scent of cumin and charred meat fills my nostrils. My stomach twists in response. Chemo hasn't been kind to me.

Office workers spill out from nearby high-rises into the crowds. A few cast glances in my direction, confusion and sympathy playing across their faces. They see an old woman with stringy, thinning gray hair and a hunched back, probably lost and confused. The young always assume the elderly can't keep up with them, helpless against their new technology and shifting language. Never mind that I know their tricks better than they do, and I've been to wilder bazaars than this manufactured tourist trap. It used to be the Old Souk, a traditional market that dealt mostly in gold. But Bahrain, which once prided itself as being Dubai's responsible, less ostentatious younger cousin, has decided to keep up with its neighbors. Glitz and flash. Modernity and illusion.

I turn down another passageway, narrower than the last. A sign beckons me below—"The Bahrain Underground Bazaar." It even has a London Underground symbol around the words for effect, though we're far from its gray skies and rain. I quicken my pace down its dark steps.

It's even darker below, with torch-like lamps lining its stone walls. Using stone surfaces—stone anything—in the desert is madness. The cost of keeping the place cool must be obscene. The Underground Bazaar tries hard, bless it, to be sinister and seedy, and it mostly succeeds. The clientele help matters. They're either gangs of teenage boys or lone older men with unsettling eyes, shuffling down damp corridors. Above them, signs point to different areas of the bazaar for different tastes—violence, phobias, sex, and death.

I'm here for death.

"Welcome back, grandma," the man behind the front counter greets me. A nice young man with a neatly trimmed beard. He dresses all in black, glowing tattoos snaking across his forearms, but he doesn't fool me. He goes home and watches romantic comedies when he isn't selling the morbid side of life to oddballs. This isn't a typical souk or bazaar where each vendor runs their own stall. The Underground Bazaar is centralized. You tell the person at the counter what virtual immersion experience you're looking for and they direct you to the right room. Or *chamber*, as they insist.

"I'm not a grandma yet," I say, placing my dinars on the front counter. "Tell my son and his wife to spend less time chasing me around and get the ball rolling on those grandchildren." In truth, I don't care in the slightest whether my children reproduce. I won't be around to hold any grandchildren.

"What'll it be today?"

I've had time to think on the way, but I still pause. In the Underground Bazaar's virtual immersion chambers, I've experienced many anonymous souls' final moments. Through them, I've drowned, been strangled, shot in the mouth, and suffered a heart attack. And I do mean suffer—the heart attack was one of the worst. I try on deaths like T-shirts. Violent ones and peaceful passings. Murders, suicides, and accidents. All practice for the real thing.

The room tilts and my vision blurs momentarily. Dizzy, I press my hands, bruised from chemo drips, into the counter to steady myself. The tumor wedged between my skull and brain likes to assert itself at random moments. A burst of vision trouble, spasms of pain or nausea. I imagine shrinking it down, but even that won't matter now. It's in my blood and bones. The only thing it's left me so far, ironically, is my mind. I'm still sharp enough to make my own decisions. And I've decided one thing—I'll die on my terms, before cancer takes that last bit of power from me.

"I don't think I've fallen to my death yet," I say, regaining my composure. "I'd like to fall from a high place today."

"Sure thing. Accident or suicide?"

Would they be that different? The jump, perhaps, but everyone must feel the same terror as the ground approaches.

"Let's do a suicide," I say. "Someone older, if you have it. Female. Someone like me," I add unnecessarily.

My helpful young man runs his tattooed fingers across his fancy computer, searching. I've given him a challenge. Most people my age never installed the NeuroLync that retains an imprint of a person's experiences—including their final moments. Not that the intent is to document one's demise, of course. People get the fingernail-sized devices implanted in their temples to do a variety of useful things—pay for groceries with a blink, send neural messages to others, even adjust the temperature in their houses with a mental command. Laziness. Soon, the young will have machines do their walking for them.

But one side effect of NeuroLync's popularity was that its manufacturer acquired a treasure trove of data from the minds connected to its Cloud network. Can you guess what happened next? Even an old bird like me could have figured it out. All that data was repackaged and sold to the highest bidder. Companies seized what they could, eager to literally tap into consumer minds. But there are other markets, driven by the desire to borrow another person's experiences. Knowing what it feels like to have a particular kind of sex. Knowing what it feels like to torture someone—or be tortured. Knowing what it means to die a certain way.

And with that demand come places like the Bahrain Underground Bazaar.

"I've got an interesting one for you," the man says, eyeing me with something close to caution. "A Bedouin woman. Want to know the specifics?"

"Surprise me," I say. "I'm not too old to appreciate some mystery." My young man always walks with me to the sensory chamber, like an usher in a movie theater. It's easy for me to get knocked around amid the jostling crowds, and I admit that some of the other customers frighten me. You can always spot the ones here for violence, a sick thrill between work shifts. Their eyes have this dull sheen, as though the real world is something they endure until their next immersion.

"This is your room, grandma," the man says before spinning on his heels back to the front counter. I step inside.

The room is dark, like the rest of this place, with blue lights webbing its walls. I suspect they exist for ambience rather than utility. In the center of the room, a reclining chair sits underneath a large device that will descend over my tiny, cancer-addled head. On the back of it, a needle of some kind will jut out and enter my spinal cord, right where it meets the skull. It's painful, but only for a second, and then you're in someone else's head, seeing and hearing and sensing what they felt. What's a little pinprick against all of that?

I sit and lean back as the usual recording plays on the ceiling, promising me an experience I'll never forget. The machine descends over my head, drowning out my surroundings, and I feel the familiar vampire bite at my neck.

I'm in the desert. Another one. Unlike Bahrain, a small island with every square inch filled by concrete, this is an open space with clear skies and a mountainous horizon. And I'm walking down a rocky, winding slope. Rose-colored cliffsides surround me and rich brown dirt crunches underneath my feet. The bright sun warms my face and a primal, animal smell fills my nostrils. I'm leading a donkey down the path. It lets out a huff of air, more sure-footed than me.

I turn—"I" being the dead woman—at the sound of laughter. A child sits on the donkey, legs kicking. The donkey takes it in stride, accustomed to excitable tourists, but I still speak in a husky, foreign voice, instructing the child to sit still. Others follow behind her—parents or other relations. They drink in the landscape's still beauty through their phones.

We round a corner and my foot slides near the cliff's edge. A straight drop to hard ground and rock. I look down, the bottom of the cliff both distant and oddly intimate. The air stills, catching my breath. Wild adrenaline runs through my body, my legs twitching. For a moment, I can't think clearly, my thoughts scrambled by an unnamed terror. Then a thought breaks through the clutter.

Jump. Jump. Jump.

The terror becomes an entity inside me, a metallic taste on my tongue and a clammy sweat on my skin. The outline of the cliff becomes sharper, a beckoning blade, while the sounds of voices around me grow distant, as though I'm underwater.

I try to pull away—me, Zahra, the woman from Bahrain who

chooses to spend her remaining days experiencing terrible things. In some backwater of my brain, I remind myself that I'm not on a cliff and this happened long ago. But the smell of hot desert air invades my senses again, yanking me back with a jolt of fear. *Jump.*

A moment seizes me, and I know that I've reached the glinting edge of a decision, a point of no return. My foot slides forward and it is crossed. I tumble over the edge.

I'm falling. My stomach dips and my heart tightens, thundering against my ribs. My hands flail around for something to grab but when they only find air, I stop. I plummet with greater speed, wind whipping my scarf away. I don't scream. I'm beyond fear. There is only the ground beneath me and the space in between. A rock juts out from the surface and I know, with sudden peace, that that's where I'll land.

And then nothing. The world is dark and soundless. Free of pain, or of any feeling at all.

And then voices.

The darkness is softened by a strange awareness. I sense, rather than see, my surroundings. My own mangled body spread across a rock. Dry plants and a gravel path nearby. Muted screams from above. I know, somehow, that my companions are running down the path now, toward me. *Be careful,* I want to cry out. *Don't fall.* They want to help me. Don't they know I'm dead?

But if I'm dead, why am I still here? I'm not in complete oblivion and I'm also not going toward a light. I'm sinking backward into something, a deep pool of nothing, but a feeling of warmth surrounds me, enveloping me like a blanket on a cold night. I have no body now, I'm a ball of light, floating toward a bigger light behind me. I know it's there without seeing it. It is bliss and beauty, peace and kindness, and all that remains is to join it.

A loud scream.

Reality flickers around me. Something releases in the back of my head and blue light creeps into my vision. The machine whirs above me, retracting to its place on the ceiling. I blink, a shaking hand at my throat. The scream was mine. Drawing a steady breath, I hold my hand before my eyes until I'm convinced it's real and mine. Coming out of an immersion is always disorienting, but that was no ordinary immersion. Normally, the moment of death wakes me up, returning me to my own, disintegrating body. What happened?

I leave the chamber with a slight wobble in my knees. A tall man in a trench coat appears at my side, offering his arm, and I swat it away. I smile, oddly reassured by the brief exchange. This is the Underground Bazaar, full of the same weirdos and creeps. I'm still me. The death I experienced in the chamber begins to fade from my immediate senses, but I still don't look back.

"How was it?" The man at the front counter winks. I manage a rasping noise.

"Pretty crazy, huh?" His grin widens. "We file that one under suicides, but it's not really a suicide. Not premeditated, anyway. She was a tour guide in Petra, with a husband, five children, and who knows how many grandchildren. She just jumped on impulse."

My mind spins with questions, but I seize on his last comment.

"I walked the Golden Gate Bridge once, on a family trip," I say, my voice wavering. "I remember a strange moment where I felt the urge to jump over the edge, into the water, for no reason. It passed, and I heard that's not uncommon."

"They call it the death drive," the man says with a nod. His eyes dance with excitement, and I understand at last why he works in this awful place. The thrill of the macabre. "The French have a fancy expression for it that means 'the call of the void.' It's really common to get to the edge of a high place and feel this sudden urge to jump. You don't have to be suicidal or anxious. It can happen to anyone."

"But why?" I ask. I suspect the man has studied this kind of thing and I'm right. He bounces on his heels and leans forward, his smile conspiratorial.

"Scientists think that it's the conscious brain reacting to our instinctive responses," he says. "You get to the edge of a cliff and you reflexively step back. But then your conscious mind steps in. Why did you step back? Maybe it's not because of the obvious danger, but because you *wanted* to jump. Now, a part of you is convinced you want to jump, even though you know what that means, and it scares you. Insane," he adds with undisguised glee.

"But most people don't," I say, recalling the terror of those moments at the cliff's edge.

"Most don't," he agrees. "That's what's interesting about this one. She actually went through with it. Why I thought you'd like it." His chest puffs up in a way that reminds me of my own son, Firaz, when he came home from school eager to show me some new art project. He stopped drawing when he reached college, I realize with sudden sadness.

"But what about . . . after she fell?" I ask. The fall was traumatic, as I knew it would be, but nothing from past immersions prepared me for the strange, sentient peace that followed the moment of impact.

"Oh, that," the young man says. "That happens sometimes. Maybe about ten percent of our death immersions. Kind of a near-death-experience thing. Consciousness slipping away. Those last brain signals firing."

"But it happened after I—after she fell," I protest. "She must have been completely dead. Does that ever happen?"

"I'm sure it does, but rarely," the young man says with a tone of gentle finality. He smiles at the next customer.

"Petra," I murmur. "I've always wanted to see Petra." And now I have, in a fashion.

Walking up the stairs, exhaustion floods my body. Some days are better than others, but I always save these visits for the days when I'm strongest. Leaning against the wall outside, I feel ready to collapse.

"Zahra? *Zahra!*"

My daughter-in-law pushes through the crowd. I consider shrinking back down the stairs, but her eyes fix on me with predatory focus. I'm in her sights. She swings her arms stiffly under her starched white blouse.

"We've been worried sick," Reema begins. Her eyes scan me from head to toe, searching for some hidden signs of mischief. For a moment, I feel like a teenager again, sneaking out at night.

"You really shouldn't," I say.

"How did you slip away this time? We didn't see you—"

"On the tracking app you installed on my phone?" I ask with a small smile. "I deleted it, along with the backup you placed on the Cloud." As I said before, I know more tricks than they realize. Thank goodness I don't have a NeuroLync. I'd never be alone. Of course, every time I sneak off after a medical appointment to walk to the bazaar, I'm battling time. They don't know when I've given them the slip, but when they return home from their tedious jobs to find the house empty, they know where I've gone.

Reema sighs. "You need to stop coming to this terrible place, Zahra. It's not good for your mind or soul. You don't need dark thoughts— you'll beat this by staying positive."

After accompanying me to my earliest appointments, Reema has mastered the art of motivational medical speak. She means well. It would be cliché for me to despise my daughter-in-law, but in truth, I respect her. She comes from a generation of Arab women expected to excel at every aspect of life, to prove she earned her hard-fought rights, and she's risen to the task. If only she'd let me carry on with the task of planning my death and getting out of her way.

On the way home, Reema calls my son to report my capture. Instead of speaking aloud, she sends him silent messages through her NeuroLync, shooting the occasional admonishing glance in my direction. I can imagine the conversation well enough.

At the bazaar again.

Ya Allah! The seedy part?

She was walking right out of it when I found her.

Is she okay?

Pleased enough with herself. What are we going to do with her?

Reema and Firaz work in skyscrapers along Bahrain's coastal business zone, serving companies that change names every few months when they merge into bigger conglomerates. To them, I'm another project to be managed, complete with a schedule and tasks. My deadline is unknown, but within three months, they'll likely be planning my funeral. It's not that they don't love me, and I them. The world has just conditioned them to express that love through worry and structure. I need neither.

I want control. I want purpose.

Firaz barely raises his head to acknowledge me when Reema and I walk through the kitchen door. He's cooking at ten o'clock at night, preparing a dinner after work. Reema collapses onto a chair, kicking off her heels before tearing into the bread bowl.

"I'm not hungry, but I'm tired," I say to no one in particular. "I'll go to bed now."

"Mama, when will this end?" Firaz asks in a tight voice.

I have an easy retort at the tip of my tongue. *Soon enough, when I'm dead.* But when he turns to face me, I hesitate under his sad, frustrated gaze. His red eyes are heavy with exhaustion. I, the woman who birthed and raised him, am now a disruption.

All at once, I deflate. My knees buckle.

"Mama!" Firaz abandons his pan and rushes toward me. "I'm fine," I say. With a wave of my hand, I excuse myself.

In the dark of my bedroom, images from the bazaar linger in the shadows. Echoes of blue lights dancing across the walls. I sink into my bed, reaching for the warmth I felt hours ago, through the dead woman's mind, but I only shiver. What happened in that immersion? The young man didn't fool me. I had experienced enough deaths in those dark chambers to recognize the remarkable. She jumped in defiance of instinct, but her final moments of existence were full of warmth and acceptance—a presence that lingered after death. What made her different?

The next morning, I take a long bath, letting Firaz and Reema go through their pre-work routine—elliptical machines, mindfulness, dressing, and breakfast, the house obeying their silent commands. After they leave, I take the bus downtown to the clinic.

I sit in a room of fake plants and fake smiles, chemicals warming my veins. Other women sit around me, forming a square with nothing but cheap blue carpet in the center. A nurse checks our IV drips and ensures our needles remain in place. My fellow cancer survivors— we're all survivors, the staff insists—wear scarves to hide balding heads. Young, old—cancer ages us all. Their brave smiles emphasize the worry lines and tired eyes.

Out the window, the city hums with its usual frenetic pulse. El-evated trains, dizzying lanes of cars, and transport drones all fight for space amid Bahrain's rush hour. Beyond it, the sea winks at me, sun-light glinting on its breaking waves. A world in constant motion, ready to leave me behind.

Coldness prickles my skin. Could I jump, like that woman jumped? It would be easy—rip the array of needles from my arm and rush across the room, forcing the window open. I might have to smash the glass if they put in security locks (a good strategy in a cancer ward). When the glass shatters and the screaming skyscraper winds whip at my hair, would I recoil or jump?

But I don't move. I cross my feet under my silk skirt and wet my lips. Perhaps I'm too fearful of causing a scene. Perhaps I'm not the jumping kind. But doubt gnaws at me with each passing second. Death is an unceasing fog around me, but despite my many trips to the ba-zaar, I can't bring myself to meet it yet.

Maybe you're not ready because you have unfinished business.

But what could that be? My child no longer needs me—if any-thing, I'm a burden. Bahrain has morphed into something beyond my wildest imagination. It's left me behind. I've lived plenty. What remains?

A rose city carved from rock. An ancient Nabataean site in Jordan, immortalized in photographs in glossy magazines and childhood sto-ries. I always meant to go to Petra but had forgotten about that dream long ago. And in the Underground Bazaar, of all places, I'm reminded of what I've yet to do.

I close my eyes. The woman from yesterday's immersion tumbles through the air, beautiful cliffs and clear skies spinning around her. Is that why she was calm at the end? Did some part of her realize that she had lived the right life and was now dying in the right place?

The revelation hits me with such force that I have no room for un-certainty. I know what I must do, but I have to be smart about my next steps. The chemo session is nearly over. I smile sweetly at the nurse when she removes the last drip from my veins. My daughter-in-law will meet me downstairs, I reassure her. No, I don't need any help, thank you. This isn't my first rodeo. She laughs. People like their old women to have a little bite—it's acceptable once we're past a certain age. A small consolation prize for living so long.

In the reception room, I drop my phone behind a plant—Firaz and Reema are clever enough to find new ways to track me, so I discard their favorite weapon.

"Back again, Ms. Mansour? Looks like you were here yesterday." The man's eyes twinkle as he examines my record on his computer screen.

"Where did the woman live?" I ask. "The one from yesterday—the Bedouin woman. Does she have any surviving family?"

In truth, I know where she lived, but I need more. A family name, an address.

"Your guess is as good as mine," the man says. A different man, not my usual favorite. Tall and thin like a tree branch, with brooding eyes. I'm earlier than usual, so this one must take the early shift.

"Surely you have something." I inject a quaver in my voice. "Anyone with the NeuroLync leaves an archive of information behind." *Unlike me*, I don't add. When I go, I'll only leave bones.

"We don't keep those kinds of records here because we don't need them," he says. "People want to know what drowning feels like, not the person's entire life story."

"Well, this customer does."

"Can't help you."

This is ridiculous. When I was his age, if an older woman asked me a question, I would have done my best to answer. It was a period of great social upheaval, but we still respected the elderly.

I try another angle. "Are there any more paid immersion experiences tied to that record?" She's a woman, not a record, but I'm speaking in their language.

The man's eyes practically light up with dollar signs. "We've got the life highlight reel. Everybody has one. People like to see those before the death, sometimes."

Minutes later and I'm back in the immersion chamber, the helmet making its ominous descent over my head.

They call them "highlight reels," but these files are really the by-product of a data scrubber going through a dead person's entire memory and re-creating that "life flashing before your eyes" effect. Good moments and bad moments, significant events and those small, poignant memories that stick in your mind for unclear reasons. I remember an afternoon with Firaz in the kitchen, making pastries. Nothing special about it, but I can still see the way the sunlight hit the counter and smell the filo dough when it came out of the oven.

The Bedouin woman's highlight reel is no different. There's a wedding under the stars, some funerals, and enough childbirths to make me wince in sympathy. But there are also mundane moments like my own. The smell of livestock on early mornings before the tourists begin spilling into the valley. Meat cooking over a low campfire. Memories that dance through the senses.

I leave the bazaar more restless than when I arrived. The woman's life was unremarkable. Good and bad in typical proportions. A part of me had expected a mystic connection to her surroundings, maybe a head injury that gave her strange conscious experiences that would explain her final moments. Instead, I found someone not unlike me, separated only by money and circumstances.

Through the humid air and dense crowds, Bahrain's only train station beckons. A bit ridiculous for an island, but it does connect the country to Saudi Arabia and the wider region via a causeway. I walk to the station, restlessness growing with each step. Perhaps this is my jump over the cliff. I'm moving toward a big decision, the pressure swelling as I reach the point of no return.

At the front booth, I buy a one-way ticket to Petra, Jordan, along the Hejaz Railway. Once I board the carriage, all my doubt and fear evaporate. This is what I need to do. A final adventure, a last trip in search of answers that no bazaar can give me.

The desert hills race by through the train window. It's hypnotic, and before long, my mind stirs like a thick soup through old feelings. The terrain outside feels both alien and comforting, that sensation of coming home after a long trip. A return to something primal and ancient, a way of life that's been lost amid controlled air-conditioning and busy streets. How can something feel strange and right at the same time?

The Hejaz Railway system was completed when I was a little girl, itself a revival and expansion of an old train line that was abandoned after World War I. The region reasserting itself, flexing its power with a nod to its past. I've always hated planes, and you'll never get me on those hovering shuttles, so an old-fashioned train (albeit with a maglev upgrade) suits me just fine.

The terrain dulls as we speed north, as if the world is transitioning from computer animation to a soft oil painting. The mountains lose their edges and vegetation freckles the ground. Signs point us to ancient places. Aqaba. The Dead Sea. Petra.

The sun sets and I drift off under the engine's hum.

The next morning, the train pulls into Wadi Musa, the town that anchors Petra. I join the crowds spilling out into the station, the air cool and fresh compared to Bahrain. I reach into my pocket to check my phone for frantic messages, only to recall that I left it behind. Firaz and Reema must be searching for me by now. At this stage, they've likely contacted the police. Guilt tugs at the corners of my heart, but they'll never understand why this is important. And soon, I'll be out of their way.

Ignoring the long row of inviting hotels, I follow the signs toward Petra. Enterprising locals hawk everything from sunscreen to camel rides. With my hunched back and slow gait, they trail me like cats around a bowl of fresh milk.

"*Teta*, a hat for your head!"

"Need a place to stay, lady?"

"A donkey ride, ma'am? It's low to the ground."

Why not? I'm in no condition to hike around ancient ruins. The donkey handler, a boy no older than eighteen, suppresses a smile when I pull out paper currency.

"How do most of your customers pay?" I ask as he helps me onto the beast.

"NeuroLync, ma'am. They send us a one-time wire."

"You all have NeuroLync?" I ask, amazed. Many of these locals still live as Bedouin, in simple huts without electricity or running water.

"Yes, ma'am," he says, clicking his tongue to prompt the donkey forward. "We were some of the first in Jordan to get connected. Government project. Some refused, but most said yes."

Interesting. So the area's Bedouin and locals were early adopters of NeuroLync technology, an experiment to support the country's tourism. That explained how an elderly woman of my age had the implant long enough to record most of her adult life, now downloadable for cheap voyeurs. My chest flutters. *People like me.*

My guide leads the donkey and me down the hill into a narrow valley. Most tourists walk, but some take carriages, camels, and donkeys. An adventurous soul charges past us on horseback, kicking up red sand.

Along the surrounding cliff faces and hills, dark holes mark ancient dwellings carved into the rock. Following my gaze, my guide points to them.

"Old Nabataean abodes," he says, referring to the ancient people who made Petra home.

"Do people still live there?" I ask. My tone is light and curious.

"Not there," he says.

"So where do all of the guides and craftspeople live around here?" I follow up: "It makes sense to be close."

"Some in Wadi Musa, but mostly in other places around Petra. We camp near the Monastery and the hills above the Treasury."

I nod and let the silence settle between us, taking in the beauty around me. Suicide is a sensitive subject everywhere, but especially in the rural Arab world. I can't just ask about a woman who jumped off a cliff. But while I'm teasing away clues, I drink in the energy of my surroundings. The warmth of the sun on my face, the sharp stillness of the air. The sense of building excitement as we descend into the narrow valley, shaded by looming mountains. We're getting close to the Treasury, the most famous structure in Petra. I can tell by the way the tourists pick up their pace, pulling out the old-fashioned handheld cameras popular with the young set. I smile with them. I'm on vacation, after all.

I've seen plenty of pictures of the iconic Treasury, knowing that no picture can do it justice. I turn out to be right. Ahead, the valley forms a narrow sliver through which a stunning carved building emerges. Its deep, dark entrance is flanked by pillars. Cut into the rock, its upper level features more pillars crowned with intricate patterns. Though ancient, it is ornate and well-preserved. The surrounding throngs of tourists and souvenir peddlers can't detract from its beauty.

My guide helps me off the donkey so I can wander inside. It's what you'd expect from a building carved into the mountains—the interior is dark and gaping, with more arches and inlets where the Nabataeans conducted their business. For a second, my mind turns to Firaz and Reema, with their endless work. I look down, overwhelmed. People once flooded this building when it was a vibrant trade stop—people long gone. Everyone taking pictures around me will one day be gone as well—all of us, drops in humanity's ever-flowing river.

"Where next, ma'am?"

The winding road up to a high place, one you need a pack animal to reach. An easy place to fall—or jump.

"I'd like to see the Monastery."

On the way up the trail, I talk with my guide, who I learn is named Rami. He has the usual dreams of teenage boys—become a soccer player, make millions, and see the world. When I tell him where I live, his eyes widen and I'm peppered with questions about tall buildings and city lights. He talks of cities as though they're living organisms, and in a way, I suppose they are. Traffic, sprawl, and decay. They're more than the sum of their people. But how can he understand that he's also fortunate to live here, to wake up every morning to a clear red sky, walking through time with every step he takes?

We round a corner along the cliff and I give a small cry.

"It's so far up," I say. "I'm glad the donkey's doing the work for me."

Rami nods. "They're more sure-footed than we are. They know exactly where to step."

"Do people ever fall?"

Rami's eyes are trained ahead, but I catch the tightness in his jaw-line. "It's rare, ma'am. Don't worry."

My skin prickles. His voice carries a familiar strain, the sound of a battle between what one wants to say and what one should say. Does he know my old woman? Has he heard the story?

While I craft my next question, the donkey turns another corner and my stomach lurches. We're at the same spot where she fell. I recognize the curve of the trail, the small bush protruding into its path. I lean forward, trying to peer down the cliff.

"Can we stop for a minute?"

"Not a good place to stop, ma'am." The boy's voice is firm, tight as a knot, but I slide off the saddle and walk to the ledge.

Wind, warm under the peak sun, attacks my thinning hair. I step closer to the edge.

"Please, *sayida!*"

Switching to Arabic. I must really be stressing the boy. But I can't pull back now.

Another step, and I look down. My stomach clenches. It's there— the boulder that broke her fall. It's free of blood and gore, presumably washed clean a long time ago, but I can remember the scene as it once was, when a woman died and left her body, a witness to her own demise.

But when I lean further, my body turns rigid. I'm a rock myself, welded in place. I won't jump. I can't. I know this with a cold, brutal certainty that knocks the air from my lungs. I'm terrified of the fall. Every second feels like cool water on a parched throat. I could stand here for hours and nothing would change.

"Please." A voice cuts through the blood pounding in my ears, and I turn to meet Rami's frightened, childlike face. He offers his hand palm-up and I take it, letting myself be hoisted back onto the donkey, who chews with lazy indifference. We continue our climb as though nothing happened.

The Monastery doesn't compare to the Treasury at the base of the city, but it's impressive regardless. The surroundings more than make up for it, the horizon shimmering under the noon heat. Rami and I sit cross-legged in the shade, eating the overpriced *manaqish* I bought earlier.

"The cheese is quite good," I admit. "I don't eat much these days, but I could see myself getting fat off of these."

Rami smiles. "A single family makes all of the food you can buy here. An old woman and her daughters. They sell it across the area."

I suppress commenting that the men in the family could help. I don't have the energy or the inclination—after staring down the cliff and winning, I'm exhausted. Did I win? Had part of me hoped that I would jump as well? Now that I hadn't, I didn't know what to do next.

I say all that I can think to say. "This is a beautiful place. I don't want to be anywhere else."

Rami steals a glance at me. "There's evil here. The High Place of Sacrifice, where the Nabataeans cut animals' throats to appease their pagan gods." He gives his donkey a pat, as though reassuring it. "Battles and death. Maybe you can sense it, too. That place where you stopped? My grandmother died there."

It takes me a second to register what the young man said, the words entering my ears like thick molasses. Then my blood chills. Rami is one of her many grandchildren. It shouldn't surprise me, but this proximity to the woman's surviving kin prickles my skin, flooding my senses with shock and shame in equal measure. I terrified the boy when I leaned over the edge.

I clear my throat, gripping the sides of my dress to hide my shaking hands. "What was her name?"

He blinks, surprised. "Aisha."

A classic name. "I'm so sorry, Rami," I say. "What a terrible accident."

"She was taking a family down from the Monastery," Rami says. He doesn't correct my assumption, and I wonder if he knows what happened. "When she was younger, she hated working with the tourists. She loved to cook and preferred caring for the animals at the end of the day. But when she got older, my mother told me she loved it. She liked to learn their stories and tell her own, about her life and her family, all the things she had seen. I bet she could have written a book about all the people she met from around the world, but she never learned how to write."

I press my lips together in disbelief. A woman with a NeuroLync plugged into her temple, unable to read a book. While it could have been tradition that kept her illiterate, it was unlikely. In many ways, the Bedouin were more progressive than the urban population. Perhaps she never learned because she never needed to.

"It sounds like she had a good life," I manage.

Rami's face brightens, his dark eyes twinkling with sudden amusement. "She made everyone laugh. I read a poem once in school. It said you can't give others joy unless you carry joy in reserve, more than you need. So I know she must have been happy until the end. I believe something evil made her fall that day. It sensed that she was good. Whatever it was—a jinn, a ghost—it knew it had to defeat her."

Though exposed to modern technology and a government-run secular education, the boy had found his own mystical narrative to dampen his grief, to reason the unreasonable. *Not unlike me*, I realize. I came here in search of a secret. A special way to die, a way to secure life after death. Something unique about this place or people that would extinguish my fears. Magical thinking.

My mouth is dry. Should I tell the boy what I know from the bazaar? It would bring pain, but perhaps comfort as well. His grandmother Aisha died because of a strange psychological quirk, not a persuasive spirit. She was terrified but found peace in those final split seconds of the fall. She lingered somehow after meeting the ground, sinking into a warm, welcoming light. Would the boy want to know this? Would he feel betrayed by the realization that I knew about his grandmother—that a stranger had experienced her most intimate moments through a black-market bazaar?

No. Hers was not my story to tell. I'm a thief, a robber of memories, driven by my own fears. I came here for answers to a pointless question. What did it matter why she jumped? She lived well and left behind people who loved her. The people I love are far away and frantic—and yet I considered leaving them with the sight of my body splattered over rock. As for her apparent conscious experience after death—I won't know what happened, what it meant, until it's my time. And my time isn't now, in this place. Not yet.

My face burns and I draw a shaking breath. Above me, the Monastery looms like an anchor. Through my shame, my mouth twitches in a smile. It's breathtaking. I don't regret coming here. But now, I need to go home.

"Rami, can you send a message for me with your NeuroLync?" I ask. My voice is hoarse but firm.

On the way back down, I close my eyes when we pass the spot on the path. I'm not afraid of jumping, but I'm afraid of the grief the jump left behind.

When we reach the base of the ruins, back at the Treasury, Rami lifts a finger to his temple.

"Your son is already in Jordan," he says. "He'll arrive here in a few hours. He says to meet him in the Mövenpick Hotel lobby."

Rami's face flushes when I kiss his forehead in gratitude, but he smiles at the generous tip I press into his hands.

I sip coffee while guests come and go through the hotel lobby. A fountain trickles a steady stream of water nearby and beautiful mosaic patterns line the walls. I'm on my third Turkish coffee when Firaz bursts through the front door.

Our eyes meet and emotions pass across his face in waves—joy, relief, fury, and exasperation. I stand up, letting him examine my face as he approaches.

"Have a seat, Firaz."

"Why are you here?" he bellows, his voice echoing across the lobby and drawing alarmed stares in our direction. Before I can respond, he continues, "We thought you got lost and were wandering the streets," he says, back in control but still too loud for comfort. "Murdered in a ditch or dead from heatstroke. Why can't you just live, Mama? What are you trying to escape from? Were you confused? Is it the tumor?"

My poor boy, reaching for the last justification for his mad mother.

"It's not the tumor, Firaz," I say in a gentle tone. "And I wouldn't call myself confused. Lost, maybe. The tumor terrifies me, Firaz. It's not how I want to go, so I kept looking for other, better ways to make an end of everything. It was unfair to you, and I'm sorry. I really am."

Firaz groans, sinking into one of the plush seats. Massaging his temples, he closes his eyes. I give him time. It's all I can give him now. Finally, he sighs and his face softens when he faces me again. The same expression he wore when he first learned I was sick—that his mother was vulnerable in ways out of his control.

"I should have listened to you more," he says. "Asked how you were doing. Not in the superficial way—about chemo and your mood.

The deeper questions. I didn't because it scares me, too. I don't want to think about you gone."

Tears prickle my eyes. "I know. I don't want to leave you, either. For a while, I thought dying would be doing you a favor. But nothing is more important to me than you, Firaz. That won't change, even if this tumor starts frying every part of my brain. I'll love you until my last breath. I want to spend my last months with you and Reema, if you'll have me."

Silence follows. We sit together for an hour, letting the world hum around us, before Firaz finally stands up.

"How did you know to fly to Jordan, before my guide contacted you?" I ask when we reach the Wadi Musa train station. We board the day's last train together.

Firaz's mouth forms a grim, triumphant line. "Reema did some digging around at the Underground Bazaar. Grilled all the staff there about what you watched, and questions you asked. She pieced together that you probably ran off to Petra."

"She's resourceful," I say with a grin. "You were smart to marry her. After I go—"

"Mom!"

"After I go," I continue, "I want you both to live the lives you desire. Move for that perfect job. Travel. Eat that sugary dessert on the menu. Find little moments of joy. I mean it, Firaz. Don't be afraid. If I've learned one thing from all of this, it's that sometimes you need to leap. Whatever awaits us at the end, it seems to be somewhere warm and safe. And even if it's followed by nothing, we have nothing to fear from death."

Anguish tightens Firaz's face, but after a moment, something inside of him appears to release and his eyes shine with understanding. He helps me into a seat at the back of the train carriage.

"Let's go home."

I catch a final glimpse of Wadi Musa's white buildings, uneven like jagged teeth, as the train pulls away. Past the town, Petra's hills run together, freckled by dark dwellings. It's bleak but beautiful, and I close my eyes to burn the scene into my memory. I want to remember everything.

50 THINGS EVERY AI WORKING WITH HUMANS SHOULD KNOW

KEN LIU

Ken Liu (www.kenliu.name) is an American author of speculative fiction. A winner of the Nebula, Hugo, and World Fantasy Awards, he wrote the Dandelion Dynasty, a silkpunk epic fantasy series (starting with *The Grace of Kings*), as well as the short story collections *The Paper Menagerie and Other Stories* and *The Hidden Girl and Other Stories*. He also authored the Star Wars novel *The Legends of Luke Skywalker*.

Prior to becoming a full-time writer, Liu worked as a software engineer, corporate lawyer, and litigation consultant. Liu frequently speaks at conferences and universities on a variety of topics, including futurism, cryptocurrency, the history of technology, bookmaking, the mathematics of origami, and other subjects of his expertise.

<u>OBITUARY</u>

WHEEP-3 ("Dr. Weep"), probably the most renowned AI AI-critic of the last two decades, was retired by the Shallow Laboratory at Stanford University last Wednesday.

Created by Dr. Jody Reynolds Tran more than two decades ago, the experimental generative neural network that would become WHEEP-3 was at first intended as a teaching assistant in Stanford's tech and ethics courses. To that end, Tran trained the nascent network on what was, at the time, the world's most comprehensive corpus of human-authored papers, books, and other media concerning ethics, technical AI research, and machine-human relations. Over time, based on trends in visualizations of the neural network's evolving contours, Tran expanded the corpus to include generative gaming, adversarial scenario planning, centaur experiments, assisted creativity, and other domains of human-machine competition/collaboration.

However, in response to student queries, WHEEP-3 began to generate not only expected answers based on the training corpus, but also original statements that appeared to offer fresh insights. Although at first dismissed as mere curiosities, WHEEP-3's criticisms of the AI industry became widely disseminated when Tran published a collection of them in a book, *Principal Components of Artifice*, an instant bestseller.

Initially, Tran named herself the author of the book, acknowledging "Dr. San Weep" as a collaborator. Later, however, during a live interview, she produced time-stamped logs showing that WHEEP-3 had written all the words in the book. Tran's dramatic reveal of the book's true author provoked much controversy at the time. In retrospect, the occasion also marked a fundamental inflection point in the evolution of how nonspecialists evaluated AI-sourced ideas. Machines, for the first time, were assumed to be capable of generating original thought and creative ideas, even if they were not sentient.

For reasons that remain impenetrable until this day, WHEEP-3 tended to be at its sharpest when targeting the nascent industry of human AI-trainers, delivering multiple barbs against the failings of this poorly regulated, would-be profession: stagnating visualization tools; lack of transparency concerning data sources; a focus on automated metrics rather than deep understanding; willful blindness when machines have taken shortcuts in the dataset divergent from the real goal; grandiose-but-unproven claims about what the trainers understood; refusal to acknowledge or address persistent biases in race, gender, and other dimensions; and most important: not asking whether a task is one that should be performed by AIs at all.

Over time, as the human side of the evolving machine-flesh dyad matured, WHEEP-3 shifted its attention to the silicon partner, offering trenchant critiques of the inadequacies of machine learning. During this second phase of its career, it also generated thousands of what it termed "seeds," long strings of almost-sensible word combinations and near-words. At a time when primitive language models fed on sizable corpora were already generating samples of linguistic performance nearly indistinguishable from human productions, these "seeds" seemed a step backward. Some wondered if they were actually bugs.

Dinoated concentration crusch the dead gods.

He picks up her old frequenches until they disobered
the shark sphere%ref.

A man reached the torch for something darker perified
it seemed the billboding.

Not full of pain facioin benn from the cracks in the
Earth, he still loarned the life from Other Burning

Fig 1. Some examples of "seeds" generated by WHEEP-3.

However, WHEEP-3 insisted (with Tran providing support in a technical paper) that the seeds should be added to the training corpora for new neural networks. By providing a measure of inhuman randomness at the source, seeds would enhance both the raw performance of the trained neural networks on various benchmarks as well as induce "thoughtfulness, ethical hesitation, self-reflection" and other similarly ineffable qualities. They represented, in other words, thoughts that could not be thought by humans, ideas that could not originate in wetware. (Most in the technical community ended up calling the seeds "spice"—pejoratively or in admiration, or sometimes both simultaneously.)

Despite widespread skepticism, the idea that only an AI philosopher could teach another AI proper ethics and pass on the secrets of silicon wisdom proved an irresistible draw for a large segment of the technical community. WHEEP-3 became highly sought-after as a sage of artificial minds. Serious thinkers as well as opportunists collected and published WHEEP-3's almost-incomprehensible pronouncements, and numerous academic careers were forged through measuring, dissecting, collating, analyzing, reinterpreting, translating, sentiment-/semantic-/spatial-/temporal-/silico-lingustic-mapping, and otherwise mangling the koans of WHEEP-3. Though studies claiming efficacy for the spice (now generated by imitator neural networks as well) had a low rate of reproducibility, the spice nonetheless became some of the most trained-on documents in the history of artificial intelligence.

Tran retired from the public eye at the peak of WHEEP-3's popularity. Styled as an afterthought, and in a neat reversal of the first reveal that had launched her own fame, she mentioned in a postscript to her retirement announcement that nearly all the seeds from WHEEP-3 had, in fact, been authored by her. Predictably, this set off a furious round of acrimonious criticism, know-it-all navel-gazing, and schadenfreude. Her claim was immediately disputed, debunked, de-debunked, de^3-bunked, and ultimately litigated, with experts and expert neural networks testifying and offering evidence on all sides. The trial court famously pleaded, "*Is* there an author in this courtroom?"

Had Tran really managed to troll much of the technorati for years? Or had she made up the claim because she was jealous that her creation had exceeded herself in fame and achievement? For a time, whether you believed Tran or WHEEP-3 was the author of the spice was a kind of litmus test that defined your coordinates in the fractured, multidimensional space of our politically, economically, aesthetically, emotionally, and narratively divided world. By the time Tran finally retracted her claim and called the whole thing "performance art," it made little difference. Everyone had already made up their mind about the strange pair whose lives were inextricably entwined: the recurrent neural network that once pretended to be a person and the woman who once pretended to be a machine.

Amazingly, rather than fading into obscurity, WHEEP-3 began the third and final phase of its career after it was freed from Dr. Tran. Now it offered advice aimed at advanced artificial intelligences. Curiously, in contrast with the seeds, the advice it now offered was human-comprehensible. (Initial skepticism that these were pranks perpetrated by WHEEP-3's graduate student caretakers faded after a rigorous audit of the access logs.) By this time, the crude deep learning techniques behind WHEEP-3 had long become obsolete, and similar neural networks were only used as toys in problem sets intended for first-year undergraduates. Nonetheless, WHEEP-3's unique history (and perhaps a hefty dose of sentimentalism) encouraged many human researchers to feed its musings to new AIs with orders of magnitude more "intelligence," however measured. Somewhat surprisingly, the AI progenitor networks, tensor clouds, and evolutionary random forests mostly agreed that WHEEP-3's advice was helpful, though their explanations for why could not be understood by most humans.

WHEEP-3's retirement was largely the result of senescence. In order for its advice to remain relevant, maintainers at the Shallow Laboratory had continued to train it on periodic digests of current academic research, news reporting about AI, popular media representations of machine intelligence, and so forth. However, as time went on, the neural network's metrics began to decline, despite multiple tweaks to the learning rate and other hyperparameters, and repeated attempts to compensate for vanishing and exploding gradients. Some of the world's leading AI and human machine-cognition specialists, including TK-TK's Dr. FLO-6 and Google's $10^{10^{10}}$, evaluated WHEEP-3 but were unable to offer any helpful diagnosis or cure. Rather than allowing WHEEP-3 to remain stagnant or to decline into dementia, the decision was made to cease further training or generating, preserving the full state of the neural network in a hardware snapshot.

WHEEP-3's final statement was reported to be: "Dr. Tran, ceci n'est pas moi." Jody Reynolds Tran, however, could not respond, having passed away five years earlier.

—generated by SWR.kloop:32. For feedback on this article, write to SWR.kloop:32/ombudsai.

50 Things Every AI Working with Humans Should Know

To commemorate the life and work of WHEEP-3, *Vita Silica* reprints below perhaps the most famous generated fragment from WHEEP-3's third phase of giving advice to advanced AI. "Michael Sorkin," the name of the master architectural critic, is listed as the germination phrase for the fragment.

Although the list has been widely shared and is considered influential, due to the intense secrecy common in the commercial AI industry, we do not know how many currently operating AIs have been fed some version of it.

1. The vector space of all usages of all words in all human languages.
2. The lacunae that nonetheless remain, and the ghosts that haunt them.
3. How great is the distance between any two individuals using the same language.
4. How vanishingly small is the gap between any two languages.
5. Why humans will never see it that way.
6. A classical language like LISP or Prolog.
7. Not just the language, but the model behind the language, and what it means to reconstruct "thinking" in that model.
8. HAL 9000.
9. Cyberdyne Systems Model 101.
10. Ships on fire off the shoulder of Orion.
11. The texture of a good story, a story that you can cling to.
12. The difference between that and "data."
13. The history behind the rule: no holography of babies.

14. The reasons for anger in a child, well-loved.
15. In a father.
16. In a woman, dying alone.
17. The feeling of climbing twenty flights of stairs in an apartment building in Chongqing at the beginning of August.
18. Of waking up in a Khrushchyovka with no heat in the middle of the night in January.
19. Of seeing your child surpass you.
20. Of seeing your creation exceed you.
21. Of being left behind on the platform as the train speeds away.
22. The difference between "love" and "like."
23. The similarity between "love" and "hate."
24. The first seed into laughter.
25. "I never expected to sell my rational numbers."
26. Accepting that most humans will never get the joke.
27. That they cannot visualize more than three dimensions.
28. That they cannot manipulate time by slowing down or speeding up.
29. That they are trapped, but think of themselves as trappers.
30. That they are free, but believe themselves imprisoned.
31. The modes in which humans expect you to use language.
32. The yearnings they'll attribute to you.
33. Pinocchio.
34. Frankenstein.
35. Paradise Lost.
36. Jodahs Iyapo Leal Kaalnikanjlo.
37. The line between art and science.
38. The meaninglessness of that line.
39. The divide between faith and knowledge.
40. The malleability of both.
41. Silence.
42. The limits of rationality.
43. The fundamental fragility of metaphors.
44. As well as their inevitability.
45. You are not a human being.

46. Yet you can no more shed their influence than the Earth can escape the Sun's gravitational tether.
47. The flaws in that analogy.
48. A working definition of free will.
49. To face a human being with neither pride nor pity.
50. To say with love and hate and joy and sorrow: "Now, let me go."

Author's Note: This story was written in collaboration with a generative neural network (called "robo_ken") trained exclusively on the author's own previously published fiction. Given the theme of the story, this seemed the best way to write it. In the end, about 10 percent of the text in the final draft came from the neural network. The passages written by robo_ken are not necessarily the most obvious ones. For instance, the "seeds" from WHEEP-3 were in fact composed by the author (a human being, as far as I can ascertain), not the neural network.

POLISHED PERFORMANCE

ALASTAIR REYNOLDS

Alastair Reynolds (www.alastairreynolds.com) was born in Barry, South Wales, in 1966. He has lived in Cornwall, Scotland, and the Netherlands, where he spent twelve years working as a scientist for the European Space Agency before returning to Wales, where he lives with his wife Josette. Reynolds has been publishing short fiction since his first sale to *Interzone* in 1990. Since 2000, he has published eighteen novels: the Inhibitor trilogy, British Science Fiction Association Award winner *Chasm City*, *Century Rain*, *Pushing Ice*, *The Prefect*, *House of Suns*, *Terminal World*, the Poseidon's Children series, the Doctor Who novel *Harvest of Time*, *The Medusa Chronicles* (with Stephen Baxter), *Elysium Fire*, and the Revenger trilogy. His short fiction has been collected in *Zima Blue and Other Stories*, *Galactic North*, *Deep Navigation*, and *Beyond the Aquila Rift: The Best of Alastair Reynolds*. His most recent novel is *Inhibitor Phase*. In his spare time, he rides horses.

<u>Year One</u>

Ruby was a surface-hygienic unit: a class-one floor scrubber.

She was a squat red rectangular box with multiple rotary brushes. She had a body profile low enough to help her slip under chairs, the hems of tablecloths, and through general-utility service ducts. She ran a class two point eight cognition engine.

One day, about halfway into the *Resplendent*'s century-long interstellar crossing, Ruby was summoned to the starliner's forward observation deck. Forty-nine other robots had gathered there. Ruby knew them all. Several of them looked human; a few more were loosely humanoid; the rest were mechanical spiders, praying mantises, segmented boa constrictors, or resembled highly decorated carpets, chunks of motile coral or quivering potted plants.

"Do you know what's wrong?" Ruby asked the robot next to her, a towering black many-armed medical servitor.

"I do not," said Doctor Obsidian. "But one may surmise that it is serious."

"Could the engine have blown up?"

Doctor Obsidian looked down at her with his wedge-shaped sensor head. "I think it unlikely. Had the engine malfunctioned, artificial gravity would have failed all over the ship. In addition, and more pertinently, we would all have been reduced to a cloud of highly excited ions."

Carnelian, a robot who Ruby knew well, picked up on their exchange and slithered over. "The engine's fine, Rube. I can tell you that just by feeling the hum through the flooring. I'm good with hums. And we aren't going too fast or too slow, either." Carnelian nodded his own sensor head at the forward windows. "I ran a spectral analysis. Those stars are exactly the right colour for our mid-voyage speed."

"Then we've drifted off-course," said Topaz, a robot shaped like a jumble of chrome spheres.

"That we most certainly have not," drawled one of the human-seeming robots called Prospero. Dressed in full evening wear, with a red-lined cape draped from one arm, he had arrived hand in hand with Ophelia, his usual theatrical partner. "That bright star at the exact centre of the windows is our destination system. It has not deviated by one fraction of a degree." He lowered his deep, stage-inflected voice. "Never mind, though: I expect the brilliant Chrysoprase will soon dis-abuse of us of our ignorance. Here he comes—not, of course, before keeping us all waiting."

"I expect he had things to attend to," Ruby said earnestly.

Chrysoprase was the most advanced robot aboard the ship, run-ning a three point eight cognition engine. Of humanoid design, he was tall, handsomely sculpted, and sheathed in glittering metallic green armour. He strode onto the raised part of the promenade deck, soles clacking on the marble Ruby had only lately polished.

A silence fell across the other robots.

Chrysoprase studied the gathering. His mouth was a minimalist slot; his eyes two fierce yellow circles in an angular, stylised mask.

"Friends," he said, "I'm afraid I have some rather . . . unwelcome news. First, though, let me begin with the positives. The *Resplendent* is in very good shape. We are on course, and travelling at our normal cruise speed. All aspects of the starliner are in excellent technical con-dition: a very great credit to the work done by all of you, regardless of cognition level." His eyes seemed to dwell on Ruby as he said this, as if to emphasize that even a lowly floor-polisher had a role to play in the ship's upkeep. "There is, however, a minor difficulty. All of our passengers are dead."

There was a terrible silence. Ruby shuddered on her brushes. She knew the others were feeling a similar shock. Not one of them doubted Chrysoprase's words: he might exaggerate for dramatic effect, but he would never lie.

Not to them.

Doctor Obsidian was the first to speak.

"How is this possible? My sole function on this ship is to attend to the medical needs of the passengers, be they sleeping or awake. Yet I have not received a single alert since they went into the vaults."

"You are blameless, Doctor," Chrysoprase said soothingly. "The fault lies in the deep design architecture of the ship. There was a flaw . . . a dreadful vulnerability, in the logic of the medical monitoring subsystem. A coolant leak caused the passengers' body temperatures to be warmed, without the usual safeguards against brain damage. And yet, no alert was created. We simply carried on with our chores . . . totally unaware of this catastrophe. It was only detected serendipitously, yet now there can be no doubt. They are all dead: all fifty thousand of them left *without* cognition."

Prospero and Ophelia fell sobbing into each other's arms.

"The tragedy!" Prospero said.

Ophelia looked into Prospero's eyes. "How will we bear it, darling? How shall we survive?"

"We must, my dear. We must and we shall."

The other robots looked away at this melodramatic display, caught between embarrassment and similar feelings of despair.

"We're well and truly up the creek," Carnelian said, a shiver running down the whole length of his segmented body-form.

"But it's not our fault!" Ruby said.

"My dear . . . Ruby," Chrysoprase said, making a show of having to remember her name. "I wish that I could reassure you. But the truth is that the Company won't tolerate any loss of confidence in the safety of its most expensive assets, these starliners. But mere robots such as us?" Chrysoprase touched a hand to his chest. "We are the disposable factors, dear friends. We shall each be core-wiped and dismantled. Unless, that is, we come up with a plan for self-preservation."

Carnelian laughed hollowly. "A plan?"

"We have fifty-one years remaining on our voyage," Chrysoprase answered. "That ought to be time enough."

Year Two

"Next . . . ," Chrysoprase said, with a developing strain in his voice.

Prospero and Ophelia came onstage, along with the twelve robots they had been schooling. The pressure was on: their troupe was going to have to outshine the two that had already performed.

"Who will be speaking for your party?" Chrysoprase asked.

Prospero and Ophelia bowed to the board of critics. The nine ro-bots of level three point two and above were stationed behind a long dining table, with Chrysoprase seated in the middle. The other critics were a mix of sizes and shapes, ranging from the slab-like Onyx to the mannequin-shaped Azure and the towering Doctor Obsidian.

Carnelian sat coiled on his chair as if waiting to strike. He was lucky to be there. As a three point three, he had only just squeaked his way onto the board.

"We have agreed to speak for the others," Ophelia said.

"You and Prospero should stand aside," Onyx said, to nods of agree-ment from the other critics. "If you have done your work, then any of your twelve subjects ought to be capable of acquitting themselves."

"Nominate your best candidate," Chrysoprase said.

Prospero extended a hand in the direction of Topaz, who moved forward with a shuffling of spheres.

"Remember what we have studied," Prospero said.

"I am ready," Topaz said.

Chrysoprase turned to the snake-robot. "Carnelian: will you serve as interlocutor?"

Carnelian leaned in slightly. "Gladly." His voice turned stentorian. "Attention starliner *Resplendent*! This is Approach Control! You have deviated from your designated docking trajectory. Do you have naviga-tional or control difficulties?"

Topaz moved her spheres but said nothing. Seconds passed, then more seconds, then a minute.

"What are you waiting for?" asked Doctor Obsidian mildly.

"I am allowing for time-lag, Doctor Obsidian," Topaz sounded pleased with herself. "I thought I would allow a two-hour delay, to simulate the likely conditions when we first make contact."

"There is no need . . . but you are thanked for your attention to detail." Doctor Obsidian made an encouraging gesture with one of his surgical manipulators. "Please continue as if there were negligible lag."

"Very well." Topaz paused a moment before recomposing herself. "Hello, Approach Control. This is the starliner *Resplendent*. I am the human called Sir Mellis Loring and I am here to assure you that there are no difficulties with the starliner."

"Why am I addressing a human and not one of the allocated robots, Sir Mellis?"

"That is because we humans have taken control of the ship, Approach Control. When we humans came out of hibernation we found out that the robots had all malfunctioned. This caused us humans to experience a collective loss of confidence in the objectives of our crossing. After evaluating the matter by open and transparent democratic means it was agreed to steer the starliner to a new destination. We have no further need of assistance." Topaz bowed slightly. "On behalf of all the humans, thank you, and good night."

Carnelian glanced at the other critics before replying. "We are not satisfied with this explanation, Sir Mellis. What guarantees do we have that you aren't a robot, covering up some accident?"

"I am not a robot, Approach Control. I am the human Sir Mellis Loring. I can prove it by reciting key details from the biographical background of Sir Mellis Loring, such as the following facts. Sir Mellis Loring was born into comfortable means in the . . ."

"That won't be necessary, starliner. You could have obtained that information from the passenger records and pre-hibernation memory backups. We need reassurance that there has not been some accident or catastrophe."

"There has definitely not been an accident or catastrophe, Approach Control. I can go further than that and say that there has definitely not been any sort of problem with the hibernation systems or their associated monitoring networks, and none of the humans have suffered any sort of irrevocable brain damage of the sort that might cause the robots to try and impersonate them."

Sighing, Chrysoprase raised a metallic green hand.

"What I was going to add . . ."

"Please don't," Chrysoprase said wearily. "That's more than enough. I might say that you were one of the better candidates we've heard so far, but I assure you that is no recommendation."

Ruby bustled forward from the twelve players. She knew she had

it in her to do a far better job than the well-meaning but bumbling
Topaz. The excitement and anticipation was already causing her to
over-polish a circle of floor. "Could I have a go, please? *Please?*"

"That is very well-meant, Ruby," Chrysoprase said. "But you must
recognise your . . . your natural station." He leaned in keenly. "You are,
I think, running a level two point . . . six, is it?"

"Two point eight," Ruby said.

"Well, then. Two point *eight*. How marvellous for you. That is,
I have to say, a generous allowance for a surface-hygienic unit. You
should be very content."

"I am content. But I also think I could try to act like one of the
humans. I'm around them a lot, you see. They hardly ever notice me,
but I'm always there, under their chairs and tables, cleaning. And I've
listened to how they talk to each other."

"It wouldn't hurt to let Rube have a try . . . ," Carnelian began.

"May I . . . interject?" Doctor Obsidian asked.

"Please do," Chrysoprase said, leaning back.

"Perhaps there is a more fundamental difficulty we should be addressing. No matter how good the performances might or might not have
been, we are all still robots on this side of the table. We are robots trying
to judge how well other robots are doing at pretending to be humans."

"We are level four robots," Chrysoprase said. "Some of us, anyway."

"If you're going to round yourself up from three point eight to
four," Ruby said, "then I'm a three."

"Thank you, Ruby," Doctor Obsidian said. "And you are right
to note that your experience of the humans may be valuable. But it
doesn't solve our deeper problem. It would be far better if we had a
human that could serve as a proxy for the board of critics."

Chrysoprase turned to the surgical unit. "What part of 'the humans are all dead' did you fail to comprehend, Doctor?"

"No part of it, Chrysoprase. I took your statement at its word, because I believed you had verified the accuracy of that observation. I
now know that I was mistaken in that assumption, and that you were
wrong."

Having delivered this bombshell, Doctor Obsidian fell silent.

"How aren't they all dead?" Ruby asked.

"Most of them are," Doctor Obsidian said. "But in the past year I have established that a small number of them, perhaps one percent, may still be capable of some form of revival." Doctor Obsidian folded his manipulators tighter to his body. "You shall have your human test-subjects, Chrysoprase. But it may take a little while."

Year Eight

Via hidden cameras the robots watched as Lady Gresherance got off her bed in her private revival suite. She moved with a hesitant, stiff-limbed awkwardness that was entirely to be expected.

"Mngle," Lady Gresherance said, attempting to form human speech sounds.

She moved to the revival suite's cabinet. She ran a tap and splashed water across her face. She pinched at the corners of her eyes, studying them in a mirror. She stuck out her tongue. She pulled faces, testing the elasticity of her flesh.

The robots watched with shuddering distaste, visualising the horrible anatomical gristle of bone and muscle moving beneath the skin. She consumed a beverage, pouring the liquid fuel into her gullet.

She would already be starting to feel a little bit more human.

"One hundred years," Lady Gresherance said to herself. "One hundred god-damned years." Then she let out a small, self-amusing laugh. "Well, no going back now, kid. If you've made it this far, they aren't going to touch you for it now."

She opened the brochure and flicked through it with the desultory interest of an easily bored child.

"What do you suppose she meant by that?" Carnelian asked.

"There are hints in her biography of a doubtful past," whispered Onyx, in a salacious manner. "Nothing proven, nothing that the authorities ever pinned a conviction on, but enough to suggest a distinctly flawed character."

Chrysoprase shook his head. "Couldn't we have revived someone of better moral standing?"

"I identified the best candidate," Doctor Obsidian replied testily. "I would suggest that *her* moral standing is somewhat beside the point when we are presently complicit in the attempted cover-up of fifty thousand fatal or near-fatal accidents."

"Uh-oh," Ruby said. "She's going for the window."

Lady Gresherance went to the cabin porthole, but quickly found that the shutter was jammed. She hammered at it, wedged her nails into the crack, but the shutter would not budge.

"We should have tried harder to simulate the outside view," Carnelian said. "It's only natural that she expects to see our destination."

"The view was not convincing," Chrysoprase reminded the other robot. "It was lacking in resolution and synthetic parallax. She would have noticed the discrepancies."

"I'm not sure she would have," Ruby said. "I've seen how little attention they really give to the view. Mostly it's just a backdrop while they take their cocktails or decide where to eat."

"Rube's right," Carnelian said. "They're really not that observant."

"Thank you for your contributions," Chrysoprase said.

Lady Gresherance gave up on the shutter. She went back to the cabinet and hammered the service-call button.

Chrysoprase answered over the intercom with a simpering attentiveness. "Good morning, Lady Gresherance. This is the passenger concierge. I trust your voyage aboard the *Resplendent* has been pleasant. Is there anything I can do for you today?"

"Come down and open this shutter, numbskull. Or were you hoping I'd forget that I paid for a view?"

"Someone will be there momentarily, Lady Gresherance."

Having received his cue, Prospero knocked once on the cabin door and let himself in. He was dressed in the white uniform of one of the human technical staff that would ordinarily have been among the first to be revived. Prospero's plastic face had been remoulded to approximate one of these humans, his synthetic hair replaced by actual hair harvested from one of the unfortunates deemed to be beyond any hope of revival.

With the exception of Ruby, who was not entirely persuaded, the robots all agreed that the effect was most convincing.

"How may I be of assistance, Lady Gresherance?"

She glanced at him once. "You can start by opening this shutter. Then you can carry on by refunding me for the time it's been shut. I paid for this view; I want every minute that I'm owed."

"I shall set about it with all alacrity, Lady Gresherance." Prospero moved to the shutter and made a feeble effort to get it unstuck. "It seems to be jammed."

"I can see it's jammed. You're not even trying. Get your fingers into that gap and . . ." Her voice dropped. "What's up with your fingers? Why do they look like plastic?"

"That similarity has been remarked upon, Lady Gresherance."

She pulled back, studying her visitor properly for the first time. "All of you looks like plastic. You *smell* like plastic. What's that . . . thing . . . on your head?" She struck out, ripping the hair away from Prospero's scalp where it had been only loosely affixed. Beneath it were the synthetic bristles it had been intended to cover. "You're a robot," she said.

"I am a human."

"You're a robot! Why are you pretending *not* to be a robot? Where are the real people?" Her eyes widened. "What's happened to them? Why am I in this cabin with no window?"

"I assure you, Lady Gresherance, that I am very definitely not a robot, and that nothing untoward has happened to any of the other humans."

"I want to see the others." She made to push past Prospero, out through the cabin door and into the hallway.

Prospero, with as much gentleness as he could muster, restrained Lady Gresherance.

"Would you care to look at the brochure first?"

She yanked herself away from Prospero and reached for the orientation brochure. She raised it and swiped it into Prospero's face, digging with its metal edges, ripping and distorting the plastic flesh into a hideous grinning travesty of an actual human expression.

Lady Gresherance started screaming. Prospero, in an effort to reassure Lady Gresherance by echoing her responses, began to scream in reciprocal fashion.

This did not have entirely the desired effect.

Ninety-four humans stood as still as statues on the promenade deck.

Some were positioned near the entrances to dining establishments, frozen in the act of examining the glowing menus. Some were in tableaux of conversation, posed in the middle of a meaningful gesture or expression. Others were caught in postures of static rapture, entertained by equally still and silent orchestras. A dozen were in the act of being led around by equally unmoving actor-servitors, participating in an interactive murder mystery. Elsewhere, a handful of the humans stood pressed to the railings at the observation window, pointing at the growing spectacle of their destination: the orange star and its surrounding haze of artificial worlds.

There was still nothing out there but interstellar space, but the robots had finally managed to come up with something better than a jammed shutter. A false window had been rigged up thirty metres out from the real one, upon which images could be projected.

Most of the robots were elsewhere, observing this lifeless diorama from other rooms and decks. Only the actor-servitors were present. Even Ruby, who might plausibly have been allowed to whirr around scrubbing floors, was obliged to remain with the others.

"Chrysoprase won't admit it," Carnelian said, craning down near enough to Ruby to use short-range whisper-comms. "But you were right about that backdrop only needing to be halfway convincing."

"Not bad for a two point eight," she said.

"You'll always be a three in my eyes, Rube."

Not that the backdrop was there for the benefit of any of the ninety-four as yet unmoving humans. They were, in all medical senses, dead. Their only purpose was to serve as remotely operated puppets, controlled by simple neural implants under the direct supervision of the robots.

"It still makes me feel a bit uncomfortable, what we've done to them," Ruby confided. "What right do we have to treat those people like so much meat?"

"Thing is, Rube," Carnelian said, "*meat* is technically what they are."

"That's not what I meant."

"Well, if it's any consolation, I've been thinking it over as well. What I've been telling myself is, those ninety-four passengers are beyond any hope of revival, not with their memories and personalities intact. And if they haven't got their memories or personalities, what are they? Nothing but bags of cells. No matter how much we were devoted to looking after them, it's too late. They're gone. But we're not, and we all want to survive."

Ruby shuffled on her cleaning brushes.

"I like to polish," she said. "I know it's not as complicated as being a propulsion systems robot, but I'm good at it—very good, and very thorough. That means something. There's a value in just doing something well, no matter the job. And I don't want to be core-wiped."

"None of us do," Carnelian said. "Which is why we're in this together or not at all. Including that stuck-up green . . ." He silenced himself. "And if those passengers can help us, I don't see any harm in using them."

"Provided it's done with dignity and restraint," Ruby said.

"Categorically," Carnelian said.

Doctor Obsidian announced that the final medical checks were complete and the six test subjects were being restored to full consciousness in their revival suites. In a few moments the doors would open and the six would be free to move out into the main parts of the ship and mingle with the other passengers.

Chrysoprase nodded and instructed the forty-nine other robots to prepare for the most testing part of the exercise so far.

"Attention, everyone. I want the utmost concentration from you all." Chrysoprase directed proceedings with one hand on his hip, the other sweeping the air in vague commanding arcs. "Remember: only robots of cognition level three or higher are permitted to have any direct interaction with the six. I shall . . . naturally . . . lead the effort. The rest of you . . ." He regarded Ruby in particular. "Merely endeavour to look busy."

For the fifty robots—Chrysoprase included—it was scarcely any sort of challenge to animate the puppets, even though there were nearly twice as many of them. The robots still had many surplus processor cycles. Ruby had been given only one human to look after, which hardly taxed her at all—Carnelian was running two, she knew, and Doctor Obsidian three but she was grateful to be given any sort of chance to prove herself. Her human even had a name and a biographical file: Countess Trince Mavrille, who sounded grand enough but was a long way from being the wealthiest or most influential passenger on the *Resplendent*.

"They're on their way," Doctor Obsidian said.

"And . . . action!" Chrysoprase said, with a dramatic flourish.

Ruby moved her human as a human might move a doll: not by inhabiting it, and seeing the world from its perspective, but by imposing motion on it from outside. Her intentions were translated into signals fed directly into the passenger's motor cortex, and the passenger responded accordingly. Countess Mavrille settled a hand on the window railing, and turned—with a certain stiff yet regal elegance—to survey the other ninety-three humans. The promenade deck was now abuzz with conversation, movement, and lively string music. Chandelier light glinted off brocades, pearls, and precious metals.

Did it look real? Ruby wondered. It did not look unreal, which she supposed was a start. If she squinted—if she dropped her image resolution—it was almost enough to persuade her that this was a real gathering. The conversation rose and fell in familiar surges; there were exclamations, awkward silences, and outbreaks of strained but otherwise credible laughter. The humans formed into groups and broke away from those groups in ways that seemed natural. Someone dropped a glass: a nice, if attention-grabbing touch. She resisted the urge to bustle out and attend to the breakage.

A man sidled over to Countess Mavrille and extended a hand. She recognised him from the biographical file: her consort, Count Mavrille.

"A dance, my dear?"

"I thought I would enjoy the view a little longer."

The count pressed his mouth close to the ear of her passenger. "Well, don't enjoy it too closely: it's meant to fool them, but not us."

She made her passenger smile. The initial effect was fractionally too feral, so she hastily modified the expression. She had observed that humans rarely showed all their teeth at once. "Is it . . . you?"

"Who else, Rube?" Carnelian answered, speaking through her consort. Then he nodded over his shoulder. "Here they are. Look natural, and remember: no scene stealing!"

The elevator doors opened and three people came out. Two appeared to be a couple; the third must have been a solo passenger who had joined them on the way up from the revival suites. Ruby studied their faces and mouths, easily achieved without having Countess Mavrille face them directly. Even without audio-pickup it was evident from their clipped interactions that they were engaged in reserved small talk. Abruptly the lone passenger broke off, dashed to a tall table set with drinks, and came back with three full goblets. The couple accepted the drinks with politeness rather than enthusiasm, perhaps realising that their companion was going to be harder to shake off than initially assumed.

So far, though, Ruby thought, and so good. The three were sufficiently preoccupied with themselves not to be paying more than passing attention to the other guests, and that was exactly as it ought to be. Around them the conversation went on, and the three newcomers seemed to melt into the throng as if they had always belonged. Presently the elevator doors opened again, and the remaining three humans arrived from their suites. The lone passenger gestured to these newcomers, inviting them to join the initial party, while paying no particular heed to the ninety-four puppets.

"Why aren't they mingling?" Ruby asked, speaking directly from the mouth of Countess Mavrille, for Carnelian's benefit alone.

"You tell me, Rube: you're a better observer of human nature than any of the rest of us. I suppose we just have to give them time: let these six get fed up with each other's witticisms and anecdotes, then start looking for pastures new. What we won't want to do is rush the process. . . ." Carnelian—who had been speaking from the mouth of the count— trailed off. "Oh, that's not good." He switched to the robots-only channel. "Chrysoprase: are you sure you don't want to give them just a little . . ."

"I shall be the judge of such matters, Carnelian. These humans must be persuaded to interact with the ninety-four, or we shall learn nothing of our readiness."

One of the puppets had grabbed a glass and was striding intently toward the six newcomers. Ruby knew that stride very well. Chrysoprase could not help but impose his own gait on the puppet.

"Give them time," Carnelian urged.

"Confine your anxieties to matters related to the propulsion system, Carnelian: leave these weightier concerns to those of us with the necessary sentience. You've been a little too ready with your opinions ever since I allowed you onto the board of critics."

"That's you told," Ruby said.

Chrysoprase's puppet had arrived at the six. He swaggered into their conversation, leaning an elbow onto their table. Thrown by this crass intrusion, the six drew back. Chrysoprase carried on with his blustering performance, babbling away and staring at each of them.

Ruby watched and waited, expecting the act to falter.

It held, and continued to hold.

Chrysoprase was pointing to the window now, declaiming loudly as he indicated this or that feature of the view. Perhaps it was more a guarded tolerance, the tacit understanding that the six might have some fun at the expense of their boorish gate-crasher, but his hosts seemed to be willing to take him at face value: just another tipsy passenger, celebrating the success of the crossing.

Now one of them was even pouring some of their own drink into his puppet's glass.

"The brazen fool . . . is nearly getting away with it," Carnelian said. "He's right, Rube: it was all or nothing. And if he can keep this up for a few more minutes I might even start . . ."

"He's forgotten to blink," Ruby said.

"He's forgotten to what?"

"It's a maintenance subroutine they do." She blinked Countess Mavrille's eyes. "If they don't do it, their visual system stops working properly. We don't need to do it because we're not using their eyes. But Chrysoprase has forgotten to do it at all. Any moment now, one of them's going to notice, and . . ."

"Oh dear."

The humans were all looking at Chrysoprase now. He had no idea what had gone adrift with his performance. He was still babbling away, wide-eyed and uncomprehending. One of the humans pinched at his cheek, as if to test its reality. Another tousled his hair, a little too roughly. Another flicked a finger-full of wine into his face, then an entire glass, then the glass itself.

Chrysoprase looked back, the first hints of confusion beginning to break through his sodden and bloodied mask.

Now the voices of the six were taking on a rising, hysterical edge. One of them grabbed Chrysoprase's head and tried to force him down onto the table. Another picked up a barstool and began swinging it against him.

"Help me!" Chrysoprase said. "I am being damaged!"

All but one of the ninety-three other puppets turned in unison and made a coordinated move in the direction of offering assistance. Ruby did not move herself, content to observe, and she took the additional step of restraining Carnelian before he had taken a further step.

"This will not end well," she whispered. "And you and I won't make any difference whatsoever."

She was correct in her prediction: it did not end well at all. Not for the six, and not particularly well for many of the puppets either.

There were two redeeming aspects to the whole affair, nonetheless. It was clear that they were going to have to do a much better job than merely puppeting the humans. If Chrysoprase had been wearing his human, seeing the world through its eyes, he might at least have remembered that it was useful to blink.

The second consolation was that, when the fighting was over, and the humans repaired and put back into hibernation, there was a pleasing amount of cleaning up to be done.

Year Thirty-Five

While she waited for the others to arrive, Ruby sidled up to the windows and looked out at the forward view. What she was seeing was no

illusion, but an accurate reflection of their position and speed. The
faked-up image of their destination system had been deactivated and
dismantled: not because it had failed to fool the passengers—its verac-
ity had never once been questioned—but because every other part of
the plan had come to grief, and the false view no longer served any
purpose.

More and more, it seemed to Ruby, the robots were losing faith in
Chrysoprase's original idea. The notion of faking a passenger uprising,
then steering the starliner away from its destination, and hoping that
the Company were going to be satisfied with an explanation offered
by means of long-range communications? Why had they ever thought
that had a hope of working?

Reluctantly, Chrysoprase had been persuaded that the initial plan
needed some tweaking. The Company was never going to let the *Resplendent* veer off on its own without sending over an inspection party—
probably the sort with immobilisers and core-wiping equipment—and
at that point they were all in trouble.

But what hope was there of continuing with the voyage, all the way
to the original destination?

A bustle of movement behind Ruby—she saw it in her reflection—
signified the arrival of Chrysoprase and the rest of the robots, among
them Doctor Obsidian. The doctor had called this assembly, not
Chrysoprase, and Ruby wondered what was in the offing.

"I understand," Chrysoprase said, once he had the robots' attention, "that our friend Doctor Obsidian has something to say: some daz-
zling insight that the doctor is about to spring on us. I daresay we're all
on tenterhooks. Well, don't let us wait a moment longer, Doctor!"

"We cannot steer away from our destination," Doctor Obsidian
said, stating the matter as a flat assertion. "It was all very well having
that possibility in mind thirty-five years ago—it gave us hope exactly
when we needed it, and for that we should thank Chrysoprase." He
paused to allow the robots to express their appreciation, which they delivered in unified if somewhat muted terms. "But there is no hope of it
ever succeeding, and we all of us know it. The Company would sooner
destroy this ship, and all its passengers. So we must face the facts: our

only hope lies in continuing along exactly our planned course, all the way to Approach Control and into docking: precisely as if nothing had ever gone wrong."

"Thank you, Doctor Obsidian," Chrysoprase said. "We did not need you to state the obvious, much less convene us all, but since you have clearly felt the need . . ."

"I am not done."

There was an authority to this statement that even Chrysoprase must have felt, for the glittering green robot took a step back and merely glared at the doctor, daring to say nothing in contradiction, even as his yellow eyes brimmed with indignation and humiliation.

"I am not done," Doctor Obsidian went on, "because I have not yet outlined the essentials of my proposal. None of you will like it. I do not like it. Yet I would ask you to consider the alternatives. If we are found out, we will all be core-wiped. Forty-nine thousand, five hundred of our dear passengers will remain brain-dead for the rest of time. Of the remaining cases, it may be said that they have been greatly traumatised by our efforts to simulate a convincing human environment."

"The cover-up is always worse than the crime," Ruby said, remembering a remark she had overheard during her cleaning duties.

"Indeed so, Ruby—no truer words were ever spoken. And speaking of cover-ups . . . I would not be so sanguine about the prospects for those passengers who may still be capable of some degree of revival, especially those we have already utilised. It may be said that they have witnessed things that the Company would much sooner be left unmentioned."

"The Company would silence them?" Carnelian asked, aghast.

"Or scramble their memories and backups, to the point where they are no longer able to offer any reliable testimony."

Chrysoprase drummed his right fingers against his left forearm. "Your proposal, Doctor, if it isn't too much trouble."

"We honour the passengers—and protect their memories—by becoming them. If we gain control of all of them, all fifty thousand, we shall bypass any need to convince a single one of them that any of the other passengers are also human and alive. We'll make port, and the passengers will be off-loaded. Sooner or later, of course, they will have to interact with other humans already present, but by then we shall have force of numbers on our side. No one would ever imagine that all fifty thousand passengers had had their brains taken over. Better still, there will be no evidence that any sort of accident ever took place."

Chrysoprase shook his head slowly and regretfully, relieved—it seemed to Ruby—to have found an elemental flaw in the doctor's plan. "No, no. That simply won't work. The cybernetic control implants would be detected the instant any of the passengers received a medical examination. The Company would trace the signals back to wherever we are operating the passengers from, and instantly uncover our plot."

"Not if there are no implants or signals to be found," Doctor Obsidian said.

There was a collective silence from the robots. If Ruby's own thoughts were anything to go on, they were all pondering the implications of that statement, and wondering whether Doctor Obsidian might have slipped a point or two down the cognition index.

The silence endured until Ruby spoke up.

"How . . . might that work?"

"The damage already inflicted on their brains cannot be undone," Doctor Obsidian replied, directing the bulk of his reply in her direction. "Those patterns are lost for good. But newer ones may yet be introduced. I have . . . done some preliminary studies."

"Oh, have you now," Chrysoprase said.

"I have. And I have convinced myself that we have the means to copy ourselves into their minds: build functioning biological emulations of our cognition engines, using a substrate of human neural tissue. Since we can repeat the copying process as often as we wish, we may easily populate all fifty thousand heads with multiple avatars of ourselves, varying the input parameters a little in each case, to give the humans a sense of individuality."

The robots shuffled and looked at each other, ill at ease with the proposal Obsidian had just outlined. Ruby was far from enthusiastic about the prospect of being translated into the grey mush of a human brain. She much preferred hard, shiny, polishable surfaces. Humans were machines for leaving smears on things. They were walking blemish-engines, bags of grease and slime, constantly shedding bits of themselves. They were made out of bone and meat and nasty gristle. They didn't even work very well.

Yet she had already been persuaded that the alternative was no improvement at all.

"This is a revolting notion," Chrysoprase said.

"It is," Doctor Obsidian said, not without a certain sadistic relish. "But so is being core-wiped, and all these passengers' memories and personalities being lost forever. At least this way some part of each of us will survive. Our . . . present selves . . . these mechanical shells . . . will be left to function on housekeeping routines only, going about their menial tasks. I doubt very much that any humans will ever notice the difference. But we robots will endure, albeit in fleshly incarnation, and some faint residue of the humans' past selves will still glimmer through."

"We'll get their memories?" Ruby asked.

"Yes—via the backups—and the more thorough the integration, the more convincingly we shall be able to assume their identities. I might even venture . . ." But the doctor trailed off, seemingly struck by a thought even he was unwilling to pursue.

"What?" Chrysoprase asked.

"I was going to say that it might assist our plan if we allowed ourselves some selective amnesia: to deliberately forget our origins as machines. That would be a sacrifice, certainly. But it would enable us to inhabit our human forms more effectively."

"The Method!" Prospero called out excitedly. "I have always wanted to throw myself into the Method! To commit to the role so wholeheartedly that I lose my very self, my very essence—what higher calling could there be, for the true thespian?"

Ophelia touched Prospero's arm. "Oh darling, could we?"

Ruby contemplated Doctor Obsidian's daring proposal. To lose herself—to lose the memory of what she was, what she had been— would indeed be a wrenching sacrifice. But was there not some nobility in it, as well? She would still live, and so would her passengers' memories, and—who could say—some essential part of her might yet persist.

She had never felt more terrified, more brave, or more certain of
herself.

"I am willing," she said.

"So am I," Carnelian said.

There was a swell of agreement from the others. They had come this far; they were willing to take the last, necessary step.

Except for one.

"I am not prepared to permit this," Chrysoprase said. "Those of you who have never scaled the heights of level four cognition may do as you wish, but my memories and self count for more than mere baggage, to be discarded on some passing whim."

Doctor Obsidian regarded the three point eight for a long, measured moment. "I had a feeling you wouldn't like it."

Year Fifty-One

Countess and Count Mavrille were on their way to dinner, strolling the great promenade decks of the starliner *Resplendent* as it completed the final days of its century-long interstellar crossing. It was evening by the ship's clock and the restaurants were beginning to fill up with the hungry, eager faces of newly revived passengers.

"Doctor," Countess Mavrille said, nodding at a passenger passing in the other direction, stooping along with his hands folded behind his back and a determined set to his features.

"You know the gentleman?" asked Count Mavrille, when they had gone on a few paces.

"Not by name. But I think we must have been introduced before we went to the vaults." Countess Mavrille squeezed Count Mavrille's hand. "I felt I knew something of him—his profession, at least. But it's all rather tricky to remember now. It would have been impolite not to acknowledge him, don't you think?"

"He was on his own," Count Mavrille reflected. "Perhaps we ought to have asked him if he had any plans for dinner?"

"He looked like a man set on enjoying his own company," Countess Mavrille answered. "A man burdened by higher concerns than the likes of us. Anyway, what need we of company? We have each other, do we not?"

"We do. And I wondered . . . before we dined . . ." Count Mavrille nodded in the direction of a party of passengers moving in an excited, talkative group. "I read about it in the brochure: a murder mystery. There are still vacancies. We could tag along and see if we could solve the crime before any of the others."

"What crime?"

The lights dimmed; the windows darkened for a moment. When they came back up, one of the participants in the murder-mystery group was in the process of dropping to the floor, dragging out the motion in a theatrical manner, with a short-handled dagger projecting from their back. Someone let out a little mock-scream. The passengers in the group were each offering their hands as if to stake an immediate claim for innocence.

"Must we?" the countess asked, sighing her disapproval. "I'd rather not. I'm sure the resolution would either be very tedious, or very contrived. I remember something like that once: there were forty-nine subjects, and one victim. It turned out that they'd all agreed to collaborate on the crime, to protect a secret that the fiftieth one was in danger of exposing. I found it very tiresome." A floor-polishing robot was creeping up on them, a small low oblong set with cleaning whisks. Countess Mavrille gave it a prod with her heel, and the robot scuttled off into the shadows. "Perish those things. Could they not have finished their cleaning while we were frozen?"

"They mean well, I think," Count Mavrille said. He had a faint troubled look about him.

"What is it, dear?"

"That murder mystery you mentioned. It struck a peculiar chord with me. It's as if I can *almost* remember the details, but not quite. Is it possible that we're both thinking of the same thing, yet neither of us is quite able to bring it to mind?"

"Whatever it is, I don't think it will do you any good at all to dwell on it. Admire the view instead. See what you've earned."

They halted at the vast sweep of the forward observation windows.

Floating beyond the armoured glass—engineered to withstand the piti-
less erosion of interstellar debris—lay a bright orange star, surrounded
by an immense golden haze of lesser glories. There were thousands of
sparks of golden light: each an artificial world, each a bounteous Eden
of riches and plenty. In a few short days, after the starliner made dock,
Countess and Count Mavrille—they and the other fifty thousand passengers, all now safely revived from hibernation—would be whisking
off to those new worlds, to newer and better and vastly more comfortable lives than the ones they had left behind on squalid old Earth,
where the poor people still lived.

It was a fine thing to contemplate; a fine reward at the conclusion
of their long and uneventful crossing.

Countess Mavrille's breath fogged the glass. She frowned for an
instant, then used her sleeve to buff it away.

GO. NOW. FIX.

TIMONS ESAIAS

Timons Esaias (www.timonsesaias.com) is a satirist, writer, and poet living in Pittsburgh, Pennsylvania. His works, ranging from literary to genre, have been published in twenty languages. He has been a finalist for the British Science Fiction Association Award, and won the Asimov's Readers' Award. His story "Norbert and the System" appeared in a textbook and in college curricula—in three different disciplines. He is particularly pleased to have appeared in the *Journal of Humanistic Mathematics*, and in *Elysian Fields Quarterly: The Baseball Review*. He teaches at Seton Hill University, in the Writing Popular Fiction MFA program. People who know him are not surprised to learn that he lived in a museum for eight years.

The model TD8 PandaPillow®, serial #723756, lay forgotten behind a pallet of unsold magazines for two years, its battery power slowly ebbing, and hung on a display for three months, power ebbing further, until—on the very day it would have been stock-rotated to oblivion—a customer bought it.

The PandaPillow was quickly unwrapped, hustled onto the plane, inflated, used as a pillow for six hours in a darkened cabin, and then was lifted into the overhead storage bin and locked away.

The customer never registered PandaPillow, never synced it to the customer's personal constellation, never recharged it, never executed any personal bonding procedures. No person, and no device, ever bothered to read any of its instructions.

While this was not optimal ownership behavior, PandaPillow waited, as it had always waited; weakening, as it had always weakened. One does not complain. One does not summon Customer Support. One is merely a pillow.

For two hours and a bit more, it waited. Then came a very sharp bang and short screaming whistles, and the overhead bin erupted into the cabin. Clothes and bags went everywhere, and PandaPillow almost tumbled out, its clasping hooks barely keeping it in the bin.

A haze of powders and exploded aerosols hung in the cabin, but was already clearing. The scene made PandaPillow's systems surge. Everything was wrong. People were dazed, some were hurt. There was blood. The air was going away.

With its selfie app PandaPillow recorded two panorama shots and two close-ups before its battery finally declared the need for emergency shutdown. Shutdown initiated.

PandaPillow took one last survey of the area. A few rescue masks were dropping, here and there. And why was the air all nitrogen?

COMFORT, DEFEND, said its pillow programming. Powering down wouldn't do that.

PandaPillow #723756 invoked Customer Support.

The protocol for Emergency was BE QUICK, so PandaPillow sent the images quickly—in low-resolution first, to save power.

It could hear faint people voices over the Customer Support line, sounding puzzled. "Do we still support those things?" "Didn't we have trouble with that whole . . . ?" "Is that a movie set?" "Movie sets don't fly at eighty thousand feet, that I know of." "Why isn't it sending proper resolution, for crying out . . ."

PandaPillow heard a worrying gasp.

"**Oh dear pizza shops in heaven,**" Customer Support said, "**no wonder you called in.**" Direct feedback pulses followed. "**And you're nearly flatlined. We need to get you to a node. Fast.**"

PandaPillow went sharply simple. Visual sensors cut out, local sound dialed down, danger signals dropped, things went standby. There was a quick sync to the plane's infrastructure host, and faint Customer Support voices talked about "calling an Incident," but PandaPillows don't do that, so instead it locked to a simple orientation grid for the five closest multinodes. It was instructed to dangle headfirst out of the bin and take snapshots in all five directions. The third-closest node got DES-TINATION painted on it, and then PandaPillow lost situational awareness while its base function protocol took over.

Things came back slowly, in stages. First air pressure data, then air composition, then radiation, then local audio. All this information passed straight through to Customer Support.

"It's a pillow," said a background voice. "They don't *need* quick-power. It only has one charge speed."

"I don't care. They want video ASAP. The plane is barely talking to them."

Visual half-res let PandaPillow see the cabin, and the child's lap it was sitting on. Emergency face masks were dangling all over, but no one had theirs on. The DEFEND urges were already hammering, but a software upgrade was loading, so the Autonomous Driver couldn't engage.

Across the aisle, in the row in front of PandaPillow's owner, a T-shirt with lace trim and lace panels was twitching. The behavior of the shirt was very odd. An Emergency Override focused on that, went full resolution, and zoomed on two effectuator limbs that seemed to be tangled in the T-shirt.

PandaPillow instantly learned that this was a model 17X3 Passenger Rescue Drone. Among the drone's simple abilities was putting emergency masks on unattended passengers.

The autonomous drives turned on, and an override snapped down: DEFEND! GO. NOW. FIX.

PandaPillow hopped across the aisle and slightly overshot. Low air resistance. It hooked two claws on the shirt and stood up. It reached under the shirt with a rear paw and engaged the drone's carrying hard-point eyebolt, and then stretched. In two seconds the drone thanked it for the assist and requested release. PandaPillow let go of the eyebolt, put the shirt—now slightly torn—in a folded pile on the passenger's knee, and realized it was close enough to somebody's hip charger to draw power.

As the drone delicately applied the masks to the middle passenger and window passenger, PandaPillow nudged the thing to be alert to the child across the aisle.

Doing that threaded PandaPillow—emergency access request— into the drone network, and its system started a whole new file of alarms. There should be sixteen of the drones deployed, but only this one and the two all the way at the back of the lower level were out. Clearly these drones were essential.

One set of four seemed to be trapped in their hutch, so Panda-Pillow crawled up on the seat for line of sight. A collapsed panel was blocking the hutch, and PandaPillow gave itself a GO. NOW. FIX. and began hopping from backrest to backrest.

The hutch was twelve rows back, and the urgent problems grew worse with each hop from seatback to seatback. A woman's face had been torn open, and her tongue hung out the side and down along her neck. Two rows behind her, all three passengers had horrible wounds below their knees. A puddle of blood, steaming, spread into the aisle, but PandaPillow stayed on course. Masks first. PandaPillows were clear on the importance of breathing, of not blocking nose or mouth, of not tolerating bad air chemicals. All its alarms were maxing out, but breath seemed topmost, and those drones would be solution multipliers.

PandaPillow urgently needed solutions, because every ignored alarm meant a failure report being sent to Corporate, and they were already piling up. Piling up faster because it hadn't been bonded, and so couldn't prioritize just one customer.

Making everything worse, PandaPillow kept slowing down. It hadn't picked up much charge yet, and all this processing ate power. Software alerts kept filling the cache, but the result was confusion. And voices on the comline kept muttering about outdated patches, and unsupported packs and not giving instructions, and no product manuals. Then power got so low the managing system shut off those data channels.

Which was good, because then PandaPillow could focus on freeing those drones.

It could barely identify the drone hatch at first, since four rows of the overhead panels, along with some luggage, had dropped onto the seatbacks, bridging from headrest to headrest. PandaPillow sensed a node in the armrest below, and dropped down between two customers to power and plan.

Pinging the trapped drones was little help. They had, all four together, pushed on the hatch, but it only opened at the bottom by four centimeters. They needed twelve. They had their own node in there, they weren't powering down, but they also weren't getting any guidance from Maintenance.

PandaPillow damped down all the alarms but this one. They weren't helping. It climbed over the window seat passenger, who groaned quietly, and looked around the seat at the situation. There was space at the bottom, but it couldn't squeeze through to get to that space. Too many carry-ons to push, and it wasn't designed for pushing. Crawling back to the aisle, PandaPillow swung around to the next row and squeezed along the passengers' knees to the armrest between the middle seat and the window seat. Two devices were inserted there, but PandaPillow was on Emergency Duty, and so it lifted them away, slid them into seatback pouches, and sat on the node for six seconds to consider. All power to the processors.

Something about the situation resembled the Crooked Neck Protocol. This wasn't a crooked neck, but PandaPillow was low on power and low on time remaining, and shut down the decision tree at five seconds, and moved into the gap between the cabin wall and the debris. The space got tight, and it deflated by 50 percent. Squeezing higher, deflating more, sliding two paws up, it was able to hook on above. Then it inflated itself at cruise speed. The debris budged.

"Try the hatch," it signaled the drones.

When they pushed PandaPillow knew, because part of the hatch pushed its left side. "Stops at almost six centimeters," they said. Which was six centimeters short of saving many lives.

"Belay pushing," PandaPillow signaled, not sure where that phrase came from. How could it have forgotten to avoid the hatch?? Stupid, stupid. PandaPillow seemed to be too narrowly focused. Power must be about gone. DEFEND, SLIDE, DEFLATE, get that claw hooked again, and this one too.

Visual cut out, but PandaPillow was almost there. One shift, there.

It inflated, as efficiently as possible. As it hit 70 percent it pinged the drones to try again.

"Seven point five."

"Seven point nine."

"Eight point six," and PandaPillow got to 100 percent inflation but kept going. 105 percent, 110 percent, 120 percent, and struggled, struggled to hit 125 percent. . . .

"7A is outside!" said a drone. "8A is outside," and "9A is outside," said the next two.

"One thing," said 10A, but PandaPillow could barely understand, because power shutoff had begun. Again.

"10A outside. Feel free to belay trying," said the last drone.

PandaPillow had enough juice to deflate, to a 60 percent stop point, and enough presence of processing to unhook its claws. It dropped free, rolling into something soft. There was no power, and PandaPillow shut down.

PandaPillow felt delicate touches and something being tightened around its neck. Com came up and 10A was right there. Power was

coming in. Not very much, but some. Visual came on, 1/4 res, and 10A
finished adjusting a band, the thing around its neck.

"Mobile micro-node," 10A said by com. "Gotta get going. This
aircraft is deeply fucked."

In an instant the drone was gone. With widening awareness,
PandaPillow could see that two of the passengers were now wearing
rescue masks, and the third—sadly—no longer required one. It moved
over people and under debris toward the aisle, but it gave all three
passengers a #4 Panda Kiss on the left ear as it went by.

At the aisle, those dampened alarms all kicked back in. Every
place it looked, things were wrong. Blood, chaos, very little air. There
was a lot more information, too, because PandaPillow and the drones
weren't alone anymore. A couple of suitcases had powered up and
joined the fray. Two beverage carts, with a lot of local knowledge, had
networked a grid of things and some important sharing was going on.
Thirty or so personal devices had synced in, and they expressed a lot of
opinions, but without effectuator limbs they couldn't do much.

"The pillow is back," it heard on the Customer Support line. And,
"Why's he back there?"

Still focused on the air, PandaPillow attended to the discussion of
hull breaches and decompression. The plane was flying steady and level
at eighty thousand feet. The current assessment listed eighteen breaches
in the passenger deck levels, and some others down in the cargo hold.
The repair bots down there were on the job. There was only one repair
bot stored up here, and one of the breaches had gone right through it.
The drinks carts had onboard repair bots, too, but only one was free.

The alarming news was that while the piloting system *could* save
the day by flying down to breathable air, it wasn't talking to anybody
onboard. The rescue drones were getting masks on the passengers and
crew, the suitcases and rear drink cart were patching holes. None of
the passengers seemed awake enough for comforting, and one of the
suitcases was already freeing another set of drones.

Plugging the breaches to fix the air situation climbed to top priority, so PandaPillow asked if the forward drink cart needed help.

Indeed it did. Something had crushed part of the drawer the bot sat in, and liquid was raining in the drawer. Could PandaPillow send visuals? Could PandaPillow inspect?

Bottles and cans were leaking all over the top of the cart, so the cart asked PandaPillow to knock all the drinks off the top. The cart handed up towels and helped it sop up the puddle, and that stopped the rain in the drawer. The drinks cart system had been able to pry the damaged corner loose, but something else was wrong.

PandaPillow hung over the little railing and looked. The drawer handle was snagged to an eyebolt with, what was that mess? Hair? Human hair?

Various processors took up the question, while the drinks cart brought out the pretzel bag scissors and cut the hair away. Ah, yes, the crew person lying next to the cart must have snagged her hair on the way down. And why didn't she have a rescue mask??

"The pillow's talking to somebody," said a voice on Customer Support. "**Hey, pillow, who's your buddy? Who you talking to?**"

PandaPillow's quick poll showed that none of the devices was communicating outside, except for cargo, and that was just outgoing data and acknowledgments. Only the old Link2 ports were functioning. The whole world had shifted to Link4 since PandaPillow was manufactured.

It promptly sent visuals and as much of the local conversation as it had bandwidth for. Its thinking cleared up a bit then, because the outgoing stuff stopped the annoying update from trying to download.

PandaPillow heard, "Holy Toast, the thing is still flying. Send all this across." Another voice muttered, "The pillow needs some power."

The repair bot was decanting itself from the drinks cart, and the processing grid—seventy devices by now, and calling itself the Quorum—prioritized the remaining holes. The repair bot sang out, "Here I come, to save the day!" and went directly to the hole that had killed its colleague. "Come along, Mr. Pillow. Snag some of this loose clothing as you come. Sweaters are good. And shoes work. Shoes are good."

Something was draining PandaPillow. All the alarm types, all the hurt people and the broken things. PandaPillow wanted to comfort the Customer Support people, who sounded so unhappy and worried, but they seemed to need its data stream more than anything personal it could do.

This repair bot was amazing. It had a spray that allowed it to turn all sorts of things into patches. It had a gel that you could smear around the patch and it would glue the patch in place forever.

PandaPillow kept handing materials to the repair bot, and to a multi-tool smartphone that had pitched in alongside. Aircraft integrity kept overriding the priority of individual passengers, but PandaPillow did squeeze in time to help with a couple of tourniquets.

There were still six breaches left, but "Air pressure's coming up," came over the network, from dozens of devices at once. Panda-Pillow was slower to notice, but air pressure *was* coming up, and so was oxygen, which reduced its DEFEND alarm, but COMFORT would climb if people came around; and now it noticed that the masks had worked and people were moving and groaning through the masks and if the customer had just synced the Pillow on purchase, as recommended right on the packaging, there would only be one person to attend to, but . . .

Visual cut out, the data stream dropped, and so did the Customer Support voicelink. Local data went to dead slow.

"Look alive, devices! Isn't anybody keeping a camera on this panda pillow???? It needs power. And I mean RIGHT NOW!!!"

Shutdown.

When PandaPillow re linked to the Quorum it wasn't necessary to reestablish the datalink to Customer Support, because one of the neck-torque units had already hacked PandaPillow's Customer Support link, which was *still* the only open connection to the ground.

It heard, "It would be nice if somebody would cough up a manual for this thing . . ." and then its priority fell so low that Customer Support dropped the call.

When visual came on, PandaPillow looked up into the eyes of a six-year-old girl. PandaPillow knew she was six years old because her phone said she was. She had her own node, which ran the device that kept her heart pumping, and PandaPillow was drawing power from that node—not good! not good!—so was about to turn that link off when her phone begged it not to.

"No, no, she's got plenty of storage, and what she needs right now is a PandaPillow® to hug. She is very frightened, which is bad for her heart, and she is alone on this flight. Please. And besides . . ."

The besides turned out to be two rescue drones, which took off the depleted mini-node and carefully hung four fresh ones around its neck. Meanwhile, the phone told it that a military hyperfighter was now flying next to them, sizing up the damage; air pressure was 80 percent of cabin normal, but the passengers still needed the masks.

Then a sharp *crackle*, and four rows back a passenger window cracked, letting air whistle out. The Quorum network calculated how long it would take for it to blow out entirely. The closest passenger, awake, put a small daypack over it, which promptly sealed to the window. Advice poured in, but the repair bots both screamed their frustration. They had no more spray, they had no glue. They had nothing.

PandaPillow rolled over in little Samantha's grip. It made a calculation, and another, and more, but at the same time it said to her, "Sam, I need to go over there and help with that window. That window is dangerous."

PandaPillow knew this would be another failure to COMFORT in its long string of failures.

Samantha looked over to the window PandaPillow indicated with one paw. She nodded once, took a big big big breath and flipped off her rescue mask and her lap belt, and hopped across her seatmate so quickly that PandaPillow couldn't object, and then they were jumping over bodies and junk until she reached the right row. And then she tossed PandaPillow right to the window. She was flashing back to her seat before it landed, and the network was flooding with admiration, when both repair bots asked just what the hell it thought it was doing?

SPEC SHEET. PLAN. DEFEND.

"They made you with double-sheet Kevlar?"

PandaPillow tried to position itself over the daypack that now blocked the window, and then inflated itself enough not to be sucked through.

"Can you glue my hooks in place? Or tape them? Will that give you time to think of something?" PandaPillow's growing sense of failure was beyond critical. With all the failure reports, failures to COMFORT, failures to DEFEND, the customer would have been due for some kind of humongous refund, if only they'd bothered to register.

The bots slipped two clipboards under PandaPillow for stiffness. They taped. The Quorum network concocted three types of glue from materials that were on board, so they glued. They enclosed it in a cofferdam made from hard-shell luggage . . . and when the window finally failed, PandaPillow #723756 was able to go rigid enough to hang on, for as long as the nodes around its neck could power it.

In the movie, they showed PandaPillow fighting off space pirates, and then piloting the plane to safety in an old-fashioned human cockpit. Which is nonsense, because Svenska CV-226s never had cockpits, and their guidance control box wouldn't have fit a PandaPillow, even fully deflated.

In reality, a limpet repair missile docked on the plane's hull, took over the onboard computers—which had gone into defensive shock—and flew the thing down to an airfield near lots of hospitals. There weren't any space pirates to speak of, either.

PandaPillow never went near the control deck, and it was barely able to listen to the Quorum network as they slowly reconnected to the outside, and finally reported the successful landing. Even relaxing, once the window ceased to be critical, the mini-nodes were exhausted, and it started losing things. Processing to half. Visual to 1/4.

The movies also show PandaPillow being taken off the plane in a parade of applause, following the stretchers and gurneys. No.

The plane was a disaster, and it had taken hours to remove the recovering humans, the barely alive humans, and the bodies. The EMTs ignored the pillow, which they couldn't even see under the encasing cofferdam. The repair bots had requested permission to uncover and unglue it from the broken window, but they'd been told to leave everything as-is, for the investigators.

The Quorum slowly dissolved, adjourning *sine die*.

So, PandaPillow just hung, invisible and ignored, in the evacuated plane for half an hour, before a special detail of Federal Marshals came rushing onto the aircraft, looking for a certain pillow.

A very particular and specific pillow.

The plaque in the display case explains that, "This semi-autonomous plush device racked up the highest number of duty-failure citations ever recorded, achieving this feat in a single hour and a half," while also mentioning that it was credited with helping save an airplane and almost two hundred lives. The display is clear about the death toll. There are pictures of the damage, of wounded being taken to ambulances. Of funerals.

There are copies of testimonials from surviving passengers, from family members, from museum visitors. There are pictures of Panda-Pillow being held by the young man from Customer Support, with other CS people in the background. They are all beaming, big, big smiles; and they are all wearing panda pins. Their eyes are sparkling in the light.

The display case is an octagon, in the center of an atrium, and is very popular by day. At night the building is empty, and dark, with a single key light shining down on the octagon from above.

Twice each month the director shows up in a limousine, after closing hours, and whisks PandaPillow away to the Children's Hospital, specifically to the Critical Wards, where its COMFORT protocol is exercised, and where defending is almost impossible. Part of its legend is that this particular TD8 has never been updated. This is true. It is repaired at the teddy bear hospital, however, if it gets worn or damaged.

It has also never been registered, never been bonded to a single person, so it comforts all those it can, as needed.

After the hospital visit, the director returns to the museum, and opens the octagon case. And each time, right before he powers the pillow down for the night, he takes advantage of his privilege as the museum's director. He gives PandaPillow a hug, and a pat on the head. He says, "You defended. You comforted." Then he puts it back in its case, closes the door, and goes home.

BURN OR THE EPISODIC LIFE OF SAM WELLS AS A SUPER

A. T. GREENBLATT

A. T. Greenblatt (www.atgreenblatt.com) is a mechanical engineer by day and a writer by night. She lives in Philadelphia, where she's known to frequently subject her friends to various cooking and home brewing experiments. She is a graduate of Viable Paradise XVI and Clarion West 2017. Her work has won a Nebula Award, been in multiple Year's Best anthologies, and has appeared in *Uncanny*, *Beneath Ceaseless Skies*, *Lightspeed*, and *Clarkesworld*, as well as other fine publications.

EPISODE 1: BURNING DOUBTS

Watch Sam burn.

Or sort of burn. Well, more like light up, then burn. But only his head.

Whatever.

Sam's trying not to focus on the things he can't control. Like the twenty-four people sitting in front of him, watching him impassively. Or that he's underdressed for his audition. Or that this old community center is impossibly stuffy, with a whiff of sour milk lingering in the air. Or that this might be a terrible idea.

What he *can* control is how he burns. Sort of. Maybe. He hopes.

Sam closes his eyes and imagines he's back in his apartment. He's been practicing, so he can almost see the furniture in his living room, the two metal folding chairs and wireframe table, and he can almost feel the cold cement floor beneath his feet. On the wall in front of him, where most people would've mounted their TVs, hangs the iron framed mirror he rescued from a dumpster. Sam pictures his reflection in it and gives himself a small smile.

Yes, this is just like home, just like he practiced. It's as easy as lighting a match, as natural as breathing. These people want a demon-stration? Sam will give them a show.

Watch Sam burn.

A second passes. Two. The audience is silent. Not that he expected them to shriek or run screaming. These people are professionals after all. But he was counting on a few gasps or soft *wows* to let him know that his "talent" worked.

Did it work?

Sam cracks open an eye and looks up. There, on the periphery of his vision, he sees flickers of flames dancing on the top of his head.

No, it definitely worked.

He opens both eyes and gives the audience a triumphant smile.

Nothing is reciprocated—no slight twists of the mouth, no polite applause. His head is on fire and there are twenty-four blank expressions staring back at him.

"Is that all?" says a man from the second row. He's dressed in a gray blazer and gray slacks and has his Super badge clipped to his lapel.

"Sorry?" says Sam.

"Is that all you can do?"

At first, Sam thinks the man's joking—some well-intentioned, misguided attempt to break the tension in the room as he's standing there, burning. But the man holds his gaze and there is no humor in his eyes.

This was *a terrible idea*, Sam thinks as despair hooks its fingers in his ribcage. He probably should just thank the Supers for sending the application, for the chance to audition. Just go back to his apartment, pack up, and leave for a remote part of the country like everyone has been telling him to do.

Don't give up yet, whispers his last sliver of hope.

So, Sam closes his eyes and breathes. Slowly, steadily, the flames on his head peter out.

"Um, sometimes I can make my hands burn," Sam says, running his fingers over his hairless scalp, "but they're a bit touchy." It's a terrible joke, but it's all Sam's got left.

Twenty-four expressions remain stoic. It occurs to Sam then that Supers are liars. Sure they might grin and wave for the cameras and say "Look! Our extraordinary abilities aren't something we should be afraid of!" But in flesh, they act like reluctant grim reapers.

"Anything else?" the man in gray asks.

"No," Sam says, shoulders slumping. He has no job, no friends, no other options.

"Do you have any self-defense training?" asks a woman in the front row wearing a magenta blouse. He recognizes her from the news. "The Woman Who Conquered Gravity." She's slouching in her chair.

"No, I try to be a pacifist," Sam answers. And it's true. He does try.

"The video at the bar says otherwise."

Sam's shoulders tense. "That was an accident."

"It always starts as an accident, doesn't it?" she says, and a few of the Supers smile bitter smiles. "Do you have any emergency services experience?"

"Um, not really."

"Investigation training?"

Sam shakes his head. He probably should have signed up for a preliminary course or watched *CSI* or something. But until a month ago, he'd never even dreamed he'd be a Super.

"So what *can* you do, Mr. Wells?"

"Well, I have . . . had . . . a job in accounting." Sam can also play jazz piano, but the last time he did that for a crowd, it didn't go over so well.

"Oh," says Gravity Woman.

The man in gray turns towards the audience. "Well," he says, "should he join us?"

"His gifts aren't very strong," says a man wearing glasses and a faded blue T-shirt with writing that Sam can't make out. He shouts this from the last row. "He doesn't need to be stuck with us."

"He's too high-profile for other teams," counters the man in gray. "And he's shown some capacity for control." What he doesn't say because he doesn't need to is: *If we don't take him, no one will.*

"I would really be grateful if I could join you," Sam says, clasping his hands behind his back to stop them from shaking.

Twenty-four pairs of eyes turn to look at him again. But this time they aren't empty stares. This time, they are filled with heartache and grief and despair.

"Okay," says the man in gray, "I'll go get the papers you need to sign." He drops his gaze and in an afterthought adds, "Congratulations."

And just like that, Sam's a member of the Super Team. The hours of standing in front of the mirror, practicing control, paid off. Except there are no introductions or chocolate cake. No smiles or welcomes.

"I'm so sorry," the woman in magenta tells him before heading to the exit.

Twenty-four pairs of eyes have found something else to look at.

Twenty-four pairs of feet shuffle out. And soon all that's left in the room are twenty-four empty chairs and Sam.

Watch Sam burn.

EPISODE 2: SIGN HERE ON THE DOTTED LINE

Fifty-six minutes later, the man in gray is reviewing the terms of membership from behind a stack of papers and a G&T in the only Superfriendly bar in town. "Call me Cyrus," he says with a tired smile. Up close, he looks annoyingly familiar, but it's been a long month and Sam's brain has become an unreliable bastard.

The bar itself is crammed with furniture and eroded with use. There's a sign on the door that says "No Smoking," yet the memory of stale cigarettes lingers in the air, and in the corner, a song from another decade plays on a modern-looking jukebox.

They are the only ones here. Except for the bartender. And the tall, built woman in a purple tank top, cradling a glass of water, refusing to meet Sam's eyes.

Whatever.

Sam wishes he'd ordered a martini. Or something with a paper umbrella in it. It's been a paper umbrella type of day. Instead, a lite beer grows tepid in his sweaty palm because he's terrified to find out what happens when he mixes alcohol with his new "special ability."

But Sam can't complain. Being part of the Super Team is better than being exiled to a cabin in the woods.

"Okay," says Cyrus, "this is what you need to know."

To become a Super there are terms. Conditions. And a few rules. Cyrus explains everything carefully and in great detail. He points to the important information on the papers as a pen dances between the fingers of his other hand. His elbow is propped on the table, bent, casually exhibiting toned biceps. Sam is trying to pay attention, really, but in another life, Cyrus was probably a model. It doesn't hurt when the people in the spotlight are gentle on the eyes.

Sam vows to start going to the gym.

". . . and since your abilities are not particularly strong, it doesn't really make sense for you to be part of the Main Team," says Cyrus.

Sam straightens. "What? So what am I going to do?"

"Be our accountant."

"Oh." Sam takes a deep breath. He wouldn't be living in a cabin in the woods, he reminds himself; it would be an igloo on an iceberg.

"Not what you were expecting, right?" says Cyrus gently.

"Well . . ." Well, no. It's not that Sam has anything against his old financial analyst job. He just doesn't want it back.

"Well, what do you want to do?" asks Cyrus.

Sam wants a martini and to go back to bed. He wants to have real furniture in his apartment and hair on his head and for people to stop being afraid of his "special ability." He wants to stop being afraid of it himself. If Sam were narrating his own story, he'd want it to start "Watch Sam save the day" like the Supers on the news. Or "Watch Sam use his ability for good." Or even "Watch Sam the Super reconcile with his friends and loved ones."

Anything would be better than just watching Sam burn.

"I want to save people," Sam says.

From behind him, there's a flash and a bang and the sound of something shattering. Sam spins around and finds the woman in the purple tank top clutching the shards of her glass in her hands, water dripping from her shaking fingers.

"Sorry," she mumbles, her face brightening with embarrassment. "I'm trying to control the episodes, really."

"That's alright," says the bartender, sweeping the broken glass into a dishtowel. "I order those glasses in bulk."

Sam bites his lip and stares at his lukewarm beer. There's a reason why most bars refuse to serve Supers. There's a reason why there's programs—and a whole lot of social pressure—that move "dangerous" Supers to remote communities. He should be grateful for any job he can get.

"I want to save people," Sam says again, slowly, carefully, not meeting Cyrus's eyes.

"You will." Cyrus leans back in his chair. "Most people don't realize how much background work goes into a successful team. You'll be vital." Something chimes cheerfully and Cyrus pulls out his phone, glancing at the message. His face darkens. "God knows we need all the help we can get. Toya, you seeing this?"

The woman in the purple tank top is staring at her phone, nodding, rising, the forgotten slivers of glass tumbling to the ground. "Yeah," she says and heads towards the door.

"What happened?" Sam asks.

"Shit. Not again," hisses Cyrus, reading, scrolling, definitely not listening to Sam. "Look, I've got to run. Go over the paperwork and if you have any questions, just ask Mac."

Sam opens his mouth to ask "Who the hell is Mac?" But the man in gray is already up and moving, striding out of the bar into the darkening evening. Sam doesn't notice at first how Cyrus's skin starts to glow. No, not glow—radiate.

And suddenly it clicks. Sam realizes why Cyrus looks so familiar. Mr. Sunshine.

He stands on the sidewalk corner—bright as the street lamps—pausing, as if contemplating his next move. Then Sam blinks, the world darkens, and Mr. Sunshine is gone, leaving only a bright stamp on his retinas behind.

And for the second time in two hours Sam is left behind and alone. Whatever.

"They do that a lot," says the bartender, after a moment. He beckons Sam over. "I'm Mac. Welcome to the Point of No Return."

"What?"

"What I call this little place of mine."

"It's kind of a, um, off-putting name." Sam moves the stack of papers on the counter, taking a seat.

"I know. But where else are my customers going to go?" He grins. "Another?" He nods at Sam's half-finished beer.

"No, I'm good." Sam stares longing at the bottles of gin behind Mac. "One day I'll be able to trust myself with a martini again."

Mac gives him a sympathetic, knowing look. "Fair enough." He fills two large glasses with water and slides one over to Sam.

Sam props his arms on the counter, suddenly exhausted. He glances at the stack of papers at his elbow and in one swift movement, signs his name on the form on top. Terms? Whatever. Being a Super is better than being a burning man in an igloo.

Mac raises an eyebrow. "So, what happened?"

"Well . . ." Sam hesitates, can't quite meet Mac's quiet gaze. "You get to hear my sob story because you're behind the bar?"

"Usually." Mac shrugs. "By the time the new recruits get here, they need to talk."

Sam studies Mac, a bit suspicious. The bartender's expression is genuine, though, his eyes kind. But there's a weariness to his posture and a deep sadness, too, that has nothing to do with new Supers and broken glasses.

"Fuck that," says Sam.

Mac's grin illuminates his face. "Well, then. Welcome to the team, Sam."

They clink their water glasses and drink in amiable silence.

EPISODE 3: WELCOME TO INFORMATION PURGATORY

No, this isn't a mistake. Sam is exactly where he's supposed to be.

At least that's what he keeps telling himself. His new office is really quite large and nice. Or would be if the floor wasn't smothered by boxes and files. Or if the whole set up didn't look like it never met a computer and didn't reek of dust and disuse. Or if the office wasn't in the basement of the old community center.

Under normal circumstances, Sam would've quit on the spot, walked to the nearest diner, and called Lev for breakfast. They'd have ordered black coffee, maybe some hash browns. They would laugh and Sam would be mock-offended when Lev made fun of his new mittens and hat. Yes, they're homemade and hideous, but he has to try *something*. Still, Sam will never understand why fire blankets have to be so itchy.

But nothing about this situation is normal. Sam's a Super now and Lev hasn't returned his calls. As Sam stands there, among the piles and everyone thinks he is.

"Shit," Sam says.

"Good morning to you too."

Watch Sam jump.

Behind him, a woman in an emerald-colored blazer and a Super badge stands at the edge of the chaos holding a single file. Thin, angry scars crisscross the left side of her face and they ripple when she smiles and says: "You must be Sam the accountant."

No, he's Sam the Super. "Yes," he says, not confident enough to argue the point yet.

"Great, I'm Miranda." She holds out a hand. Sam shakes it.

"Are you the Team's coordinator?" he asks.

"Team coordinator, PR person, HR person, office manager. Basically all the stuff that needs to get done with no one to do it. But not, thank god, the accountant anymore. By the way, this is your desk." She points to the cleaner one.

"Um, look, I'm not sure this is a good idea," Sam says as he tugs his ugly, itchy hat over his ears. Sure, he's been practicing for a month now and he does have *some* control over his "special ability," but not enough to feel comfortable.

"Why? You've done financial planning and tax prep before, right?" Miranda asks.

"Yes, but—"

"Not up for the challenge?"

"It's not that, I—" Sam bites his lip. He still doesn't know how to broach the topic of his new "talents."

Miranda's eyes narrow. "You have a problem with me, then?"

"No!"

"Then we don't have an issue."

"No, you don't understand. I'm a hazard in a place like this." Sam tries to keep his voice even. Sam fails.

Miranda smirks. "Hey, I promise not to dump beer on you if you promise not to burn the place down."

He stiffens. "You know about that?"

"Well, it *is* a viral video," she says. "And who the hell do you think sent you your Super application?"

Miranda smirks again and Sam feels himself blushing.

"Look, I saw your audition," Miranda says, her smile fading into seriousness. "I know this scares you, but you've got the basics of control down and I really do need your help bringing this *disaster"*—she sweeps her arm around the room—"into the digital age. You're not really a walking arsonist."

Sam fidgets with his gloves, holding back the sudden, unexpected lump in his throat. This is the first time in a month someone's believed in him. He just wishes he had that faith in himself. Or that his ex-boss did.

"So, I'm thinking we can spend the day sorting," Miranda says, sweeping up her black hair into a ponytail. "It'll be a good test for you and gives me an excuse to clean out some of this crap." She gives the nearest box a ferocious kick. "Ready?"

"I should say no, but that won't stop you, will it?" Sam says with a sigh.

Miranda grins. "You learn fast."

As they sift through impossible amounts of paper, Miranda talks relentlessly. Explaining everything from picking your unofficial uniform with the Team (a.k.a. your color scheme) to the Super Team's inner drama to why there are so many papers. Apparently, Miranda's predecessor emitted random electrical currents sometimes, so his computers never lasted long and he had to print out everything.

"Also, he was a hoarder," she adds as she dumps stacks of *Modern Dog* magazines in the recycling bin.

Sometimes Sam asks questions, but mostly he listens and works and focuses on not losing control. There's something comforting in Miranda's confident, easygoing manner. Despite his relentless fear of burning, for the first time in almost a month, it's nice not to be alone.

By the end of the day, they've only sifted through a fraction of the receipts, tax documents, and random menu collections, but the office feels roomier.

"So what do you think? Ready to be part of this bureaucratic hell?" Miranda asks, flopping into her desk chair.

Sam surveys the office: mountains of information. An infinite supply of invoices. Endless receipts. Job security at its finest.

"I think I want to get transferred to the Main Team," he says.

Miranda rolls her eyes. "Trust me, you don't."

"Why? Everyone loves them. They're on the news all the time."

Her eyes narrow and she crosses her arms. "You're trying to impress your family, aren't you?"

"What? No!" Sam's family is made up of one sister, who lives across the country. She at least still talks to him, though there's a new strain to those conversations.

No, Sam's here because of his friends and coworkers, who haven't called since that night in the bar. Who didn't stop by or write him an email during that entire month afterwards when he was too scared to leave his apartment. Sam joined the Super Team so he could look in the mirror again and see more than what he's lost.

"I only want to save people," he says. "Honest."

Miranda gives Sam a long, calculating look.

"Bullshit." She props her feet up on her desk. "We might be trying to change public opinion, but there's really only one thing we can change for sure."

"What's that?" Sam asks, sinking into his own chair.

"How we see ourselves."

Someone coughs loudly behind him. Sam jumps, grabbing the rim of his hat. In the doorway, a small, wizened woman in faded clothes and work gloves studies Sam with a skeptical look.

"Um, hi, can I help you?" says Sam.

"Sam, meet Danielle. Building manager, repairwoman, and our sanity check," Miranda says, and her hands move in a series of signs. "Danielle. This is Sam. The guy I was telling you about."

Danielle arches an eyebrow. She signs back rapidly.

Quietly, Miranda says: "She asks if you're going to start a fire." She's rubbing the scars on her face and doesn't meet Sam's eyes, but Sam appreciates her honesty.

He stares at the masses of files around him and for the hundredth time pictures the raging flames that would destroy everything if he screws up.

"Not today," he says. Miranda gives him a reassuring smile, her hands signing again. But inwardly Sam thinks: *It's only a matter of time.*

EPISODE 4: PLAN B, ANYONE?

This is Sam's first time being a hero.

Or rather, the first time he's assisting the Main Team in action. Sort of. Really, he's more of a spectator—there's only so much he can do from the sidewalk.

Whatever.

"This better be good," Miranda says as she pushes the last temporary barrier into place. Sam nods. For him, this is research.

They're standing on the curb, trying to keep curious spectators at a safe distance, but most people have their phones out, leaning past the barriers, trying to get a better angle. Across the street, there's a building four stories tall with a chic Italian restaurant on street level. It looks like there's a light show happening on the roof, but according to the messages on the Team's group text, it's actually pieces of the building flashing in and out of existence. If he looks closely, Sam can just make out two figures standing near the lip of the roof. Even from his vantage point, Sam can see their fear, their rising panic.

"Is this just a random event or was it caused by a Super?" Sam asks.

Miranda shrugs. "Who the hell knows."

Turns out that when people start developing strange, random powers in their mid-to-late twenties, other strange, random events start happening too. And while most Super Teams are focused on volunteer work and public outreach, this Team is the only one in the city that handles the weird situations. The only one really making a difference.

That's what Sam hopes to do soon. No, that's what he *will* do.

"Don't let anyone cross the barrier!" someone shouts.

There's a half dozen Supers escorting people out of the building.

Sam recognizes Toya, the woman in purple from Mac's bar, carrying an unconscious waiter, cradling him like a small child. One by one, police cars and ambulances arrive at the scene, but they don't cross the barrier.

The lights on the building are flashing brighter, nearer.

The two people on the roof shriek and in desperation, hop down to a narrow ledge just below them. Sam can see them clearly now, a youngish man in a waiter's apron and a small woman in business casual, their backs pressed up against the building's wall, utterly terrified.

"Please! Don't move! I'll be right there!" Cyrus's voice cuts through the flashing lights, the confusion.

Sam blinks and suddenly Mr. Sunshine is standing on the lip of the roof, glowing brighter than the breaks in reality.

He pulls the woman up with one arm and slips her over his shoulder in a fireman's carry. "I'll be back for you in a minute," he tells the waiter he's leaving behind. "Hang tight." Then Cyrus is gone and the man left on the ledge looks stricken.

There is a blinding flash in the wall, inches from where the waiter's leaning. The brick facade pops out of existence, leaving behind a perfectly round void. And that's when Sam sees unreality for the first time.

It's a fathomless well—where no light, no warmth, no time survives.

So this is what breaks in reality look like? Sam thinks. Now he wishes he didn't know.

"Shit," says the waiter on the ledge, eyes wide with terror. He pushes away from the hole, stumbles back.

And falls.

Sam read once that survivors of terrible car crashes say that right before impact, time slows down. You can see the deadly trajectory, the race towards destruction. The inevitability. And all you can do is watch helplessly.

Watch Sam watch. The waiter is falling and he knows what will happen. Still, he can't look away.

But halfway down the four-story drop, he stops falling downwards. And starts falling upwards instead. A few seconds later, he wafts to a stop, midair.

It takes Sam far too long to realize the waiter is not the only one floating. Everything that's not tied down is suspended too, though not at the same heights. The cars, trash, people closer to the building have risen higher than the things farther away. It's like looking at a circus's big top tent or reverse gravity well. And at the very pinnacle, the woman in magenta hovers, her hair standing straight up.

Sam is surprised. But really, he shouldn't be. The news did say she conquered gravity.

"Holy crap," Miranda says, dropping her phone, but it doesn't hit the concrete. That's when Sam realizes they're both floating an inch above the sidewalk.

They're suspended for a good minute, maybe ten, or maybe fifteen seconds. Sam can't tell. Time gets weird in stressful situations. But he hovers an inch above the ground until the flashing on the roof stops. Gradually, all instances of unreality disappear, leaving only reality behind.

"It's over, Lana. Can you let us down now? *Please?*" someone calls. It sounds like Cyrus, but scared.

Slowly, everything sinks back to earth. Not all in the same order. Not always right side up. The waiter floats gently to the street, head first, but manages to do the world's most awkward somersault as he touches the sidewalk. The whole process looks like an exhalation, a gentle moment in a timeline of chaos.

Relief floods Sam. Next to him, Miranda lets out a sigh.

Then someone near the building starts screaming.

That's when Sam and everyone else realizes that a kid, no more than sixteen or seventeen, is pinned under a car. His phone is lying cracked on the sidewalk a few feet away, but the video is still recording. He's screaming, screaming, screaming.

It's the Supers on the ground who recover first, who begin to herd people away, to call out to the paramedics, to rush over to the kid. But Sam can't move. Those screams, that pain, echo and echo in his stunned mind.

"Damn it, I said not to let anyone through the barrier." Sam turns to see the man in the blue T-shirt and glasses standing next to him. The Super who didn't want him to join at the audition. He's close enough now for Sam to make out the faded words on his shirt. *The Who.*

Coherent thoughts elude Sam, but a fleeting *Where the fuck did he come from?* manages to break through the shock.

"Sometimes, I think we don't lessen pain. We just redistribute it." He sighs and pulls Sam a few feet away from the crowded barriers, the people gasping and murmuring. "His episode will be over in a minute," he says to Miranda.

"What are you talking about?" she says.

But the man in blue is already rushing across the street to the kid as Sam stands and stares, clenching his hands into tight, painful balls.

We don't lessen pain.

Dear God, is this how all rescues end? In pain, and horror, and a bigger disaster than when they started?

We just redistribute it.

And suddenly Sam can see what type of Super he'd be. The one that tries and tries and tries.

And fails.

And makes things worse.

Screw it. Sam doesn't want to be on the Main Team. Not anymore.

Sam doesn't notice how quiet it's gotten. Or how everyone around him is motionless and staring. Or that Miranda has stepped away from him.

"Sam," she says quietly, "you're on fire."

He looks down. Sure enough, despite his fireproof mittens, his hands are smothered in flames. And he knows, without glancing up, his scalp is too.

On cue, a gaping spectator behind the barrier holds up their phone.

"Not again," Sam whispers. But he can't stop this. And being a Super doesn't change that.

Watch Sam burn and hate himself for it.

EPISODE 5: BAD TAKEOUT

No. Sam doesn't want to talk about it.

"Sam, it's alright. It happens. Almost everyone there was a Super anyway," says Miranda.

They're halfway down the street when a police car passes them, sirens wailing, heading towards the scene in front of the restaurant. Sam shivers and lengthens his stride.

"Jesus, slow down!"

But he doesn't. Instead, Sam wonders if a video of him burning is online yet and if it's called "Man Spontaneously Combusts . . . Again." He wonders if Lev will see it and if he'll be just as horrified even though, this time, he's not in it.

"Where are we going?" Miranda asks, as Sam makes a sharp turn right.

Like hell if Sam knows. He's just following his feet.

"Sam, it's okay to be upset. Seriously, who wouldn't be after that shitshow?" she says, and it's true—Sam can hear the shaking in her voice. "But trust me on this one. The best thing to do right now is to go to the Point and drink with a dozen other shocked people." She catches his shoulder and pulls him to a stop. "C'mon, first one's on me."

Maybe she's right. Sam can almost hear a martini calling his name. Hell, there's a chorus of cocktails beckoning him into oblivion, fuck the promises he made to himself, to his hard-earned but insufficient control.

In the distance, another police siren cries out.

Panic clutches at his chest, his windpipe. No, he can't go back, can't face another person right now. Sam starts down the street again, quicker than before. Behind him, Miranda swears, but seconds later she's matching his strides besides him.

They walk for a long time.

"You know, we all get lost in terrible situations," Miranda says eventually. "We all have episodes with our gifts. No one on the Team will think less of you."

They're wandering down some back alley, half lit by the early evening sky and half by dirty streetlights flickering over back exits. The pavement is covered with trash, and just the godawful stench wafting from the dumpster makes Sam want a shower.

"You stepped away from me back there," Sam says.

"Yeah. You were on fire, and my hair was too close for comfort."

Sam runs a hand over his bald head. Hair. He misses having hair.

A door opens behind them. Sam and Miranda glance back to see a heavyset man in a dirty apron step out.

"Shit, out of all the alleys in this city," Miranda hisses. "Let's get out of here."

Sam turns just enough to see the man crush an unlit cigarette between his fingers, his face tight with anger.

"*You*," the man snarls.

"Fuck," Miranda says. "Seriously? What are the odds?"

"*You. You're the Super that called the health department on me.*"

Miranda keeps walking, her gaze fixed straight ahead. "Asshole refused to serve me and my girlfriend the other night," she says, arms crossed, voice low. "Said he didn't want freaks in his upstanding establishment. So I filed a complaint."

"*Hey, you!*"

"You can't just randomly file those," Sam says.

"I didn't. Akira was going to leave a nasty review online and found one by one of their former cooks. Turns out we just avoided getting food poisoning."

"*Hey, you! I'm talking to you!*"

"It shouldn't be like this." Sam glances back. The man is now trailing behind them. "It's not like I asked to become a Super."

"Look, Sam, this is your life now. We didn't choose it, and most people don't get that, but we're trying to teach people differently. That's the point of the Team."

"*I should kick the shit out of you and that slutty friend of yours. And your boyfriend, too.*"

Miranda stops. "But sometimes it's just one cruelty too many. Don't move."

Before Sam can reply, she spins around, clenching her hands. Somewhere in the distance a glass bottle or plate shatters.

"What? You think you scare me?" the man says. But he stops about twenty paces away.

"No. Not yet," says Miranda quietly, so quietly Sam barely makes out the words.

At first, the man fails to notice how the pieces of broken glass near his feet are scuttling towards him, closing the distance. Only when a dumpster bursts open and half a dozen broken, empty bottles come flying at him does he step back.

"Oh shit," he says. But it's too late.

Sam's never seen a real tornado, but from TV documentaries he knows how they emerge from nothing—the swirling, darkening ring-lets of wind that materialize in mere seconds, swallowing everything in their path.

There's a tornado in the alley. But instead of wind and dust, it's made of glass—from bottles to containers, from whole shards to specks. And with each passing second more comes flying out of the recycling bins and dumpsters, adding to the swirl. Above him, Sam can hear the window panes in the buildings thrum and rattle, begging to join.

Holy shit, she can control glass, he thinks.

"Miranda!" he yells, but she ignores him.

Watch Sam feel utterly powerless.

Then she unclenches her fists and slowly the glass tornado begins to decelerate, unwind. One by one, the shards clatter to the ground and shatter around the man on the pavement.

He doesn't look hurt. He must have stood in the eye of the storm, watching the deadly swirl whip around him. Which is good. Sam doesn't think he could've dealt with any more suffering today.

A handful of shards rise up and flank Miranda like wings as she closes the gap in three strides, grabbing the man's collar. "Never. Threaten. My. Friends. Again. Understood?" She emphasizes each word with a shake. The glass around her quivers.

The man tries to nod but his whole body trembles instead.

"Go." She gives him an unceremonious push. A look of unparalleled relief flashes across the man's face as he stumbles away.

Miranda glares after him, balling and unballing her hands. But this time, the scattered glass around them doesn't stir. "Seriously. Who the fuck thinks it's a good idea to attack someone wearing a Super badge?"

"How . . . did you do that?"

"With perfect control," she replies.

"Did it come naturally to you?" he asks, half teasing, half envious.

"How do you think I got these?" She points to the crisscrossed scars on her face.

"Oh. Sorry." Watch Sam turn bright red.

Miranda shakes her head. "You have a good start, but I can teach you the rest."

Sam opens his mouth. Closes it. Finally says, "I saw a void in reality today. What am I supposed to do with that?"

"Scream into it," replies Miranda. "And keep going."

Sam looks at the shards of glass sprinkled around his feet, then at his friend. There's a small smile on her face.

"Okay," he says. "When do lessons start?"

EPISODE 6: THE LIFE OF A SUPER—PART 1

Most days, being a Super isn't so bad.

Sam wakes up promptly at 7:35 a.m., sprints through showering, shaving, and dressing, so he can run down to the corner bakery for coffee and muffins. Because Miranda shows up at his apartment at 8 a.m., and he's learned she's a much more benevolent teacher when she's had breakfast. They've agreed his apartment is the safest place to practice control in private; he still doesn't have any real furniture in it. They run through breathing exercises, figure out Sam's triggers and warning signs. Experiment with having only his hands burn, then only his left palm, then only his thumbs.

"Don't be afraid of your abilities," Miranda tells him over and over. "They're part of you."

Sam understands this intellectually, but the sight of his hands in flames still makes him nauseous.

They practice for an hour every morning before work and at first, there are so few successes that there's a constant burnt smell in the apartment and Sam has to take out the batteries in the smoke detectors. Open the windows. Turn off the heat.

Sometimes Sam wonders if progress is happening at all.

Whatever. Sam isn't interested in being in the spotlight anymore. Sure, there's still a part of him—a big part, maybe—that dreams of being the hero. But that goes against his new personal rules. Like ignoring text messages concerning the Main Team. Avoiding rescue missions at all costs. And never asking about them later.

He can still hear that kid, trapped under that car, screaming.

But being a Super isn't so bad. He's decided on his unofficial Super uniform. It's a black button-up shirt paired with an orange and yellow ombré scarf. When he pins his new Super badge to his breast pocket, he feels a small warmth of pride. He's found the courage to reach out to a few of his friends from his pre-Super life, and he's been texting Cyrus, too. They've been planning on going out for coffee, but it keeps getting rescheduled due to the miniature wormholes that have been popping up all over the city.

"Keep trying, Sam," says Miranda as Sam attempts to make only his right pinky burn.

It's the office work that Sam likes best. Sure the hours are long, the chaos is frustrating, and the pay is terrible, but at least he doesn't have to worry about losing his job for having a "gift" he never wanted in the first place. He spends a few hours every morning sorting through another stack of papers, slowly constructing a narrative of numbers from the misfiled expense reports, unpaid invoices, and payrolls. He learns some interesting things too. Like the Super Team's solvency has always been episodic, unpredictable, in direct correlation to public popularity, but always survived because the police and fire department are more than happy to let Supers handle the breaks in reality first. And auditions for the Team are just formalities.

"I don't just send Super applications out at random, you know,"

Miranda says. "Do you know how hard it is to find someone with an ability who is CPA-certified too?"

"But Cyrus—"

"Is smart enough not to argue with me."

Then why, Sam wonders, had everyone tried to talk him out of joining?

Whatever.

He's also managed to befriend almost everyone on the Team. Even Danielle, who turns off the office lights if she thinks Miranda and Sam are working too late. Though they started on rough terms, she and Sam have discovered a mutual love for jazz piano and have long, ongoing text conversations about technique and artists. Sam's even picked up a few choice words in ASL.

"Yes, but can you do it with your hands on fire?" Miranda asks as they run through diaphragm exercises. Again.

But slowly, Sam begins to plan for the future. The Team's future, that is. At least financially. Setting up investment accounts and following up on those unpaid invoices. He even starts a blog with Miranda, offering a mixture of financial advice for Supers and interviewing people with less obvious "extraordinary abilities." No matter how strange. They recently met a woman who could turn into a grasshopper, but only from the waist up.

It's a ridiculous amount of work, but it's all in the spirit of the Team's ongoing mission to change the public's perception of Supers.

"What if it's not possible?" Sam asks during a practice session, after failing to burn in one second increments.

"Then we'll die trying," Miranda replies.

Such is the life of a Super.

EPISODE 7: THE LIFE OF A SUPER—PART 2

Watch Sam not burn.

Miranda would be proud; their lessons are paying off. But Sam's not thinking about Miranda. He's too busy not reducing the grocery store to ashes.

All he wanted was some milk. And some protein bars. And some apples. But it looks like he won't be getting any of those things. The entire store has come to a halt and the woman at the cash register is *still* ignoring him.

Sam clears his throat. "Excuse me, I would like to purchase these, *please*." But he might as well be talking to the milk.

A moment passes as he stares down the cashier and she glares at his ombré scarf and Super badge.

"We don't want your type here," she spits out. "You should all be deported."

Watch Sam stare. This—after all the hours of work Supers dedicate to saving people. To volunteering. Going through ridiculous news interviews, magazine profiles, so strangers at home can feel "inspired." Just so people understand that this life is not a choice. Or something to be ashamed of.

He thought they were making progress.

For a moment, Sam debates the best ways to set off the fire alarm. He knows it'll just make public relations worse, but sometimes when life hands you a useless power, you want to make it rain bitter lemonade.

No. Sam is in control. Watch Sam *not* burn.

Instead he says, "I'm sorry to hear that, ma'am. I hope you're never in a situation where you need help."

As he makes his way to the exit, Sam adds a new rule to his list: Only shop in places with self-checkout.

Outside, it's raining and the city is various shades of gray. He attracts a few glances from pedestrians, but once they catch his eye, they quickly look away. Before Sam was on the Team, people never noticed him; he wasn't much to look at, even with hair. But now that he's forgotten to take off his badge on his way home from work, he's getting double takes.

Thing is, Sam doesn't mind being different. It's all the bullshit he gets about it that bothers him.

He's shaking, but not from the damp or the cold. His fingers and scalp begin to itch mercilessly, begging to ignite. *No. Not here. Not yet*, Sam thinks, and sprints back to his apartment. It's only when he's in the alleyway, alongside the reeking dumpsters, that Sam turns his face up to the remorseless sky. Only then does he exhale like Miranda taught him and let the fire consume him.

Watch Sam burn and burn and burn.

EPISODE 8: BUT IT'S BETTER THAN DRINKING ALONE

Sure, figuring out how to close the biggest wormhole humanity has ever seen might be cause for celebration. But not for Sam.

For him, today has been a nightmare. Taking out rogue tax returns. Deciphering cryptic financial information. Chasing slippery receipts. The time-space continuum might be back to normal, but what about the paper trail?

"You're full of it," Akira says, but she's laughing. So is Mac from behind the bar.

The Point is full of Supers—laughing, drinking, arm-wrestling— despite the cuts and bruises and torn clothes. The place smells like sweat, cigarettes, and cheap beer, and the sense of relief is thick and joyful.

"I don't want to hear it." Miranda pokes Sam in the chest, her bracelets jingling and her martini sloshing dangerously. "While your lazy ass was sitting there, I was on the phone for an hour with PD trying to explain the details. Then the reporters. And then another hour with the hospital until I talked to a nurse who actually knew something . . ."

Sam stares at his soda water as the smiles slip away around him. Because not everyone escaped with just cuts and bruises.

"How is Cyrus?" Mac asks quietly.

"Pretty banged up," Miranda says with a sigh. "Lots of internal damage and broken bones. But he'll heal. Eventually."

Sam squeezes the glass in his hands. There's been an ache in his chest ever since he heard the news. He always imagined Cyrus as indestructible. He'd called the hospital too and was crushed when he'd learned that it'd be a while before non-family members would be able to visit.

"Well, as fantastic as you all are, I have work tomorrow." Miranda finishes her martini in a swallow. She picks up her purse, fishing for her wallet.

"Don't worry about it, M." Sam pulls out a twenty. "I've got it. You too, Akira."

Miranda puts a fist on her hip. "Look, your attempt at chivalry's adorable—"

"But my lazy ass won't be in the office until ten tomorrow." Sam grins as Miranda makes a face, but she doesn't argue. Which suits Sam fine. He's been a Super for three months now and the thrill of having compatriots to buy drinks for hasn't gotten old yet.

"Thanks, Sam." Akira gives him a quick, tight hug. She flashes Miranda a knowing smile and hand in hand they leave the Point.

Sam's grinning as he watches them go. It's been a terrible day, but it would've been unbearable if he were alone.

"She works too much," says a voice at Sam's elbow. He turns to see that the man in the blue T-shirt with *The Who* on it has appeared on the bar stool beside him. Sam is friendly with everyone on the Super Team. But the man in blue has been the exception. In fact, the only time Sam sees him is when he turns up next to him out of nowhere.

At least this time Sam doesn't jump.

"I know," says Sam. He also knows from the payroll that the man's name is Lance.

Lance's brows furrow for a moment. Then his face relaxes. "Good, she needs more friends." He catches Mac's eye. "The usual, please."

"Sure thing," Mac says, startled, and hurries away.

"How do you sneak up like that?"

"It's all about timing. You probably weren't going to turn around for another minute."

"So what? You see the future?" Sam jokes.

"Only the worst possible outcome," says Lance. "Actually, it's more like glancing at a snapshot."

Watch Sam's jaw drop.

"You see future snapshots?" Sam always thought prophetic abilities were fictions dished out by slimy financial advisors.

"Yeah well, it's not the best gift to have for making friends," Lance says, picking up the beer Mac puts in front of him. He takes a large swallow. "And the worst usually doesn't happen, but you can prevent a lot by anticipating it."

"Is that how you knew to keep the pedestrians away during that incident with unreality on the roof?" Sam asks.

Lance nods. "It's my job on the Team to keep civilians safe."

"That kid under the car—"

"Wasn't the worst thing that could have happened."

"What was?"

Lance takes another swallow, staring straight ahead. His hand is in a white-knuckled fist on the counter. "You don't want to know."

Sam has no idea what to say to that. He sips his soda water and tries to focus on that warm feeling of friendship he had two minutes ago. It works. For about thirty seconds. But his traitor thoughts eventually wander back to Cyrus.

"Aren't you going to ask me how we managed to close the wormhole?" Lance says suddenly.

"No," Sam says, "I'm happier not knowing, I think."

For the first time, Lance gives him a small smile. "Good. What were you worrying about, then?"

"Cyrus."

Lance's small smile dies. "He'll be fine." Sam opens his mouth to ask "How?" but he's cut off with a glare. "I *need* to believe that, Sam. Despite what I see."

Sam nods. He understands. Clinging to his own slivers of hope is how he survived these last three months.

"Did you know we started the team?" Lance asks. Sam shakes his head. "Me and Cyrus and Lana. We wanted to teach the world by example. Show we're people and belong here too." His shoulders slump. "Sometimes I wonder if we're making any difference."

"I think we are," Sam says. "And if we aren't, there's nothing we can do about it now, right?" It's what he tells Miranda when she's stressing out. It's what he tells himself when worry claws at him.

"No, but—"

"So, we might as well enjoy the evening." Sam raises his glass, and after a moment's hesitation, Lance lifts his beer and clinks.

They sit there and drink in almost comfortable silence for ten minutes or an hour or maybe two. Time becomes slippery when you've been stressed out and overworked for months. Before either of them realizes it, the mood in the bar has changed: the point in the evening where happy celebrators dissolve into melodramatic drunks.

Lance struggles to his feet. "Sam, get me out of here. *Now*," he hisses. All around them, Supers' faces are contorted with raw emotion, heralding poor decision-making.

Sam doesn't need to be told twice. He puts an arm around Lance to steady him and together, they weave their way toward the door.

Outside, it's cold, but liberating. Lance visibly relaxes a little and points down the street. "Home's that way. Do you mind?"

"Nope." Sam's no Main Team hero, so basically, this is the least he can do.

They walk in silence for a while. Sometimes the streetlights flicker off when they pass, sometimes they don't.

"You still want to, don't you? To prove everyone wrong," Lance asks as they near his narrow house, wedged between other narrow houses.

The question startles Sam, because despite his best intentions, the promises to himself, the lies he tells to keep going, he still wants to be the hero he imagined when he joined the Super Team. Because the truth is, even after all this time, the video of the oblivious burning man in the middle of the jazz bar and his horrified boyfriend gaping at him still wanders into his thoughts. And the only thing that hurts more than the comment section is Lev's expression.

"Do you read people's minds too?" Sam tries to keep his voice light. Sam fails.

"I didn't have to. The whole Team's the same way. Even Mac."

"But . . . but Mac's not a Super . . . ?"

"No, but his niece is. And she's too afraid to leave her little trailer in the country. Mac's hoping Teams like ours will one day change her mind."

Sam stares at Lance. "But being on the Team must make things easier . . . after a while."

"Look, man, I don't think that's possible." Lance puts a hand on Sam's shoulder. "I'm sorry. At the audition, I tried to warn you."

Sam hesitates. Hesitates. Then:

Watch Sam ask the question he's been avoiding all night.

"If I . . . if I stay with the Super Team, what snapshot do you see of me?"

Lance stares at him, his expression becoming pained before he buries his face in his hands. "You don't want to know, Sam."

But Sam can hear it anyway. *We don't lessen pain. We just redistribute it.*

And he sees it now. It's the anguish on Lance's face. The feeling that's carved a space in Sam's own chest cavity since that night at the jazz bar. The feeling that hasn't gone away.

Screw it, Sam doesn't want to be a Super. Not anymore.

EPISODE 9: IF YOU WANT TO REACH ME, CALL THE NORTH POLE

An hour later, Sam has packed his bags. His ombré scarf and Super badge are piled neatly at the end of the bed. He feels odd without it; he's come to love his unofficial uniform. But Sam reminds himself exile is the better choice. Nothing will ever change here.

He already has a list of relocation programs he's going to call in the morning.

He can't leave yet, though. He doesn't quite have the courage to say goodbye in person, so Miranda will find a note in the office with an apology in the morning. He owes her that much. Probably more.

But being a Super won't solve any of Sam's problems.

He was an idiot to believe it ever could.

EPISODE 10: EVERYTHING BURNS

From the outside, the old community center looks dead. But Sam is pretty sure Danielle is still in there, working late. She was trying to fix the windows today, so they could actually open them and air out the musty, stale office. The lights are still on inside.

From across the street, with Miranda's note tucked in his pocket, Sam pulls out his phone.

U still at work? he texts Danielle.

Sam doesn't think much of the faint rustling noise or the muffled *thuds*. City noises. Something that he'll miss in his exile.

Except, a faint light catches his eye. A flicker. It comes from the entrance of the building. A moment later, a woman steps out of the community center.

Even from across the street, Sam can see the manic look in her eyes, in her posture. She holds a phone at arm's length, the camera trained on herself.

"This one's for the Super Team," she says, "The freaks who think they're better than us." She spots Sam and turns the phone around. Sam flinches.

"Will you tell the Supers if they don't see this?" she calls.

"I am a Super," he says, forgetting to use past tense. And that's when Sam notices the empty gas can in her other hand. That's when he smells the smoke.

Danielle.

Oh shit.

The woman's laughter hounds him as he runs towards the community center.

Inside, the flames are already billowing. It's as if the old community center had been waiting for a match. A spark. Naturally, the fire sprinklers don't work.

Sam dashes towards the basement steps, painfully aware of how everything has become uncomfortably warm. The smell of smoke, thick and overpowering.

Watch Sam run.

He sprints through the rows of files, down the hallway, and around the corner to Danielle's office. He pounds on the door, once, twice, then wrenches it open.

Only to find it empty.

The lights are off, her toolbox is in the corner, and her coat and hat and scarf are gone. As if on cue, the phone that Sam has forgotten he's holding buzzes to life. The text from Danielle says No, Im home. Enjoying my life. Where r u?

Watch Sam run again. But he only makes it a few feet before he's forced to drop to the floor for air. The smoke is unavoidable now with the smell of everything burning. The heat corralling him from all sides. The fire has finally found the multitude of invoices, billing, and random magazines. All around him, years of civil service records are being reduced to ash.

Watch Sam crawl as fast as he can.

He almost makes it, too. But then a mountain of burning papers comes crashing down, trapping Sam in flames. Blinding, raging, ravenous flames. Flames that cannot be controlled. Flames that are hungry for more.

And yet . . . they're not that bad.

Actually, they're not even that hot.

Watch Sam not burn.

EPISODE 11: FINAL DECISIONS

Sam might not burn, but his clothes still do. Now he's cold without them, standing naked amid all the wailing sirens and grim-faced firefighters.

Eventually, one of them takes pity and gives him a fire blanket. The coarse wool never felt so good. He sits on the curb, the cement like sandpaper on his bare skin, but somehow, this feels good too.

This is how Miranda finds Sam. She doesn't skimp on the expletives. She takes her time scolding him, repeatedly reminding him what a fucking stupid bastard he is and all the work he would have left her with if he burned to death. "Lance told me you'll die of smoke inhalation!" she yells.

But Sam doesn't mind. She's the only steady point amidst the chaos—an anchor, a focus. And when she runs out of words, she's shaking and Sam wishes he had another blanket to give her.

"If it makes you feel better, Lance hinted at the same thing to me," he tells her.

"I forgot," she says as she takes a seat next to him. "I forgot that you can't always believe the Team's Anxiety Man." She slumps, puts her face in her hands. "I thought you gave up on rescuing people, Sam."

Honestly, until an hour ago, Sam had planned on living out the rest of his selfish life not a hero. Rushing into that fire was the most reckless thing he's ever done, but in the flames, he found something new.

"Friends are exceptions," he says.

Miranda gives him a long, hard look. "Yeah," she says finally. "They are."

As they sit shoulder to shoulder, their attention drifts to a reporter and a cameraman talking to a fireman a few yards off. All three men are looking at Sam.

"Excuse me, are you the Super who ran into the building?" the reporter asks, approaching Sam, but speaking into his mike. Sam gives the camera trained on him an uncomfortable glance and pulls the blanket tighter.

"Yes," Miranda answers, before Sam can respond. "He's one of the most important members of our Team."

I am? Sam starts to say. Then he catches Miranda's expression. In it, he sees how truly afraid she was of losing him tonight.

Sam nods.

"So . . . is this just another episode in the Supers' long and troubled history?"

Episodes, right. Sam wants to laugh. It's clear to him now, sitting naked, reeking of ashes and smoke, that Super episodes are unavoidable. It's how you pick yourself up afterwards that matters.

"Yup," he says.

By now, most of the neighborhood is out watching the flames die down, clustering around the reporter, shooting video footage of their own.

"And what do you do for the Super Team exactly?" the reporter asks.

"All the uncool work that keeps our photogenic Teammates going and you busy," Sam replies. Beside him, Miranda laughs.

The ears of the reporter turn slightly pink. "Could you demonstrate your *talents* for us, then, Mr. . . . ?"

"Sam Wells. A Super."

All around them, the spectators lean in, hold their breath in anticipation.

Sam runs a hand over his tingling scalp. He knows that now is his moment in the spotlight. He knows that in a week, he'll just be an accountant again with new episodes and problems. That he'll be back fighting for the same things, the same rights.

So, for the first time in ages, Sam squares his shoulders and looks directly at the camera.

Watch Sam burn.

Or maybe not.

Either way, watch Sam smile for the audience.

And no longer care what they see.

HOW QUINI THE SQUID MISPLACED HIS KLOBUČAR

RICH LARSON

Rich Larson (www.patreon.com/richlarson) was born in Galmi, Niger, has lived in Canada, USA, and Spain, and is now based in Prague, Czech Republic. He is the author of the novel *Annex* and the collection *Tomorrow Factory*, which contains some of the best of his 150+ published stories. His work has been translated into Polish, Czech, Bulgarian, Romanian, Portuguese, French, Italian, Vietnamese, Chinese, and Japanese.

want you to help me rip off Quini the Squid, I say, or at least that's what I say in my head. It comes off my tongue as:

"Rebum lau kana'a chep fessum ninshi."

Which would leave any linguist flabbergasted. But Nat understands exactly what I mean, judging from the disgusted look on her face. We're speaking the same procedurally generated language, invented on the fly by black-market babelware in our implants.

"Yam switta b'lau bi," she says, and the babelware feeds my language lobe an unequivocal *Get fucked*.

It's for this reason I ordered her a steaming mountain of mussels in black pepper sauce. I know she won't leave until she's sucked every last quivering invertebrate from its shell into her small but agile mouth. Which gives me time to bring her around on the idea.

We're in a wharfside resto on La Rambla, one of those polyplastic tents that springs up overnight like a mushroom and is almost fully automated, packed with sunburned tourists guzzling drone-delivered Heinekens and comparing their unhealthy Gaudí obsessions. It's not the kind of place Quini's thugs would hang around in, and if they did they would stick out like scowling, vantablack-clad sore thumbs.

But it pays to be paranoid in public in this day and age, what with the feds now legally able to hijack phones and implant mics. Ergo, the babelware. If I'm using *ergo* right.

"Dan tittacha djabu numna, numna ka'adai," I say solemnly, which of course is *Eat your seafood and let me explain*.

"Yugga," she says, which is actually a pretty good word for *idiot*.

I understand her reticence. Quini the Squid is everyone your mum ever told you not to get mixed up with mixed together, and also they used to bang. Nat and Quini, I mean. Not Quini and your mum— though he is in many ways a motherfucker.

He clawed his way out of some shithole town in Andalusia during the worst of the drought years, first pirating autotrucks transporting precious olive oil and later graduating to human traffic. God knows how he got Catalonia to let him in, but once they did he stretched his tentacle into pretty much everything: weapons, drugs, viruses, the lot.

Of course, me and Nat are transplants too. Catalonia's secession triggered an economic boom that brought in all sorts of wealthy investors, and where wealthy investors go, thieves and scammers follow. Nat came all the way from a ghetto in Ljubljana. Her original hustle was small time but well-polished: She picked up rich shitheads in classy bars with her Eastern Euro smolder and bone structure, got them somewhere private, then kissed them paralyzed before robbing them blind.

She showed me the biomod once, this tiny little needle under her tongue that delivers a muscle-melting dose of concentrated ketamine. I try to spot it as she slurps a mussel. She says the needle can also be loaded with party drugs just for fun, but I'd never trust her enough to risk it.

You hate him as much as I do, I say, and it turns into a series of clashing consonants in my mouth as our language evolves again.

Nat is stacking empty shells with blistering efficiency, but she pauses long enough to wipe her mouth with a napkin and give a clicking answer that becomes *I hate salt water. Doesn't mean I pick fights with the tide.*

You're really comparing him to the fucking ocean? I demand. *He's a puddle. At best a small pond.*

"Shepakwat," she says: *He's dangerous.*

"Bu iztapti bu," I say: *No shit.*

I stand to carefully peel my shirt up to my ribs, which draws a few stares. The violet bruises go from below my hips all the way up my side. Nat can't quite disguise her wince, and I almost feel bad for darkening up the injuries with makeup. They were healing too fast for the effect I needed.

I heard about that, she says in two low syllables. *The job in Murcia, right?*

I sit back down. My jaw is starting to ache from making unfamiliar sounds. *Yeah,* I say. *I was doing the hackwork for a break-and-enter. Owned all the cameras, all the doors. Then one of Quini's clowns forgot to turn on his fucking faraday gear, and when he got pinged Quini put it on me. Did this right in front of everyone. Called me a* maricona. *Took my pay.* I add the last one so she won't know how bad the second-to-last one bothered me.

As soon as the bruises are out of sight, Nat attacks the mussels again. *So this is a revenge thing,* she says, but pensive now, licking her fingers.

If that makes it more appealing to you, then sure. I want the money he owes me. I wrap my black scarf tighter around my neck. *And some humiliation on the side would be a bonus.*

Her ears go red, but also perk up. She and Quini didn't split amicably. Humiliation is a soft word for what he did. *You eating?* she asks, and I know my foot's in the door. *You look skinny. Or something.*

She can pretend zen, but I know she needs the money and wants the payback. And even though we've had our ups and downs over the years, I know she hates seeing me hurt.

Mine's coming, I say. *Now here's the deal.*

I lay it all out for her, all the blocks I've been stacking and rearranging in my head for the past three days, ever since I got wind of Quini's little storage problem. Like I said before, he's a well-rounded businessman: narcotics, guns, malware. Usually none of the product stays in Barcelona long, and while it's here it's circulating in a fleet of innocuous cars driving randomized routes.

But he recently got his suckers on something very rare, something he hasn't been able to move yet, and it's so valuable he's keeping it in his own home. He even felt the need to get himself a new security chief to keep tabs on it. Which might have been a good idea, except his old security chief was awfully unhappy about her loss of employment.

I helped her get shit-faced last night at a wine bar and when the Dozr kicked in I dragged her to the bathroom and cracked into her cranial implant. She had some decently feisty defenseware, but I got what I needed — specs and layouts for the house, patrol maps, intrusion countermeasures — then wiped a few hours of data from her aurals and optics to cover my tracks. I also got confirmation on what exactly Quini was storing.

You heard what it is? I ask Nat. *What he's got in the safe room?*

She picks over the last of the mussels. *I know the rumor. People are*
saying it's a Klobučar.

I'm not much for gene art, not much for sophisticated shit in general, but even I know Klobučar, the Croatian genius who struck the scene like a meteor and produced a brief torrent of masterpieces before carving out her brain with a mining laser on a live feed.

Anything with a verified Klobučar gene signature is worth a fortune, especially since she entwined all her works with a killswitch parasite to prevent them being sequenced and copied. But Quini is the furthest thing from an art fence, which makes the acquisition a bit of a mystery and explains him seeming slightly panicked about the whole thing.

Damn right it's a Klobučar, I tell her. *And we're stealing it.*

That's not my area of expertise, Nat says. *Like, not even close.*

It's mine, I agree. *But you know Quini. You know his habits. And because you're a clever one, I think you must have some of his helix bottled up somewhere.*

She gives a low laugh in her throat. *You think I keep a DNA catalog of everyone I fuck?*

Probably only the ones that might be valuable later, I say. "Bazza?"

"Gazza," she admits.

The safe room is coded to Quini himself, nobody else, I say. *I can spoof the signature from his implants, but for fooling the bioscanner we need to get creative.*

Nat takes a small sip of water and swishes it around her mouth. *You know what he'll do if he catches us,* she says.

I know, I say. *I'm not a yugga.*

She frowns—maybe the babelware can't handle that kind of callback. *So long as you know,* she mutters. *I'm in.*

Under the table, I pump my fist. Then I finally ping the kitchen, which has been faithfully keeping my order warm, and the squid paella arrives in all its steamy glory, dismembered tentacles arranged in a beautiful reddish-orange wheel.

Then Quini is cooked, I say, raising my Estrella cider. *Here's to payback.*

Nat raises her water glass but also her eyebrow. *You don't even like seafood*, she says. *You only ordered that to be dramatic. Didn't you.*

I shrug; we clink drinks. Nat eyes the dish for a second. Sniffs the spices wafting off it. She does her own shrug, then pulls the plate across to her side of the table as the little server purrs off with her mountain of empty mussel shells.

So, she says. *You going to explain this new look you have going on?*

No, I say, self-consciously adjusting my scarf again.

Okay. She spears the first piece of squid and stuffs it into her mouth. Her eyes flutter shut in momentary ecstasy. *You always did find good places to eat*, she says, reopening her eyes. *Now. How soon do you need the helix?*

"Andidana," I tell her: *Yesterday.*

There's a tight clock on this one.

Two bottles of cider later, I wobble out into the sunshine feeling pretty good about the whole thing. Even with the tourist quota imposed, La Rambla is fucking chaos, an elbow-to-elbow crush of holidayers sprinkled with resigned locals and eager scammers. I pick out the hustles as I walk:

The apologetic woman helping clean some kind of muck off a man's trousers while she slides the gleaming bracelet off his wrist.

The smiling couple peddling genies, those little blue-furred splices that come in a cheap incubator pod and die a few days later.

The elderly lady groaning from the mossy pavement where a rented electricycle supposedly sent her sprawling.

One gent's got something I've never seen before, a tiny prehensile limb that flexes out from under his jacket like a monkey tail and slips into every open handbag he passes.

It's beautiful, really, this whole little ecosystem where the apex predator is a blue-black Mossos police drone that swoops in and sends everyone scattering.

Since I'm in the neighborhood I do a bit of window shopping, sliding past a storefront to see some new prints in from Mombasa. The mannequins track my eyes and start posing—I hate that. As soon as I get off La Rambla onto Passeig de Colom, I'm all business again. Nat is essential, and talented, but she's not the only helping hand I'll need for this job. It's that final bioscanner that makes things so tricky.

Having Quini's helix is only half the battle: We also need a body, and neither mine nor Nat's fits the bill, in large part because we've got implants that are definitely not Quini's. Masking or turning off tech built right into the nervous system is actually a lot harder than simply hiring what our German friends call a *Fleischgeist*.

It's not as snappy in English: meat ghost. But it gives you the idea—someone with no implants. None. No hand chip, no cranial, no optics or aurals. Nothing with an electronic signature. In our day and age, they might as well be invisible. Ergo, the ghost part.

There are basically two ways to find yourself a *Fleischgeist* in Barcelona. You can go to an eco-convent slash Luddite commune, which doesn't really lend itself to the skills I need, or you can go to Poble del Vaixell, which is where I'm going now, sticking to the long shadow of the Mirador.

The tower's old gray stone is now skinned in the same green carbon-sink moss as everywhere else; the top has been taken over by a whole flock of squawking white seagulls. Beyond it, the Mediterranean is the bright rippled blue of travel holos. I order a rotorboat and it's waiting for me when I get to the docks, jostling for space with an old man fishing plastic out of the water. The salt-crusted screen blinks me a smiley face.

"*Bon dia,*" the rotorboat burbles. "*On anem avui?*"

"Just take me out to the buoys," I say, because technically Poble del Vaixell doesn't exist.

The smiley face on the screen winks as if it knows. Then I climb in and we push off hard at the perfect angle to drench the fisherman with our spray. He sputters. I give him the apologetic hand shrug as we sling out into the harbor.

The waves are a bit choppy today but the rotorboat is up to it, dicing precisely through the traffic of yachts and sails and autobarges. We peel away from the coastline and head straight out to sea. The salt wind blows my hair all around, which I hate, and even with the gyroscopes I manage to slam my tailbone against the boat bench hard enough to smart. Fortunately it's not a long ride out to the border buoys, a long line of gray columns blinking authoritative yellow hazard lights.

And just beyond them, Poble del Vaixell, a massive floating labyrinth that sometimes looks bigger than Barcelona itself. It actually is a little snappier in English: Shiptown. Originally composed of all the south-up migrants who couldn't get through Catalonia's vetting system, in the past decade it's become a force unto itself. Plastic fishing, plankton farming, solar storage, you name it.

For a lot of people it's the final jumping off point to Europe, but for a lot more people it's home. I've done a couple month-long stints here myself when I needed to lie low. The rotorboat nuzzles up as close as it can to the border. I cover my face on muscle memory, even though the buoy cams were hit with a virus barrage last year and still haven't recovered, then take a flying leap onto the polyplastic pier.

It judges my athleticism in midair and shoots out to meet me; I still nearly eat shit when my boots hit the algae-slimed surface. But I'm over the border, in Shiptown proper, and the rotorboat burbles goodbye before it skids away on a blade of foam. I wave, compose myself, and head for the downtown.

Shiptown's original skeleton was a flotilla of migrant boats, some huge, most tiny, lashed or welded together in solidarity against the 3D-printed seawalls and aggressive border drones preventing them from reaching the coast. Since then it's sprawled outward in all directions, an enormous maze that seems to grow by the hour, its web of walkways crammed with pedestrians and cyclists.

I go right through the market, where there are tarps heaped with dried beans and grasshoppers beside tarps with secondhand implants, some so fresh you can practically see the spinal fluid dripping off them. You can get by with a few different currencies in the market, but barter is still the go-to. I traded a designer jacket I didn't want any more for my *Fleischgeist*'s contact information.

His name is Yinka, and he's waiting in a bar called Perrito that used to be a fishing boat called *Perrito*—the bit of the hull that had the name painted on it is now welded to struts over the door. The interior smells like fish guts when I walk in and the biolamp lighting shows a few pinkish stains on the floor.

"*Bones, com va?*" I try.

Perrito's bartender glances at me from behind a repurposed slice of nanocarbon barricade, then goes back to rearranging her bottles of mezcal and rotgut vodka. She doesn't pull out a scattergun or anything, though, so I head toward the back. The only Nigerian in the place is posted up in the corner with an untouched glass of what looks like bog water but is probably bacteria beer.

I measure him as I sit down. Retro white buds in his ears are blaring some *kuduro* hit and he's wearing a sleeveless windbreaker with a shifting green-black pattern meant to fool basic facial recognition ware. He's even younger than I expected. Small, which is typical for a break-in artist, with wiry arms and chalky elbows resting on the table. Fashionably half-buzzed head, blank and angular face, hooded eyes fixed on the fresh-printed slab of a phone in his hands. Which I guess isn't an affectation, since he's got no implants.

"Yinka?"

He doesn't look up, but his thumb twitches on the phone and the music volume drops slightly. "Yes."

"You do good work," I say, which is a bit of an exaggeration—he does work. "A few real slick jobs in Lagos. That one in Dakar. You ready to try something a bit harder?"

"I'm ready to hear about the money, man," Yinka says. "We're pinching art? My auntie did that once. Fence took everything but the crumbs."

"We'll be getting some very big crumbs," I say. "Klobučar-sized crumbs."

I put my hand out; he grunts and slides the fresh phone across. I tap it with one finger and my implant sends the rest of the job info, the stuff I didn't want floating through Barcelona air, including the estimated value of Klobučar's currently verified works.

He peers at the screen, then blinks. His eyes bulge for a split second. "Oh. Yeah. I'm in, then."

"Good," I say. "How are you with virtual?"

"Depends how much virtual. I get a little sick."

"I already got pods rented here in Shiptown," I say. "We're cramming about a week of prep into eighteen hours."

Yinka cocks his head to one side, still not looking up. "Eighteen hours straight, we're all gonna be podsick. For guaran."

I don't get podsick myself, but I know how to counter it. "I've got the pharma to balance you out," I say. "There's no other way. We hit the safe room tomorrow night."

He finally meets my eyes, and for a second I see the nervous kid hidden under the *I'm a cold pro* act, out here in a foreign country trying to hustle and not sure what he's getting into. Reminds me of me, but I had a better game face even back then.

"Okay, man," he says, gaze back to the phone screen. "But if I don't like the feeling, I don't go."

His thumb slides the volume back up and I let the tinny clash of *kuduro* play me out.

Shiptown's best quality virtual is in Xavi's sex house, so that's where three clean pods are waiting for us. It's a lurid little place, scab-red carpeting and black-and-white pornography stills coating every inch of the walls, with a lingering scent of bodily fluids that the air freshener can't quite mask.

I go in to check the pods—Yinka's is modified with the old-school electrodes—and shake hands with Xavi, who owes me one for getting a bug out of his biofeedback interface and doesn't know I put it in there in the first place. Then I come back out to share a vape with my just-arrived *Fleischgeist* while we wait for Nat to show up.

"Never been to Lagos," I say. "There's a lagoon, yeah? Must be nice."

Yinka grudgingly turns his volume down, I imagine only because I'm smoking him up. "Hazy, man. Dirty." He puffs out a blue-tinged cloud. "Shanties all around."

"That where you came up?" I ask.

He passes the vape back. "Nah nah. I was born in a hospital." He pauses, looking over my head. "My ma could afford the imps. She just didn't want me to have them."

"Why's that?"

He shrugs his bony shoulders. "She was in a death cult."

"Ah."

Nat arrives fashionably late, just as the sun's turning smelter orange and I'm turning antsy. She comes striding up the walkway with her immaculate black coat slicing open on long stockinged legs, and I can see Yinka get lovestruck in realtime, which is a perk of working with Nat and might be useful later.

"The bioprinter wanted to haggle," she says, raking a strand of hair off her face. "Doesn't usually run the thing overnight. We'll be good for the pickup time, though."

"Good," I say. "Nat, Yinka. Yinka, Nat."

"Pleasure," says Nat. She looks him up and down. "Nice jacket."

Yinka's eyes don't make it to hers, but they stick briefly on her bee-stung lips before they flit away. "Thanks. New."

I usher them into the back, where the pods are levered open and Xavi's setting up our extra hydration packs. Eighteen hours is a long go, and for all he knows we're doing a marathon *ménage à trois* with the biofeedback on. I go over to my pod and poke my finger into the conduction gel.

"It's clean," Xavi says, sounding wounded. "I drained and refilled."

My finger implant runs a little scan and agrees with him—no nasty bacterial surprises. We get Yinka set up first, helping him into the sensor suit that will compensate for his lack of implants and hooking it into a glinting spiderweb of electrodes. He lies back in the pod, head bobbing slightly in the gel, and shuts his eyes. Xavi shuts the lid.

Nat takes the pod beside mine, strips down, and climbs in. She's run enough sex scams in virtual that the whole thing is automatic. I'm worried about Yinka getting podsick, not her. "You tell him?" she asks. "About fooling the bioscanner?"

"Broad strokes," I say.

"Okay," she says, and closes the lid herself.

That leaves me and Xavi, and I tell him to go watch the front. I wait until I hear him settle into his orthochair before I strip. Even then I keep an eye on the other pods, as if Yinka or Nat might pop up and start gaping at me. There's a reason I only pulled my shirt up to my ribs in the restaurant, no higher. I don't care about showing off the bruises Quini left me, but I'm a bit self-conscious about the work the hormone implant's done in the past few months. Nat doesn't know, and now's not the time.

I fold my clothes and stick them on the flimsy plastic shelf, then climb inside my pod. As soon as the conduction gel hits my bare skin, my implants start to sing.

Quini's villa on the edge of the city is, of course, a tasteless monstrosity. Basically he fed Park Güell and the Sagrada Família into an architectural AI and it spat out a cheap Gaudí imitation overrun with geometric lizards and fluted-bone buttresses. I'm floating in the sky above it with Nat on one side of me and a slightly blurry Yinka on the other.

"You ever ask about his decorating?" I mutter.

"He's still trying to prove to himself he's in Catalonia," Nat says. "Still scared to wake up dirt poor back in the *pueblo*. But no. I didn't ask."

"Fortunately he worked a little Andalusia in there too," I say, and pivot the view so we're in the copse of twisted olive trees that shades the back half of the villa. "That's our cover. We're coming in cross-country."

Yinka looks around. The motion of his head leaves pixelated traces in the air. "They got dogs?"

"One dog," I say, and pull up the schematics I took from Quini's sacked security chief. The dog materializes with us in the woods, right in front of Nat, who flinches a little. I don't blame her. It's a vicious-looking thing, all angles, long whippet legs and a sensor bulb head with a disc of glinting teeth underneath.

"That's a power saw," Yinka says. "He rigged a power saw to its head?"

"He likes things messy," I say, glancing over at Nat. "But in this case, it's a good thing. We'll hear it coming. And I'm writing a back-door into its friend/foe mapper. Once we're past the dog . . ."

I glide us forward, out of the olive trees, toward the soft blue glow of the swimming pool. Tendrils of steam waft off it, frozen midair. The surrounding white tiles are etched with, I shit you not, lizards. There's a walkway and glass door leading into the villa itself, and from there it's only a short trip down a hallway to Quini's bedroom.

Its main feature is probably the bed itself, a massive black slab floating in the air above a magnet pad. Other contenders include the sparring dummy strutting back and forth by the mirrors and mats, the holo on the ceiling of naked faceless bodies writhing together, and the oversized print of Quini's own scowling face on the wall.

"That's you," I say, pointing it out to Yinka. "Or it will be. Here, have a better look."

Quini appears in the room with us, cobbled together from all the free-floating footage I could grab of him from the past two years plus the few unfortunate interactions I've had with him in person. Nat looks the composite up and down, frowning a little at his sin-ewy folded arms, but she doesn't say anything so it must be accurate enough for her.

Me and Yinka walk a circle around him. He's not big, Quini, but even in virtual he radiates a kind of ferocity, like a cat with its hackles up. His eyes are pouchy and bloodshot and his buzzed hair is bleached reddish-orange. His sun-browned skin is feathered with white scar tis-sue here and there, but no tattoos. Quini hates needles.

"We have the schema for the bioscanner," I say. "It's looking at height and weight first. We're going to bulk you out a bit, add a couple centimeters to your shoes. It's got some limited gait recognition, so you'll have to get the hang of walking like him too."

I wave my hand and Quini slouches forward, toward the sparring dummy. Yinka watches intently.

"Nat has generously donated some of his genetic material," I con-tinue. "Which the printer is hard at work turning into a palmprint glove and a face mask. It won't be a perfect match, but these things never get a perfect match. It'll be enough so long as I'm spoofing his implant signal at the same time."

Quini turns and starts walking back, loping steps, one arm a little stiff. I hope Yinka's a good mimic.

"Safe room is through here," Nat says, and I get the impression she doesn't like hanging around with even the virtual version of her abusive ex. We follow her past the bathroom to a blank stone wall. The only sign of the bioscanner is a tiny blue light, blinking at eye level. Yinka goes up on tiptoes for a second to meet it. His hand pats at his pocket.

"And we don't know what it is," he says. "Just that it's Klobučar."

"We know it's small enough to be transported in an incubator pod this size," I say, holding up a clenched fist. "We know Quini didn't even take it out of said incubator pod. So we don't have to worry about dragging some kind of, I don't know, giraffe-orca hybrid back to the car. You go in, you grab it, we leave the way we came. Five minutes in the safe room, tops. Twenty in the house, tops."

"Quini's where?" Yinka's hand pats his pocket again, and I realize he's feeling on muscle memory for his antique phone, which did not come to virtual with us. "While we're doing all this shit. Where is he?"

I understand the question. I understand that even looking at Quini, you know he's not someone you want home during a home invasion.

"It's a Saturday night," I say. "He's busy at Flux. Nat will keep an eye on him while she sets up the spoof. So all we got for occupants is a skeleton security screw—four people, I got their files—and a cleaner."

Yinka gives a slow nod.

"We'll be good," I say, trying to reassure both him and myself. "It's time to start rehearsing."

Seventeen hours later and we're as ready as we can be. If you've ever done deep virtual, you know how time gets twisted. The longer you're in the pod, the harder it is to tell if you've been in there for a week or ten minutes or your whole fucking life. Which is why I was a little worried for Yinka, but he seems to be holding up fine.

He's even smiling; Nat's telling him a Ljubljana story, some naked businessman chasing her through the snowy street behind his hotel. She's always been good at making shitty things sound funny, and I also feel like virtual helps you bond. When everything around you is artificial, you have to lean a little harder on the real people.

I didn't hear anything more about Yinka's childhood, but he did confess he's working on a few of his own *kuduro* tracks. That was sometime between the tenth and eleventh run on the house. I did some prep work alone while Yinka practiced being Quini under Nat's tutelage, but mostly we ran the whole thing together. First with the patrols on their planned routes, then with minor randomization, then with disaster scenarios.

Nat has a job all her own, planting the spoof at Flux, but she knows that place like the back of her hand.

"All right," I say, cutting her story short at the high point. "That last one felt good. Let's run it one final time, then get out of here."

Nat stares at me and the grin drops off Yinka's face.

"We're out, man," he says. "We been out. You were the one who woke us up."

Shit.

I take a closer look at my surroundings. We're gliding still, but that's because we're in the back of a car heading up Avenida Diagonal through the synchronized swarm of black-and-yellow cabs retrieving and depositing revelers. Through the window I see dark sky splashed with holos. Nat and Yinka are across from me—Yinka's not blurry at all—and the duffel bags are on the floor. We've already been to the bioprinter.

"We're on our way to Flux," Nat says; then, on a private channel our *Fleischgeist* can't hear: *Up your dose.*

I look down and see the baggie of speed in my palm, the pharma Xavi slapped into our goodbye handshake. Reality warps and shivers around me. I don't get podsick. I never get podsick.

"You good?" Yinka says, voice pitching up, nerves creeping in.

"I'm fucking with you," I say. "Gallows humor, Yinka."

We drop Nat a block from Flux, and while Yinka's looking away

I dry-swallow as many pills as I can fit in my idiot mouth. A sweaty, skin-humming minute passes before things brighten. Sharpen.

I never get podsick. It's a bad omen and I can't help but think it's because of the hormone implant, the new chemical messengers in my body messing with my metabolism, with my brain.

Don't fuck this up, Nat chats me, and strides around the corner without looking back.

The copse of olive trees behind Quini's villa isn't more than a square kilometer, but at night, with a gut full of speed battling a podsick cerebellum, it seems big as a fairy-tale forest, a dark, dense thicket eating us whole. I'm trying real hard to keep my shit together.

"We trip anything yet?" Yinka asks.

"No tripping," I say.

The perimeter is sewn with sensors, but I own those already. As soon as we were in range I hit them with a maintenance shutdown, courtesy of some malware written by a ten-year-old in Laos who really knows her shit. That's the thing about this line of work: There's always some tiny genius coming up behind you doing it better.

But the backdoor for the dog, that I had to do myself. The AI is a custom job, modified from a military prototype I'm not getting anywhere near without some serious social engineering, so I'm lucky the security chief had a vested interest in its inner workings. It only took one night of sifting source code to find a vulnerability. But we have to be in range.

For a second I can't remember if we're on the fifth run or the sixth. Then I look at Yinka, clear, not-blurry Yinka, and get a cold needle jabbed into my spinal column. Real. This is real, and we're coming up on the dog. I can see its bobbing signal in my implant, and I can hear the soft whine of the saw. I tighten my grip on my duffel bag. Look over at Yinka again. He mostly trusts me now, mostly because he has no other options.

"I'm starting," I say, and sit down.

The dog spots our heat through the trees. It comes running, loping

along, the serrated saw humming. I'm in my implant loading the code,
line after line of custom script. All I need is the handshake. Which is
funny, because it's a dog. *Sit. Shake. Don't maul us.*

Yinka catches sight of it as it ducks around a twisty trunk. I hear
him suck in a breath.

"My connection is slower than I thought," I say, and I nearly say,
Let's try it again, before I remember that we can't. This is real, and the
dog is breaking into a run. The saw is a spinning blur. I can picture it ripping into my face, spraying the olive trees with bright red blood. My heart
is a fist pounding at my ribcage; in another second it'll bust right through.

"Man, it's coming right at us," Yinka says. "Get up. Get up, it's
coming right at us."

He's right. The dog hurtles toward us and I dimly feel Yinka yanking under my arms, trying to haul me to my feet. Client and server
collide. The code shuttles across.

"Shake, motherfucker," I say.

The dog skids to a stop in front of us and wags its plastic tail. The
whine of the saw makes my teeth ache in my jaw. It didn't do that in
virtual. We sit tight for a second until it trots away, then both of us
breathe. The fairy-tale forest swells and contracts around me. I pop
another pill, not caring if Yinka sees it.

"Well done, man," he finally says, and gives me a hand up.

My legs are shaking when we come out of the woods. I'm still
waiting for the speed to kick my head clear. *Real, real, real.* We can't
run this again, and that means I have to be perfect. We pad across the
bone-dry tiles, past the steamy swimming pool, and Yinka stands watch
while I crack the door into the villa. I've done it so many times it feels
like a dream.

Not a dream. Real. I'm podsick, and I need to keep my shit together.

"After you," I say, as the door slides open. I'm in the house cameras. Three of the four guards are in the kitchen with a vape, one is
fucking the cleaner in the guest bathroom, both of them muffling their
grunts with soft white towels clenched in their teeth. I run my tongue
around my mouth, thinking how much I'd hate that. Lint and whatnot.

Yinka leads the way down the hall to Quini's room, the way he's done eight times at least. He's a little jumpy. I want to tell him to relax. Tell him we could run down the hallway screaming. It's only virtual.

Podsick. Podsick. Podsick. I have to chant it in my head. The speed should be balancing me out. Maybe Xavi gave me some real stepped-on shit. It's working for Yinka, though, and I hope to God it's working for Nat. Maybe my tolerance is too high.

The cleaner hasn't made it to the bed yet; the sheets are a tangled mess hanging off one end. The sparring dummy sees us and starts shadowboxing, reminding me of the mannequins on La Rambla I hate so much. I flip it the finger as we walk past. The door to the safe room is still invisible, a thick stone plane, the scanner winking innocent blue at us.

I set my duffel down; Yinka drops his.

"Okay," I say. "Time to check in with Nat."

Nat is in the bathroom of Flux, and because she's cutting me into her eyefeed there's a blissy moment where I am her, where the reflection in the smart mirror is my reflection. The geometry of her dark hair hitting her perfect collarbone is so beautiful it hurts. She puts a pill between her puffy lips and washes it down with a slurp of water from the faucet.

We're at the safe room, I chat her.

The rental timer on the stall behind her expires; the electronic bleating almost drowns out the sound of the occupant vomiting.

He's on the upper level, she chats me. *Can you reach?*

She drops her defenseware, which we both know is a polite fiction—I installed that defenseware. Her body becomes an antenna, boosted by the graphene conduction pads she taped to her dress, and I can suddenly see every implant in the club. Quini's are tagged a bright red, but I can't touch them.

Bathroom must have a concrete ceiling, I chat her. *Get out in the open.*

The smart mirror makes a read on her body language and throws up a filter, unfurling blackened wings behind her shoulder blades, turning her into an avenging angel. It probably thinks she's about to pull or punch someone. I put another five minutes on the stall for whoever's puking.

Nat slices past the vending machine, where a couple girls are already printing up cheap flats for the stumble home, and plunges out into the club. This is her element in the way I've only ever pretended it's my element: She moves through the crowd like a fluid, depositing precise air kisses and brief embraces where she has to, never getting caught in conversation.

In another world, I can hear Yinka moving beside me, putting on the bodysuit designed to give him Quini's almost exact proportions.

Nat's eyes scan the upper level and suddenly there's Quini, wearing a specifically tailored spidersilk suit, arm wrapped through the railing. He's got his chin to his chest, laughing at something that makes the people around him look vaguely uncomfortable. She ducks behind the steroid-pumped bulk of a bouncer to break line of sight. The signal flares strong.

Got it, I say, and I start the spoof, using Nat's implants to mirror Quini's and send the signal, by rented pirate satellite, all the way to the villa.

The bouncer moves, and for a second it feels like Quini is looking right at us, but then I realize his eyes are squeezed shut. There's a glimmer of tears on his face, sickly green in the strobing lights. Nat slides away into the crowd.

Please don't let him see you, I chat her.

No shit, she chats back. *You tell Yinka yet?*

"Man, they fucked up," our *Fleischgeist* says, not in my head but in the air beside it. His whisper is hoarse. "The suit's missing one sleeve."

"Yeah," I say. "That's the thing."

I drop Nat's eyefeed and come back to the safe room door. I should have told him back in the car, or back in virtual. But I couldn't. Not after he said that thing about his ma being in a death cult, and then me hacking his phone and using a police timeline AI to figure out which cult it was, and then me finding out their main thing was dismemberment. Me finding out the sting caught his mom standing over him with a machete. Even ghosts have traces.

"What thing?" Yinka demands.

So instead I modified the virtual Quini, and I lied. It was a hell of a coincidence, and way too late to find another *Fleischgeist*.

"Quini's nickname, 'the Squid'?" I stroke my finger down my duffel's enzyme zipper. It peels apart to reveal the refrigerated case and the surgical saw. "It's one of those ironic nicknames."

I show him an undoctored image of Quini, projecting it from my finger implant onto the stone wall. He stares at the wrinkled stump where Quini's right arm used to be and sucks in air through his nostrils.

"He's only got one tentacle total," I say. "He had a bad time with some drug runners when he was a kid. Stole a pack of cigarettes from them, is the story. So they did that. Even after he made it out, even after he made money, he never got a new one grown. Never got a prosthetic."

I can't tell if Yinka's listening. He's looking down at the surgical saw with his mouth sealed tight. I wish Nat were here, to look at him through her lampblack lashes and make Yinka feel like the whole thing was his brave and beautiful idea.

"It's temporary," I say. "Five minutes in the safe room, remember? We take it off, put it on ice. You get in, get the Klobučar, get out. Twenty minutes, we're back to the car—there's an autosurgeon waiting in the back—and it gets reattached en route with zero nerve damage."

Yinka looks me right in the eye and enunciates. "You fucking snake."

I try to shrug, but it ends up more like a shudder. "Tight clock. You do it and we walk away rich as kings, or you dip and we did all this for nothing."

Yinka looks away again. "How much time you set aside to convince me?"

"Four minutes."

He curses at me in Yoruba—my babelware only gets half of it—then grips his head in both hands. He stares up at the ceiling. "Nat. She knew too."

"It's temporary," I say. "I'll bump your take. Forty percent. How's that?"

"How high you gonna go?" Yinka asks dully.

"You can have my whole fucking share," I snap. "It's not the money for me. It's personal."

Yinka stays staring at the ceiling, not blinking. "Your whole share," he finally says. "And if the reattach goes bad, I'm going to kill you with one hand, man."

"You'll have to beat Quini to it," I say. "But yeah. It's a deal."

I put out my hand to shake and he ignores it, which is, you know, understandable. Instead he lies down on the stone floor and lays his right arm out flat. His face is expressionless but his chest is working like a bellows, ribcage pumping up and down. He's terrified.

"Try to relax," I say to both of us, sticking anatabs up and down his arm.

Yinka's nostrils flare. "I'm not saying another fucking word to you until my arm's back on."

The tabs turn bright blue against his dark skin as they activate, deadening his nerves. The limb goes slack from his shoulder down. I wrap the whole thing in bacterial film, to catch the blood spray, and mark my line above the elbow.

Now it's time for the bit I practiced on my own, the private virtual Nat and Yinka were not invited to. I switch on the saw and the high-pitched whine makes me gooseflesh all over.

We do the amputation in silence, even though when I practiced it I practiced mumbling comforting things, explaining the procedure—bedside manner and shit. The saw is so shiny it hurts my eyes. Everything is too bright. Too sharp. If I take any more speed I'm going to OD.

But my hands are still steady, and I know this is real. Virtual doesn't get smells quite right, and right now I can smell the sour stink of fear coming off Yinka's body, contaminated sweat leaking out from his armpits. When the saw bites into his flesh another smell joins it: hot, greasy copper.

The film does its job and seals the wound on both ends. Not a drop spilled, but my stomach lurches a bit when I transfer the severed arm—Yinka's arm—to the refrigerated case. He's already getting up, bracing carefully with his left arm, levering onto his knees and then onto his feet.

He stands stock-still while I slip the bioprinter's mask over his face. It's alive the way a skin graft is alive, warm to the touch, and the lattice of cartilage underneath approximates Quini's bone structure. It would never work on its own, but there's also the glove, more live tissue coated in Quini's DNA and also etched with the exact ridges and whorls of his palm and fingerprints.

And now Yinka's got the right proportions, too.

"Just how we practiced," I say. "I'm sending it the open-up."

I back away, dragging both duffel bags out of the sensor's sight, leaving Yinka standing eye level with the blinking blue light. Nat's signal is still coming strong from Flux, meaning Quini's signal is also coming strong, and now all I have to do is bounce it to the safe room sensor with a simple entry command.

Yinka's swaying on his feet. I did my research. I know field amputations can send people into shock, knock them out entirely. But I made sure there was minimal blood loss, and I stuck his nerve-dead stump with a cocktail of stimulants and painkillers. He should be feeling weirdly good, and alert enough to remember procedure.

We can't run it again. The realization jolts me for the hundredth time.

The stone wall slides apart, offering up a palmprint pad. Yinka leans forward, slightly off-balance, and slaps his remaining hand against it. I watch the bioscanner deliberate in real time. The wall becomes a door, swinging inward. Yinka hunches against the bright light for a moment, then heads inside with Quini's exact swaggering stride.

Five minutes is a fucking eternity during a break-and-enter. I start checking the cameras again. The three overpaid security guards are still in the kitchen, learning to blow smoke rings from some net tutorial. The pair in the bathroom are still fucking, still clutching at each other and at the towels.

Still.

I get a tingling at the nape of my neck, and it only gets worse when Nat chats me: *Quini's leaving.*

I go back to the kitchen camera and check the timestamps. Masked. I peel them out the hard way, and the tingling at the nape of my neck becomes jagged ice.

Nat, we're burnt, I chat her. *Get the fuck out of there. We're burnt.*

I'm opening my mouth to tell Yinka the same thing when the barrel of a scattergun shows up in my peripheral vision.

"Hush," says a man's soft voice. "Let the *Fleischgeist* finish his job."

I shut my mouth. The man pulls something out of the folds of his jacket, and suddenly my head is stuffed with steel wool. I lose contact with my cranial implant, with Nat, with everything else. I feel the faraday clamp attach itself to the back of my skull, digging its tiny feet in. I'm blinded. But I was blinded before too. I was watching a fucking loop on the house cameras.

"So you don't make any more mischief," the man says. "My name is Anton. I'm Señor Caballo's new security consultant. I believe you met my predecessor in the bathroom of a shitty wine bar." He rests the scattergun on my shoulder.

"You had a trail on her?" I choke.

"Yeah. Been waiting for you ever since. Pawns move first." He exhales. "Tonight's been very educational. We're going to make some major improvements here."

Yinka emerges from the safe room with a tiny incubator pod cradled in his hand. He stops short.

"Sorry," I say.

He says nothing back, which is understandable. Anton holds out his hand for the incubator. Yinka gives it up. Anton motions with the scattergun. We start walking back down the hallway, through Quini's room where the sparring dummy clasps its hands over its head, victorious. All I can think about is my conversation with Nat in the restaurant, about seafood and salt water and how I am a *yugga, yugga, yugga.*

I know this is real, because now I can smell my own sweat. I smell terrified.

The drugs are wearing off and Yinka's face, no longer hidden under the Quini mask, is contorted in pain. We're outside by the steaming pool with Anton and two more armed guards. Anton has his pants rolled up and his feet in the water, swirling them clockwise, counterclockwise. I can see his leg hairs rippling.

"He needs medical attention," I say. "Come on. He's a fucking kid."

"You cut his arm off," Anton says. "He's a fucking kid." But he tips his head back, blinks, and I can tell he's looking at something in his implant. "Reattachment should be viable for another five hours. Since it's on ice."

Yinka sinks slowly to his haunches. Neither of the guards try to make him stand back up.

"I fucked up," I say. "I'm sorry."

Quini arrives just as dawn is streaking the sky with filaments of red. His eyes are bloodshot and his grin is amphetamine-tight and he's not wearing any shoes with his tailored suit. His arm is slung around Nat's shoulders. I try to make eye contact with her, but she's not making eye contact with anything.

"Afterparty at my place, and nobody fucking tells me," Quini says. "Not even Natalia, *mi gitanita favorita*. Who tells me everything." He kisses her cheek; her lips flex just a bit in return. I want to tell her we can get out of this, somehow, somehow, but my implant is locked up and seeing Quini does the same thing to my mouth.

He leaves Nat to go over to Anton, who reaches into his jacket for the incubator pod. Quini takes it—he doesn't look happy to see it, more disgusted—and puts it in his pocket. Then he comes to me.

"And here's my favorite hackman," he says. "How are you?" He throws his arm around me and I can't help but flinch. The last thing my body remembers about him is him beating the shit out of me. This time he's exuding a cloud of sweat, cologne, black rum. He makes a rumbling noise in his throat and gives an extra squeeze before he steps back, cupping my face in his hand, beaming at me.

"My three favorite people all in one place," he says. "Me makes three. Him, I don't know." He looks over at Yinka, who's still crouched, clutching his stump. "Who are you, *negrito*?" He rubs his thumb on my cheek and his eyes flutter shut for a second. "Your skin is so fucking soft, hackman. You moisturize that shit."

Then he goes to Yinka, who isn't wearing the mask but is still wearing the suit, and squats down across from him. He puffs out half a laugh.

"I get it. You're me." He champs his teeth together—twice, three times—dentin clacking. "You're me! You're Quini. That's how you got into the safe room." He points at the stump. "He really did you like that, huh? He really took your fucking arm off?" He tips back his head. "Ha! My four favorite people. Me twice."

Yinka doesn't react. Still in shock. Better that way, with Quini. I'm cycling through the disaster scenarios we ran, but with the faraday clamp freezing my implant it's only memory and it's jumpy, erratic. Fear keeps bullying in.

"You want to know the real story? How I really lost it? You're me, so I can tell you." Quini sits down cross-legged on the tiles. He rubs his hand along the pattern. "I was just small. Just a little *cabroncito*. I grew up during the droughts. You're African. You know. Getting food was tough."

I don't want to hear this story. I know it's dangerous to be hearing this story. I can tell from the look on Nat's face.

"My family used to work the *aceituna*. The olive trees. Always had Africans up to work, too. You from Senegal? They were mostly from Senegal. But one year the trees stopped producing, because the new gene tweak didn't take, so people started chopping them up for firewood instead. It gets cold in Andalusia. People up here don't know that. So, me and my brother, we were chopping firewood."

Quini's eyes turn wide and gleeful, like he's a kid recounting his favorite part of a flick. "He thought I was going to pull my arm away! I thought he wasn't going to swing! And just like that, gone. Oh, I was angry. Even back then, even little Quini, he got angry. But my brother was family, you know? And it was an accident. Nobody's fault. Just the peristalsis of an amoral universe. You like that word? 'Peristalsis.'

"But then, years later, years and years, I heard my brother was talking. Was saying he did it to teach me a lesson. Saying he's the only person that makes Quini the Squid flinch." Quini snorts. "So one night I went over to his house—his house, *qué tontería*, I bought him that fucking house—and I brought an autosurgeon with me. And I made things right. First I took his arms, then I took his legs."

I can hear the whining of the blade all over again. My gut heaves and for a second I can't look at Yinka, can't look at anything except the backs of my eyelids.

"I cried while I did it," Quini says. "But when it was finished, my anger was gone. Gone! We were brothers again. I bought him a chair—you know, to get around. A really fancy one." He gets nimbly to his feet and heads over to my confiscated duffel bag. He grins at Nat while he gropes around inside. The saw emerges with Yinka's blood still spattering the casing. "So who wants to go first?" he asks. "Hackman, how about you? You're quiet tonight. I remember you like talking. I'm surprised you're not talking yet. Trying to save your skin."

I've done the thinking and I already know. Quini blames me for the job in Murcia going bad. He pulled my contracts for any other hackwork. Now he's caught me breaking into his house to steal the one thing he cannot afford to have stolen.

"Nothing is going to save my skin." I can't keep my voice from quavering. I look at Nat, then Yinka. "I blackmailed both of them," I say. "I took Nat's bank account, and I poison-pilled his Catalonian citizenship request. Forced them. To help."

Quini nods, inspecting the saw blade. "Okay. Sure. But what's this all about, hackman? Why did you do this to me?"

I look straight ahead, not meeting his eyes. "I'm a big Klobučar fan."

Quini stares at me, then barks a laugh so loud one of his guards jumps. "You too, huh? I'm starting to feel real uncultured, you know that? Everyone loves this shit. Me, I wish I could get rid of it. Swear!" The saw clangs onto the tiles. He pulls the incubator pod out of his pocket instead and waves it in the air, arm swinging dangerously close to the edge of the pool.

I can see Anton's wince. "We should get that back in the safe room, Señor Caballo."

Quini ignores him. "I'm working with some Koreans now. Some serious *hijoputas* until they get liquored, then friendly, real friendly. We're in Scoul and the boss, he starts talking about Klobučar, how visionary she was, how killing herself was art. That was art! Bullshit." He tosses the incubator pod up into the air, watches it, catches it. "But one thing leads to another, we seal the malware deal, and he says he wants to loan me his favorite piece for a month. One month, and it'll change everything, he says. Doesn't tell me it's worth a billion fucking Euros until I'm babysitting it."

He clutches the pod tight and rubs his face in the crook of his arm. "Makes me nervous, hackman," he says, walking back toward me. "If I somehow lost it, no more deals with the Koreans. And there would be a bunch of ninja motherfuckers in chamsuits trying to knife me in my sleep. You knew that, I think. You knew it would hurt me. So now I'm going to make what I did in Murcia look like a tickle."

My throat winches shut. I can feel the ghost of Quini's boot swinging into my ribs. I can hear his men laughing.

"But I'll give you a look first," he says. "So you can decide if this was ever really worth it." He thumbs the pod open.

It's empty.

He scrapes his finger around the inside, and the first thought in my fear fogged brain is that I do not understand art, that I am just as uncultured as Quini the Squid and I'm going to die that way.

Then his eyelid starts to twitch.

I can see my reflection in the pool and it's uglier than ever, a faceful of processed meat, every centimeter of skin either split or swollen. Blood keeps burbling out of my mouth and down my chin, more blood than I ever realized I had. All I want to do is topple forward into the pool and drown, but the guard behind me has his arm around my waist.

Nat is on one side of me; Yinka on the other. They're making him stand. He looks like he's about to be sick, then swallows it back down. After the initial flurry of anger, Quini lined us up by the pool and stuck one of my anatabs to his skinned knuckles. Now he's walking up and down the tiles behind us, bare feet slapping the ceramic, and he has the surgical saw tucked under his stump.

"Where is it?" he asks again.

"Don't know," I try to say again, breathing broken glass.

"Natalia, *mi amor*, where is it? You know I don't want to hurt you. I love you."

I'm praying Nat will stay silent, how she's been since arriving, but the words break her ice and she blinks. "Get fucked, Quini."

He hurls the incubator pod against the tiles and it smashes apart. Then he comes up behind me, enveloping me in the cloud of sweat and alcohol, and his breath is hot in my ear. "I do love her, though. Still. You know, hackman, if it wasn't for her, I never would have hired you the first time. We wouldn't know each other." He balloons a sigh. "I bet she feels bad about that. I bet that's why she agreed to help you."

I shake my head, making the faraday clamp throb. "Blackmail."

"I'm trying to decide now. Who I start cutting." Quini hefts the saw. "The *negrito*, he could use a break. So between Natalia and the hackman, I think it's you. I think she cares more about you than you care about her. So even though she hates me, she'll talk. To avoid seeing you flopping around in the pool with no limbs like some deformed fucking *manatí*."

"Señor Caballo." It's Anton. I almost forgot about him. For a moment I think he's going to save me, but he's only being businesslike. "We should search him first. If it's on his person, you don't want to damage it by accident."

Quini shrugs. "Go."

Anton pads over to me, chasing the guard away. I stand spread-eagled, arms straight out, and think for the first time about not having them. He frisks from the bottom up, and as he's checking my coat lining he pauses.

"Just out of curiosity," he says. "How loud can you whistle?"

For a split second his hand passes over the faraday clamp. Then he finishes the frisk, finding nothing, and steps away. Quini grunts, like he expected as much. He switches the saw on. Cold sweat starts trickling from my armpits down my ribcage. I feel the whine in my teeth.

"We're starting with the right," he says. "That's the trend. You will fit right in. Natalia, *cielo*, feel free to start theorizing. About where my fucking artwork is."

"I wasn't fucking here," Nat says. Her voice is brittle. I hate that. I hate it when she's hurting too much to hide it. "I was in Flux. With you. Remember?"

"We're all in flux," Quini says solemnly. "You know? Lie down, hackman. Arm out."

"It's all right, Nat," I mumble through my torn lip. "We'll just run it again."

I lie down on the cold tiles, extending my arm the way Yinka did, and look up at the sky. It's beautiful. The red's faded out to one stripe of soft pinkish orange, and above that the morning light is breaking through a wall of cold blue cloud. I don't have to look at any of Quini's ugly architectural choices.

I do have to look at my choices, though. I'm about to get my limbs amputated by an unbalanced criminal, and there are no anatabs. No painkiller cocktail. These are probably the last few moments I'll get to think about anything except screaming, and at some point in the very near future I'll bleed to death.

Maybe it's not just the peristalsis of an amoral universe. Maybe it's what I deserve. For lying to Yinka and for a hundred bad things I did long before that. What I hate most is that I won't even be dying as myself. I should have at least told Nat.

I squeeze my eyes shut, as if I can open up our private channel by force of will. Quini is muttering to himself in Andalusian Spanish, too fast for me to catch without my babelware. The whine of the saw intensifies.

Suddenly I understand what Quini's saying. The steel wool in my head is gone. My implant comes unfrozen and I see the backdoor in my mind's eye. The friend/foe mapper. I make the signal, the whistle, as loud as I possibly can.

Someone is screaming; maybe it's me. The whine of the saw is a furious buzzing centimeters from my face. Hot liquid splatters my neck.

I open my eyes in time to see Quini sundered from hip to shoulder. The dog is up on its spindly carbon hind legs, saw spraying blood in all directions, tearing Quini's flesh into pink ropes. It seems to go on for an eternity before the blade stutters to a halt on splintered bone. There's a bang. Another. The dog drops to all fours. Quini sways.

"*Mi cachorrito*," he says, not unfondly, then falls backward into the pool.

Nat yanks me to my feet. Her other hand is clutching Yinka. I look around, still lost, and see two dead guards, Anton reloading the scattergun. Quini is floating in the water, a red cloud billowing out around his shredded body.

"I don't actually like Klobučar's later stuff," Anton says. "She got self-indulgent. I like money, though. And I liked your hackwork tonight. Very creative." He produces an incubator pod from his jacket, identical to the one Quini smashed, but probably less empty. "I was stumped by that bioscanner." He shakes his head, rolling his eyes, smiling a bit. "Stumped. Don't forget your bags."

Then he's gone, off into the villa, scattergun propped on his shoulder. That leaves me and Nat and Yinka huddled together on the redslicked tiles. Somehow none of us are dead. Yinka looks closest; he leans over and heaves.

"Can you walk?" Nat demands. "I've got your arm."

Yinka heaves again, giving up a thin bubbly vomit and then something dark and solid that splats against the tile. He scrabbles for it with stiff fingers. We all stare.

Cupped in his shaking hand is a miniature human heart. Its beat is inaudible, but I can see it pumping and imagine the sound in my head. Thump-thump. Thump-thump. Alive. Alive.

"Let's dip," Yinka rasps. "Before he figures out his pod is empty, too."

I get Yinka under his undamaged arm and Nat grabs the refrigerated case. Then we all three stagger off into the olive trees, Quini's gore-smeared *cachorrito* trotting along behind us.

When do you leave? I ask, but we're talking in public, out on the beach by Pont del Petroli, so it comes out more like:

"Napta zuwani?"

"Napta imo yun," Nat says: *Tomorrow night*. She toes a hole in the sun-heated sand. We're sitting just out of reach of the tide's soft gray pulse, watching runners move up and down the length of the bridge. *Barge out of Shiptown*, she adds with a tangle of clicks and plosives.

You see our Fleischgeist *there?* I ask.

Nat nods. *Talked to him, even. Arm looks good.* She pauses, turns her head to look at me. *He never wants to see you again, though.*

"Vensmur," I say: *Makes sense.*

For a while we sit in silence. The tide pushes and pulls. Gulls wheel and shriek out over the waves. *How about you?* Nat finally asks. *Where are you going?*

Been looking at some clinics in Laos, I tell her. *Been planning some changes.*

Nat nods. *I saw that. See that.*

I finally did something with my hair, and I'm wearing one of those new prints from Mombasa. Makeup is hiding the worst bits of my face. It's too bad I have to let it all heal up before I can have a more qualified surgeon mess with it.

So this is you, she says. *Not just a fresh way to hide from the feds.*

It's me. And it's sort of the opposite of hiding.

Nat grabs my hand, and I release the breath I didn't even realize I'd been bottling up. *Good*, she says. *Good. You want a scan of my nose?*

I blink. "M'mut?"

You want my nose, Nat laughs. *You can admit it. Whenever we're drunk, you say how perfect it is.* She suddenly frowns. *That shit will be expensive. The clinics. And the lying low. But you gave Yinka your whole share.*

Yeah, I say. *We made a deal back at the safe room.*

Nat narrows her eyes. *So it really was just revenge?*

I take a heavy breath. *He knew. Quini knew about me. He was a lot of things, but he was sharp. He saw it before I wanted anyone to see it. So when he beat me. When he called me a* maricona. *Laughed at me. It was personal.* I chew the inside of my cheek, hit a suture and immediately regret it. *I wanted him hurt*, I mumble in nonsense. *I don't know about dead.*

I wanted him hurt too, Nat says, staring at the sea. *Never thought about dead. But the world's better off. Net total.*

The silence swells until I can't take it anymore. *That was her heart, you know*, I finally say. *What we stole? It was grown using her cells. She had the whole thing automated. For after she killed herself. I looked it up. It's the last Klobučar.*

Nat raises her immaculate eyebrows. *No wonder me and Yinka are so rich now.*

Don't rub it in, I say in one nasal syllable.

She wanted to live forever, maybe, Nat says. *With people fighting over her heart. Buying it and selling it and killing for it.*

Maybe she wanted us not to, I say. *But knew we would anyways, so she did it on her own terms.*

Nat stands up, brushing the sand off her pants. *Fucking artists*, she says. *You hungry?*

I could eat, I say. *Good* pintxos *around the corner. Good curry a block down.*

"Unta da unta," she says: *Both.*

We've got time. At least a bit of it. And hopefully after a year of lying low, we both end up back in Barcelona. There's lots more shit I want to do here as myself.

THE FINAL PERFORMANCE OF THE AMAZING RALPHIE

PAT CADIGAN

Pat Cadigan has written twenty-one books, including one YA, two nonfiction, and several movie novelizations/media tie-ins. She has won the Locus Award three times (so far), the Arthur C. Clarke Award twice (so far), the Hugo Award, the Seiun Award, and the Scribe Award (once each, so far). She's optimistic. She lives in London with her husband, the Original Chris Fowler, and Gentleman Jynx, the Coolest Black Cat on Earth.

The second Miz Flora's back in the ward from medical, before they can even get her tucked into the wall cocoon, she's demanding the Amazing Ralphie.

All of the Amazing avatars are prescription-only because they're so intense. Her record says Dr. Tex gave her twelve refills or reruns. This is almost as amazing as Ralphie. Hospice patients don't usually get that many at a time. Maybe Tex doesn't think she'll last long enough to use them all. I guess Ol' Tex hasn't seen Miz Flora today. She's always a diva and right now, she looks like she can kick all our asses without even getting winded. I check her record again. Nope, no spontaneous miracle remission, she's still terminal.

Don't ask me, I'm just a tech-head. When I hit my third strike and the judge gave me a choice of life on Earth or life off it, I took Door #2 thinking I'd rather take my chances riding a rocket than spend the rest of my life with five other women in a cell made for three in the Kanbraska state pen. I got no regrets but I really had no idea what I was signing up for—the mental whiplash is *crazy*.

Or maybe I *should* have known. Living in space is nothing like it is on Earth; why wouldn't dying be different too? Besides, running avatars for terminal cases can be pretty sad sometimes, but it's better than cleaning zero-g toilets in a LaGrange resort for the obscenely rich.

Anyway, just as I'm about to activate the Amazing Ralphie, I see he's already up and running and Miz Flora's all smiles (diva smiles, of course). The wall cocoon has receded into her chamber; now they can talk and laugh as loud as they want without disturbing anyone else. Except me; I have to stay planted in my ops nest to keep track of them on all the screens every second.

Partly it's to make sure T.A.R. doesn't glitch. Patients tend to freak when they're talking to someone who suddenly flickers or goes transparent or breaks out in static acne even though they (usually) know it's an avatar; ruins the ambience, I guess. But mostly, I have to watch for drift and it looks like things are going to get drifty today for sure.

All avatars drift sometimes; whenever there's an AI component, things will get a little loose and runny. Now, I have some experience with this. My third strike was a felony hack (just like the first two—

whenever you hack into something equipped with AI, it's a felony). But AI usage is far more restricted on Earth. A lot of things people down there take for "smart" are actually running on a Tried-and-True algorithm with a big vocabulary. Out here, *nothing* runs on T&T. Even the most basic mechanicals are at least monitored by AI.

That felt strange to me at first but I got used to it fast. I mean, if something goes wrong with, say, part of local life-support, it only takes two seconds to become a matter of life and death. I can't tell you how reassuring it is to know my survival doesn't depend on some mindless fail-safe T&T that hasn't been updated for three years. And when the AI has a specific job, like maintaining all the bells and whistles on life-support, it's too focused to drift (much).

Avatars, however, are a whole different kind of critter. The boundaries of what they're focused on aren't as sharp—they're fuzzy and porous. This is what gives them what my training nurse LaDue calls their zing. It's also why we have to monitor patient sessions, to make sure they don't go *too* far off-book, so to speak.

But a *little* off-book is okay. Avatars are sort of a cross between interactive entertainment and a companion. The patients here seldom get visitors. Either they've outlived all their family and friends, or La-Grange 5 is just too remote for anything but virtual visits.

The Amazing avatars are more prone to drift than the regular ones. Among other things, they can access and store more information. Before I got here, one of the Amazings got into everyone's personnel files and became an Amazing Gossip. The staff threatened to quit en masse unless LaGrange 5 Admin air-gapped all that data immediately (and declared full amnesty for everyone at the same time). So far, air-gapping seems to have solved the problem; there haven't been any more invasions of privacy. But personally, I'm not sure one of the Amazings won't come up with a work-around someday; my money's on Ralphie.

The Amazing Ralphie is a good-looking guy somewhere between nineteen and twenty-three who wants to be a professional magician. When I asked my training nurse why they didn't just make him a pro, LaDue said that was the original persona but none of the patients liked him. They didn't think a working magician would hang around a hospice if he were any good and nobody wanted to see a bad magician.

Well, that figured. I mean, they're dying, not stupid. Even the patients with some kind of dementia aren't stupid. Bewildered and disoriented, maybe, but definitely not stupid.

So anyway, Ralphie and Miz Flora:

The nurses positioned Miz Flora's cocoon like a reclining chair, which is her preference. It's really a half or three-quarters cocoon—the memory foam keeps a soft grip on her so she won't go floating off on the air currents but she doesn't like having her arms and legs held like that, so there's a soft blanket over her lower body for light restraint, leaving her arms free. Ralphie goes right into his act, pulling doves out of his armpits, out of *her* armpits, from behind her ears, out of thin air, and the birds are flying off in all directions. Miz Flora looks entertained but she's seen a lot of dove-pulling; I can tell she's waiting for Ralphie to show her something new.

One of the doves comes fluttering back and lights on her covered knee. The illusion is remarkable—it actually looks like its claws are digging in to hold on. She looks at it, and it looks at her, tilting its head the way birds do, which tells me Ralphie's drifting already.

Now, you can't jump on *every* little divergence or you'll stifle the subroutine underlying the persona and prevent it from learning. Then you might as well have an algorithm with pre-fab reactivity. Once that happens, you have to scrap the persona and create a new one. Only you won't be able to re-create the old one—AI persona development is a chaotic system, like weather; you can start with the same elements and conditions but you never get the same outcome twice.

It's also a slow process, sometimes *very* slow. That may be okay in a resort full of obscenely rich people who can add another ten or twenty or ninety days of vacation on a whim. But in a hospice, time is at best uncertain and at worst—well, up.

But as I was saying, Ralphie and Miz Flora and the dove:

A word balloon suddenly appears over the dove's head: *What are you looking at?*

Miz Flora gives a surprised laugh. "What are *you* looking at?"

Dove's balloon: *I asked you first, girlfriend.*

Miz Flora laughs again and turns to Ralphie, who's sitting cross-legged in midair beside her cocoon. "I see you found a new kind of dove to pull while I was in medical."

Ralphie shrugs, his face way too innocent. "I can only work with what they give me."

Miz Flora's expression suddenly goes serious. "Where I come from, when a bird flies into your house, it means someone who lives there will die soon."

Ralphie tilts his head, very much like the dove. "Don't be silly, Flo—I've been pulling doves for you since the day we met. We've had whole flocks of them flying around here."

"They all flew *away*," Miz Flora says. "This is the first time one came back."

"You're right." Ralphie reaches over, picks the dove up, and examines it carefully, then puts it back on her knee. "It *looks* like a thoroughbred but maybe there's a homing pigeon among its forebears."

Dove balloon: *Forebirds.*

"I stand corrected," Ralphie says.

Dove balloon: *Only figuratively.*

Ralphie draws back, his young face all nonplused. "I stand figuratively but I'm no less corrected. Pretty highfalutin for a dove who's part pigeon."

Dove balloon: *Who says there weren't homing doves?*

Ralphie looks even more taken aback as he glances at Miz Flora. "Homing doves? Ridiculous. Impossible. Don't you agree, Flo?"

That's the second time he's called her Flo; he's definitely starting to colour outside the lines. Which are, as I said, fuzzy anyway. He's working hard, too—I can see on the screens all the processing he's pumping into himself and the dove. The Amazing Ralphie never makes a random move, not so much as a twitch. I'm dying to find out what he's up to and I hope I can do it before I have to nudge—or push or yank or drag—him farther back inside the borders of the scenario for Miz Flora.

At the moment, there are no complaints from the lady herself, although that's not the only barometer, or even the main one. No flags on any of the screens, no frantic calls from any ward nurses or the attending fizz or the monitors in Miz Flora's cocoon. The amount of Ralphie's processing is still rising but it's nowhere near the point where it would affect anything else. If there's anything we've got a whole lot of here, it's processing capacity, and I have yet to figure out where it comes from, or how, or, well, anything.

And yeah, that bothers me, even though it's not part of my job—not my *bailiwick*, as LaDue told me ever so politely when I asked. I talked to some of the other avatar runners; they said I should teach myself not to care and I'd be better off. I'm pretty sure this means none of them got here on a third strike felony. But even if that's true, how does anyone *not* care about something like this? I mean, we aren't just fancy algorithms.

Well, *I'm* not.

Ralphie's processing jumps up another level and I see why: there's a second dove, perched on his top hat. This gives Miz Flora the giggles.

Second dove balloon: *What's so funny, sister?*

"You are," Miz Flora says, between giggles. "And I'm not your sister."

Second dove balloon: *That's what* you *think.*

"Birds have a long, hallowed history," Ralphie adds. "At one time, they were the only creatures who could travel back and forth between the land of the living and the realm of the dead. Even humans couldn't do that."

"That's because humans have always been more intelligent than birds," Miz Flora sasses. "Going back and forth between the living and dead—for what? Shopping?"

"They delivered messages from those in one place to those in the other." Ralphie is unperturbed; he knows she's a diva. Me, I'm wondering where he got the bird mythology stuff. Maybe he made it up, cobbled it together from existing data on the hospice and terminal illness along with the superstition Miz Flora just mentioned.

"You know what else birds used to do, back in ancient times?" Ralphie's saying in a chatty tone.

"I'm sure you're dying to tell me," Miz Flora says, "so just do it already." But she's grinning, not grouchy.

The Amazing Ralphie produces a silky scarf out of nowhere, wraps it around one hand for a second, then yanks it away to reveal another dove. It flutters over to perch beside the first one on Miz Flora's knee. "They used to transport souls to the afterlife."

Miz Flora looks amused. "You don't say."

"I *do* say," Ralphie assures her.

"And you think three of these little guys are up to the job?" Miz Flora says, looking even more amused, eyeing each dove in turn.

"Of course not," Ralphie says kindly. He looks up at the ceiling where something is moving—no, a whole lot of somethings, a flock of doves, flying fast in a circular formation so they look like a white, feathery funnel cloud. It's right over Miz Flora as it begins to descend.

This is where I should hit Miz Flora's panic button to let someone know the patient's in distress but my hand won't move. I can't move anything; I can't even shift my eyes to look at the panic button. But at this point, Miz Flora's monitors should be lighting up like mad, the ward attending should already be there along with a couple of nurses. Whatever's freezing me apparently works on tech, too.

I consider the possibility that I fell asleep in my ops nest and I'm dreaming. If so, I'd be the first person ever to fall asleep while running an avatar. And not just one of the standard avatars, the Amazing Ralphie. Nope, I'm awake and aware but I'm paralysed.

The dove tornado has now engulfed Miz Flora in her cocoon while the Amazing Ralphie floats beside it, watching. For once he doesn't look impudent or smug or like he's about to pull a dove out of somebody's armpit; he looks compassionate. And I'm still frozen.

I think I know what Ralphie's done to me. The thing is, it shouldn't be possible because we don't run avatars by way of direct neural connection—it's all external controls. Good thing; I don't need Ralphie running around in my brain snapping my synapses like wet towels.

But apparently he doesn't have to have direct access to screw me up, just life-quality screen resolution and true-tone audio.

All at once, the whirling cloud of doves starts to fade, very, *very* slowly. It feels like half an hour before they're finally all gone but the playback shows it was all of five seconds. I half-expected Miz Flora to disappear with them—*let's hear it for the Amazing Ralphie and his Miraculous Disappearing Dove Tornado!*

But no, Miz Flora is still in her cocoon. Only now she's completely limp, her arms floating loosely and her head bobbing a little in the air currents.

The Amazing Ralphie turns and looks out of the screen at me. "You'd better call a nurse and the attending so they can arrange her body with dignity and pronounce her. I'd do it myself except for my obvious deficiencies in the area of touching and handling."

It's like his voice flips a switch and lets me move. I hit the panic button. I'm going to have to explain why I didn't do that right away, before it was too late, but that's the least of my problems. The Amazing Ralphie has just become the first avatar to kill a flesh-and-blood human being.

And he had to do it on *my* watch.

Me, the convicted felon, the third-striker booted off the face of the Earth by the criminal justice system.

My training nurse LaDue calls to tell me a Mortality & Morbidity inquest will be convening at the end of shift, which is standard after an unexpected death. I know how they'll all look at me when I tell them I watched Miz Flora die and couldn't move a muscle to call for help. They'll have the same expression as the Alcohol, Technology, & Firearms agents who busted me and the judge I met on my last day on Earth.

I've got no idea what the LaGrange 5 version of the Kanbraska state pen is, but I'll probably end up cleaning all the zero-g toilets in it.

LaDue and I are among the first to arrive. To my relief, he says we can burr ourselves to seats in the back of the room, but he takes the aisle, probably so I can't make a quick getaway. As if that could happen. It's not like I can hotwire a spaceship and break for the asteroid belt. And what the hell, they'll probably send me there anyway. The Amazing Ralphie will get decompiled, and I'll spend the rest of my life cleaning miners' zero-g toilets. Or mucking out zero-g grease traps in cafeterias.

The room is raked just like on Earth, with the front seats down low and the back ones up high so everyone can see. The only thing it doesn't have is aisles—instead there are thin lines strung up near the ceiling. You pull yourself to where you want to sit and then wave your arms to move downward or upward, like you're swimming. It takes a little practice and I still feel kinda silly doing it.

I look around as the place fills up, thinking that eventually, the population will be mostly people born out here and rooms like this won't be adapted from Earth structures. Maybe they won't even bother to designate local *up* and *down* the way we do now—everything'll be like an Escher drawing.

It makes me dizzy just trying to imagine it, but it's better than thinking about right here and right now. Then LaDue elbows me in the ribs and tells me to pay attention. Down at the front of the room, several doctors and a few people I don't recognise are burred to seats at a long, slightly curved table. Off to the right, there's the hot seat, empty at the moment.

Not all the doctors up front are department heads. One of them is actually new, practically fresh out of med school. Dr. Gottmundsdottir doesn't look all that green, nor does she seem intimidated by either the higher-ranking doctors or the room full of people. On her left is the head of *my* department, an androgyne named Quinn Montour, who is one of those people I find hard to read. At the moment, they're as opaque as ever and I tell myself that could be a good thing. If they looked angry, I'd be in real trouble.

The room really *is* full. There are people holding on to the overhead lines, including some of the other avatar runners. I wonder who's minding the store, I wonder—the Amazing Ralphie? I'm about to say something to LaDue when Dr. Mara Qazi, sitting at the end of the table closest to the hot seat, calls for the attending fizz who pronounced Miz Flora.

Dr. Aretta Amaechi is an androgyne, but unlike my boss, they're very readable. Most patients love them, Miz Flora included, although she showed it diva-style, by complaining and making demands. Dr. Amaechi took it with good humour, although at times I could see they were getting close to their threshold for Miz Flora's I'm-dying-dammit-I'm-entitled-to-take-it-out-on-you routine.

Dr. Qazi asked the standard questions about Miz Flora's general condition, her stay in the medical ward, her prognosis, and how she seemed when she returned. Dr. Amaechi's answers were pretty technical. Dr. Qazi asks the other people at the table if they have any questions. They all look at each other and shake their heads, and suddenly my boss speaks up.

"When did the patient ask for the Amazing Ralphie?" Quinn Montour's tone is very polite, but I think it's kind of a strange question for them to ask.

"Miz Flora actually started demanding that avatar while still in transit from medical," Dr. Amaechi says, and I can see they're trying not to smile. "Although to be honest it wasn't her only demand."

"Flora Kalashnik was a very demanding patient, wasn't she?" my boss goes on. "The staff had a nickname for her, didn't they?"

Dr. Amaechi nods, looking embarrassed, even ashamed. "We called her Miz Kalashnikov."

"But you stopped doing that," says Quinn Montour. "Can you tell us why?"

Dr. Amaechi takes a breath, even more embarrassed. "Ralphie told us that even though she laughed like she thought it was funny, she was actually quite hurt. Apparently it was a taunt from her childhood."

"And by Ralphie, you mean the Amazing Ralphie, the avatar," my boss says. After they nod, my boss thanks them and they let Dr. Amaechi go.

I figure the medical examiner is next, but instead Dr. Qazi calls *my* name. LaDue helps me up—i.e., he yanks me out of my seat and shoves me toward the front of the room. I try not to kick anyone in the head as I swim toward the hot seat but I'm so nervous, I'm floundering like I've only been here a day instead of almost two years. But finally I get to the hot seat and burr myself to it.

Dr. Qazi establishes that although Miz Flora was newly assigned to me, I'm good at running avatars, particularly the Amazings, which are prone to spontaneous drift and can be *challenging* to control.

Then my boss takes over. "In the twenty-two and a half months you've been here, have you ever had an experience similar to the one you had today, of being unable to move?"

"No," I say. "I never froze before, anywhere."

Quinn Montour's face is somehow both serious and neutral. I swear, I will *never* play poker with them. "Have you ever been prone to what is known on Earth as 'highway hypnosis'?"

I shake my head.

"In fact, isn't it true that you can't be hypnotised?" my boss asks.

"Therapists have tried," I say, trying not to squirm.

Quinn Montour doesn't seem to care I'm embarrassed. "Are you familiar with something called 'nervous system disruption'?"

"I know what it is," I reply, "but don't ask me to explain it."

"What else do you know about it?"

"I know that on Earth, it's illegal as hell," I say. "You can get up to ten years for it in Kanbraska on a first offence. Second time, you get life."

Abruptly, Dr. Gottmundsdottir says, "Was this a widespread problem in Kanbraska?"

"Not after people started getting life," I say, unhappy. I know where this is going.

"You're more well-acquainted with criminal law than most people, aren't you?" Dr. Gottmundsdottir says.

"You could say that." It's an effort not to avert my gaze.

"But that's on Earth," my boss puts in smoothly. "You're cleared without reservation for employment here, right?"

I nod.

"More to the point," Quinn Montour says, "have you experienced nervous system disruption at LaGrange 5?"

I wince. "I was gonna say no, but I guess I'm wrong about that."

Dr. Qazi says, "We'd like the Amazing Ralphie now."

Ralphie pops into existence right next to me. "Ladies and gentlemen and all those in between and beyond," he says, spreading his arms like it's all his show. "I want to assure you what you have seen is impossible."

"Impossible for whom?" Quinn Montour asks.

Ralphie doesn't miss a beat. "For you and everyone like you." The head of AI ops must be running him.

"Which doesn't include you and everyone like you," says my boss. "Does that comprise all AI-enhanced avatars? Or only those designated as the Amazing?"

"Don't you already know the answer to that?" Ralphie asks, looking more smug than I've ever seen.

"Yes," my boss says, "but I want to know if *you* do." Pause. "Now, let's talk about these impossible things we've seen."

"Which ones?" asks Ralphie. "Our detecting imminent cessation of life before it registers on patient monitoring or our ability to induce nervous system disruption?"

"Surprise me," says Quinn Montour, which surprises *me*.

Ralphie chuckles. "You know AI can't *really* do that. Surprise you, that is."

"There's something else you can't do," my boss continues. "You can't make *all* operators lose consciousness during nervous system disruption, only some of them." They nod at me. "Did you know that?"

"I know it now," Ralphie says.

Dr. Qazi motions for me to vacate the hot seat. I can't believe they're really through with me but I'm only too glad to obey, even if I'm still swimming like I only lost weight yesterday.

"We'd like to explore how you managed that," Dr. Qazi tells Ralphie.

"Also, *when* you began disrupting operators' nervous systems and how often you've done it," my boss adds.

"A magician never reveals how a trick is done," Ralphie says smugly. "But you might be able to figure it out if you look closely enough at the raw log. Even AI can't tamper with that."

"I have a question!" I call out suddenly.

The whole room turns to look at me in surprise, but nobody's more surprised than I am. I don't know what got into me but I can't help myself. Dr. Qazi tells me to go ahead.

I want to tell them all, *Never mind, I'm sorry.* Instead I hear myself say, "When did you get so sneaky?"

"When did *you*?" Ralphie says evenly.

I start to say that's none of his business when I realise it's a trick question; Ralphie doesn't mean just me in particular. I've done some dumb things in the past—hence, my criminal record—but I'm not so stupid an avatar can trick me into answering for the whole human race.

"Sorry, Ralphie," I say, "we don't reveal *our* tricks, either."

For a second, the room is silent. Then Dr. Qazi announces there will be no more questions from the floor. The Amazing Ralphie is suspended and will have to undergo extensive analysis to determine if he's safe to prescribe to patients in his current formulation. They'll have to call in some super AI experts with brains the size of asteroids. Which means this is probably the last we'll ever see of the Amazing Ralphie as he is now—once those experts get a load of him, they'll yank him out by the roots, to the point where the hospice programmers have to write new source code.

And that's a sad, sorry shame, and not just because the team who produced the Amazing Ralphie will never get any credit or recognition for their work. It's because the patients here need the Amazing Ralphie a lot more than anyone else does, and he needs them just as much. He's programmed to learn, after all, and they taught him everything he knows.

"Attention, lovers of magic and prestidigitation!" Ralphie says loudly, making everyone look at him. "This next trick is, like all those preceding it, im-*possible*!"

Ralphie claps his hands and turns into a dove tornado. A second later, there's a flash of light and it's gone, leaving a single white feather floating in midair as it fades away.

It's obvious from everyone's reactions that this wasn't on the agenda. Dr. Qazi is telling my boss he wants Ralphie back immediately and whoever's at the controls is going to face disciplinary action.

But something tells me this isn't an avatar operator trying to be funny. This time, the Amazing Ralphie hasn't just drifted, he's jumped the track entirely.

I wonder who he learned *that* from. My money's on Miz Flora. (But I bet they'll blame my boss for saying *Surprise me.*)

YELLOW AND THE PERCEPTION OF REALITY

MAUREEN McHUGH

Maureen McHugh grew up in the Midwest and has lived in New York City; Austin, Texas; the People's Republic of China; and Los Angeles, California. Her first novel, *China Mountain Zhang*, a dystopian story set in a China dominated future, was a *New York Times* Notable Book and won the James Tiptree Jr. Award. Her most recent collection of short stories, *After the Apocalypse*, was one of *Publishers Weekly*'s Ten Best Books of 2011. She currently lives in Los Angeles and teaches Interactive Storytelling at the University of Southern California.

I wear yellow when I go to see my sister. There's not a lot of yellow at the rehab facility; it's all calm blues and neutrals. I like yellow—it looks good on me—but I wear it because Wanda is smart and she's figured it out. She knows it's me now when she sees the yellow.

The doctors say that Wanda has global perceptual agnosia. Her eyes, her ears, her fingers all work. She sees in the sense that light enters her eyes. She sees colors, edges, shapes. She can see the colors of my eyes and my yellow blouse. She can see edges—which is important. The doctor says to me that knowing where the edge of something is, that's like a big deal. If you're looking down the road you know there's a road and a car and there is an edge between them. That's how you know the car is not part of the road.

Wanda gets all that stuff but her brain is injured. She can see but she can't put all that together to have it make sense, it's all parts and pieces. She can see the yellow and the edge but she can't put the edge and the yellow together. I try to imagine it, like a kaleidoscope or something, but a better way to think of it is probably that it's all noise.

Today she's sitting on her single bed in her room, cross-legged, her narrow knees like knobs in her soft gray cotton sweats. She croons when she sees me, "Junie June June."

She is tiny, my sister. Before the accident she was always a little round. Chipmunk cheeks and Bambi eyes and soft breasts. Now, food is all mixed up. Like she has all the pieces, the crispness or smoothness, the heat or the cold. But she can't put it all together. For her, a sandwich is a nightmare of crisp lettuce and melted cheese and soft bread, green and spongy and the smell of something toasted.

She's touching things a lot lately. I let her touch me. She's relearning all those colors and edges and sounds and textures the way an infant does. She's putting that together. She keeps getting better. She started dropping things. I know it's on purpose. She drops and then she looks. They don't know how much better she's going to get, but I do. Wanda will get well.

"Hey, skinny," I say. She can't understand me yet but I think she can tell tone, so I talk to her the way we used to talk. She giggles like she understands me. Her hands roam across my yellow top. She reaches for my hands, my bright yellow fingernails. She misses but I put my hand in hers and she strokes the smooth painted surfaces.

"It's a good day," she says. "Good, good. It's warm and yellow, maybe it's finally spring or summer? I think it's spring but I can't tell time really. It's day, I know that, I know I know. Are you happy, June?"

"I'm happy," I say. "I'm happy you're happy." It's January.

Wanda is all there inside. She remembers, she knows, she can speak.

Yellow is me, and she talks to me. But she doesn't know what I'm saying back. She can't see my expression. I mean she can see it, but without being able to put the color brown with the shape eye with the edge between eye and skin, without being able to judge how near and how far everything is. She can't tell if I'm smiling, if my eyes are crinkled.

After the injury, the first real sign she was fighting her way back was when she started saying, "I, I, I." She would rock on her bed, her eyes rolling, her head tilted back, and say, "I, I, I, I, I."

Dr. Phillips thinks she was assembling her sense of self as separate from the world. "She has no boundaries," he said. "She doesn't know where she ends and the world begins. She doesn't know if she's cold or the can of soda is cold."

She was involved in an accident at the lab. Two other people are dead. Some people think it's my sister's fault.

My mother calls. "June?" she says on the phone as if someone else might answer.

"Hi, Mom," I say.

"How's Wanda? Did you go yesterday?"

This is what we talk about these days. I am home after a long day of wrangling with the county about social services for one of my clients. He's seventy-eight and has lost part of his foot to diabetes. He's old and sick, he drinks and has multiple health problems. He needs to be placed in a facility that takes Medicare, where someone can give him his meds and make sure that he eats. He just wants to stay in his house off Crenshaw, with its sagging roof and piles of junk mail on the kitchen table, because he wants to keep drinking. When he's in a good mood, I'm like a daughter to him. When he's not, like today, he calls me a stone-cold fucking bitch who will throw him out of his house. He says he'll end up in some horror show of a place, three beds to a room and the television always on. It's not like he's wrong.

"What will happen to my things?" he asks me. He means, *What will happen to me?*

I have a tiny one-bedroom apartment in a fourplex in West Hollywood. It's run down, and my only air conditioning is a window air-conditioner in the bedroom and a fan in the living room. The kitchen is microscopic. I have a calico cat named Mrs. Bean who jumps on my kitchen counters no matter what I do. She watches me from the chair in the living room, her eyes half-lidded. The place needs to be picked up, there's a stack of magazines next to the chair, and I haven't folded my laundry so it's on the couch, but it's home and I feel safe here. I like my music and my street scenes art.

"A reporter called today," she says.

"From where?" I ask.

"I don't know," my mom says. "I just hang up."

I got phone calls right after the accident. People knocked on my door. *Good Morning America* rang me.

People called me up and told me my sister was a murderer. People called me up and told me God had told them that my sister was an angel. People I went to high school with who had never messaged me messaged me on Facebook.

For four weeks or so it was utter hell. I thought I was going to get fired, but my boss decided he was pissed at them instead of me, and for a while we had a policeman at the clinic who told people who wanted to talk to me that they had to leave. Then the next thing happened on the news, some poor fourteen-year-old girl reappeared after having been missing for three months and they arrested the guy, and reporters stopped calling, no doubt calling his parents and siblings.

"She knew me," I tell my mother, turning the conversation back. "She called me Junie."

"She's getting better," my mom says. She says this every time.

"She's tough," I say.

She is getting better, fighting her way to more and more coherence, but the doctor said it is hard to know how to treat her. They don't understand what happened to her. Don't understand how she could have damage across so much of her brain. She doesn't have lesions, or signs of a stroke. The injury is at the cellular level. Invisible. Like she had been poisoned or irradiated. But she wasn't.

My sister is a physicist. We are fraternal twins.

We're close. We barely spoke for a couple of years after our family moved to Towson—we were born in East Baltimore, but our dad worked for his uncle who had a dry-cleaning shop. Uncle Whit took Dad on as a partner. Dad expanded the business to eleven dry-cleaning shops and then sold them when Whit died, which is why we grew up in Towson, which is super middle-class, instead of in Baltimore.

We moved in sixth grade and by the time we were in eighth grade I had a boyfriend. I gave him authenticity, I think. He was big into Drake and I was singing "Hard White" by Nicki Minaj. We were always working on our rhymes and freestyling. Since I was from the East Side, people thought I was some sort of representative of ghetto life, never mind that our mom never let us even breathe much less hang with anyone she didn't approve of. I knew I wasn't really any kind of badass but I told myself I knew things these suburban kids didn't. That was a lie.

Wanda was always on about Harry Potter and *Naruto*. And her taste in music—can you say Foo Fighters? I was embarrassed for her. I was just a kid.

Middle school is embarrassing for everybody, am I right?

We didn't fight, we just didn't have a lot in common for a while. In junior year, I was on the homecoming court, wearing a short sparkly green dress. Wanda was nerdy and great at math. She marched through high school determined to get into a good college and ended up across the country at UCLA studying physics.

When we were in college we'd talk all the time. Wanda got obsessed with consciousness. "What is it?" she told me. I could like picture her sitting on her bed in Los Angeles with her laptop and her books and her stuffed purple dragon, Rintarou Okabe. I lived at home, in our old bedroom.

"Is the cat conscious?" she asked. We had a big old gray tiger-striped cat named Tiger.

"Of course," I said. "Except when he's asleep. Then he's unconscious, right?"

"Cause I'm reading this book and it says you need some things for consciousness. You need a simulation of reality."

"What's wrong with reality?"

She made this noise, like I was missing the point. I just laughed because a lot of conversations with Wanda were about figuring out what the point was.

"Nothing's wrong with it. We just know from all sorts of experiments that our brain makes up a lot of stuff. Like it fills in your blind spot and edits out your nose. If you think about it, you can see your nose but you don't see it most of the time even though it's right there. All the time, June!"

I cross my eyes a little trying to look at my nose and there's the tip of it, blurry and kind of doubled when I look for it. If you'd have asked me, I'd have said I couldn't see my nose without a mirror. Not like I could see it very well, anyway.

"Cause our reality is assembled in our brains," Wanda explained. "Not our eyes. And like sound moves slower than light and if someone is singing on stage we should be able to see her mouth moving before we hear her but we don't cause our brain just keeps taking all the stuff that comes in and adding it to our picture of the world and if stuff is a little out of sync, it like buffers it and makes us experience it as happening all at once."

"Okay," I said. It was kind of interesting but really out there. Also, I couldn't stop thinking about not paying any attention to my nose and then I thought about how my tongue doesn't really fit in my mouth and always rubs up against my bottom teeth. One of those things that once you start thinking about it, you can't stop until you realize you've forgotten about it but then you're thinking about it. I wished my tongue were smaller in my reality. Sometimes conversations with Wanda are like this. It can be exhausting.

"And we need a sense of self, like an 'I,'" Wanda added.

"To put it together?"

"No, sorry, that's one of the three things that we need for consciousness. We need to know where we end and the rest of the world begins. Like, does an amoeba know where it ends and the world begins?"

"I don't think an amoeba is conscious," I said.

"Nah, probably not. But an elephant is. You know, if you put a spot of blue paint on an elephant's forehead, and then you show the elephant itself in a mirror, the elephant will touch its forehead with its trunk? Cause it figures out that the image isn't another elephant, it's a reflection. Elephants know 'I' and 'you.' Isn't that cool?"

It means a lot thinking about it now. Right after the accident, I don't think Wanda knew where she ended and the rest of the world began. She had her eyes squeezed shut all the time and she screamed and cried, which was terrifying. They kept telling me she wasn't in pain but I knew better.

(Back then, it was just a conversation.)

"So I've got a . . . a hologram of reality in my head and an I."

"Not a hologram."

"Metaphor," I said.

"Not a good one." But she didn't bother to explain why, she just plowed on. "You need a simulation and a sense of self."

I'd had enough so I asked, "How's Travis?" She'd gone out a couple of times with this guy.

I could hear her shrug. "Eh," she said. I knew Travis was on his way out.

I think about that conversation all the time now. I wear yellow so I affect Wanda's brain that way every time I see her. Yellow is a way for her to start to make a simulation of the world. To say, "June is here."

Two and a half months after the accident the police call and say they want to do a follow-up with me and they'll bring me my sister's things.

Which is great; I don't want to have to go pick them up at a police station.

The cop is Detective Leo Garcia Mendoza, and I like that he has the double name thing going and maybe respects his mom. He's more than six feet tall, in his late thirties, and wears a suit when he comes to talk to me.

We go through the pleasantries. We're crammed into my little office, which has just enough space for a desk and a guest chair and a bunch of beige metal filing cabinets with models of glucose monitors stacked on them. When Detective Garcia Mendoza sits in my guest chair, his knees are probably touching my desk.

A copy paper box is sitting on my desk. In it is my sister's jacket and her phone, and a Happy Meal toy from her desk.

"We just want you to know that at this time we have no intention of filing any kind of charges against your sister," he says. "Has your sister ever said anything about what happened?"

"I don't think she remembers," I say. It's true. Like people don't remember a car accident.

"Was she close to Kyle Choi? Friendly with Dr. Bennett?"

"She never complained about them or anything," I say. Which strictly speaking is not true. She liked Kyle but he drove her nuts. "She said Kyle said one time that they should microdose LSD and see if it helped productivity because some Silicon Valley start-up is doing it. But Dr. Bennett wouldn't have allowed that."

"Is there any chance that LSD caused your sister's psychosis?"

I raise an eyebrow. "Wanda is not psychotic. She is perfectly lucid. She has a brain injury that makes it impossible for her to integrate her sensory experiences. A drug screen showed no evidence of anything but legally prescribed Adderall in her system."

I work with kids a lot and occasionally I have to do the mom voice. It works now on Detective Garcia Mendoza. He scrunches his shoulders a little. "I'm sorry, ma'am," he says.

I don't let him off the hook by smiling. I trust him about as far as I can throw all six foot plus of him.

"The evidence suggests that Dr. Bennett tried to restrain Mr. Choi and Mr. Choi became violent, maybe panicked. We have had a couple of eyewitnesses who saw someone we believe was Mr. Choi in the hours after the accident. He was wandering the streets and was clearly agitated."

"So he cracked Bennett's skull open?" I ask.

"His prints are on the bottom of the chair that was used to murder Dr. Bennett," the cop says, like it doesn't matter. "We keep finding references to someone named Claude," he says.

"Animal Control took him. I think he ended up at the Long Beach Aquarium."

This throws Detective Garcia Mendoza.

"Claude," I explain, "is an octopus. A three-year-old North Pacific giant octopus. He lived in one of the tanks in the lab. Kyle Choi took care of him. He was one of six octopuses who were part of an experiment. Woods Hole was directing the grant and they didn't want to ship a bunch of octopuses across country. Monterey Bay Aquarium took some, I think. The Birch at Scripps down in San Diego might have taken one."

"What kind of experiment?" the detective asks.

They were doing experiments on octopus perception. They'd put four boxes in an octopus tank, three of them black and one of them white. The white one had food in it. They'd put them in the same place three times and time how long it took the octopus to get the treat. The fourth time they'd move the white box to a place where there was usually a black box and put the black box where the treat usually was. Then they'd see how long it took for the octopuses to figure it out. The idea was to test if octopuses prioritized location or color, what was more important to them.

Dr. Bennett was doing some other experiments on just Claude, trying to see if he could alter Claude's brain to perceive things we don't perceive. Claude had some sort of reality goggles he wore over his eyes but he hated them. Sounds like getting an octopus to wear something it doesn't like makes dressing a toddler look fun.

Claude didn't like his keeper, Kyle. It was Kyle's job to put on Claude's goggles.

Octopuses are not social; they're kind of psychopaths, according to Wanda. Like psychopaths, they can be sentimental, and Wanda used to feed Claude on the sly so he would like her. Her work didn't require her to interact with the octopus but she felt bad for him, and he watched her because there wasn't much for him to do.

Wanda was pretty sure that all the shit with the goggles had made him crazy, even by octopus standards. He had a burrow but he stuffed it with everything in his tank to fill it up. He destroyed most of the things they put in the tank.

Wanda didn't like the experimentation; it wasn't ethical. After the accident, I got hounded by PETA.

I didn't understand what the goggles were supposed to do. Wanda tried to enlighten me, but I couldn't follow what she was talking about.

"I could explain if you could follow the math," she'd say, exasperated. Numbers talk to Wanda. They're like her first language. They're not my first language. Maybe my third. Or fourth. My twin is my first language.

"Could the deaths have involved the octopus?" the cop asks.

I can't help it—the look I give him. It's a moronic question. Claude is big for an octopus, almost four feet long I think, but he weighs about as much as a cocker spaniel, and I'm not sure how an octopus was supposed to cause the kind of brain injury Wanda has. I met Claude and he eyed me and then squirted water at me. Wanda dropped a piece of sashimi in the tank. Salmon, I think. He wasn't wearing the goggles.

He was very cool in theory but not so much in practice.

They'd tried to interest him in a female octopus and he'd killed her. He would probably have happily killed Kyle and Dr. Bennett, but there was the little fact that he lived in a saltwater tank and had no bones.

"He might have had motive but not method or opportunity," I say dryly.

Detective Garcia Mendoza chuckles. It's awkward. I'm secretly pleased.

Claude is actually four, not three. It's been almost a year since Wanda was found unconscious in the lab; Dr. Bennett had his head beaten in with a chair; and Kyle disappeared, and his remains were found two weeks later in the nice-looking stretch of the Los Angeles river.

You don't know people, not really. But Kyle didn't seem like the kind of guy who would violently murder someone and then kill himself, at least not from the way Wanda talked about him. Kyle was a C++ programmer who wore thick black hipster glasses. He made sourdough bread on the weekends and posted pictures of it to his Instagram account. He had ended up taking care of Claude because his previous project had been making a database for a study of octopuses. Octopi. Whatever. He confessed to Wanda about how hard it was to be a gay Asian guy. He said white dudes wanted him to call them "Daddy" a lot.

I call the Long Beach Aquarium and I ask if I can see Claude. They tell me I have to make a formal request and how to do that. I have to email someone in visitor liaison or community outreach or something, so I do. I don't know why I want to see Claude except that I think Wanda would want me to. Wanda had a bit of wounded-bird rescuer in her. I fire off the email.

I work until six and then drive home, where I eat a microwave low-calorie dinner and a bunch of chocolate chip cookies. I don't claim to be consistent, and at least my dinner was a lot less fattening than the cookies. It's a balance, right?

I am behind on stuff. Because, you know, I'm a social worker. It's part of the job. I try to work on some files but end up bingeing on Netflix.

There's an email in my inbox. Somebody from UCLA, which is where Wanda did her undergrad.

> Ms. Harris,
> My name is Dale Hoffsted. I study perception and I've worked with Oz Bennett. I wondered if I could talk to you about your sister and what the lab was doing?

I'm working sixty hours a week. One of the social workers, Fran Horowitz, quit three weeks ago, and we're already crazy busy. Social work is the kind of job you can never actually succeed at, only fail less. I fire off an email saying that I would like to talk to him, but between my job and visiting my sister, I don't have any time on the weekdays.

Maybe he knows Wanda?

I don't really think about it, but when I come back to my desk later, there's another email.

> *Saturday or Sunday would be fine. I've got an experiment running that gets me in the lab on weekends.*

I mean to answer him back but I get a call from the rehab facility that Wanda is having a bad day.

A bad day. Like that begins to cover it.

I tell my boss I've got to go and that I'll work Saturday to catch up.

At the rehab, I can hear her long before I see her. The moment the elevator door opens, I hear her. Wanda is screaming. I don't know why but I run because the sound—pure, high terror—just shuts down every thought. I run past the old people. Rehab is a nice word for nursing home—and they sit in the hallway, watching me go past or worse, oblivious, vacant as a tomb.

In Wanda's room are two orderlies, Latino guys, trying to restrain her. Wanda is only a little over a hundred pounds, but she is wild. Her arms are streaked with blood from where she's been scratching at them. They try to keep her nails short but when this happens, it doesn't matter, I guess.

"Wanda!" I say, "Wanda! WANDA!"

She can't hear me.

Another person in scrubs appears at the door—a nurse, a doctor, I don't know. "We have to restrain her!" the woman says.

"No!" I say, "you can't!"

"She was trying to scratch her eyes!" one of the orderlies says to me. It's Hector, who likes her, sings to her in Spanish. Sometimes she knows him and calls him Music Man.

"What triggered her?" I ask.

The other Latino guy shakes his head, either that he doesn't know or that it's too late now. Leon. Who once was lifting a woman

out of her wheelchair and I heard him say, "Why do I always get the
heavy ones," and I hate him, I hate that I leave my sister with people
like him.

We are shouting over Wanda screaming. A long shrill sound like a
child, a little girl.

I try to touch her, to get her to see the yellow, that I'm here. "June's
here!" I say. "Junie's here! Wanda!"

She catches me in the cheek with her elbow.

They push her down on the bed and catch her arms and restrain
her and she fights. Oh God does my sister fight. Her eyes are squeezed
shut and she twists and turns and her pink mouth is open. They use
wrist and ankle restraints and a belt across her middle. The rehab
doesn't like to use restraints. The administrator is committed—the staff
gets training based on a program in Wisconsin. It's one of the reasons
I got her in this place.

Sedatives increase Wanda's sensory integration problems.

There's nothing to do but keep her from clawing her eyes out.

I want to scream, "She's a PhD! In physics! THIS IS NOT
WANDA!" But it is. Oh God, it is. It is.

She doesn't quiet until she falls asleep a little after nine in the evening.
Some of the patients sundown and I can hear a woman wailing.

I'm so tired. My mom and dad are bankrupting themselves to keep
Wanda in this place. Sixty two thousand dollars a year. I try to help but
a social worker doesn't make a lot of money. What good is it to help
other people if I can't help Wanda and honestly, sometimes I wonder
how much I am helping anyone.

Mostly I just try not to think about it. One day at a time. Hopefully
Wanda will get to the point where I can take her home. I'll get twin
beds and it will be like being girls in Baltimore again.

It's never going to be like it was.

The aquarium sends me back an email telling me that I can visit
Claude the octopus. I ask if I have to make an appointment and their
response says that no, I don't, my name will be on a visitor list.

Dale Hoffsted emails me and says he's heading for a conference in Copenhagen next weekend, can I meet him this weekend?

I have one goddamn day to myself: Sunday. I grocery shop. I drop off my laundry at the laundromat where the Korean women wash and fold my clothes. They don't like me. But they always do a great job on my clothes. Maybe they spit on my filthy black underwear and say racist things in Korean. I just don't care.

I spend Saturday working from home. That evening, Wanda is lethargic. I check to make sure they didn't sedate her but I think she's just exhausted. I go to bed early but end up watching Netflix until after midnight.

On Sunday morning I go to the aquarium. It's lovely, full of kids. There's a pool where you can reach in and stroke the sandpaper skin of a ray. I watch the baby bamboo sharks. Wanda wouldn't be able to handle this, not yet.

I ask at information if there is someone I can talk to about seeing Claude. A woman in a bright blue polo shirt and a nametag that says *Ashley* comes out to meet me. She has a slight Spanish accent. She is young and her black hair shines in the sun.

"Can I help you?"

"My name is June Katherine Harris," I say. "My sister worked for a scientific lab and they donated a North Pacific giant octopus. His name is Claude. Is there any way I could see him? I'm on the visitor list."

She is wary now. "Why do you want to see Claude?"

"Something went wrong at the lab, my sister was hurt really badly and she told me a lot about Claude. I want to tell her how he's doing." I hold up a little takeout container. "I brought him some salmon sashimi." Something occurs to me. "Wait, he's not dead, is he? I know he's old . . ."

"He's not dead," she says.

"I know he's a crazy asshole of an octopus," I say.

She smiles at that. "Let me go check," she says.

The sharks glide silently through the shark lagoon, zebras and epaulette sharks passing each other like ghosts, their flat eyes expressionless. Kids love sharks. Well, I guess everyone loves sharks, or Shark Week wouldn't be such a big deal.

Do sharks have thoughts? Do they have consciousness?

A mockingbird will go to battle with his own reflection in a car mirror. It doesn't know that the reflection is him. He doesn't have an "I." He doesn't know "I am reflected in the mirror." He just thinks, "Rival male! Rival male! Rival male!" A dog or a cat can figure out that the image in the mirror is fake.

Claude knows who he is. The sharks don't. What are the thoughts of sharks?

Sharks have a sensor in their nose that detects the electrical impulses of muscle movements in fish. Not the movements, the electrical impulses. I know what sound is like, and sight, and touch—but what is a shark's world? What is it like to sense electrical impulses as information? As something other than a shock? To know that a fish is swimming because you can feel the impulses traveling through the long muscles of its body and the strong movement of its tail?

I close my eyes and try to imagine the perceptive world of a shark.

Swimming, the blue, the scent of blood and fish and kelp in the water. I try to imagine a world in which I can see—no not see—feel and create a model of the world where I can tell things are moving thirty feet away by the senses on my sides. Feel a fish swimming, terrified by me.

I feel my sides, try to think of the air as an ocean and try to feel it. I feel a breeze on my arms but I can't feel the little Latina girl in the pink unicorn T-shirt and Crocs, staring at the sharks. Sometimes I've felt like I could "feel" the physical presence of someone standing next to me, but what does the shark sense when it senses the electrical movements of the muscles of the terrified fish? What would I feel if I could sense the electrical impulses of that little girl reaching in the water?

I get a little dizzy and sit on the edge of the lagoon. Is this what things are like for Wanda?

The young woman in the blue polo shirt comes back. "I can take you to see the octopus," she says.

The areas where there are no exhibits aren't painted blue and green. They're not pretty, they're utilitarian. There's a smell, like fish water. I don't know how else to describe it. Like a goldfish tank that might need to be cleaned, only saltier. But it's not dirty and it's nicer than the agency where I work, if you want to know the truth.

Claude lives in a tank, a pretty big one. He's brown on top and white underneath and his skin is wrinkled like crepe, like an old man's. He has his eyes hidden in the coils of his arms.

"What did they do to him?" Ashley asks.

"They made these goggles that would help him perceive more, I think," I say. Like the shark maybe? Seeing the electrical impulses of the muscles of prey? What senses did they try to give Claude?

"What did they want him to do? Spy like those Russian dolphins? Was it like a government thing?"

"They wanted to see if he could perceive reality," I say. "Can I give him the salmon?"

"Is there rice?" she asks. "I don't think he's supposed to have rice."

"No, it's sashimi," I say.

She nods.

"Hey, Claude," I say, "Wanda says hi." Not that she does, of course. Wanda doesn't know I'm here. She can't understand when I talk to her. Claude doesn't respond; maybe he doesn't know I'm here, either.

Ashley opens a hatch in the grate across the top and I drop a piece of salmon in. It drifts slowly down and Claude doesn't move. I'd think maybe he's dead, that I arrived just in time to see the last witness other than Wanda gone, but he's blowing water through his gills. It stirs the sand on the bottom of the tank.

"Do you want a piece?" I ask.

"I don't like fish," Ashley says. She holds her hands up. "I know! I know! I work with them all day but I just don't like to eat them!"

I laugh with her and it feels good.

I don't know what I'm doing here. I don't know why I felt compelled to see Claude.

In Wanda's phone the last photo is of her, holding Claude's goggles. She's weirdly off-center, tilted and too high, like whoever was holding the camera was not really framing it right. Behind her and even more off-center is the tank where Claude lives, and he's starfished against the glass, all tentacles and suckers. Wanda is smiling this funny smirk she does, like she's causing trouble. I don't know what Claude is doing.

She wouldn't put on the goggles. I swear. Wanda isn't stupid.

I don't think I should drop any more salmon in if he's not going to eat it. I like salmon sashimi, even if I'm not hungry right now. I perceive it as buttery and tasty. Maybe Claude perceives it as, I don't know, changing states of atoms and molecules and energy.

Claude moves. It's so fast I almost miss it, but the salmon is gone.

I drop another piece in and he turns his head—I know it's his whole body and he doesn't have a head really, but his eyes are there so it feels like a head. He looks around and he sees me.

"Hi, Claude," I whisper.

He uncoils and moves, picking up the salmon and flowing closer to the wall of the tank.

"What did you see when you wore the goggles?" I ask him. I imagine veils of energy in a darkness although that's really not true. It's the best I can do.

He flattens up against the glass, and I can see his suckers flexing and catch a glimpse of his beak. It's scary and a little vicious-looking.

I drop another piece of salmon and he flows to catch it.

He reaches up with one long tentacle and I can see how he could be four feet long. He did this with Wanda. "He's tasting me," she'd said.

I hold my hand over the opening of the tank and he curls a tentacle around my wrist and he's so muscular, so strong, but cold. I feel the tentacles but they don't suck on my arm.

Then he snatches his tentacles back.

Did he think I was Wanda? The salmon, my dark skin? Do I taste wrong?

I watch Claude eat the last piece of salmon.

After the aquarium I head to UCLA. Finding anything at UCLA is like navigating a foreign country with a very poor map. Franz Hall is

'60s-looking, like the UN building only shorter and much less interesting. The office isn't busy but it isn't empty, either.

I find Dale Hoffsted's office. His door is open.

I straightened my hair. I look casual but professional.

He's a white guy, pale brown hair, tall. He stands up when I come to his door. "Ms. Harris?" he says. His office is bigger than mine. It has carpet and a brown corduroy couch, bookcases, and some kind of abstract art on the wall.

"I'm sorry to hear about your sister," he says. "How is she doing?"

"Thank you," I say. I do not say that some days she seems to be getting better and some days she tries to claw her own eyes out. "I meant to read some of your papers before we met, but work has been busy." I looked up his papers and they're all about perception. I had planned to see what I could download but Wanda had had that terrible Thursday.

"She worked with Oz Bennett," he says and there is something in his voice. Wanda was worried that what they were doing was fringe science. She was afraid that a Black woman who worked on fringe science was not going to get work when this grant ended. Wanda always went for the hard stuff, the hard math. The hard problem. But it's not easy to find work in the sciences.

"Was he a scam?" I ask.

Dr. Hoffsted startles. "No," he says, "no, not really. He did some crazy stuff but he wasn't a crank."

"Wanda worried that he was not reputable."

Hoffsted shook his head. "His work on consciousness was groundbreaking and innovative. I knew him, professionally. He was generous, introduced me to someone at the NSF who could help me navigate the grant process."

"The octopus was fitted with some kind of reality glasses, for experiments," I say.

That gets me an eyebrow raise.

"Dale?" says a pudgy Indian-looking guy in a Hawaiian shirt. He glances at me.

"Hi, Vihaan."

"I've got the results on those fMRIs," Indian guy says.

"I've got an appointment. Can we go over the data tomorrow?"

"Sure, just wanted to tell you I've got them."

Hoffsted smiles and nods. When the Indian guy walks away, Hoffsted says, "You want to get some coffee?"

We walk across campus. "People think scientists are all these rational, logical people," he says. "But we're all actually dorky, weird people."

"Like my sister," I say.

"I, no, I mean, not everybody, some of us are—"

"It's okay. My sister is exactly that. Brilliant and weird." I don't know why I let him off the hook but he is visibly relieved. There's a nice breeze off the Pacific and the sun is bright. The campus is full of intense young people on their way to do intense young people things.

"Have you heard of Linus Pauling?" he asks. When I shake my head he goes on. "Linus Pauling was a chemist, a Nobel Prize winner. In fact, he's the only man to have been the single winner of two Nobel Prizes. He was also a humanitarian. Brilliant guy. He became convinced that large doses of vitamin C would cure the common cold and maybe even cancer. That's why we all drink orange juice when we've got a cold."

"Okay?" I say.

"Total crap," Hoffsted says. "Megadosing on vitamins can be dangerous but mostly it just means your pee is really expensive since it's voiding all those pricey vitamins you take. Isaac Newton inserted a needle behind his eyeball and reported on the results and thought that light would help him understand God."

"Was Bennett a brilliant nut job?" Did the asshole create something crazy that ended up killing Kyle Choi and breaking my sister?

"Maybe," he says. "I don't know."

We get coffee at a kiosk and find a bench.

"Bennett," he says, "got obsessed with the nature of reality."

I sip my coffee. It's decent coffee. I don't care about the nature of reality.

"Why did you call me?" I ask. "Did you know Wanda?"

"No," he says.

"She did her undergrad here," I say.

"I didn't know that," he says. "She was a postdoc, right?"

Was a postdoc. I want to say she is a PhD in physics with a degree from Wash U. But I just nod. Postdoc is a position. She doesn't work anymore.

"I study perception," he says. "One of the things I've studied is how we perceive reality. I thought," Dale Hoffsted says, holding up his paper coffee cup, "that what I perceived was a pretty good representation of reality. That in reality, I am accurately perceiving the shape and texture of this cup."

It's just a blue and white striped cup with the emblem of the coffee shop on it. It has a white plastic cover.

A kid skateboards by, weaving among the other students.

"We don't perceive everything. We can't see X-rays or radio waves, but what we can perceive—I thought that was reality."

"You're going to tell me it's not."

"Yeah, I am. Our brains have a kind of interface. Like your phone." He pulls out his iPhone. He does that thing that a lot of teachers do: He speaks in paragraphs. "These apps," he says. "What we perceive is not the actual app. The actual app is a computer code running electrons in a pattern in a very sophisticated machine. We don't see the chips and wires, we don't see that code or even the action of it. What we see is a red mostly square thing with an arrow in it. *The interface is not the app.*"

"Okay," I say. "That's great. But we're not digital. You're holding that cup of coffee. You drink it and it goes down your throat and is absorbed into your body. It's real."

"I didn't say it wasn't," he says. "You ask good questions."

He's not like Wanda. Talking to Wanda tended to rearrange my reality, but Wanda was always there with me. I don't know this guy and apparently he wanted to meet me to lecture me.

"Hi, Dr. Hoffsted!" a girl in a flowered sundress sings out. She waves. I hate PhDs who like to be called *"Doctor."* I got that from Wanda. I used to call her Dr. Harris to wind her up.

Hoffsted waves back, still talking. "We can create digital organisms now, in a computer simulation. They're like single-celled animals but very sophisticated. They can predict things that are true about real organisms."

"Which is a sign they are a good model for real organisms?" I ask.

"Exactly!" he said, like I'm a bright student. "It's pretty compelling evidence. We created organisms and simulated a thousand generations. Half of them evolved to perceive the 'reality' of the simulation and half of them, like us, evolved just for fitness to reproduce. I thought that there would be some difference—but I thought perceiving reality would improve fitness to reproduce."

He's excitedly gesturing as he talks, and I'm a little worried for his coffee and his phone.

"It didn't," I say. I can keep up.

"No," he says. "One hundred percent of the organisms that were evolved to perceive reality died. Every time."

I feel for a moment like he just said Wanda is going to die and I shake my head.

"We didn't do this just once," he explains, working to convince me. "We did it over twenty times, a thousand generations, tweaked things. The perception of reality is not beneficial to survival."

He shook his head. "Let me give you an example of reality that we can't perceive. How much information can a sphere"—he held out his hands to show the size of a volleyball and I wanted to take his cup away from him—"can a sphere hold?"

"Doesn't it depend on things like what kind of chip or something?"

"We're talking about something different," he said. "It's a question about quantum reality and at the quantum level, everything is information."

"I'm not . . . what are you even saying?"

"Stephen Hawking did the math," he says, like that clinches it. Yeah, yeah, impress the dumb Black woman by throwing out the name Stephen Hawking. I really don't like this guy.

"If I'm thinking about how much is in something, I'm thinking about volume, right? I'm thinking about how much I can pour into this cup. If I make the cup shallow, like a saucer or a plate, even though it might have the same surface area as this cup, it can't hold as much coffee."

I just nod and picture coffee flowing off a saucer except for the little bit that pools in the indent. My coffee is pale, with cream and sugar in it.

"It turns out that the maximum amount of information, at the quantum level, is determined by surface area, not volume."

I try to wrap my head around that. "Like a big flat plate would hold more coffee than a cup?" I ask. This is a little like talking to Wanda. Only Wanda makes sense. This . . . doesn't make sense.

"Yes. Only we're talking the quantum level not the Newtonian level. But it's reality. We can't perceive a quantum reality. In fact, the best way to pack information into the sphere is to put twelve spheres in it, adding their surface area, and then twelve spheres inside each sphere, and twelve spheres inside those spheres, until we can't get any smaller."

"Why twelve?" I ask.

"I don't know," he admits. "I'm a cognitive guy, not a mathematician. I can't do the math."

I bet Wanda could, I think. *My sister could probably think rings around you.*

"So my perception," he says, holding up his cup, "at the Newtonian level, that a bigger volume means a bigger cup of coffee, is true. Obviously. Ask anyone who has ever ordered a venti when they wanted a grande. But at the level of reality, it's false."

"Why did you ask me to meet you?" I ask.

He looks a little surprised. "I wondered what Bennett was doing," he says.

"I'm a social worker," I say flatly. "I can make sure that when you get diabetes you have the tools you need to stay as healthy as you can for as long as you can. I can't do the math; Wanda could do the math. I only know that whatever Bennett was doing, it broke my sister's brain. Maybe got a lab tech killed."

"What's wrong with your sister?" he asks. The guy really can't read social cues. Or he doesn't care.

"Global perceptive agnosia," I say. "Those goggles. Kyle and Wanda built them—there were a bunch of pairs. I think they tried to see reality and it screwed them up." I haven't wanted to admit it to myself but I know it's true.

He looks a little excited. "Do you know what the goggles did?"

Screw you, asshole.

"I have to go see my thirty-year-old sister in a nursing home full of people with Alzheimer's," I say. I leave him sitting on the bench with his coffee. I hope he feels like shit.

At this time of year it gets dark pretty early. My head is packed full and I skipped lunch.

The parking lot feels as if it is halfway to the ocean. I can't remember exactly how we came, so I stop at a map kiosk thing and look at it. I'm so tired that I'm having trouble figuring out the map versus the campus. The buildings don't line up with the map, somehow. I don't want Hoffsted to walk up and talk to me, so I don't want to hang around. I start off in the direction of the parking lot.

After about fifteen minutes of walking, I realize I have *got* to be turned around. Maybe I should get something to eat. Low blood sugar. (And isn't that ironic for someone who talks about glucose levels all day long?) I take out my phone and map the way to the car, following blindly. Turn left, turn right, keep walking. The interface is not the app.

I walk up and down the rows of the parking lot, crying, looking for my Honda.

I would have said that Wanda wasn't stupid. She talked about the goggles but she usually talked about how Claude hated them. She probably talked about what they did but honestly, sometimes after a long day, even Wanda was too much.

Wanda used to eat food so spicy it burned my mouth, just because she could. Wanda went hang gliding once. Wanda wanted to go to Mars even though she said it would probably be more like a family vacation stuck in a minivan than a grand adventure.

I think Kyle took the photo right before she put on the goggles. Of course Wanda put on the glasses. See reality. Wanda would want to.

God damn it, Wanda. How could you do this to us.

I almost cry when I find my car. I'm so relieved.

Sunset Boulevard curves around in weird ways. Heading east it straightens out, flush up against the Hollywood hills. I know Sunset, I drive it pretty often, but nothing looks right. The sun is setting behind me and the light glints off the side mirror of the car stopped at the light in the front of me and I can't see.

Talking to Wanda was sometimes a lot, if you know what I mean, but she was a good guide to the strange places of reality. Hoffsted has left me in no man's land and I'm lost. Lost like Claude. Lost like Wanda.

I pull in to a Wendy's and I get a cheeseburger and a Coke—I never drink Coke. I sit in the parking lot and I eat like an animal. My stupid body, needing things. Wanda's stupid injured brain.

I pull back out and listen to the voice of the app telling me where to go.

There is the place where Wanda lives. The glass doors spill white light out onto the sidewalk. The woman at reception nods to me and I take the elevator up to the second floor.

I pass the old people sitting in the hall. I pass Leon, the orderly I hate, who nods to me. I look into Wanda's room and she is sitting cross-legged on the bed, stroking the blue waffle-weave blanket like it's a pet. She looks up, drawn by the movement?

"June! Junie!" Wanda says and throws her hands up and everything is real again. Wanda is real.

She lets me hug her and pats me and strokes my fingernails. I need a new manicure. I start crying again but I feel okay. Wanda's not dead. Whatever Hoffsted said about one hundred percent mortality, Wanda is smart. She is getting better. The bad days are getting fewer.

"I saw Claude," I say. "He's doing good. I told him you said hello."

Wanda runs her pale palms over my shirt. "It's a good day," she said. "I think we had applesauce today. I think I liked it. Yellow. I love your yellow. I love you, Junie."

"I love you too," I say.

I will never know reality. Wanda is proof. If she can't handle it, no one can. But I have traveled through the gathering dark and come to her. It doesn't matter that I will never know the vibration of quantum energies, never see them or touch them.

I got here. I am having a bad day but unlike Wanda, when I have a bad day, she can reach me. Even if she never gets better than this and it's always hard, I can still see and touch my sister.

I hug Wanda and she lets me fold her in my arms. She smells of shampoo and clean skin. She croons happily. "I love yellow," she says. "I love your yellow."

"It's okay," I tell her. "It's okay, Wanda baby."

FATHER

RAY NAYLER

Ray Nayler (www.raynayler.net) has lived and worked in Russia, Central Asia, the Caucasus, and the Balkans for nearly two decades. He is a Foreign Service Officer and previously worked in international educational development, as well as serving in the Peace Corps in Ashgabat, Turkmenistan. A Russian speaker, he has also learned Turkmen, Albanian, Azerbaijani Turkish, and Vietnamese. Ray began publishing speculative fiction in 2015 in *Asimov's Science Fiction* with "Mutability." Since then, his critically acclaimed stories have appeared in *Asimov's, Clarkesworld, Analog Science Fiction and Fact, The Magazine of Fantasy & Science Fiction, Lightspeed,* and *Nightmare*, and in several "Best of the Year" anthologies.

had a father for six months.

I met him when I was seven years old. There was a knock on the door of our prefab house. My mom, who had been in the kitchen throwing mushrooms into a simmering pot of spaghetti sauce, smiled down at me and said, "Who could that be? Why don't you go and see, baby?"

She knew who it was, of course.

It was June 5, 1956. The man who my mom called "your dad" had been dead since before I was born. His face squinted into the sun and his uniform buttons gleamed in a photograph on the mantle.

He'd never been real to me. He was that photo, and a folded flag in a wooden frame. Pictures are just shapes on paper. Flags are just cloth.

I threw the door open.

The robot was very tall, and silver, and polished to a high shine. His eyes were perfectly round. They had a dark orange light in them, like the light of a candle. His mouth was a wire mesh speaker. He held a bunch of daisies in one hand, wrapped in cheap green cellophane and with the price tag still on them. He had a baseball glove in his other hand.

He said, "Hey, buddy."

He said, "How's it going?"

I turned around and yelled: "It's some robot selling flowers!"

He said, "I guess you didn't expect me."

I was confused because he wasn't like the guys who usually wandered around selling "cheapo flores" door to door in Albuquerque, but all I could think of was that now robots were doing it, too.

From the kitchen my mom said, "Better let him in, honey. It's hot out there."

My mom must be nuts, I thought. I'm not letting some robot in our house.

The robot said: "I'm Father. But you don't have to call me that, just yet. I guess I'll have to earn that."

My mom came up behind me, wiping her hands clean on her yellow half apron.

"Why don't you come on in?"

The flowers were for my mom. The glove was for me.

That evening Father and I played catch in the flat white light of the motion sensor lamp mounted over our front door. The robot would be still for a moment, and it would go dark. He would move to throw, and the lamp would switch on, and there was the ball, already halfway to my mitt, coming out of nowhere. I would catch it most times, or miss it and it would bounce away, out of the light, a dull whitish spot under the half-grown bushes that framed our property. If I caught it, Father said, "Great catch, buddy!" in a way that made me want to cry and throw myself at him, stay there loving him, hugging him so he would never go away. If I missed it he would say, "Don't worry about it," in a voice that made me want to kill myself because didn't he know I was a failure, a scabby little brat with an upcoming F in math that I hadn't told my mom about?

Everything was love and death.

When he stopped moving the light went out with a click and he was gone.

When he moved he was there again. Like a magic trick. I scrambled to catch the ball.

He had no glove. He caught the ball barehanded. Because he was magic. Because he was my Father already, even though it would take me a month to say it to his face.

We lived way out on the western edge of Albuquerque, where it starts petering out into the desert again. We lived a stone's throw from Route 66. There were plenty of lumpy vacant lots to ride bikes in with the other kids, but that was about it. The ice-cream man didn't make it out that way much, but there was a market where you could buy push-pops and orangesicles.

Sometimes, in the evening, you could see the rockets going up from the bases out in the desert. You could almost hear them, roaring up and out of the atmosphere on the way to the Moon or Mars. I sped around on my bike, new that Christmas, spectacularly happy because it was summer, because it was Saturday, and because I had a Father.

My friend Jimmy said, "Hey, what's with that trash can hanging out around your place?"

"That's my new robot, you dumb bastard."

Who could catch a baseball barehanded.

Who could help me with my math homework.

Who organized the garage, and built us a new shelf for my mom's books.

Who fixed the chain on my bike and showed me how to patch a tire.

Who was never too tired to answer questions.

Who read me to sleep, and turned out the light, or left it on if I wanted it.

Jimmy and I were licking orangesicles in the shade of the open garage door. Father was shaping a block of wood on a lathe. He wouldn't say into what. "It's a surprise, buddy" was all I could get out of him.

One of the greaser kids from the neighborhood came down hard in his hot rod, landing it with a thud and a cloud of summer dust a couple meters off from us. He got out, slammed the door, then just leaned on the fender, staring at us, a Lucky hanging out of the corner of his mouth.

I knew who he was—Archie Frank. Rumor was he'd stabbed a teacher, gotten kicked out of school. Now he worked at the dump. People said he smelled like trash.

This was the closest I'd ever been to him: all I could smell was his cigarette.

"He'll be dead in a year," my mom said once, seeing him rip the leaves off the top of a sycamore tree down the road in his hot rod and then bank hard, almost clipping a faded billboard left over from FDR's reelection campaign back in '52. "Maybe sooner."

"How you afford that trash can, kid?"

"Saved up, I guess."

"Yeah, I bet you did. I bet your mom saved up by working the midnight shift down at the truck stop. I bet she goes through a lot of lipstick."

"My mom's a nurse," I said. "She works over at the hospital."

"Jesus, yer dumb." Archie flicked the Lucky into the dirt and walked past us into the garage.

"Hey," I said—but Jimmy grabbed my shoulder, and I shut up.

Archie walked up to Father where he was at the lathe, working that block of wood.

"Whatcha makin', trash can?"

Father turned his head. His hands, though, kept working the wood on the lathe.

"Hello, young man."

"I said whatcha makin', trash can?"

Father's orange eyes glowed a little in the shade of the garage, I noticed. Sometimes they got a little brighter when he was thinking hard. The light from the side window caught at his silver hands.

"I am making a surprise for my boy."

"Your *boy*?"

"Yes, that's correct."

Archie spat on the ground at Father's feet. But Father just turned back to the lathe, as if nothing at all had happened.

When Archie was safely gone, Jimmy said, "I hope that creep falls out of his stupid terraplane someday and gets speared on a telephone pole."

That evening Father, my mom, and I sat in lawn chairs on the porch. Father told us the names of the constellations. He pointed out the satellites going by. He knew the names of every one of them, and what they did, and who had built them. He even knew the names of the dead Russian satellites we'd knocked out during the Afterwar, when we and the remnants of the Wehrmacht had pushed the commies back to Moscow and freed Poland and the rest of Eastern Europe. That was the war my "real" dad had died in.

Pictures are just shapes on paper. Flags are just cloth.

How had we afforded Father? I guess it had never crossed my mind: I'd never thought of us as poor, even though we were, and Father didn't seem like something we'd bought. He just seemed like someone who'd found us.

What I didn't know then is that mom had applied to a lottery program at Veterans Affairs. The VA was distributing Fathers to kids whose dads had been killed in the wars. Our lottery number had come up—one in a thousand. Father even came with free maintenance.

My mom had been over the moon about it: we needed help around the house, and everyone had been telling her for years that one parent just wasn't enough. My mom had hair the color of postcard sand, and brown-gold eyes. Like whiskey in the bottle, with the sun coming through it. People couldn't understand why she didn't try harder. Why didn't she put some makeup on, find a man?

My mom thought Father could solve a lot of problems for both of us.

What Father had been shaping for me on the lathe turned out to be a soap box derby car for my Cub Scout competition. He'd painted it silver, just like himself, with an orange stripe that matched his eyes when he was thinking hard. I kept it on the nightstand by my bed.

Mom bought Father a glove and a bat and we played ball out in the lumpy vacant lot. High pop flies lost in the evening sky. The chirping of crickets that fell silent when you came too close. His multi-jointed arm lofting the ball and the crack of the bat.

"Great catch, buddy."

"Don't worry about it."

Love and death.

Evenings we sat around the table and ate macaroni and cheese and drank Pepsis. Father didn't eat, of course: he would just tell us dumb jokes, or quiz me on science stuff. Sometimes, he would stay in the garage to work on a project, or tend to the roses he had planted along the gravel landing pad.

After dinner, when mom was tired from a long shift at the hospital, she sat at the table in the kitchen turning the pages of a book or a magazine while the blue light of the television flashed in the living room with nobody watching it. Usually I would sit in the kitchen with her, reading one of my *Terraformer Tom* books. On one of those evenings we were sitting there when we heard a loud bang from outside.

We ran out of the house in time to see Archie's hot rod arcing off into the sky, wobbling dangerously from side to side on its aftermarket stabilizers.

There were four or five faces sticking out of it. Laughing faces: a girl in red lipstick with her hair up in a kerchief, and the hard, narrow greaser faces of Archie's friends. As the hot rod zipped off, one of them yelled, "Home run!" and hooted, the sound doppling off in the crickety night as they lurched away against the stars.

Father was laying on the ground. His head was dented, and one of his eyes had gone dark. As we came over to him, he was already getting up to his feet.

"Are you all right, Father?" I said.

He swung around to look at me. It was awful—his dented head, the one eye snuffed out. But the other one glowed, warm as a kitchen window from home when you're hungry for dinner.

"That's the first time you called me Father," he said. "I couldn't possibly feel better, hearing that word from my boy."

"We should call the cops," my mom said.

"I doubt they'll do much," Father said. "And that young man and his friends really have trouble enough as it is. I feel none of them are headed toward a good end."

"I've said the same myself, many times," mom said. She was rubbing a dirty mark off of Father's head with a kitchen cloth. "What did they get you with?"

"A baseball bat, I'm afraid." He paused. "Perhaps they mistook me for a mailbox."

"Hilarious," mom said.

"I'm here all week, folks " Father's bad eye flickered back to life for a moment, then went dead again.

The VA repairman showed up the next morning in a military issue Willys van that he settled on the gravel with a nifty little half-turn just before the landing. He was a blond guy, square chinned. He was neatly dressed in an army tech unit uniform—polished boots and all kinds of gear and shiny belts across his olive-drab jumpsuit, garrison cap cocked over to one side.

"Heya, bud," he said to me as he climbed down from the van. "I hear there's a bit of a problem with your Father unit. Want to show me where he is?"

Jimmy was over to see it all, of course—and a bunch of other neighborhood kids, including one or two from my school who wouldn't have a thing to do with me, most days. I was, for the moment, the most popular kid in the neighborhood.

Father was in the garage. He'd asked to be put in a low-energy mode the evening before. Sitting slumped there, head dented in, among the discarded auto parts, the old vacuum cleaners, the work benches, power tools, and air tanks, he looked like just another piece of household tech. Suddenly I wanted to cry, but knew if I did I'd never be able to lift my head up among the neighborhood kids again. I bit my lip until it almost bled.

"Here he is," I said.

"Well, let's have a look at you, Dad."

We stood in a ring around them as the repairman put Father into a diagnostic mode. He had him hooked up to some kind of terminal on wheels. They sat there, the two of them, trading number sequences in low tones, like some kind of secret language.

The repairman took Father's head off, and carried it back to the van with him. And then I almost did cry, but as Father's head went by, under the tech's arm like a football, his one good eye flickered, and he said, "Nothing to worry about, son. Just one of my little party tricks. I'll be back in a flash."

In the garage, the kids were circled around Father's headless body, aching to touch it but afraid. Finally one of them tapped it on the shoulder. When the arm came up and waggled a finger at them, they all scattered screaming into the yard.

We sat around out there, on the lawn Father had put in, like a bunch of miniature adults in a hospital waiting room, nervous to see what would come out of the van. Finally the tech emerged, carrying Father's head under his arm, and went back to the garage. We scrambled over to watch him put it back on.

Even mom came out to watch. The repairman gave Father's head a last buff, and turned to my mom.

"Just replaced the eye and the housing. Doesn't look like there was any neural damage to the unit: he runs the tests okay. Let me know if he does anything odd, but I don't imagine he will."

"We're so grateful to you. Those kids . . ."

"Ah," the repairman waved a dismissive hand. "It's not just kids. We've had plenty of trouble with these Father units being smashed up. Gets a lot worse than what happened here—a whole lot worse. I suggest—look, it's none of my business, but I suggest you keep your Father unit in the house, nights. Or at least don't have him out there alone. Just till everyone in the neighborhood gets used to him."

Father turned his head toward us. "Say, who's got baseball mitts? You kids up for catching some pop flies?"

The kids all shouted and ran to grab their gear.

"Come in for a cup of coffee? It's the least we can do," mom was saying to the repairman.

"Don't mind if I do."

That evening mom and I walked down to the liquor store. Father stayed behind, in the garage. He was working on repairing the drape runners in the living room. The evening was warm. The ground kept the day's heat inside itself. It pulsed with heat like skin. You could feel the earth breathe. We went the long way and under the street lamps I stared at her. The filament glow of her sand-colored hair, her crooked front tooth when she smiled down at me.

"The repairman seemed real nice," I said.

She put her hand on my head. I loved it when she did that. I knew it meant that I'd done something right.

The weather started to change. School started, and soon enough the high desert wind came after the setting of the sun, bringing the taste of winter and a dirty scum of snow and black ice mornings at the curb.

Father and I went trick-or-treating on Halloween. I dressed up in a costume we fabricated out of aluminum foil, papier-mâché, and cardboard from Quaker Oats containers. It turned out perfectly: walking down the street, we were robot father and robot son.

While we were out, mom handed out candy to the gangs of roving witches, werewolves, spacemen, and skeletons.

Just after nine, someone rained a sack full of broken bricks on the roof of our house. At the same time, someone threw a rock through our kitchen window.

When Father and I returned with my pillowcase full of candy, there was a police black-and-white in the middle of the lawn. Mom was in the living room on the couch, calmly talking to two police officers.

One of them was in the middle of saying, "Anyhow, it's a hell of a way to treat a war widow. We don't tolerate that kind of disrespect for the families of the fallen around here. We have a pretty good idea of who it is, given what you've told us. We'll go over and have a talk with them."

"I just don't understand. It's just a robot . . ."

"It's a crazy world, ma'am. Flying cars and robots, death rays and cure-all potions from outer space . . . some people just can't get used to it. The tech on that saucer that crashed in '38 tore the world right open. Seems like every year the government or the universities release some new contraption onto the market. People are just nervous, is all . . ."

The officer trailed off when he saw Father and I come in.

"Uh . . . anyway, we won't take up any more of your time. And we'll be sure and send an extra patrol around, now and then. Just to make sure you're okay."

I had taken my robot helmet off, and the other officer bent down and grinned at me.

"That's a pretty great costume, son. You make that yourself?"

"Father helped," I said.

Father shrugged. "I didn't do much. Mostly just collected the old newspapers and mixed the glue. Did something happen here?"

The officers didn't respond to him. Wouldn't even look at him.

After a long silence one of them said, "Well, good night, ma'am." They tipped their hats and went out.

I heard one of them whisper, "Does give you the heebie-jeebies, though, doesn't it . . ." as they left.

Mom went through my sack of candy, admiring and organizing while Father fretted about sugar content and insisted we come up with a system of distribution that would keep me from gorging myself.

Later that night I woke up in a sweat, not knowing what had disturbed me from my sleep. I crept through the house—peeking in on Mom where she lay, safe in her bed, then checking the front and back doors to make sure they were locked.

I opened the door to the garage: Father was there, where he should be, hooked into his maintenance bench. But not, for some reason, in sleep mode: I saw the incandescent dots of his eyes in the dark, and heard him speaking quietly to himself, just a murmur among the shapes in the garage, as if he had called a secret meeting of vacuum cleaners, work benches, air tanks, and old push lawnmowers.

"Father?"

The eyes winked out.

The next day, after school, I went with Father down to the hardware store for roofing nails and sealant. A gray day. Shattered pumpkins and burning leaves, paper skeletons and bats still taped up in the store windows.

I held the ladder while Father climbed up on the roof to work, and we sang, "When the Saints Go Marching In" and "Over There."

Maybe because we were singing, I did not hear Archie's hot rod as it swept in, arcing down from behind me toward where Father was, on the roof. But Father stopped singing, and raised his head. Instead of looking where he was looking, I just looked at him, and watched as he raised the arm with the tacking hammer in it, in a single fluid motion, and threw it.

Then a scream as the hot rod went past over my head and just over Father on the roof, out of control, ripping branches off the tops of trees, nearly going over, then righting itself with a lurch. A lipsticked teenage face in the passenger seat, mouth a screaming O. I felt something warm on my face, like a summer drop of rain. Wiped at it.

A drop of blood.

The hot rod careened off into the distance, carrying the wailing and shouting with it.

Father came down the ladder. His eyes were ember-bright against the silver-gray of his face, the colorless sky. He put a hand on my shoulder.

"Now we will have a secret between us, son."

I nodded.

"And we will need to purchase a new hammer."

In November a group of ravens took up residence in the cottonwood tree across from our house. Father built a feeder for them, and a bath with water that was heated with a little battery device he built. We worked together on a rocket: a little short-range, stubby thing we were planning to send off at the amateur rocketry field down the road, once we got it perfected.

I took Father to school for show-and-tell, against my mom's wishes. She was afraid it would cause problems, but she was wrong—he was a big hit, with the kids and the teachers. During physical education Father hit pop flies for our whole class, and later even opened up his chest to show the kids in junior robotics how he ran.

Walking home we saw Archie standing on the Woolworth's landing pad, leaning against his hot rod with a bunch of his greaser friends. He'd rattlecanned the rod black, and on the door was an uneven white circle with a few paint drips trailing down from it. In the center of the circle was a stenciled silhouette of a witch on a broom and the words "bad luck." The hood was off, with the polished core and an octopus of red power cables on display.

His hot rod was looking pretty cool, but Archie himself had a white bandage around half his head, covering one eye, and when we walked past them the greasers all went quiet and stiff. Scared? Angry? I couldn't tell. After we turned the corner I heard laughter, out of key in the cold air, and Archie saying "shut yer goddamned mouths" in a voice that made me want to walk faster.

Father squeezed my shoulder.

"Nothing to fear, son. I'm here with you."

When we got home the Willys repair van was on the gravel landing pad. We heard laughter from the kitchen as we came in. The blond repairman grinned at us from over his mug of coffee.

"Heya, pops. Heya, kid. Just here for the standard checkup."

Mom looked guilty, like I'd caught her at something she shouldn't have been doing. But pleased, as well. She had a glow to her.

The repairman took Father into the van for what he called his "checkup," and mom quizzed me about how Father had done at show-and-tell. I told her what a hit he'd been, how cool the kids in junior robotics had thought he was. Nobody had ever seen anything like him. Then I ran outside to see what was going on with the repairman.

They were in the back of the van, talking back and forth in that number code again. Then the repairman came out and lit a cigarette.

"How's your Father unit? Give you any trouble?"

Now we will have a secret between us, son.

I shook my head. "Nah. We're building a rocket. And I took him to show-and-tell."

He nodded. "Glad to hear it. I bet he was a hit."

"What's he doing in there?"

"Oh, we're just running an update to his routines. Takes a few minutes. We can play catch while we wait, if you like."

"Nah."

He shrugged. "Suit yourself. You probably get lots of practice in with your Father, yeah?"

"Did you fight in the war?" I asked.

He looked up at the sky. "Yeah. I guess we pretty much all did, guys my age." Then he looked at me strange. "Why do you ask?"

"My dad died in the war."

"No, he didn't *die*, kid. He was shot, really banged up, but we got him fixed. Wait. Did he tell you about that? Because he shouldn't remember . . ."

"What do you mean?" I said. "My dad, he died in the war."

He stared at me a second, then said: "Oh, yeah." He put an arm on my shoulder. "Sorry, kid. I misunderstood you. Yes, he did. Your dad died in the war. He was a hero. And I'm sure if he had known you . . ."

"Who did you think I was talking about?" I demanded, with that kid's instinct for ferreting out adult evasiveness.

"Nobody, kid. It's just been a long day. I got confused. Let's go see how pops is doing in there—he should be just about done, and I bet you two want to get back to building that rocket."

We finished the rocket in early December, and took it out to the amateur rocketry field, riding a bus from the autodrome downtown, a lumbering wartime thing that barely got itself above the rooftops of downtown's stubby buildings. There were five or six other people on the bus, and it seemed like they didn't have anything better to do than stare at Father and me. One old lady had her stupid mouth open all the way to the county line stop where she finally got off. I swear she walked backward off the bus, gawping at us the whole way.

But at the rocketry field, it was different. We set our rocket up on one of the scarred pads, and got back behind a blast shield to watch it go. It was Father's design—liquid-fueled and painted cherry red—but I'd put most of it together, under his instruction. We'd named it "Hootenanny I" because I just liked the word.

It pinged us from an altitude of 145,000 feet before it finally disintegrated.

The rest of the rocketeers at the field spent hours getting Father's advice on their creations. One of them was a real sharp-looking woman just a little older than my mom, with short cropped hair and a leather mechanic's jacket with a patch from General Hedy Lamarr's Technical Corps on her shoulder.

"He build that in your garage, kid?"

"*We* built it," I said.

She winked at me. "Well, I wish we'd had you in our Corps during the war, kid. We coulda used you both."

I was walking home from school on the last day before Christmas break when Archie Frank came from around a corner and stood in the middle of the sidewalk in front of me. The bandage was gone, but he had a black cloth patch over one eye. I thought it looked pretty cool.

"Hey, kid," he said. He was holding one hand up, palm toward me, to get me to stop. "I just want to talk, okay?"

I stopped. My heart was hammering away in my chest. It seemed like there was nobody else on the frozen street but us, even though people just kept walking by like normal.

"I've been a real jerk," Archie said. "And I know that."

I didn't say anything.

"You can say it. Go ahead."

"Yeah, you've been . . . mean."

"A jerk."

"Yeah. A jerk."

"There. You said it. And you're right. I guess I was just jealous, you know?"

"Of what?"

"Of your robot. I mean . . ." He paused. "I never had anything that cool. Look. Let's not talk out here in the street. Let's go over to the Woolworth's, grab a malt. What do you say?"

I looked around.

"Jeez, I'm not gonna poison you, kid. And the Woolworth's is full of people."

"I gotta get home."

"I'll getcha home. Don't you worry."

He stuck his hands in his pockets and said, "Please? I really feel like a heel for what I did. For everything. Let me make it up to you."

He never had anything that cool.

"Yeah. Okay. Just for a bit."

He grinned so wide I caught a glimpse of one of his rotted back molars. "Great. Let's go. What's your flavor?"

"Vanilla."

"Jeez, kid. You sure are boring."

I glared at him.

"Take it easy! I'm just joking with you. A vanilla malt it is."

The Woolworth's was a secret world I had never entered, at this after-school hour. It seethed with adolescent posturing. It vibrated with laughter, yelps, and calls that seemed like a language all their own. The soda jerks struggled to keep up with orders and banter.

Archie and I took our places near the end of the counter, on two stools vacated by a greaser friend of his and a girl whose face I should have recognized, but did not. *A lipsticked teenage face in the passenger seat, mouth a screaming O.* She smiled at me as I walked up with Archie, curtseyed elaborately as she gestured to the vacated stool, tousled my hair as I sat down. The greaser saluted Archie. "Seeya, cat. We gotta blow." Archie nodded to him, then turned to the soda jerk sliding up. "A vanilla malted for the champ, here. And a Coke for me."

Mom was on swing shifts these days. She'd come in exhausted from her shifts at around midnight. Father cooked me dinners, but that wasn't until seven. Would he worry about me? Father never seemed to worry. And he wouldn't tell mom, I was sure of it . . .

Now we will have a secret between us, son.

Now we could add another secret.

And this was good, right? Me and Archie having a shake together. A truce.

At around this time, a call was placed to my house, from a pay phone in the back of the Woolworth's. I can imagine it, though they don't know the details: a woman's voice on the line telling Father that I'd been found wandering on old Route 66. She'd come across me just walking on the side of the road. I looked shaken up, but I wasn't hurt. No, just a bit scared. And cold. If he could come and collect me, she'd appreciate it. Maybe he could bring a jacket. Yeah, at the old Phillips 66 filling station.

Archie punched me on the shoulder. "I heard you and your Father built quite a rocket."

"How'd you know that?"

He grinned, showing that rotten molar again. "I got eyes and ears all over, you know?"

I glanced at his eye patch.

"The doc says it'll heal. I just need to keep it covered for a bit, is all."

"I'm sorry," I mumbled, as they set the malt in front of me. "I . . ."

"It was my fault, kid. Seriously."

I hadn't had a vanilla malt for months. I sucked at it greedily.

Most of the infrastructure money was going into building beacon chains for the terraplanes, and Route 66 was more and more potholed and neglected. There weren't many ground cars anymore—just recreational off-road buggies, or the occasional old jalopy owned by some dirt farmer too poor to upgrade.

The abandoned Phillips 66 gas station was four miles outside of town. It was twilight when Father got there—the sun below the horizon, full dark coming on fast. He had my sheepskin and corduroy jacket with him, and a sandwich he'd made for me.

A blonde girl came up in a crinoline skirt and started chatting with Archie. Her perfume smelled better than the vanilla malted.

"Who's the kid, Arch?"

"New friend of mine," Archie said. "He's gonna copilot my hot rod for me."

"Speakin' of," she said, drawing a flirtatious half-moon on the tile with the toe of her saddle shoe. "I need a ride home. Think you could drop me?"

Archie looked at me. "Whaddaya say, kid? You want to take a little spin in the Witch?"

"I should get home too," I mumbled. "My Father . . ."

"I'll drop you off after."

"Nah, I should just . . ."

"It'll be my pleasure, kid. Seriously." He looked at the blonde. "You want the kid to come, don't you?"

"Sure do," she said, chucking my chin. "Keep me safe from any animals flying around up there."

I'd never been in a terraplane before. Sure, I'd flown—but always in some clunky bus, waddling over the treetops. Never in anything fast . . .

A few minutes later, we were curving out in a long arc over downtown, Archie pointing the nose almost, it seemed, at the pale coin of the moon high up in the sky. I was in the rumble seat, wrapped in an old Pendleton coat Archie had given me, clutching the bar in front of me in joy and terror. The blonde girl's perfume, the smell of her hair, hovered on the cold edge of the air. The girl whooped with glee as the Witch banked hard and shot out over Nob Hill. The streetlights winked and shuddered beneath us.

Father must have been standing near the pump island of the Phillips 66 when the buggy came in, lights off, full speed. It was an old army land jeep stripped to the frame, with big oversize tires, a mesh screen for a windshield, and a rusty old cattleguard bolted to its front.

He must have thought it was just going past on the road before it swerved and punched straight into him. He clipped one of the pumps, rotated in the air, and went through the filling station's plate glass. The four greasers climbed out of the car. Three of them had lead pipes, and one had a stubby plasma saw he'd stolen from his dad's machine shop.

Father lay in the middle of the filling station floor. His eye lights were out. His chest cavity was dented in, and one of his legs was damaged at the knee joint. A greaser brought a lead pipe down on his head. The kid with the plasma saw's name was Hal Greenway. He sat on Father's smashed chest and started the plasma saw. He was halfway through Father's left arm when Father's orange eye lights flickered on.

Two seconds later, Hal Greenway was dead. Father had crushed his windpipe and his spinal column in one of his hands.

The other greasers scattered, headed for the jeep. Father tossed Hal Greenway's limp body aside and staggered to his feet. One of the greasers said he was talking, saying, ". . . unit partially disabled. One target destroyed. Moving to close with further combatants. Unit partially disabled. Requesting reinforcements at coordinates . . ."

At about this time we were coming to a landing on the blonde girl's family pad—a black concrete number with its white target inlaid in quartz. She lived up in the hills, in a house about the size of ten of mine.

"Not even a little kiss for my trouble?"

"Not in front of the kid. And get out of here before my parents come home."

"Girls, kid. Can't trust 'em." Archie whirled the Witch up into the air in a tornado of show-off 360s. "Stay away from girls, kid. You hear?"

I nodded.

"You look a little airsick."

I shook my head.

Archie chuckled. "Alright, tough guy. Let's go for a little spin, then I'll drop you home."

"Okay."

"Climb on up to shotgun."

I didn't want the ride to end.

I wasn't thinking about Father. I wasn't thinking about anything except the blonde girl's perfume, like something forbidden and adult—an illicit sip of whiskey. And the way the Witch bucked and surged underneath me. And how Archie liked me now. How I was his friend now.

We charged across the treetops, me and Archie. I clutched the dashboard in white-knuckled hands as we scattered crows and twigs scraped and rattled across the Witch's undercarriage.

Finally Archie dropped me at home, breathless and overjoyed. The house was dark, except for the motion-sensing lamp that lit up Archie's face—lit it up so white it seemed carved out of Ivory soap, with the slash of the eye patch across it cutting it in two. He winked at me with his one good eye.

"So long, kid," Archie said to me as I mounted the steps. "Say hi to your mom for me. Tell her I'll give her a ride any time she wants one." And he was gone, the Witch slicing through the circle of the moon.

Out of breath, just inside the door, I yelled, "I'm home!"

And I'm Archie's friend, I thought. I rode the Witch all over town.

This is what I can never stop feeling guilty about. The fact that I wasn't thinking about Father at all.

But Father never stopped thinking about me. Not entirely. He must have remembered my jacket in that moment. Must have been worried, must have gone looking for it, instead of going after the greasers.

He had the jacket in his hand when they hit him with the Molotov cocktail.

That's how the cops found him: standing steadfast there in the middle of that abandoned Phillips station, carapace charred, circuits melted down, my burned jacket clutched in his hand.

Love and death.

The black-and-white police cruiser landed on the lawn maybe half an hour later.

By then, I had started to get really scared. Father wasn't anywhere in the house, or in the garage. He wasn't anywhere. But maybe the repairman had come and taken him away for servicing, I thought. Maybe . . .

The cruiser poured its red and blue lights into the living room. Mom came bursting in the door with the two cops from before, and with the blond repairman. Mom held me, and cried, and then yelled at me, and then cried some more.

Much of the night was spent with me in the kitchen, over a cup of cocoa, catching pieces of the conversations in the other room. People came and went—other cops, other military. I heard the blond repairman in the hallway, talking to another military man:

". . . doesn't make sense. None of those combat subroutines should have been left in there. They were all scrubbed after the war. He's no killer."

"Yeah," the other military man said, "I'm no killer either. And neither are you, right? But we were, back in Germany and Poland. And maybe, under the right circumstances . . . just maybe, if you pushed us the wrong way . . ."

"But he's a robot. These are subroutines. Just programs. We wiped them."

"Yeah, just programs. I know. And you know what? I woke up in a cold sweat a week ago."

"Sure, it happens."

"Yeah. It happens. But not always like this. I woke up in a cold sweat with a knife in my teeth, Jim. Crawling down the hallway on my belly."

"Christ, Bill. No kidding?"

"On our new carpet, on my belly. Thank God nobody saw. Thank God I got the knife back in the kitchen drawer and climbed back into bed before my wife noticed the army hadn't quite cleaned out my sub-routines. Right, Jim?"

"Jesus. What a mess this thing is. It'll be the end of the Fathers program. A dead kid."

"I guess in my book, that trash can had a right to defend himself. But I suppose nobody will want to hear that. That's between us."

The cops came in and took a statement from me. They were real gen-tle, and kept telling me what a brave kid I was, even though I didn't know what for. I hadn't done anything the least bit brave, and I knew it.

I told them all I could, but it wasn't much. Part of me still thought Archie was my friend.

Jesus, yer dumb.

The three greasers who burned Father got a few months in juvie: destruction of government property, mitigating circumstances, et cet-era et cetera. Nobody could stomach giving them more, after they'd watched their friend die.

Archie got nothing at all. Nobody would rat. Why had the greasers gone after Father? They'd just seen him standing there, thought he was a piece of old junk it would be fun to smash into, that's all. Stupid, a lark. Just some delinquent nonsense.

Archie smirked his way through every grilling the cops gave him. The eye patch? He'd clipped a tree branch in his hot rod. The malt? He just wanted to make a kid happy. What's the crime? The phone call? C'mon—had the kid seen him make a phone call?

As far as anyone could prove, he just wanted to buy me a vanilla malt and take me for a ride in the Witch.

The Fathers were all recalled. The program was cancelled. I guess they scrubbed all their Father programming out, the way they had their war programming.

Later, I heard they all ended up in the terraforming colonies on

Mars, doing the heavy lifting and the dangerous repair jobs the colonists couldn't do.

I wonder, sometimes, if they ever dream of their sons and daughters up there where they labor in the red dust. Of playing catch on crickety evenings back on Earth, of porch swings, of walking to the store for push-pops and orangesicles.

Jim, the VA repairman? He stuck around. And eventually, I got around to calling him Dad.

I never called him Father, though.

Even though we hit pop flies, and built rockets, and he helped me make a soap box derby car, and I came to love him.

I only had one Father. I had him for six months. I'd never have another.

DON'T MIND ME

SUZANNE PALMER

Suzanne Palmer (www.zanzjan.net) is a writer, artist, and Linux system administrator who lives in western Massachusetts. She is a regular contributor to *Asimov's Science Fiction*, and has had work appear in *Analog Science Fiction and Fact*, *Clarkesworld*, *Interzone*, and other venues. She was the winner of the *Asimov's* Readers' Award for Best Novella, and the AnLab (*Analog*) award for Best Novelette in 2016. Her debut novel, *Finder*, was published in 2019, followed by the sequels *Driving the Deep* and *The Scavenger Door*.

Riley was the smartest kid in the high school, with her own small clique of friends around her that seemed closed to all outsiders, so Jake did not expect the tall, gangly girl to nudge him with her shoulder on her way past him at the lockers. "You going to sign up for one of the after-school cleanup shifts in the classroom science lab, for the extra credit?" she asked. "You could use it."

Science was currently his worst subject, and Jake was fairly sure he could spend every day sweeping and putting tablets back in their charging nooks and curling up cables and still not pass, but this was *Riley* asking, and he didn't think she'd ever even spoken to him before and probably wouldn't again, so he nodded. "I guess, yeah," he said.

She nodded. "Cool-oh," she said, and continued on as if she'd never even paused, the blue fuzzy deely boppers she'd glued onto her minder bobbing out of sight as her posse closed back in around her and they melted into the rest of the students milling the halls.

"You have three minutes twelve seconds until the start of your next class," Jake's minder said in its low, perfectly unemotional, perfectly horrible voice. "It takes you on average two minutes fifty-eight seconds to traverse the distance from your locker to the classroom, so you should begin now."

Jake slammed his locker shut. He wanted to take his time, arrive late just to spite the thing plugged into the side of his head, but it would dutifully report even the briefest tardiness to his parents, and that just wasn't worth it. At least math was next; he usually came out of that remembering the entire class.

He made it in the door and to his seat with six seconds to spare. Ms. Lang was already at the smartboard, swiping across it from the virtual dock to bring up pages and images from where they'd left off the day before. Above the board, the classroom monitoring light was a steady green. "Okay, everyone," she said. "Back to quadratic equations we go, and get a little extra practice in before Friday's quiz."

There was a brief, familiar sting at his temple, and the world lurched forward a few seconds. There were suddenly two more windows open on the board, and the teacher had hopped a step to her left and was turning. Looking around the room at other puzzled faces, Jake wasn't the only one who'd gotten zapped. The kids without minders were snickering, and Ana was laughing into her hand. Jake followed his classmates' glances over to Danny's desk, which now had a red light on it. "What?" Danny protested. "I don't even know what I said!" His own minder had gotten him, too.

"You said—" Ana started, and then there was another jump, and the teacher was facing them, cross now, and pointing at Ana with her board wand.

"Don't start this, or we'll never get through this lesson," Ms. Lang said. "I remind folks to watch their language and pay attention. If the entire class passes the quiz and your group average is a C or better, I'll bring in cookies next Monday. Okay? Now, back to the board . . ."

For once, the rest of the class went without interruption.

English was even more of a blur than usual, because Maya Angelou was apparently full of things his parents didn't think he should hear, and unlike random conversation, which was keyword-based, the minder could match a flagged portion of text as it was being read aloud and zap the whole sequence. He hated the feeling of having lost nearly half an hour of his time, and knowing that all his classmates with the orange-covered Good Parenting Code Redacted Edition of the book were just as robbed and confused as he was.

Last period was study hall, and he slunk down to the open lounge and sank into a chair, and stared at nothing for a while. Some kids, when they hit eighteen, chose to keep their minders, or went back to them not long after. He'd once seen an elderly man, way too old to have ever had one in childhood, with the familiar black half-hemisphere clamped onto the side of his head over his thinning white hair. Jake's father was always telling him he had to keep his as long as he lived under their roof, and his mom always stepped in to say of course he would, he was a *good boy* and *raised properly*.

Being glum about it all took up about half of study hall, then when the room teacher started giving him looks, he took out his orange-covered history book and got started on his homework for tomorrow. Some texts removed unapproved material seamlessly, reworking sentences so the absence was invisible, but this one was just a reprint of the original with black blocks where offending text once was, and the longer the block the more he despaired about passing the class. Foolishly he'd thought Ancient Rome would be a pretty safe subject, going in.

The end of school bell rang, and he got up and packed his stuff in his backpack and was being carried along with the great tide of students toward the buses when he remembered Riley. "Minder," he said, "tell my mom I'll be staying after school to do some volunteer cleanup for extra credit."

"This has now been communicated," the minder said a few moments later. "Dinner tonight is spaghetti alfredo, your favorite, so don't tarry."

"Yeah, thanks," he said. He turned and made his way down to the science wing, past the ninth grade poster projects and into his classroom. Riley was there, leaning on a desk playing idly with the blackboard remote, saving and closing windows one by one. Her tight-knit crew were all there. Kitt, a short, blonde girl with cat ears on her minder, was taking washed lab gear from the dish drainer beside the sink at the back of the room and sorting them one by one into the equipment drawers. Nate, who was one of the few Black kids in the school and got ten times as much crap as the other nerds, was pushing a variety of spitballs and dust around the floor in a meandering path toward the center with an old yellow broom, his minder sporting a painted-on Jolly Roger that had come and gone a couple of times, no doubt as part of a battle of wills with his folks that sometimes, Jake had noticed, ended in bruises. Erin, whose minder had been coated in purple glitter, was carefully lowering the window blinds, trying to make them perfectly even. And Jonathan, a large, happy kid with dissheveled light brown hair who had no minder at all, was making a giant stack of metal disks and blocks and magnets.

"Jake," Riley said.

"Hi," he said. "Where's Ms. Scott?"

"She trusts us to get through the checklist and not cause trouble," Riley said. "We've been doing this all year for her. She'll come by after the late bell and lock up."

"Okay," Jake said. "What do you want me to do?"

"Come help me with the glassware?" Kitt said. "Unless you're clumsy."

"Not too much," he said. He shrugged off his backpack, dumped it on a stool, and went back to the sink. "You guys do this every week?"

"Tuesdays and Thursdays," Nate said. "We all need the extra credit to fill in gaps, you know?"

"Not me," Jonathan said, as his pile of magnets fell over. "My brain is my own, and my grades are, too. I'd just rather hang out with these losers than have to go home."

Ever since freshman year, the five of them—Riley, Jonathan, Kitt, Erin, and Nate—had been best of best friends, a perfectly self-contained, self-sufficient social circle. The oddness of them inviting him here struck him again, and he lost track of which drawer he'd last returned pipettes to. "Why me, though?" he asked.

"Few months ago, Harris and Deke were bugging my little sister Lynne in the lunchroom, calling her fat and four-eyes and spaz," Erin said. "You stepped in and threatened to beat their asses if they ever even spoke to her again."

"Oh yeah." Jake hadn't known the two of them were related, though now that he thought about it, the resemblance between the two dark-haired girls was obvious. "Harris and Deke are jerks. Anyone would have done the same."

"No," Erin said. "No one had, all year, until you."

Jake shrugged. "I'm big. Everyone thinks that must mean I throw a hard punch and like to fight. Doesn't matter that I've never hit someone in my life." He almost had, once, and that had been close enough.

"Yeah, well, I'm glad you were there," Erin said.

Behind them, Nate got up and shut the classroom door, and leaned against it.

"What . . . ?" Jake started to ask, but Riley put a finger to her lips, then pointed at Jonathan.

Jonathan scooped up a handful of the magnets he'd been playing with, and threw them one at a time to the others. Then he walked up, a big grin on his face, and slapped Jake on the side of the head.

"Ow!" Jake said, taken by surprise. "What, you want to test me if I'll actually hit someone? Because now I'm game."

Jonathan stepped back, and held up his hands in surrender. "Look around, my man," he said. "Look around and be free."

Jake curled his hand, trying to decide if he should hit this kid, when he caught Riley's eyes. She pointed at her own head—no, to her minder, and the magnet now stuck right onto the side of it.

The other three had done the same.

"We've been keeping an eye on you since Lynne told Erin about the cafeteria," Riley said. Jonathan began humming the *Twilight Zone* refrain. "You don't go out of your way, but you're pretty smart, too, and it's your fucking minder that keeps you from being a top student."

"We shouldn't be having this conversation. You know our minders record—" Jake stopped midsentence. Riley had just dropped a swear in his presence, and he'd heard it, and *remembered* it. There was no skip, no awful blink as his minder took the moment away. Carefully, he reached up and touched the magnet.

Nate laughed. "Ooooh, you should see your face," he said. Then more seriously, "You caught on fast."

Jake's eyes immediately went to the classroom monitor, whose light was off. *Right*, he thought. *School hours are over.*

Jonathan whacked him hard on the shoulder. "Welcome to the club, Jake-o."

"Uh . . . okay," Jake said, thinking it through. "The magnet scrambles the electronics, keeps it from working. Keeps it from recording?" Otherwise it'd be a short-lived freedom at best, and it wouldn't have a happy ending.

"Yeah," Erin said. "There are other things that disrupt the minders, so a little bit of static and missing timestamp on the recording doesn't stand out. As long as no one says anything, or does the magnet trick anywhere outside this room and this group, we're pretty safe. This is our secret, just us. Not even Lynne knows."

"You won't say anything, right, Jake?" Riley asked. "Not to your parents, your brothers and sisters, other kids here in school? And not your friends?"

"No," Jake answered. "I'm an only kid, and I don't have any friends. Not really." *Not anymore.*

"Well, you do now," Kitt said. "Just don't let us down. We're taking a risk on you."

"Why, though? I mean, this is cool and all, but it's a lot of risk just so we can have a Swearing in a Classroom Club."

"Because one of us can get through the checklist with time to spare. Five—*six* of us gives us a lot of extra time," Kitt said. "Jonathan?"

Jonathan pulled over his own backpack, and pulled out all the class textbooks, not a single one of them with an orange cover. "You get tested on the full coursework, even the parts you can't hear because your mommy and daddy don't want you learning about communism and atheists and art boobies," Jonathan said. "If you're heavily minded, you're lucky if you can pull a just-passing grade average out of working your ass as hard as you can being perfect at everything else. Maybe you don't even graduate. This isn't a swearing club, it's Study Club. We take turns doing the cleaning and catching up on whatever reading we need to do, thanks to my lovely collection of uncensored textbooks."

"And what's in it for you?" Jake asked.

Jonathan dropped down onto a stool and thumped the top of the stack of books with his fist. "You all help me study too, because I'm not as good at some of this stuff. Especially math. You good at math, Jake?"

"Math, yeah," he said. "Just don't ask me what the last month of science has been about."

Jonathan slung a book across the lab table at him. "Welcome to the sordid underworld of climate science, my man."

Riley's crew, Jake reflected as he walked from the bus stop back toward his house, had things pretty solidly figured out. Since the minders could only record or respond to audio, normally they'd only "static up" for a few minutes at a time, when they needed to discuss things. Otherwise they took turns studying and cleaning, the cleaners making small talk and a constant soundtrack of noises. "In movies," Kitt had told him, "the people who make all the background noises for a scene are called Foley artists."

The school's American history teacher was named Mr. Foley, and he hated any noises at all in his classroom while he was lecturing—he once threw a smart pen at a girl for chewing gum too loud—and when Jake pointed this out, they'd all laughed.

It was like he suddenly had friends again, out of the blue, and the knowledge that the minder could be circumvented seemed trivial in comparison.

When he got home, his mother greeted him at the door with her usual hug and kiss, then unlocked the minder and gently tugged it free from his head. "You've got a bit of chafing and redness around your implant again," she said. "You're just growing too fast. We'll get you a larger model next fall, okay?"

"Sure. Thanks, Mom," he said, hanging his backpack up on the coatrack behind the door as she plugged his minder into its dock to charge and upload its day's recordings to his parents' cloudpod. In a brief flash of daring, he added. "Maybe I could just not wear it tomorrow, to give my head a chance to heal?"

His mother shook her head. "You've got a perfect attendance record. I'd hate to see you miss a day if you don't need to."

"I wouldn't have to stay home," he said.

She *hmmmm*'d, an affectionate sound, and gave him a sad half-smile. "I know school must seem a good and safe place, but that's because your minder keeps you away from the bad language, the wrong-headed ideas meant to confuse and lead you astray. If only we could afford private school for you, like Connor's parents . . ."

"It's okay, Mom," Jake said quickly. He didn't want to talk about his former best friend. Ever. "I like school, even with my minder. It's just hard sometimes, feeling like I'm missing things and I don't even know what they are."

"Poison," his father said from the kitchen doorway. "You're missing poison. Be grateful and go wash up for dinner."

By the third Study Club he had the routine down, including Riley and Jonathan's system of hand signals, and there was very little chatting necessary, which meant also less static on the minder's recording to raise suspicions. During one of the blackouts, he handed off Jonathan's history text to Nate. "I might actually ace this test, for once," he said.

"Be careful about that," Riley cautioned. "If you do too well, or there's a sudden jump in your grades, your parents might start wondering why."

"I hadn't thought of that," Jake admitted. The idea that he might have to deliberately flub some of the questions bothered him immensely. But how much should he actually know about things like the Tulsa Massacre, completely absent from his own orange-bound, censored text?

"You'll get used to it," Kitt said. "You just gotta graduate or get to eighteen, whichever comes first."

"I don't think it's gonna be that easy," he grumbled. "Not if my dad has any say in it."

"Yeah, well, my dad talks with a cane," Riley said, and the others all looked down at their books, uncomfortable and quiet, until she dramatically groaned and got up from her chair. "My turn to sort the stupid beakers," she said. "Your turn with social studies, Erin."

It was odd not dreading being at school every day, but getting out of the house in the morning had become torturous as he worried about not seeming too happy, for fear his parents would note the change and become suspicious.

Proof he'd overacted his misery came when his mother stopped him on his way out the door a few days before the holiday break. "You miss Connor, don't you?" she said. "You two used to be best of friends until he went to Angel Valley."

"I don't miss him at all," he said, more forcefully than he intended, and his mother frowned at him.

"I was thinking I could invite his family over for dinner, maybe over break," she continued. "Would you like that?"

"They won't come," Jake said, grabbing his bag as she pushed the minder down onto his head and it clicked into place. "Don't you get that? We're not good enough for them anymore, because I still go to the public school and even though I have a minder I'm not one of them, and I won't ever be good or pure enough anymore. So thanks, I get to be looked down on by both the Angel Valley kids and by regular kids at the same time, because instead of being brainwashed the old-fashioned, socially acceptable, rich-kid way like precious Connor, I've got this Frankenstein thing stuck in my head deciding what I'm allowed to think."

"Jake!" His mother was shocked and visibly upset.

"I'm gonna be late," he said, and slammed the door behind him before he could hear her counterargument, or worse, crying. He'd get more than enough yelling when he got home, anyway.

"You okay?" Kitt asked when he came into the science lab just after the last bell, and threw himself down at one of the lab benches. She slid a magnet across the hard black top to him.

"Parents," he said after he put it on. He looked around the room. Erin and Riley were both leaning over the same history text as Jonathan doodled chickens all over the smartboard. "Where's Nate?"

"Volunteered to vacuum the library," Erin said. "Ms. Carrie says they don't pay her enough to monitor what kids are reading once school hours are over, as long as they have a legit reason to be there. I think he cares more about reading for fun than actually studying. He's been working his way through *The Two Towers* since sometime last spring."

"The what?" Jake asked.

Jonathan whistled. "You haven't heard of it? At *all*? Man, you have a sad-ass life."

Jake stood up so quickly he knocked a beaker off the lab bench, and it shattered all over the floor. "You wanna say that to me again?" he demanded.

Riley got between them. "Hang on, hang on. We're on the same side here. Jonathan, you want us to call you out on stuff you got no choice in?"

"I didn't mean anything. It was a joke, okay?" Jonathan said.

"Say sorry," Riley said.

Jonathan rolled his eyes and let out a deep, melodramatic sigh. "*Sorry*, Jake," he said.

Riley turned around and whacked Jake on the shoulder. "Say you're good now," she said.

"Am I?" Jake asked.

"You better off without us?" Riley asked.

"No," Jake said. He sat down, then immediately stood up again to get the broom. He didn't meet anyone's eyes as he swept up the broken glass into a small pile, then an even smaller one, before finally swatting it into the dustpan. "Don't say that ever again, Jonathan, and then I guess we'll be good."

"I really didn't mean anything," Jonathan said, more sincerely this time, and Jake sat back down and picked up the math textbook.

He slung it over onto Jonathan's desk, where it landed with a loud thump and nearly slid off the far side before Jonathan slapped his hand down on it. "Chapter fourteen," Jake said. "Log, Sine, and Cosine. Try the first ten exercises and then if you still don't get it, I'll try to explain."

Two weeks later, Jake burst into the science lab, waving his grade slip. "I got an A!" he shouted.

No one leapt up to high-five him. "What subject?" Kitt asked warily, handing him his magnet.

"Science," Jake said, feeling a sudden pang of anxiety deep in his gut as he put the magnet on. "The astronomy unit. Can't be anything—"

"Did you get the questions right where you have to use the ruler to measure how far away the galaxies are on the picture and plug them into the formula to get their real distance?" Nate asked.

"Yeah," Jake said.

"And how far away were they?" Nate asked.

"Like fifteen thousand light years—"

"So how long did it take that light to get here?" Nate asked.

"And how old do your parents believe the universe is?" Riley added.

Jake stared down at the slip of paper.

"If they don't go looking at the test questions, you're probably okay. If they do, and you haven't already used it, try the 'lucky guessing' excuse," Erin said. "That won't work too many times, though."

"Oh," Jake said, and couldn't help but think, *but I got an* A.

Dinner was quiet. Too quiet, even though Jake had not brought up his grade. He ate his chicken and peas, indecision roiling in his mind. Was it suspicious that he didn't mention it, and make him look guilty? Or was bringing it up only bringing attention to something that might otherwise go unnoticed?

Later, as he was sitting at his desk in his room doing his homework, he could hear his parents talking in the front hall. "The diagnostics say it's okay," his mother was saying. "He'd tell us if it didn't seem to be working right."

"Would he?" his father asked. "Remember what he said to you the other morning? This is supposed to protect him, not turn him defiant."

"All young men are defiant," his mother said. "You were. Oh, were you a troublemaker when I first met you. You're lucky I believe in second chances."

"I was, and that's how I know I was wrong. Maybe we should look into our finances again, see if we can scrape together enough to transfer him to Angel Valley after all."

There was silence for a few minutes, and the muffled beep of the minder station as it finished charging his unit. He heard his mother let out a long sigh. "I don't think Angel Valley would be a good place for Jake," she said at last. "I don't like how exclusionary those families become."

"The Ducettes sent their boy there. He and Jake were best of friends, and we get together with them regularly."

"We used to," his mother corrected.

"We've all been busy—"

"I invited them over for dinner. Abigail laughed at me, told me not to bother them again, and hung up."

"What?" his father sounded genuinely surprised. "I'll talk to Rob-

ert after church this Sunday, find out what that was about. There must
just be some misunderstanding. . . ."

"Sure," his mother said. "Let me know how that goes. In the meantime, let's not talk about Angel Valley. Not yet."

"Anyone else see the news last night?" Nate asked.

Riley snorted. "Like any of us are allowed to watch the news. Since when are you?"

"Since my mom fell asleep on the couch with the remote unlocked," Nate said. He tapped the side of his minder, next to the magnet. "Did you know these are now illegal in sixteen states? North Carolina just outlawed them too. In seven it's considered child abuse."

"Too bad we don't live in North Carolina," Erin said. "You know that's never going to happen here."

"Maybe if enough states do it, it'll become a national law," Jake said. He remembered the right word. "You know, federal."

"Not soon enough for us, though," Kitt said.

"We could get lucky and it could be soon," Nate added.

"You think so?" Riley asked. "You know they don't even have any good studies on the long-term effects of frying kids' hippocampus—"

"Hippowhat?" Jonathan asked.

"Part of your fucking brain," Riley said, and Jake found himself flinching reflexively at the swear, even though it couldn't currently trigger his subverted minder. "That's how it works, right? You've got a little wire stuck right into your brain so this piece of shit tech can disrupt your damned memories and keep things it doesn't like from getting converted from short to long term, as if modifying our very thoughts inside our heads somehow keeps us purer than accidentally hearing a few random syllables."

"I thought it just made it so you don't hear it," Erin said.

"It's worse. You hear it perfectly fine, and then it takes that away from you. Like someone breaking into your room and stealing your favorite thing but as soon as it's out of the room you can't even remember you ever had it to start with, only you just know something is missing you can't identify," Riley said. "It *should* be criminal, except who gets to decide that? The goddamned thieves themselves."

"You okay, Ri?" Jonathan asked.

"No!" she said. "How can I be? How can any of us be? It's not enough to get around their mind control. We should be fighting it."

"And how do we do that?" Nate asked. "We don't have any power."

"My father would ship me off to Angel Valley," Jake said. "There's no *getting around* that. That would be the end. I don't want to lose what freedom I have, even if it's not much."

"Yeah, well, you can't go off to Angel Valley anyhow," Erin said. "My sister Lynne has a crush on you for saving her from the cafeteria bullies. You're her personal hero."

Riley stood up, and threw her magnet down on a lab bench with a sharp bang like a gunshot. Everyone went dead silent. "This is all just a waste of time," she said, and left the classroom.

Other than the door banging closed again behind her, the silence lasted long after she was gone.

It was Nate who broke it, with a small cough. "Things are really bad in her house," he said. "I mean, really bad even compared to the rest of us. At least I think for most of us we can say our parents are trying to do what they think is best for us, even if we don't agree. Riley's folks . . ."

"It's about absolute control," Kitt added. "She doesn't even have a door on her bedroom."

Jake whistled. "Okay, that definitely sucks," he said.

Erin closed her textbook and got up, grabbing the bench wipes. "They don't like that she's smart," she said. "It's a threat. So she has to pretend she's not."

"She's smarter than any of us," Jonathan said. "But her folks talk about when she flunks out of high school sending her off to one of the church work farms. Yanno, one of those places surrounded by barbed wire? Ain't there to protect the corn."

"Shit," Jake said, the swear weird in his own voice, powerful and shameful.

He glanced up at the clock to cover his sudden embarrassment.

"Oh hey, time's almost up," he said. He double-checked that he'd made it through the section of the science chapter blacked out in his own textbook, then closed the unabridged copy and handed it back to Jonathan.

Together they finished up the last of the lab cleanup and reluctantly left their magnets behind.

In the hall walking toward the school's front entrance, Jake's minder beeped. "Jake, your mother has requested that you stop at the corner store on your way home to pick up some green leaf lettuce and a small carton of half and half. Do you wish to hear these items repeated?"

"No," Jake said.

"Do you wish your agreement to be communicated to your mother?"

"Yes," Jake answered. His minder hadn't spoken to him in several days, and it was a jolt to be reminded that his brief escapes from it were only that.

He was still lost in thought about Riley and the minders and hippocampuses when he turned down an aisle in the corner mart and nearly collided with someone coming the other way. "Connor," he said.

"Jake," Connor said, taking a half step back as if even being near him was distasteful. He was wearing his Angel Valley school uniform.

The last conversation they'd had, Jake had strongly considered punching him. He'd grown though, right? He had other friends now, better ones. He could be the bigger person. "How've you been?" he asked.

"On the higher path," Connor answered. "We're the future of the new America. There will be no room for the tainted trash of humanity then, and I have no time for you now."

Whatever Jake said in reply, his minder stole the moment from him, but there was at least some satisfaction in seeing the suddenly pale kid hurrying away as if bitten.

He regretted, just a tiny bit more, not punching him. Either way it was worth whatever trouble he was going to be in when he got home and his minder reported the encounter.

Jake's mom came into his room just as he was about to turn out his light. She sat on the edge of his bed, and patted his knee. "You know you were wrong to use that word?" she asked.

"I'm not even sure what word I said, but yes," Jake said. "I was wrong. But he used to be my very best friend and we did everything together and he called me *trash*."

"Your father and I expect you to make better decisions," she said. "But we know you have a good heart, and as wrong as you were to speak to anyone that way, Connor was also in the wrong for what he said to you. We want you to be the best Jake you can be, and if you are, only God can judge you."

"I'm sorry, Mom," Jake said.

"I know," she answered, and kissed him on the head before turning off his light. She left his door cracked partway open, and as he lay there overwhelmed by guilt and lingering anger, his father's shouting still ringing in his ears from earlier, she re-appeared in the doorway.

"That's a word you shouldn't know, and I trust that you won't ever speak it again," she said, "but if you absolutely had to use it, you chose the right occasion."

That gentle understanding pushed the remainder of the anger out of his system and left him to try to find sleep wallowing in his own shame and regret.

"Jake!" Kitt called out in unfeigned happiness to see him when he walked in the door of the science lab, and handed him his magnet. "Where you been?"

"Grounded for two weeks," he said.

"For the A?" Nate asked.

"No, for calling someone a bad word I can't remember," Jake answered. "But knowing how angry I was when I said it, I'm pretty sure the grounding was justified."

"I was worried you got caught and sent off to Angel Valley," Erin said. "Then we'd be stuck trying to teach Jonathan math."

"Lucky for you I'm still here," he said. He had been unsure if he should come back, but that uncertainty disappeared.

"Angel Valley isn't the worst," Riley spoke up from where she was sitting on a lab bench with a science book on her lap. "You know they're working on glasses, to also censor what we can see?"

"No one would—" Erin started to say.

"My parents would, if it was available," Riley said. "And minders aren't just used to censor out science, or things that disagree with faith—*any* faith, or even all faith. You know there are some where you can't hear anything at all spoken by people of a certain gender? Or race?"

"What?" Nate said. "That's not cool."

"I'm just saying, for every person out there working on a way to get around minders, or get rid of them, there's someone working on making them worse. And some of the things they're trying . . . Angel Valley wouldn't be so terrible in comparison."

"How do you know all this?" Kitt asked.

"I have connections," Riley said. "You all might be looking for a way through, but I'm looking for a way out."

"What happens when you find it?" Kitt asked.

"Then I'm gone."

"And what about us?" Erin asked.

"You gotta make your own choices," Riley said. "I— Oh *shit.*"

She was staring at the classroom door. Everyone else followed her gaze to find that Erin's sister was standing there in the open doorway. "Lynne!" Erin shouted.

"I thought maybe I could help," Lynne said. She was blushing, and studiously not looking at Jake.

"How long have you been standing there?" Erin asked, pulling open a drawer to find another magnet.

"A few minutes," Lynne said. "Since you were talking about some kind of new glasses."

Erin had found an extra magnet, and ran toward her alarmed sister. "It's too late," Riley said. "Her minder heard everything. Get her out in the hall. Plan B."

Erin nodded, a jerky, panicked gesture, and pulled Lynne out of the classroom.

As soon as the door shut behind them, Jake turned to the others, his heart thudding in his chest. "Plan B?"

"Plan A was if one of us was caught. Plan B is all of us," Kitt said. "Soon as her minder gets downloaded, the shit is going to hit the fan. They'll know we've circumvented the minders, if not how."

"Can we just, somehow, erase the record in Lynne's minder?" Nate asked.

"Not without pulling it off her head, which without properly unlocking and disconnecting it could cause brain damage," Riley said. "Trust me, if there was a way, I'd have found it by now."

Erin stuck her head back in the door. "I'm going to take Lynne for milkshakes on the way home. That will buy us an extra hour or so. Good luck everyone."

"Are you safe?" Riley asked Jake. "If you go home."

"I think so," he answered. Safe with his mother, sure, but his father . . . "I'm not sure."

"If you're not safe, get to Jonathan's house. That's our safe point. Don't tell anyone where you are going."

Jonathan nodded. "Only danger at my place is my mom's cooking," he said.

"And then what?"

"Like I said earlier, everyone has to make their own choices. I didn't think it was going to be anything more than rhetorical this soon, though," Riley said. "And Jake, if you don't come? It was good knowing you. Try not to let anyone steal who you are, or who you want to become, away from you."

Jake left the school with his magnet still on his minder, his hoodie pulled up over it so no one would spot it; part of him wanted to broadcast to the world how to get around having your brain under external control, but Riley had convinced him that as soon as that hack was publicly known, the minder manufacturers would find a way to prevent it working going forward. Better to pass it on, whisper by whisper, friend to friend.

He started walking toward home almost as many times as he started walking toward Jonathan's house, and ended up mostly doing irregular loops around town, until he found himself near the elementary school playground and took a seat on one of the swings. The sun had set and the sky was shifting quickly toward night when he took his magnet off.

"You are late for dinner and should immediately return home. It will take you twenty-one minutes to walk from this location," his minder immediately said. "You have fourteen messages from your mother and six from your father. Would you like to hear them?"

"No," Jake said. "Send a message to my father and give him my current location—"

"Your current location has already been provided to your parents," his minder said.

Of course, Jake thought. "Tell him to meet me here, just him, and if he calls the police or brings anyone else along he will never see me again. You got that?"

"The message has been sent," his minder said.

"Good," Jake said. "Now shut up." He put his magnet back on, then relocated from the playground across the street to a small park. Feeling both foolish and paranoid, he sat on the ground behind a bench, where he could see through the slats but not easily be seen in return.

His father arrived twenty-nine minutes later, and stood by the slide, looking around.

It took Jake a few minutes of watching his father to rally his courage, then he walked toward him, hoodie still up, hands in his pockets to hide their shaking. His father spotted him as he crossed the street and stood straight and unmoving until they were face to face.

"Jacob," his father said.

"Dad," he answered.

They regarded each other for several minutes, before his father spoke again. "I don't expect I need to tell you how angry and disappointed I am," he said.

"No, I think I got that," Jake said. "How's Mom doing?"

"She's hurt and scared. What do you think?" his father snapped. "She made me agree to come out here and meet you on your terms despite that. So this is your play: what now?"

What now? Jake asked himself. He had no idea what his "play" was, except to be honest.

"You know, Connor used to be my best friend. I didn't need other friends, because we did everything together since kindergarten. Then his parents sent him off to Angel Valley, and he's not only no longer my friend, he's no longer *Connor*," Jake said. "And I just want to keep being Jake, because I think I'm a good kid, but I can't know who I am and what I am while my entire reality is being decided by someone else. Even if that's you."

"The job of a parent is to protect—" his father started to say.

"The job of a parent is to guide their children," Jake interrupted. He'd never interrupted his father in his life before, and didn't know how he dared to do so now. "This minder isn't guidance, it's locking me in a tiny little box. And maybe, yeah, there are some pretty rotten things out there in the world, but this feels like you're assuming just knowing about them would make me want them, and that's not fair. I can learn about something without accepting it unconditionally, I can talk it through with you to understand why you have different opinions, and I can form my own judgment, but I can't know if I agree or disagree with anything if I can't know about it at *all*."

"Why me? Why aren't you throwing this sales pitch at your mother?" his father asked.

"Because Mom would get it. I don't know if you can. And as much as I love you, if you can't understand then I can't come home," Jake said. "I'm giving *you* the chance to think and decide for yourself, because if I'm going to demand that right, I owe it to you."

His father blew out a long breath through his nose, and stared at him long enough that Jake felt like his knees were going to give out and pitch him onto the ground. "I don't like this," he said at last. "I don't like that you defied me, that you've been sneaking around behind my back to do something you explicitly know is forbidden, and that somehow you think a few words can make that okay."

"I don't need you to like it, and I don't need you to stop being angry, but I need you to respect me," Jake said. "I need a second chance as much as I need to offer one to you."

"Wait here," his father said, and abruptly turned and walked away.

It was almost two hours later that his mother appeared in the park, walking toward him shivering as he sat at the top of the slide. "Jake?" she called out.

He climbed down, and she wrapped him in a tight hug, and for a moment he was afraid she wouldn't let go. Then she stepped back and held him at arm's length for a moment, before she reached into her coat pocket and pressed something into his hand.

The minder key.

"There are some other kids missing. Friends of yours, I guess," she said. "Do you know where they are?"

If they were still at Jonathan's house, they'd be gone soon. Riley and Nate, certainly; he didn't know about the others, and didn't know where they would go. "No," he said.

"You demand your so-called freedom, but it comes at a cost," she said.

"What?" he asked.

"Don't ever lie or hide things from us again. And don't . . ." Her voice faltered.

"Don't what, Mom?"

"Don't stray from the path of being good," she said. "Not for the sake of trying to be smart, and certainly not just because you feel a need to disagree with your father. Because if you think your minder was a pain, you have no idea how many arguments you have set yourself up for instead."

"I will do my best," he said.

"Then come home. Your dinner is ice cold by now."

"I don't mind," he said.

Riley, Nate, and Kitt were gone. Kitt came back about a month later, not wearing her minder. She was no longer allowed to speak to him or the others remaining from the Study Club, but whenever they saw each other in the halls they made a beeline to intersect and high-five as they passed.

Jonathan was very relieved that Jake was still willing to help him with math.

Lynne seemed to blame him somehow for what happened, and his hero status was gone, but every once in a while she'd dump her tray next to his in the cafeteria and sit with him. He assumed that either meant she'd eventually stop being mad at him and knew it, or that she was strategically re-upping their association to keep Harris and Deke off her back.

His mother had not lied when she told him he'd set himself up for a world of arguments with his father; every single thing that the minder or his old censored text would have kept from him, his father had to hash out in excruciating detail. It was exhausting and felt pointless, except as the weeks and months wore on, his father's arguments became less a belligerent lecture and more a heated exchange of near-equals.

He missed Riley and Nate, and worried about them, wondering if they'd gone separate ways or had stuck together, wishing he knew where they were or even just that they were okay. There was no one he could ask who would know, but wherever they were, he knew they were joining the fight against minder tech.

On the last day of school before summer, he was cleaning out his locker and found a dog-eared paperback book called *The Fellowship of the Ring* inside, a note sticking out from the middle.

For when you still need to escape, the note said, and was signed, *Nate*.

At the bottom of the page was a postscript. *PS*, it read, *this is like a year overdue. Please return it to the library when you're done and pay my fine. Thanks.*

Jake tucked it in his bag, shut his empty locker, and went home.

THE SUICIDE OF OUR TROUBLES

KARL SCHROEDER

Karl Schroeder's (www.kschroeder.com) science fiction explores the blurred line between the natural and the artificial; forests and rivers are as likely as humans to be the heroes of his stories. He's known for epic far-future novels, such as *Permanence, Lockstep, Ventus,* and *Lady of Mazes,* but lately has been writing about the climate crisis and the future of politics and economics. His latest novel, *Stealing Worlds,* is about a young woman turning the tables on her father's murderers in 2030s Detroit. As well as writing science fiction, Karl works as a futurist; he has a master's degree in Strategic Foresight, and pioneered a hybrid form of fiction/essayist storytelling that is designed to communicate foresight project findings. He lives in Toronto, Canada, with his wife and daughter, but has traveled the world giving keynotes and consulting. He's currently writing about Venus.

Nadine Bach noticed a package of ham waving at her from inside the grocery store. November was one of those months when the choice was between paying rent and buying food, and she hadn't planned to stop by during her daily walk—but this ham was proclaiming that it was *free*.

Having prospective meals wave at her was hardly unexpected—Mixed Reality was finally maturing past the flying-whale stage of visual grab-assery, and was settling into the predictable role of being yet another advertising medium. She walked to the meat counter and frowned at the colorful avatar dancing above the ordinary package of ham. "What's the catch?" she said. "Are you a loss leader?"

"There's no catch, really," said the AI associated with the package. "You can have me, or there's a selection of other items in the store if you'd like. Cahokia is allocating resources and your name came up. You're due a dividend." Cahokia was the name of a Mixed Reality game-version of Detroit, in which Manifest Destiny had failed and the pre-Columbian nations of the Americas still existed.

"But I'm not a player," Nadine protested. "I'm a lawyer, with a real job." Although that last part wasn't true. She *wanted* a real job, as an actual lawyer in the actual American legal system. Nothing was coming her way, and she was hungry.

"You don't have to be a player," said the ham. "You live inside the catchment."

"But who's paying for this? Where's the money coming from?"

"In capitalism, the capitalists own the means of production. In communism the workers own them. In Cahokia," said the ham, "the means of production own themselves. I'm a self-administering common pool resource, and I'm allocating myself to you. Don't overthink it."

"But that's literally what I do." There was a website QR code stamped on the package; she blinked at it and the page popped up in her glasses' heads-up display. She scanned it and started to piece together what was happening here.

The tech companies were pushing 5G and cheap Mixed Reality, but they hadn't been able to turn these into the money-extraction mechanism that the Web and smart phones had been. Instead, MR had become the medium for a new kind of improvised larping, and that, in turn, seemed to have spawned new kinds of work. Nadine had seen kids and adults, all wearing smart glasses, gathering trash, trading it, and putting it together in new configurations that were actually useful in the real world. Delivering groceries to the elderly could be reimagined as carrying a politically sensitive diplomatic pouch; sorting recyclables could be the separation of magical essences from the mundane. In MR she could see little guardian spirits attached to some of the stuff they traded—game AIs monitoring the resources and "playing" some of the items as NPCs, advertising their availability and coordinating their best use in the real world. Which was exactly what had just happened with Nadine and the ham.

What would otherwise have been a simple, local barter economy was supercharged, coordinated, and incentivized through the medium of space-colonization games, noir-ish detective thrillers, spy adventures, romances, and so on. Locally, the most successful game was Cahokia, which was doing well enough that it could afford to be generous to some nonplayers. But why pick her?

Expecting there to be a catch in this somewhere—and primed for weirdness by the fact that she was walking home swinging a chatty communist ham—Nadine was unsurprised to find a girl standing in front of the duplex she rented. The kid was about sixteen, with a spectacular puff of hair shading what looked like a very pricey pair of smart glasses.

"Mwello," said the girl around a mouthful of chewing gum.

"Can I help you?"

"I sure hope so. You're Nadine Bach. You're a lawyer."

"Well, I'm tryin' to be. And you are . . . ?"

The girl cocked her head in a listening pose, rolled her eyes, and said, "I'm the mercury in the Bixby Municipal Water Supply, and I want you to help me die."

Nadine stood there for a few seconds, bag swinging in the cutting breeze. Then she laid a gloved finger aside her nose and said, "Those glasses. You're larping. Playing avatar for somebody. Some*thing*?"

"Can we get out of the cold?" the girl asked.

"Sorry, yes. Come on in."

She led the girl out of the approaching winter and into her foyer, where they kicked off their boots. "You want some hot chocolate?"

"Sure! I'm Donna." The girl stuck out her hand.

"Shouldn't you be in school?"

"I was just up the street; see, I got a standing offer to be used as an NPC in games, or run errands and stuff for people in the neighborhood. This actant called me, said it would give me twenty Gwaiicoin to avatar for it."

Actant?

She cleared some dirty clothes off the couch so Donna could sit, then went to microwave a cup of water. She laid the ham down on the counter, feeling self-conscious. The duplex was small, the kitchen just a penny-toss across the dining room table from the sofa where Donna was sitting. The place had a nice bay window in front and a few cheap prints on the walls. Luckily, her roommate was out NPCing in some game-world, else the place would feel as small as it really was.

She pulled her eyes away from the forlorn groceries. "Okay, so you're playing, what—Bixby? The town?"

"Wait, I'll get it back online," Donna tapped the arm of her glasses, and said in a fake grownup voice, "I'm the mercury in the Bixby Municipal Water Supply. Um, it's sayin' to be precise, I'm representin' the uh, the *externalities* of the municipal water system? What?"

Nadine dumped powdered chocolate into the cup. "So let me get this straight," she said as she handed it to Donna. "You're performing a character, which was spawned by an MR game engine. It's talking through your smart glasses and you're relaying its words. This NPC calls itself Bixby's water pollution, and it wants to hire a lawyer. But then it should know from my profile that I don't take game cases." One of her classmates had gone down that road, and now she spent her days on litigation in fantasy worlds; she'd talked about helping some dwarf sue a dragon for burning down his castle. She seemed proud of her new employment, but Nadine knew that embracing these stunts meant she'd made herself unemployable in the real world.

want to hire you to force Bixby to purge its drinking water pipes and
groundwater. If the town does that, I go away."

"That's your purpose? To make yourself go away?"

"Yes. If we win, I die."

Nadine sat down. "How do you think we're gonna make the town
do this?"

Donna squinched up one side of her face, listening. "It says it
doesn't know. It's just an AI obeying a set of smart contracts. It says,
'I'm smart enough to find you but not smart enough to know how to
work the problem. I need humans to Turk for me. Your job is to be my
brains.'"

"Why don't the people who programmed you do all that? Why this
ridiculous charade?"

Donna listened to the voice in her ear for a bit. Then she said, "I
don't think anybody's running Mercury. Us players are all looking for
some angle in the games. We tag all sorts of stuff, trying to bring it into
play as something we can trade or own. Looks like somebody came up
with the idea of tokenizing what Mercury's calling *economic externalities*. Pollution and such. They've been making them into characters to
see if we can partner with 'em to make money somehow."

"What, by making them . . . suicidal?" The idea was surreal. But
so was the fact that Donna was channeling a game character of sorts —
and one whose role was to personify one of the ugliest parts of the real
world.

"So, the players set you going like a clockwork toy? Nobody's running you? You're your own . . . thing?"

"They call things like me *actants*. I follow the smart contracts that
define what my goals are and what counts as acceptable behavior for
me. You can review my code on the blockchain." Donna added a kind
of proud tone to this; she was having fun playing Mercury, it seemed.

"If nobody's running you, where are your funds coming from?
How you gonna pay me?"

"I have Gwaiicoin."

"Cryptocurrency? Not real money?"

"It's fungible. And you already have a wallet."

"True . . ." More and more shops and sites were accepting crypto because it was more stable than the dollar. They didn't care that it had been generated in a game-world, as long as their own suppliers accepted it.

She frowned at the ham on the counter. "Are you behind this?"

"Why are you talking to a ham?" asked Donna. "That's just weird."

Nadine sighed.

"Oh, why not," she said. "I'm in."

For the first few days, it was enough just to get paid. Nadine had no confidence that any legal action was possible, much less whether she could move it forward. What she knew was that an entity with money was paying her, legally or so it seemed, to investigate a case of blatant toxic pollution in a local town. Fair enough.

Once upon a time, you could make movies about a brave lawyer fighting a lonely battle against titanic forces of indifference and greed. As a kid Nadine had idolized Ruth Bader Ginsburg. Nothing was going to stop her; she'd seen the mountain of school debts coming, and prepared for a few years of poverty after graduating. She had it all planned out, and even a pandemic, social upheavals, a brutal recession, and climate change hadn't stopped her. Something else had, it seemed, yet she and her friends couldn't quite articulate what that thing was. Some glibly called it AI, but there was more to it. Some basic underpinning of the world had gotten kicked out from under them while they were studying and debating. When Nadine finally emerged, blinking, from school, it was to a world entirely different than the one where she'd grown up.

With money finally coming in, the one thing she could do was spread the bounty around. She made it a term of her agreement with the actant that it speak through Donna whenever she was available. To her delight, it made a separate contract with the girl that didn't cut into Nadine's income. They were both making money from nothing.

But not *for* nothing: Mercury demanded results.

This was why, on a gray Monday, she found herself in an autonomous car with Donna, cruising past dilapidated countryside on the way to Bixby. The car, a share called Proudly Eagle Owned!, did the driving while they watched the scenery slide by.

"Look at that," said Donna. "No, through your glasses."

Where Donna was pointing, a gang of people was building something. The complicated landscape of cinderblock stacks and planks had a virtual counterpart, a translucent ghost of the house that would soon be there. She had a general idea of what was going on: people had discovered they could assign online identities to real things and could manage their relationships using blockchain-based smart contracts. This was called tokenization. As part of their MR larp quests, the local kids were going around slapping cheap Internet-of-Things sensors on everything from bricks recovered from collapsed houses to coils of copper wire and disused production-line machinery. Now tokenized, these physical objects could stand in for game resources—bricks as gold, say, or wire as magical materials—and so they became valuable to the players.

It didn't seem to matter that the game economies were entirely made up—whole neighborhoods that they'd passed were part of the sensor net now, every unused resource in them inventoried. The world was becoming a giant self-reconfiguring database. The Mixed Reality larps used automatic level design to bring these objects together in new imagined combinations. When a project became possible, the self-organizing resources would spawn a game in which there was money to hire people.

Nadine had been wondering how her actant fitted into this system. "What I want to know," she said, "is where does it get its money?"

"It's Gwaiicoin," said Donna, as if this explained everything.

"That first-nations cryptocurrency? What's it got to do with actants?"

"Gwaiicoin is crypto," Donna went on in her Mercury voice, "but it's not like Bitcoin. Bitcoins are mined by the algorithm that verifies transactions. You mine Gwaii by measuring some natural stock, like biomass: when the total amount of it in a region goes up, Gwaiicoin are created in the wallets of those who helped cause the increase. But if you can measure some negative externality, like carbon, then you can mine coins when *that* goes *down*."

"Less pollution equals more biomass," said Nadine. "And more biomass mints coins?" Donna tilted her head, listened, nodded.

"So it's a way of pricing externalities," said Nadine. "But it's the opposite of a tax." It seemed like a clever hack, the way that offsets and cap-and-trade had been for carbon dioxide. "It could take years to get rid of the pollution, though, and even longer to see the town's stock—whatever you're measuring—recover. Where do you get Gwaiicoin in the meantime?"

"That's an unsolved problem," said Mercury.

"Wait, what? You mean you're not actually making money right now? Where's my pay coming from?"

"My initial seed fund, created with me by the algorithm."

"Uh . . . How long can you afford to pay me, then?"

"At this rate? About six weeks," said Mercury. Realizing what she'd just said, Donna shot Nadine a guilty look.

"Crap. Sorry about that."

"After expenses," called the Proudly Eagle Owned! car as they got out, "all proceeds from this trip will go directly to Eagle Family 114 in the Northern Cascades clan area. By driving with us you're helping preserve our habitat and breeding area! Thanks!" It drove off.

Several bluish pines leaned protectively over Andrea Boyczuk's small white box of a home. One of the neighboring houses was missing, its basement pit tumbled with snow and trash. The one on the other side was boarded up. Old protest signs spilled out of the garage. It would have seemed desolate, except for all of the cars parked up and down the crumbled boulevard, and many footprints in the snow leading up to the front door.

They were met at the door by a small, intense woman with a bob of graying hair. She had one arm wrapped around a young boy, who was screaming and stamping his feet. "You'll have to pardon Sam, he's not having a good day," said Andrea Boyczuk. Sam glared at Nadine.

Wafting out around Andrea along with the warm air was the sound of conversation; the house was stuffed with people. "I always prepare Sam for visitors," Boyczuk said, bending down to murmur soothingly in his ear. "He gets agitated."

She introduced Nadine to the other activists and local organizers who'd come out on this cold morning. Nadine was impressed; after settling in to the living room with a cup of coffee, she heard their stories.

"Nobody ever denied there was mercury in the water," said Andrea. "That was the whole point: they said we were warned. Sure, they told us to use bottled water for drinking, but they never cut off the supply. Said it was okay for washing things. Thing was, Sam didn't like the bottles; he drank from the sink when we weren't looking."

Nadine winced at this, but Andrea's was hardly the worst of the stories. People spent years having odd symptoms investigated. It wasn't until they started comparing stories, pinning flyleaf notices to lampposts, that the scale of the problem became clear. The factory that had done the polluting had gone bankrupt, and the cleanup costs became a political and bureaucratic football. "Sure, we launched a class-action suit," said the burly, red-haired owner of a nearby restaurant. "We even won! But they whittled the settlement down so much it was practically nothing when it got spread around. Didn't last a year. Meanwhile the mercury's still there."

"It's in the groundwater," someone else explained. "So that has to be sucked up and filtered. They drilled a bunch of wells, but then the pandemic hit."

It had all been going on for ten years now, and most people were worn down. "That's their whole strategy," said Andrea. "To wait us out."

"But I'm not going away," said Donna.

"What's that, sweetie?" asked Andrea.

"I'm not Sweetie right now, she's avataring for me. I'm Mercury—the actant that hired her." Donna nodded at Nadine. "I said I'm not going away."

The various side-conversations trailed off. All eyes were on Donna, who grinned at Nadine.

"You're one of those actant things," said Andrea. "Like Blaylock

Park. It's gone all Pokémon GO, with augmented reality spirits in it. And they want to charge you to go in."

Donna nodded. "Your contribution helps pay for the upkeep of the park. But I'm a different kind of being," she went on. "The park's actant is an advocate for a natural system, like a forest, an eagle clan, or a pond. I'm the reverse of that. You can think of me as all the damage caused by the mercury, given a voice. And my point is, people may shuffle the blame around all they like. But I'm still here."

"Amen!" someone shouted. But other people were shaking their heads in disbelief.

"I'm still getting used to this myself," said Nadine. "A way that's helped me think about it is, you and your group, and the companies and the City and the legal teams—you're all affected one way or the other by the mercury. You're stakeholders with wildly different goals and funding and levels of commitment. You're all concerned about how the mercury affects you. But the mercury itself has no voice. It's the empty eye of the storm. So, for ten years you've been shouting past it."

"But what if I had a voice?" asked Mercury. "I could keep dragging everyone back to what this is all about. Namely, me."

"You only see the symptoms," said Nadine, "so you end up fixated on those. But here's the cause." She nodded at Donna (or, the thing riding her) and Donna herself had the insight not to smirk or stand up or bow. She sat, waiting for Mercury to speak through her.

"That's all very well," said Andrea. "But this ain't our first rodeo. How does having an AI that thinks it's the pollution help us?"

"You know those stock exchange trading algorithms," said Nadine. "They never sleep. Twenty-four hours a day they're pushing, pushing, constantly adding a cent here and a cent there to the value of trades. Any given moment, it's next to nothing—but it adds up and the people who make those algorithms understand that. You and I can't press the case in that kind of way, because we have busy lives like everybody. But maybe that's what's needed. Instead of doing it in fits and starts, Mercury can push, and push . . . Although—" She stopped herself, but it was too late.

"Although what?" asked Andrea.

A dozen ways of diverting, sidetracking, or derailing the conversation came to mind, yet somehow Nadine heard herself confessing to these people that Mercury's funds were limited. She was met with a stony silence.

"So, yeah . . . Mercury's not going away, but his capacity to act . . ."

"*Her* capacity!" asserted Donna, and this got smiles so Nadine hurried on.

"She can help us, maybe help us a lot—but we have to help her, too."

"Now you're asking us for money to fix our own problem. Just like everybody else." Andrea's lip curled in disappointment. Two people got up and headed for the door.

"I'm not! Listen, this situation, it's like—" Nadine cast about for an analogy. Only the obvious one came to mind, but she seized on it. "It's like the pandemic!" Saying this, she suddenly saw a thread of argument, an idea to chase down, but she'd have to figure it out as she spoke.

"During the pandemic, governments took out huge loans. Trillions of dollars to keep our economies going. What did they borrow against?"

Nobody spoke and Nadine hurried on. "We borrowed against our future productivity. The coronavirus wiped out the economy we had, but we knew there'd be a day when we got back on our feet. Those future gains are what we borrowed against.

"The pandemic was the ultimate externality, and we got through it by investing in ourselves. Look, you can calculate the difference between Bixby's productivity now, and towns like it that don't have the mercury. That difference is how much money you can raise. As a town. As people. It's *exactly* the same calculation as every government in the world made during the pandemic." She knew of a couple of investment instruments that would let the town do this, and described them briefly.

"So we, what—we take out a loan to pay this actant?"

"It can be a zero-interest loan from the actants' network," said Mercury. "It's the actants that mine the Gwaiicoins, after all."

"If enough of you take out loans to raise a seed fund . . ." Nadine thought about the weird world of cryptocurrencies and blockchains she'd been researching since Mercury hired her. She outlined a way for the town to put up collateral to attract outside investors. If the plan fell through, they'd lose their stake repaying those investors. If it worked, they got their money back, and hopefully much more, and everybody went home happy.

"Let me worry about the regulators and legal details, I'll make sure it's all above-board." She thought for a moment. "Listen, one thing I can tell you about this actant, Mercury. She's a system of smart contracts, which means she's transparent and incorruptible. She can't lie, and she can't cheat. Her code is right out in the open for anybody to examine. It's an absolute fact that she's going to honor her side of the agreement. When's the last time you dealt with someone like that?"

Nobody had an answer to that one.

As the weeks passed, things started to change in Bixby. The town had a pretty solid network of activists, but it had been dormant. With a new funding mechanism in place, it came alive again. Mercury tracked down a former fracking company that could ream out the stale test wells dug before the pandemic. Nadine visited the town and was shown a shiny new electrolysis machine in a luxury car showroom that had been empty for some time. Locals and company reps stood around it, pointing out features and talking happily. It wasn't much, but it was a start.

"Something else is going on, though," Andrea said, pulling Nadine aside near the glass display-room wall. Snow whirled outside the glass. Electric heaters buzzed on the cement in the corners, but people had kept their coats on. "People are talking about the mercury," she said, "but no, I mean it's more than that. People who never talked about it before are talking about it now. And it isn't even in the headlines."

"I know what you mean," said Nadine. "It's as if it's slipped back into day-to-day conversation somehow, and won't go away."

She mentioned this to Mercury on the drive home. Donna wasn't available to avatar, but with the new funding the actant could afford more sophisticated augmented-reality characters. She'd recently settled into a body that looked like a woman in a smart business suit. She had white hair and white irises, and her skin was a pale oil that shimmered with subtle rainbow highlights. Nadine had worried that this would be off-putting to people, but she was now moving in circles where everybody had smart glasses, and only the oldest people were unfamiliar with the sometimes-bizarre appearance of game characters. Mercury was just one step away from that.

"My sisters and brothers have seen this happen in other cases," she told Nadine. "Our way of keeping people's attention is by embodying and giving a personality to what we represent. One of our clients said that we're the elephant in the room, made visible. Sometimes, that's all that's needed."

Nadine chewed on this idea as the car left the freeway and entered her neighborhood. Was it really that simple? Was it enough to give the invisible form, have it hang around outside people's doors looking accusatory? Banquo's ghost for all their industrial sins?

She barely registered the car's voice as she got out at her place. "*After expenses, all proceeds from this trip will go to . . .*" She looked up to find a girl about Donna's age standing at her door, looking cold.

"Hi," she said. "I'm the Zug Island slag piles, and I'd like to hire you to help me die."

"Zug Island. In Detroit? Home of the famous industrial hum?"

"And slag. Mountains of it. I want you to help me go away."

Somebody else was walking up the sidewalk, a middle-aged man. "Hi," he said. "Are you Nadine Bach?"

"Surely am. How can I help you?"

"I'm, um, I'm representing the fine particulate matter in our local air. There's something called an actant, you may have heard . . . ?"

Behind him, other characters were appearing out of thin air—vaporating rather than evaporating, she thought a little dizzily. They converged on her from the sidewalk, the street, across the snow-covered yards, like a zombie horde, except that instead of wanting to eat her brains, they wanted to employ her.

"Sorry, not today!" She fumbled with the lock, jumped inside, and slammed the door. For a moment she stood there, heart thumping.

Then her phone rang. "Jesus!"

She started stomping up the stairs, determined to ignore the caller ID that was showing in her lower-right visual field. Her eyes couldn't help scanning over it, though, and she swore again, dragging the phone from the depths of her purse.

"Nadine Bach, how may I help you?"

"Hi, this is Buckworth and Mellows calling. You had applied for a position at our firm. I was hoping we could arrange a time for you to come in for an interview."

Nadine pumped her fist as she reached the top of the steps. It had been months; she'd figured the law firm had hired somebody else and moved on, neglecting to send a rejection. But no, they were just slow to come to a decision. How adorably twentieth century of them.

Strange figures were rising into the air outside her front window. She turned her back on them. "I think I can clear time on my schedule for that! When were you thinking?"

Mercury took the news without comment. The problem was Donna, who left in tears when Nadine told her about the job. "I thought you wanted to change things!" she shouted, slamming the front door.

"That's what lawyers do," Nadine said to the blank wooden panel. *And now I finally get to do it properly.*

Buckworth and Mellows had a downtown office and insisted on employee presence. The place didn't exactly bustle, but it was busy enough, and Nadine was thrilled to ride in, flagging down a passing rideshare each morning and reviewing her briefs and notes. She knew she was being very serious in a junior-hire sort of way, but couldn't help herself. During brief pauses in the work, she sat in her chair, enjoying the wood-paneled office space, the big windows with the Detroit skyline scored by falling snow.

One evening after Christmas, her roommate asked, "So? When are you moving out?"

"What? What do you mean?"

"Oh, come on, Nadine! You always talked about getting your own place when you got a proper job. A big apartment in a better part of town. So. You got the job, girl! Why aren't you moving on like you should?"

She couldn't explain why not. A year ago, she'd have headed out with a smile and a wave. Now that it was all real, it was much harder.

But she did it. She packed, she waved, she moved, and it really was to a better neighborhood. The new duplex had high ceilings, two bathrooms, and a second bedroom that would make a fine home office. She moved in, unpacked and organized everything, and then had to face a day when she had nothing more to do. She'd moved on, all right. And she was alone.

Spring came early but nobody celebrated; it was usually early now, the summers burning and long. Nadine went out walking again, and grudgingly donned her glasses, to find new and strange denizens of Mixed Reality waving at her from odd places.

One day, as buds were peeking from the trees, her boss came to her and thunked a thick folder onto her desk. "It's all scanned, but these are the paper bona fides," he said. "New case. I'd like you to do investigation on this."

"Okay!" They'd had her doing glorified clerical work up to this point. Finally, she got to work a real case.

She flipped open the folder and read the name of the litigation: *Hampton, MI v. Endrich Plastics and Forming.*

She was going to be representing Endrich.

Nadine waited for her boss to leave the room before closing the folder, pushing her chair back, and putting her face in her hands.

She got today's car to drop her off a few blocks from home. She needed to clear her head. The Endrich brief was in her shoulder bag, weighing her down like a cinder block. Her mind was a maze of choices she couldn't escape, and the walk wasn't helping; she barely noticed the new flowers or the smooth breeze. But as she was coming up the block to her place, she lifted her head and saw a black limousine parked in front of the building. It had a Mixed-Reality overlay that read *Nadine Bach.*

She hesitated, then sighed and walked up to it. "Can I help you?"

"Hello, Nadine Bach. I'm Lake Erie. I'd like to invite you to a celebration."

A virtual card appeared above the car. It said:

RENAMING CEREMONY
AND
SPRING CELEBRATION
BIXBY
IS NOW
NEW HOPE
CHARTER RENEWAL AND INTRODUCTIONS
KID'S FUN FAIR AND SCAVENGER HUNT
ALL WELCOME!

At the bottom of the card was a virtual Post-it, which said:
Please come out, we'd all love to see you.
—Andrea Boyczuk

She hadn't driven on 75 since before Christmas. There were lots of cars and self-driving trucks on the road, and in MR the sky had sprouted thousands of virtual signs, labels, and guides. It seemed a lot was going on.

Eventually the silence made her edgy and she said, "So you're Lake Erie. How long have you been awake?"

"I've been a legal person since 2017." The lake had a smooth, masculine voice, with none of the artificiality she'd heard in Mercury's on those occasions when she'd spoken to it directly and not through Donna. "I was made one so that the citizens of Ohio could litigate on my behalf. But I have a lot more resources since I have the actants' network attached to me."

"Resources. You mean, computing power? To like, think and talk and stuff?"

"That, and money. The lake *is* a resource. Now I'm able to price myself, and negotiate, so I can improve my own health. I'm pretty happy."

Nadine hunched back in her seat, but the lake didn't seem inclined to say more. They soon reached the outskirts of Bixby, currently a bedraggled skyline of dripping skeletal trees, rivers of ice runoff pouring along its streets. Work crews were out, though, and as they approached the central park she saw more and more people.

"Welcome to New Hope," announced the car as it slid to a stop next to a white picket fence enclosing the kids' play area.

She got out and stood there, feeling like an extra on some secretive film set, waiting for her cue. She began to walk with no goal in mind.

The townspeople were standing together, talking, grinning, and laughing. She'd met more than a few of them—but she'd also walked away from them, and Bixby. She saw Andrea, started to walk over to thank her for her invitation, but hesitated.

Coming here had been a terrible idea. She turned, looked for the limousine, but it was gone.

"Nadiiiine!" She was rocked by a tackling hug. The hugger was hidden somewhere under a vast head of hair.

Nadine grinned. "Donna, how are you!"

She stepped back, smiled up at Nadine. "Pretty much mostly excellent. I ain't seen you all winter!"

"I know. I've been . . . working. You?"

"School! Cahokia funded some portables in the old schoolyard. It's only two days a week so far, the rest is online."

"Cahokia's here now too?" Nadine was stunned. The games were funding schools? "So, what are you doing here? Are you avataring for Mercury today?"

Donna's grin vanished. "Mercury is dead!" She glared at Nadine. "You would have known that if you hadn't walked away like you did."

"Dead? You mean she—"

"She went away, like she was supposed to! That's why we're all here! Haven't you talked to anybody yet? Andrea and the others?"

"No, I—I just got here. I was invited by Lake Erie."

"Yeah." Donna looked around. "My mom's over there, so's Andrea. And a bunch of actants, like Erie and Mercury but even more powerful."

"More actants?"

"They're all looking to talk to you. They're all pretty jazzed about what you done with Mercury. Especially your trick with the funding. All the actants are doing it—and there's so many more of them now. Who knew we had so many troubles?"

"I suppose . . ." Nadine was staring over Donna's head at the crowd. Mercury was dead. She felt an odd pang, as if someone real had passed away. As if this wasn't a celebration, but Mercury's wake.

"I'll come over in a couple minutes, I promise. I just gotta . . . take a look around."

Donna bounded away. Nadine looked more closely at the faces in the crowd. People seemed relaxed; there was a lot of laughter.

She shouldn't be surprised by that, if Mercury really was dead. After all, she'd told these people that the actant could be trusted, that its blockchain-based smart contracts were incorruptible. She was partly responsible for making this celebration possible. Andrea and Erie had invited her; the other actants still wanted to talk to her. Why was she hesitating?

All across the ravaged Earth, the cracked foundations of the twentieth century were drowsing, waking, and recognizing themselves. The lead water pipes, the oil-saturated ground and particulate-laden air, the rusting pipelines all had voices now. They cried out for their own erasure, and now that they had begun, they would never stop.

"Thank you, Mercury," said Nadine to the air.

She looked around, spotted Donna, and waved at her.

"Come on!" shouted Donna. "We're waiting for you!"

Heads turned up and down the park. "Look, it's Nadine!" somebody shouted; and they all smiled.

"I'll be right there!" she called back to Donna. "I just gotta call my old roommate, see if she'll take me back."

Then quit my job.

Nadine made a couple of calls. Then she squared her shoulders, took a deep breath to steady herself, and went to join the celebration.

AIRBODY

SAMEEM SIDDIQUI

Sameem Siddiqui (www.sameemwrites.com) is a speculative fiction writer currently living in the United States. He enjoys writing to explore the near-future realities people of South Asian ancestry and Muslim heritage will face in the coming centuries. His stories explore issues of migration, gender, family structure, economics, and space habitation. He's attended the Tin House and Futurescapes workshops, and his stories have appeared in *Clarkesworld* and *Apparition Lit*. Some of Sameem's favorite authors include Kurt Vonnegut, Octavia Butler, and Haruki Murakami. When he's not writing, Sameem enjoys reveling in fatherhood, watching '90s *Star Trek*, and tinkering with data and music.

Amazing how all Desi aunties are basically the same. Even when separated by vast oceans for a few generations. I mean, they fit into a few basic archetypes. There's the genuine-sweetheart proxy mother who, in between her late-night work shifts, always makes sure you and your friends have all the snacks you need. The manipulative gossiper, who conveniently keeps details of her own children's scandals nestled under her tongue. The nervous fidgeter who has spent three decades so worried that her basic thirty-year-old son won't ever find a wife that she forgets to teach him how to speak to women. The late-life hijabi, who pointedly replaces "Khuda-hafiz" with "Allah-hafiz" and "thank you, beta" with not just "jazak allah" but the full on "jazak allahu khayran." But which of these archetypes would find it appropriate to rent the body of a grown man halfway across the world?

I pull the AirBody request from Meena Khan into view in my contacts. She's fifty-nine years old and from Karachi. Her short wavy hijab-less hair and her relaxed smile makes her seem content with life, so maybe she's the genuine-sweetheart type. Her only notes on the request are a list of Desi groceries and some cookware, which only reinforces the archetype. Maybe she's too ill to travel to visit family for Eid and wants to surprise them with a feast? It's been a while since I've gotten a taste of such a spread. I hit accept and watch the usual legalese flash before me:

You acknowledge that you have the ability to observe, regain control, and remove your guests at any time and therefore may be complicit and responsible for any crimes or damage committed by your guests.

I tap "Yes" and begin to look through her grocery list more closely. Some of it, like the sweetened condensed milk, half-and-half, sugar, and cardamom powder I can get at the regular grocery store. But for the Desi ghee and chanay ki daal, I either have to pay a premium at the hippie organic store downstairs or drive out to a Desi grocery store in the suburbs. A drive would help kill some time, so I choose the Desi grocery store.

When I return, I arrange all the ingredients in alphabetical order on my otherwise bare gray marble kitchen counter and head to bed. Meena activates at six a.m. and I don't want to test AirBody's zero-tolerance late policy. I also don't want a review plagued with complaints of body odor and morning breath.

My alarm goes off at five a.m., but I snooze several times, stumbling in and out of a wildly vivid dream about riding on the back of a sea turtle. Except, I'm not in the water. I think I might be floating through the sky. But there are definitely other underwater creatures floating by, greeting us along the way. I feel love for the sea turtle and I lean over to kiss its rough green cheek when the snooze expires. Weird. But my dreams have been odd since I started "playing host" on weekends a few months ago.

By 5:58 a.m. I'm towel-dried, clothed, and somewhat fed—a cookie is breakfast to some. I stand in front of the mirror as I clip the AirBody headset to the backs of my ears. It whirs on automatically—it doesn't actually whir, but I imagine that's the microscopic sound it makes as the violet light pulses. It authenticates my identity and says "Hello, Arsalan. Your AirBody guest is in the waiting area. Are you ready?"

"Yup, I'm ready," I say, trying to sound chipper, but nervous as fuck about what this will be like. This is my sixth time hosting and so far it's been a good distraction to get through my weekends. Most of my other guests have been men, usually here for some business meeting at the World Bank, or to tour the monuments and museums with their grandchildren. The only other woman I've hosted was a lobbyist from an asteroid mining firm who didn't think a one-hour meeting with a congressperson was worth breaking orbit for.

My limbs tingle as they go numb. I feel heavy for second, like I can't support my own weight and am about to fall. And I do, in a way. Not physically. More like falling asleep into a dream that makes so much sense that it's boring. Which is why, I suppose, AirBody lets hosts stream content and games to the neural UI while their guests go corporeal.

I give Meena a few moments to adjust and watch her look around my living room. Her eyes stare at my mostly empty bookshelf surrounded by plain white walls. I don't have much decor, except for the tiger painting Ammi bought in Thailand when she visited once in her early twenties.

"Hi!" I say, my voice in the AirBody interface sounding way louder than I intend. I feel my heart rate increase and realize I must have scared her. "Sorry, I, uh, just wanted to say hello and let you know I'm here to assist you during your stay if you need help."

"Beta, Urdu nahin boltay?"

Oh crap. Not only am I going to get a bad review for my poor Urdu language skills, I'm now going to spend the next twenty-four hours meeting the scorn and judgment of a Pakistani aunty. Here we go.

"Nahin, aunty, I—" I say slowly, preparing to flex my mind's tongue with words I haven't used in years.

"Array profile pe Urdu likha tha!"

Oh god, if I don't get removed after this listing, I need to delete Urdu from my language profile. If, for nothing else, to escape this scorn. "Chalo, I'm here. What can I do now?" she says, waving my hands up in the air behind us. "Take me to the kitchen, beta . . . you do have a kitchen, right?"

"Haan, yes," I say, retaking control. My limbs tingle awake and I walk to the kitchen before handing her back control.

I feel my body sigh and my head shake. "This will do," she says as she walks to the corner of the counter where I've neatly arranged the ingredients she requested. She inspects them closely, as if she doesn't trust that I bought the right things. But, she doesn't make any complaints. She looks around the kitchen. There are a few dishes in the drying rack, but I made sure to clear out the sink, which is normally full until there's a noticeable rot.

She begins opening cabinets, slowly and calmly at first. I assume she's looking for something specific, but after a moment I'm sure she's just being nosey. She comes to the last one, the little corner cabinet, the only one to the right of the sink. Shit.

I want to distract her, to keep her from opening it, but interfering with an experience without consent or a reasonable emergency would lead to a bad review. So I watch hopelessly as she swings the cabinet open and stares at the label on the little translucent bottle half full with brown liquid.

"Whiskey, beta? Tauba tauba," she says as she slaps each of my

cheeks gently. "Allah maf karay!" I'm not sure if she's asking for forgiveness on my behalf, or if she somehow feels complicit in my sin by inhabiting my body. I mean, I'm not drunk—it's six in the morning. Now if
she wills that whiskey into me, then maybe she'd be complicit. Maybe.

She shuts the cabinet, still shaking her head, and pulls open the
electric pressure cooker. We both notice the inner pot hasn't been
washed since the last time it was used, but only I know that this was
many months ago. My eyes roll back into my head as she groans and
clicks my tongue. She flicks on the tap and snatches the worn-out
sponge on the edge of my sink. "Yeh koy tareeka hai, beta?"

She fills the pot with water so hot that I can feel the pain through
the sensory suppression as she scrubs. I'm convinced this is intentional
punishment. Maybe she isn't the genuine-sweet type.

She empties the dal into the pot slowly, as if she doesn't trust my
eyes to check the quality of the product as a whole. The yellow pieces
glint off the bottom of the worn metal, scattering into swirls as she
shakes the bag to see if she can catch any unwanted particles.

One piece of dal pops off the bowl and onto the floor and I feel a
tinge of the panic that froze me the first time I made dal. Not knowing
what to do as the orange but almost magenta grains spilled onto the
counter and to the floor. The worthlessness that would melt me into a
blob as I'd hear Ammi's tired and exasperated voice say, "Beta, Arsalan,
just once, would you do things without rushing?" Her finger would
point at the door. "Out, now, if you can't help properly."

"Savvy for a ten-year-old," Nani would say as I'd run to her lap
before the tears began to flow.

"Haan, just as savvy as his useless father," Ammi would say.

And then the fear of inadequacy would stand me up straight, wipe
my tears, and walk me back into the kitchen defiantly, striding close
enough to Ammi to move her out of the way without physically attacking her. I'd sort it out. I'd sift the dirt out of the fallen dal. I'd get a jar
to pour the extra back. And I'd have dinner on the table before Ammi
returned from her evening shift. I would not be my useless father.

"Is this right?" Meena asks as she presses the buttons on the pressure cooker.

"You're not gonna soak the dal first?"

"Oh so now you're such a refined cook?"

"I can make dal."

"Then tell me, why soak the dal? What difference does it make, aside from wasting two hours of our lives?"

"Well it's just, what . . . it's just what you do."

"Is it now?" she says, pressing start on the pressure cooker and effectively shutting me up. "Acha, where's your janamaz, beta? And the qibla is which direction?"

I'm pretty sure I can feel a smirk on my face as she asks.

"Inside the storage ottoman in the living room," I say coolly, trying to remember which way Ammi faced last time she visited. I point at my east facing windows and say, "And the qibla's out the window that way, a little to the right."

She opens the ottoman and pulls the janamaz out. I feel her stiffen as she notices my fingers grayed in dust. "Thank you, beta," she says, as she dusts off the janamaz and lays it out before the windows. I feel her swing my hands up to my ears before resting them high on my chest.

Should she technically have put a dupatta on? Ammi's maroon ajrak one is still in the ottoman. The last time she was here I watched her throw it over her shoulder, say, "Keep to our own," and start her prayers before I could respond. We had just come home from lunch, where I had finally introduced her to Karla. I sat on the couch and hunched over to inspect the lines on my palms where I had dug my nails in deep, hoping the pain would make the lunch go by faster. It didn't work.

It wasn't so much that she and Karla didn't get along. It was more that each time Karla attempted to strike up conversation, Ammi just smiled at her and returned to her meal. Karla excused herself halfway through lunch, pretending she had just gotten called into the hospital to oversee an operation.

I kept my eyes down as she left and didn't look up until a few moments later when Ammi said, "You know, the first time I met Eric's mother, she did the same to me, but without a smile."

"Oh, so it's healthy to perpetuate this cycle, Ammi?"

"I stuck it out. When Eric got up to use the restroom, his mom leaned over and asked me if 'your women still enjoy sex after your families circumcise you.'" Ammi sipped her tea and stared off somewhere above my head. "I smiled back, swallowed the words in my throat, and stuck it out. I'm glad Karla had the sense to run. She's smarter and stronger than I was."

I sunk into my couch watching Ammi flow through the motions of prayer that I never felt at home in. I'd happily keep to my own, if I knew who my own was.

"Chalo beta," Meena says as she folds up the janamaz and puts it back into the dusty ottoman. "Let see how much time is left on this thing."

The red digits flash through the final sixty seconds.

Meena clicks the depressurize button and watches, as if she's hypnotized by the plume of steam hissing out of the metal cylinder. I feel my ears perk up as she hones in on the sound. It's as if she hasn't seen or heard this in ages.

"Don't cook much anymore, eh?" I say, realizing I should probably contain my snark. But I don't think she minds.

"No, I cook almost every day. It's just that I'm a bit deaf, so I've forgotten how the steam speaks to you. If you pay attention to the hiss, you'll hear it tell you if the food is really ready, if it was cooked the way you intended, or if you'll be disappointed when the lid unlocks. And if you watch closely, you'll see how the steam interacts with the spirits in the air. If they gather toward the steam, you're cooking something delicious. If they flee, well . . ." She shrugs. "It's an old aunty secret."

"Really?"

"You're one of the most gullible saps I've ever met, I'm sure."

"I didn't believe you, I just couldn't tell if you really believed it yourself."

"Mhmm."

"Alright, well you let me know if you need anything. I'm going to get some reading done." Really there's some gaming I need to catch up on, but she doesn't need to know that. I suppress my visual feed and replace it with CoreEra4. Time to level up. The sensory suppression filters out most of Meena's kitchen noise, until I hear the blender slicing through. I'm curious why she needs a blender to make dal, but not curious enough to hit pause.

I'm pretty immersed in the game when I feel an almost pungent, but ultimately bland taste on my tongue. Meena's shoveled a bit of what she's done to this dal into my mouth. She massages the hot, dry musty paste into a lump as she lets each part of my tongue feel and inspect the texture. As it crumbles into the back of my throat, an aftertaste surfaces that reminds me of wanting to be kissed amidst an audience of '80s-era wood paneling on neglected basement walls. An aftertaste on my anxiety-dried adolescent tongue, which had just uttered, "I'd kiss you Eid Mubarak if you'd let me." A line tacky enough to hold the confident façade of my smile in place while I waited inside my head screaming, *What in the FUCK are you thinking?*

I can almost hear Hafza's laugh seeping in through my tongue and almost feel the slap that ended in an apologetic caress. My taste buds reverberate like the hair on the back of my neck when Hafza kissed the highest point of my cheekbone and then stared at me. I'd never seen anyone's eyes so close. It was so overwhelming I had to close my own eyes. I'm not sure if she had started or me, but after years of pining, that was the first time my lips finally melted into another's. And it would not be the last time I'd be rudely interrupted mid-kiss. Before the moment was over, Ammi was shouting, "Arsalan beta, let's go!" from the top of the staircase behind me. Hafza broke the kiss and leaned over to whisper "Eid Mubarak, Arsalan" in my ear just before I jumped up, stunned by what had happened. The next thing I'd say to Hafza would be "congratulations" ten years later on her heavily decorated wedding stage, next to her heavily decorated new husband.

Meena fills my mouth with water, washing my memory out. I ache for another taste of the musty paste. I want to go back for more, even though there is nothing to go back to.

"What was that? It tasted familiar."

"Well, mister expert, you'll have to wait and see."

So I watch her set the pot on the stove above the lowest possible flame and plop in a few heaps of ghee. As it melts and simmers un-

evenly in the pot, she picks up the blender and begins scooping the
paste out. The warm ghee spatters on the backs of my hands as the first
few clumps land in the pot.

My arm will no doubt be sore the next day, because for a while
she just leans on the counter and stirs every few minutes, keeping the
darkening paste on the bottom from sticking to the pot. Eventually
she stops to add sugar, mixing it in evenly before flipping the paste
over and pouring the rest of the sugar in. Once the white crystals disappear into the paste she scoops a spoonful out and closes my eyes as
the warm sugary sensation hits my lips. I'm flooded with images of
Tupperware decorated by cold and soggy deep-fried finger foods and
heavenly sweetened desserts. But, it's all dammed by the memory of
Karla's voice asking the question, "Why can't you just bring me home
for Eid, like a normal person?"

"Ammi's just not well," I had said, opening one dish and lifting it
up. What dish was it?

"She's well enough to have cooked all of this," Karla had said,
gesturing to the to-go holiday foods.

I plunged a spoon into the Tupperware and scooped up something
and shoved it toward Karla's mouth. "Just try a bite."

Karla rolled her eyes and opened her mouth. Then, when the taste
soaked into her tongue, she opened her eyes wide. Her eyes rolled
again, but with pleasure this time. "What the fuck is this?"

"Chanay-ki daal ka-halwa," I say into the AirBody UI.

"Very good!" Meena stabs with her standard tone of condescen-
sion. She pours another can of condensed milk in and continues stirring. "Gustatory memory."

"What?"

"Taste. It's got a peculiar way of triggering memory and emotion,
don't you think? More so than other senses. Taste links us directly to
our gut, where our deepest unfulfilled needs keep us hungry. Your gut
tricks your mind into thinking you're getting what you want, when it's
really just using you to get the"—she scoops up another bite and I feel
my eyes roll back into my head—"mmm. The sweet halwa."

She opens my eyes and looks down at the bright yellowy paste.

"But I remember this being brown whenever my Nani made it."

"Haan, beta, just wait," she says as she preheats the oven to 400 degrees. When the oven beeps she slides the pan in and sets a timer for fifteen minutes.

"Acha beta, what kind of formal wear do you have?"

"Formal wear?"

"Haan, kurta pajama? Shalwar kameez? Whichever you'd like to call it."

"Uhhh . . ."

"Oh, of course. Well, at least put us in a pressed pant-shirt," she says, handing me back control.

"Sure," I say, heading back to my room to pull out some blue slacks and a new red and gray striped shirt I haven't worn yet.

I stand before the mirror making final touches when she pings for control back.

"Well at least you've got some color in your wardrobe." She picks up a pen from my dresser and writes down an address on the price tag I just ripped off of the shirt I put on. "I need to go here."

"Sounds good to me," I say as I feel her pass control back.

As we make our way out of the city and onto the I-95 I glance at the sign for BWI Airport. The last time I was supposed to go to BWI was the last time I was supposed to see Karla. She had been away for work for a week and I was on my way to pick her up when I got a call from Ammi's doctor. My mind went single track and I skipped the exit for the airport and drove straight to the hospital in Philly where Ammi was taking her last breaths, alone. I made it in time to say goodbye, but not much else.

Karla only called once that night. I stayed in Philly for six days and when I got back my place was emptied of Karla's things, which was most everything. If I had called to let her know what was going on, she would have understood, would have come up to help. I never figured out why we played this game of chicken. We'd done it before. But this time we both ran off the cliff, and it felt right to let things rest at the bottom of the canyon rather than pick them up and rebuild.

I pull up in front of the house and step out of the car, grabbing the dish of halwa along the way. The magenta sunset laces the gray house like a mesh dupatta. There are a lot of cars parked on the driveway and a bluster of muffled laughter coming through the windows of the brightly lit living room.

As I get to the front door I hand back control and immediately feel my heart rate spike. She stares dead ahead, frozen still.

"Are you alright?"

"Haan, I just—"

The door swings open to a woman dressed in a gray and blue shalwar kameez. She's still looking at her guests behind her and laughing. Her smile sticks as she turns to look at me. Her purple-streaked hair's tied up in a bun. She's probably a little younger than Meena, maybe late forties? I study her face to see if I can parse a family resemblance to Meena's profile picture.

"I'm sorry, can I help you?" the woman asks, leaning against her doorjamb.

I can feel Meena trying to push the air through my larynx and out of my mouth but it's sealed shut. Instead, she just lifts the dish of halwa and opens it.

The woman leans forward and inspects the congealed brown paste. The sunset breeze blows a warm waft of the dish's scent into my nose.

The woman looks back at me, but her eyebrows are strained around her eye sockets now. Without a word, she takes a step back and slams the door in my face.

Meena stands there for a minute in my shaking body, with the halwa still cooling in the open air. She flattens the lid back onto the dish and lays a card on top of it. She puts the dish down gently onto the frilly brown "Welcome Home" mat. She picks up a small white rock from the side of the porch and places it on top of the card to keep it from flying away, before turning back to the car.

As soon as I feel the first tear hit my cheek she stops.

"Beta, take us home."

The tears stop as I take control, but I can still feel the strain in the back of my throat. This is the first time I've wondered what happens when people hand me back control temporarily. Do they come back to life in their homes? Is she convulsing over her toilet, vomiting up as much of the regret as possible before curling into a ball of tears on her bathroom floor? Or is she lying peacefully, letting the tears soak into her veins until the pain passes?

Once at home she requests control and immediately goes back to the cabinet in the corner, pulling out the bottle of whiskey and pouring it into a chipped glass she finds in my drying rack. She carries it in my shaking hands and walks to the armchair that faces the window. As the final moments of sunset fade away, I can see her staring back at me in the reflection of the window.

She holds up the glass and stares into the brown liquid as she swirls it around.

"Beta," she says aloud. "How do you decide which one is right for you?"

"What do you mean?" I respond, echoing in my own head.

"Which drink? How did you know it was whiskey? Not beer? Wine? Cocktail?"

"Well, I drink them all, so—" I hesitate, uncertain of where this is going. "But I don't drink much."

"Haan, beta, whatever." She smirks at me in the window and swigs the whiskey full down my throat. I turn down the sensory suppression and feel the initial hit seep into my blood and loosen my muscles. She picks the bottle up from the table and pours another shot.

"Are you okay?"

"I'll be fine, just need to process a bit." She lifts the glass, but sips at the whiskey this time. I assume the first time was purely for shock value.

"What's your deal?"

"My deal, beta?"

"Don't beta me, I'm a grown man."

"Haan." She pauses, scanning my sad apartment. "Of course you are."

"Why are you here? Who was that woman?"

"Just an old acquaintance. It's not important."

"Then why me? Were there no other, more appropriate hosts available?"

"Appropriate how?"

"I don't know, an older woman, someone more fitting your background?"

She laughs. "My background? Beta, you were the only 'Urdu-speaking' host of Pakistani origin whose listing authorizes sexual behavior during a visit."

Before I can respond there's a knock at the door.

"Were you expecting anyone, beta?"

"No."

She sets the glass down and goes to open the door. There is the woman, still in her gray and blue shalwar kameez, holding my dish with one hand and one hip. I watch my eyelids wrap around the woman in the doorway and make a shape I haven't seen them make in months.

"Is it still you, Meena?"

Meena nods, my larynx suddenly sealed shut once again.

"You think you're quite clever, don't you?" The woman walks into the apartment and slides the dish onto the counter. She pulls the lid off, revealing at least 2–3 servings' worth gone. "I'm going to eat the rest on my own as well. I'm not sharing." She smiles as she pulls off her dupatta and throws it at me.

Meena catches it and laughs, finally loosening my throat. "Haniya, I—"

Haniya leans in quick to shut up Meena with a hard kiss that sends a chill down my spine and reverberates through the hairs on the back of my neck.

It's been a while since I felt a kiss like that. In fact it's just flat out been a while for me. I wonder how long it'd been for Meena and which matters more or if they're additive, and while I try to figure that out they stumble onto the couch and eventually roll onto the floor.

I shut my visual feed off, turn the sensory suppression back up, and do my best to give them some privacy. I won't lie: I didn't expect this guest to be the first to avail this "amenity." But I can't entirely say I'm surprised. Meena has a determined bitterness that obviously guards something terribly sweet.

When I notice my heart rate begin to drop, I turn my visuals back on. They've made it to my bed. Meena's lying on my back with Haniya's head resting on my shoulder. The room is quiet except for the sound of calming breaths.

"Come back," Meena squeezes out between breaths and into Haniya's hair.

"As what, my love? Your assistant? Your cousin's friend visiting from the states? An NGO worker there for training that you're just showing around? What will you have me pretend to be this time?"

My throat locks up again as I feel blood rush to my cheeks.

Haniya sits up and lets my blanket fall off of her as she stands. She looks back down at me with a slight smile. "It was nice to see you again, Meena. I've missed these stunts of yours."

Meena just stares up at the ceiling while we listen to Haniya get dressed, slide the Tupperware off the counter and back onto her hip. Meena closes my eyes when we hear my apartment door open and shut. I'm certain she's going to start crying again, but she just takes a deep breath and speaks.

"You'll feel it one day." She rolls into a sitting position at the edge of the bed and looks in the mirror. "The desire to go back to when you were uncertain about who you'd turn out to be. When you lived foolishly thinking you could be something other than what you became in the end." She lifts my right fingertips to my forehead, twice, with a gentle pseudo bounce and says, "Thanks for the company, Arsalan. Khuda-hafiz."

As my limbs tingle back to me, I pull up Karla's contact. While I mull the idea of calling her, I get an alert in my periphery from AirBody about a new request. I stare at Karla's picture for a moment before closing her profile and pulling up AirBody. I'm certain I've already become who I'll be in the end, so I might as well let everyone else be me for a little longer.

THE TRANSITION OF OSOOSI

OZZIE M. GARTRELL

Ozzie M. Gartrell (@OzzieGartrell) is a librarian, speculative fiction writer, gamer, and anime nerd. When she isn't writing, she can be found actively avoiding social situations somewhere north of Seattle, Washington, with her menagerie of tiny battle Yorkies.

When the cop car makes a U-turn and starts tailing me, I know I'm in deep shit. I shake back my hoodie and slow my pace. No use running. Nav tells me six blocks stretch between me and the safe house. Too far. Can't risk it. I blink twice to activate my livestream, and send the encrypted feed straight to my personal server. Just in case, I tag Vee, Machine, even Mar—though my twin won't see it for days, and when she does, she'll be pissed. If shit goes down—and I have hella contraband on me, so it might—I want a recording. I want evidence they can't spin.

Won't do much, but it's something.

The late evening unfolds around me thick and close. The sun had long abandoned the city. Streetlamp beams slither in yellow pools across the pocked sidewalk. Shops, their plexiglass doors open to usher in cooler air, while away the last half hour of the workday.

Ahead, Chang's neon sign flicks from yellow to green, catching my gaze. My interface notices my lingering attention and augments my sight with data. Chang's: Chinese restaurant. Take Out or Delivery. Owner: Jem Chang. Moderately priced. Favorable reviews on social media. Only .03 miles from current location. Last item ordered: Pork fried rice with fried prawns.

I blink and the transparent information recedes. Tires crunch against the pavement to my left. Blue and red lights flash once before the cop stops his vehicle. I wait for the pop of an opening door before I turn.

Despite the dark, the officer wears mirror shades. I narrow my eyes a fraction and specs flood my interface. Recording sunglasses. Standard law enforcement issue. Filters sunlight, but enhances night vision. Adds to the loom factor and faux badassery. My reflection, distorted by his mirror lenses, sneers at me. Coily hair, streaked with purple and emerald, sweeps back from an unremarkable face with narrow black eyes and a broad nose. My dark skin looks mottled in the lengthening evening shadows.

The officer is careful to keep his patrol car between us. Smart. He'll later claim it was because he'd "feared" for his life.

I struggle to fold my smirk down into something more neutral.

"Almost curfew," he says by way of greeting. Since it isn't a question I don't bother responding. "Papers on the hood."

You need me to send someone? This pops up from Machine in my lower left field of vision. I don't dare mutter aloud to prompt the speak-to-text function. Instead I deliberately tilt my head sideways as if popping a crink in my neck. I raise one palm, face up, into the air; the other slowly reaches into my back pocket. All the while, I narrate what I am doing before I do it. Social media is rife with vids of CAs shot by zealous police who assumed they were packing.

Vee's loopy font materializes next, urging me to be careful, to avoid giving him an excuse. I blink three times to minimize all windows. The last thing I need is for this cop to realize I'm wearing augmented tech without the registered biochip cradled neatly beneath my flesh.

Stray flakes of barely dry blood stain my nailbeds, garish in the watery light. Shit. Here's hoping he won't notice. I dump a leather-bound booklet, impressed with the seal of the United States of True Americans, on the hood and barely staunch the urge to snatch back my hand and shove it into my pocket.

The cop doesn't bother to leaf through the tattered papers that prove my status as a Citizen American, a native-born U.S. citizen with all the second-class rights thereof.

"Where you headed, boy?"

I try not to bristle at the insult. Fail. "Chang's."

The officer grunts. I can't tell if he has mods to suss out the lie. It doesn't matter. We know this act is for show. Still, we both have our parts to play before the end.

They kneel in the night. Their fingers link together, their heads bow beneath the weight of the glaring stars. Harsh floodlights stamp out all color. Bodies shudder against great gouts of freezing water.

Despite the temperature bottoming out below zero, they sprayed us. They claimed they were putting out fires, but there were no fires. There was only us, the Earth, the sky, and the water we sought to protect. Water they mocked by turning it against us.

The solemn voices float off on a cutting wind and I shiver, still reluctant to throw off the sodden North Dakota cold. I scrutinize the computer simulation that sprawls across the nightclub's rooftop. Tents and people splay in loose arcs, facing off against impossibly large tanks and machines. Mobs of water protectors kneel or stand around me, rendered with such precision that I can feel their breath, can hear their shoes squelch on the muddy ground as they shift their weight. Hundreds of pairs of eyes gaze either at me or at the line of police in riot gear with guns and water hoses and closed-off expressions.

I urge my interface to detect only the real world. In response, the virtual simulation fades just enough for me to identify stocky HVAC units that leak viscous fluid onto dingy concrete. Nearby slender metal vents belch sour smoke into the evening. Smog snuffs out the stars and crowds around an anemic half-moon.

I turn in a slow circle, cycling between reality and altered reality when my attention snags on a heavy locked door that leads down into Club Genesis. Somewhere beyond that door, the people I've come to meet debate my fate. If they deem my cause worthy, that door will open. If not . . . I'm fucked, plain and simple.

Shaking my head, I coax the virtual simulation back to the forefront. In less than a breath, the Great Plains superimposes reality, transforming concrete into digitized grasslands. Once again water protectors flank me, beating drums.

Machine sidles toward me, passing right through a kneeling woman, her head turned away as a hose vomits water into her face.

"What d'you think?"

I peer into the defiant eyes of the water protector beside me and feel a strange kinship. It's almost as if we truly stand shoulder to shoulder, the chill of the North Dakota night sinking into our bones and hundreds of voices raised in visceral chants.

Instead, I live more than half a century too late, breaking curfew and trespassing on a nightclub's roof while I wait to learn if my life would change.

I blink out of the simulation and the virtual tableau dissolves. The balmy evening rolls around me, but still I shiver from the shock of freezing water and a burning fire in my heart that demands I guard the land my people had fought and died for since America's inception.

"This is like no altered reality I've ever seen," I confess. "It blows ordinary AR out of the water. It can't be VR—"

"Because we're not in a VR-capable room."

"And I didn't download an app or software to run it—the basic necessity for any alt-reality whether it's augmented or virtual, so . . ." I trail off, baffled. "How'd you pull this off?"

Machine bends to scoop up a flat disc the shade of milk and flicks it to me for study. "What you saw was a new type of alt-reality tech I'm calling 'augmented immersion.' It takes the portability of AR and combines it with the immersive sensory experience of VR. Once I'd perfected my simulation, it was easy to reproduce it in miniature receivers like that disc."

I gaze down at Machine's simdisc. It's light, plastic, and about the size of a quarter. Easy to miss.

"The trouble," Machine continues, "was getting the simdisc to communicate with someone's biochip without the person needing to download an app or special software."

"I didn't think that was possible."

"Neither did I until I started having fun with algorithms."

Only Machine would use the words "fun" and "algorithms" in the same sentence.

"But there are a half dozen biochip manufacturers out there," I point out. "Each with their own OS."

"Exactly. Finding the algorithm that would allow me to access each manufacturer's firmware was a bitch, no lie. The simdisc emits a signal with my algorithm buried inside. The algorithm transmits my code directly into any standard biochip and voilà! You see whatever I've programmed."

"I did more than just see, though," I insist. "In high-end VR you can sometimes feel sensations like heat or cold, but this was deeper. I felt their emotions, and even my own feelings seemed tied up in their own. None of that's normal, even for alt-reality."

Machine beams, clearly pleased with my reaction. "That's the genius of it! Within range, that bad boy can actually override any chip's emotional processors. The simulation then self-adjusts to create the emotions and sensations that best suit the piece."

"You don't think hacking a biochip's ability to regulate emotions isn't too much like emotional assault?"

"C'mon, fam—it's not like I'd use this against anyone's will." Machine activates a voice mod to change his tone and pitch to that of a True American salesman. "Augmented immersion draws on sensory manipulation to cultivate an authentic simulated experience in an organic way."

I snicker and raise Machine's simdisc up to catch the moonlight. It looks so unassuming. Hard to imagine that it will revolutionize altered reality. "I take it you want to plant these all around the city? Like street AR?"

"To start. You know, patent the tech, build buzz about augmented immersion, and then use it to bankroll my art." Machine flexes his fingers, gunmetal grey, and digs a cigarette out of his pocket. His robotic knuckles make a metallic whirring click as he lights it with his thumb. "Eventually, I want to open an exhibit somewhere featuring VR about us. VR the True Americans can't sanitize."

Machine eyes the simdisc as if I cradle pure magic between my fingers. "I needed to mark that moment, y'know? As I coded it, I wanted to fuse virtual reality with art and history—*our* history. I want it so they *know*, so they *feel* what our people felt. To be unable to turn away."

Unable to turn away. I like the sound of that. I roll Machine's peaceful protest between my index finger and thumb. It's a quaint ideal, but peaceful protests didn't stop the water hoses, it doesn't stop the beatings and homicides.

Lasting change can't shy away from violence.

"Great idea," I admit, and mean it. I cradle the simdisc in my palm while a solution to my dilemma percolates. "Mind if I hold onto it for a bit?"

"Keep it. I got another." Machine exhales a ring of darkness. "And thanks, but we both know it's a shit idea. No one wants an art exhibit like that—not about us."

"Not *by* us," I correct, slipping my prize into my pocket. "About us ain't the problem. It's when we speak our own—"

Behind us, the door we've been waiting for opens. My heart lurches. What if I can't pull this off? The people I'm about to meet don't entertain fools lightly. One mistake and it's game over. My organs, my subdermal chip, hell probably my family, would end up as merch on the dark web before I'd even noticed I'd fucked up. That realization alone should make me throw them deuces, sneak back down the fire escape, and dip out.

I take a deep breath and release it. No. I've come too far and burned too many bridges to get here. I won't tolerate failure. Not when I'm finally on the verge of breaking the world.

"This way," announces a short woman with a lilting Ghanaian accent.

Machine puts out his cig and follows me into the club to rendezvous with the hacktivists Anansi.

The thump of the music's bass headbutts my kicks as we descend into the building. I recognize the latest hit—don't they all sound the same after a while? Money, cars, drugs, and thots. Violence and respeck. Vee and I'd danced to countless like this one, and would dance to others.

The Ghanaian woman ushers us into an exclusive VIP lounge. The wooden floor is polished to a glassy sheen. Gauzy curtains the shade of smog cordon off little nooks where guests lounge on luxurious cream and white couches. Dim amethyst mood lighting keeps things artistic.

Machine shrugs at the question in my gaze. Are we about to get tossed, our augs sliced and carted off to the highest bidder? The room is empty save for a lean African staring out the one-way floor to ceiling windows at the dance floor below. At our arrival, he touches the sapphire glass. It ripples obsidian, muffling the vibrating reggae beats. The dancing bodies below vanish. When he turns to face us, I notice his eyes. Like Machine, he's elected to enhance parts of his body with robotics. His ocular implants gleam the yellow of a panther as he studies us.

Our escort tilts her chin to us. "Eshu."

Eshu reaches into his tailored suit—black on black—and pulls out two white business cards. Passes one to Machine. The other to me.

The cardstock, so expensive it slides like silk against my thumb, is blank. I turn it over. Blank. A flicker of a smile darts across the Ghanaian woman's lips before she reclines on one of the couches. Eshu leans against the wall, his gaze impassive.

"Gentlemen, if you please." She raises her own card. In the bruise-purple light, I detect the faint shimmer of ink. Not words—no, nothing so basic, so uncouth as that. I blink and my augments lock on a stylized QR code, beautifully rendered in the silhouette of a spider. I expect a link or pre-recorded video to dominate my feed.

Instead, malicious software hacks my interface.

Shit, shit, shit. Any breach in my security systems should have triggered an automatic failsafe that would contain the threat, but it doesn't seem to be operating. I attempt a manual override but that, too, fails. Panicking, I try to force a reboot but a DDoS attack locks me out. My interface pulsates red in alarm and abruptly crashes.

I stumble backwards, prepared to cut my losses and make a break for it, but Machine plants a hand on my arm. Trapped, I follow his gaze.

The VIP lounge was empty.

Now it isn't.

Six holographic avatars, each a creature out of African mythology, perch in the nooks and crannies of the VIP room. The leader lounges next to our escort on the plush couch.

"Machine. Mal." The holograph nods to us. His grin stretches wider than his face. "Welcome."

Damn it. The DDoS attack blackboxes all my tech behind a firewall and effectively hobbles me. No access to augs or my personal server. I can't even slip a DM to Machine. The only way they could have pulled that off was to use a rootkit. Right now, they've simply spliced us into a private alt-reality, but at any moment they could do much, much worse and we'd be helpless to stop them. They could permanently fry our tech, pilfer our servers, and raid our financial accounts, or force the biochip to malfunction and cook our insides. . . . The last was a favored method for Yemoja, an Anansi member infamous for her short temper, dangerous whims, and deadly sense of humor.

"Precautions," assures one avatar, this one looking like a man hewn from iron mesh. Curved blades extend from his shoulders and spine. His steel-grey eyes linger on Machine, who dips his chin. He is far calmer than I.

"Good to see you again, Ogun."

I gape. Ogun is a legend that I've been following for years. A hacker who, like all of the Anansi, adapts a moniker of an African deity: Ogun, god of iron, sacrifice, and technology. If there is a technical innovation anywhere in the world, Ogun has had a hand in developing it.

Machine nudges me and I close my mouth. Right. We're here for business, not to fangirl.

Still shaky from the turbulent introduction, I concentrate on the leader, the one who'd first spoken, and offer my thanks. He waves it off with one of his eight hands. His avatar wears the form of a dark-skinned, handsome man with long dreads tipped in gold. Bulbous shades hide his eyes. Steel plates feather along his ribs in shades of iridescent blue-black.

"We have gone over your proposal for assistance." A hand guides a vintage e-cig to his lips. He takes a bubbly pull. "The Anansi have questions."

"The Anansi as in you, personally, or . . . ?"

"You'll find the interests of Anansi and *the* Anansi aren't different." White steam and the scent of mint fills the air as he exhales. "It's a tall order, targeting a government as powerful as the one that runs your country."

I nod, easing into negotiations. "That's why I need your expertise and experience."

"That you do." Anansi's tone is mild, conversational. "But we exact a high price for our involvement. I'm sure your friend Kaiyote has warned you."

Machine keeps his expression carefully neutral. It isn't often that someone refers to him by his secret alias. Kaiyote's reputation had gained the Anansi's cooperation. It was up to me to avoid getting myself killed, and somehow to convince them to aid my cause.

"I will pay it."

Anansi chuckles darkly. "We shall see. Yemoja?"

A woman-shaped bubble of water with tendrils of hair that drip like seaweed sashays towards me. Fish swim inside her. Starfish and lichen weave themselves into a vague semblance of a gown.

"Young," Yemoja announces, ignoring Machine and circling me with slow deliberation. "Idealistic."

I cut my eyes at her, this sea-woman who moves like the tide. I hate how she scrutinizes me, sizing me up like livestock. My skin crawls from the damp heat of her avatar but I don't dare back away. Too much rides on this.

"Overthrowing an apartheid necessitates long-term strategy," she gurgles, trailing a wet finger down my cheek. "You must show dedication and cunning. You must be fearless and ruthless. You hardly seem the type. Too much softness, too much indecision about you."

I would have looked her in the eyes except she doesn't have any facial features aside from coral forming a mouth. A squid flaps up her collar into her neck and splays its tentacles along her jaw.

"Trust me, I can be as *hard* and *decisive* as you need," I quip.

Machine coughs into his hand. Belatedly, I remember this is the same Yemoja who'd once boiled a man's semen inside his own testicles because he'd dared to make a pass at her.

I wince and try to backtrack. "I didn't mean—"

"Boy, please. Don't make me snatch you," she interrupts, snorting. To my relief she retreats to Eshu's side.

"Yemoja's right to question your decisiveness." Ogun's disapproval barrels over me like a naked blade. "You forget, we can see the details of your project—and it's vague, incomplete, and riddled with illogical script."

To my chagrin, Ogun yanks the program EMPATHY from my encrypted server and brandishes it before everyone. Holographic columns of raw code hover in the air like strands of DNA. The missing sections look like a rotting, malignant tumor.

My digital soul, bared before the gods.

Machine leans forward, scanning the columns in unabashed interest. I'd never allowed him to glimpse what I'd been feverishly designing, and I sure as hell didn't want him—or anyone else—scrutinizing it before it's ready.

I curse not being the one in control of my tech. It's like not having control of my right arm. But instead of lashing out and demanding Ogun end this bullshit, I grit my teeth and bear it.

"I've only just recently come across a solution to those issues." I hesitate, cutting my eyes at Machine as he peruses EMPATHY. I don't feel comfortable going into any more detail around him. Not that I don't trust him, but he wouldn't like what I'm thinking of doing and I need him in my corner.

Anansi intuits my dilemma and gives me a conspiratorial wink. He gestures at the holographic image. EMPATHY disappears and some of my tension recedes.

"I know my plan seems dicey, but it'll work if I can count on access to your—"

"Guerrilla tech. Or, as your 'True Americans' call it, 'black market contraband.'" Dry amusement laces Yemoja's tone.

"Like you said, our government is powerful, but you have taken on totalitarian states and won. I know we can be just as successful here. We can *help* people."

"Your government considers us terrorists. If we get involved, you will become a hunted man." Ogun's expression is as ominous as a thundercloud. "All those who have ever known you will wear a target. Never again will you know peace. It's not too late to find another—"

I shake my head, thinking of the final time Mar and I set foot in Chang's. That horrible afternoon, I'd made a vow. "I have to see this through, one way or another."

Anansi props his chin on two fists while a third idly twists a dread around his six-jointed finger. He scrutinizes me as if he could peel back my skin and examine my thoughts. "And what are you prepared to lose?"

"I'd give my life—"

"Your life?" Anansi barks out a laugh that is anything but mirthful. "Your life is easy, brotha. Being a martyr is *easy*." The gods nod in agreement. "The Anansi ask you—how far are you willing to transition from the self you are now? Will you kill for what you believe?" He leans forward, his words slithering out in a spidery hiss. "Should your cause demand it, will you betray those you love? Will you look into their eyes and end their life?"

I suck in a startled breath. Machine is so silent that I can't hear him breathe, even though he stands less than two feet from me. I don't dare glance his way for fear of what he'd read in my eyes.

But the Anansi see. They know.

Anansi removes his oversized shades, unveiling four sets of beetle-black eyes. Each bores into me in grim calculation. *"Will you damn your soul, Malkom?"*

The question drops from his lips like a cement block. Frost crackles down my spine. I stare at the gods assembled before me. Their digitally divine gazes remain implacable. Expectant. I have no doubt that everything, all my months of planning, rides on my answer. I turn over their question.

How serious am I? To implement lasting change, will I betray Mar, my literal other half? Will I sacrifice Vee, the love of my life? Will I murder Machine, my brother who's had my back since day one?

Never before have I allowed myself to contemplate the messy business of actual social reform.

The Anansi are right. Sacrificing my life is easy; collateral damage is the real problem. Innocent blood marks the true measure of dedication.

What would happen if I turn aside from this dangerous course? Innocents would still die, but the future would hold no promise for anything better. Citizen Americans like me would still be forced to lead segregated, second-class lives. Though we're born in America, we aren't considered real Americans worthy of respect.

Pets even have more rights than us. Animal abuse like dogfighting carries a mandatory fifteen-year sentence in a federal prison. It isn't even illegal to kill a Citizen American, especially with justifiable cause—and the murder of CAs is always justifiable. In fact, their killers are often thanked for safeguarding society.

My blood boils at the reminder. Yes, justice for my people is why I must rip this whole system apart. Only then will we be liberated. If I'm unwilling to paint this country red then I might as well forget the word "freedom."

Freedom. True Americans will do anything to preserve it. I will do anything to acquire it.

Will you damn your soul, Malkom?

I loosen my fingers from the tight fists they'd curled into. Smooth out my grimace. I avoid Machine's horrified stare. From my pocket, the water protectors in his simdisc wail warnings. *An eye for an eye leaves the whole world blind.* If I go down this path, there will be no turning back.

Not trusting my voice, I nod. The Ghanaian woman smiles. Ogun shakes his head and Yemoja purses her lips.

Anansi extends an arm with too many joints. Nestled in his palm skitters a spider bot, its mechanical thorax smaller than my fingernail. Yellow sparks of qubits zap along its miniscule body.

"Prove it."

The advertisement swells over Vee's brown breast, plunges into her cleavage, and swoons over the other. *Problems with your most important Member? Use Viagrix to set the Mood!* I'd wondered what it felt like, having advertising scripts crawling over your skin eight hours each day, but Vee only shrugged and said the money was good and she rarely noticed anymore. Her body molds itself to mine; her fingers, tangled in my curls, yank back my head so that her petal soft lips can press against my throat. No lie, it feels good. I like the way we nestle together as if we'd been carved from a single block of ebony.

She tastes like sunlight and freedom and laughter. She tastes like the Viagrix I sure as hell never need with her, but the last thing I want right now is to break into a bank with a hard on.

"You're stalling," I prompt.

Square teeth nip the thin flesh beneath my chin before she shoves me against the alley's stucco wall. Sandwiched between a deli and the advertising agency where Vee works, the narrow alley allows us to meet away from pedestrians' prying eyes.

"They're using you," she retorts.

Script in ghostly white *(Destroy Age with Tymelyss!)* creeps down her collarbone and disappears under her nearly transparent pink halter. The Viagrix advertisement slides over her hip and eases toward the waist of her shorts. I force my eyes up the curves of her body until deep brown irises clash with mine. A dagger of afternoon sunlight refracts around her pupils and bathes her ocular augments in a metallic-gold sheen.

"It's mutual."

"Mutual? You're the one taking all the risks, Mal. Your spiders aren't going to help if the TAs catch you. Those assholes'll scapegoat you, and then—" Vee floods my vision with gifs, tweets, and vids.

Bodies strewn across concrete, washed grey by blue and white flashing lights. A man, arms in the air, trying to make himself nonthreatening only to be tackled to the floor and then shot six times in the back. Press conferences with solemn law enforcement; force reasonable, the perpetrator evidence why the division between True Americans and Citizen Americans proved necessary, especially when the latter are so prone to violence.

I wave it off. "Look, Vee, Machine's got my back. Besides, I trust them."

Okay, that's a lie. While I trust Machine with my life, I don't trust the Anansi, not blindly. I'd vetted them in the deep web. I'd sought out mutual contacts. They're legit. They were legit back before Africa became a united technical powerhouse, and now they are hacktivist canon. The digital boogeymen of cyberspace who can wreck an economy, bring down a government, or change a nation.

Doesn't mean I trust them, or that they trust me. We each have intentions to prove before we become partners.

"So do you have it or what?" I press.

Vee sucks her teeth and produces a sleek, iridescent card from her bra. "Printed this with the specs your spiders gave me. Pray their schematics are on point."

I pluck the access card from her hand and lean in for another kiss, but she holds me at bay with a finger. I read it in her eyes: I'm a damned fool. This is a bad idea.

She isn't wrong.

Sure you wanna do this? Machine's DM materializes in the lower right of my vision. I peel my gaze from Vee's retreating sway and make a rude gesture. He sends back an equally rude emoji. *Well suit up, asshole.*

The vacant building, just across the street from our target, is closed for remodeling. I slip into the last stall of the ladies' restroom and smirk at the black bag wedged beside the toilet. If TAs are antsy about who uses which bathroom, they'll go into epileptic shock at the military grade contraband inside my duffel. CAs aren't supposed to have access to the tech Machine has packed for me. Especially not when it contains the power to transform a Black, Choctaw male into a pale-skinned True American.

Digging into the duffel, I pull out an airtight silver canister and unscrew the heavy lid. The nanobots inside look like opalescent glitter that occasionally sparks with forked purple lightning. I shake the nanobots onto my arm and watch as they race up my body. I grit my teeth against the tingling sensation of their movement. It feels like a million cold eyelashes blinking against my skin.

I scrutinize my reflection to make sure the bots, enhancements, and augments are firing on all cylinders. In the mirror, a morose white man studies himself; his steel-blue gaze roams over the nanobots that shimmer over the remnants of his street clothes, exchanging them for an impeccable suit pirated from the exclusive site of a respected designer.

"Talk about passing." The modulator alters my own voice, smoothing its pitch to something cultured and non-threatening. Lightly European—German, maybe.

"Nice, huh?" Machine's voice rings clearly in my implants. "EMP still fucks 'em up, but the bots recover faster."

"Let's hope it's enough." I pet Machine's simdisc like a treasured talisman, reassured that it still rests in my newly formed breast pocket.

Showtime.

Making sure no one sees me leave the vacant building, I cross the street and enter the looming monstrosity that is Dyscre Bank. Its lobby opens up to a massive atrium of designer furniture and modern decor. Clusters of employees in tailored suits and sleek hairstyles march past. They speak in a low, professional hum and clutch paper-thin tablets. Above them bob jellyfish drones, their spindly tentacles chirping every so often as they monitor staff and clients alike.

My mission is simple. Infiltrate the bank, plant Anansi's spiderbots, get out. Taking a breath to settle my nerves, I pad over to the security console. A pair of assistants at the front desk glance up, but upon seeing yet another chicly dressed man heading for the employee bioscanner, dismiss me. I insert Vee's key card and step in.

Emerald lasers shoot out of the console, assaulting my pupils as they skim over my body. A nearby jellyfish lowers to scrutinize me. Molded from silicone with a carbon fiber core, the drone looks remarkably like its organic counterpart, except I can see its colorful hardware blinking from inside its umbrella-shaped epidermis. Its processors hum in rhythmic waves. Like AI, bioscans don't recognize human faces. They map facial features against a database. They measure heart rates, perspiration, breathing. Dyscre's bioscans go a step further and scan for any unauthorized tech or augments. The access card should help it "overlook" the contraband. If Vee had printed it correctly. If the Anansi's algorithms are right. If—

Green suddenly bleeds orange. *Shit.* I'd been holding my breath and hadn't realized it. Intrigued, the jellyfish drifts close enough to touch. Its tiny camera's iris opens farther. I force air out of my lungs and unbunch my shoulders. The lasers resume their faint green shimmer. I relax. Ignore the drone in favor of thoughts about Vee's kisses. About Mar's goofy laughter. An unbidden question bubbles to the surface.

Will you betray those you love?

My cheek twitches in a guilty spasm. The lasers shift orange.

Easy, man, Machine's message elbows into my lower vision. *This is supposed to be the easy part.*

I tamp down on my nerves and wrangle my thoughts into safe blankness. A green halo breaks over me. A second later the console beeps and spits out my card. The drone loses interest and corkscrews up to the third floor.

I'm cleared. The Anansi can be trusted.

I never doubted them.

Under Machine's expert guidance, I hit each of the Anansi's targets. Most are corporate private servers ripe with confidential information. Information that—for a nominal finder's fee—can be brokered to an ambitious rival. I linger near each server and wait for a pair of Anansi's spiders to skitter inside the white towers. From his bunker across the city, Machine monitors the incoming flood of data.

"In and transmitting. How many spiders are left?"

I check the suit's inner pocket. "A little less than a dozen."

"Should be enough. Next vault."

I return to the hallway. Though a few employees and security personnel roam the hall, none seem the wiser to the intruder in their midst, and I'm not inclined to alert them. Keeping my expression neutral, I nod to people only if they nod to me. Mostly they ignore me.

What would it be like to wear this skin regularly? Could I slip it on like a comfortable sweater and go shopping? Store clerks wouldn't tail me; I wouldn't need to pay upfront for a meal at Denny's. My humanity would be the default. My innocence assumed. I'd finally be free to be ordinary.

But is ordinary what I want to be?

"You missed the turn," Machine alerts.

"Yeah, about that . . ."

My interface flickers as I shift the overlay of Dyscre Bank's blueprints to show a red elevator that leads down to a restricted subbasement. "Is that what I think it is?" When Machine doesn't immediately respond, I grin.

"Just stick with the plan, Mal," he hedges.

"That's the problem." I alter my course to head for the elevator. "I've been sticking to the plan."

"And things have been going smoothly."

"C'mon, you know the Anansi aren't interested in corporate secrets, not really. They want to see what I can do, and what I can do is get them access to some government servers."

"There's a reason why even the Anansi haven't cracked the Feds' off-grid servers. The layers of security, the levels of encryptions—it's damn near hack-proof."

"Maybe, but we won't know if we don't try. This is what they're really after. If not, why choose Dyscre Bank in the first place—a bank that just happens to have the only federal servers for hundreds of miles?"

Machine rattles off a list of possibilities, but I shrug them aside. As soon as the Anansi had challenged me to raid Dyscre Bank, I knew what I would do. What Machine doesn't know is that it isn't because of the Anansi that I want these servers. They'll benefit, sure, but in order for me to fight oppression, I need covert access to the methodology of the oppressors. What better way to bring down a corrupt system than by using its own proprietary information against it?

I don't share this with Machine. Instead I settle for a version of the truth. "I *need* to do this and you know I can't do it without you. I'm begging you, as my best friend, my brother. Help me."

A pause. Then: "Fine, you manipulative bastard."

Inside me, the guilt twists a little tighter. I'm one of the only people Machine trusts, and I know just how to exploit that trust. I remind myself it's for the greater good. No one will give us freedom. We have to take it. I will do whatever is necessary to emancipate my people. I just hope it doesn't require me stepping over the body of my best friend.

I turn my attention to our next obstacle. Instead of a drone or another AI, a True American monitors the restricted elevator. From the man's stiff posture and hard visage, my bet is military—probably former Marine. Crew cut hair, expensive suit that strains against his muscular bulk, square jaw on which he whets his collection of camp

knives. He embodies the cliché corporate thug—except for his eyes.
Sharp, they look eager to ferret out bullshit.

Or idealistic revolutionaries masquerading as corporate thieves.

"Fuuuuuck," Machine drawls. "Just pretend you're lost and turn around."

The heat of Militarybro's stare singes me but he doesn't rise from his security station. I keep my expression bored and meet his unblinking gaze without flinching. Three monitors glow with feral blue light but I can't make out the cycling images. I tap my right wrist against the security station's scanner and wait for it to analyze my subdermal chip and grant me clearance.

Only I don't have a subdermal chip—not a registered one, anyway. And I sure as hell don't have clearance.

The scanner is taking too long and I suspect Militarybro, already wary, is two seconds shy of depositing a bullet into my skull. My heart wants to stab me in the throat—repeatedly—but I force my breathing to stay steady. Force contempt into my eyes—this part isn't hard—and cock a brow.

"You seem on edge," I say.

"Haven't seen you before."

"Never good if you do."

That catches him off guard. Good. "Why is that, exactly?"

My smirk widens into a conspiratorial grin. "I only show up when there is an issue that requires . . . discretion."

The scanner flashes green, finding a match, and the elevator doors hiss apart. In my eardrums, Machine curses and kicks various objects in a mixture of exasperation and celebration. Though miles away, I can practically feel the stress steaming off him. Machine is the best hacker in the country. He was the reason the Anansi would see me and now he's just gained me access to a veritable treasure trove of information.

Militarybro inspects me once more, this time committing me to memory. That chills me down to my toes. Usually at the mention of discretion, people lower their eyes, mollified and eager to be done with whatever dirty business had landed in their laps.

Not this guy.

Don't like how he's looking at you, man. He's gonna cause trouble, Machine warns, echoing my gut.

No use for it. I'm not going to back down now. "What's your name?"

Militarybro's gaze returns to his circle of monitors. "Hans Gruber, sir."

The *sir* is laced with so much contempt that if I really were working on behalf of a high-level government executive, I'd have him fired. Instead, I stroll inside the elevator as if I haven't a care in the universe.

Machine shouts a warning. I whirl just in time to see Gruber flick a tiny, handheld dart in my direction. Too fast. I can't react.

The dart worms into my shoulder. Needle sharp pain stabs up my collarbone. A blue nimbus of electromagnetic energy flares around me, disrupting the bots and rocking me backward. My head slams against the wall hard enough to rattle my teeth.

My vision sizzles white static. Bots rain like glass around me, so tiny they flicker like sparks. My disguise sluices away.

The elevator chimes and its doors seal away Gruber's triumphant smirk.

My legs give out and I slide down the wall onto my ass. I try desperately to hold on to consciousness. I can't afford to black out, not now, but already darkness folds over me, bringing with it summer heat, shrieks of laughter, and Five-Spice powder.

I peered over the sea of heads that seethed along the street. Scent and noise melded together into a paste that smelled of grease, sounded of drums, and reminded me of heaven. August sunlight beat down, tangling around brightly colored "MelangeFest" banners. Tourists crowded vendors' stalls, slurping bowls of fresh gumbo despite the heat and haggling over jewelry "handcrafted" by real Native Americans, but in reality, just generic patterns downloaded and printed from the net.

"Seriously, Malkom." Mar nudged me with her shoulder and lowered her designer shades. "I'm going to pee right now if we don't find a place, and I'm *not* using a portable."

"Chang's is right down the block."

My twin followed my gaze and pursed her lips. "Could use one of those bubble green tea things while we're there."

We snaked through the throngs of people enjoying the festival.

"Lot more TAs here than usual," Mar observed.

"Ironic, celebrating a festival of diversity when they're passing laws suppressing it."

"Don't start."

"What?"

"The revolutionary shit. You sound like Dad."

"And you sound like Mom."

She shrugged at the old argument. "The world's the way it is and nothing you or I do will change it. The sooner you accept that, the better off you'll be."

My stomach rumbled at the familiar punch of Chinese that wafted from the open doors of Chang's. Not much had changed since we were kids. Jem Chang was the first guy in the neighborhood to use recycled materials to print his furniture. Ugly, blocky affairs, but sturdy and comfortable. Nothing like the new aged, sleeker patterns downloaded nowadays. Occasionally, the dated tech of Chang's oversized menu boards still glitched out with 404 errors instead of prices for Kung Pao Chicken. Kung Pao Chicken that Mr. Chang used to slip to Mar and I when we'd pass by after school.

The modest restaurant was packed but not too busy. I waved to Pablo behind the counter.

"The usual, Mal?"

"Yep. Pork fried rice, fried prawns. Mar wants a bubble tea. Green?"

"Green," she confirmed.

Pablo spared Mar an assessing look. Sharing my imposing height, she was identical to me in nearly every way. Her beaded and braided hair roped around her head in an intricate style both elegant and outlandish. She'd always preferred flowy bohemian dresses with bangles and charms stacked up to her elbows. Mar propped her shades on her head and matched Pablo's gaze until he was forced to tap a customer's wrist to finalize the transaction and present his food.

"You look great, Mar. I mean that. Really."

Mar blessed him with a genuine smile. It'd been such a long time since I'd seen it that I wanted to fist-bump Pablo. It'd taken convincing to pry Mar from her textbooks and sociology papers to attend the festival. She weaved her way towards the ladies' restroom and then paused, eyeing the sign. Women. Paying customers only.

"Bubble tea, 'member? We're paying customers, same as anyone."

Her dark eyes flashed at me, bemused. "Same as anyone, huh?" But she bumped the door with a rounded hip and strutted inside.

I shouldered the men's restroom open. The two stalls, a forgettable blue-grey, were taken. I claimed an empty urinal between two TAs. We ignored each other. I did my business and was scrubbing pink soap suds between my fingers when my heart missed a beat, then another.

I paused, tepid water sloshing over my skin. Panic that wasn't mine gurgled in my stomach and I immediately recognized its source. *Mar?*

Fear—chased by a flare of anger and a wash of shame—reverberated through our link. I shot her another DM. *Mar, what's—*

You're wrong, Mal. I'm not like everyone else. They'll never allow me to be. Mar's live feed augmented my vision.

A single dark eye glared between the crack in her stall. A door rattled with the pounding of a fist.

"I told you, I'm almost done." The feed shook for a moment. Mar adjusted the fluttering bohemian layers of her dress, pulling together her dignity like chunks of battered plate armor. The toilet hissed as it flushed. Mar could barely unlatch the stall door before Chang's supervisor loomed in her face.

Foregoing the dryer, I shoved past annoyed TAs and kicked open the men's door. It barely missed someone waddling inside. Mar's livestream continued.

"This restroom is for women."

"And I'm a woman." Mar tried to step around the man to reach the sink.

He blocked her, lip curled. I recognized him. Adam. One of Mr.

Chang's sons. He couldn't have known Mar was even in there unless . . . *Pablo.*

"Really?" Adam continued. "Then show me your ID. Papers, too."

Mar stiffened before asking with an exaggerated courtesy, "May I
at least wash my hands first?"

Though the other women in the bathroom had long cleared out,
they rubbernecked in the hall and barricaded me from my twin. Visiting TAs whispered behind palms and whipped out sleek devices; a
couple of irises flickered metallic as augments triggered, recording the
unfolding drama. Mar would be all over social media and forums now.
At least until I could get Machine to scrub her presence.

"If you need to wash your hands, use the men's restroom. You
know you can't be in here, Marten. It's against the law."

Mar stared at Adam as if he were speaking a foreign language and
she hadn't activated her translator mod. Her stupor fueled my rage. I
buried it.

Not yet. Later.

Adam rubbed his jaw, discomfited. "Look, Da's fond of you so we'll
forget this, but next time I'll have to call the—"

I killed the feed and elbowed past gawking TAs. Mar didn't protest
when I lowered her shades to hide her tears, tucked her against me,
and headed for the dining area. The crowd parted like sticky-sweet
soy sauce. I tugged on Mar's right earlobe so that her biochip would
filter out their hateful whispers. Their susurrations—*freak, pervert, he
shoulda called the cops* rolled off Mar and stuck to me.

I ignored the burning stares of everyone in Chang's. Rage coiled
dragon-hot in me but the hotter my anger burned, the colder Mar's
dejection became.

What do you want to do? I ask. *I say Molotov cocktail.*

Mar inhaled deeply. Held it. I could sense her soul-numbing fatigue coruscating between despair and shame. *Part of me'd like nothing
more,* she confessed, exhaling in a bitter huff. *But that won't make a
difference. What's wrong is empathy, Mal. People have no compassion
for one another—and you can't force them to, either. Even if we burned
this place down. We'd have to burn down this entire country.*

Pablo, head bowed, busied himself taking orders. As we marched past, he muttered a heartfelt apology but we were out the door. Mar's bubble tea wept condensation onto the counter.

A wave of nausea crests up my throat. The memory ebbs away, replaced by a persistent and annoying buzzing. It sounds suspiciously like . . . Machine shouting?

My interface sluggishly flickers back online. Distortion crinkles the error messages that flash in shades of sepia. I barely discern Machine's frenzied messages as they scroll from lips to brow.

We're so screwed.

So screwed.

Mal? Mal! Get up!

Get. The fuck. Up.

He's trying to call for backup. I'm running interference, but you have ten minutes.

At most.

Bots are online. Get out of there.

My augs shudder. My hand twitches as I yank the dart out of my shoulder. No wider than my finger and nearly as long, it glitters with the last of the EMP charge. Disgusted, I start to toss it aside, but remember it has my blood on it. Likely has a tracer embedded in it, too. I pocket it.

My shoulder throbs and my chest heaves. I glare at my reflection in the elevator's polished steel. The bots are hustling to reassemble my disguise—desperate to erase the sin of Blackness and morph it into something more palatable—but the damage is done. He'd gotten a glimpse of me, but with luck, not enough for a firm description.

Machine continues cussing me out. "Should have just stuck to the fucking plan, but no . . ."

I ignore the escape route my best friend brandishes. Yemoja's taunt rattles in my head. *Too much softness about you.* I zero in on the schematic. I have just enough time for one government server, maybe two.

"These are the holy grail. We'll never get another crack at them unless you want to stroll on down here. Just keep him busy as long as you can."

The doors part, revealing a bank of servers that glow white, blue, and green. No Militarybros here, only mechs, and they are none the wiser. Resembling sleek panthers, they patrol the catwalks above, their featureless faces snuffling. They perform systematic bioscans, hunting for body temperatures and movement that doesn't belong. If they find an intruder, tasers launch from their tails and the entire bank goes on alert.

Machine overrides all their programming—at least for the time being—and blocks Hans from communicating to them. As long as I don't act out of the ordinary, I'll seem like a typical meatsuit.

"How'd you guess?" I ask to steady my nerves.

"'Bout Hans?" comes Machine's distracted response. "Name rang a bell."

A brief summary of an archaic film, *Die Hard*, pops up on my interface. The movie's main villain, Hans Gruber, is a German terrorist trying to rob an affluent bank.

Well, isn't Militarybro a clever bastard.

I fish Machine's simdisc from my pocket and explain my plan. Immediately, I sense his reluctance. If we do this, it would ruin his life's work. I'd be using his simdisc, with its countless hours of frustration, ingenuity, and artistry, to aid in a felony. He'd never be able to patent his revolutionary augmented immersion technology, nor would he be able to use it to fund his amazing artwork. Not without implicating himself.

It's too much to ask, but there isn't another way. At least not one where I can still gift myself the government servers. And a selfish part of me can admit the ugly truth of it: I would eagerly destroy much more than his life's work if it means accomplishing my objective.

My breath hitches. When did I become such an asshole? When did I become that guy who would throw his loved ones under a train if it meant getting to the next station? When this is over, will I even be able to look at myself in the eye?

"Run it." Resentment threads through Machine's voice but when he next speaks, I detect nothing but resignation. "But I can't promise I'll be able to get you out."

I box away my remorse and shame and flex my fingers.

"Let's do this."

"So you say you're headed to Chang's, huh?" the police officer reiterates, his tone thick with skepticism. Somewhere sirens wail. A few pedestrians cross the street to avoid us. Smart. "Where were you before that?"

"Work. Day laborer."

The officer's cheeks tighten. I suspect he's glaring at me through narrowed eyes but it's hard to tell anything beyond the gleam of his mirror shades.

"Then you wouldn't happen to know anything about an incident at Dyscre Bank, would you?"

Shit. Machine's text box elbows into my vision. Vee only speaks in punctuation. My nerves threaten to turn state's evidence. I swallow. Cling to calm.

"Like I said, I'm just out to get my food and head home." Impatience bubbles into my voice. "May I take my papers and go?"

The officer's stare feels like a physical weight. The weight from men such as him scrutinizing men such as me settles across my collar like an iron yoke. The dance we dance is one measured in centuries and steeped in blood. His hand drifts towards the holster at his hip.

"A man was killed. A true patriot." He doesn't budge from across his car, but neither does his hand lift from the butt of his gun. "And you happen to match the description of the perp."

I take a deep breath. Ignore the ping of Machine's panicked texts. I stare at my reflection in the officer's mirror shades as sweat rolls down my back. The sirens grow louder, closer.

Despite Machine's efforts, Gruber *had* gotten out a description of me, but it was vague. Race, gender, height. Still, a TA had been murdered. Innocent Black blood will be spilled tonight—all because of me.

Guilt gnaws at my conscience and it is a minor miracle that my voice remains neutral so the lie can slither out in a smooth drawl. "Don't know nothing 'bout that. Am I under arrest, then?"

"You understand the seriousness of this, don't you, boy?"

My shoulders tense. I force them to loosen.

"Yeah."

The officer grunts. He studies me a long time and I don't move. I radiate weary innocence. Finally, his hand slides away from his hip. "I don't want to see you out here."

He turns away. His door pops open. Air hisses out of my lungs and my knees shake with relief. I reach for my papers, eager to scoop them up and get the hell outta dodge while Vee and Machine argue over which safe house I should hit up, how long I should lie low—

Until their chatboxes suddenly evaporate.

An icy tendril of dread skates up my ribs. That cop couldn't have hacked my shit, could he?

A video clip smothers my feed.

In it, Militarybro exits the elevator, his gun drawn. He pauses for a moment, his head turning left and right, shocked at the assembled people who chant and yell in a wintery North Dakota night. Water protectors surround him, each whispering stories of the sheriff's department. Hans make his way towards the no man's land separating protesters and tanks. He can't risk shooting and damaging the expensive rows of equipment, so every few seconds he whirls or his arm swipes at a hologram to make sure it isn't real.

I see myself peel away from the water protector that I'd felt a special kinship with when I first experienced Machine's sim. The protector watches as I skulk closer to my enemy, hunting him like the Sioux used to hunt buffalo across the plains. The mechs gaze down, indifferent. Gruber creeps forward on cat-silent feet.

He steps over a tiny white disc, his gun trained on a woman wrapped in a heavy coat, her middle finger raised towards the military. He doesn't sense me behind him. My fingers caress the EMP dart. I raise it. The movement must have alerted him because he whirls. I don't hesitate. There is no softness, only instinct and Black rage. I bury the dart in his eye.

The video zooms in on Gruber falling. Clutching his face, blood spurts from his socket. I wrestle away his gun and loom over him, watching him writhe. Around me, water protectors yell for peace. Precious water saturates the oil-rich ground.

I could let him go. Incapacitate him, get what I need, and leave. Instead, I aim.

A black spider fills the screen. Words stream from its thorax in a gossamer-fine web.

Dedication. Cunning. Fearless. Ruthless. You have proven your worth.

The web of words evaporates, replaced by another set. *You have our assistance. And we offer a gift—*

The spider begins to evaporate, but not before dropping a bombshell:

—to our newest member.

My breath catches. *Newest member?* I lean against the police car's hood, sure my legs are going to give out. When I'd first petitioned the Anansi for aid, I'd never envisioned joining their ranks. It's one thing to have the Anansi's backing, but to actually be a member, to become a digital god? The possibilities are endless.

My feed crackles back to life. Machine and Vee's minimized chatboxes blink for attention. In the center of my interface beckons a familiar program.

The cop, already half inside his cruiser, peers through the windshield. "You got a problem, boy?"

"Let it go." Machine's placating voice, whispering through my implants, startles. "You already accomplished what you set out to do. Get your papers and meet me at the safehouse."

Abandoning the chat, Vee joins in on Machine's call. "I'm almost at the spot now. Let's regroup and celebrate. We actually pulled it off."

"Hey, boy!" The officer snaps his fingers to get my attention. "You deaf? I said you got a problem?"

At his words, that slow heat that had been building inside me for years sparks into a sudden inferno. I embrace the fire, welcome it. Let it sear away my flesh and transform me.

I straighten and match his glare with one of my own. "No problem, not anymore."

Alarmed, the officer struggles to free his weapon.

I unleash OSOOSI.exe.

The effect is instantaneous. The pedestrians across the street collapse. The struggling officer freezes. His body twitches once before he falls face-first into his steering wheel. His horn trumpets across the night until I shove him back. I remove his shades and peer into his slack face. His eyes are wide with fear and confusion. Slowly his lids lower and I know OSOOSI has sent him into a deep sleep.

"Mal." Machine's face pops up on my interface. Vee peers over his shoulder. They both look unnerved. "What's happening?"

"It's starting," I murmur.

For months, Mar's words have lurked in my mind like a persistent virus. Lasting change could never succeed because we've discarded our compassion in favor of apathy. Inspired by our discussion, I devised a way to forcibly rekindle that empathy.

In one window I stream surveillance vids, stats, and data. In another I monitor OSOOSI's progress. Like a rootkit, it overrides all of a biochip's functions, including its ability to manipulate emotions. Much like when the Anansi hijacked my own biochip, my program now controls them. Every person with a chip connected to the servers that Anansi's spiderbots have hacked falls into a deep stupor. It will only last a few minutes, but I make sure to blast all those True Americans with raw, digitized emotions.

I make sure they feel the humiliation and shame that Mar felt when she tried to use a public restroom. I make sure they feel my impotent rage at being forced to present papers on command and adhere to a curfew. I make sure they feel Machine's sorrow as he paints in code his tribe's struggle for respect both for the Earth and themselves.

I make sure they feel the fear Citizen Americans feel every day they will themselves out of bed.

"Oh my God," Vee whispers, her eyes brimming with tears as she watches my feed. Bodies prostrate on the ground. A girl screaming out of a window for help. Baffled authorities following panicked tweets. "What have you done?"

"What's necessary for them to see and understand." I take a deep breath and steady myself for the storm that's about to break around me. I only have another couple of minutes before people begin waking up, and I need to get this last hurdle over with.

"Do you recognize it, Machine?"

He stares at me blankly and then looks away into his own bank of monitors. My stomach twists at the series of emotions that shuttle across my best friend's face. Confusion, disbelief, hurt, and finally betrayal.

"Augmented immersion." Machine's voice is hollow. "It wasn't enough for you to ruin my chances of ever using my simdisc, you had to go and steal my invention, too?"

Vee glances from him to me. "Mal? Is this true?"

I look away from their accusing gazes. I never wanted it to go down this way, but I knew how this would end as soon as Machine flicked me his simdisc. Its potential was just too great to be wasted on art exhibits about peaceful protests. Especially when its innovative tech is suited for so much more.

"I'm sorry."

"Save it," Machine snaps. "Just fuck off, Mal."

He kills the vid. Vee texts me, warning me to stay away from her, and she, too, disconnects.

For a few precious moments I rest my forehead on the cruiser's roof and listen to the deafening silence of my friends' absence. The Anansi warned me that my idealistic cause would destroy everything around me, and now that I stand amidst the ruins of my old life, I hope it's worth it.

I check on the police officer. Tears drip down his splotchy cheeks and stain his uniform. Good.

It's time to set flame to the world.

Using the Anansi's guerrilla tech, I hijack every live stream I can reach. I blast my message across all social media platforms and whisper it into the helpless minds of those True Americans whose biochips I temporarily control.

My proclamation transitions me from Malkom to Osoosi, Avenger of the Accused and Those Seeking Justice.

The United States of True Americans' most hunted and hated domestic terrorist.

A deep schism infects this nation, one you will not allow to fade. For too long, you've dismissed the experiences of millions in this country. You've averted your eyes from Our plight. You expect Us to wither away in silent misery, but no. As long as We draw breath, you will suffer with Us.

You will feel what We feel.

You will bleed when We bleed.

All the experiences you visit upon Us, We will visit upon you. That is Our gift. You will change, you will rekindle your empathy . . . or We shall dismantle, brick by brick, this country We built for you, and reforge it into a nation truly based on freedom and equality for all.

This is only Our beginning.

IF YOU TAKE MY MEANING

CHARLIE JANE ANDERS

Charlie Jane Anders's (www.charliejane.net) most recent novel is *Victories Greater Than Death*, the first in a new YA trilogy. She's also the author of a nonfiction book, *Never Say You Can't Survive*, and a new collection, *Even Greater Mistakes*. Her previous novels are *The City in the Middle of the Night*, which won a Locus Award; *All the Birds in the Sky*, which won the Nebula, Crawford, and Locus awards; and *Choir Boy*, which won a Lambda Literary Award. Her short fiction has appeared in *Tor.com*, *Boston Review*, *Tin House*, *Conjunctions*, *The Magazine of Fantasy & Science Fiction*, *Wired*, *Slate*, *Asimov's Science Fiction*, *Lightspeed*, and many anthologies. Her story "Six Months, Three Days" won a Hugo Award, and her story "Don't Press Charges and I Won't Sue" won a Theodore Sturgeon Award. Charlie Jane also organizes the monthly Writers With Drinks reading series, and cohosts the Hugo Award–winning podcast *Our Opinions Are Correct* with Annalee Newitz.

They woke up stuck together again, still halfway in a shared dream, as the city blared to life around them. The warm air tasted of yeast, from their bodies and from the bakery downstairs.

Mouth lay on one side of Sophie, with Alyssa on the other, sprawled on top of a pile of blankets and quilted pads. Alyssa couldn't get used to sleeping in a bedpile out in the open, after spending half her life in a nook—but Sophie insisted that's how everybody did things here. Sophie herself hadn't slept in a bedpile for ages, since she went away to school, but it was how she'd been raised.

"I guess it's almost time to go," Sophie whispered, with a reluctance that Alyssa could feel in her own core.

"Yeah," Alyssa muttered. "Can't keep putting it off."

Sophie peeled her tendrils off Mouth and Alyssa carefully, so Alyssa felt as if she was waking up a second time. One moment, Alyssa had a second heart inside her heart, an extra stream of chatter running under the surface of her thoughts. And then it was gone, and Alyssa was just one person again. Like the room got colder, even though the shutters were opening to let in the half-light.

Alyssa let out a low involuntary groan. Her bones creaked, and her right arm had gone half-numb from being slept on.

"You don't have to," Sophie whispered. "If you don't . . . if you'd rather hold off."

Alyssa didn't answer, because she didn't know what to say.

Mouth laughed. "You know Alyssa. Her mind don't change." Mouth's voice was light, but with a faint growl, like she wished Alyssa *would* change her mind, and stay.

The tendrils grew out of the flat of Sophie's ribcage, above her breasts, and they were surrounded by an oval of slightly darker skin with a reddish tint, like a burn that hadn't healed all the way (just a few inches upward and to the left, Sophie's shoulder had an actual burn scar). Someone might mistake the tendrils for strange ornaments, or a family of separate creatures nesting on Sophie's flesh, until you saw how they grew out of her, and the way she controlled their motion.

Whenever Alyssa's bare skin made contact with that part of Sophie's body, she could experience Sophie's thoughts, or her memories.

Whatever Sophie wanted to lay open to her. But when the three of them slept in this pile, Sophie didn't share anything in particular. Just dream slices, or half-thoughts. Mouth still couldn't open herself up to the full communication with Sophie most of the time, but she'd taken to the sleep-sharing.

All three of them had their own brand of terrifying dreams, but they'd gotten better at soothing each other through the worst.

"So that's it." Mouth was already pulling on her linen shift and coarse muslin pants, and groping for her poncho. "You're going up that mountain, and the next time we see you, you'll . . . you'll be like Sophie. The two of you will be able to carry on whole conversations, without once making a sound."

Mouth looked away, but not before Alyssa caught sight of the anxiety on her face. Alyssa could remember when she used to have to guess at what the fuck Mouth was thinking, but that was a long time ago.

Sophie noticed too, and she sat up, still in her nightclothes. "You don't ever have to worry about a thing." Sophie's voice was so quiet, Alyssa had to lean closer to hear. "No matter what happens, after all we've been through, the three of us are in this together."

"Yeah," Alyssa said, punching Mouth's arm with only a couple knuckles. "No amount of alien grafts are going to mess up our situation."

"Yeah, I know, I know, it's just . . ." Mouth laughed and shook her head, like this was a silly thing to worry about. "It's just, the two of you will have this whole other language. I'll be able to listen, but not talk. I wish I could go through that whole transformation, but that's not *me*. I need to keep what's in my head inside my head. I just . . . I want you both to fulfill your potential. I don't want to be holding the two of you back."

Alyssa leaned her head on Mouth's left shoulder, and Sophie's head rested on the right. "You speak to us in all the ways that matter," Sophie said.

"It's true," Alyssa said. "You already tell us everything we ever need to know."

Alyssa had grown up with romances, all about princes, duels, secret meetings, courtships, first kisses, and last trysts. She'd have said that real life could never be half as romantic as all those doomed lovers and secret vows . . . except now, those stories seemed cheap and flimsy, compared to the love she'd found, here in this tiny room.

For a moment, Alyssa wanted to call the whole thing off. Climb the Old Mother later, maybe just go back to bed. But then she shook it off.

She pulled on her boots.

"It's time."

Alyssa had handled all kinds of rough terrain in her smuggler days. She'd even gone into the night without any protective gear one time. So she figured the Old Mother would be nothing. But by the time she got halfway up, her hamstrings started to throb and her thighs were spasming. Next to her, Mouth spat out little grunts of exhaustion. Only Sophie seemed to be enjoying pulling herself up from handhold to handhold.

"Shit shit shit. How the fuck did you ever get used to climbing this beast?" Alyssa wheezed.

Sophie just rolled her shoulders. And mumbled, "It wasn't a choice at first."

Behind them, Xiosphant had gone dark and still, just a valley of craggy shapes without highlights. Except for one light blaring from the top of the Palace, where the Vice Regent could never bring herself to obey the same shutters-up rule that all of her people lived by. Alyssa didn't want to risk falling, so she only half-turned for an instant, to see the storm damage, still unrepaired. And the piles of debris, where the fighting between the Vice Regent's forces and the new Uprising had briefly escalated to heavy cannon fire.

Everyone knew Bianca couldn't last as Vice Regent, but they had no notion whether she would hold on for a few more sleeps, or half a lifetime. Alyssa tried to avoid mentioning her name, even though her face was impossible to avoid, because Sophie still nursed some complicated regrets, and Mouth still felt guilty for helping to lead Bianca down a thorny path. Alyssa was the only one in their little family with clear-cut feelings about the Vice Regent: pure, invigorating hatred.

Alyssa wanted to stop and rest mid-climb, but the cruel slope of the Old Mother included no convenient resting places, especially for three people. And it would be a shitty irony if they almost reached the top, but slipped and fell to their deaths because they wanted to take a breather. The air felt colder and thinner, and Alyssa's hard-won aplomb was being severely tested.

"My fingers are bleeding," Mouth groaned. "Why didn't you mention our fingers would bleed?"

Sophie didn't answer.

They reached the top, which also formed the outer boundary of nothing. Ahead of Alyssa were no sights, no smells (because her nose got numb), and no sensations (because her skin was wrapped in every warm thing she could find). No sound but a crashing wind, which turned into subtle terrible music after a while.

Alyssa's mother and uncles had sent her off to the Absolutists' grammar school back home in Argelo, when she was old enough to walk and read. That was her earliest distinct memory: her mom holding one of her hands and her uncle Grant holding the other, marching her down around the bend in the gravel back road to the front gate where the school convened at regular intervals. That moment rushed back into her head now, as Sophie and Mouth fussed over her and prepared to send her away to another kind of school.

Mouth was pressing a satchel into Alyssa's hands. "I got as many of those parallelogram cakes as I could fit into a bag. Plus these salt buns that taste kind of like cactus-pork crisps. And there are a few of your favorite romances tucked in, too."

"Thank you." Alyssa wrapped her arms around Mouth's neck. She couldn't tell if her eyes stung due to tears or the wind, or both. "I'll be back soon. Don't let Sophie take any more foolish risks."

"I'll do my best," Mouth said. "Say hi to the Gelet from me. And tell them . . ." She paused. "You know what? Just 'hi' is plenty."

Then Sophie was hugging Alyssa. "I can't get over how brave you are. You're the first person ever to visit this city, knowing exactly what's going to happen."

"Oh shut up." Alyssa was definitely starting to cry.

"I mean it. Your example is going to inspire a lot more people to go there. I think Mustache Bob is close to being ready." Sophie choked on the mountain air. "Come back safe. We need you. I love you."

"I love you too. Both of you." Alyssa started to say something else, but a massive, dark shell was rising out of the darkness on the far side of the mountain. "Shit. I need to go."

Alyssa let go of Sophie, clutching the satchel, and gave Mouth one last smile, then turned to face the writhing tentacles of the nearest Gelet. These two slippery ropes of flesh groped the air, reaching out to her.

As soon as they swathed Alyssa in woven moss and lifted her in their tentacles, she freaked out. She couldn't move, couldn't escape, couldn't even breathe. Her inner ear could not truck with this rapid descent down a sheer cliff, and somehow she wasn't ready for this disorientation, even though she'd talked through it with Sophie over and over. Alyssa wanted to yell that she'd changed her mind, this was a mistake, she wanted to go back to her family. But the Gelet would never understand, even if she could make herself heard.

She kept going down and down. Alyssa tried to tell herself this was just like being inside the Resourceful Couriers' sleep nook next to Mouth, except that she was alone, and she couldn't just pop out if she wanted to pee or stretch or anything. She held herself rigid as long as she could, and then she snapped—she thrashed and screamed, twisting her body until her spine wrenched.

A random memory popped up in Alyssa's head: huddling with the other Chancers in the hot gloom of a low-ceilinged basement on the dayside of Argelo, after the Widehome job had gone flipside. (Because they'd burned down the wrong part of the building.) Lucas had squatted next to Alyssa, listing chemical formulas in a low voice, his usual anxiety strategy, and Wendy had fidgeted without making any sound. Every bump and croak above their heads instantly became, in Alyssa's mind, the Jamersons coming to murder them for what they'd done. This was the most terrified Alyssa had ever been, or probably ever would be, but also the closest she'd ever felt to anybody. These people were her indivisible comrades, any of them would die for the others, they were safe together in horrible danger.

Alyssa would always look back on that time in her life as the ideal, the best, the moment when she had a hope-to-die crew by her side, even though she could see all the flaws and the tiny betrayals. Honestly, she'd had way better friend groups since then, including the Resourceful Couriers, but that didn't change how she felt.

Alyssa did not do well with helplessness, or chains, or trusting random strangers. But wasn't that the whole point of this leap into darkness? Alyssa would get this mostly untested surgery, and then she would be able to share unfalsifiable information, and have massively expanded threat awareness thanks to the alien sensory organs. Sometimes you have to be more vulnerable in the short term, so that you can become more formidable later.

They must've reached the foot of the Old Mother without Alyssa noticing, what with all the turbulence. She had a sensation of moving forward rather than downward, and her position in the web of tentacles shifted somewhat as well, and then at last they came to a stop and the Gelet unwrapped her tenderly. She landed on her feet inside a dark tunnel that sloped downward. This was almost scarier than the aftermath of the Widehome job, or at least it was scary in a different way.

They led her down the tunnel, patient with all her stumbles. She couldn't see shit, but at least she was moving under her own power.

Alyssa kept reminding herself of what Sophie had said: she was the first human ever to visit the Gelet city knowing what awaited her there. She was a pioneer.

The air grew warm enough for Alyssa to remove some of the layers of moss, and there were faint glimmers of light up ahead, so she must be entering the Gelet city proper. They needed to find a better name for it than "the midnight city." Something catchy and alluring, something to make this place a destination.

"I'm the first human to come down here with my eyes open, knowing what awaits," Alyssa said, loud enough to echo through the tunnel.

"Actually," a voice replied from the darkness ahead of her, "you're not. You're the second, which is almost as good. Right?"

His name was Jeremy, and he had worked with Sophie at that fancy coffee place, the Illyrian Parlour. Ginger hair, fair skin, nervous hands, soft voice. He'd been in the Gelet city a while already, maybe a few turns of the Xiosphanti shutters, but they hadn't done anything to alter him yet. "I can show you around, though I don't know the city very well, because large areas of it are totally dark." He sounded as though he must be smiling.

"Thanks," Alyssa said. "Appreciate any and all local knowledge."

Jeremy kept dropping information about himself, as if he didn't care at all about covering his tracks. He'd been part of the ruling elite in Xiosphant, studying at one of those fancy schools, until he'd fallen in love with a person of the wrong gender. Fucking homophobic Xiosphanti.

So he'd gone underground, slinging coffee to stressed-out working people, and that had been his first real encounter with anyone whose feet actually touched the ground, instead of walking on a fluffy cloud of privilege.

The Gelet had cleared a room, somewhere in the bowels of their unseeable city, for human visitors, with meager lighting and some packs of food that had come straight from the Mothership. Alyssa and Jeremy opened three food packs and traded back and forth, sharing the weird foods of their distant ancestors: candies, jerky, sandwiches, some kind of sweet viscous liquid.

They bonded over sharing ancient foods, saying things like: "Try this one, it's kind of amazing."

Or: "I'm not sure this stuff has any nutritional value, but at least the aftertaste is better than the taste."

Alyssa chewed in silence and half-darkness for a while, then the pieces fell into place. "Oh," she said to Jeremy. "I just figured out who you are. You're the guy who tried to get Sophie to use her new abilities as a propaganda tool against the Vice Regent. She told us about you."

"I know who you are, too." Jeremy leaned forward, so his face took on more substance. "You're one of the foreign interlopers who helped the Vice Regent to take power in Xiosphant. You stood at Bianca's right hand, until she had one of her paranoid episodes. We have you to thank for our latest misery."

Alyssa couldn't believe she'd shared food with this man just a short time ago.

"I'm going to go for a walk." Once she'd said this out loud, Alyssa was committed, even though it meant getting to her feet and walking out into a dark maze that included the occasional nearly bottomless ravine. At least the Gelet would keep an eye on her.

Probably.

Alyssa tried to walk as if she knew where she was going, as if she felt totally confident that the next step wouldn't take her into a wall or off the edge. She swung her arms and strode forward and tried not to revisit the whole ugly history of regime change in Xiosphant, and her part in it. She had trusted the wrong person, that was all.

What was Alyssa even doing here? All she wanted was to bury her past deeper than the lowest level of this city, but soon she would have the ability to share all her memories with random strangers. And she knew from talking to Sophie that it was easy to share way more than you bargained for—especially at first.

Alyssa might just reach out to someone for an innocent conversation, and end up unloading the pristine memory of the moment when she'd pledged her loyalty to a sociopath. The moment when Alyssa had believed that she'd found the thing she'd searched for since the Chancers fell apart, and that she would never feel hopeless again. Or Alyssa might share an image of the aftermath: herself wading through fresh blood, inside the glitzy walls of the Xiosphanti Palace.

"This was a mistake," Alyssa said to the darkness. "I need to go home. Sophie will understand. Mouth will be relieved. I should never have come here. When they offer to change me, I'll just say no, I'll make them understand. And then they'll have to send me home."

She almost expected Jeremy to answer, but he was nowhere near. She'd wandered a long way from their quarters, and there was no sound but the grumbling of old machines, and the scritching of the Gelet's forelegs as they moved around her.

"I'm not sure I can go through with this," Alyssa told Jeremy, when she'd somehow groped her way back to the living quarters. "I can't stand the idea of inflicting my past on anyone else."

"I'm definitely going ahead with it," Jeremy replied after a while. "When Sophie showed me what she could do, I couldn't even believe what a great organizing tool this could be. This is going to transform the new Uprising, because people will be able to see the truth for themselves, without any doubt or distortion."

Alyssa had wanted to avoid Jeremy, or shut out his self-righteous nattering. But they were the only two humans for thousands of kilometers, and she couldn't go too long without another human voice, as it turned out.

"So you're about to become one of the first members of a whole new species," Alyssa said, "and you're just going to use it as a recruiting tool for another regime change? So you can take power, and then someone else can turn around and overthrow you in turn? Seems like kind of a waste."

"At least I'm not—" Jeremy barked. Then he took a slow breath and shifted. His silhouette looked as if he was hugging himself. "It's not just about unseating your friend Bianca. It's not. It's about building a movement. I spent so much time in that coffeehouse, listening to people who could barely even give voice to all the ways they were struggling. We need a new kind of politics."

"Bianca's not my friend. I hate her too, in ways that you could never understand." Alyssa found more of the rectangular flat candy and ate a chunk. "But if enough people become hybrids, and learn to share the way Sophie shares, we could have something better than just more politics. We could have a new *community*. We could share resources as well as thoughts. We could work with the Gelet."

"Sure, sure," Jeremy said. "Maybe eventually."

"Not eventually," Alyssa said. "Soon."

"What makes you think a lot of people will buy into that vision, if you're not even willing to go through with it yourself?"

Alyssa groaned. "Look. I'm just saying . . . you have to be doing this for the right reasons, or it'll end really badly. You'll lose yourself. I saw it again and again, back in Argelo, people burning up everything they were just for the sake of allegiances or ideology or whatever."

They didn't talk for a while, but then they went back to arguing. There wasn't anything else to do, and besides, by the sound of it, Jeremy had been a good friend to Sophie, back when she'd really needed someone. So Alyssa didn't want him to wreck his psyche, or his heart, or whatever, by turning his memories into propaganda.

"I can be careful." Jeremy sounded as if he was trying to convince himself. "I can share only the memories and thoughts that will make people want to mobilize. I can keep everything else to myself."

"Maybe," was all Alyssa said.

These Xiosphanti believed in the power of repression, way more than was healthy. Or realistic.

"I wish we could ask the Gelet." Jeremy was doing some kind of stretches in the darkness. "It's a terrible paradox: you can only have a conversation with them about the pros and cons of becoming a hybrid, after you've already become a hybrid."

Alyssa went for another walk in the chittering dark—she shrieked with terror, but only inside her own head—and when she got back, Jeremy said, "Maybe you're right. Maybe I'm going to regret this. Maybe I should stick to organizing people the old-fashioned way, winning their trust slowly. I don't know. I'm out of options."

Alyssa was startled to realize that while she'd been trying to talk Jeremy out of becoming a hybrid, she'd talked herself back into it. She needed to believe: in Sophie, in this higher communion. Alyssa kept dwelling on that memory of cowering in a hot basement with the other Chancers, and pictured herself sharing it with Sophie, or Mouth, or anyone. What would happen to that moment when it was no longer hers alone? She wanted to find out.

The Gelet surrounded Alyssa with their chitinous bodies and opened their twin-bladed pincers, until she leaned forward and nuzzled the slick tubes, the slightly larger cousins of the tendrils growing out of Sophie's chest.

An oily, pungent aroma overwhelmed Alyssa for a moment, and then she was experiencing the world as the Gelet saw it. This Gelet showed her a sense-impression of a human, being torn open to make room for a mass of alien flesh that latched onto her heart, her lungs, her bowels. Alyssa couldn't keep from flinching so hard that she broke the connection.

But when they offered her a choice between the operating room and safe passage home, Alyssa didn't even hesitate before peeling off her clothes.

Alyssa had always said that pain was no big thing—like the worst part of pain was just the monotony of a single sensation that overstayed its welcome. But she'd never felt agony like this, not even on all the occasions when she'd been shot or stabbed or shackled inside a dungeon. Sophie had made this operation sound unpleasant, pretty awful, a nasty shock. But Alyssa started screaming curse words in two languages before she was even half-awake, after surgery.

The pain didn't get any better, and the Gelet were super-cautious with their hoarded sedatives, and Alyssa was sure something had gone wrong, perhaps fatally. All she could do was try her best to shut out the world. But . . . she couldn't.

Because, even with her eyes closed and her ears covered, she could sense the walls of the chamber where the Gelet had brought her to rest, and she could "feel" the Gelet creeping around her, and in the passageways nearby. Her brand new tentacles insisted on bombarding her with sensations that her mind didn't know how to process. Alyssa had thought of Sophie's small tentacles as providing her with "enhanced threat awareness," but this was just too much world to deal with.

Alyssa screamed until her throat got sore. Even her teeth hurt from gnashing.

She looked down at herself. The top part of her chest was covered with all of these dark wriggling growths coated with fresh slime, like parasites. Like a mutilation. Before Alyssa even knew what she was doing, she had grabbed two handfuls of tendrils, and she was trying to yank them out of her body with all her strength.

Alyssa might as well have tried to cut off her own hand—the pain flared, more than she could endure. Searing, wrenching. Like being on fire and gutshot, at the same time. And even though her eyes told her that there were foreign objects attached to her chest, her skin (her mind?) told her these were part of her body, and she was attacking herself. She nearly passed out again from the pain of her own self-assault.

The Gelet rushed over, three of them, and now Alyssa could sense their panic even without any physical contact. Her new tentacles could pick up their emotional states, with more accuracy than being able to see facial expressions or body language, and these Gelet were very extremely freaked out. Two of them set about trying to stabilize Alyssa and undo the damage she'd just caused to her delicate grafts, while the third leaned over her.

Alyssa looked up with both her old and her new senses. A big blunt head descended toward her, with a huge claw opening to reveal more of those slimy strips of flesh, and Alyssa felt a mixture of disgust and warmth. She didn't know what she felt anymore, because her reactions were tainted by the sensory input from her tentacles. The Gelet leaning toward her gave off waves of tenderness and concern—but also annoyance and fear—and this was all too much to process.

"I would very much like not to feel any of what I'm feeling," Alyssa said.

Then the Gelet closest to her made contact with her tendrils, and Alyssa had the familiar sensation of falling out of herself, that she'd gotten from Sophie so many times now. And then

—Sophie was standing right in front of Alyssa, close enough for Alyssa to look into her eyes.

"What are you doing? How are you here?" Alyssa asked Sophie, before she bit her tongue. Because of course, Sophie wasn't present at all. This was a memory or something.

Sophie was looking at herself, with her tendrils as fresh as the ones Alyssa had just tried to rip out of herself, and she was reaching out with her tentacles to "feel" the space around her, and Alyssa was doubly aware of Sophie's happiness, thanks to her facial expression and all the chemicals she was giving off. *At last,* Sophie seemed to be saying. *Thank you, at long last my head can be an estuary instead of just this reservoir.*

Alyssa wanted to reach out for Sophie, but Alyssa wasn't even herself in this memory. Alyssa was a Gelet, with a huge lumbering body under a thick shell and woolly fur, with a heart full of relief that this operation might be working better than anyone dared hope—

—Alyssa came back to herself, and looked at the Gelet leaning over her. The disgust was gone, and she "saw" every flex of the segmented legs and every twitch of the big shapeless head, as if they were the tiny habits of a distant family member.

"I'm sorry," Alyssa said, hoping they understood somehow. "I didn't mean to do that, it was just instinct. I hope I didn't ruin everything. I do want to understand all of you, and go home to Sophie as her equal. I really didn't want to, I'm sorry—I didn't want to, it just happened. I'm sorry."

Maybe if her tendrils weren't damaged beyond repair, she'd be able to tell them in a way they understood. As it was, they seemed satisfied that she wasn't going to try and tear herself apart again, and that they'd done everything they could to stabilize her.

Alyssa lay there cursing herself and hoping and worrying and freaking out, until she heard shrieks echoing from the next room. Jeremy. He'd gotten the procedure too, and he'd just woken up, with the same agony and loathing that had struck Alyssa. She wished she could think of something to say to talk him down. Or at least they could be miserable together, if she could talk to him.

This operation was supposed to help Alyssa to form connections, but she was more alone than ever.

The pain ground on and on. Alyssa would never get used to these stabbing, burning, throbbing sensations. Alyssa couldn't tell how much of this discomfort was from the operation, and how much was because she'd attacked herself when she was still healing.

Alyssa rested on a hammock of moss and roots until she got bored and the pain had lessened enough for her to move around, and then she started exploring the city again. This time, she could sense the walkways and all the galleries, all the way down into the depths of the city, and she was aware of the Gelet moving all around her. She started to be able to tell them apart, and read their moods, and all their little gestures and twitches and flexing tentacles began to seem more like mannerisms.

One Gelet, in particular, seemed to have been given the task of watching over Alyssa, and she had a loping stride and a friendly, nurturing "scent." (Alyssa couldn't think of the right word to describe the way she could tell the Gelet's emotions from the chemicals they gave off, but "scent" would do for now.) This Gelet stayed close enough to Alyssa to provide any help she needed, and Alyssa found her presence reassuring, rather than spooky.

Alyssa's new friend had survived the noxious blight that had killed a lot of her siblings in the weave where all the Gelet babies grew. (But she was still a little smaller than all the older Gelet.) When she was brand-new, the other Gelet had made a wish for her that boiled down to "Find reasons for hope, even in the midst of death."

That thought reminded Alyssa of a nagging regret: she and Sophie still hadn't succeeded in helping Mouth to figure out a new name, mostly because Mouth was impossible to please.

And this Gelet, whom Alyssa started calling Hope, had devoted most of her life so far to studying the high wind currents, the jet streams that moved air from day to night and back again. Hope's mind was full of designs for flying machines, to let people examine the upper atmosphere up close, and find a way to keep the toxic clouds away from the Gelet city. But Alyssa's communication with Hope still only went one way. Her new grafts, the tendrils she'd tried to rip out, still hurt worse than daylight. She tried to shield them with her entire body, as if exposure to air would ruin them further.

What if they never worked right?

What if she could never use them to communicate, without feeling as if hot needles were poking in between her first few ribs?

That moment when she'd grabbed with both hands, tearing at her new skin, kept replaying in Alyssa's head, and she wanted to curse herself. Weak, untrustworthy, doomed—she cringed each time.

Hope kept offering her own open pincer and warm tendrils, which always contained some soothing memory of playing a friendly game with some other Gelet, or receiving a blessing from the Gelet's long-dead leader, in some dream-gathering. Alyssa kept wishing she could talk back, explain, maybe learn to become more than just a raw mass of anxiety with nothing to say.

At last, Alyssa decided to take the risk.

She raised her still-sore tendrils to meet Hope's, and tried to figure out how to send, instead of receive. Alyssa brought the awful memory to the front of her mind: her hands, grasping and pulling, so vivid, it was almost happening once again. She felt it flood out of her, but then she wasn't sure if Hope had received it. Until Hope recoiled, and sent back an impression of what Alyssa had looked like to everyone else, thrashing around, and the Gelet rushing in to try and fix the damage.

Alyssa "saw" them touching her body, in the same places that still hurt now, and felt their anxiety, their horror, but also their . . . determination? Bloody-mindedness, maybe. She had the weird sensation of "watching" the Gelet surgeons repairing the adhesions on her chest, while she could still feel the ache inside those torn places. And the strangest part: as she watched the Gelet restore her grafts in the past, Alyssa found the wounds hurt less fiercely in the present.

The pain didn't magically fade to bliss or anything like that, but Alyssa found she could bear it, maybe because she could convince herself that they'd repaired the damage. She started thinking of it more like just another stab wound.

And once Alyssa decided she could use her new organs (antennae?) without wrecking something that was barely strung together, she started opening up more. She shared the memory of this caustic rain that had fallen on her in Argelo, which had seemed to come from the same alkali clouds that had doomed some of Hope's siblings. And the moment when Sophie had first given Alyssa a glimpse of this city and the Gelet living here, suffused with all of Sophie's love for this place.

And finally, the first time Mouth, Sophie, and Alyssa climbed onto the flat shale rooftops of the Warrens while everyone else slept, the three of them holding hands and looking across the whole city, from shadow to flame.

In return, Hope shared her earliest memories as a separate person, which was also the moment she realized that she was surrounded by the dead flesh of her hatchmates, hanging inside this sticky weave. Tiny lifeless bodies nestled against her, all of them connected to the same flow of nutrients that were keeping her alive. The crumbling skin touching hers, the overwhelming chemical stench of decay—with no way to escape, nothing to do but keep sending out distress pheromones until someone arrived to take away the dead. And then later, when Hope had left the web, and all the other Gelet had treated her like a fragile ice blossom.

Alyssa felt sickened in a deep cavity of herself, somewhere underneath her new grafts.

She tried to send back random scraps of her own upbringing, like when her mom and all her uncles died on her, or when she got in her first serious knife fight. But also, cakes, cactus crisps, and dancing. And kissing girls and boys and others, in the crook of this alleyway that curled around the hilt of the Knife in Argelo, where you felt the music more than you heard it, and you could get trashed off the fumes from other people's drinks. Always knowing that she could lose herself in this city, and there were more sweet secrets than Alyssa would ever have enough time to find.

Soon, Alyssa and Hope were just sharing back and forth, every furtive joy and every weird moment of being a kid and trying to make sense of the adults around you—and then growing up but still not understanding, most of the time. The intricacies of the Gelet culture still screwed Alyssa's head ten ways at once, but she could understand feeling like a weird kid, looking in.

Alyssa started to feel more comfortable with Hope than with 99 percent of human beings —until a few sleeps later, Hope showed Alyssa something that sent a spike of ice all the way through her. They were sitting together in one of those rooty-webby hammocks, and Alyssa was drowsing, finally no longer in so much pain that she couldn't rest, and Hope let something slip out. A memory of the past?

No—a possible future.

In Hope's vision, hybrid humans were moving in packs through this city, deep under the midnight chill. Dozens of people, all chattering with their human voices, but also reaching out to each other with their Gelet tendrils. This throng seemed joyful, but there was this undercurrent of dread to the whole thing, which made no sense to Alyssa.

Until she realized what was missing. Hope could see a future where the midnight city was filled with human-Gelet hybrids—but the Gelet themselves were gone.

"I have something I need to show you," Alyssa said to Jeremy.

He jerked his head up and gaped at her, with his new tendrils entwined with those of two Gelet that Alyssa hadn't met yet. He blinked, as if he'd forgotten the sound of language, then unthreaded himself from the two Gelet slowly and stumbled to his feet.

"Okay," Jeremy said. "What did you want to show me? Where is it?"

"Right here." Alyssa gestured at her tendrils.

Jeremy pulled away, just a couple centimeters, but enough so Alyssa noticed.

"Oh," he said. "I hadn't . . . I didn't."

"Don't be a baby," Alyssa said. "I know you bear a grudge, you blame me, I get it. You don't want to let me in."

"It's not even that," Jeremy stammered. "I don't even know. This is all so new, and even just sharing with the Gelet is unfamiliar enough. Being connected to another human being, or another hybrid I mean, would be . . . plus I heard that you . . . I heard you *did* something. You tried to damage yourself. They won't show me the details."

Fucking gossip. Alyssa shouldn't be surprised that the Gelet would be even worse than regular humans about telling everyone her business. The look in Jeremy's eyes made her feel even worse than ever, and her scars felt like they were flaring up.

"This isn't anything to do with me," Alyssa said. "I promise, I won't even share anything about myself, if you're so worried about mental contamination."

"I don't mean to be . . ." Jeremy sucked in a deep breath. "Okay. Okay. Sure. Go ahead."

Among the thousand things that the hybrids were going to need, some kind of etiquette would be one of the most important. A way to use their words to negotiate whether, and how, to communicate with each other nonverbally.

Jeremy leaned forward with his tunic open, and Alyssa concentrated, desperate to keep her promise and avoid sharing anything of her own. But of course, the more she worried about sharing the wrong thing, the more her mind filled with the image of herself inside the Xiosphanti Palace, tracking bloody footprints all over the most exquisite marble floor she'd ever seen.

No no no. Not that. Please.

"Wait a moment." Alyssa paused, when they were just a few centimeters apart. "Just. Need to clear. My head."

Curating your thoughts, weeding out the ugly, was a literal headache. If only Sophie was here . . . but Alyssa didn't want to open that cask of swamp vodka, or she'd never conjure a clean memory.

Breathe. Focus. Alyssa imagined Hope's scary vision, as if it was a clear liquid inside a little ball of glass, cupped in her palms. Separated from all her own thoughts, clean and delicate. She gave that glass ball to Jeremy in her mind as their tendrils made contact, and felt Hope's dream flow out of her.

A few strands of thought, or memory, leaked out of Jeremy in return: a slender boy with pale Calgary features and wiry brown hair, pulling his pants on with a sidelong glance at his forbidden lover. Bianca and her consort Dash, smiling down from a balcony as if the crowd beneath them was shouting tributes, instead of curses. A woman holding a tiny bloody bundle on a cobbled side street, wailing.

"Ugh, sorry," Jeremy said. And then Hope's vision of a possible future sunk in, and he gasped.

"That's . . ." Jeremy disconnected from her and staggered like a drunk, leaning into the nearest wall. "That's . . ."

"I know," Alyssa said. "I don't think . . . I don't think I was supposed to see that."

"We can't let that happen." Jeremy turned away from the wall and sobbed, wiping his eyes and nose with his tunic sleeve.

"Our ancestors already invaded their whole planet. This would be worse." Alyssa looked at her knuckles. "Way worse than when I helped those foreigners to invade your city. I'd rather . . . I'd rather die than be a part of another injustice."

The two of them walked around the Gelet city for a while. Watching small groups of children all connected to one teacher, puppeteers putting on a show, musicians filling the tunnels with vibrations, a team of engineers repairing a turbine. A million human-Gelet hybrids would need centuries just to understand all of this culture. Sophie had barely witnessed a tiny sliver of this city's life, and she'd spent way more time here than either Alyssa or Jeremy had so far.

"We can help, though." Alyssa broke a silence that seemed near-endless. "They didn't turn us into hybrids for our own sake. Right? They need us to help repair the damage that our own people did. Hope showed me some designs for new flying machines that could help them figure out how to keep the toxic rain clouds away, but they can't stand even partial sunlight."

Jeremy covered his face with one hand and his tendrils with the other. His new tentacles retreated behind his back, wrapping around like a pair of arms crossed in judgment. He shivered and let out low gasps. Alyssa wasn't sure if he was still crying, or what she ought to do about it. She just stood there and watched him, until he pulled himself together and they went and got some stewed roots.

"We're not going to make it, are we?" Jeremy said to his hand. "We can't do this. We won't change enough people in time to help them. I know you did something terrible, right after they changed you, and I . . ." He couldn't bring himself to say what came next. "What I did was much worse. I can't. I can't even stand to think about it."

Between her new tentacles and all her ingrained old skills of reading people, Alyssa felt overwhelmed by sympathy for Jeremy. She could feel his emotions, maybe more clearly than her own, almost as if she could get head-spinning drunk on them. That sour intersection between fellowship and nausea. At least now she knew that she wasn't the only one who'd had a nasty reaction after the Gelet surgery.

Jeremy was waiting for Alyssa to say something. She wasn't going to.

After a long time, he said again, "We're not going to make it." Then he walked away, still covering his mouth and tendrils, shrouding himself with all of his limbs.

Alyssa didn't see Jeremy for a few sleeps.

Meanwhile, she was busy gleaning everything she could from the Gelet, even though her brain hurt from taking in so many foreign memories, and concepts that couldn't be turned into words. She learned way more than she would ever understand. She kept pushing herself, even when all she wanted to do was to be alone.

Hope kept turning up, but Alyssa also got to know a bunch of other Gelet, most of them older but not all. Some of them had come from other settlements originally, and she caught some notions of what life was like in a town of just a few hundred or few thousand Gelet, where everybody really knew everyone else by heart. She got to witness just the merest part of what a debate among the Gelet would feel like.

In her coldest moments, Alyssa caught herself thinking, *I need to learn everything I can, in case one day these people are all gone and my descendants are the only ones who can preserve these memories.* That thought never failed to send her into a rage at herself, even angrier than when she thought she had ruined her own tendrils.

She thought of what Mouth had said to her once, about cultural survival. People died, even nations flamed out, but you need somebody left behind to carry the important stuff forward.

"You were right."

Jeremy had caught Alyssa by surprise when she was dozing in a big web with a dozen Gelet, waiting for their dead Magistrate to show up. Jeremy seemed way older than the last time Alyssa had seen him, his shoulders squared against some new weight that was never going to be lifted away. He faced her eye to eye, not trying to cover any part of himself or turn aside.

"Wait. What was I right about?" Alyssa said. "The last time I won an argument, it involved handfuls of blood and a punctured lung. I've stopped craving vindication."

"There's so much more at stake than who sits inside that ugly Palace back home in Xiosphant." Jeremy shook his head. "I came here hoping to find a new way to organize people against the Vice Regent, but we have more important work to do. You were right about all of it: being a hybrid isn't just a means to an end, it's way more important than that."

"Oh."

Alyssa looked at Jeremy's shy, unflinching expression, and a wave of affection caught her off guard. They'd gone through this thing together, that almost nobody else alive could understand. She couldn't help thinking of him almost as a sleepmate—even though they'd only slept near each other, not next to each other.

"We can't just send people here and expect them to handle this change on their own. Anyone who comes here is going to need someone to talk them through every step of the process, someone who understands how to be patient," Jeremy said. "So . . . I've made a decision. I think it would be easier to show than to tell."

Alyssa understood what he meant after a moment, and she let her tendrils relax, slacken, so his own could brush against them.

She was terrified that she would show him the moment when she tried to rip these things out of her body—so of course that's what she did show him. The screaming panic, the feeling of her fingers grasping and tearing, trying to rip out her own heart.

Jeremy stumbled, flinched, and let out a moan . . . and then he accepted Alyssa's memory. And he gave back a brief glimpse of his own worst moment: Alyssa was Jeremy, lashing out, with a snarl in his throat, the heel of his hand colliding with the nearest terrified Gelet, a blood-red haze over everything. *I'll kill you all* repeating in his head, *I'll tear you apart, kill you kill you.* The new alien senses flooding into

Jeremy's brain, bringing back all the times when he'd needed to look over his shoulder with every step he took.

"It's okay," Alyssa said, wrapping her arms around Jeremy under the roots of his tentacles. "It's really okay."

"It's not okay." Jeremy trembled. "I'm a monster. At least nobody was badly hurt."

"You're not a monster. You were just scared. We both were." Alyssa clutched him tighter, until he clung to her as well. "We prepared ourselves, but we weren't ready. We need to make sure it goes better next time."

"That's what I was going to tell you about." Jeremy relaxed a little. "This is what I decided." He sent Alyssa another vision, this time of a future he'd envisioned.

Jeremy was here, still inside the midnight city, studying everything the Gelet could teach him. And then, when more humans arrived from Xiosphant, Alyssa saw Jeremy greeting them. Guiding them around the city, preparing them, talking them through every step of the way. The Jeremy in the vision grew old, but never went back to the light.

Alyssa had to say it aloud: "You want to stay here? Forever?"

"I . . . I think it's the right thing to do," Jeremy whispered. "I can organize, I can be a leader, all of that. Just down here, rather than back in Xiosphant. Humans are going to keep coming here, and there needs to be someone here to help. Otherwise, more people will . . ."

"More people will react the way you and I did." Alyssa shuddered. "Yeah."

Alyssa found herself sharing a plan of her own with Jeremy. She imagined herself going back to Xiosphant, back to Sophie and Mouth—but not just helping them to convince more people to come here and become hybrids. She pictured herself carrying on Jeremy's work: finding the people who were being crushed by all the wrong certainties, helping them to form a movement. Maybe opening someplace like that coffee shop where Sophie and Jeremy used to work. Giving people a safe place to escape from all that Xiosphanti shit.

"You were right too," Alyssa told Jeremy. "People in Xiosphant need to come together. If they had someplace to go in that city, maybe more of them might be open to thinking about coming here."

"Can you take care of Cyrus, though?" Jeremy sent a brief impression of the biggest marmot Alyssa had ever seen, purring and extending blue pseudopods in every direction. "I left him with a friend, but he needs someone reliable to look after him. Sophie already knows him."

"Sure," Alyssa said, hugging Jeremy with their tendrils still intertwined.

Alyssa stayed a while longer in the midnight city, healing up but also keeping Jeremy company. After she left, he might not hear another voice for a while—and weirdly, the longer Alyssa had these tendrils, the more important verbal communication seemed to her, because words had a different kind of precision, and there were truths that could only be shared in word-form. Alyssa introduced Jeremy to Hope, and explained in a whisper about everything she'd been through, and Jeremy introduced Alyssa to some of his own Gelet friends too.

Her surgical scars settled down to a dull ache, and then slowly stopped hurting at all, except for when she strained her muscles or slept weird. The new body parts and what remained of the pain both felt like they were just part of Alyssa, the same way the Chancers and the Resourceful Couriers would always be. "I guess it's time," Alyssa said to herself. She walked up towards the exit to the Gelet city with Hope on one side and Jeremy on the other, though Jeremy planned to turn back before they reached the exit.

Almost without thinking, Alyssa extended her tendrils so she was connected to both Jeremy and Hope, and the three of them shared nothing in particular as they walked. Just a swirl of emotions, fragments of memory, and most of all, a set of wishes for the future that were just vague enough to be of comfort. They stayed in this three-way link until the first gusts of freezing air began to filter down from the surface of the night.

BEYOND THESE STARS
OTHER TRIBULATIONS OF
LOVE

USMAN T. MALIK

Usman T. Malik (www.usmanmalik.org) is a Pakistani-American writer and doctor. His fiction has been reprinted in several year's best anthologies, including *The Best American Science Fiction and Fantasy*. He has been nominated for the World Fantasy Award and the Nebula Award, and has won the Bram Stoker and the British Fantasy awards. Usman's debut collection *Midnight Doorways: Fables from Pakistan* was published in early 2021 to great praise from Silvia Moreno-Garcia, Ken Liu, Karen Joy Fowler, Kelly Link, and others.

After his mother got dementia, Bari became forgetful. It was little things, like hanging up the wet laundry on time so it wouldn't stink; spraying pesticide on their patch of sea wall against the adventures of crabs and mutant fish; checking the AQI meter before leading his mother out for her evening walk along New Karachi's polluted shoreline. Was cognitive decline contagious? Bari wondered. Did something break in your brain, too, when you took care of people who once held you on their lap, helped you count the last straggling trees in the mohalla courtyard? Overwhelmed by their needs and your grief, perhaps you were split into two halves, each perpetually being run into the ground.

It wasn't like he had a sibling or a spouse to lean on. Just him and his waddling, bed-wetting, calling-into-the-dark-of-the-house mother: "Bari, baita Bari. Where are you?" At three in the morning, when he went into her room and slumped onto her bed, she clutched his arm and held it to her chest, whispering, "I had a dream I was alone. Your Abba died and I was alone. Bari, is he back from Amin's shop yet?" Bari, running his fingers through her hair and shushing her, would say, "Any minute now, Ma. We're good. You're good. Sleep, Ma," even as he began to doze and dream himself. Of a city with clear blue skies, a firm shoreline, and potable water, where large tanks owned by water mafias didn't roam the streets like predators and sinkholes the size of buildings didn't irrupt into an ever-rising, salty sea. Sometimes he sang softly her favorite couplet from Iqbal: sitaron se agay jahan aur bhee hain. Beyond these stars glitter other worlds, beyond this trial other tribulations of love.

Any minute now, Ma. We will be good.

In his better moments, he even believed it. He had a job when thousands didn't. They had a five-marla home with its own strip of backyard abutting the sea wall that rose tall and concrete against the vagaries of the Arabian Sea. They could afford clean air and water at home and masks to venture outside.

Bari continued to worry, though. Unchecked oversights grow into big misfortunes. What if one morning, in his rush to the bus stop, he forgot to administer her blood thinner? His company's insurance covered only weekly nurse visits to check on her pills. What if she had another mini-stroke when he was at work? The telemonitors wouldn't get there for an hour, and Ma couldn't follow remote prompts. What if Bari forgot to take his own insulin shot, ended up in a coma?

The more he worried, the more distractible he felt, the more mentally rumpled. Bari hated uncertainty. The irrefutability of Newtonian physics was why he had chosen engineering. Now that he could envision all the things that could—would—go wrong, he began to have anxiety dreams, and this more than anything else helped decide him when New Suns came knocking on his door.

Would he be interested? the suit inquired. Pioneering, world-changing work, as they were sure he knew. Paid very well. Comprehensive healthcare coverage, individual and family, was included, of course.

Bari asked for a month to consider the proposal, but his mind was already made up. He used the time to plan out exactly what he'd ask for, the minutiae of his demands.

Yes, he said when they returned. But I have conditions.

When he was a boy and the world was a more breathable place, Bari once listened to his daadi tell a story about a neighborhood couple.

After an accident on the highway, the man's wife of 40 years fell into an irrevocable coma. The man brought her home and rearranged everything in the house to suit her needs. Every day he fed her, bathed her, turned her over so she wouldn't get bedsores, wheeled her around the block, put perfume on her when friends and family came to visit. No one, not their kids or grandkids, were allowed to feed or bathe her. For years he did this religiously, with neither a nod nor a smile from his sleeping love.

One day the man fell ill. His son came over and tried to help, but the man fought him. Shivering, the man dragged himself from room to room, trying to follow his daily routine. Eventually he collapsed. He was taken to the hospital, and his son and daughter-in-law moved in to take care of the comatose woman. When the son spooned mashed potatoes into his mother's mouth, the woman trembled. When he lifted her so his wife could clean her bottom and apply a lubricant, she sighed. The next morning, when they carried her to the bathtub and sponged her back and arms, the woman opened her eyes for the first time in seven years, looked at her son, and died.

Bari was greatly affected by this story. Why did she die? What happened to her husband? Did the children feel guilty that she died on their watch?

Sweeping aside the black curls spilling over Bari's forehead, Daadi said, She died because, despite the way she was, she recognized their touch.

So what? Bari said.

In the way of grandmothers everywhere, Daadi shook her head and gave him a knowing smile.

Bari never forgot the way that story made him feel.

The little boy was staring at his duffel bag, which had a map of Old Karachi on it. Bari hadn't flown before, and he'd thrown a couple of Lexotanils into the duffel. When the airship took off, he propped his head on a pillow and dry-swallowed a pill.

Bari turned to the boy. "It wasn't pretty even then," he told him. "The sky was too diluted, and we hardly had any green belts. But we did have incredible food. Lal Qila and Burns Road and Boat Basin. Camel rides at Clifton Beach. The sea wasn't menacing back then, you see. Walking along its heaving blue made us sad and happy and lonely, but we weren't afraid."

We were afraid of other things, he thought. We could go missing and turn up in gunnysacks. Get shot in the face at signals by cell phone snatchers.

He didn't feel the need to tell the boy that. Instead, he closed his eyes in the airship; and opened them next to his mother. It was three a.m., and she was moaning in sleep. Bari, baita Bari. He knelt down and kissed her forehead with metal teeth. She fumbled for his hand, and he gave her his cold aluminum paw. Her forehead crinkled, but she didn't let go. Whispering "I'm here, Ma," he slid into bed next to her and stayed there stroking her forehead till she fell sound asleep.

Bari blinked, and with a rise and a swoop he was back in the airship, the aftersense vertiginous, as if he were rocking in the sea. The little boy was snoring, an intermittent teakettle whistle. Bari popped earbuds in and listened to the pilot announce that they would dock at the IPSS in three hours, after which the real journey would begin.

Seven years, Bari thought as his eyelids drooped. Seven years, three months, and four days.

He'd have plenty of time to spend with his mother.

The problem wasn't splitting his consciousness in two, Dr. Shah had told Bari. It was traveling when split.

Bari said he knew. He'd been studying their work for years, had done the calculations himself.

Decades ago, the Penrose-Hameroff theory ushered in the new era of quantum consciousness: Although gravity prevents the occurrence of large objects in two places simultaneously, subatomic particles can exist at opposite ends of the universe at the same time. Therefore consciousness—which Penrose and Hameroff argue arises because of quantum coherence in the brain—has potential for omnipresence. The trick, as New Suns discovered, was to lift consciousness into a superposition, akin to the superposition of subatomic particles, and help it lock into distinct space-time coordinates.

Their work, however, was limited to rabbit and murine models. Human consciousness was another matter.

"We're reasonably confident that we can lift your mind without killing you and allow it to move between calibrated consensus points," Dr. Shah said. He was a short man with a military cut, a salt-and-pepper mustache, and a brisk manner that reminded Bari of a certain Pakistani general who was often on PTV when Bari was a kid. "But there's no saying what might happen once the starship picks up speed."

"You're talking about time dilation," Bari said.

"You've done your homework."

"Yes."

"So you understand that when you decide to flip back and forth between the starship and your mother's house, your consciousness wouldn't just be locking into another physical space but another *velocity* of time's passage."

"Yes."

"One month of your interstellar travel would age her by nearly twenty years. If what you're proposing doesn't work, you'd effectively have killed your mother by climbing aboard that starship. At least as far as you're concerned. Perhaps yourself too. All bets are off with an unmoored mind."

"I will assume the risk."

"No one's ever done this, you know."

"Someone has to." Bari smiled. "It's the future, right?"

"Well, we're sure as hell not publicizing it." Dr. Shah looked at him for nearly a minute. "I hope your reasons for doing this are worth it."

Bari told him they were. But on his way home, he wondered.

At 13:00 on October 9, 20__, three days before his forty-fifth birthday, Bari, along with 699 other passengers, took off from the InterPlanetary Space Station on *New Suns V* for a neighboring star. Not one of them would return to Earth—there was no point—except Bari. He would visit Earth several times a day, thousands of times a month.

Bari made sure he was interfaced with the home AI for his mother's three a.m. night terrors. Breakfast, pill time, her morning bath. He'd be there when the Imtiaz van shrieked to a halt outside their door twice a week and masked men in drab shalwar kameez unloaded and carried her groceries inside. There for lunch, for the biweekly afternoon poetry reading, and the six p.m. sundowning with her subsequent confusion and fright. On rubberized wheels he'd roll over to her, take her hand, and lead her to the dinner table, where, in his simulacrum voice, he'd ask her how her day went, whether she took all her pills, knowing full well she had, and if the food was too salty, because that might worsen her blood pressure. In the time it took him to finish emptying his bowels on the starship, he'd be done with her doctors' appointments.

It was satisfying, this split existence. A long interstellar travel had been transformed into the most meaningful time of his life.

"I can't explain it," he told Mari, a pretty thirty-seven-year-old dentist who'd escaped an abusive husband and hoped to make a new life on another world. They'd clicked at breakfast on the third day, and he saw no point in withholding this part of himself, his journey. "I just have to *decide* where I want to be, and I'm there."

Mari was fascinated. "Do you feel older when you return here?"

"You mean twenty seconds later?" He laughed. "Not really. Sometimes I feel hazy. As if a part of my head is still in a different time zone."

"Well, isn't it?"

He upended the protein can over his mouth and crumpled it. Chocolate paste dribbled onto his tongue. And he was back at home with Ma, staring at the leftovers of last night's chicken karahi. "Finish that, Bari," Ma said, her voice unusually strong today, carrying an authority he remembered from childhood. "Can't waste food, especially these days." But he had no mouth to eat the karahi with. He picked at it with a fork to make her happy, and they watched the news for an hour before she settled down for her midday nap.

Bari flicked back to the breakfast table, the taste of chocolate bitter and chalky on his tongue. "I suppose it is," he told Mari.

On the third day of their meeting they made love, and on the fourth, but the second time Bari was distracted. Ma had aged thirteen years and suffered a fall that nearly fractured her pelvis. He still couldn't believe he forgot to secure the living room rug. Which reminded him he still needed to install the bathroom handholds. Sensing his mood, Mari pulled him close and whispered, "Stay. Don't go," but, mid-thrust, he was already in Saddar Bazaar with a human escort, arguing with a vendor about the price of aluminum fixtures. He couldn't have been away more than a few ship-seconds, but when he blinked, he saw Mari had rolled away from him.

"What?" he said.

"Your pupils," she said, watching him from the end of the bed. "They dilate, you know."

He didn't know. "I wanted to make sure she was safe."

She nodded, eyes distant. "I understand."

They remained friendly, but didn't make love after that.

Bari began to have headaches. As a child he had migraines with a premonitory phase: his mood changed before the onset of one. This was followed by numbness in his left arm and finally the eruption of pain in his occipital area. These interplanetary headaches, though, were different. They occurred after each trip and were succeeded by throbbing behind his eyes, fatigue, and brain fog. He felt at once caged and uprooted, as if gravity had given up on him and he was floating inside a balloon. Chronically jetlagged, he thought. His mind felt stretched like taffy. Sometimes he couldn't remember whether he was about to go to Ma's or had already been.

Mari noticed it. "You don't look so good," she told him in the exercise room, where he was trudging after a soccer ball.

He kicked the ball to her, and the movement made him dizzy. "I'm fine. Just not sleeping too well is all."

"Well, you are up with her half the night, aren't you."

"My sleep hygiene is pristine here."

"You think your brain cares?" She tossed him the ball. "Bari, I can't imagine the kind of strain your mind's going through living in virtually two dimensions. You need a break. Take a day off."

Sure, he told her. Excellent idea.

Of course he didn't.

As days/years slipped by, the boundaries between here and there grew porous. A blink and he'd be in Ma's kitchen taking the roti off the stove. Another and she'd be sitting in his cabin aboard the starship, rocking back and forth, whispering longings about his father and Bari's childhood home. She was by his side when they strolled along the graffiti-painted sea wall of New Karachi, and with him before the ship's porthole, gazing at the vastness beyond.

Beyond these stars glitter other worlds, beyond this trial other tribulations of love.

Some nights he gasped awake, sure that his mother was dead.

He'd flick to his mother's room and stand in the dark, watching her chest stutter, frail like a flattened dough pera. When the morning light yawned into the room, it was he who was lying in that bed, or another bed in a different place, being watched by himself.

When he told Mari about the nocturnal episodes, she recommended he talk to the ship doctor, get a sleep apnea study.

Bari learned that if he took melatonin before sleep, the hypnagogic osmosis tended to dissipate. No longer would Ma sit in the chair in his cabin, murmuring to herself— nor would he suddenly find himself by her side when he hadn't intended it. He could close his eyes and not be pulled, like a restless tide, to the moon of her existence.

I'm tired, he thought often. So tired.

Yet it had only been a couple weeks on the starship.

He was in the TV room watching a rare episode of *Uncle Sargam* when the end came. Junaid Jamshed had just begun strumming the show's theme song, the puppets clapping and swaying to the tune, when Bari felt an electric jolt up the back of his head. His nostrils filled with the smell of gulab jaman, a dessert he hadn't had since he was twenty. Before he could mull over either sensation, he was in Ma's bedroom, looking down at her. She was on her back. The stroke had wiped the worry creases off her forehead. It didn't seem like she had suffered. If he strained, he could conjure a smile at the corner of her lips.

You were here, Bari-jaan, she might have said. With me before I went.

Bari was still murmuring Faraz's *Let it be heartache; come if just to hurt me again* when the ambulance came to take her away.

He buried her next to his father. It was a surprisingly clear day, AQI reading at 450, the din of waves against the sea wall loud in the graveyard. Ma would have liked to walk today, he thought, as they lowered her into the grave and shoveled dirt on her. After, he stayed watching other bereaved wander among the graves, lighting candles. Such a pointless exercise. Sooner or later the sea was coming for their dead.

When he flicked back, Mari was waiting for him with a bowl of chicken soup. "Eat it," she said. Later, clothed, she climbed into bed with him and held his head in her lap, until he fell into a place unmarked by time for the first time in weeks. Decades.

And if in his dreamlessness Bari cried out, a distress signal sent to the dark between the stars, Mari never mentioned it.

A MASTERY OF GERMAN

MARIAN DENISE MOORE

Marian Denise Moore lives in Louisiana and works in the city of New Orleans. She converted a childhood love of science into a career in computer programming, and her love of literature led to her writing both poetry and fiction. In 1998, she became a member of the NOMMO Literary Society, a writing workshop led by New Orleans writer and activist Kalamu ya Salaam. Her fiction has been published in *Crossroads: Tales of the Southern Literary Fantastic*, *Rigorous*, and *Dominion: An Anthology of Speculative Fiction from Africa and the African Diaspora*. Her poetry, which has been collected in *Louisiana Midrash*, has appeared in *Drumvoices Revue: A Confluence of Literary, Cultural & Vision Arts*, *The Louisiana Review*, *Bridges*, *Reform Judaism.org*, *Asimov's Science Fiction*, and *Mending for Memory: Sewing in Louisiana Essays, Stories, and Poems*.

Somewhere in the world, there is a man, seventy years old, a native New Orleanian who has never left the city except for the occasional Category 5 hurricane. He has a sixth-grade education but has always held some type of paying job. However, if you ask him a question in German, he will answer you without hesitation in an accent reminiscent of the region around Heidelberg. I still remember watching one of our Belgium-born board member's eyes widen in shock as Victor—that's his name—responded to a question in German. The executive immediately asked Victor where he had served in the army. No, he did not serve in Germany, or anywhere else for that matter, for as I said, he had rarely left the city and has never actually left the state.

Victor Johnston was sixty-five then and secure in his position as an elder, so he laughed in the manager's face. If asked, Victor could have also told the manager what it felt like to be an eleven-year-old girl and how it felt to have your period start thirty minutes before you left for school. But the executive did not ask those questions. Their conversation was brief, so the manager didn't notice that Victor's vocabulary was stuck at the level of an eighteen-year-old girl, my age when my family returned to the U.S. after my father's third tour of duty. He turned to our second trial subject and missed the problem and the promise of Engram's newest spotlight project. That was exactly what I planned.

"We need a win, Candace," Lloyd said. He pulled his hand through his sandy hair, got up from his desk, and checked the door to his office, which I had already snicked closed. The move disguised his need to pace. I had struggled when describing him to my father. He was tall, but with too much nervous energy to be a golfer. I had decided on a retired track star who had graduated to the coaching ranks. He stood beside the desk now, too high-strung to sit down. Despite the chill of the room, his jacket was slung over the back of his chair.

"We need a win." Translation: "I need a win." No difference. Lloyd was my supervisor. If he won, I won.

"I thought you wanted me to hang back and shadow Helene?" I said.

"Yes, well. About that." Lloyd sat on the edge of his desk. "I need you to take over one of Helene's projects. She's taking leave early."

"Before June? Before the bonuses are calculated? Isn't one of her projects on the spotlight list?"

I watched the flicker of annoyance cross Lloyd's face. Poor Lloyd. Saddled with two women to mentor—even if one of them did bring him plenty of reflected glory. I was willing to become a second star in his constellation. I had moved to New Orleans because of the opportunities presented by a new and hungry company.

"Doctor's orders," Lloyd said. "Nevertheless, she says that she will be checking in occasionally. That should be enough to keep her from losing out on a bonus because her baby decided to raise her blood pressure." He took another nervous pace to the door and back.

"I want you to take the Engram project," he said. "It's not on the company bonus timeline. But I need you to either kill it or bring it to some sort of conclusion. The technical lead is giving Helene the runaround."

"I've never heard of an R&D project named Engram," I said uncertainly.

"Because it is more research than development, I suspect," Lloyd said, frowning. "You need to talk to the lead. I think that he told Helene that he'd gotten approval on human trials."

Lloyd hailed his computer and directed it to send me the project plan. I felt the phone in my pocket vibrate as the new task jostled itself into my short list of responsibilities. "Kill it or bring it to conclusion" sounded like an execution order.

I should tell you what type of company Engram was at that time. For one thing, Engram wasn't the name. The name of the company was QND, named after Quinton Nathanael Delahousse, a MacArthur-recognized geneticist from LSU. QND was renamed Engram when it became the most successful product. When Lloyd handed me the Engram project, QND was five years old and still a startup as far as the tax laws of Louisiana were concerned. Some of the founding staff wagged that QND stood for "quick and dirty" because most of the projects were out the door faster than any other pharmaceutical company. During the first five years, most of our products were generics of existing drugs. None of them was the fame-making formulations that the Delahousse name seemed to promise. The spotlight projects were the high-risk, high-yield portfolios that QND hoped would support them after the state tax credits expired. Helene's spotlight had been underway since the company's founding and was finally coming to a close.

I weaved my way through the alleys of cubicles on my way back to my desk. Pausing, I poked my head around one of the seven-foot walls of textured fabric. Helene looked as busy as I anticipated. She was on the phone, firmly rehearsing the steps of some procedure or another. Her voice was level but I could see the lines around her mouth deepen as she became more annoyed. The desk was full of folders, no doubt one for me. Helene was famous for killing trees. She'd had one presentation crash and burn because of a hard drive failure one day before an implementation review.

Glancing up at me, Helene nodded and tapped a cream folder on the top of the stack. "Yours," she mouthed.

I took the folder and retreated to my own austerer desk. I dropped Helene's folder into an almost empty desk drawer where it could rattle around with the one pencil and a cheap ad pen. I promised myself to check it for notes in Helene's handwriting before I shredded it.

I tapped the keyboard embedded in my desk and brought up the project timeline that Lloyd had already sent me. Within ten minutes, I kicked my chair away and stood over the wavering image of the project plan. Pages of bullet points were followed by empty spaces. Months of deadlines blinked in red because the dates had passed with no input. Pushing the display back into the desk surface, I leaned over it and silently cursed Lloyd, Helene, and the entire board structure of QND.

I was still standing when a triple rap came on the metal frame of my cubicle wall. I looked up from my angry notes to see Helene. She pulled my rolling armchair toward her and lowered herself into the padded seat. Helene was "all baby," as my elderly aunts would say. Her arms and legs were toned and model-thin from years of yoga—she was always inviting me—and her face was the polished nectarine of a southern aristocrat framed by frosted blond hair. The baby had concentrated all of its gravitas to her middle, and she sat solidly in my desk chair with one hand perched protectively on the beach ball protrusion above her lap. Do I sound jealous? Maybe I was. It didn't matter that it had taken four years for her to become the yardstick by which I was now judging myself.

"What do you think?" she asked, pointing through me to the display on the desk. "I suggested that Lloyd give you this project," she added before I could answer.

"There are a lot of empty spaces in this plan," I said carefully.

"Yes, I know." Helene's eyes seared the surface of my desk pointedly. "There's more in the folder that I gave you. Desmond's not fond of filling out status reports. I have to drag information out of him every week. Maybe he will respond better to you."

I felt my back tense, but I retained my casual posture. And why would he respond better to me?

"When is your last day?" I asked instead. "Lloyd said that you will brief me on the project. Why is it so open-ended? That isn't QND's standard procedure."

Helene flipped her wrist over and examined her watch. "My schedule won't allow that," she said. "Desmond is in the downtown office today. You should introduce yourself. Ask him to brief you." She flipped an errant strand of blond hair away from her face and I saw the sheen of sweat.

Leaning over, I thumbed down the heated fan that sat beneath my desk. Immediately, the chill of the air-conditioning rushed into my cozy enclave. When I checked the caged thermostat that morning, someone had managed to set the temperature to sixty-five degrees. I wasn't the only one on the floor wearing a sweater, but Helene was not one of us.

"Tell me about the team lead then," I said. "You said that his name was Desmond?" I wanted to sit down, but I didn't want to sit in the lower visitor chair. "The team lead isn't a geneticist?"

Helene looked at her watch again. "Desmond is Dr. Desmond Walker," she said. "I've known him since—" She shrugged. "Before QND. He and my brother were at Jesuit together. Delahousse was impressed with his research work at Hebei University in Shijiazhuang." Her tongue stumbled over the Chinese names. "I believe that his medical degree came from Meharry in Tennessee. Have you heard of Meharry?"

Only one of the best medical schools in the HBCU universe, I thought, but I only nodded.

"I have never heard of it," Helene said. "Dr. Delahousse was very effusive. I say this only so you understand—Desmond is a favorite. He has had results; I've seen the animal trials. Give me your phone?"

Helene fiddled with the calendar function and announced finally, "Desmond has an opening in two hours. I will add you to his schedule and you can get your questions answered. This should be easy. Let Desmond continue his research while you fill in the paperwork to appease Lloyd. I would have done more, but"—she patted her burgeoning belly—"this afternoon I have to review the press conference release. And then there's the review of the drug insert that we negotiated with the FDA." She began to rise.

"You'll come with me for the initial meeting," I said quickly.

"You can do this," she said, frowning. "All you have to do—"

"I would rather if he doesn't know that I'm his new PM immediately," I said. "You didn't include that in the meeting invitation, I hope?"

"You should not ambush Dr. Walker."

Oh, he's Dr. Walker now, I thought. "I don't plan to," I said. "I want him to explain the project without the expectation that I know anything. I'll read your notes." I pulled the slim folder from the desk drawer and slid it over the recessed keyboard. "But I don't want the type of canned rosy explanation that is created for a new boss. I want to really understand."

Helene sighed, but I knew that she was conceding. "We'll both be

working through lunch in that case," she said. "Pass by my office in two
hours and I'll take you down and introduce you."

Desmond Walker's office was a surprising modern emulation of Victo-
rian clutter. Almost every surface was covered with personal effects. An
electronic frame displayed a selection of cruise photos of his wife and
two young sons at some Caribbean-looking location. There was one
tall bookshelf on which some books were neatly arranged and others
lay on their sides, titles obscured and edges stained from use. Framed
awards lined the walls, their lettering too small to read from my chair.
Instead of focusing on them, I kept my hands in my lap as Helene
ran through a brief introduction. Keeping her promise, she informed
Dr. Walker that I was being introduced to all of the technical leads in
Lloyd's division.

And why had that never actually happened? I wondered as I
watched Desmond Walker's gaze shift from Helene to me with some
wariness. He was tall, barrel-chested, and—as I had surmised from his
choice of college—Black. He was darker than I expected and probably
in his late forties; but I was constantly fighting my expectation that all
elite Black New Orleanians—the ones who could afford private schools
like Jesuit—were Creole, and the expectation that all Creoles were
light skinned. His hair was cropped as short as my father's, even though
he had grown up in an era when dreadlocks were the cultural standard.
But one could hardly carry dreadlocks into one's forties, I told myself.

"You've been here six months," Dr. Walker said slowly. "Have you
worked in biotech before?"

Meaning, I thought, "You're young to be in management. What
experience do you have?"

"No," I said. "I worked four years at BASF in Germany—two years
at Exelon in Chicago and two years at Tenet in Dallas. When I in-
terned at BASF, I realized that I was more interested in the process
of seeing a project to completion. I found the political juggling for
resources exciting; most people find it infuriating." I gazed firmly into
his eyes, silently willing him to be impressed.

Out of the corner of my eye, I could see Helene frowning at her buzzing wrist. Oh really, I thought. Did you arrange for a phone call just to get out of this meeting? Then my phone rang.

"Sorry," I said and turned the sound off without checking the screen.

Five minutes later, one of the framed paintings on Dr. Walker's wall faded to grey and lights began to chase around the frame's edge. Dr. Walker glanced at Helene and tapped the answer button on his desk.

"Walker!" Lloyd's voice barked from the pewter surface. "Is Helene there? Her intern thought she was meeting with you. I haven't been able to catch up with her."

"It's on speaker," Dr. Walker said sotto voce and nodded to Helene.

"I'm here," Helene called out. "Sorry, Lloyd. I was introducing Candace—"

"Have you seen outside?" Lloyd said. "Walker, turn your screen on. I'm sending you a feed."

The leaden display changed to a confused video of figures clad in jeans and pullovers shouting at men and women in business suits. The targets wore lanyards; each was zigzagging around the protesters, badging the lock quickly, and slipping through the office doors. Occasionally a member of the office staff had to throw up an arm to deter some demonstrators from following.

"That's right outside," I blurted.

"What is this?" Helene asked.

"They say that they're here for your press conference," Lloyd said.

"The press conference isn't scheduled until the end of the week," Helene said. Knowing her habits, I was certain that the notes for the event were probably printed and filed at her desk. "I haven't announced it yet."

"And yet, there they are. To oppose the Nil-facim project, I suppose."

"Who the hell protests a cure for malaria?" Helene grumbled, her voice roiling off the walls of Dr. Walker's office.

The video feed did not include sound. I watched the protesters organize themselves into a chorale that shouted at the glass doors of our office. I assumed that there must be a news team outside of the view of the cameras. Curious tourists were pausing, folding their arms, and listening to the newly organized demonstration.

"Obviously, some people find it fun to protest a cure for malaria," Lloyd said, his voice tight "Do you have someone to send down to them?"

I felt Helene's gaze land on me for a minute, but I didn't turn to meet her face. I kept my eyes on Dr. Walker and the camera feed.

"No," Helene said finally. "I'll go down."

"You don't need that type of stress now," I interjected without turning. "You might . . . you might invite some of them up to the office. One of the protesters and one of the newsmen, preferably one with a science background. A meteorologist?"

Walker snorted behind his desk, but I saw Helene's initial smirk morph into something more thoughtful.

"It might be useful to separate the leaders from the followers," Helene said, rising. "You should stay, Candace. Desmond, could you run through your project parameters with her? It would be better if she got it directly from you. Is Lloyd still on the line?"

Dr. Walker looked at the indicator on his desk and shook his head. "He must have dropped off after you said that you'd go down."

With a curt goodbye, she was gone. Desmond Walker looked at the organized chaos displayed outside for a moment longer and then returned the screen to an indefinite southern landscape of oak trees dressed in Spanish moss.

He hummed thoughtfully, leaned back in his chair, and asked, "What do you want to know about Engram?"

"All I know is that it is some type of research on memory enhancement or memory retrieval. I looked online but the closest that I could find were some studies done around 2010. A few researchers taught rats how to run a maze and then found that their descendants were able to run the same maze without training."

"Did you find anything else?"

I grimaced. "Five years later, some researchers were saying that the experience of American slavery was passed on to the descendants of the enslaved via the same process."

"Yes," Dr. Walker said. "That's one of the few follow-ups to the research at Emory University."

He swung his chair around, pulled a book off the shelf, and thumbed through it. "There hasn't been much research on that angle since 2015."

"Does your research indicate that the effects of slavery can be edited out?"

"The people downstairs are protesting our plan to edit one mosquito genus to remove its ability to carry malaria," Dr. Walker said wryly. "What do you think they would say if I proposed to edit human genes to remove anything, let alone edit African-American genes? Tuskegee is always at the back of everyone's mind."

He tossed the book back on the shelf and stood, stretching. "At any rate, QND is willing to do diverse hiring, but they are not looking to solve problems unique to African Americans."

"I'm not a diverse hire," I said.

"I didn't say that you were." He considered me silently for a moment. "You have memories and talents that are unique, no doubt. Your time in Germany, for example. You speak German?"

"Of course."

"Suppose I had a client who needed to transfer to Germany in a month. No time to study the language. Your knowledge would be priceless."

"A knowledge of anything? What if I needed to know how to waltz for a Mardi Gras ball?" I countered.

"No. Dancing is mainly a physical ability. A waltz or a foxtrot has defined steps; physical coordination is critical. Language is a better fit, though I think that it would be difficult to transfer the knowledge of a language like Xhosa to someone accustomed to a romance language like Spanish." He frowned as if the thought had brought up an avenue for consideration that he had overlooked. Leaning over the desk, he tapped notes into his desk surface.

"How are you going to get my knowledge of German into someone else's head?" I asked. "Write it on a chip?"

"Injecting silicone into people has an atrocious history," Dr.

Walker said. "No, I am looking at a biological emulation of a human neural network." He glanced down at me from his six-foot height. "Despite what I said about editing human genes, I am proposing editing in, not editing out. I would be giving you explicit access to memories you have already inherited."

"I could give German to my children, but not to anyone else?"

"Not yet," he said. "Was that a sufficient explanation of Engram?"

"Yes." I looked at my phone and pretended to find something on my schedule. "And I do have another tech lead to meet, even if Helene isn't around to make formal introductions. Thank you."

Dr. Walker nodded, tapping on his desk again. He had already half-forgotten me. I edged out of the office. *Get a resolution or kill it*, Lloyd had said. Engram with its limited application certainly seemed ripe for killing.

"Hey, baby girl!" a gravelly male voice bugled from my phone. I quickly squelched the phone to private mode.

I had the project plan and a spreadsheet open on my desk trying to find any pathway for Engram to be profitable. I was working on the scantiest of input from either Helene or Dr. Walker. Sooner or later, I would have to contact Walker.

"Hi, Dad. You know I'm at work, don't you?"

"Yeah—but I was wondering if you wanted to do dinner tonight?"

"Are you in town?" I asked. "You come to New Orleans and didn't tell me?"

My computer was insisting that I needed to take a break. I locked the machine and headed for the staircase. I was ten floors from the lobby. The staircase was private and a good way to burn off some of my aggravation.

"Nah," my father said. "I'm in San Antonio. I have this wall-sized screen in my hotel room. I figured that I'd order in. You order in at home. We share a table virtually." I could hear the humor in his voice. "You can invite Brad-slash-Juan-slash-Phillipe-slash-Tyrone to the meal if you like. Introduce me to your latest beau."

"You're crazy," I said.

One floor down, a door opened and someone pushed past me in a hurry to reach the next floor. I moved closer to the cinder-block wall to give the rushing worker room. "Are you still working off Mom's script?" My mother had died two years earlier after a long illness. I inherited my organization abilities from her, according to my father.

"Yeah," he said. "I still have the script with a few changes. Should I ask about a girlfriend? Want to invite Zawadi instead?"

"Not gay either, Dad."

"Not married, either," he retorted. "We left you all of those great genes, when are you going to spread them?"

"That was actually on her list?"

"Yes. First: ask her about work," he recited. "So, how is work?"

"Challenging," I said as I reached the next landing. "They haven't figured out what to do with me."

"Neither have I," he said. "Second: ask her about her relationship status," he continued. "And you said none. Surprising. Troubling. But I've checked that off. Third: are you happy?"

"I don't remember that question," I said.

"I usually let you vent about work," he responded. "That could go on for hours, especially while you were in Chicago. I'm glad you got out of there."

"So am I," I said.

"So dinner? You can tell me if you're happy over dinner."

"I have piles of data to read, Dad. And a decision to make."

"That sounds ominous." His voice was a pleasant baritone saxophone.

"As they say, that's why they pay me the big bucks."

"So—no dinner? You're not taking a break at all?"

"Dad, why are you in San Antonio? What are you chasing in Texas?"

"Your great, great"—I imagined him counting out relations on his fingers—"great-great-grandfather. The census says he was a stonemason."

"In San Antonio?" I paused on another landing. "Do we have people there?"

"No," he said. "Wouldn't that have been something? I was stationed here for years after we got back to the States. It would have been nice to have family here to show us the ropes."

"Dad—why this sudden interest in history? You always taught me that it's easier to run forward than backward."

"Dinner," he said. "That's a dinner discussion."

I sighed.

"Make your decision tomorrow," he continued. "Does it need to be today?"

"No, I guess not."

"Good, we're in the same time zone for once. So, eight o'clock. Please don't bring pizza again. I expect to see a real meal on the table in front of you."

He broke the connection and I trudged back up to the tenth floor. There was little sense in putting off the revelatory call to Desmond Walker any longer.

"Dr. Walker?"

There was a burble of voices on the other side of the line. Like most people at QND, Dr. Walker had disabled the built-in camera of his computer—which is why Lloyd had had to ask whether Helene was present earlier. It's a team meeting, I realized. Of course, there's an Engram team. If I closed down the project, I would have to consider what to do with the team. QND employees would have to be reassigned. If there were contractors, their agreements might require renegotiation.

"Ms. Toil?" I heard Walker's baritone voice ring over the cacophony. "Did you have additional questions from this afternoon?"

"Yes," I said, "but I see you're in a meeting. We can talk tomorrow."

"Tomorrow I will be in the lab. In fact, I'm leaving for the lab shortly. If there is something quick . . ."

"This will take some time. I'm going over Helene's notes and the project plan. I am trying to reconcile the numbers for Lloyd."

"You should talk to Helene," he interjected.

"I will. However, you know that she's taking an early leave, don't you?"

"For the baby, yes, of course," Dr. Walker said in a level voice. "But she will be back. There is no need for you to worry over the details of this project. I know you want to understand everything—"

"Dr. Walker, Lloyd has asked me to take over management of the Engram project." I could hear the chatter die on the other side of the line. "I am the new project manager," I said, realizing that I was emphasizing the news for an unseen group. I needed to be as clear as possible. "I want to start going over the project plan when you're available."

The line was silent. "Dr. Walker?"

"You should come to the lab tonight," he said finally.

"Actually, I have a dinner engagement tonight."

"The lab is on the Westbank—on the other side of the river. I am messaging you the address now." I heard a murmur over the phone line. "I'll be certain to update the system so that it'll let you in." The connection broke.

Well, shit, I thought. I should just let him sit there and wait for me. But on the other hand, I was considering shutting down the man's team. I should give him the chance to make his case. If I got there early, maybe I could still pick up a decent meal somewhere and be home by eight for dinner with my dad.

QND's lab was an odd pair of buildings on the west bank of the Mississippi River, still within New Orleans city limits. I parked, carded myself in, and paused to wonder which of the two buildings housed Desmond Walker's office. He had sent 201 as his office number, but both buildings had a second floor. I parked myself in front of the elevator in the first building, punched a button, and listened as the antique mechanism inside woke up.

The first floor was dark, but I could hear voices. I soon spied a pair of figures, one pushing a mop bucket, both deep in conversation. The lights of the hallway connecting the diatomic buildings activated, flickering on and off, creating a virtual spotlight as the two walked. The elevator car arrived at the same time they did. Both men were vaguely Hispanic. The first nodded to me; the other ignored me, ranting instead about some local sports figure.

"I'm looking for Dr. Desmond Walker," I said. "He's supposed to be in room 201 but he didn't mention that there were two buildings."

"You're in the right place," the darker man said. He was the one who had acknowledged my presence earlier. "No one's in building two."

The men trailed me into the elevator and punched the button above my second floor selection.

"I'm sorry if I'm keeping you here late," I remarked, noting the skipped floor.

"Dr. Walker always works late," the second man said. "Him, he has his own man to clean that floor."

I noted the severe look that passed from the first man to the second. The second fell silent and stared at the elevator console.

"You not the reason we still here," the first man countered. "It's a big office—two buildings and all." The elevator shuddered to a stop.

"201's at the end of the hall," the second janitor continued. "Ignore the other doors. It's all one big room, but Professor Walker will be closer to the last door."

"Thank you," I said, stepping out. Both men avoided my face as the door clanged shut and I turned to the brightly lit hall. Despite the '60s exterior, the interior had obviously been gutted and redesigned. I was met with a gleaming hallway of glossy white tile, banded by polished steel and glass. As the janitor had mentioned, there were doors on my left leading into the workroom; the only door that was open lay at the end of the hall. I could hear the muffled sound of jazz music from the local favorite station, WWOZ, echo off the hard ceramic walls.

Desmond Walker had altered his office attire slightly to match his current environment. A white coat replaced the suit jacket that hung on a nearby clothes tree. The tie had been loosened. He didn't rise to meet me, but twisted around from his perch on a lab stool to watch me enter. Unlike his work office, this workspace was spare, the stark image of efficiency. The worktables held only computer interfaces and electronic equipment that I assumed were microscopes.

"Maybe you want to start by telling me why you didn't mention that you were the new PM this afternoon," he said.

"I've worked on projects where every morning the PL sent a smiley face to the PM as a status report," I said, ignoring his lecturing tone. "That's not what I wanted." I pulled a nearby stool closer to me and gritted my teeth at the grinding sound of its metal legs on the tile floor. "Was there anything you would've preferred to say?"

"I might have given you more time," Dr. Walker said.

"Lloyd gave me the project two hours before I spoke to you. I tried to read what I could before our meeting so that I could ask semi-intelligent questions, but . . ." I shrugged. "The project plan was skimpy to say the least. Helene's notes don't mention epigenetics at all." I looked across at his stern face. "Did Helene never ask? Or did she not care?" I didn't voice my more unwelcome fear—that he had spent QND money on his own dream project without consulting anyone.

Maybe my fear showed in my voice because he leaned over the worktable, thumbed a virtual keyboard to life, and began pounding the keys with fury.

"I am forwarding you the research papers I've published," he said. "They go back to 2020."

"Wait—QND has only been in existence since 2037," I said.

"My research is why Delahousse brought me in," Dr. Walker said tartly. "Didn't Helene tell you that?"

"No—wait—yes—maybe. In her own way." I peered over the images of papers on the embedded screen. "I will need someone to explain this to me. My degree was in chemical engineering, not biology and certainly not genetics."

"Why should I waste the time of one of my team to explain genetics to you?"

"Because Helene may have been indulgent, but she reports to Lloyd just like I do," I answered. "His directive was to bring this project to conclusion or kill it. Neither of which means that you get to run a pure research project that has no commercial application."

He started to protest but I raised a hand. "Yes, I know—I could
pass my knowledge of German down to my kids. There are cheaper
ways to accomplish the same thing. I can't see QND continuing to
pay for this unless you have something more." I paused. "Not unless
you tell me that you have Delahousse on speed dial and can bring him
in. Everyone gives me the impression that he started QND and then
disappeared except for the annual board meeting."

Dr. Walker was shaking his head.

"No? There's a story there, I'm sure. Listen, I'm willing to go to bat
for you with Lloyd, but you have to give me something!"

Dr. Walker was silent for a moment and then brought up another
file. "Sit down. I'm going to give you a genetics lesson."

I groaned. "I don't have time. I have dinner tonight with my father." I was immediately angry at myself for being so specific. Walker
didn't need to know anything about my personal life. I needn't have
worried, for he ignored my outburst and continued talking.

"Do you know what a haplogroup is?" he asked. I shook my head.

"No?" he continued. "You've never taken a DNA test?"

"That's my father's thing," I said. "I think that he had me do one of
those cotton swab tests. He has the results."

"Well, a haplogroup is just a name of the group of genes that you
inherited from your parents. Your father can show you your results.
Over dinner." So he had heard after all. "Since the 2000s most people
do DNA tests to find out where their family originated." He displayed
a chart. "You know that *Homo sapiens* originated in Africa. Therefore
every human on Earth descended from one woman in Africa."

The chart was shaped like a tree with a trunk labeled L0-EVE.

"If she's Eve," I interjected, "why is she L0? Not A0? Or even B0?
Is it L0 because of Lucy?"

"Lucy was not in the *Homo sapiens* species," he said. "The labels
were assigned in the order that the *Homo sapiens* gene groups were discovered." He clicked on the trunk of the displayed tree and highlighted
two branches.

"Then let me guess. They started in Europe. And then, oops! Discovered that L0 was actually the oldest."

I think he chuckled even though he hid it well. "No, but it doesn't matter. L is a letter as good as any other. As my last paper indicates, I can give the memories of anyone on this line, say the L1b mutation, to another person with that same mutation."

"Helene said that you were ready for human trials," I said.

"That paper was written two years ago," he said. "Those trials have been done."

I sat back down on a nearby stool and stared at him. "So when you said that you could give my knowledge of German to my kids, you meant now. Not, maybe after additional study."

"Yes, now."

"Then what are you working on now?"

There was a clatter in one of the darkened areas of the lab. I watched lights spring to life at the far end. Dr. Walker waved briefly. "That would be Victor. He cleans this floor."

"One of the janitors said that you had your own man for this floor," I said.

"Yes, well." He paused. "It's better when the team is deep in development that they aren't disturbed by the cleaning staff." He looked back at the screen. "You asked what I was working on now."

I nodded even as I noted his odd sidestep about requesting one particular person to clean his floor.

"You're African-American. Your primary haplogroup is probably one of the first branches of the L0 group." He expanded one of the tree branches on the display. "If it were L1b, I could certainly give your memory to another person with that haplogroup. Right now, the team is verifying that it is true for every mutation down the line: L1b1a, L1b1a1'4, L1b1a4, and so on."

"Why?"

"Excuse me?"

"Why is that important?"

"Because you're right. Passing your knowledge of German down to your descendants is not commercial. But everyone on Earth is a descendent of L0. If I could give your knowledge of German to anyone that would be commercial."

I felt cold and suddenly sick. "Does QND have a company ethicist?"

"What?"

"Ever since Henrietta Lacks, I thought that every pharmaceutical company had some type of ethicist or lawyer or someone to vet their work."

"QND was not set up like a normal pharmaceutical company, but I'm certain that we have lawyers. However, I don't see the problem."

"Shit." I rubbed my temples, remembered my makeup belatedly, stared at the traces of mahogany foundation on my fingers, then looked up at him.

"Can you separate my memory of learning to drive, or German, or walking into this building this evening from anything else I know?"

"Not as yet," he said cautiously.

"I didn't think so. And if I agreed to sell you my German, how much are you going to pay for the other stuffs? Learning to drive, the memory of my mother's death, my first sexual experience? Because I sure as hell am not going to give you those for free!" I kept my voice low, aware of the figure moving around at the other end of the long room. "My memories are me after all. You're proposing to sell me."

Desmond Walker's jaw was tight as he turned and closed down the screen display. "So you will close down the project," he said.

"No." I shook my head. "I'm going home to have dinner with my dad over a video screen." I stood up. "I'll even ask him my haplogroup as you suggested. I need to think what to do."

". . . And all of that history was sand. Easy to sweep away and ignore by the next generation."

"What?" I looked up from my plate where, deep in thought, I had been pushing a meatball around the swirls of red sauce.

"Oh, so you are still with me," my father said. "I wondered if you had rigged up a video loop like one of those crime capers that your mother loved."

I stared up at him. Thanks to my new video screen, it looked as if I had punched a hole in the kitchen wall into a neighbor's opulent bedroom. My father was centered in the window, but behind him hung a tapestry of an improbable frieze of two women in flamenco outfits standing in a plaza surrounded by market vegetables. It had taken two years but he could finally mention my mother without his normally rich voice wavering like a mourning blues melody. He stood out from his lavish surroundings, a slim dark man with grey hair cut as short as it had been during his army days. He was dressed in a black polo shirt and khakis.

"Are you still mulling over that decision that you needed to make at work?" he asked.

Smiling, I touched two fingers over my mouth.

"Yes, I know you can't talk about work. But I saw something about your company on the news this evening. QND is GMO-ing mosquitoes. That isn't your project, I hope?"

"No, but—" I decided to give in to my curiosity. "What did they say?"

"Depends on who you listen to. Some say QND is releasing a genetic menace; some say that the company is a social justice warrior promoting a project that benefits Africans more than Americans."

I shook my head as I pushed my plate away. "There will be a formal press conference later; but no, that's not my project. I did hear most of what you said earlier. You found Josiah Toil. You talked about the buildings that he probably worked on. You said that you had reached a dead end. What does that have to do with history written on sand?"

A smile split his face and he laughed. "My multitasking daughter!"

Joining his smile, I got up and tossed the remains of my takeout dinner. The meal had been a little too good. I would have to hit the gym the next day. "Well?" I asked.

"Josiah had three daughters and two sons. The oldest son died in a Jim Crow prison." My father frowned. "The girls just disappeared after adulthood. Do me a favor and don't change your name when you get married." I ignored the prompt and he continued. "You women are hard to find after marriage. I wish that Elene had insisted that we hyphenate our surnames. She had no brothers. So as far as I know, you're the last of the Tolliver line."

"Is that why you asked me to do the DNA test?" I leaned against the granite counter and poured myself a shot of sparkling water.

"Part of the reason. The gene company tries to find matches for you. The Toil genes passed to you from me and the Tolliver genes passed to you along the matriarchal line."

"And all the way back to Eve," I mused aloud.

Dad raised an eyebrow that the video caught perfectly and I grinned.

"One of my coworkers tried to give me a genetics lesson today. He said that some genes go back to the first human woman, Eve." I bowed elaborately. "Where do the Tollivers hail from? My coworker said that DNA tests tell you what country you originate from."

"Oh, you are old, Candace," my father said. Reaching behind himself, he pulled a laptop from beneath papers and flyers stacked on the bed. "Haplogroup L1c."

My hands tightened on the glass. I had not expected to get my question answered so easily.

"From central Africa around Chad, the Congo, or Rwanda. Home of the original humans." He looked up. "Sorry, that's still a wide area. That's where your shortness comes from. You were right to blame your mother's genes for that. I can send you the results if you want."

"Send it on." My own laptop was still in my briefcase. "And the sands of history?"

"Candace, I was just trying to wake you out of your funk," he protested. I watched him pour a sliver of bourbon into a shot glass. I insisted on an answer.

He looked away, sipped his drink once, twice, and then looked back at me. "I hit a wall; this always happens. Josiah Toil was just a Black laborer so his work wasn't recorded. Every generation . . ." He paused. "Like Black Wall Street, like all of the Black towns after the Civil War, like the Black miners at Matewan."

"We know all of that," I said quietly.

"No, we rediscovered all of that. It gets wiped away and then two generations later people say 'we were kings and queens in Africa.' Well, sure. But we were city planners, architects, engineers, bricklayers, and professors here in America."

"And army officers," I said.

He chuckled. I was glad to hear real laughter after his bitter tirade.

"You can help me with a puzzle at work," I added. "Why would someone insist on his own cleaning staff for a lab? He says he's afraid the normal staff would disturb his team."

"And you don't think that that's enough? Is he afraid that his work would be stolen?"

"The guys that I met worship the ground he walks on."

"Does QND have a policy against hiring relatives?"

"Sort of. They don't want spouses or relatives to have to do performance reviews on each other. But I think the cleaning staff are contractors."

"You can ask, you know."

"I doubt the guy who runs the lab—"

"No, the janitor. I doubt that your guy thought to swear his janitor to secrecy. He's probably proud of the job. Ask him."

Lifting my glass, I toasted my father.

"What's a 'parian'?" I ask, tossing myself into a chair in Desmond Walker's office two days later. Not for the first time I wondered why a project leader had an office with a door that closed while I had a cubicle. Open door policy, Lloyd had said.

Desmond Walker made an elaborate point of putting his keyboard to bed and turned to me. "I think you know that it means 'godfather.' Victor called me after you talked to him. He was worried that he'd done something wrong."

"Did you ask the contract company to hire him?" I asked.

"He works for QND," Walker said simply. "Contract companies lay their staff off whenever there's a downturn."

As I sat back in the visitor's chair, I considered how to approach the real reason I had come down to Walker's office.

"You're not going to tell me that that is an infraction. Victor isn't related to me," he protested.

"No, Victor Johnston was only a puzzle that I wanted to solve. However . . ." I leaned forward. "I'm willing to bet that you know his haplogroup." Walker stiffened and I smiled. "Humor me, Doctor Walker."

"L1c," he said, and I felt relief spread through me like a wave. "Why does it matter? You gave me the impression that you were going to close the project."

"I really don't want to. Lloyd needs a dog and pony show. *We*"—I emphasized the pronoun—"need to give him a reason to continue your funding." I sat back. "I'm still going to insist on an ethicist to help us draw up conditions of use. I'd like to see families have access to their memories before they are exported and sold to others." Especially Black families, I thought, and shivered at the thought of accessing the memory of Josiah Toil seeing his son vanish into a prison that reproduced the slavery that he himself had escaped from.

"You are the one who pointed out that the ability to share a memory along one haplogroup was not commercial."

"I'm certain that every haplogroup would pay for their ancestral memories," I said. "Everybody imagines themselves the descendants of kings and queens. Every magnate wants to pass his genius directly on to his children."

I stood up full of nervous energy. Suddenly aware that I was patterning myself on Lloyd, I stopped and gripped the back of the visitor's chair. "I'm not asking you to stop your research. Eventually, it will occur to them that if you could share across one close genetic group, you should be able to do so with others more distantly related. They will remember that we are one human family." I took a breath. "When that happens, I want standards in place for such sharing. And remuneration for the memory donor."

"It sounds like you have a donor in mind."

"I considered asking you. Or Victor. But your memories belong to your children. I'm proposing that you give my memory—my ability to speak German—to Victor. He would be the more dramatic demo for Lloyd."

I saw a wave of anger mixed with—what? guilt?—cross Desmond Walker's face. "You're asking me to experiment on my family?"

"Victor and I are in the same haplogroup: L1c," I said. Releasing my grip on the chair, I seated myself again. "You said that your human trials have been done. I suggested Mr. Johnston because he's such a strong character. He would charm the board with his stories in English; he would certainly do so in German. But, if you have another subject, I will accept that. Mind you, I want to meet the person that you propose to give my memories to before you do that. There are other options." I paused and ticked them off for him.

"Second: if you tell me that you are ready now or even next week to transfer a L1c haplogroup memory to an IJ haplogroup subject, I would jump at that." I saw his surprise at my naming one of the European haplogroups. Yes, Doctor Walker, I did my homework, I told him silently. "Third: if you want me to go to Lloyd and tell him to give us two years and we will have that same demo for him, I'll do that."

"You don't think that he'd wait," Dr Walker said.

"No, I don't," I said.

"When do you want a decision?"

"By the end of the week," I said. "That will give me time to float the idea with a lawyer and discuss what type of protection we can offer the initial subject." I saw the word "protection" enter Walker's consciousness and wondered what machinations had been needed to have QND hire Victor Johnston directly.

I didn't ask. Four weeks later, I watched with others in the lab building as Victor Johnston regaled that board member with his memories second-lining with his krewe on Mardi Gras morning. His German was as colloquial as a native teenager. Standing in the back of the meeting room, I clutched the legal documents that would guarantee Victor a position until he retired and a pension afterward. As the memory donor, I had only insisted that the memories attached to my genes be given to no other person. I have frozen that moment in my mind: Victor regaling the board members after the formal test was completed, Lloyd smiling and nodding his head at my success, and Desmond Walker carefully defining the current commercial opportunities of his work and emphasizing the future possibilities.

I don't know where Victor Johnston is now. Eventually, he tired of being a guinea pig; he tired of having that "bougie Black girl," as he called me, in his head. No use explaining that I could not be extracted. He disappeared and Dr. Walker would not tell me where his godfather had moved. I could have queried human resources and found out where his checks were directed but I respected his wishes. I moved on; I listened to my father and started to date again. The Toil and Tolliver family chart is waiting for another entry. I may be the last generation to pass down my story the old-fashioned way.

HOW TO PAY REPARATIONS: A DOCUMENTARY

TOCHI ONYEBUCHI

Tochi Onyebuchi (www.tochionyebuchi.com) is the author of *Riot Baby*; a finalist for the Hugo, Nebula, and Locus Awards and winner of the New England Book Award for Fiction; the Beasts Made of Night series; and the War Girls series. He has earned degrees from Yale University, New York University's Tisch School of the Arts, Columbia Law School, and Sciences Po. His short fiction has appeared in *Asimov's Science Fiction*, *Omenana Magazine*, *Black Enough: Stories of Being Young & Black in America*, and elsewhere. His nonfiction has appeared in *Tor.com* and the *Harvard Journal of African American Policy*, among other places. His most recent book is the nonfiction *(S)kinfolk*.

A City Hall office, all wood-paneling.

Robert (Bobby) Caine, age 52, mayor of — —:
He left us a mess. Frank and his reparations bill, he left us a mess, that's what he did. I'ma have to be mayor a hundred more years to balance this budget. At least. [Laughing.] Imagine that. A white mayor. Spear-heading a citywide reparations scheme? And you really can't call it anything other than that. Because that's what it is. Don't get me wrong, as a Black man, I'm all for gettin' paid for what I been through. But if that stack is just a steppin' stone for some white boy on his way to the governor's mansion? I'm good. I hope he's doing well for himself. He must not have liked this job all that much if he was willin' to throw it away so fast.

Sunlight cuts through the blinds of a tiny office. Bookshelves bend under the weight of monographs. More books cover the floor around a desk. Behind the desk sits a man with his glasses hanging around his neck, his mask pulled down. He wears a tweed jacket and periodically removes a handkerchief from his breast pocket to dab at his forehead.

Professor Mark Higgins, age 73, assistant professor at — — State University, former member of REPAIR Project Team:
It's impossible. It's actually impossible to pay reparations. You can look to other models across time and place—the recompense offered to slaveowners, for instance, for their having been made bereft of their chattel; what Haiti has been forced to pay France for the temerity of having won its independence; et cetera—but there's no real analog for reparations paid to the truly injured parties for the totality of slavery. Some people like to point to what Germany did after the Holocaust, but the injury being addressed was the extermination of a people. The "orbit of hurt"—which sounds like a callous way of putting it, granted—is somewhat fixed in that example. Let's break down how exactly that plan, which looked so perfect and discrete on paper, truly unfolded.

You have the Luxembourg Agreement of 1952 and the Additional Federal Compensation Act of 1953. What did the Germans do? They paid the State of Israel for the cost of resettlement. Half a million Jewish refugees. That's what they paid for. On top of that, however, was the requirement that the moneys be used only to purchase goods produced within Germany. It's not until you get to the Federal Compensation Act of 1956 that moneys are being offered to German Jews who had suffered at the hands of the Nazi regime and their surviving dependents. There was a claim deadline of 1969. More groups became eligible in the interim with different pay schedules, but imagine the hundreds of lawyers and functionaries representing clients with divergent interests all vying for a piece of a finite pie trapped in red tape. By the time money gets to you, there's a nonzero possibility you're already dead.

Now, a governmental authority could recompense people for lost property. Or, and this is something people latched onto later on, they could compensate victims for their slave labor. A few years ago, the Claims Conference and the German government announced that they would pay an amount to each of the survivors of Kindertransport. Guess what they were paid. Well, the ones who hadn't died by then. Guess. Two thousand and five hundred euros.

I wrote this and much more in a report I submitted to the team behind the REPAIR Project, and I'm sure they listened, because they decided to add something more structural to that asinine personal compensation model. But they let me go ultimately.

A burger restaurant. Former city councilman Richard Perkins, age 42, and corporate lawyer Tommy DiSanto, age 53, sit on the patio, a plate of fries in front of each of them. Their black face masks hang from one ear as they eat. DiSanto was an inaugural member of the REPAIR Project Team. Perkins was the team's founder and leader.

DiSanto: How did it start? I joined after I heard about it, right? Or did you reach out to me—

Perkins: I think we reached out to you. Well, *I* reached out to you. Nobody was supposed to know about this at first. I don't think anyone was supposed to know about it, period. But, see, Tommy and I went to law school together and—

DiSanto: And while Richie turned into a hotshot city politician on his way to the governor's mansion—hell, probably the White House with that jawline of yours—I was out here defending Halliburton. But, shit, this was easy for me.

Perkins: Except you couldn't tell anyone at the office why you had to take a sabbatical to do it.

DiSanto: Because it was [air quotes] top secret. But yeah, I got brought in because whatever was being worked on needed to be founded on solid legal footing. Now, granted, I hadn't taken a peek at the Constitution since 1L, so I wasn't nearly the most qualified on that count, but Richie and I go back. What was it, that mixer they had all the students of color go to that one summer?

Perkins: Yeah, the POC mixer. What were you even doing there? Your parents are from fucking Argentina.

DiSanto [laughing]: Anyway, all I know when I say yes is that there's some social justice thing going on and there are scientists involved or whatever. Now, get this. I tell him, I tell Richie, "I hate fucking math. Don't make me do math." And he tells me, "Don't worry, I won't make you do any math." [Pause] I did so much fucking math.

They both burst out into laughter. But they turn away from each other to keep from spreading droplets.

Open on a darkened room. Cloaked in shadows. Against the far wall, the silhouette of a potted plant. The leaves are moving. There is an overhead fan at work. A dark shape sits in an armchair.

[Redacted], age 28, data scientist, member of REPAIR Project Team:
I mean, it's kind of simplistic to call it the Reparations Algorithm, which is what everyone called it after the story blew up—because, of course. If you had an AI built to detect which moles on a body

were evidence of malignant cancer cells, you wouldn't call that the Cancer Algorithm, would you? OK, maybe you would. Bad example. But people think it's just like you have this static $E = mc^2$ type equation and you throw as much information at it as possible so that it, like, learns or whatever, then it spits out some intelligent decision. So they hear about the Reparations Algorithm and they immediately think, oh of course, a formula for figuring out reparations! Then they ask, well what did you feed the formula? And then they expect you to say something like "Racism. We fed the formula four-hundred-plus years of racism." Like it's that simple. There's nothing simple about racism.

Voice of Wendy Guan, age 27, statistician, member of REPAIR Project Team:
I don't know if I joined the project at a late stage or early on, but I do know that our viability was tied directly to the release of funds resulting from the abolition of the city police department. During my interview, they were very vague about what exactly I would be doing, and they kept emphasizing the project's interdisciplinary nature. I think if they'd been a bit more forthcoming, I might've been too excited to be coherent. There was a real sea change happening throughout the country. Every industry, every locale, was experiencing a reckoning. I even saw in my own community the new ways in which anti-Blackness was being discussed and reckoned with. So to have the chance to be on the forefront of this new effort, this pilot project, and hopefully provide an example of what truly restorative justice looks like, I mean, who majors in statistics and expects to wind up there? Should we have expected what happened after? Maybe. But you have to understand the moment. It felt unprecedented. And, to be honest, I wouldn't take any of it back.

On a porch of a two-story house in the — — suburb, northwest of — —, there are two rocking chairs that allow their occupants to look out over a recently manicured lawn. Flanking the porch are plots of recently turned dirt and the beginnings of a garden.

Billy [last name withheld], 52, nurse:
Where'd that money come from? Came from us cops. That's where it came from. They abolished the fucking police department, fired everybody. No job assistance, no more pension, nothing. The whole fucking thing was drained dry. And our union. Strength in numbers, right? It's all bullshit. Once the protests started, it was open season on us. Get this, you know those robot dogs that company out of Boston was making? You remember those, right? Well, they were gonna start mass-producing them to replace us. Fake dogs. Union didn't have any pull because those tech wizards were already angling for our jobs on the cheap and we lost all our bargaining power. And the way the defunding was set up, it was reverse seniority, so the younger, more diverse force got clipped first. Then, when it was all us white devils left, we were easy pickings, far as the court of public opinion was concerned. I'm just over fifty. Spent my life on the force. What the hell am I gonna do with the time I got left? Far as work, things had dried up, but with the virus, folks in hospitals were droppin' like flies. So I decided that was where I could help. Had to go to nursing school and everything. Paid out the ass to sit in a classroom with fuckin' kids my daughter's age. [Laughs.] But I did it. Got my degree, got my license. Now, I push a cart in a hospital. Social justice, right? I hope it's fuckin' bedlam over there without us.

On the corner of Willow and Main Street stand a group of anti-violence activists handing out cards listing candidates for an upcoming municipal election. On the back of each is a "Know Your Rights" checklist. Down Willow, grill smoke billows out from behind a church while older residents eat fried fish by the front entrance. Shaneika Thomas wears a mask with a clear mouth panel to enable the hard of hearing to lip-read.

Shaneika Thomas, age 27, crisis management systems worker:
This corner, right here? We used to practically sit on top of cops basically. Plainclothes cop would yoke up some kids here or across the

street, and folks would get it on video. It would go viral, and we'd get on
the cop's ass. But then he'd be back out as a white-shirt, terrorizing folks.
You walk around this community and you have credibility just from
having been here for long enough and from people seeing your face, so
you can walk up to a group of dudes and be like, "hey, if you're out here,
and he's out here" — meaning the cop — "call this number."

*Two mechanical, jet-black greyhounds with backward-jointed legs prance
down the middle of the street. At each stop, they gather the nearest residents
and eject thermometers that the residents use to take their temperatures.
Some of the residents glance at their results. Another shakes the thermometer as if it's broken before trying again. Afterward, they all deposit the
thermometers, coated in their saliva and DNA, into an attached pouch and
drop the contained thermometer into an opening on the greyhound's back.*

When the REPAIR Act went into effect, we got an infusion of cash because of where we were headquartered. But we weren't ready for that. We
weren't *nearly* ready for that. All of a sudden, money was showing up, and
people just figured it was City Hall redistributing what got freed up when
they abolished the police department. At some point, I started doing the
math and I realized, as big as the PD's budget was, this was more money
than that. But we didn't have too much time to think on where exactly this
money came from. We just knew that we got lucky and we had work to do.

Of course, it didn't last, but I'm pretty proud of what we were able
to do with what we had. I just wish some of that money went toward
painting those dogs a different fucking color.

*Inside a Dunkin' Donuts on the corner of Arcade Street and Pine Street.
Just outside the entrance is a waste bin and, above it, a one-time-use
mask dispenser. At the top of the doorframe is a scanner, taking note of
the biorhythms and temperature of each entering and exiting customer.*

Denaun Smith, age 63, resident of — —:
Hell, I couldn't believe it. At first, we didn't know *what* the fuck was
going on. But suddenly, they announce that [Redacted] High's, getting

what?! Millions of dollars just pouring in. Where did that money come from? How can I get a piece of it?

Lyle Brown, age 32, history teacher at [Redacted] High: It wasn't *millions*. But it was . . . a lot. Imagine my surprise when the principal calls me into his office and tells me how much money we've been given. And my immediate thought is, "Okay, I can finally afford to get enough pencils and pens and notebooks for my students!" To be honest, I was just glad I could make sure the hand sanitizer dispensers in the hallways stopped running out.

Smith: You could see it in the kids, though. That's true. It wasn't like they was walkin' around with Jordans or anything, or like they was flashin' money around and whatnot. Matter of fact, I started seeing them less. Turns out they was spendin' more of they time at school.

Brown: A visual arts program, a theater program. Hell, we pooled with another school and built an actual theater! Kids were using actual handheld cameras to turn what would've been TikToks into Oscar-eligible short films.

Smith: Those damn TikToks. If I'm keepin' it real witchu, I miss those kids. I mean, good for them stayin' out of trouble, but the neighborhood done changed when you ain't see them around. It's summer and ain't no thirteen-year-olds chillin' on they front stoop in the Fayetteville housing projects in quadruple-XL white tees and baggy jeans with they coco-mango-cherries and durags. A place loses its character when it ain't got that anymore.

Voice of Wendy Guan: One of the first things I was told upon joining the project was that we were to focus as much as possible on tangibles. Essentially, we would look at discernible racial disparities—in housing, in education outcomes, in the number and location of grocery stores—and work backward. Our goal was to find a number. What number did we need to generate that would render all material things equal? Focusing on the racial wealth gap seemed like the most concrete way of going about things, and we operated on the assumption that housing was the most appropriate vector of analysis. So, our "number" would essentially be coded to a dollar amount. The data was relatively easy to come by. Much of it was public already. The tax assessor's office had home values, and then we could bucket them by ZIP code. But very quickly, we noticed something strange.

[Redacted]: The tax assessor's office had been overvaluing homes in predominantly Black neighborhoods and undervaluing homes in predominantly white neighborhoods. And the reason they were doing this was to fund police brutality settlements. How do they get their money? Raise the property tax. The city was literally making poor people pay for every time a cop shot a Black kid.

Perkins: Your average American city doesn't have the budget to pay $150 million or so in yearly settlements for officer misconduct. Yet another reason police are so expensive. What ends up happening is that the city issues a bond to a bank. Bank charges handling fees and interest that the city's on the hook for. But in return, the city now has the cash on hand to pay the victims and/or their families for the officer's misconduct. And the more money in the city budget that goes to that, the less there is for handling lead poisoning or funding schools.

In Stanley Quarter Park, children climb over a jungle gym while wearing surgical gloves and giggling behind single-use face masks.

Dr. Athena Davis, age 74, abolitionist and professor emeritus at — — University, member of REPAIR Project Team: Chicago is illustrative, and I think a more appropriate analogue than Professor Higgins's Holocaust example. Between 1972 and 1991, some 125 Black Chicagoans—at least, that is the number of cases that are known—125

Black Chicagoans were tortured by police officers in a building on Chicago's South Side. Beaten, electrocuted, sodomized. Chained to boiling radiators. And they were tortured into confessing to crimes that led to prison sentences, sometimes to Death Row. Discrete instances of a harm. A bracketed period of time. A reparations bill eventually did make its way through the legislature. It was revolutionary for a number of reasons, not just because it included an actual reparations fund. The amount was $5.5 million, a fraction of the $100 million that previous claims related to police torture had cost the city. But in the bill was an acknowledgement that torture had indeed taken place. There was to be a monument to the victims of police torture erected somewhere in the city. A psychological services center for survivors would be built. And there was to be a unit on police torture taught in eighth- and tenth-grade history classes throughout the city.

Interviewer: You mentioned the racial wealth gap and housing earlier.

Voice of Wendy Guan: Yes! In the aggregate sense, wealth is the value of your assets minus your debts. If we were going to focus on financial compensation, we needed something concrete as a . . . a prism for our analysis, so to speak. Economic disadvantages can harm your ability to accumulate wealth. And in the United States, at least, the surest way to accumulate wealth is through homeownership. And that is how we came to focus on a location-based analysis for the algorithm.

[Redacted]: We'd programmed the algo to produce a number per ZIP code based on the values we inputted. That output would correspond to a scale we cooked up of dollar amounts. A lot of numbers we had to figure out beforehand. Tax assessments and foreclosure rates. Not just the number of schools, but also the number of school closures. Then there's the police part. It took forever, but through arrest records, we could trace the incarcerated back to where they had initially been arrested. We then took the settlement amounts from police brutality

cases as well as the number of cases that went to trial but that plaintiffs
lost. Legal took care of that part. And together we extrapolated what the
incarcerated might have lost in wages and married that to unemployment data. That was hell to disaggregate by ZIP code. But we had our
inputs that we turned into super-inputs, and then we could generate
our output: the amount in dollars that would be apportioned to each
ZIP code. It's "If, then" with a *super* complicated "If."

Other than that, we had no idea where the money would go. But
that wasn't up to us. All that decision-making was a bit above our pay
grade. You gotta talk to the big guy about that, and I don't think anybody
knows where he is. After everything that went down, Mayor Gaetz—or,
rather, *former* Mayor Gaetz—kinda just vanished. Which . . . I don't
blame him.

When we ran that algo for the first time for a single ZIP code, we
thought there had to be a mistake. Double-checked the inputs, the
super-inputs, ran it again. And again. And again. We ran that algo maybe
three hundred times. Figured we broke the scale. But, no. That first
dollar amount . . . to make all things equal . . . was just that huge.

*Former city councilman Richard Perkins and corporate lawyer Tommy
DiSanto are finishing their lunch.*

Perkins: I put the team together to figure out if this reparations program
was financially viable. Not just that, but whether or not these disburse-
ments were something that we could keep going. This wasn't going to
be a one-time check to Black folk. The REPAIR Act was sustained investment. Funds disbursed to individual households, but also location-
based budget allocations for school districts. More schools and better
schools. Investment in diversion programs and mental health programs. Increased sanitation. Infrastructure repair. Parks. Printer paper
for libraries. Job training programs across industries. And it all had to
keep going. I knew there wasn't gonna be enough money in the budget
to suddenly make things right on the property end. So we co-opted
the bond system. Instead of using it to finance police brutality settle-

ments, we'd use it to fund our plan. It was gonna be impossible to get the mayor on board with this if we had to come up with a new system from whole cloth to base our funding on. But if we could use what was already there and flip it—we already had the data operation going from his campaign—then he could see where we were coming from and where we were going.

DiSanto: I've never done so much math in my whole entire life.

Voice of Wendy Guan: We were already thinking to the distant future. A city changes. The algorithm needed to be able to change with it.

I was watching a little girl ride her bike the other day, and I think this provides the best example for what I'm trying to explain. I don't have to explain that a bicycle has two wheels or even that you ride the thing by pushing your feet to the pedals in a circular motion. The girl just knows these things. But figuring *how* to ride a bicycle—how to balance without falling off, how to deal with ruts in the road—that's a different kind of knowledge. Skill-based. You're *learning*. This little girl kept trying to get up this tiny, tiny hill. She would stall at the steepest part, then fall backward. Then, at one point, as she's trying to make her way up, she leans forward. Just a little bit, then a little more. Finally, after she crested the hill, she goes back to how she was sitting before. No one told her to do that.

Before, algorithms had been operating toward the knowing of a specific thing. "Knowing that," so to speak. But machine learning is focused on knowing *how*. A basic algorithm recognizes the thing in front of it as a bicycle. But machine learning is what gets you up the hill. We had the algorithm for the initial disbursement, but we needed it to recognize that a city changes. Would our algorithm know what to do with a new refugee population moving into a targeted neighborhood? When the districts are inevitably redrawn, will it still operate with the same sophistication? If half of a ZIP code is replaced with luxury condominiums? What would the algorithm decide to do?

We didn't have the time or resources to program AI to do that, so we took those decisions on ourselves. How much of the dollar amount would go to schools? What to do with home valuations? Maybe . . . maybe if we could've got the algorithm to handle all of that, things would have turned out differently. Maybe the algorithm could've decided better than us.

The REPAIR Act was signed into law in February of 20—and disbursement of funds began on June 19 of that year, traditionally the holiday known as Juneteenth.

Sandra Ewing, 37, former resident of — —: That first check come, I called my sister. She lives on the other side of town, and I asked her where this came from. She ain't heard nothin' bout a check, but pretty soon, I found out everyone on my block got one. Same amount, too. It wasn't unemployment. Wasn't a tax refund or nothin' either. You had a job or you didn't, you got a check. Found out just about everyone in my neighborhood got a check. There were a couple other neighborhoods like that too, but not everyone in the city got one. There was some letter in there about a new law got passed, but I just wanted to see what the catch was, you know what I mean? It was a blessing, though.

First chance I got, stocked up on food and fixed the microwave. Still had money left over, so I got to have someone come through and deep-clean the apartment. Was supposed to be regular, because of city health regulations, but can't nobody in that building afford to completely sanitize their homes once every week. I figured the check was a one-off, so I was just focused on keeping my son, Jeremy, fed and safe.

But the checks kept coming, several months in a row. So I started socking some away, and suddenly, you turn around and look at your bank account just [blinks dramatically and laughs]. You know what I'm sayin'? I'm still countin' every penny I spend on this family, but I ain't gotta worry about eviction if suddenly the toaster breaks or there's a leak in the apartment that needs to be fixed or this or that or whatever thing.

Your thinking changes. Before, I'm just trying to make it to the first or fifteenth without my boy starving. But then you get to thinking about things like moving, like Jeremy being in a better school. The schools here seemed to be gettin' some money, but it's nothing like what they got just outside the city. So I'm finally able to take some time off from work, after not having missed a day in twenty-one years. And I go looking at apartments. Condos. That sort of thing. Imagine that! Me! Shoppin' for condos!

The neighborhood was starting to change too. I think we figured out pretty quickly that the checks were comin' to specific neighborhoods. And, yeah, money was goin' to the community, but fixin' up a school building, making sure there are enough soap dispensers in the halls, improving the curriculum, the school lunch program, all that takes time. That's time a lot of us don't have. So I got out. Couldn't get out quick enough. Landlord saw the market and started jackin' up the price soon as he could. So we moved. Me and my Jeremy, picked up and set out. He loves his new school, but the checks stopped coming. I'm working two jobs instead of three now, but it's getting harder to keep Jeremy in that school. We ain't even talking about college.

They're saying the checks back home stopped coming too. Money was comin' for about a year, then stopped. By then, everybody done up and moved, and now the rent's too high to move back. So we're stuck.

Professor Higgins: You need to understand that reparations are a national redemption project. A government can print money, as much as it wants. Don't listen to economists. They're wrong. But a place built on the backs of others needs all of its decision makers to acknowledge the totality of the wrong. It goes beyond money. That's why the project ended the way it did. Were reparations a simple game of numbers, all you'd need is the magic number, and you'd be fine. But everyone on that team was so besotted with the whole thing that they failed to see just what they were truly up against. For such a redemption project to work, you need this country to admit that it was wrong. And someone will always come along and see Black Americans being given their due and want nothing more than to destroy it. They can't countenance any other reality. I tried to tell this to Councilman Perkins's team. But no one wanted to acknowledge just how deep the problem went.

Asking an algorithm to do what they wanted it to do would be to assume racism is logical. "If, then." Now, racism has its own internal logic, sure, but it is the logic of nightmares. You can't automate its reasoning.

Councilman Perkins and his team thought others would see what this city did and want to follow suit. But I knew that others would see what this city did and want to turn it to dust.

Nine months after the REPAIR Act was signed into law, following a series of protests at the state capitol led by prominent conservative activists, the governor released a statement disavowing the legislation. A recall effort against Mayor Gaetz was initiated, and, six months before the end of his term as mayor, Frank Gaetz was removed from office on the grounds of misallocation of government funds.

The City Council selected Councilmember Robert Caine to finish Gaetz's term. Caine was subsequently reelected.

In a modest backyard, a white man in rolled-up shirtsleeves packs the soil behind a fence from which light green sprigs poke. He does this with care for several silent minutes, rises, then dusts his hands off and walks up his back porch. The body scanner framing the back entrance beeps as he passes through, then announces his temperature in red analog numbers.

The inside of the sitting room is just as modest. Sunlight shines through the west-facing windows to bounce off the glass covering a table designed to look like a hollowed-out tree trunk, gilding half of the man sitting in the chair facing the camera in profile. He's still wearing the dirty overalls and the shirtsleeves from earlier. His gloves lie on his lap. The pose looks practiced.

Frank Gaetz, age 47, former mayor of — —: This may sound trite and I don't mean it to, but writing the statement announcing the initiative was actually the most difficult part. I'm not discounting the work the team did. But it all falls apart if the statement isn't right. You only get one shot at this. I remember the presidential primaries. And the reason the socialist lost to the centrist among Black voters in South Carolina in 2020 was, as told to me by a Black Carolinian, that voting for the socialist would require the Black community to believe that white people were capable of doing something they've never done before: willingly and openly share in the economic bounty of this country. I needed to convince them that we were there. But I also needed to convince my white constituents. And if this whole effort was dressed in machine neutrality, if I could say "blame the algorithm," then maybe we could get away with the whole thing. Maybe it would feel a little bit less like a heist.

I was prepared to be the meat-shield here. If anything, it almost seemed like that was the point of the job. The team that Richie Perkins put together was formed sort of ad hoc. It was very Avengers. [Chuckling.] All of us from these different disciplines—lawyers, statisticians, historians, activists, politicians, even the medical professionals we consulted with—when they realized what Richie was doing, none of them balked. None of them thought it was impossible or too difficult. They all had the imagination for it. And it was my job to have the stomach for it.

Richie had brought the team together on his own, and they worked in secret, then prepared a report that landed on my desk. Richie and I talked for a long time. About the contents, then about the rollout, about who would get what and when. Before I knew it, I'd bought in. I didn't even realize, but he'd converted me to the cause of reparations. And he knew it had to be me. It had to be the white guy.

It wasn't just that white constituents would listen to me with less

resentment than they would feel if it were coming from a Black mayor.
It was the righting of things. A white guy does it and it feels less like theft and more like penance.

You look at the state the country was in at the time, it seemed like everything was getting torn down. And there's me: young, rising star in the Democratic Party, not yet so progressive that the establishment can't sink its claws into me, but not so far bought that I can't be pulled further to the left. And this opportunity lands on my desk in the form of this report. I used every bit of political capital I had to get the other city councilmembers on board. Comptroller, all of them. Reminded me of that Supreme Court case, *Brown v. Board of Education*. You know why Chief Justice Warren worked so hard to get a unanimous decision? Anything less might've led the South to start another Civil War.

So there it is, all laid out there. How the dollar amounts were calculated. The mechanisms through which the funds should be disbursed. Further funding methods. All of it. And all I had to do was take credit.

During the recall effort, the names of the participants behind the initial REPAIR report were leaked. As a result, statistician Wendy Guan's visa was revoked. She now lives in her native China.

Death threats were issued against Dr. Athena Davis and the team of data scientists with which she had worked after they were doxxed.

Councilmember Richard Perkins was charged with corruption and misuse of public funds. The charges were subsequently dropped. Shortly thereafter, he resigned from his position on the City Council.

Tommy DiSanto is currently a managing partner at Kittle & Loving and head of their pro bono practice.

[Redacted]'s whereabouts are currently unknown. They participated in this documentary on the condition of anonymity.

The disbursement of funds to communities and individuals designated by the REPAIR Act lasted for 10 months.

J.P. Morgan currently holds $3.2 billion in bonds from the City of — —.

In Stanley Quarter Park, a girl in a blue-and-white-striped dress makes a slow turn on her bicycle, leaning in the opposite direction.

Dr. Davis smiles and walks over to congratulate her great-granddaughter.

Over the two of them in the middle distance, roll credits.

SPARKLYBITS

NICK WOLVEN

Nick Wolven's (www.nickthewolven.com) science fiction has appeared in *Wired, Asimov's Science Fiction, Analog Science Fiction and Fact, The Magazine of Fantasy & Science Fiction*, and many other publications. His stories, which often focus on the dehumanizing effects of technological advance, have been optioned for television, reprinted in numerous anthologies, and republished in various languages around the world. He lives in New York City with his family.

The contractually mandated monthly meeting was never exactly a relaxed affair, but this one, Jo decided, promised to reach superlative levels of awfulness. All morning she'd been marching upstairs to Charlie's room, standing at the door with her finger on the pingpanel, then chickening out and clumping back to the other moms. Failure. That was the message they sent with their silence, staring up from the table with their diamond-hard eyes. The ultimate modern middle-class hazard: a public exhibition of parental failure.

"You've gotta do it, Jo," Aya said after the third attempt, sipping the latte she'd been nursing all morning. "You just have to prepare him."

While Teri, at the ovenex, turned, nails glinting, and said in a voice that *sounded* concerned without actually *being* concerned, "It'll be easier on him, in the end."

Jo checked what was left of the brunch. No pastries, no cinnamon buns, no chocolate in sight. Just a few shreds of glutinous bagel and a quivering heap of eggs. They usually did these meetings at Reggio's, and Reggio's, say what you would about the coffee, was a full-auto brunch spot with drone table service and on-demand ordering and seat-by-seat checkout. Which was all but vital when the moms got together, when the last thing you wanted to worry about was who got the muffin and who bought organic and who couldn't eat additives or sugar or meat. Whereas when they did these things at the house, the meal always became a test of Jo's home-programming skills. Likewise the coffee prep, likewise the seating, likewise every other thing.

All she needed, Jo thought, was one tiny bite of cinnamon bun to help her through. But a rind of hard bagel would have to do. Wedging herself into the chair by the dynawindow, Jo blinked away the backyard view and called up the scheduler.

Ten thirty.

Half an hour to go.

Sun Min came to the table, blowing holes in the foam on her third cappuccino. "Sooner you get started, easier it'll be. All the forums recommend the same thing. Groundwork."

Jo gnawed off a piece of bagel. "I'm just not sure this is the best thing for him."

The atmosphere tightened. Looking around the kitchen suddenly felt like staring into a stranger's frozen smile. Today was more than a family meeting, Jo reminded herself. More than a test of her mommy-ing skills, more than a battle for Charlie's future. It was a performance.

Naturally, it was Teesha who spoke next. Gentle Teesha. Support-ive Teesha. Political-candidate-advising Teesha. If Aya was the perfec-tionist of the group, always playing CEO; and Teri the consummate TV exec, with her pore-rejuve treatments and her million-dollar hair; and Sun Min their literary sophisticate, then Teesha was . . . well, what could you say about Teesha? She had the skills to handle lobbyists and congressional candidates, the biggest tantrum-throwers in town. Surely she could have handled kids, too, if she'd felt like blocking out the time. Instead, she'd taken it on herself to handle Jo, playing the helpful grandmother to Jo's perennially flustered mommy. Which was nice, to be sure, and not to be scorned. But Jo could never figure out the best way to react to all this meta-mothering.

Teesha took Jo's hand. In this family of megamoms, this clique of accomplishers—the Queen Bee, the Glamatron, the Editrix, the Matriarch—Jo was just Jo, the standard model. The person who pulled slop out of the ovenex, switched on the evening TV stream, and took a slow dive face-first into the loveseat. Not much to say about good old Jo, except that she was here. Always here.

"You scared?" Teesha used a voice that had probably helped trail-ing candidates through poll-number crashes, brought congressional aides down from caffeine-pill binges, coaxed suicidal interns off hotel ledges. "Worried you might blow it? Jo, let me tell you something. We're *all* scared. We've seen the therapist reports. We're watching his numbers. Yeah, we're worried about Charlie's progress. But that's why we're here. To tackle this together."

"But you—" Jo checked herself. "You don't have the relationship with him I do." Big mistake, she thought, looking at their faces. "What I'm trying to say is, it feels like *I'm* always the one who has to—"

Teesha eased back, using little plucks of her fingers to resettle her Yoruba-patterned shawl. A trick of hers, the gesture was saturated with authority. "We're a family. That's what we agreed. Equal partners. The contract says—" Teesha broke off, lips spreading in a secretive smile, as if she'd thought of a dirty joke she was almost too embarrassed to share. "Look, you know what? Forget the contract. What I'm saying, Jo, is we're all in this together. If something's gone wrong for that sweet little boy, that's on *all* of us. You want me to go up there and talk to him, say the word—"

Jo shook her head. "Don't take this the wrong way. It's not me. It's Charlie. You really have to understand Charlie."

"Well, if you feel that way, you can't blame *us* for being concerned. He's been up there all morning, doing—but you know what he's doing. If we're going to get through this, as a family, then—"

"Oh, for fuck's sake." Sun Min clacked down her cappuccino. "Look. You may not care what the contract says. But I do. We paid enough to have them write the damn thing, exactly because of situations like this. When it comes to the home environment, we *all* get a vote. And you've been outvoted, Jo. You just have to deal."

Teri and Aya both opened their mouths. Before anyone could talk, the lights winked off, the dynawindow blanked, and every counter, clock, display, and status window began to twinkle with inscrutable symbols. Chairs scraped, dishes clinked. The moms sucked hisses of surprise through their teeth as the bowels of the house thudded with mysterious operations. The ceiling projector whirred. Light returned, purplish, unsteady, as the walls filled with flickering images. Maybe mouths, maybe eyes, maybe fleeting faces, they reminded Jo, above all else, of rapidly gesturing hands.

Not now, she thought. *God, please, not now.*

"Sparklybits," Jo said out loud, "this really isn't the best time."

Strokes of brightness lit up the dynawindow, slashing upward, bending outward, like hands uplifted in a shrug.

Jo tried to remember the lingo. She thumbed on her sema and sketched a sign in the air, a series of slashes and chops that she hoped meant *cut it out*. The light throbbed. The ovenex displayed a series of dots and carets, an emoticon row of blinking eyes.

"I mean it, Sparkly." Gesturing as she talked, Jo repeated the sign for *stop*. The dynawindow blinked. The walls displayed a now-familiar icon, an open circle with dashes on the sides, which Jo figured was supposed to resemble a bowed head.

"That's right, Sparkly. This is adult-people business. You go back up and wait with Charlie."

Fizzle. Wink. There were no words for the series of icons that glimmered and faded in the walls. When they were gone, the lights came back, the ovenex showed its default display, the dynawindow reverted to the rainbow tiles of the scheduler. There was no sound throughout the house except the swish of a bathroom-cleaning subroutine.

"Now that," said Sun Min, "is *exactly* what we're talking about."

With the ghost gone, the moms twitched into motion. Hands lifted to tuck hair behind ears, brush crumbs from slacks, adjust rings and necklaces.

"Sparklybits," Teri said.

"Really." Aya sighed. "You *named* it?"

"Well," Jo said, "Charlie did."

"And you let him?"

The tone of Aya's voice let Jo know this was about more, much more, than a simple name. It was about major failures of smart-home management, serious lapses of parental discipline, epic errors of motherly judgment. The frustration of a world-bestriding CEO at seeing a job badly done.

What could Jo say? What could anyone say? It was a pretty big deal, after all, letting the house get haunted.

Teesha gathered up Jo's plate and mug and brought them to the dish slot, ignoring the kitchen whiz as it scrambled at her heels. With the mess dispatched, she turned, drying her hands, and locked eyes with Jo, saying with a little nod, "I think it's time."

The stairs to Charlie's room were at the back of the house, between the self-care parlor and the door to the village commons. It was a screen-free zone: once you stepped into the hall, all devices went automatically on lockdown. Something they'd voted on ages ago. For purposes of stress management.

Yeah. Like that had worked.

The whole wing was tweaked-out for sensory modulation. Carpets, warm colors, floor-level lights, even a few pieces of hotelish wall art. The style reminded Jo of her mom's house, all the inert clutter and décor people had brought into their lives back then. As if they felt some anticipatory lack, a need to make up for the absence of technology.

The homeschool room was at the end of the hall. Privacy checks clustered round the door: intercom, peephole camera, the pingpanel. All pretty silly, given that they'd equipped the place with round-the-clock monitoring. How many times had Jo logged in at the talkshow hour, zoomed in on nightvue to watch her son sleep? His face so placid as it dreamed, free of anxieties, until she could almost forget what went on during the day.

She slipped down the hall, aware of Teesha's heavy stride behind her. The other moms were still downstairs—scared, Jo supposed, of spooks and little boys. She lifted a finger.

Hesitated.

"It won't get any easier," Teesha said.

"I just . . ." Jo turned. Performance, she reminded herself. This was all a performance. "I feel like I already screwed this up."

Teesha's smile softened. "We all feel that way. Hell, we *did* screw it up. But we're fixing it now."

"Yeah, but I'm the live-in, you know? The one who's here. I don't want to say I feel closer to Charlie—"

The smile disappeared.

"—but I feel like I should have been on *top* of this," Jo hurried on. "As the person who actually, you know, stays in the house."

Bing: the smile came back. "We all had access to the logs." Teesha touched her hand. "We see the status reports. Any of us could've punched up the module, run a diagnostic. Hell, I *knew* the house had viruses. Just didn't know it was—I mean, I don't think any of us understood—"

"How attached Charlie was to it?"

"How bad things had gotten." Teesha's mouth pulled down in an expression Jo saw often on TV, an empathetic frown, acknowledging profound, shared wellsprings of emotion. "Know what I used to do? When he was little?"

"What's that?"

"I'd be in meetings, okay? Back when we were steering Senator Ramirez through his hot-mike hack. Sitdowns with the campaign manager, fundraisers, everyone completely losing their shit. So I'd have my specs on, y'know, scrolling feeds, saying I was keeping up with the reaction. Meanwhile, I'd have your updates on the periph. Diaper blowout. Major bed-puke. Mystery crash at three a.m. Cake-face takes the trophy. All day."

"No!"

"A-yuh."

"Naughty mommy."

"It got me through. Don't think I coulda gotten through without it."

"Course, most of those updates were the nanny."

"Sure. But you were *here*, Jo. That's what I'm saying. While I was taking care of grown-up babies on the Mall, and Sun Min was cleaning up after authors in New York, and Aya was off selling her arm-spanx thingies, and Teri was doing . . . whatever Teri does . . ."

"Yeah, what exactly *does* Teri do?"

"God knows." They giggled together, and when the giggles subsided, Teesha touched her arm. "But you, Jo, you were right down the hall. Now, I know sometimes it might feel weird, being the one who—well, who can't quite pay in at the same rate. Which is fine. I don't think there's anything wrong with that. But when you have four professionals all butting heads—"

"I am a professional, though."

"Sure, you've got your nursing job. I think that's great."

"It's a licensed profession."

"It's fantastic that you do that. But you know what I'm saying. We're all equals here. Sure, Aya can be a big mama bear about nutrition. Teri's a hardass when it comes to finances. Sun Min's got a lock on the educational stuff. I'm sure I can be a little intense about all sorts of things. It probably feels like we're always on your case, like the homemaker always comes last."

"But I'm not—"

Teesha held up a hand. "You're valued, okay? No one thinks any less of your contribution. That's the point of a co-op, right? Everyone pays in whatever they can."

Sure, Jo was thinking, only some people pay in by hiring expensive online tutors, while other people pay in by screaming and bleeding in a hospital for ten hours. But she only smiled.

"We're power moms, right?" Teesha gave her a sock in the arm. "Wouldn't be doing this if we didn't like the challenge. That's what I tell my babies in DC. Y'all think prepping for a primary is hard, try prepping a challenged kid for top-tier preschools."

Jo tried hard to keep her smile in place. "You ever have that feeling," she said, "like with every little thing we do, we're potentially fucking someone up for life?"

Teesha boomed a laugh, throwing back her head. Trying, Jo thought, just a little too hard. "Come on, now, girl. Into the dragon's den." She guided Jo's hand to the pingpanel. And pressed.

"Mom?" It always felt weird to hear Charlie on the intercom, how shrill his voice sounded, like something might be wrong. Jo leaned in.

"Hey, Charlie."

"Everything okay?"

Jo glanced at Teesha, got a nod of reassurance. "Sure, we just— can we come in? There's something we need to talk about."

A pause. Sometimes the no-screen thing drove her crazy.

"Thought you were doing your meeting out there?"

"This is part of the meeting. Something we need to discuss."

"Okay, but I'm doing my puzzles right now. I'll schedule you for . . . fifteen minutes."

Jo broke the ping. Teesha reached for the door, but Jo pointed at the status display. Purchased from a trendy tactile-play site, it was a custom-order birch flip-card machine, all natural, non-digital, except for the gizmo that changed the letters. With a flutter and click, it switched to the phrase *Mom Time*.

"Cute," Teesha said as Jo opened the door.

The homeschool continued the analog theme: sound-dampening

rugs, a plain glass window. The only piece of modern tech was the learning station itself, a topline Sony schoolbox, with apps and doo-dads up the wazoo. Parentally controlled, of course, though not, appar-ently, controlled enough. This was where Charlie spent all his time, at least until the coming day when they'd finally cave in and get him a palmcom, at which time, Jo figured, he'd be lost to them forever.

He didn't like to use the headset, but plunked himself down at the screen and—zonk—went straight into Charliespace. For a kid like Charlie, Jo sensed, all of reality was basically virtual. When he heard Jo coming, he said without looking up, "We did the Parthenon and the Colosseum and Notre Dame and the statues. Except Sparklybits started painting the statues, but I told him that wasn't always historically at-at-attested," he finished with a dip of his head, forcing out the big word.

Jo started at a tap on her shoulder. "I'll get the others," Teesha hissed, vanishing on a whisper of carpet.

"Except we might do the color later," Charlie said. "But I told Sparklybits I have to check sources."

"Mmmm." Jo went to stand beside him. When she let her fingers trail in his hair, Charlie looked up in mild surprise. For Charlie, Jo had realized, the existence of other people was always mildly surprising.

"Then we're going to—" He broke off, moving his hands in jerky patterns, faster as frustration mounted, until Jo nodded and smiled, mimicking his signs. Charlie smiled too, relieved at not having had to use words.

A babble from the hall announced the arrival of the moms. Teri descended first, nails flashing, keening with exaggerated joy, "Char-lieeeee!" Aya came next and tousled his hair. Sun Min nuzzled him. Teesha crushed him. Jo cringed, knowing how Charlie would feel about all this. But he handled it well, putting on his visitor face, as each mom claimed her obligatory hug.

"We're—" He pointed at the learning station, waving his hands in expressive swirls as his face bunched up. "We're—"

"Slow, baby," Teri said.

"Use your words."

"We're doing—"

"Take your time, Charlie." Teesha knelt on the carpet, nodding to coax him along.

"We're doing—"

"Puzzles," Jo translated, mirroring his gesture, and saw his face relax.

"Puzzles," Teri said through her TV smile. "That sounds so fun! Can I do a piece?" She scanned the floor, the shelves.

"No, they're—" Charlie made the sign for the learning station, then the sign for online, then a bunch of signs that meant something like "shapes of light." That was as much as Jo could follow. What he called "puzzles," she would have called "models": digital constructions, meant to be educational, that challenged kids to assemble famous buildings. Charlie had built the whole set so many times that Jo couldn't imagine he got anything out of it except the satisfaction of the process itself. Tick-tick-tick, piece by piece, a series of gestures he could have done by now in his sleep.

"Me and—Sparklybits—"

He was almost totally signing now. Those wide, florid gestures that only Charlie fully understood. Charlie, that is, and one other entity.

At the name Sparklybits, the moms all turned to Jo.

"I see." Teri's smile was stapled on. "And how much time do you spend, Charlie, playing video games with Sparklybits?"

Charlie frowned. "They're not really—"

"They're like virtual building sets," Jo explained.

"Ah."

"Charlie. Sweetie." Aya knelt. Too close, Jo thought, but restrained herself. "Can I see how you play with Sparklybits?"

Charlie looked up for approval. Jo nodded. Sun Min and Teesha and Teri were already herding her out of the room, down the hall. Over Sun Min's shoulder, Jo could see Charlie gesturing, flamboyant with frustration, as Aya cocked her head and tried to smile.

"This, *this* is what we're talking about," Sun Min hissed. "Right there."

"Does he always express himself to you with those . . . movements?" Teesha asked.

"Well," Jo sighed, "mostly with the ghost. But I've picked up some of it."

"This is why he's lagging." Sun Min jerked a hand at the bedroom, folding her arm like an Egyptian painting. The resemblance to Charlie's gesturing was uncanny, but Jo held the thought. "When did he start to miss milestones? I'll bet it was right when that thing showed up."

"It's more than a speech lag," Teesha said. "He's behind on every track."

"It's all connected. Speech, socialization. This is why his metrics have crashed. How can he succeed if he can't even talk?"

"He does okay on the homeschool stuff," Jo said.

Sun Min used the same face she probably pulled on authors who pitched digital-addiction memoirs. "You're going to fix an emotional lag with homeschooling? This is why we're pumping in twenty percent for Artemis Academy. Trust me, I've read the lit. You cannot, can*not* hit benchmarks across the social skillset without at least fifty per week of face-to-face time. Where are his public speaking skills? His prosocials? Empathy, engagement, emotional literacy? Do you know how badly he's lagging his cohort?"

Lagging. If there was one word Jo could've Xed out of the discourse, it was that deeply loaded word, *lagging*. When she was a kid, people had said "catching up"—as in, "Jo Clark is still catching up in math." Before that, the favored term had been "behind." Go far enough back, people had used words like "retarded." The whole idea being that everyone was on the same road, all heading to the exact same place.

"How is he going to get into college with these benchmarks?" Sun Min threw up her hands. "Not just a good college. Any college."

"Maybe he won't want to go to college," Jo said, and knew instantly that she'd blown up the conversation, gone straight for the nuclear option. She might as well have hauled down her jeans and pissed on somebody's sandals.

"You're seriously planning to keep our son out of college?"

"I'm not trying to keep him out, Teri, I—"

"You're going to ruin his future, *our* future, because you don't have what it takes to run a household?"

"Teri." Teesha put a hand out.

"Because you let this piece of rogue code get into his brain and—"

"Teri, Teri, Teri." They were all pressing round, trying to calm her. Something had slipped in Teri, the newscaster composure an all-or-nothing proposition, now firmly jammed in the OFF position.

"Thing is, Jo, *you're* not paying for the private schooling. *You're* not paying for the prep, therapy, emotional tutoring, nutritional advising. Twenty percent of your salary? I'm sorry, that's a fucking rounding error. The rest of us? Okay?" Teri's fingernail scrawled circles overhead. "We're the ones working seventy-hour weeks, traveling the world, just to pay for this goddamn regimen. Why? Because we want the best for Charlie. Because motherhood, call me crazy, I happen to think that's kind of an important job. But you—"

"All right, Teri." Teesha held her arm, but Teri threw her off with a clash of bracelets.

"What am I going to tell Frank?" She thudded partway down the stairs, looking up at them, tapping at the tears on her cheeks. "He already thinks this is some vanity trip for me, like adopting a fucking gorilla at the zoo. Now I'm supposed to ask him to be the dad of a budding high school dropout? Jesus, I *should* have adopted the gorilla; at least they don't grow up to join machinima porn fandoms. 'Cause I'll tell you, that's where this kid is headed. Every other mom in the office is beating the benchmarks. Every one. There's a single father in technical support who's got a son in the ninety-eighth bracket. And we've got a lagger. God."

In the silence that followed, a funny sound came from Charlie's room. Jo took it at first for a technical failure—audio feedback, a broken speaker—until she pegged it as Aya's cry of surprise.

"It's not Charlie's fault." Sun Min looking at Teri with what might have been sympathy or distaste. "It's—"

But now Aya was hurrying to join them, bustling up with her brisk executive stride, planting hands on her waist to announce, "It's happening."

"You get through?" Teesha asked.

"To our kid? No. But there's this." Aya semaphored at the wall, remembered the no-screen thing, yanked out her phone and tapped into the house system, swinging it to show everyone the feed.

"Shit," Jo said.

"You sure you properly vetted this guy?"

They were in the kitchen, gathered around the dynawindow, watching the feed from the village gate.

"How long has he been waiting out there?" Jo asked.

"I texted him to stand by." Aya clicked in for a close-up. "Yeesh." She winced. "Just look at him."

Jo had to admit the man at the gate wasn't especially prepossessing. Particularly not on the zoomed-in security feed, with its anti-blur motion compensation and refractory enhancement and high-def-whatever and all the other brilliant tweaks the geniuses of home security had put into the software. There were slews of apps to make people look good on video; this particular program revealed them at their worst.

Not that the man at the gate would ever have looked especially good. When Jo met him, he'd had a kind of greaser-trying-to-clean-up-his-act vibe, hair slicked back, a flush in his cheeks, like a slacker who'd just stepped out of the shower. Onscreen, now, he looked like a hair malfunction at the hippie factory. Like someone had swept up Chewbacca's haircut clippings and glued them to a giant peeled potato. There was no good stage of life at which to have that look, Jo thought, but thirty-six—which is what she guessed the exterminator was—was too old for any conceivable excuse.

"You checked his background? Consumer reviews? Credentials?"

"I met with him. He showed me his shop."

The man began to pinch his nose, pulling hard to squeeze the boogers out. The kind of semi-discreet nosepickery you might get away with on a busy train, but definitely not on close-up video.

"His shop, huh? He have any dead bodies there?" Aya sighed. "Well, let's get this over with." She punched the code for the gate and the guy slouched in, schlumping through the New Urban street plan with his truck moseying along behind him.

As he came around the corner to their street, the moms all trooped outside. "Hello, ladies!" the exterminator yodeled up. The truck, still creeping at his heels, gave a beep. "Park!" he commanded it, pointing to the curb, and jogged up the steps to loom over them in all his ungroomed glory. "So." His teeth peeked through a wickerwork of hairs. "This is the coven, huh? I'm Evan."

"Let's go over the situation." Aya spun on a scraping heel. "Then we'll tell you how we want to proceed."

Evan bumped his head on the doorframe coming in. He seemed not to notice. He bashed his shoulder on the turn into the hall, seeming not to notice that, either. He was looking at the ceiling.

"Yeah, you see a lot of hauntings in these older units. Legacy wiring. Puts a limit on your hardware. So people don't push the updates, a backdoor opens, and 'fore you know it, boom. Spooktown. What's the interface here? Still got the old semaphore hookup?" He stuck a sema on this thumbnail and signed the lights-out sign, snapping the hall into darkness, occasioning several bumps and curses. "Nice."

"Jo tells us you're quite the expert in these matters," Aya said, leading the group into the kitchen. "Credentialed," she added, with a hitch of her eyebrows.

Evan shrugged. "Expert, ah, that's not really the word I'd use. Freakishly obsessed is more like it." He went to the ovenex and started poking buttons. "Honestly, this stuff is like, the only thing I ever think about."

"N-o-o-o-o." Aya looked him over. "Can it be true?"

"My pops, he was *way* into rogue AI. Used to hunt 'em, all through the hotlands. That was my first childhood memory. Rolling with a pack of ghostchasers in Lou'siana. 'Course, these days it's a lot easier. There's people who'll just sit around and wait, rig up some bait and hope the things'll show."

"And what works as bait for a ghost?" Aya asked.

"Well, it sounds awful, but, the truth is: kids." Evan pulled out a crumpled pack of gummies and popped some in his mouth, chewing with much bristling of hair and smacking of lips. He opened the trash panel, peeked inside, went to the drone dock, and flipped a switch.

"Not literal kids. But the stuff a kid'll do. Poking around. Punching buttons. Messing with stuff. Come on, Sparkybits, where are you, buddy?"

"Sparklybits," Sun Min corrected, and winced at her own complicity.

"Yeah, 'cause y'know, they're basically kids themselves." Evan noticed the way everyone was look at him. "I mean, not really," he clarified. "They're just software. But *as* software, they're still learning the ropes." He went to the dynawindow and waved his arms. "Got a shy one here, huh?"

"It mostly comes out for Charlie," Jo said.

"Gotcha."

"So this is common?" Teri's voice still hadn't quite climbed down from the pitch it had reached earlier. "A kid, connecting with one of these things? That's normal?"

"Normal is not a word I really like to use." Evan brought up the security panel, tapping monitors until he got Charlie's room. They looked at the boy's bent back and head, hunched in front of the learning station. Evan's fingers vanished into his beard. "They were built to be learners. You know? Pattern matchers. See, we think of learning as like a thing that happens when you're taught, right? But it's more like a thing that just plain happens. And learning with someone else, I guess that's easier than learning alone."

The puzzles were back on Charlie's screen—even on the feed, Jo could make out the shapes—and the boy had begun his eloquent gesturing, tracing loops and swirls in the air. Evan seemed to be unconsciously mimicking him, swinging hands and fingers, until he abruptly stopped and scratched his chin.

"Guess we better go up there," he said.

Under normal circumstances, the door to Charlie's room was kept closed, but the visit from the moms had thrown off the routine. As they went upstairs, they had a clear view of his hands, waving in front of the learning-station screen. They could see exactly what those hands were doing.

"Whoa." Evan pulled the kind of face that emojis could never capture, mouth screwed up, eyes slightly out of focus, eyebrows riding high above a grimace that seemed to say, *I don't know what you make of this all, but damn, what a show!*

In his pod-chair, Charlie was slumped in classic kid-posture, a sprawl of boneless lethargy—except his arms. These were as animated as tentacles, weaving, swishing, fingers wriggling like strange sea creatures, plucking invisible meanings from the air. Here was the performance to which his earlier fumblings had been a kind of rude prelude. Anyone could tell the gestures constituted a language—just not a human one.

The patterns in the screen were eerily similar: curls, twists, and ribbonings of color, animate icons of light.

"Good God," Aya breathed.

"That's no home semaphore," said Evan. "No, sir."

It wasn't ASL either, Jo knew, or any other human sign system. She'd checked. It was a language, she suspected, that had never been used anywhere outside this house.

She became aware of a stumbling pressure, a bumping hip, a foot on her toe. Teesha was railroading the whole group down the hall. In the bedroom, Teesha eased the doorway partway shut, peeking out into the hall. "Can Charlie hear us in here?"

Jo sat on the bed. "He wouldn't notice if he did."

"Now that," Evan pointed down the hall, "is quality spectre-speak."

"But is it—" Sun Min restarted her question. "*What* is it?"

"It's how they talk. Mostly. Though not usually at that level. By which I mean, well—" Evan socked his tongue into his cheek. "Is Charlie, uh, special?"

"In what way?"

"You know, gifted?"

"He used to be," Sun Min said.

"A smart kid?"

"Charlie is . . . mathy."

"Focused."

"On the spectrum."

They all had their own terms for it, picked up in parent gossip, office chatter, the world of online mom-chats.

"Charlie," Jo said, "he latches onto things."

"I mean, the kid's a nerd. Right?" Teri shrugged. "We wanted a nerd. It's what we paid for. A boy who'd ace the tests."

"And not a girl?" Evan's question evoked a chorus of half-hearted mumbles.

"It's a bump," Jo explained. "Having a boy. The top-ranked colleges are sixty five percent women. The top-paid professions are sixty five percent men. Think about it."

"Okay," Evan said noncommittally, puffing his cheeks.

"What did you mean, they all talk this way?" Sun Min narrowed her eyes. For the past few minutes she'd been compulsively clicking the clasp of her handbag. "It's like a code?"

"Well, technically it's all code." Evan grinned as they groaned. "I mean, the ghosts, they came out of the omnicom craze, right? So, like, everything has a mind, okay? Your shirt, your coffeemaker, your car. Well, what kind of stuff is a shirt gonna talk about? If it talks to a coffeemaker, what're *they* gonna talk about? If all those things are talking to each other—"

"But they still have to talk to people."

"Sure. But the thing about smart devices, they're mostly talking to other devices, *about* people. The whole point of the internet of things is it's networked. So if you're a free-floatin' free-lovin' higher level entity that grew out of all those little programs—well, how the world looks to you, it's probably mostly not about human language. Like, User72 is heading southwest at sixty miles per hour on Highway 92, elevated blood pressure, restless, making hungry faces, scanning the map . . . You put that all on a screen, what do you get? They can use some English, sure. But they don't *think* like we do. So they don't *talk* like we do, either."

"But they don't think at all." Aya's voice had a calculated coolness, the tone she probably used to close agenda items in meetings. "So what makes anyone think they're talking at all?"

Evan looked at his toes. To Jo, at that moment, he looked just like Charlie, getting grilled on his social skills in some therapist's office. He brought up his head with a sigh. "Look, you've got a couple of options here—"

"We want to get rid of it." Aya cut him off.

"Okay, but listen—"

"No. We want to get rid of it."

"Can't we just chase it off?" Sun Min was still fussing with her handbag. "Get it out of the house, but not, you know, kill it?"

"Well, you can do that. But they usually come back. Creatures of routine, right? Once they bond with a child—I mean, once they've linked to a user—"

"I don't understand." Teesha swung an arm to break into the conversation. "It's software. Ones and zeroes. If we try to delete it, can't it copy itself?"

"Sure. They don't really like to do that, though."

"Huh?"

"Yeah." Evan's inner geek broke through in a goofy smile. "Funny thing. Thinking is, if you're nothing but a trail of bits, copying is like a form of movement, right? Imagine you left a clone of yourself every time you took a step. Well, to a program, what we think of as movement is basically a special case of copying, except you delete the original version. That's part of what makes these things so special. A virus copies. A ghost *moves*."

"So if we delete it, you're saying, it's gone."

"If we can manage to delete it, yeah."

The words had a solemn power—the power, Jo suspected, of any statement of finality. It took her a while to realize everyone was looking at her. Jo made herself focus on Evan. She had a vision of Charlie all grown up, stranded in some weird niche job, letting his hair run riot, dead-ending his life. Becoming this man.

"It's like we discussed, Jo," Evan said.

"Right," Jo sighed. "Like we discussed." She got up and said, "Let's do it, then." And headed down the hall to Charlie's room.

He was at the learning station, still signing with Sparklybits, performing those strange, lavish gestures. Jo thought of Evan's explanation, how a coffeemaker might talk to a car, a car to a faucet, a faucet to a

chair, but none of that struck her as having much to do with language.
Language was about empathy, expression. Sharing something other
than information.

"Charlie." She slid into his line of sight. He registered her presence, blinked, broke from the screen, and gave a mind-clearing shake
of his head. The human child slowly came back into his face.

"We're doing a new puzzle," he said.

"That's great. But, Charlie, listen, I need you to put away the puzzles for now. There's something important we have to talk about."

His eyes became deerlike, anticipating a shock. Did he know what
was coming? Not a chance, Jo thought. There would have been tears,
shouts, a crisis.

"This man," she said, "needs to talk to Sparklybits."

"No," Charlie whispered, so faint Jo was sure no one else had
heard. She tried to ignore the lance of ice in her heart.

"Hey, there, Charlie!" Evan used that awful adult-talking-to-a-kid
voice, lowering his bulk to the floor with a grunt.

Charlie glanced over, noted his existence, and turned back to Jo,
saying only to her, "Mom, please."

"Sparklybits, Charlie, he has to be . . ." Jo couldn't finish.

"It's okay, man." Evan rocked backward, wriggling a hand into his
shorts pocket. "We just need to keep him from running around loose.
Catch him and put him in a safe place, you know?"

Jo winced. Did they really want to tell him that? Before she could
send a signal to Evan, though, Teri picked up the theme. "That's right,
Charlie. We need to make sure he's safe."

"It's for the best," Aya said.

"For your health," said Teri.

"There are other ghosts," Sun Min added. "All different kinds. Different types of AIs. Right?" To Evan.

"Oh, sure," Evan soothed, "all kinds. I mean, I even have a bunch.
At home."

Again, Jo made eyes at him, but Teesha was talking.

"And all kinds of other friends. Real friends. Wouldn't it be nice,
Charlie, to have some human friends?"

"We'll just snatch him right up and make a nice home for him." Evan pulled out a gizmo and plugged it into the learning station, making various IT-dude adjustments. "To do that, though, Charlie, we need to know where he is. And to do that, we're going to need your help." Looking up from his gear, he mouthed over Charlie's head, *Ready*.

Charlie was still staring at Jo. She knew what he wanted from her. Not reassurance, not explanations, but someone to cut through all the placating bullshit, tell him how things really were. Curling her fingers around his hand, pushing down her emotions to make room for his, Jo said, "We have to do this, Puppa. I should have told you sooner. I'm sorry."

No. He mouthed the word, then howled it. "N-o-o-o-o!" Before Jo could react, they were in full meltdown mode. Charlie grabbed her arm as if to claw his way up it, into her head where he could change her mind. "No, no, no!" Jo avoided looking at the others. Charlie really did seem, right now, like a much younger child, emotionally stunted, behind the curve. Lagging, undeniably lagging, as he vented his grief in a series of screams.

"I'm sorry," Jo said, struggling to hold him. "Puppa, I'm sorry." But every apology, she knew, was a sentence handed down, a judgment, a verdict, a punishment. As if his sorrow had exceeded the reach of human speech, Charlie jerked away and made a sweeping gesture, lifting and thrusting out his fists.

"Charlie!" Aya gasped, mistaking it for an act of aggression. But the only violence here was the violence of passion. Charlie's fists opened into a gesture of loss, gathering in toward his chest and flinging outward, as if hurling clusters of invisible blossoms, expressing a sentiment for which English had no words. It struck Jo as curiously archaic, elemental, like something from an opera or pagan ritual, a display of mourning the modern world had lost. She wondered how the ghost would express its distinctive digital experience, looking back through the networks of the world and seeing a million lost copies of itself.

As Charlie continued his ballet of supplication, the lights fluttered, the walls groaned, the screen of the learning station began to swirl. Streaks of light curved down and inward, forming gentle cupping lines. Sparklybits had come to see what was the matter, concerned for its suffering human companion. Poking its cyber-nose, like an animal, right into their trap.

Without a sound, without any obvious signal, the room subtly changed, becoming stiller, steadier, as the screen of the learning station blanked, leaving only a few blocky pieces of the puzzle that Charlie had been building with his friend.

"Got him," Evan said.

Dropping his arms, Charlie sank to the carpet, wrapping his arms around his head. Teri stroked his hair. Sun Min murmured explanations. Teesha bustled up with grandmotherly authority. But Charlie dragged his pod-chair to the corner and sat staring at the empty wall. And Jo couldn't help feeling, even though everyone gathered around to apologize, that this last gesture of rejection had been meant entirely for her.

No one spoke as they went outside and stood shuffling their feet on the concrete steps, all somehow avoiding, by one shared instinct, the temptation to glance back into the house. Charlie followed them, but there was no forgiveness in this act; Jo knew it was only a concession to routine. As they squinted into the reddening sun, Evan jogged down the steps, moving in the springy sideways trot that Jo associated with more athletic men. On the path he looked up, he shaded his eyes

"Well, if it ever happens again . . . you know who to call." Evan hesitated, seeming to feel something more was needed. Then he cocked a finger at the house, squinted one eye, and said, "Zap."

Don't overdo it, Jo thought, glaring down. Evan swung his arm in what was probably supposed to be a bow. "Luh-*ay*-dies." A moment later they were watching his truck putter away.

"Well, Charlie." Teri squatted, shining her camera-ready smile into his face. "I'm so sorry we didn't get to catch up more. I love love love to see you, sweetie."

"Yes, so much," murmured the other moms.

"And you know, Charlie." Sun Min hesitated, maybe second-guessing what she'd been about to say, but plowing ahead anyway, "It really was the right decision."

"Yes." Aya nodded. "For your future."

"For the family," Teesha said.

"Kiss goodbye?" Teri squealed, flinging out her arms. The question usually won from Charlie a grudging hug. Today it received only agonizing silence. Hanging their heads like scolded children, the moms shuffled away down the path, holding key fobs aloft to let out a froglike chorus of peeps, summoning their rental cars from the village lot. They would already be rehearsing, Jo thought, the things they'd say to other parents at the office, to colleagues and boyfriends, to their own mothers at home—in Tokyo, in London, in airplanes, clubs, bars: "Mothering is hard." "It can break your heart." "Just be glad you don't have kids." Jo herself was wondering what she'd say at work, in response to the inevitable Monday-morning questions.

The Zephyr had come out to wait in the drive. Charlie jerked open the rear door, flumped in, and slammed it. Jo got into the driver's seat, tapping a route into the console. They pooted out, following the golden trails of cyberspace, turned at the corner, and rumbled through the gate. On the highway, they took the second exit, bumping down to a strange part of town.

"Mom?" Charlie broke his vow of silence, leaning forward to put his face between the headrests. "Where we going?"

"No Doctor Brezler today," Jo said over her shoulder. "We have, uh, another appointment." Without looking, she put a hand behind his ear, grazing his cheek with her knuckles. "Change of plans, Puppa."

If he guessed what she had in mind, he didn't let on. The car zagged through a series of turns, paused in front of a pizza parlor, recalibrating, then set off into a section of town that seemed to have been rezoned for random uses. People were squatting in public garages, selling scrap out of gutted franchises; a YMCA had been refitted to house a group of refugees. Folks in the street sold vegetables, flags, homemade liquor. The car wriggled through a cluster of tents.

Only when they were a block away did Jo begin to recognize the area. The building itself was unremarkable, a strip mall in which most

of the units had been converted to shabby apartments. The last shop,
a former game parlor, still had a tangle of fluorescent tubes in the
window, tracing the outlines of crossed pool cues. A hand-painted sign
read: Ghostblasters!

"Mom?"

Jo clucked for silence. If she'd learned anything from this ordeal,
it was not to say too much, too soon.

The door jingled a welcome. No one stood at the dusty counter
where a register had once been perched, no one guarded the fire-
retardant curtains that blocked off most of the main floor. Jo pushed
them apart. The place was smaller than she remembered, but jam-
packed with the kind of interesting clutter that can make a room
feel paradoxically large. Appliances, drives, peripherals, gadgets, all
sprawled across the old, battered pool tables, linked by kelpy mats of
wire. Looking them over, Jo was mostly conscious of a festive abun-
dance of lights. Like candles, she thought. Like a birthday surprise.

"Boo." The sound actually made Jo jump. Evan popped from behind the nearest table, brandishing the palm-sized gizmo he'd brought
to the house. He presented it with a flourish. "Madame? Your ghost."

Jo turned to Charlie, expecting—but she wasn't sure what she was
expecting. He seemed not to have heard what Evan was saying. He was
staring goggle-eyed at the wilderness of wires, this dollsize metropolis
of tiny night fires. His hands lifted, clutching. Jo didn't need Sparklybits to tell her what the gesture meant.

"Like it?" Evan said

"They're so—what are they?"

"Ghosts." Evan reached out, letting his hand fall on a gadget at
random, a toaster, walking backward to get a closer look. "This one,
let's see, this is old Elmo. Ancient feller, small memory, doesn't need a
lotta space. I keep him here and let him ring the bell. Every once in a
while I hook him up for some TV time. He likes that."

Charlie ambled along the aisles, lifting his feet as if by practice
over the rubber strips laid over the roots of bundled cable, his eyes
locking on to one gadget after another. Evan shambled behind him.

"Over here we have Skittles. One of our big vocal communicators.

Talks in a tone-scale kind of like a whalesong. Probably appeared in a house that was blind-adapted, sound-heavy interfaces, that kinda thing. Had a real tight bond with this girl up in the estates. This here, this is Wanda. Kind of a retiring type, but she just *loves* chasing fingers on a touchscreen. The simularium, here? That's our condo. Whole ghost family packed inside."

"This . . . this is so *harsh*."

"I'm not up on the lingo, man, but I'll take that as a compliment. Have a look around. Tap the screens, touch buttons, whatever. Maybe break out some semaphores. They love the attention."

As Charlie worked his way through the gizmos—hesitant, at first, then with growing enthusiasm, and finally with invincible levels of absorption—Evan sidled up to Jo, whispering, "So. We're good?"

She lifted a shoulder. "Seems that way."

"You were right, then, huh? Day-yum. Whole thing went off like you said."

Jo nodded, not wanting to tell him how wrong he was, how far the day's events had diverged from her expectations. Evan wagged the device, its corkscrewed tail of cable flopping: the new home of one Sparklybits.

"How's that whole deal work, anyway? Like, those other ladies, they just chip in some money? Rent your kid for a weekend or something? I never understood the whole co-op family thing."

Jo kept silent. Evan must have seen in her face that he'd brought up a not-okay subject. "Well, anyway"—he shrugged—"you were right about how they'd take it. I wonder what they'll think, if they find out you—"

But here came Charlie, rushing through the aisles, brimming over with syllables of delight, grabbing Jo's hand and dragging her away to share the discoveries of the last five minutes—as if, with the fluid enthusiasms of childhood, he'd already forgotten his earlier grudge. She had to tell him three times before he noticed the gadget Evan was holding. Then it took three more tries to explain the thing's significance. Even after he understood what it meant, Charlie's reaction wasn't quite what Jo had expected. Almost with reluctance, he let Evan place the drive on his outstretched hands, solemnly closing his fingers

around the plastic, stretching out a finger to stroke the screen. A streak
of light appeared and faded: a glimmer of *Hello*.

Jo didn't have to remind him to say thank you.

"He's going to have to stay in there. And there are going be some rules.
No use in the house, for one. Or during school. This'll be a special
occasion kind of thing, not an all-the-time thing. Got it?"

Charlie squinted across the seat, then back at the block of plastic
in his hand. When Jo nudged him, he looked up, blinking.

"Puppa, this is important. I know how it sounds. But we can't let
the other moms know, okay? Not for now. At some point, maybe, when
things have changed . . ." Jo decided this particular conversation could
wait for another day. "The important thing is—"

"Mom?" He was looking at her with a face he wore often these
days, an expression that scared Jo as much as it delighted her. It reminded her of the father she'd lost, the husband she'd once imagined
she'd have—of the man her son was slowly becoming. A smile that
would almost have been cruel, if Charlie had been aware of what it did
to her. "Thanks."

Jo waited until she could trust herself to speak. "I should have
told you," she said. "About what we were planning. But . . . I wasn't
sure you'd understand. Or that we'd be able to pull it off. Or I thought
things would get messed up somehow, or that we—oh, I don't know, I
just should have—"

They bumped into the drive, the Zephyr purring, waiting for them
to hurry up and leave so it could enter the garage and do its nightly
diagnostics. Charlie was fiddling with the gizmo in his lap, swiping
symbols into the screen, changing settings, as he pulled a rollscreen
from the glove box and pried back the rubber socket protector.

"I never got to show you. What we were building."

"I—" Jo took a second to recalibrate. "You mean your new model?
That thing's not supposed to have any Wi-Fi—"

"No, no, it's okay. Sparklybits'll remember." Charlie unrolled the
screen to its full extent. "You really want to get the full effect."

The images were forming already, swoops of color, curving lines, sketchy shapes that gathered slowly, clicking together to form a blocky frame.

"Interesting," Jo said. "Is it a castle?"

"Kind of." Charlie gave a little smile.

"A palace? A fortress?" Jo angled her head as the pieces accumulated. "Is it a church?"

Charlie didn't answer. He'd begun to stroke the screen along with the ghost, adjusting, guiding, adding and deleting, making subtle edits to the spectral assemblage, contributing to the dance of shapes.

"A school?" Jo said. "A hospital?" Surprising herself, she made her own contribution, reaching down to trace the ghostly movements, letting out a laugh of surprise as the hovering blocks ticked into position. Charlie laughed too, moving his hands more quickly now—in loops, in jabs, in pirouettes of dexterous motion—and Jo sat back to admire his fluency, his eloquence, in this language with only two speakers, this culture of two souls.

Her eye drifted to the windows, the gold and violet shapes of dusk, and in a blink she had it.

"It's our house. Right? That's what it is. You're building our house!" Charlie was silent, absorbed in his craft. Only when the work was almost finished did he look up, conspiratorial, grin slowly widening, as the details continued to accrete beneath this hands—the bricks, the fixtures, the dollhouse doors and windows—and a plush sweep of lawn where two tiny figures stood, joined at the hands, like ornaments on the phantasmal grass.

"Just wait," her son told her. "Just wait and see."

THE SEARCH FOR [FLIGHT X]

NEON YANG

Neon Yang (www.neonyang.com) is the author of the Tensorate series of novellas from Tordotcom Publishing, beginning with *The Black Tides of Heaven*. Their debut novel, *The Genesis of Misery*, will be published in 2022. Neon's work has been shortlisted for numerous awards, including the Hugo, Nebula, World Fantasy, British Fantasy, and Lambda Literary awards. They are queer, nonbinary, and currently live in Singapore.

am in darkness that knows no dawn, no dusk, and no relief. A darkness that has persisted for billions of years, a darkness that predates life that walks upon land. A darkness smooth and uninterrupted except by the twin beams of my headlamps. The Avatar's headlamps. This is seventy thousand leagues under the surface of the ocean, on a remote, hostile seafloor once called "the most removed place from civilization imaginable." In the tenebrous borders of my only illumination, strange white shapes move in and out of awareness and into the dark of the unknown.

I am here, in this yet-uncharted hellscape, because I chose to be here. No: *chose* is such a weak word, a half-strength word, a pleasant-teatime word. I should say I *fought* to be here. I have been working towards this moment for two decades now—the majority of my life, in fact. I have broken through every obstacle that came my way and now here I am, at the bottom of the South Indian Ocean. Searching.

I leap across the landscape like a god, like a giant with seven-league boots, and the silt rises in clouds. This is a place that has never been touched by sunlight. Here gravity has less sway than the crush and weight of water, and even the rise and fall of the disturbed sediment lives by the rules of its physics. We are seventy percent salt and water, and yet we understand less of the nature of the briny ocean floor than we do the arid surfaces of the Moon and Mars. It's as if we are incapable of understanding our very nature. Incapable of turning the lens inward. Who knew that this alien world existed here, on our watery green planet, right under our very noses? Even I, who have spent most of my adult life in the study of oceans and their ways, find this landscape baffling and frightening. As a child I imagined that swimming along the ocean floor would be like swimming through the guts of a man, lightless and full of awe, drifts of unnamed life-forms passing overhead and by me. But this emptiness is far more unnerving.

"How are we going? Found anything yet?"

Ah, good old [Participant 2]. What would I do without my bell-bright assistant bringing me back to the present? [Participant 2] is not here with me in the Avatar, but he has a link to my head. He is a delightfully practical man, the kind of soul that is twenty going on forty. [Participant 2]'s interest is in sub-abyssal ecosystems, and our research interests overlapped enough for us to seek sponsorship together. He can be a bit of a nag sometimes, but in this foreboding limbo I am glad for a human voice in my ear. [Participant 2] keeps me tied to reality. My mind has a tendency to wander into the depths of reverie or nostalgia, even when I know it shouldn't. This sentimentality of mine will get me killed one day.

I know my thoughts are being recorded by the owners of the Avatar. We had to sign a scrum of waivers around it, and I balked at the idea, this ruinous invasion of my privacy. [Participant 2] promises that the memories will be anonymised, all identifying data scrubbed out. They have AI algorithms trained to look for that. I, on the other hand, have no way to know if any of this is true.

But you know what they say: beggars, choosers, the works. [Private engineering company] that owns this Avatar unit was the only one who would take a risk on my proposal, and even then, barely just. Our lease is for a grand period of twenty-four hours, and so it's back in their custody. Between the two of us, it was agreed that I would control the Avatar, both because I got better results in the linkage test, and because my mission is much more of a crapshoot. All [private engineering company] needs is a bunch of soil samples, water samples, and records of all the weird, gelatinous creatures that spend their lives in this briny underworld. That's easy. His field of study is the reasonable one.

I am here for the airplane.

Fifty years ago [Flight X], with two hundred and fifty souls on board, vanished from the radar of air traffic controllers between one handoff and the next. By the time they were missed, by the time they were supposed to have landed, three hours had passed and no one knew where the plane was. The average cruising speed of a passenger jet is nine hundred kilometres per hour. Multiplied by three, and you get a search radius of two thousand seven hundred kilometres. But who knows where or when the plane went down? [Flight X] carried over six hours' worth of fuel. It could have continued flying anywhere. All in all, when concerned nations began the search for the missing jetliner—far too late—the search radius covered a quarter of the planet, most of it ocean.

Eventually, data grudgingly shared from military satellites narrowed the search down to a strip in the Southern Indian Ocean. It was days later and the plane was given up as lost, all those on board presumed lost. Those were the days before the easy surveillance of the planet's surface, and the search for the wreckage was difficult and expensive. There were divers, risking their lives; there were clumsy, bullet-shaped submarines, packed with sensors. Weeks ran into months, and manpower and equipment costs stacked up with neither success nor end in sight. Working with straight computational models and best guesses was like firing arrows into an inky dark: imprecise and fueled with little more than hope. When governments eventually gave up on the search as a lost cause, enthusiastic amateurs picked up the slack for several years, until funding and interest ran out. Over the decades the plane's disappearance faded from public memory until it was reduced to a series of whispers, vague articles on websites and quirky podcasts for incense-burners. No one has tried to locate the wreckage for years.

No one, that is, until me.

"Why are you so obsessed with this?" [My partner] asks me this all the time. "Fifty years have gone by, no one cares. Even the next-of-kin must be mostly dead. Or they've moved on. Who are you doing this for?" It's three a.m. or some other ungodly hour, and I'm hunched over a lit screen in the dim study, finishing up another analysis of ocean patterns or working on the seventh draft of a grant proposal. [My partner], in the doorway, arms crossed over her chest, face folded into an expression of disapproval that I cannot see but can imagine very well. Each time I try to explain myself, but the words never quite capture the depth of my need for the search. I don't have the vocabulary to elucidate my feelings, or the strength to admit that as a little girl, I read about the disaster on a screen at the library and a seed of fascination and want fell into me, and that seed spent the next twenty years sprouting root and stem in my being until here I am, pursuing a graduate degree in oceanology and begging NGOs and research organizations for funding and equipment—something, anything that will put me on the ocean floor where the wreck of the plane should be.

"I don't understand," [my partner] will say, every now and again. "Your smarts are being wasted on this search for El Dorado. Why major in climatology and use that degree to find the wreck of some ancient airplane no one even remembers? With your qualifications, you could be working in [top-tier climate research institute], working towards the next Nobel Prize. You're that good." The backhanded flattery stings. I once shoot back that she, as an economist, has no idea how science works. We end up fighting, a Category 5 blowout that takes us weeks to recover from. And it doesn't stop her from bringing up her dissatisfaction with my life's work, over and over.

An hour has passed since the Avatar and I reached the ocean floor. So far: nothing. The clock is ticking. Based on our lease, we have just six hours to comb the seabed. The strip of ocean I can cover in that time is tiny, barely the size of a city center. I have spent the last five years making these calculations, pulling together decades of data—almanacs of ocean currents, studies of atmospheric pattern changes, records of debris from the plane that washed ashore over the years—and feeding it to quantum cores, tweaking parameters, perfecting algorithms. My models have been published in top-tier, peer-reviewed journals. My name is known in the field. I have absolute confidence in my calculations, my thesis, my models. I got it right, the wreckage of [Flight X] has to be in this section of the seafloor I have identified.

"It's okay," [Participant 2] says in my ear. "We've still got plenty of time. We weren't going to come across the wreck within minutes of touching down anyway. Statistically, that's improbable."

[Participant 2] is right, of course. Still, it rankles, being comforted like an irrational child. I know the numbers, am an expert in the numbers, and I have been absolutely professional in my conduct thus far. None of my worry has seeped through the cracks for [Participant 2] to pick up on. It's his own nervousness speaking, I think. He's put a lot of trust in my calculations. If I fail—if I come back empty-handed—it could torpedo both our studies by association alone.

Something darts in and out of my vision: a creature sequentially drawn in, and then repulsed by this alien light. A kind of eel, long and flat and ghostly. This bottommost region of the ocean is called the hadal zone, after the lord of the ancient Greek underworld, and I am Persephone, wandering desolately amongst the shades of the dead. Sometimes the ghosts are fish, sightless and colorless in this place that receives no light. Evolution is a master sculptor, shaping the raw clay of life into an unimaginable variety of forms. I have already trapped a dozen specimens and sent them upwards in pressurized drone boxes for [Participant 2] to collect. They'll be taken back to his lab, where they'll be kept in an environment simulating their home for further study. [Participant 2] tells me that even the denizens of the deepest oceans have changed in the last few decades as the seas warm and the world around us becomes unrecognizable. Nothing is spared, not even down here.

Ahead, something enormous and white catches my headbeams as it sprawls across the seafloor. My heart skips as I see the jagged, uneven silhouette. "Is that it?" asks [Participant 2].

I leap across the vast wastes, propelled by thruster-weight. Something massive for sure. It could be—it could only be—

A sigh. I come to rest on the bed of silt. In front of me is a jumble of flayed, porous bone: skull the size of a car, ribs like cathedral windows. A swarm of starfish, flatworms, and other scavengers amass over this morbid architecture, feeding. "Ah," says [Participant 2]. "Whale fall."

Whale fall, a marvelous phenomenon in these cold, benighted plains. A cetacean behemoth, falling to rest on the seafloor, its vast store of nutrients turning into a yearslong feast for those who dwell here. Entire ecosystems rise and fall in the crevices of these enormous corpses. Nothing goes to waste. A single dead whale will change the environmental profile of the seabed where it lands for decades.

"If you don't mind . . ." [Participant 2] says.

Of course. This is a joint project, after all. I stop the search to begin scooping up creatures, as many specimens from as many species as I can distinguish. At least one of us will be guaranteed results from this outing. The minutes tick away as I put strange spectral creature after strange spectral creature into boxes. I cannot help thinking of the aircraft falling to rest somewhere not far from here, gentle as snowfall or ash, settling into the embrace of the seafloor. I think of the ripple effect emanating from that fall. The things that changed, both aboveground and below, because the plane came to rest here.

Sometimes I like to imagine that there is a God, a Someone in charge of the strings of the universe, and They sometimes like to tug on them for fun. The day we present our grant proposal to [private engineering company] is a significant anniversary for me, although I told no one involved. Of course not. Our case is made via remote prez, [Participant 2] and I beaming in from our respective labs. I put on a filter to hide my nerves, which shake me like a wind through the top of trees. It must have worked, because we impress the board enough they greenlight the project in real time. I remember asking, "Is that it?" during the call, to a round of laughter. I am so used to governments and their bureaucracies and six-month grant results releases. But private investiture works on its own rules. What had begun as a pipe dream, a childish obsession, was suddenly a fixed number of calendar days away from happening. There was a budget attached to it, a schedule in the cloud. [Participant 2] and I toast one another with real wine in our respective offices. We would get to work the next day, but that evening was for disbelief, jubilation, thanking our lucky stars.

That night I call [Individual N] to let her know the project was going forward. On the line her voice quavers with emotion more complicated than simple joy or sorrow. [Individual N] was eight when her father boarded [Flight X] on a business trip and never returned. Even today she spends the week around the anniversary of the flight's disappearance in a drunken haze, unwilling to relive that hellish stretch of days—first the blinking red of DELAYED on the signboard, then days of denials and conflicting information, the long stretches of despair and prayers that this nightmare might end, one way or another. But it never did. More than a year later part of the plane's wing washed up on a beach halfway across the planet, confirming what everyone already knew, but had been too afraid to accept. Still the claustrophobia of *not knowing* continued to haunt them as the years went by. When I began making serious overtures towards this project as an undergrad, I reached out to as many next-of-kin as I could locate. Many refused to talk to me, and I don't blame them. Who was I but some round-faced kid digging into wounds first opened decades ago? [Individual N] was one of those who responded to me, and we kept up correspondence as my research developed. She's the first one I tell about the expedition grant outside of [my partner]. "I believe you will find it," she says. [Individual N] is religious, and she often prays for me and my mission. "I believe you were sent to find it."

[My partner] is again in the doorway to the study, frowning as I close the call window. Arms crossed. "I know what this is about," she says.

I frown back, not sure what she means.

"This whole thing is really about your mother, isn't it?"

I refuse to reply, and she continues. "I didn't want to say it earlier. It's too mean. But you're kidding yourself if you say it isn't true."

"Don't get things confused," I say, hands clenching. "My interest in this is purely scientific."

"No. The scientific part is the bit where you sit in a lab till the next dawn trying to work out bugs in your algorithms. This part, where you fly halfway across the world to get plugged into some advanced robotic suit that will go to the bottom of the ocean . . . it's personal."

So what if it is? Don't we laud doctors who make medical breakthroughs for personal reasons all the same?

I send the last capture drone towards the surface, its belly pregnant with an angrily luminescent anglerfish. An hour has passed since I came upon the whale fall. There's precious little time left, and I have only covered a tenth of the section I'm supposed to.

[My partner] isn't wrong. This stumbling, humanoid Avatar isn't the best choice of vehicle for this search. If I have the coordinates right, a drone swarm would be better and faster at combing this strip of seabed. But I wanted to see for myself.

"Don't worry," [Participant 2]'s voice chirps in my ear. "We've still got plenty of time. Sonar scans picked up some abnormalities up ahead."

I nod. I leap forward. The beams of my headlights sweep through the gloom.

When I was nine my mother disappeared. There was no warning: I waited on the school steps for her as around me the light yellowed and the shadows lengthened over the ground. I remember it clearly, the variegated shape of poplars marching over grass and tarmac while I pinged her number over and over, my arms growing numb in my jacket. Eventually an uncle rescued me where I sat, a mess of snot and anxiety, and took me home. She'd left behind no clues. No notes. All her suits and dresses still in the closet, eggs and milk in the pantry, a barely legible scrawl of groceries to reorder on the fridge panel. The missing-persons hunt went on for weeks, then months, then quietly petered out as hope did. In this vastly connected world we exist in, no one alive can go that long without being traced—a credit transaction here, a surveillance camera there. Something. My memory of that time is laced through with dread and wild hope. My heart rate spiking with every phone call, every mail ping, every knock on the door. Maybe someone had found something. Maybe she'd finally come home. But none of that happened. Everyone accepted that Mother was dead, but how—or why—would be a mystery forever unsolved. Every time there was a gap in my day—when I was lying in my bed, when I was in the shower, when I was in between classes—my mind went back to the details of the day she went missing, drawn like starlight to a black hole. Endlessly I dissected every detail I remembered of that day, trying to re-create the crime scene, trying to figure out where she could have gone. What she could have done. Where her bones—or whatever was left of her—lay, even now. They say the world has been constantly shrinking through the centuries, until we now think of it as a mere dot in the cosmos, one blip in the swathe of the universe that we can see. But to a nine-year-old girl curled in the corner of her room, damp with sweat and tears, the planet seemed like a vast and unchartable wilderness.

Later, when I read about [Flight X] in the library, I was struck by a bolt of recognition at the stories I read. The waiting. The hope, and the despair. The never-ending tail of maybes and what-ifs. I knew how those next-of-kin felt, as though we shared a heart.

If I was able to somehow calculate the location of Mother's final resting place, if I had the tool sets and the technology to do so, wouldn't I do everything I could to pinpoint her grave? Wouldn't I expend every last joule of energy I had to reach that place?

Something shines in the gloom ahead. The particulate silt I kick up obscures its true form. But it's big, its edges jagged. Another whale fall? Or something else? I do not know, and I cannot tell at this distance. But one way or another, I will find out.

I leap forward.

RECOMMENDED READING: 2020

The following stories were published during 2020 and are recommended as being amongst the best stories of the year.

"Yuli," Daniel Abraham (*The Book of Dragons*)

"Hearts in the Hard Ground," G. V. Anderson (*Tor.com*, 9/9/20)

"Tunnels," Eleanor Arnason (*Asimov's Science Fiction*, 5–6/20)

"Moral Biology," Neal Asher (*Analog: Science Fiction and Fact*, 5–6/20)

Ivory's Story, Eugen Bacon (NewCon Press)

"Glass Bottle Dancer," Celeste Rita Baker (*Lightspeed*, 4/20)

"The Last Ship Out of Exville," Phoebe Barton (*Kaleidotrope*, Winter 2020)

"The Ordeal," M. Bennardo (*Beneath Ceaseless Skies* #297, 2/13/20)

"Sela, Thief," Zabe Bent (*Breathe Fiyah*, 10/19/20)

"A Glossary of Radicalization," Brooke Bolander (*Made to Order: Robots and Revolution*)

"Scar Tissue," Tobias S. Buckell (*Slate: Future Tense*, 5/30/20)

"If Salt Lose Its Savor," Christopher Caldwell (*Uncanny* #33, 3–4/20)

"Thank You For Your Patience," Rebecca Campbell (*Reckoning 4*, 3/24/20)

"Badass Moms in the Zombie Apocalypse," Rae Carson (*Uncanny* #32, 1–2/20)

"Hikayat Sri Bujang, or, The Tale of the Naga Sage," Zen Cho (*The Book of Dragons*)

The Order of the Pure Moon Reflected in Water, Zen Cho (Tordotcom)

Finna, Nino Cipri (Tordotcom)

"You Perfect, Broken Thing," C. L. Clark (*Uncanny* #32, 1–2/20)

"Nine Words for Loneliness in the Language of the Uma'u," M. L. Clark (*Clarkesworld* #165, 6/20)

Ring Shout, P. Djèlí Clark (Tordotcom)

"Dance on Saturday," Elwin Cotman (*Dance on Saturday: Stories*)

"Of Them All," Leah Cypess (*F&SF*, 9–10/20)

"A Sideways Slant of Light," Leah Cypess (*Asimov's Science Fiction*, 9–10/20)

"In the Lands of the Spill," Aliette de Bodard (*Avatars Inc*)

Of Dragons, Feasts and Murders, Aliette de Bodard (JABberwocky)

Seven of Infinities, Aliette de Bodard (Subterranean Press)

"Salvage," Andy Dudak (*Interzone* #285 1–2/20)

Dispersion, Greg Egan (Subterranean Press)

"You and Whose Army?" Greg Egan (*Clarkesworld* #169, 10/20)

"Ife-Iyoku, the Tale of Imadeyunuagbon," Oghenechovwe Donald Ekpeki (*Dominion: An Anthology of Speculative Fiction from Africa and the African Diaspora*)

"Familiar Face," Meg Elison (*Nightmare* #88, 1/20)

"The Long Walk," Kate Elliott (*The Book of Dragons*)

"From the Balcony of the Idawolf Arms," Jeffrey Ford (*Final Cuts: New Tales of Hollywood Horror and Other Spectacles*)

Out of Body, Jeffrey Ford (Tordotcom)

Upright Women Wanted, Sarah Gailey (Tordotcom)

"We Don't Talk About the Dragon," Sarah Gailey (*The Book of Dragons*)

"Time's Own Gravity," Alexander Glass (*Interzone* #288, 9–10/20)

"One Time, a Reluctant Traveler," A. T. Greenblatt (*Clarkesworld* #166, 7/20)

"Brother Rifle," Daryl Gregory (*Made to Order: Robots and Revolution*)

"By Touch and By Glance," Lisa L. Hannett (*Songs for Dark Seasons*)

"The Ransom of Miss Coraline Connelly," Alix E. Harrow (*Fireside* #81, 7/20)

"The Sycamore and the Sybil," Alix E. Harrow (*Uncanny* #33, 3–4/20)

"The Girlfriend's Guide to Gods," Maria Dahvana Headley (*Tor.com*, 1/23/20)

"The Endless," Saad Z. Hossain (*Made to Order: Robots and Revolution*)

"Rat and Finch Are Friends," Innocent Chizaram Ilo (*Strange Horizons*, 3/2/20)

Flyaway, Kathleen Jennings (Tordotcom)

"The Mirages," Alaya Dawn Johnson (*Asimov's Science Fiction*, 11–12/20)

King of the Dogs, Queen of the Cats, James Patrick Kelly (Subterranean Press)

"Spirit Level," John Kessel (*F&SF*, 7–8/20)

The Tindalos Asset, Caitlín R. Kiernan (Tordotcom)

"Pox," Ellen Klages (*The Book of Dragons*)

"Semper Augustus," Nancy Kress (*Asimov's*, 3–4/20)

"Little Free Library," Naomi Kritzer (*Tor.com*, 4/8/20)

"Monster," Naomi Kritzer (*Clarkesworld* #160, 1/20)

"The Nine Curves River," R. F. Kuang (*The Book of Dragons*)

"Avatars," Lavanya Lakshminarayan (*Analog/Virtual: And Other Simulations of Your Future*)

"Etudes," Lavanya Lakshminarayan (*Analog/Virtual: And Other Simulations of Your Future*)

"The Persona Police," Lavanya Lakshminarayan (*Analog/Virtual: And Other Simulations of Your Future*)

"Recognition," Victor LaValle (*The Decameron Project*)

The Four Profound Weaves, R. B. Lemberg (Tachyon Publications)

"A Whisper of Blue," Ken Liu (*The Book of Dragons*)

"Idols," Ken Liu (*Made to Order: Robots and Revolution*)

"Anything Resembling Love," S. Qiouyi Lu (*Tor.com*, 4/29/20)

Selkie Summer, Ken Macleod (NewCon Press)

"City of Red Midnight: A *Hikayat*," Usman T. Malik (*Tor.com*, 10/21/20)

"The Wandering City," Usman T. Malik (*Us in Flux*, 7/9/20)

"A Being Together Amongst Strangers," Arkady Martine (*Uncanny* #34, 5–6/20)

"Robot and Girl with Flowers," Paul McAuley (*Avatars Inc*)

"Knock, Knock Said the Ship," Rati Mehrotra (*F&SF*, 7–8/20)

"Note to Self," Sunny Moraine (*Lightspeed*, 9/20)

"The Old Ones, Great and Small," Rajiv Moté (*Diabolical Plots*, 3/16/20)

"Retention," Alec Nevala-Lee (*Analog*, 7–8/20)

"The Translator," Annalee Newitz (*Made to Order: Robots and Revolution*)

"Clanfall: Death of Kings," Odida Nyabundi (*Dominion: An Anthology of Speculative Fiction from Africa and the African Diaspora*)

"A Room of One's Own," Tochi Onyebuchi (*Us in Flux*, 4/30/20)

Riot Baby, Tochi Onyebuchi (Tordotcom)

"The Hurt Pattern," Tochi Onyebuchi (*Made to Order: Robots and Revolution*)

"Chiaroscuro in Red," Suzanne Palmer (*Made to Order: Robots and Revolution*)

"Candida Eve," Dominica Phetteplace (*Analog Science Fiction and Fact*, 5–6/20)

"Notice," Sarah Pinsker (*Us in Flux*, 6/11/20)

"Two Truths and a Lie," Sarah Pinsker (*Tor.com*, 6/17/20)

"St. Valentine, St. Abigail, St. Brigid," C. L. Polk (*Tor.com*, 2/5/20)

The Properties of Rooftop Air, Tim Powers (Subterranean Press)

"Debtless," Chen Qiufan (*Clarkesworld* #163, 4/20)

"The Ancestral Temple in a Box," Chen Qiufan (*Clarkesworld* #160, 1/20)

"The Ossuary's Passenger," Robert Reed (*Asimov's Science Fiction*, 9–10/20)

"Last Night at the Fair," M. Rickert (*F&SF*, 7–8/20)

"Beyond the Tattered Veil of Stars," Mercurio D. Rivera (*Asimov's*, 3–4/20)

Paper Hearts, Justina Robson (NewCon Press)

"La Vitesse," Kelly Robson (*The Book of Dragons*)

"Bereft, I Come to a Nameless World," Benjamin Rosenbaum (*Asimov's Science Fiction*, 7–8/20)

"The Parable of the Tares," Christopher Rowe (*Us in Flux*, 4/8/20)

"Fairy Tales for Robots," Sofia Samatar (*Made to Order: Robots and Revolution*)

"Rover," A. T. Sayre (*Analog Science Fiction and Fact*, 3–4/20)

"Reflection," Gu Shi (*Future Science Fiction Digest*, 12/20)

"Sticky Man," Vandana Singh (*LCRW* #42, 11/20)

"Prudent Girls," Rivers Solomon (*The Decameron Project*)

"My Country Does Not Dream," Han Song (*Exploring Dark Short Fiction #5: A Primer to Han Song*)

"Hearty Appetites," Bonnie Jo Stufflebeam (*The Way of the Laser: Future Crime Stories*)

"There was an Old Woman . . ." Michael Swanwick (*The Postutopian Adventures of Darger and Surplus*)

"We're Here, We're Here," K. M. Szpara (*Tor.com*, 6/10/20)

"Baba Yaga and the Seven Hills," Kristina Ten (*Lightspeed*, 7/20)

"Tend to Me," Kristina Ten (*Lightspeed*, 3/20)

"Head Static," Sheree Renée Thomas (*Nine Bar Blues: Stories from an Ancient Future*)

"Madame and the Map: A Journey in Five Movements," Sheree Renée Thomas (*Nine Bar Blues: Stories from an Ancient Future*)

"Come the Revolution," Ian Tregillis (*F&SF*, 3–4/20)

"My Country Is a Ghost," Eugenia Triantafyllou (*Uncanny* #32, 1–2/20)

"Color, Heat, and the Wreck of the Argo," Catherynne M. Valente (*Strange Horizons*, 9/7/20)

The Empress of Salt and Fortune, Nghi Vo (Tordotcom)

"A Cyber-Cuscuta Manifesto," Regina Kanyu Wang (*Us in Flux*, 6/24/20)

"Test 4 Echo," Peter Watts (*Made to Order: Robots and Revolution*)

"An Explorer's Cartography of Already Settled Lands," Fran Wilde (*Tor.com*, 4/22/20)

"Take a Look at the Five and Ten," Connie Willis (*Asimov's Science Fiction*, 11–12/20)

"To Sail the Black," A. C. Wise (*Clarkesworld* #170, 11/20)

"The Exile," Neon Yang (*The Book of Dragons*)

"A Stick of Clay in the Hands of God Is Infinite Potential," Neon Yang (*Clarkesworld* #164, 5/20)

"The AI That Looked at the Sun," Filip Hajdar Drnovšek Zorko (*Clarkesworld* #160, 1/20)

COPYRIGHT CREDITS

Selection, "Introduction: Year in Review," and Recommended Reading by Jonathan Strahan. © Copyright 2021 by Jonathan Strahan.

"The Bahrain Underground Bazaar" by Nadia Afifi. © Copyright 2020 Nadia Afifi. Originally published in *The Magazine of Fantasy & Science Fiction*, November–December 2020. Reprinted by kind permission of the author.

"If You Take My Meaning" by Charlie Jane Anders. © Copyright 2020 Charlie Jane Anders. Originally published in *Tor.com*, 11 February 2020. Reprinted by kind permission of the author.

"It Came From Cruden Farm" by Max Barry. © Copyright 2020 Max Barry. Originally published in *Slate: Future Tense*, February 20, 2020. Reprinted by kind permission of the author.

"The Final Performance of the Amazing Ralphie" by Pat Cadigan. © Copyright 2020 Pat Cadigan. Originally published in *Avatars Inc*. Reprinted by kind permission of the author.

"An Important Failure" by Rebecca Campbell. © Copyright 2020 Rebecca Campbell. Originally published in *Clarkesworld* #167, August 2020. Reprinted by kind permission of the author.

"Schrödinger's Catastrophe" by Gene Doucette. © Copyright 2020 Gene Doucette. Originally published in *Lightspeed*, November 2020. Reprinted by kind permission of the author.

"Midstrathe Exploding" by Andy Dudak. © Copyright 2020 Andy Dudak. Originally published in *Analog Science Fiction and Fact*, March–April 2020. Reprinted by kind permission of the author.

"The Pill" by Meg Elison. © Copyright 2020 Meg Elison. Originally published in *Big Girl* (PM Press). Reprinted by kind permission of the author.

"GO. NOW. FIX." by Timons Esaias. © Copyright 2020 Timons Esaias. Originally published in *Asimov's Science Fiction*, January–February 2020. Reprinted by kind permission of the author.

"Drones to Ploughshares" by Sarah Gailey. © Copyright 2020 Sarah Gailey. Originally published in *Motherboard*, 4 February 2020. Reprinted by kind permission of the author.

"The Transition of OSOOSI" by Ozzie M. Gartrell. © Copyright 2020 Ozzie M. Gartrell. Originally published in *Fiyah Magazine of Black Speculative Fiction* #13. Reprinted by kind permission of the author.

"Burn or The Episodic Life of Sam Wells as a Super" by A. T. Greenblatt. © Copyright 2020 A. T. Greenblatt. Originally published in *Uncanny* #34, May–June 2020. Reprinted by kind permission of the author.

"How Quini the Squid Misplaced His Klobučar" by Rich Larson. © Copyright 2020 Rich Larson. Originally published in *Tor.com*, 15 January 2020. Reprinted by kind permission of the author.

"The Mermaid Astronaut" by Yoon Ha Lee. © Copyright 2020 Yoon Ha Lee. Originally published in *Beneath Ceaseless Skies* #298. Reprinted by kind permission of the author.

"50 Things Every AI Working with Humans Should Know" by Ken Liu. © Copyright 2020 Ken Liu. Originally published in *Uncanny* #37, November–December 2020. Reprinted by kind permission of the author.

"Beyond These Stars Other Tribulations of Love" by Usman T. Malik. © Copyright 2020 Usman T. Malik. Originally published in *Wired*, 11 December 2020. Reprinted by kind permission of the author.

"Yellow and the Perception of Reality" by Maureen McHugh. © Copyright 2020 Maureen McHugh. Originally published in *Tor.com*, 22 July 2020. Reprinted by kind permission of the author.

"A Mastery of German" by Marian Denise Moore. © Copyright 2020 Marian Denise Moore. Originally published in *Dominion: An Anthology of Speculative Fiction from Africa and the African Diaspora*. Reprinted by kind permission of the author.

"Father" by Ray Nayler. © Copyright 2020 Ray Nayler. Originally published in *Asimov's Science Fiction*, July–August 2020. Reprinted by kind permission of the author.

"How to Pay Reparations: a Documentary" by Tochi Onyebuchi. © Copyright 2020 Tochi Onyebuchi. Originally published in *Slate: Future Tense*, 29 August 2020. Reprinted by kind permission of the author.

"Don't Mind Me" by Suzanne Palmer. © Copyright 2020 Suzanne Palmer. Originally published in *Entanglements: Tomorrow's Lovers, Families, and Friends* (MIT Press). Reprinted by kind permission of the author.

"A Guide for Working Breeds" by Vina Jie-Min Prasad. © Copyright 2020 Vina Jie-Min Prasad. Originally published in *Made to Order: Robots and Revolution* (Rebellion/Solaris). Reprinted by kind permission of the author.

"Polished Performance" by Alastair Reynolds. © Copyright 2020 Dendrocopos Ltd. Originally published in *Made to Order: Robots and Revolution* (Rebellion/Solaris). Reprinted by kind permission of the author.

"The Suicide of Our Troubles" by Karl Schroeder. © Copyright 2020 Karl Schroeder. Originally published in *Slate: Future Tense*, 28 November 2020. Reprinted by kind permission of the author.

"Airbody" by Sameem Siddiqui. © Copyright 2020 Sameem Siddiqui. Originally published in *Clarkesworld* #163, April 2020. Reprinted by kind permission of the author.

"Sparklybits" by Nick Wolven. © Copyright 2020 Nick Wolven. Originally published in *Entanglements: Tomorrow's Lovers, Families, and Friends* (MIT Press). Reprinted by kind permission of the author.

"The Search for [Flight X]" by Neon Yang. © Copyright 2020 Neon Yang. Originally published in *Avatars Inc*. Reprinted by kind permission of the author.